Jon Glover was born in 1943. He was educated at the University of Leeds, where he read English and Philosophy. After research for an M.Phil. at Leeds and a period working in the United States, he moved to Bolton Institute of Higher Education, where he is a Principal Lecturer in Literature and Head of the Division of Humanities. He has taught courses on the literature of the war and has written on the relationship between Owen's poetry and Barbusse's *Under Fire*. His poetry has been published widely and broadcast on *Poetry Now* (BBC Radio 3). Collections of poetry include *The Wall and the Candle* (1983) and *Our Photographs* (1986). He has been associated with the literary magazine *Stand* for more than twenty years. He is married and has two daughters.

Jon Silkin was born in London in 1930, and after two years as a national serviceman, when he was a sergeant instructor in the Education Corps, he became a labourer in London for six years. In 1958 he was awarded the Gregory Fellowship in Poetry at the University of Leeds and went on to take his degree in English there. It was during this period that he first met Jon Glover. Jon Silkin co-edits the literary quarterly *Stand* (which he founded in London in 1952). He has published nine collections of poetry, one of which, *Nature with Man*, was awarded the Geoffrey Faber Memorial Prize in 1966. His most recent collections of poetry include *The Psalms with Their Spoils* (1980), *The Ship's Pasture* (1986) and *Selected Poems* (1988). He has edited *The Penguin Book of First World War Poetry*, and his critical book on the poetry of the First World War, *Out of Battle*, has recently been reissued. He is married to the fiction writer Lorna Tracy, with whom he edits *Stand*. He has also written a verse play based on the life of the First World War poet and composer Ivor Gurney, which is called *Gurney* (1985).

THE PENGUIN BOOK OF
FIRST WORLD WAR PROSE

Edited and with an introduction by
JON GLOVER AND JON SILKIN

PENGUIN BOOKS

PENGUIN BOOKS

Published by the Penguin Group
Penguin Books Ltd, 27 Wrights Lane, London w8 5tz, England
Viking Penguin, a division of Penguin Books USA Inc.
375 Hudson Street, New York, New York 10014, USA
Penguin Books Australia Ltd, Ringwood, Victoria, Australia
Penguin Books Canada Ltd, 2801 John Street, Markham, Ontario, Canada l3r 1b4
Penguin Books (NZ) Ltd, 182–190 Wairau Road, Auckland 10, New Zealand

Penguin Books Ltd, Registered Offices: Harmondsworth, Middlesex, England

First published by Viking 1989
Published in Penguin Books 1990
1 3 5 7 9 10 8 6 4 2

This selection copyright © Jon Glover and Jon Silkin, 1989
All rights reserved

The acknowledgements on pp. xi–xvi constitute an
extension of this copyright page

Printed in England by Clays Ltd, St Ives plc

CONTENTS

ACKNOWLEDGEMENTS

—

Many people have offered suggestions and advice concerning the choice and balance of texts. We would particularly like to thank John Wardle, David MacDuff, Lorna Tracy Silkin, Elaine Glover, Burton Delroy, Malcolm Pittock, Roger and Janet Whitehouse, Cecil Davies, Barry Wood, Watson Branch, Martin Booth, Tricia Wood and David Levy.

Dr Gerry Bryant gave valuable advice on military aspects of the war and made his excellent collection of First World War books available. The help of the Research Committee of Bolton Institute of Higher Education is gratefully acknowledged and we would like to thank the staff of the British Library, the John Rylands Library (University of Manchester), the Library of the University of Newcastle and the Newcastle upon Tyne Public Library.

Norma Willescroft, Barbara Higham, Jean Flinders, Abigail Glover and Rhiannon Glover helped to put the manuscript into order. Special thanks are also due to Paul Keegan and Nick Wetton.

We are indebted to the copyright holders for permission to reprint the following:

Richard Aldington: to The Hogarth Press and the author's Estate for *Death of a Hero*; to Rosica Colin Ltd for *Roads to Glory*, © Madame Catherine Guillaume.

Paul Alverdes: to Martin Secker & Warburg Ltd for *The Whistlers' Room*, translated by Basil Creighton.

Enid Bagnold: to William Heinemann Ltd and Speechly Bircham (Solicitors) for *A Diary without Dates*.

Henri Barbusse: to Janet Whitehouse (translator) for *War Diaries*, translation © 1965; to J. M. Dent & Sons Ltd for *Under Fire*, translated by William Fitzwater Wray (Everyman Library Series).

Rudolf Binding: to Unwin Hyman Ltd for *A Fatalist at War*.

Edmund Blunden: to A. D. Peters & Co. Ltd and Collins Publishers for *Undertones of War* (William Collins Sons & Co. Ltd); to A. D. Peters & Co. Ltd for *De Bello Germanico* (Hawstead: G. A. Blunden).

Gordon Bottomley and Paul Nash: to Oxford University Press for *Poet and Painter: Being the Correspondence between Gordon Bottomley and Paul Nash 1910–1946*, edited by Claude Colleer Abbott and Anthony Bertram (1955).

Vera Brittain: the extracts from *Testament of Youth* are included with the permission of her literary executors and Victor Gollancz Ltd, and Virago Press; published by Virago Press Ltd 1978, copyright © Literary Executors of Vera Brittain 1970.

Richard Carline: to Faber & Faber Ltd for *Stanley Spencer at War*.

Willa Cather: to Virago Press and Alfred A. Knopf, Inc., for *One of Ours*.

Louis-Ferdinand Céline: to Chatto & Windus Ltd for *Journey to the End of the Night*, translated by John Marks.

Guy Chapman: to A. D. Peters & Co. Ltd for *A Passionate Prodigality* (MacGibbon & Kee Ltd).

Humphrey Cobb: to Viking Penguin, Inc., for *Paths of Glory*, copyright 1935 by Humphrey Cobb; copyright renewed © 1962 by William Cobb and Alice Cobb.

Colette: to Martin Secker & Warburg Ltd and Farrar, Straus & Giroux, Inc., for 'Les Heures Longes' from *Earthly Paradise*, translated by Herma Briffault, edited by Robert Phelps, © 1966 by Farrar, Straus and Giroux Inc.

Borys Conrad: to John Calder (Publishers) Ltd and Riverrun Press, Inc., for *My Father: Joseph Conrad*.

Jessie Conrad: to the trustees of Jessie Conrad's Estate for *Joseph Conrad as I Knew Him*.

John Conrad: to Cambridge University Press for *Joseph Conrad: Times Remembered*.

E. E. Cummings: to Liveright Publishers and Grafton Books for *The Enormous Room*; to André Deutsch Ltd for *Selected Letters*.

Roland Dorgelès: to Éditions Albin Michel for *Les Croix de Bois*; English translation published by William Heinemann, 1920.

V. M. Doroshevich: to Constable Publishers for *The Way of the Cross*, translated by Stephen Graham.

John Dos Passos: to Elizabeth Dos Passos for *1919*.

Pierre-Eugène Drieu La Rochelle: to Writers and Readers Publishing, Inc., for *The Comedy of Charleroi*. Copyright Writers and Readers Publishing, Inc.

Georges Duhamel: to Unwin Hyman Ltd for *Civilisation*; English translation by Florence Simmonds.

Ilya Ehrenburg: to Jack and Rowna Barnett and the Estate of the Hon. Ivor Montagu for *People and Life: Memoirs of 1891–1921* (MacGibbon & Kee), translated by Anna Bostock and Yvonne Kapp.

Florence Farmborough: to Constable Publishers for *Nurse at the Russian Front*.

William Faulkner: to the author's literary Estate and Chatto & Windus Ltd, and Random House, Inc., for *A Fable*; to Curtis Brown Ltd and Random House, Inc., for 'Victory'.

Ford Madox Ford: to The Bodley Head Ltd, David Higham Associates Ltd and Janice Biala for *A Man Could Stand Up* from *The Bodley Head Ford Madox Ford*, Vol. IV, © copyright renewed 1954 by Janice Biala.

Leonhard Frank: to Leonhard Frank and Trans-Cyrus Books for *Carl and Anna*.

Ernst Glaeser: to Martin Secker & Warburg Ltd for *Class 1902*, translated by Willa and Edwin Muir.

Stephen Graham: to Macmillan, London and Basingstoke, for *A Private in the Guards*.

Robert Graves: to A. P. Watt Ltd on behalf of The Executors of the Estate of Robert Graves for *Goodbye to All That*.

Uri Zvi Greenberg: to Associated Book Publishers for 'Naming Souls' (translated by Jon Silkin and Ezra Spicehandler) from *The Ship's Pasture* by Jon Silkin (Routledge & Kegan Paul).

Ivor Gurney: to Humanities Press International, Inc., the Mid Northumberland Arts Group and Carcanet New Press, with the permission of J. R. Haines, the Trustee of the Ivor Gurney Estate, for *War Letters*, edited by R. K. R. Thornton (MidNAG).

Sir Ian Hamilton: to the Trustees of Sir Ian Hamilton's Literary Fund for 'The End of War?', published in *Life and Letters*, Vol. 3, No. 18, 1929.

to the author and Chatto & Windus Ltd for *The Spanish Farm Trilogy*.

John Middleton Murry: to George Sassoon and the *New Statesman* for extracts from Siegfried Sassoon's war verses, reprinted in John Middleton Murry's review, 'Mr Sassoon's War Verses', in *The Nation*, 13 July 1918.

Robert Musil: to Tanja Howarth for 'Diaries' (translated by David McDuff and E. M. Valk) from *Gesammelte Werke*, copyright © 1978 by Rowohlt Verlag GmbH, Reinbek bei Hamburg.

Paul Nash: to the trustees of the Paul Nash Estate for *Outline*.

Wilfred Owen: to Oxford University Press for *Wilfred Owen: The Collected Letters*, edited by Harold Owen and John Bell (1967).

Arthur Ransome: to Jonathan Cape Ltd and the Arthur Ransome Estate for *The Autobiography of Arthur Ransome*, edited by Rupert Hart-Davis.

Herbert Read: to David Higham Associates Ltd and Horizon Press, New York, for *The Contrary Experience*, copyright © 1963 by Herbert Read. To Carcanet Press Ltd and New Directions Publishing Corporation for *The Collected Poems of Hilda Doolittle, 1912–1944*.

Erich Maria Remarque: to David Higham Associates Ltd for *The Road Back* (The Bodley Head), and *All Quiet on the Western Front* (The Bodley Head); English translations by A. M. Wheen.

Ludwig Renn: to Aufbau-Verlag for *Krieg*, © Aufbau-Verlag AG Berlin und Weimar; English translation by Willa and Edwin Muir, published by Martin Secker 1929.

Frank Richards: to Faber & Faber Ltd for *Old Soldiers Never Die*.

Jules Romains: to Souvenir Press Ltd and Editions Flammarion for *Verdun*, © Flammarion 1984; English translation by Gerard Hopkins.

Isaac Rosenberg: to Chatto & Windus Ltd for extracts from the letters of Isaac Rosenberg from *The Collected Works of Isaac Rosenberg*, edited by Ian Parsons.

Siegfried Sassoon: to Faber & Faber Ltd and K. S. Giniger, Inc./Stackpole Books for *Memoirs of an Infantry Officer*, and *Siegfried's Journey, 1916–1920* (Stackpole Books), © 1967 by Siegfried Sassoon.

Laurence Stallings: to Harcourt Brace Jovanovich, Inc., for

Plumes, copyright 1924 by Harcourt Brace Jovanovich Inc.; renewed 1952 by Laurence Stallings.

Herbert Sulzbach: to Penguin Books Ltd for *With the German Guns* (Frederick Warne Ltd).

Helen Thomas: to Carcanet Press Ltd for 'Under Storm's Wing' from *World without End*.

Ernst Toller: to Carl Hanser Verlag and The Bodley Head Ltd for *I was a German*, from *Gesammelte Werke*, Vol. IV, edited by Wolfgang Fruehwald & John M. Spalek, © 1978 by Sidney Kaufmann; English translation by Edward Crankshaw, published by The Bodley Head in 1934.

H. M. Tomlinson: to H. C. Tomlinson, Margery Dickinson, Dorothy Bailey for *All Our Yesterdays*. Copyright Reserved.

Rebecca West: to A. D. Peters & Co. Ltd and Virago Press for *The Return of the Soldier*, published by Virago Press Ltd 1980, © in the original edition Rebecca West 1918, © in the revised edition Rebecca West 1980.

Edith Wharton: to Watkins/Loomis Agency, Inc., for *Fighting France* (Charles Scribner's Sons, 1915) and *A Son at the Front* (Charles Scribner's Sons, 1923).

Henry Williamson: to Macdonald Publishers for *The Patriot's Progress*.

Edmund Wilson: to Farrar, Straus & Giroux, Inc. for 'Lieutenant Franklin' from *A Prelude*, © 1967 by Edmund Wilson.

Arnold Zweig: to Barthold Fles for *The Case of Sergeant Grischa*, copyright 1956 by Viking Penguin, Inc.; English translation by E. Sutton.

The publishers regret that their attempts to trace the copyright holders of *The New Book of Martyrs* by Georges Duhamel, *Russia and the World* and *The Challenge of the Dead*, both by Stephen Graham, and *Outline* by Paul Nash, have been unsuccessful. Due acknowledgement will gladly be made in later editions if the relevant information is forthcoming.

What pure peace allows
Alarms of wars, the daunting wars, the death of it?

Gerard Manley Hopkins, 'Peace'

INTRODUCTION
A Prose Version of the First World War

PART ONE
The Writing of Britain and America

In retrospect, the writing that emerged from the war that was supposed to have ended all wars seems distinctive. No other poetry became, ultimately, as centred in its commitment to exposing the horror and absurdity of war; no other, with the exception of Shelley's, so committed to infusing compassion with a determination to expunge war: 'And am I not myself a conscientious objector with a very seared conscience?' (Owen). Even the experienced, sacred tenderness of Whitman's poem 'Reconciliation' contrives to anticipate Owen's 'Strange Meeting', so consistent and characteristic is the poetry of the war. This is as true of the poets of the trenches on the Western Front, such as Rosenberg, Owen and Sassoon, as it is of, say, the poet Uri Zvi Greenberg,[1] who fought under different conditions in Galicia, as a soldier in the army of the Austro-Hungarian Empire. It is the same army in which the good soldier Švejk served.

The response to war of the poet as combatant is, eventually, as consistent in its confidence that war is morally wrong as the newly enlisted soldier's first response, which was that the Cause was sacred, the war therefore just. The Cause, that is, seemed blessed in its own way despite the developed scepticism of European peoples. Two years later many in the United States were to see their entry into the war similarly as a Great Crusade – with a special fervour derived from the conviction that the New World was destined to cleanse and uplift the Old. And this moral assurance, at first supportive of a 'just cause', and then directed against the War and its Cause – 'nothing can justify war' – is characteristic of the poetry and its development in the War. Anne, Countess of Winchilsea's poem, 'A Soldier's Death', seems as if it were written in support of that moral outrage and compassion which is constituent of the later poetry of the Great War.

The Spanish Civil War does not 'distil' a poetry moral and

I

pacific but moral and political. There is one right Cause, and war is to be erased in the defeat of that Other. Implicit in Picasso's *Guernica*, for instance, is not only the conviction that war is obscene, but that it is the Cause of the fascists. This position is underlined by the story that during the Second World War, when the Nazis in Paris demanded of Picasso concerning *Guernica*, 'Did you do this?', he answered 'No, you did.' It is not only the sacred passion of Isaiah for beating swords into plough-shares but also the stamping of that ploughshare 'anti-fascist', 'use only in humane causes'. And the monopoly of moral right-eousness which Davie [2] claims the left believes itself to possess, and which therefore so nauseates him, is balanced perhaps by the alliance of Franco with the Spanish 'wing' of the Catholic Church, as well as with the fascists of Europe.

The Second World War again united the political impulsion with the moral. Day-Lewis claimed that the bad (the Western Alliance) were fighting the worse (the Axis Powers); [3] yet in the West few doubted that fascism had to be fought even though war was morally wrong. One product of this position was the exemplary poem by Herbert Read, 'To a Conscript of 1940': 'To fight without hope is to fight with grace . . .'

But if some writers found that the Second World War required new moral positions this should not be seen as a modification of a simple pacifist conviction. After 1918 many American novelists adopted a bitterly anti-war stance – Humphrey Cobb in *Paths of Glory* (1935) and Laurence Stallings in *Plumes* (1924), for ex-ample. Even so, in the *prose* of the First World War, that was not the whole picture. Selecting poems for an anthology of First World War poetry, [4] I began with the belief that most of the best poetry of the period I had read opposed and condemned war. Such a common denominator of belief is, I am convinced, shared, if in a more differentiated way, by poets of the Second World War. Consider, for instance, Roy Fuller's poem 'Spring 1942'.

The prose of the First World War is not – amongst the Americans at least – as unified in its attitudes, nor is the possession of excellence so clearly in the hands of those opposed to the war. In his scrupulous *World War 1 and the American Novel* (1967), the late Stanley Cooperman advances the idea that the closer to the experience of the war the writing was, the more bitter its expression against it. It is true that the bitterness is to some extent dissolved in the passage of the years but even so

2

Cooperman's formula is not absolute. The range of response comes as much from those who had been in Europe during the war, whether as combatants or observers (Hemingway, Cummings, Wharton, John Reed), as from those who had remained in America. Many non-participants (Scott Fitzgerald, Katherine Anne Porter and Dalton Trumbo, for example) continued to write about the negative effects of war with angry conviction. Despite (or perhaps because of) the thousands of miles that lay between American families, communities and politicians, and the actual battles, there is here a literature of the 'return'; and in the aftermath grew a vigorous imaginative and social commitment rarely found in England. Unable to include all of those writers in this anthology I have chosen William Faulkner to represent a particular American response. He was not a participant, although in later years he liked to be thought one, but he wrote his first novel, *Soldiers' Pay* (1926), and one of his last, *A Fable* (1954), about the war. Surprisingly, these great American writers seem to have found the deformity left in the psyche by the barbarity of war more central to their writing than many of their British counterparts.

In contrast to the position of these novels, there is also Edith Wharton's *A Son at the Front* (1923), which Cooperman thinks fairly well of, its ideology notwithstanding, and Willa Cather's more ambiguously aligned *One of Ours* (1922), of which Cooperman thinks less well (I would reverse the order of preferences). Both fictions are by, as is said, writers of distinction; and the Great Crusade which took hold of the American imagination and which, in consequence, suffered a greater disillusion than the more sceptical European mind – this crusade is convincingly offered as America's moral imperative. In saying this, one is admitting to the strength of the conviction, not its substance. Even so, Willa Cather does not balk at reporting the excesses committed against the American-German communities in the name of patriotism, which disfigured those whose moral fervour was otherwise 'acceptable'. In order to dislodge Cather's novel, against which he displays a clear animus, Cooperman is obliged to claim that Claude, the hero, whose marriage all but terminates in sexual failure, finds erotic fulfilment in combat and ultimately in death. This overstates the case. Claude's unfulfilled, brief relationship with Mlle de Courcy brings out, I think, not violence as an erotic alternative to sexual fulfilment, as Cooperman suggests, but potential sexual and emotional fulfilment. It is this

3

potential which Cather makes Claude realize in his espousal of the French woman's Cause.

Edith Wharton, on the other hand, explains her commitment to the Cause by offering a sour view of French culture and society (Jamesian in its dubiety over European morals) together with an overview of French societal care and provision for the alien. Campton is American, and his son George virtually so. Yet the father has lived most of his adult life (now a successful and fulfilled one as a painter) in France, and his son has been brought up within the provision of that culture. Thus although father and son are still American they owe a debt to France which, in the context of the war, only death can repay.

The American 'testimony' is especially interesting because of its range of talent: from Cummings to Hemingway; from Stallings and Dos Passos to Wharton and Cather; from John Reed to Edmund Wilson. The range is of talent divided upon ideology and, as I have said already, the majority of the talent is aligned upon the anti-war, anti-militarist positions; even so there is a significant minority otherwise aligned.

In England, the range of ideological attachment and its contingent spread of talent is less pronounced. More people professed to hate the war – Graves, for instance, and Sassoon. Yet where in the war Sassoon showed a moral courage as astonishing as his physical valour, when he protested against the waste of war by refusing to serve any further in the army, it seems that Robert Graves,[5] probably Sassoon's most intimate army friend, outwitted him and effectively annulled his protest: 'No doubt I should have done the same for him if our positions had been reversed.'[6] Additionally, Graves shows not merely respect for but an interest in regimental history and its pride. Although this may not be difficult to appreciate, it is hard to couple it with Graves's detestation and grief at the destruction of war. By sending up the bullying militarist strut and self-esteem of his French jailers, or even their simple brutality, Cummings manages a greater consonance between his attitudes and the uses to which he puts his style and his hatred of war; if such bullying ceased to be respected, he suggests, how could *organized* warfare or any such military activity continue. The courage required to oppose American moral righteousness, and its corresponding self-esteem, must have been considerable; as considerable as that required by Sassoon to speak from within,

4

but against, the interests of the English caste system and its militarization during the war.

There are, however, ambiguities in some English prose writing of the war that go beyond Graves's eccentric care for the regiment. Frederic Manning's *Her Privates We* (1930) is perhaps the most curious mosaic of all. On the one hand there is the fastidious ranker, educated and almost delicate, who grows wild when 'the kid' is destroyed in battle, and becomes after all – in manly paradigm – almost more brutal than those who practise a straightforward blood-lust. And in contradistinction to this tacit endorsement of the caste system – a system more subtle perhaps than Prussianism, but every bit as pervasive and powerful – in contrast to it, there is the 'homo-erotic' relationship between the huge (and tender) Weeper – who turns out to be intelligent as well, despite his size – and the hero of the book, who is finally destroyed. Given such contrasts, one might ask what values this writing upholds. To whom does it speak, and for whom is it intended?

Another strange gathering of seemingly opposed modes is found in the prose of Blunden's *Undertones of War* (1928). In *New Bearings in English Poetry* (1932), F. R. Leavis wrote of his poetry:

> The peculiar poise that constituted Mr Blunden's distinction has proved difficult to maintain. On the one hand, the stress behind the pastoral quiet becomes explicit in poems dealing with mental conflict, hallucination, and war-experience; on the other, the literary quality ... He was able to be, to some purpose, conservative in technique, and to draw upon the eighteenth century, because the immemorial rural order that is doomed was real to him.
>
> (pp. 59 and 61)

If 'the immemorial rural order ... is doomed', this may be seen in the tension Blunden sets up between his account of war and his expression of a rurality that bears the imprint of pastoral. It is a peculiar, fine achievement not found in any other writer of the war in England – not, for instance, in the work of Edward Thomas. And what makes Blunden's achievement so distinctive is that odd blend of the English rose and the English military phenomenon; or, to put it differently, between immemorial arcadia and an English army at war: the one seemingly eternal, the other mortal. Fussell writes in *The Great War and Modern Memory* (1975):

An ancient tradition associates battle scars with roses ... Roses were indispensable to the work of the imagination during and after the Great War ... (pp. 243–4)

and then quotes Northrop Frye:

In the West the rose has a traditional priority amongst apocalyptic flowers ... [it] is connected not only with the risen body of Christ and the sacramental symbolism which accompanies it, but with the union of the red and white roses in the Tudor dynasty.

Fussell then adds:

Skulls juxtaposed with roses could be conveniently employed as an emblem of the omnipotence of Death. (pp. 244 and 246)

'Under the auspices of a government scheme,' Bernard Bergonzi writes in *Heroes' Twilight* (1965), Ford Madox Ford 'produced two books of a somewhat didactic kind, one attacking Prussia and the other praising France.' His poem 'Antwerp', an apologia on behalf of Belgium and its peoples, is, in the main, clumsy and transparent; his fiction, certainly the *Parade's End* trilogy (or tetralogy if one counts in *The Last Post*), published between 1924 and 1928, is altogether different. The poetry offers a single-minded commitment to the 'war effort' and the prose creates a complex debate. Ford's prose narrative blends, with greater power and complexity, the same sort of pairings-off that inform *Her Privates We*. Ford's Tietjens is a landed aristocrat from the north-east. He has 'brains', and he selflessly uses his intelligence to subserve a greater good. He forces himself to become a conscientious *soldier*, and, in the process, finds respect for those whom war tries to the utmost and who nevertheless remain 'good soldiers'.

The connection between a middle-class utilitarian intelligence and the courage of an aristocrat more or less indifferent to self and the fate of that self is commemoratively fused in the figure of Tietjens. Tietjens has not only brains and courage but 'enormous physical strength' which (like Weeper Smart in *Her Privates We*) he uses to save the diminutive child-like officer Aranjuez. By contrast, the draper's assistant and the milkman need help and instruction in the art of digging with shovels as they try to save another buried soldier. The contrast is ironic and unexpected (the stoic, grinning ordinary soldiers are 'not good with shovels') and the active, high-minded, down-to-earth courage of Tietjens is placed in a nice conjunction that is made to commemorate a social order which itself seems doomed. It is one founded on an

English-speaking union called up in time of crisis to bear beyond those divisions of class or caste which would otherwise in peacetime be invoked. Ford uses these unions in the subtlest way to celebrate (not unlike Mottram in his *Spanish Farm Trilogy*, (1927), the endurance and achievement of the English at war. Ford makes a fine celebration of that – less bloodied perhaps than some – but he calls out his praise not, I think, for war but to salute the life forces of courage. And because Ford does not appear to be inventing – as he does in his time-serving poem 'Antwerp' – but drawing on coexistences of which he seems to have prior, deep understanding, he manages to produce one of the most supple, concentrated prose works of the war. There is no other work, English or American, unless it is Blunden's *Undertones*, that weaves in and out of the war, yet in which the war is always present, and in which the prose concentrates itself on the war.

——

Berserkers: Icel. *berserkr*, prob. = 'bear-coat', otherwise explained as Baresark.
Baresark, in a shirt only, without armour, *Shorter Oxford Dictionary*

In a recent conversation with Henry Merritt, a lecturer in Old English, I learned a few disturbing facts to do with the word *berserk*. The warriors called *berserkers* were those inspired in combat with divine fury. Under that same influence they had, in the course of their lives as warriors, destroyed a wild bear, and because of this feat they were permitted to wear the skin of the creature they had killed. A further aspect of this act was that these warriors were supposed to have destroyed the creature with the strength of their bodies alone; in this combat they used neither armour nor weapon. This act put these men in a special moral position within their tribe, since all would value the act and acknowledge that it required great physical strength coupled with determination and courage. These were evidently attributes valued within the cultures of the northern tribes and their kingdoms, and we would be foolish if we refused to recognize the power of such acts, whatever valuation we chose to put on them. Finally, I learned that the England of the eighth century AD, 'highly civilized and highly violent', also valued these same attributes, and that Beowulf was reputed to have possessed all three.

Beowulf's generosity and his almost credulous trust in his followers in no way contradicted the ferocity of his martial behaviour; on the contrary, these were qualities seen to complement his prowess. And because the condition of the berserk was set alongside those attributes of loyalty and generosity, it would indicate that the berserk state was approved by the tribe.

Nothing Henry Merritt suggested concerning this culture and its outlook could contrast more with our own. Robert Graves pinpoints this when, out of his experience of the First World War, he writes:

> Until the unendurable moment struck –
> The inward scream, the duty to run mad.
> ('Recalling War')

It is not that, as Herbert Read has indicated in 'The Happy Warrior', we do not know how to run mad, but that our culture needs to legalize and sanction such behaviour, which is otherwise ordinarily unacceptable. Even in boxing, for instance, a controlled ferocity is today preferred.

What Henry Merritt told me seems relevant to an understanding of the First World War. 'The Spirit of the Bayonet' lectures were intended, as Graves, Blunden and Sassoon separately testified, to inculcate extremes of aggressive and uncontrolled behaviour – which could only be realized by one's rejecting all those civilized constraints that had been developed with such care. Yet in pointing to the rejection of these constraints and in indicating, at the same time, the power of modern weapons, we sometimes offer the argument that 'today' we are uncivilized where before, in an age such as Beowulf's, we were not. Our combat, it is argued, is uncivilized where before it was heroic. David Jones says as much in his Preface to *In Parenthesis* (1937):

> Some of us ask ourselves if Mr X adjusting his box-respirator can be equated with what the poet envisaged, in
>
> > 'I saw young Harry with his beaver on.'
>
> ... for [the old authors] the embrace of battle seemed one with the embrace of lovers. For us it is different ...

and

> The wholesale slaughter of the later years [of the First World War] ... knocked the bottom out of the intimate, continuing, domestic life of small contingents of men, within whose structure

Roland could find, and, for a reasonable while, enjoy, his Oliver. (my italics – pp. xiv–xv and ix)

It is a familiar-enough argument. In *In Parenthesis* David Jones attempts to infuse the unheroic beastliness of modern combat with a degree of the past's more intimate, allegedly more heroic, behaviour in the war. Yet this is no more than a repetition of the similar arguments made in an earlier age. For the purposes of discrediting what might be called the democratization of war through such weaponry, the aristocracy deplored the use of gunpowder:

> The social argument was that gunpowder was a coward's weapon which destroyed the dignity of knighthood by allowing a common soldier to kill a gentleman from afar. Ariosto's apostrophe
>
>> Through thee is martial glory lost, through thee
>> The trade of arms become a worthless art:
>> And at such ebb are worth and chivalry
>> That the base often plays the better part.
>
> was paralleled by the French marshal Blaise de Monluc's reference to 'poltroons that had not dared look these men in the face at hand, which at distance they had laid dead with their confounded bullets'. ('War and public opinion in the fifteenth and sixteenth centuries', John Hale, *Past and Present*, no. 22, July 1962, p. 29)

The point I am making is that if we speak of the 'brutishness' of modern war in contrast to its earlier practice, we must also reckon with the *berserker*, and those attitudes which once accredited his behaviour. All war is horrible, and it is unlikely that the spilling of one's opponents brains through the blow of an axe, or the crushing of him to death, is any more palatable than shooting or gassing him:

> ... The thief
> Fell in battle, but not on my blade.
> He was brave and strong, but I swept him in my arms,
> Ground him against me till his bones broke,
> Till his blood burst out.
> (*Beowulf*, trans. Burton Raffel, 35, ll. 2504–8)

Gassing one's enemy is cold-blooded, but so too are the attitudes that approved the berserker.

Jon Silkin

PART TWO
The Writing of Europe and Britain

The war was appallingly destructive and, arguably, unnecessary. Yet, to immerse oneself in the literature it produced is, in a strange way, heartening. Great writing emerged from the war's brutally enforced actions, which were, for the individual, supremely alienating and uncontrollable. However, these actions provided experiences of extraordinary challenge that were physically and morally repeated innumerable times and, in effect, shared. This sense of terrible community was, and is, vital. In that state of uneasy, unasked-for self-awareness that comes in the face of acute, incomprehensible danger, the desire, and the ability, to record, to express and to communicate testifies to what those involved refused to abandon of their humanity. To the modern reader the point is, perhaps, that even if the languages of Europe were not common, language itself was, and in a world in which the individual was valued only as expendable material words affirmed that the individual existed and was capable of independent action. The war *demanded* a written response and the very act of articulation formed the basis of an imaginative self-assertion that might develop into a common bond of protest and warning.

To say that, despite all, language 'won' is facile. Yet the war was, at least in part, a drama of language. If political rhetorics, persistently unrelated to the destructive potential of industrialized warfare, helped to set the war going, it is the verbal testimony of what 'actually happened', the substitution of realistic languages, which struggled to bear witness to the results of the outworn vocabularies of monarchy and militarism, that may have helped to end it. Of course, it would be naïvely inaccurate to claim that every participant turned against it and that every piece of prose in this volume constitutes an explicit protest. But in looking for the message behind this vast body of literature one cannot but notice the way in which the demands of experience force language to break away from the rehearsed formulae of tawdry nationalism. It is worth recalling here that Wilfred Owen's poem 'Dulce et Decorum' has, at its heart, a point about the misuse of language.

What are the experiences of the Great War that became manifest in the prose of so many letters, memoirs, semi-fictional autobiographies and novels? What will we see in the prose that we cannot find in the poetry? Firstly, we are almost invariably confronted with descriptive detail which contributes to an expansive, sometimes unstable, realism. Duhamel's Breughel-like view of the surroundings of Verdun in *The New Book of Martyrs* and Barbusse's surreal vision from the mountains over the 'great livid plain' of Europe are informed by shocking, unexpected observation which insists that this 'really happened'. Significantly, Barbusse's perspective from the comprehending detachment of the sanatorium starts *Under Fire* and only lasts a few pages before writer and reader are pitched into the battle. On the other hand, in Thomas Mann's *The Magic Mountain* the principal character is abandoned in about four pages of war after seven hundred pages (and seven years) in his sanatorium.[7] The comparison only makes a rhetorical point, perhaps. But it is true that, for the participants, the powers of literary vision, and therefore of organization, were undermined by the knowledge that each day's fighting could match the worst, most private dreams of the author. Events could not be manipulated and structured to fit a literary mould; the meaning of life was given by shells and mud, politicians and generals.

Secondly, we follow the physical and moral education of individuals or groups as the various new worlds of war are revealed. Identifiable stages continually recur: recruitment and training, the journey to the front, initial battle experience. And then, usually horrifyingly, the appearance of the dead, the experience of injury, hospitals and nursing. This prose, sometimes by the women involved, concerning injury, treatment and what was for many a first ironically brutal sharing of physical contact between men and women, is particularly moving. The effort to kill and the struggle to save and survive are starkly witnessed. Not surprisingly, in a world so prepared by death for the unnatural, episodes that one might expect to be welcomed as a reminder of conventional reality such as visits to a restaurant, meeting a woman, or periods of leave or convalescence are treated as absurd, inadequate and disillusioning. For those who survived and knew the outcome, descriptions of victory or defeat and return to their respective countries are interesting but often tantalizingly inadequate.

Thirdly, one is confronted with a series of contradictions that are partly in the works themselves and partly in our perception of them. On the one hand we see the continuity and repetiveness of each individual's experience, the dreary and harrowing progression from recruitment to almost certain injury or death. It is a common, shared pattern, and, to some extent, the soldiers themselves were aware that it was like that from the English Channel to the Swiss border – on both sides. On the other hand, it is important that although we can recognize the repeated dubious logic of war we must also recognize what is revealed by the episodic, unorganized nature of even the semi-fictional works. So much of the experience of war highlighted unprepared moments of confrontation and hate but also pity, selflessness and moral growth. Clearly the authors valued the discoveries of these brief, unstructured events and the fact that they returned to them so often means that we should look for the logic of the short story – an undervalued form in Britain – rather than the novel. Of course there are dangers. Response to experience of the absurd can become morally careless, technically random. The very richness of incident packed into those four terrible years provided seemingly infinite material for plotless but detailed stories. The modern reader may simply feel surfeited by too much of a bad thing. While boredom may not be a danger in a work like *The Good Soldier Švejk*, in others one longs for a clearer sense of literary purpose. (The *Švejk* stories were begun in 1911, of course; Hašek's vision of benign idiocy conceived in the story of a Czech who wanted to be proved fit for military service when everyone else wanted to prove they were unfit survived the assassination at Sarajevo!) Even in works written long after the war there remain problems of selection and organization. Many people lived to read the published accounts of others before beginning their own but still did not feel impelled to register individual response in terms of formal innovation. Only the really accomplished, such as Conrad, Zweig, Mottram, Ford and Drieu la Rochelle manage to vary the moral and technical predominance of the first person point of view.

But, perhaps we should beware of simplistic literary evaluations. After all, this selection hints at both the problems and opportunities of dealing with the material of war in different technical ways. Sassoon not only wrote great poetry but important letters, diaries and various forms of autobiography. Graves, Mottram, Williamson, Barbusse, Duhamel and Toller all kept 'returning' to the war, often in different forms, finding it to be unfinished and unfinishable business. When the first desire to communicate and protest had been transformed into the need to remember, re-examine and warn, and when other wars confirmed that neither the Great War nor the protests had ended all wars, still the literary spring did not wind down.

We can see a particularly fascinating case of differing styles struggling with the same material in the group of extracts from works by the Conrad family. Joseph Conrad himself gives us the spontaneous and personally involved response of his letters, then the cooler, more thoughtful overview of 'Poland Revisited', which sets his experience of war in a more (British) political context, and finally, a short story, 'The Tale', which characteristically weighs in the balance of his literary discipline the supposed wartime ideals of duty and patriotism against justice, mercy and personal integrity. Not surprisingly, 'The Tale' manipulates the narrative point of view to enhance the author's dark, ambivalent detachment. Conrad's wife and two sons add accounts (in 1926, 1970 and 1981) of their struggle to escape from Poland in the early months of the war.

This strange, nagging persistence in the desire to get things right is, perhaps, mirrored by the equally strange way in which the literary response to the war was, necessarily, unprepared. What actually happened was as surprising for writers as it was for the military. It is a point that Conrad makes. Asked what he thought would happen after the murder of Archduke Ferdinand he replied: 'Nothing . . . It fitted with my ethical sense that an act cruel and absurd should be also useless.' Conrad's perplexity is important since the writers in this anthology were all faced with the unprecedented moral and literary problems of making sense of million upon million of 'useless' but 'cruel and absurd' acts. Dominant ideologies had created the war, but they could not provide writers with ready-made feelings when confronted with actual involvement in overwhelming human conflict. This prose experimentally marks out an ideological challenge as each writer was forced to discover a response to 'useless' suffering. (Yeats's famous judgement of Wilfred Owen denies the possibility of such a response.[8]) Moreover, in so far as the attendant contradictions were actually experienced, rather than merely imagined, we, perhaps, have a key to the energy and fascination each writer found in continually retelling his story. It would, of course, be wrong to claim that all writers were 'made' by the contradictions of war – far from it, since Duhamel, Barbusse and Hašek, for example, were already writing before 1914. But the war did provide both a personal and a literary opportunity for the writer to discover his own principles, and the most successful let such discoveries emerge raw in the writing rather than try to batter the material into pre-1914 codes of morality and artistic expectation.

Whether or not the work was written during the war, the attempt to make sense of things through inherited political convictions sits uneasily. Sometimes, the refusal to respond to, or learn from, the facts of war amounts to ugly arrogance. More often, the reader senses a bitter, if understandable, irony, when, for example, Barbusse's squad's hopes for a better world are pinned on Karl Liebknecht. Some writers, like Roger Martin du Gard, managed to make the sense of being let down by political beliefs part of the subject of their work. Near the end of *Summer 1914*, Jacques stares across the Rhine at the country that had suddenly become a mysterious enemy and realizes that the brute fact of impending war was outside the control of language and that dreams of European socialist unity were as hopeless as his own gesture of scattering leaflets appealing for peace from an aircraft over both sides. Even if we now disagree with du Gard's view embodied in Jacques Thibault, it is the inclusion of such problems in the structure of works such as *Summer 1914* that marks off the genuinely novelistic treatment of the war from the memoirs and semi-fictional autobiographies.

What else is there for the reader in the specifically European works? It will be hard to forget the picture in Isabelle Rimbaud's *In the Whirlpool of War* of ordinary French people escaping from the invading forces in their best clothes in order to 'score off the enemy'. There is a similar picture in Duhamel's description of the Verdun area, and his laconic association between civilization and the giant, steaming hospital sterilizer is compelling. Remarque's *All Quiet on the Western Front* and Frank's *Carl and Anna* portray civilian life in Germany during the war. And both Renn and Sulzbach evoke an experience quite unlike anything we are used to in British accounts: the final retreat and the painful, and, to the ordinary soldier, incomprehensible orders to the army to elect democratic representatives following political changes in Germany. We have been able to find relatively little about the Eastern Front readily available in English but Zweig's Sergeant Grischa preparing to escape to Russia and Arthur Ransome's visits to the Russian Front hint at that other side of the war. It was, after all, a *world* war. Stephen Graham, John Reed and V. M. Doroshevich add to our sense of the appallingly vast cultural and geographical space that was involved.

For the British, the Western Front marked out the war's relatively simple geographical identity. We are reminded in the passages from John Reed and Ilya Ehrenburg of some of the more complex and racialist aspects. Reed found the Russians using the war as a cover for more pogroms. Ehrenburg caps this with the absurdity of Russian Jewish emigrés, in France to escape persecution at home, volunteering to fight for the French and being ridiculed and finally executed for their pains. For the indigenous population of Flanders, Alsace-Lorraine, parts of eastern Europe and the Middle East, and for minorities everywhere, the Great War was just one more episode in a continuing and familiar fight for survival.

One final point. It is a convention that the British literary consciousness is insular. The fact that so many of these translations are now out of print indicates the way in which the modern British memory has made the Great War its own. This anthology should help to change that assumption. On the other hand it is remarkable that so many translations, including those from German, were published, particularly during the 1920s and 1930s. Perhaps British insularity, literally enforced by the Second World War, has helped more recently to diminish interest in the wider aspects of the Great War. The European war of 1914–18 with its horror, boredom, fear, absurdity and agonies of national and individual identity recorded in this literature deserves our attention today.

Jon Glover

1. See Greenberg's poem 'Naming Souls'.
2. In 'A Rejoinder to Jon Silkin', Donald Davie wrote: 'To speak for myself (though I think and hope for a thousand others), it is just this that I find intolerable and diseased in the rhetoric of the British Left: the constant need for self-righteous indignation, as for a stimulating drug.' (*Stand*, Vol. 20, no. 2, 1979)
3. It is the logic of our times,
   No subject of immortal verse,
   That we, who lived on honest dreams,
   Defend the bad against the worse.
       'Where Are the War Poets?'
4. *The Penguin Book of First World War Poetry*, ed. Jon Silkin (1979).
5. *Goodbye to All That*, Robert Graves (1929).
6. *Memoirs of an Infantry Officer* (1930); *The Complete Memoirs of George Sherston* (1937) by Siegfried Sassoon.
7. A passage whose style in translation only makes sense in relation to those previous seven hundred pages. In context its impact is tremendous but we decided not to include it here.

A NOTE ON THE EDITING

Nearly all of the authors in this anthology participated in the Great War in some way, although there are a few civilian reactions and a few imaginative recreations of battle experience. In effect, we are charting the war's representation in prose from some of the earliest reactions in letters (Sorley) through diaries and autobiography written at the time (Edward Thomas, Musil, Barbusse) and on to various levels of 'faction', autobiography and fiction. Soon, the impact of the war had found its way into novels of non-participants either dealing with events 'at home' (Rebecca West) or with the fighting and its aftermath (Wharton, Cather, Faulkner). The reader can trace, therefore, how the now familiar images of modern war entered the 'civilized' literary consciousness.

We agreed that an anthology of snippets – of choice lines, of pithy utterances and apophthegms was not desirable. Both editors worked on the British works. Jon Silkin made most of the selections from the United States and Jon Glover from Europe. In certain cases the former tended to choose smaller parts from one work and bring these together while the latter tended to take a single, longer passage as representative. In no cases have selections from one work been conflated with those from another.

As to what makes a writer 'important', it is the usual question of insight and comprehensive grasp. But it is also, as it is with poetry, not just what the writer inadvertently reveals of experience, and his or her attitudes to it in the choices of language and diction; it is also a question of what each writer achieves by such choices which make up the complex of intention. Sassoon's recorded experience – of physical valour and, equally, of moral courage – is crucial. But so is the exemplary religious drama that informs Faulkner's *A Fable*.

The editors were agreed on the kinds of themes, and wide range of attitudes they wanted represented, each made his selection, and then together put in order a composite view of the war. The task of choice became increasingly daunting as every new book seemed to lead on to a dozen more. A. G. S. Enser's *A Subject Bibliography of the First World War* (London, André

Deutsch, 1979), contains references to more than five thousand non-fiction works. We soon decided to exclude journalism in uncollected form, political speeches, pure historical accounts and the innumerable memoirs whether by generals or privates that merely listed regimental movements, strategic plans and the actions of individuals, and which give no flavour of individuality. We have also avoided the vast number of 'adventure story' books: they are, of course, worth studying but they are, in their way, almost more depressing than the more honest prose that we have chosen. Arguably, drama, particularly from post-war Germany, should not have been excluded but it will be agreed that there are particular problems in taking excerpts from plays.

Some of the chosen works are readily available, others we are particularly pleased to be bringing back into print after many years. The European texts have nearly all been drawn from existing translations, some of which may not be ideal. However, it was interesting to discover just how much European work had been translated and had enjoyed considerable popularity. The history and nature of these translations is a subject for study in its own right, reflecting, as it does, the various ways in which the English-speaking world responded to what was, after all, a European conflict. The passage from Barbusse's *War Diary* has been translated especially for this volume, as have Rosa Luxemburg's Letters.

In selecting texts we concentrated on author and work. In other words we did not wish to illustrate a historical thesis or to provide a literary history of the war. In consequence, the reader will not find five neat paragraphs by different hands on Verdun followed by five more on the Somme. Each writer's work, even from widely differing points in his or her life and in different modes such as diaries, memoirs and fiction, has been kept together, and this allows the importance and integrity of each excerpt to be judged as literature. This is not to make an artificial division between art and life in this most 'historical' of writing; rather, in rediscovering so much neglected prose, we hope that the reader will reach his or her own conclusions about the relationship between the experience of war and the impulse to write.

The reader will, however, find thematic developments and we have attempted to place the authors so as to show a gradually evolving sense of the war's moral, political and emotional impact. Inevitably, some passages describing the end of the war come before another author's description of his first journey to the front. The disadvantages of this were thought to be outweighed by the advantages of showing changing response and experience in terms of each individual writer.

———

'My subject is War, and the pity of War,' Wilfred Owen wrote in the Preface to his 'war' poems published after his death on 4 November 1918. Not every contribution echoes this, even if many writers were in broad agreement with the position held in the Preface, that war is morally indefensible: 'All a poet can do today is warn. That is why the true Poets must be truthful.' For all the writers war seems to have been an intensifying experience out of which they asked what values, if any, inhered in human life. They asked what kind of survival was possible – for whom and for what end. These answers, they made – many of them tentative – remain relevant.

We begin the selection of texts with a poem which records the intensely explored relationship between man and God in time of war, and between the horror, warning and tribute integral to the great prose writing that follows.

URI ZVI GREENBERG

Uri Zvi Greenberg (1896–1981). Born in Galicia and brought up in Lvov. In 1915 he was drafted into the Austrian army. In this year also he published his first volume of Yiddish verse. Deserted in 1917 and returned to Lvov where he witnessed the Polish pogroms (see John Reed and Florence Farmborough below). He emigrated to Palestine in 1923. He continued to write and became active in politics. This poem is translated from the Hebrew by Jon Silkin and Ezra Spicehandler.

Source: Uri Zvi Greenberg, *Anacreon at the Pole of Melancholy*, 1928.

NAMING SOULS

An hour is held deep, in the underneath of time.
In the religion of purification
men's innerness
stands, stripped of garments, in the dusk
and prays to see God's image. Ah, if only I could bear up
the cup of bitterness,
my eyes turned inward, I would drink to the terror in the eyes
of soldiers, brothers whom I fought with
and reached the Sawa's water.

They fell, tangled on the wire,
their feet raised high,
and that wail, essence of their dying, lasted only
a moment; they died, then,
very dark.

I stood on my own, the last
of the species that fight,
seeing these brothers, with feet turned upwards, growing
until they reached the sky, in death,
to kick it. I saw
the moon like an animal
rub a silver face on the worn nails in the boots
of upturned soldiers.

This fearful glowing on the nails in the boots of the dead
who kick at God, electrified
my being with a terror
that shone as if I were dying. With the flesh's
eyes, I saw the divine
in fear's mystery, in men falling. I cried
then, as if I were the last to cry
who never again in life
will cry what I wept
on the Sawa's water.

CHARLES HAMILTON SORLEY

Charles Hamilton Sorley (1895–1915). Born in Old Aberdeen and educated at Marlborough (see also Siegfried Sassoon). Before taking up a scholarship to Oxford he went to Germany and enrolled briefly at the University of Jena. His poems were published posthumously as *Marlborough and Other Poems*, 1916, and reprinted several times. His *Letters*, from which excerpts appear below, were collected by his father, W. R. Sorley, and published in 1919. Sorley's battalion left for France in May 1915 and he served mainly around Ploegsteert. He was killed in action at the battle of Loos on 13 October 1915.

Source: Charles Hamilton Sorley, *The Letters of Charles Hamilton Sorley*, Cambridge, Cambridge University Press, 1919.

To The Master of Marlborough   July 1914
                                                            [Jena]

... Another point in your letter leaves me unconvinced. You say that the 'corps' aren't bad really. But they are! Black-rotten! The sooner one dispels the libel on German universities that the corps student is the typical student, the better. They comprise only a third of the total number of students at Jena: and Jena is the most traditional of all German universities. They are the froth and the dregs. We, the 'nicht-inkorporierten', the other two thirds, are the good body of the beer. We live in two feet square bedsits, we do a little work (impossible for the first three semesters for the corps students), and pretty soon we can mix with one another without any of the force and disadvantages of the artificially corporate life. A peculiarly offensive form of 'fagging' for the six youngest students in each corps: compulsory drunkenness; compulsory development of offensive and aggressive behaviour to the outsider; and a peculiarly sickening anti-Semitism are their chief features. The students with whom I mostly go about are Jews, and so perhaps I see, from their accounts of the insults they've to stand, the worst side of these many-coloured reeling creatures. But they're dying out. Their place is being taken by non-combative and non-disciplinary Verbind-ungen. One or two will still remain – for they're picturesque enough and their singing is fine: and I like a little froth to my beer. But please dòn't think they're typical of us. We've most of us outlived that Sedanish spirit here. . . .

To Miss M. M. Smith   26 July 1914
                                                       [Jena]

. . . I'm so glad you're going to visit Germany again after your stay in Sweden. I don't think any one could help it who has been there once. But I hope you'll still like Berlin. I liked it least of what I have seen of Germany. Too much of Prussian officialdom and red tape, I thought. I'll allow it to be called the capital of Prussia – but of Germany, no . . .

We are having an exciting time with the various Abschied-fests. It is a fine sight to see all the corps dressed up in their old-fashioned costumes, carrying torches, singing through the town at midnight. It almost makes one wish that one was an 'in-korporierter' too. Tonight, I'm afraid, they are making a war-demonstration and shouting 'Down with the Serbs'. We are altogether having a thrilling time at present: with new editions of the papers coming out every hour, each time with wilder rumours. It is curious that the one person who would have leapt with joy at this new war is the murdered Crown-prince, whose death has been the means of bringing it about. I hope you'll find a pacified Germany when you come south from Sweden.

So both the sides of the channel we are pretty 'angespannt'.[1] And the gunpowder seems to have caught fire. The next week should bring exciting things.

To A. E. Hutchinson   10(?) August 1914
                                                      Cambridge

Having proved my identity at home as distinct from the gar-dener's, I investigated my (a-hem!) 'papers' and found, among old receipts for college clothes and such like, a lovely piece of paper, which I daresay you have got too, which dismissed me from the corps. Only mine had EXCELLENT written (in the Major's hand) for my General Efficiency. Yours can have had, at most, 'very good'. I took this down to a man of sorts and said 'Mit Gott für Kaiser und Vaterland, I mean, für König und

Mutterland: what can I do to have some reasonable answer to give to my acquaintances when they ask me, "What are *you* doing?"?' He looked me up and down and said, 'Send in for a commission in the Territorials. You may get something there. You'll get an answer in a fortnight's time, not before.' Compromise as usual. Not heroic enough to do the really straight thing and join the regulars as a Tommy, I have made a stupid compromise [with] my conscience and applied for a commission in the Terriers, where *no* new officers are wanted. In a month's time I shall probably get the beastly thing: and spend the next twelve months binding the corn, guarding the bridges, frightening the birds away, and otherwise assisting in Home Defence . . .

. . . But isn't all this bloody? I am full of mute and burning rage and annoyance and sulkiness about it . . .

. . . I could wager that out of twelve million eventual combatants there aren't twelve who really want it. And, 'serving one's country' is so unpicturesque and unheroic when it comes to the point. Spending a year in a beastly Territorial camp guarding telegraph wires has nothing poetical about it: nor very useful as far as I can see. Besides the Germans are so nice; but I suppose the best thing that could happen to them would be their defeat . . .

To A. J. Hopkinson   October (?) 1914
                                              Shorncliffe

I thought the enclosure from [your] Uncle peculiarly interesting and return as you must want to keep it. He put the case for Prussian (as distinct from German) efficiency far more fairly than I had ever thought of it before. I think his transatlantic criticism of England's 'imaginative indolence' and consequent social rottenness most stimulating in this time of auto-trumpeting and Old-England-she's-the-same-as-ever-isms. Also I suppose he is to a certain extent right that we have temporarily renounced all our claim to the more articulate and individual parts of our individuality. But in the intervals of doing and dying let's speak to one another as two pro-Germans, or nearly so, who have tramped her roads, bathed in her Moselles, and spent half-a-day in her cells.

The two great sins people impute to Germany are that she says that might is right and bullies the little dogs. But I don't think that she means might *qua* might is right, but that confidence of superiority is right, and by superiority she means spiritual superiority. She said to Belgium, 'We enlightened thinkers see that it is necessary to the world that all opposition to Deutsche Kultur should be crushed. As citizens of the world you must assist us in our object and assert those higher ideas of world-citizenship which are not bound by treaties. But if you oppose us, we have only one alternative.' That, at least, is what the best of them would have said; only the diplomats put it rather more brusquely. She was going on a missionary voyage with all the zest of Faust –

> *Er wandle so den Erdentag entlang;*
> *Wenn Geister spuken, geh' er seinen Gang;*
> *Im Weiterschreiten find' er Qual und Glück,*
> *Er, unbefriedigt jeden Augenblick!* [2]

– and missionaries know no law. As Uncle Alder says, her Kultur (in its widest sense) is the best in the world: so she must scatter it broadcast through the world perforce, saying like the schoolmaster or the dentist 'though it hurts at present, it'll do you no end of good afterwards'. (Perhaps she will even have to add at the end of the war 'and it's hurt me more than it's hurt you'.)

So it seems to me that Germany's only fault (and I think you often commented on it in those you met) is a lack of real insight and sympathy with those who differ from her. We are not fighting a bully, but a bigot. They are a young nation and don't yet see that what they consider is being done for the good of the world may be really being done for self-gratification – like X who, under pretence of informing the form, dropped into the habit of parading his own knowledge. X incidentally did the form a service by creating great amusement for it, and so is Germany incidentally doing the world a service (though not in the way it meant) by giving them something to live and die for, which no country but Germany had before. If the bigot conquers he will learn in time his mistaken methods (for it is only of the methods and not of the goal of Germany that one can disapprove) – just as the early Christian bigots conquered by bigotry and grew larger in sympathy and tolerance after conquest. I regard the war as one between sisters, between Martha and

Mary, the efficient and intolerant against the casual and sympathetic. Each side has a virtue for which it is fighting, and each that virtue's supplementary vice. And I hope that whatever the material result of the conflict, it will purge these two virtues of their vices, and efficiency and tolerance will no longer be incompatible.

But I think that tolerance is the larger virtue of the two, and efficiency must be her servant. So I am quite glad to fight this rebellious servant. In fact I look at it this way. Suppose my platoon were the world. Then my platoon-sergeant would represent efficiency and I would represent tolerance. And I always take the sternest measures to keep my platoon-sergeant in check! I fully appreciate the wisdom of the War Office when they put inefficient officers to rule sergeants. Adsit omen . . .

To A. E. Hutchinson   14 November 1914
                                       Shorncliffe

. . . England – I am sick of the sound of the word. In training to fight for England, I am training to fight for that deliberate hypocrisy, that terrible middle-class sloth of outlook and appalling 'imaginative indolence' that has marked us out from generation to generation. Goliath and Caiaphas – the Philistine and the Pharisee – pound these together and there you have Suburbia and Westminster and Fleet Street. And yet we have the impudence to write down Germany (who with all their bigotry are at least seekers) as 'Huns', because they are doing what every brave man ought to do and making experiments in morality. Not that I approve of the experiment in this particular case. Indeed I think that after the war all brave men will renounce their country and confess that they are strangers and pilgrims on the earth. 'For they that say such things declare plainly that they seek a country.' But all these convictions are useless for me to state since I have not had the courage of them. What a worm one is under the cart-wheels – big clumsy careless lumbering cart-wheels – of public opinion. I might have been giving my mind to fight against Sloth and Stupidity: instead, I am giving my body (by a refinement of cowardice) to fight against the most enterprising nation in the world . . .

To Professor and Mrs Sorley   23 November 1914
                                                             Shorncliffe

... I don't like your Tommy friends sneering at the French courage, when every able-bodied Frenchman is in the field. It is possible that the majority of the French lack that 'cauld deidly' courage: but these are the less favourable specimens, I feel sure, whose corresponding types in England are still watching football on Saturdays. I think your Irish friend should see that our own house is in order before making comparison between our 'contemptibly little' army (note the emendation) and that of our ally, whose spirit is at any rate willing.

To Professor and Mrs Sorley   30 November 1914
                                                             Shorncliffe

... Hardy explains in the preface to one of his former books of poems that they are expressions of moods and are not to be taken as a whole reading of life, but 'the road to a true philosophy of life seems to be in humbly recording divers aspects of its phenomena as they are forced upon us by chance and change'. And I don't think he writes these poems [for the reason] you suggest, but with a view to helping people on that 'road to a true philosophy of life'. Curiously enough, I think that 'Men who march away' is the most arid poem in the book, besides being untrue of the sentiments of the ranksman going to war: 'Victory crowns the just' is the worst line he ever wrote – filched from a leading article in *The Morning Post*, and unworthy of him who had always previously disdained to insult Justice by offering it a material crown like Victory. I think in looking through it you must have missed a verse like:

> Yes, I accompany him to places
>   Only dreamers know,
> Where the shy hares show their faces,
>   Where the night rooks go;
>
> Into old aisles where the past is all to him,
>   Close as his shade can do,
> Always lacking the power to call to him,
>   Near as I reach thereto!

I have been lately reading a great deal in *The Dynasts*, which I bought three weeks ago. His poetry there is at its very best, especially in the choruses and battle-songs, perhaps because the comprehensiveness of the task did not allow him to introduce himself and his own bitternesses, as he can in his lyrics. It has a realism and true ring which 'Men who march away' lacks . . .

To A. E. Hutchinson   25 January 1915
                                       Shorncliffe
. . . War in England only means putting all the men of 'military age' in England into a state of routinal coma, preparatory to getting them killed. You are being given six months to become conventional: your peace thus made with God, you will be sent out and killed. At least, if you aren't killed, you'll come back so unfitted for any other job that you'll have to stay in the Army. I should like so much to kill whoever was primarily responsible for the war. The alarming sameness with which day passes day until this unnatural state of affairs is over is worse than any so-called atrocities; for people enjoy grief, the only unbearable thing is dullness . . .

. . . We talk of going out in March. I am positively looking forward to that event, not in the brave British drummer-boy spirit, of course, but as a relief from this boredom (part of which, by the way, is caused through Philpott having been away the last three weeks in hospital).

We don't seem to be winning, do we? It looks like an affair of years. If so, pray God for a nice little bullet wound (tidy and clean) in the shoulder. That's the place . . .

To Mrs Sorley   March 1915
                                       Aldershot
. . . I talked a lot (in her native tongue) to the hostess with whom I was billeted, and her sensible German attitude was like a cold bath. She saw the thing, as German hausfraus would, directly and humanly and righteously. Especially sensible was she in her remarks against the kind ladies who told her she ought to be proud and glad to give her sons to fight. After all, war in this century is inexcusable: and all parties engaged in it must take an equal share in the blame of its occurrence. If only the English from Grey downwards would cease from rubbing in

27

that, in the days that set all the fuel ablaze, they worked for peace honestly and with all their hearts! We know they did; but in the past their lack of openness and trust in their diplomatic relationships helped to pile the fuel to which Germany applied the torch.

I do wish also that people would not deceive themselves by talk of a just war. There is no such thing as a just war. What we are doing is casting out Satan by Satan. When once war was declared the damage was done: and we, in whom that particular Satan was perhaps less strong than in our foes, had only one course, namely to cast out the far greater Satan by means of him: and he must be fought to the bitter end. But that doesn't alter the fact that long ago there should have been an understanding in Europe that any country that wanted Weltmacht might have it. The Allies may yet score a victory over Germany. But by last August they had thrown away their chances of a true victory. I remember you once on the Ellerby moors telling us the story of Bishop What's-his-name and John-Val-John from *Les Misérables*. And now, although we failed then of the highest, we might have fought, regarding the war – not, as we do regard it, as a candle to shed light upon our unselfishness and love of freedom, but – as a punishment for our past presumptuousness. We had the silver candlesticks and brandished them ever proudly as our own, won by our valour. Germany must be crushed for her wicked and selfish aspiration to be mistress of the world: but the country that, when mistress of the world, failed to set her an example of unworldliness and renunciation should take to herself half the blame of the blood expended in the crushing.

To Mrs Sorley
28 April 1915
Aldershot

I saw Rupert Brooke's death in the *Morning Post*. *The Morning Post*, which has always hitherto disapproved of him, is now loud in his praises because he has conformed to their stupid axiom of literary criticism that the only stuff of poetry is violent physical experience, by dying on active service. I think Brooke's earlier poems – especially notably *The Fish* and *Grantchester*, which you can find in *Georgian Poetry* – are his best. That last sonnet-sequence of his, of which you sent me the review in the *Times Lit. Sup.*, and which has been so praised, I find (with the exception of that beginning 'These hearts were woven of human joys and cares, Washed marvellously with sorrow' which is not about himself) overpraised. He is far too obsessed with his own sacrifice, regarding the going to war of himself (and others) as a highly intense, remarkable and sacrificial exploit, whereas it is merely the conduct demanded of him (and others) by the turn of circumstances, where non-compliance with this demand would have made life intolerable. It was not that 'they' gave up anything of that list he gives in one sonnet: but that the essence of these things had been endangered by circumstances over which he had no control, and he must fight to recapture them. He has clothed his attitude in fine words: but he has taken the sentimental attitude . . .

To Arthur Watts
23 May 1915
Aldershot

. . . We profess no interest in our work; our going has lost all glamour in adjournment; a weary acceptance of the tyranny of discipline, and the undisguised boredom we feel toward one another, mark all our comings and goings: we hate our general, our C.O. and men; we do not hate the Germans: in short we are nearing the attitude of regular soldiers to the army in general . . .

To Arthur Watts
1 June 1915
[France]

. . . But this is perfect. The other officers have heard the heavy guns and perhaps I shall soon. They make perfect cider in this valley: still, like them. There are clouds of dust along the roads, and in the leaves: but the dust here is native and caressing and pure, not like the dust of Aldershot, gritted and fouled by motors and thousands of feet. 'Tis a very Limbo lake: set between the tireless railways behind and twenty miles in front the fighting. Drink its cider and paddle in its rushy streams: and see if you care whether you die tomorrow. It brings out a new part of one's self, the loiterer, neither scorning nor desiring delights, gliding listlessly through the minutes from meal-time to meal-time, like the stream through the rushes: or stagnant and smooth like their cider, unfathomably gold: beautiful and calm without mental fear. And in four-score hours we will pull up our braces and fight. These hours will have slipt over me, and I shall march hotly to the firing-line, by turn critic, actor, hero, coward and soldier of fortune: perhaps even for a moment Christian, humble, with 'Thy will be done'. Then shock, combustion, the emergence of one of these: death or life: and then return to the old rigmarole. I imagine that this, while it may or may not knock about your body, will make very little difference to you otherwise . . .

To Arthur Watts   16 June 1915
                                                      [France]

. . . So one lives in a year ago – and a year hence. What are your feet doing a year hence? (For that feeling of stoniness, 'too-old-at-fortyness', and late afternoon of which you speak, is only you among strangers, you in Babylon: you were forty when I first saw you: thirty, donnish, and well-mannered when you first asked me to tea: but later, at tennis, you were any age: you will be always forty to strangers perhaps: and youthen as you get to know them, be they knowable. And after all, friends are the same age.) All this in a bracket: but where, while riding in your Kentish lanes, are you riding twelve months hence? I am sometimes in Mexico, selling cloth: or in Russia, doing Lord knows what: in Serbia or the Balkans: in England, never. England remains the dream, the background: at once the memory and the ideal. Sorley is the Gaelic for wanderer. I have had a conventional education: Oxford would have corked it. But this has freed the spirit, glory be. Give me *The Odyssey*, and I return the New Testament to store. Physically as well as spiritually, give me the road.

Only sometimes the horrible questions of bread and butter shadows the dream: it has shadowed many, I should think. It must be tackled. But I always seek to avoid the awkward, by postponing it . . .

To Mrs Sorley   10 July 1915
                                                      [France]

. . . All patrols – English and German – are much averse to the death and glory principle; so, on running up against one another in the long wet rustling clover, both pretend that they are Levites and the other is a Good Samaritan – and pass by on the other side, no word spoken. For either side to bomb the other

30

would be a useless violation of the unwritten laws that govern the relations of combatants permanently within a hundred yards of distance of each other, who have found out that to provide discomfort for the other is but a roundabout way of providing it for themselves: until they have their heads banged forcibly together by the red-capped powers behind them, whom neither attempts to understand. Meanwhile weather is 'no bon': food, 'plenty bon': temper, fair: sleep, jamais.

Such is 'attrition', that last resort of paralysed strategy of which we hear so much.

I hate the growing tendency to think that every man drops overboard his individuality between Folkestone and Boulogne, and becomes on landing either 'Tommy' with a character like a nice big fighting pet bear and an incurable yearning and whining for mouth-organs and cheap cigarettes: or the Young Officer with a face like a hero and a silly habit of giggling in the face of death. The kind of man who writes leading articles in the *Morning Post*, and fills the sadly huge gaps in his arguments by stating that the men at the front either all want conscription or think that Haldane should be hanged, is one step worse than [the people] who think that our letters concern our profession and not our interests. 'I hate a fool' . . .

To Arthur Watts   26 August 1915
                                                   [France]

. . . Health – and I don't know what ill-health is – invites you so much to smooth and shallow ways: where a happiness may only be found by renouncing the other happiness of which one set out in search. Yet here there is enough to stay the bubbling surface stream. Looking into the future one sees a holocaust somewhere: and at present there is – thank God – enough of 'experience' to keep the wits edged (a callous way of putting it, perhaps). But out in front at night in that no man's land and long graveyard there is a freedom and a spur. Rustling of the grasses and grave tap-tapping of distant workers: the tension and silence of en-counter, when one struggles in the dark for moral victory over the enemy patrol: the wail of the exploded bomb and the animal cries of wounded men. Then death and the horrible thankfulness when one sees that the next man is dead: 'We won't have to *carry* him in under fire, thank God; dragging will do': hauling in of the great resistless body in the dark, the smashed head rattling:

the relief, the relief that the thing has ceased to groan: that the bullet or bomb that made the man an animal has now made the animal a corpse. One is hardened by now: purged of all false pity: perhaps more selfish than before. The spiritual and the animal get so much more sharply divided in hours of encounter, taking possession of the body by swift turns.

And now I have 200 letters to censor before the post goes ... You'll write again, won't you, as soon as the mood comes – after tea? And good health to you.

1. Strained.
2. *Faust*, II, 6820–23.

COLETTE

Sidonie-Gabrielle Colette (1873–1954). Perhaps best known for the *Claudine* series of novels. She was in St Malo at the outbreak of war, which she describes in the passage below. Her husband was immediately mobilized and she followed him to Verdun after helping to organize a hospital in St Malo. Her reports for the *Matin* were collected in *Les Heures Longues* and she built up an impressive reputation for her writing from the war. The war also features in her letters and later novels.

Source: Colette, *Les Heures Longues*, Paris, Arthème Fayard, 1917. (This passage is translated by Herma Briffault; it appears in Colette, *Earthly Paradise*, ed. Robert Phelps, London, Martin Secker & Warburg, 1966; Penguin Books, 1974.)

Saint-Malo, August 1914

The war? Until the end of last month, it was nothing but a word, enormous, stretching across the pages of the lethargic newspapers of summer. The war? Yes, perhaps, very far away, on the other side of the world, but not here ... How could anyone imagine that even the echo of a war could make its way through these rocky ramparts, forbiddingly wild, the wildness accentuating the quiet calm at the foot of the cliffs – the waves, the sparse dune grass, the sand embossed by the tiny claws of birds ...? This paradise was not made for war, but for our brief holidays, for our solitude. The reefs hidden beneath the sea are unfriendly to boats; the vigilant sparrowhawk has almost banished birds from these parts. Every day he climbs the sky and is slow to return to land; our field-glasses discovered him on high, wings widespread and pressing against the wind, and his beautiful glowing eye did not gaze down at the earth ...

Yet a war was on, there were signs of war. For instance, that Cancale fishwife who last month stopped gossiping with customers and no longer smiled but demanded her pay in silver and copper coins, refusing banknotes, and stood gazing out to sea as if expecting the arrival over that sea of a succession of days without bread or cider ...

The war had come, and it was the grocery boy on a bicycle who relayed the news, to the merry tinkle of the bell, that food was getting scarce and that certain things should be stocked: sugar, salad oil, and paraffin.

The war was a fact. In Saint-Malo, where we ran to hear the news, a bolt fell from the blue just as we arrived: reserves had been called up.

How can I ever forget that hour? Four o'clock on a beautiful summer day at the seaside, the sky misted over, the golden-yellow ramparts of the old town facing the sea, which near the shore was green but on the horizon was blue – the children in red bathing-suits leaving the beach for their teatime snack, and climbing the choked streets ... And in the centre of town, the uproar bursts forth all at once: alarm bell, drum, the shouts of the crowd, the crying of children ... There is a press of people around the town drummer, who reads aloud the edict: no one listens to him because they know what he is announcing. Women leave the groups at a run, stopping short as if struck, then running again with a look on their faces that seems to say they have gone beyond some invisible boundary and have plunged into another world. A few of the women burst into tears, then as suddenly stop weeping and stand, open-mouthed, to reflect. Some young lads grow pale and stare straight ahead like sleep-walkers. The car in which we are riding stops, wedged into the crowd, and the crowd congeals against the wheels. Some people climb up on it, the better to see and hear, then get down without even having noticed us, as if they had climbed a wall or a tree – in a few days, who will know whether this car is yours or mine? The details of that hour hurt me and are necessary, like the details of a dream that I would like both to leave and avidly to pursue.

A dream, a dream. More and more a dream, since the farther I go from town, the closer I come to the countryside, which is being swept by the startled wing of the tocsins. And these fields, these harvests, that drowsing sea are no more than a stage setting interposed between me and reality: the reality that is Paris, Paris where half of me lives, Paris which is perhaps blockaded now, Paris grey and suffocating beneath its August mist, full of shouts, fermenting with heat and fury, anguish and derring-do.

Will it be my longest evening of the war, the one I am spending here, waiting to leave, this evening when the dead

34

calm drops the image of the purple cliffs down into the sea? All night long the sea is quiet, without a wrinkle, without a breath of life, imperceptibly swaying all the umbrellas of the crystal-blue jellyfish open in a milky phosphorescence . . .

Paris: the wounded

Three o'clock . . . The beautiful glacial moon has left the sky, and two more hours will be needed to colour the windows blue. It is the darkest time, and the quietest, in the college hospital ward. Beneath the dimmed electric lights the eight wounded men have gone to sleep. They are asleep, but not silent. Sleep liberates the moans they proudly repress during the day. The pleurisy patient whimpers regularly, in a sweet voice like a woman's. The man with the shattered jaw and eye says, from time to time, 'Oh!' with an accent of dismay and disgust. A thin, fair-haired young man whose leg was amputated four days ago sprawls on his back, arms widespread, and his sleep seems to have renounced all signs of life. A bearded man with an arm in a plaster cast tries to find, sighing, the place in bed where he will suffer less. Is that a death rattle from that other man with the bandaged throat? No, he's snoring, half suffocated . . .

Since last night, they have only sampled crumbs of rest in the intervals of fever, thirst, lancing pain. One after another they have implored a glass of herb tea, hot grog or hot milk, a hypodermic, especially the hypodermic . . . And now there they are, these brave lads, vanquished by the long night. Miserable as they are, will they ever awake?

Yes, they will! When the sparrows cheep on the frozen white lawn, the eight wounded men will also salute the red dawn with a sharper cry, a deeper sigh, a muffled oath in which life and laughter reappear. They are the scions of a stout race, which resuscitates and bounds up with the light. Sitting in his bed and smelling the aroma of coffee, the poor monster with the shattered, scarlet head will give me a wink with his single eye and will speak to me from his half mouth, banteringly:

'Admit it, I certainly have what could be called a ruddy mug!'

And he will demand his double ration of breakfast, alleging that liquid nourishment doesn't stick to the ribs.

Raising his heavy arm in plaster, the man in the next bed, a true Gaul whose humour is broad, will rejoice in Rabelaisian style, and the young fellow with the amputated leg, cadaverous, preoccupied with his stump, with the blond beard that is darkening his cheeks, with his future, poor handsome boy, will once more interrogate me.

'I say, tell me ... Tell me how he was amputated, your father? Higher up than I am, wasn't it? And he could walk, couldn't he? And, I say, did he run? ... Like a rabbit, you say? And it's true he found a girl who would marry him, all the same? Yes? A pretty girl? Is that so? What was she like, his wife? Tell me about her, will you?'

'How's The Head?'
'The Head is none the worse.'

He is sitting on his bed, in one corner of the white room, and his eye follows us, bright and intelligent in the midst of the crisscrossed bandages, the miles and miles of bandages ... He sighs hungrily at the passage of the odorous veal scallops and fried potatoes; his hearty countryman appetite despises the liquid nourishment which is the only nourishment his frightful wound will allow ...

When he came to, after a long blackout, he had his face in a puddle of water. He told himself: 'Well now, I'm not too badly hurt ...' Then he noticed quite a big morsel of his tongue, all his teeth, and various other fragments of himself floating in the puddle. And he told himself, 'Yes, I'm not badly hurt.' Slowly he got to his feet and began to suffer. Step after step he walked among the silent bodies and the groaning bodies, covering two kilometres, until he came to a village in ruins, where some of the inhabitants exclaimed in horror at the sight of him:

'Oh, poor fellow! In what a state ... But we can't give you first aid here, and our army is down there at X, twelve kilometres away!'

Mute, the wounded man walked the twelve kilometres. He could not say in how many hours. At X, he was led to the commanding officer, and he wrote on a piece of paper: 'Sir, will you be so kind as to lend me your revolver.' And he signed.

'Never! Not on your life!' the officer exclaimed. 'They'll fix you up, my boy, they'll cure you, you'll be amazed! Where do you come from?'

The reply was written.

'Why, that's twelve kilometres from here! How does it happen you didn't meet any ambulances? Didn't you meet any?'

'Yes, several,' wrote The Head.

'And they didn't see you?'

'Yes, sir,' The Head wrote calmly. 'But the ones they were picking up were so much worse off than I was, for I could still walk. And so *I didn't believe I ought to ask them to pick me up.*'

WALTER LIPPMANN

Walter Lippmann (1889–1974). Born into a comfortable New York City German–Jewish family. Educated at Harvard and went into political writing rather than active affairs. Widely respected for his unclassifiable independence of mind and judgement. His newspaper columns were widely syndicated. His blunt, clear prose indicates an intellectual reaction to the coming of war quite different from those found in Europe.

Source: Walter Lippmann, 'Force and Ideas', *New Republic*, New York, 7 November 1914.

FORCE AND IDEAS

Every sane person knows that it is a greater thing to build a city than to bombard it, to plough a field than to trample it, to serve mankind than to conquer it. And yet once the armies get loose, the terrific noise and shock of war make all that was valuable seem pale and dull and sentimental. Trenches and shrapnel, howitzers and forts, marching and charging and seizing – these seem real, these seem to be men's work. But subtle calculations in a laboratory, or the careful planning of streets and sanitation and schools, things which constitute the great peaceful adventure of democracy, seem to sink to so much whimpering futility.

Who cares to paint a picture now, or to write any poetry but war poetry, or to search the meaning of language, or speculate about the constitution of matter? It seems like fiddling when Rome burns. Or to edit a magazine – to cover paper with ink, to care about hopes that have gone stale, to launch phrases that are lost in the uproar? What is the good now of thinking? What is a critic compared to a battalion of infantry? This, men say, is a time for action, any kind of action. So, without a murmur, the laboratories of Europe are commandeered as hospitals, a thousand half-finished experiments abandoned. There was more for the future of the world in those experiments than we dare to calculate. They are tossed aside. The best scholarship has turned press agent to the General Staff. The hope of labor is absorbed, the great plans built on the surplus of wealth are dropped, for the armies have to be financed. Merely to exist has become a problem, to live finely seems to many a derelict hope.

Yet the fact remains that the final argument against cannon is ideas. The thoughts of men which seem so feeble are the only weapons they have against overwhelming force. It was a brain that conceived the gun, it was brains that organized the armies, it was the triumph of physics and chemistry that made possible the dreadnought. Men organized this superb destruction; they created this force, thought it, dreamed it, planned it. It has got beyond their control. It has got into the service of hidden forces they do not understand. Men can master it only by clarifying their own will to end it, and making a civilization so thoroughly under their control that no machine can turn traitor to it. For while it takes as much skill to make a sword as a ploughshare, it takes a critical understanding of human values to prefer the ploughshare.

That is why civilization seems dull and war romantic to unimaginative people. It requires a trained intelligence to realize that the building of the Panama Canal by the American army is perhaps the greatest victory an army ever won. Yet the victories of peace are less renowned than those of war. For every hundred people who can feel the horrors of the battlefield, how many are there who feel the horror of the slum? For every hundred people who admire the organization of war, how many are there who recognize the wasteful helter-skelter of peace?

It is no wonder, then, that war, once started, sweeps everything before it, that it seizes all loyalties and subjugates all intelligence. War is the one activity that men really plan for passionately on a national scale, the only organization which is thoroughly conceived. Men prepare themselves for campaigns they may never wage, but for peace, even when they meet the most acute social crisis, they will not prepare themselves. They set their armies on a hair-trigger of preparation. They leave their diplomacy archaic. They have their troops ready to put down labor disputes; they will not think out the problems of labor. They turn men into military automata, stamp upon every personal feeling for what they call the national defence; they are too timid to discipline business. They spend years learning to make war; they do not learn to govern themselves. They ask men to die for their country; they think it a stupid strain to give time to living for it.

Knowing this, we cannot abandon the labor of thought.

However crude and weak it may be, it is the only force that can pierce the agglomerated passion and wrong-headedness of this disaster. We have learnt a lesson. We know how insecurely we have been living, how grudging, poor, mean, careless has been what we call civilization. We have not known how to forestall the great calamity. We have not known enough, we have not been trained enough, ready enough, nor radical enough to make our will effective. We have taken the ideas that were thrust upon us, we have believed what we were told to believe. We have got into habits of thought when unnecessary things seemed inevitable, in panic and haste we stumbled into what we did not want.

We shall not do better in the future by more stumbling and more panic. If our thought has been ineffective we shall not save ourselves by not thinking at all, for there is only one way to break the vicious circle of action, and that is by subjecting it endlessly to the most ruthless criticism of which we are capable. It is not enough to hate war and waste, to launch one unanalyzed passion against another, to make the world a vast debating ground in which tremendous accusations are directed against the Kaiser and the financiers, the diplomatists and the gun manufacturers. The guilt is wider and deeper than that. It comes home finally to all those who live carelessly, too lazy to think, too preoccupied to care, afraid to move, afraid to change, eager for a false peace, unwilling to pay the daily costs of sanity.

We in America are not immune to what some people imagine to be the diseases of Europe. Nothing would be easier for us than to drift into an impossible situation, our life racked and torn within and without. We, too, have our place in the world. We have our obligations, our aggressions, our social chasms, our internal diseases. We are unready to deal with them. We are committed to responsibilities we do not understand, we are the victims of interests and deceptive ideas, and nothing but our own clarified effort can protect us from the consequences. We, too, can blunder into horror.

D. H. LAWRENCE

D. H. Lawrence (1885–1930). *Kangaroo* was mainly written in about six weeks in Australia during 1922. The chapter entitled 'The Nightmare' is partly based on Lawrence's experiences in England during the war. However, Richard Aldington notes in his Introduction to the novel 'In fact, he was never in any danger of conscription since he was so ill with consumption that he was instantly exempted; but the spiritual battle was to be fought, and he did not shrink.' (See also Lawrence's *Letters*.) While Richard Lovat Somers is visiting Australia, Nationalists and Communists try to persuade him to join their movements. Richard finally rejects them because he is reminded by both of the atmosphere of fear and suppression, 'mob-spirit', which he lived through during the war years in England. Somers recalls the war in the excerpts from 'The Nightmare' below.

Source: D. H. Lawrence, *Kangaroo*, London, Martin Secker, 1923; Penguin Books, 1950.

THE NIGHTMARE

But now the two began to be hated, hated far more than they knew.

'You want to be careful,' warned one of the Cornish friends. 'I've heard that the coast-watchers have got orders to keep very strict watch on you.'

'Let them, they'll see nothing.'

But it was not till afterwards that he learned that the watchers had lain behind the stone fence, to hear what he and Harriet talked about.

So, he was called up the first time and went. He was summoned to Penzance, and drove over with Harriet, expecting to return for the time at least. But he was ordered to proceed the same afternoon to Bodmin, along with sixteen or seventeen other fellows, farm hands and working men. He said goodbye to Harriet, who was to be driven back alone across the moors, to their lonely cottage on the other side.

'I shall be back tomorrow,' he said.

England was still England, and he was not finally afraid.

The train journey from Penzance to Bodmin with the other men: the fat, bragging other man: the tall man who felt as Somers did: the change at the roadside station, with the porters chaffing the men that the handcuffs were on them. Indeed, it was like being one of a gang of convicts. The great, prison-like barracks – the disgusting evening meal of which he could eat nothing – the little terrier-like sergeant of the regulars, who made them a little encouraging speech: not a bad chap. The lounging about that barracks yard, prisoners, till bed-time: the other men crowding to the canteen, himself mostly alone. The brief talks with men who were for a moment curious as to who and what he was. For a moment only. They were most of them miserable and bitter.

Gaol! It was like gaol. He thought of Oscar Wilde in prison. Night came, and the beds to be made.

'They're good beds, clean beds, you'll sleep quite comfortable in them,' said the elderly little sergeant with a white moustache. Nine o'clock lights out. Somers had brought no night clothes, nothing. He slept in his woollen pants, and was ashamed because they had patches on the knees, for he and Harriet were very poor these years. In the next bed was a youth, a queer fellow, in a sloppy suit of black broadcloth, and down-at-heel boots. He had a degenerate sort of handsomeness too. He had never spoken a word. His face was long and rather fine, but like an Apache, his straight black hair came in a lock over his forehead. And there was an Apache sort of sheepishness, stupidity, in everything he did. He was a long time getting undressed. Then there he stood, and his white cotton day-shirt was long below his knees, like a woman's nightgown. A restless, bitter night, with one man cough, cough, coughing, a hysterical cough, and others talking, making noises in their sleep. Bugle at six, and a scramble to wash themselves at the zinc trough in the wash house. Somers could not crowd in, did not get in till towards the end. Then he had to borrow soap, and afterwards a piece of comb. The men were all quiet and entirely inoffensive, common, but gentle, by nature decent. A sickening breakfast, then wash up and sweep the floors. Somers took one of the heavy brooms, as ordered, and began. He swept his own floors nearly every day. But this was heavier work. The sergeant stopped him. 'Don't you do that. You go and help to wipe the pots, if you like. Here, you boy, *you* – take that sweeping brush.'

And Somers relinquished his broom to a bigger man.

They were kindly, and, in the essential sense, gentlemen, the little terrier of a sergeant too. Englishmen, his own people.

When it came to Somers's turn to be examined, and he took off his clothes and sat in his shirt in the cold lobby: the fat fellow pointed to his thin, delicate legs with a jeer. But Somers looked at him, and he was quiet again. The queer, soft, pale-bodied fellow, against Somer's thin delicate whiteness. The little sergeant kept saying:

'Don't you catch cold, you chaps.'

In the warm room behind a screen, Richard took off his shirt and was examined. The doctor asked him where he lived – where was his home – asked as a gentleman asks, treated him with that gentle consideration Somers usually met with, save from business people or official people.

'We shall reject you, leave you free,' said the doctor, after consulting with the more elderly, officious little man, 'but we leave it to you to do what you can for your country' . . .

———

. . . And so this morning the voice struck into his consciousness. 'It is the end of England.' So he walked along blindly, up the valley and on the moors. He loved the country intensely. It seemed to answer him. But his consciousness was all confused. In his mind, he did not at all see why it should be the end of England. Mr Asquith was called Old Wait-and-See. And truly, English Liberalism had proved a slobbery affair, all sad sympathy with everybody, and no iron backbone, these years. Repulsively humble, too, on its own account. It was no time for Christian humility. And yet, it was true to its great creed.

Whereas Lloyd George! Somers knew nothing about Lloyd George. A little Welsh lawyer, not an Englishman at all. He had no real significance in Richard Lovat's soul. Only, Somers gradually came to believe that all Jews, and all Celts, even whilst they espoused the cause of England, subtly lived to bring about the last humiliation of the great old England. They could never do so if England *would not be* humiliated. But with an England fairly offering herself to ignominy, where was the help? Let the Celts work out their subtlety. If England *wanted* to be betrayed, in the deeper issues. Perhaps Jesus wanted to be betrayed. He did. He chose Judas.

Well, the story could have no other ending.

43

The war-wave had broken right over England, now: right over Cornwall. Probably throughout the ages Cornwall had not been finally swept, submerged by any English spirit. Now it happened – the accursed later war spirit. Now the tales began to go round full-tilt against Somers. A chimney of his house was tarred to keep out the damp: that was a signal to the Germans. He and his wife carried food to supply German submarines. They had secret stores of petrol in the cliff. They were watched and listened to, spied on, by men lying behind the low stone fences. It is a job the Cornish loved. They didn't even mind being caught at it: lying behind a fence with field-glasses, watching through a hole in the drystone wall a man with a lass, on the edge of the moors. Perhaps they were proud of it. If a man wanted to hear what was said about him – or anything – he lay behind a wall at the field-corners, where the youths talked before they parted and went indoors, late of a Saturday night. A whole intense life of spying going on all the time.

Harriet could not hang out a towel on a bush, or carry out the slops, in the empty landscape of moors and sea, without her every movement being followed by invisible eyes. And at evening, when the doors were shut, valiant men lay under the windows to listen to the conversation in the cosy little room. And bitter enough were the things they said: and damnatory, the two Somers. Richard did not hold himself in. And he talked too with the men on the farm: openly. For they had exactly the same anti-military feeling as himself, and they simply loathed the thought of being compelled to serve. Most men in the west, Somers thought, would have committed murder to escape, if murder would have helped them. It wouldn't. He loved the people at the farm, and the men kindled their rage together. And again Somers's farmer friend warned him, how he was being watched. But Somers *would* not heed. 'What can they do to me!' he said. 'I am not a spy in any way whatsoever. There is nothing they can do to me. I make no public appearance at all. I am just by myself. What can they do to me? Let them go to hell.'

He refused to be watchful, guarded, furtive, like the people around, saying double things as occasion arose, and hiding their secret thoughts and secret malignancy. He still believed in the freedom of the individual. – Yes, freedom of the individual! . . .

HELEN THOMAS

Helen Thomas (1877–1967). Two of the principal national
biographies have no entry for Helen Thomas, née Noble. Her
account of her husband's departure to the war is one of the most
moving personal documents to emerge from the war. *As It Was*
was published in 1926, and *World without End* in 1931. The
excerpts below are taken from the latter. Myfanwy Thomas
gave a key to the names used, in her edition of 1972: 'David' –
Edward Thomas (1878–1917); 'Jenny' – Helen Thomas; 'Philip'
– their son, Philip (1900–1965).

Source: Helen Thomas, *World without End*, London, William
Heinemann, 1931.

But now indeed things were bad for us, and after our friends
sailed back to America taking Philip with them for a year,
David became torn in his mind as to what he ought to do. There
was hardly any literary work to be had, and we were hard put to
it to keep going. He got one or two commissions for special
articles having an indirect war interest, but naturally the papers
did not want his reflective and critical essays, and reviewing had
almost ceased. Besides the anxiety of providing for us all, there
was the deep conviction that he ought to enlist. He hated the
newspaper patriotism. He saw through the lies and deception of
the press as he had always seen through untruths. He was not
even carried away by the abnormal condition of the national
emotion. Indeed his attitude to the war was inexplicable to his
father who was roused to fury by what he thought was his son's
disloyalty when David suggested that the Germans were as
brave as the English, and that 'cold steel' would bring fear to the
hearts of any man, be he German or English. The old antagonism
broke out again and was never healed.

One day when he was in London ostensibly looking for work,
he sent me a telegram telling me he had enlisted in the Artists'
Rifles. I had known that the struggle going on in his spirit would
end like this, and I had tried to prepare myself for it. But when
that telegram came I felt suddenly faint and despairing. 'No, no,
no,' was all I could say; 'not that.' But I knew it had to be and

that it was right. He was – so the telegram said – to come home in a few days a soldier.

During our life there had been many bitter partings and many joyous homecomings. The bitterness of the partings has faded from my consciousness; I know it was so, but I forget how and why. But the memory of the joy and hope and happiness of the reunions has stayed with me, and for ever, so it seems to me, part of me will stand at the gate and listen for his step, watch for his long stride; feel the strong embrace of his arms, and his kiss . . .

. . . The platform was crowded, the town band was there, with the town officials. It seemed right and natural to me that there should be all this fuss, and it accorded with my own joyous excitement, but I stood away from the crowd at the end of the platform. The crowd could have their hero, but I wanted my soldier all to myself. The train came in.

I did not see the official welcome of the V C, for David got out just where I stood. I noticed with a shock that his hair was cut very short, and that the thinness of his face was accentuated, but that he looked trim and soldierly in his uniform.

As he stooped to kiss me I smelt for the first time that queer sour smell of khaki, so different from David's usual smell of peaty Harris tweed and tobacco. What a difference the clothes made! The stiffness and tightness too were so strange after his easy loose things. I could not now walk with my hand in his pocket and his hand over mine.

I looked up at his face as we walked along, and in a flash I saw the sensitiveness, the suffering, the strength and the sincerity which had determined for him the rightness of this step. I was proud of him, and my heart silently responded to the cheers with which the crowd welcomed their hero. I passed again the woman who had spoken to me. 'You be luckier than us,' she said, 'with a V C all of your own.' David saluted her, and I nodded in acknowledgement of the truth of what she said . . .

. . . The school as a whole stood for pacifism, and though the roll of honour in the school hall lengthened each day as old boys fell, the spirit of the place was anti-war. Young athletic men in sweaters and shorts carried on the great work of coeducation, and at the village debating society tried to hold their own against the onslaughts of the more instinctive villagers and

46

landed proprietors. I could hardly believe in the sincerity of the men who said they would not fight for anything, and if they were sincere I thought them even more contemptible. When I told a leading member of the staff that David had enlisted, he said disapprovingly, 'That's the last thing I should have expected him to do.' How I hated him for that remark, and hated more the schoolmaster smugness from which it came. So by degrees I became antagonistic towards the school people and all they stood for. I felt stifled – especially at that agonizing time – by the self-confident righteousness, by the principles which proved so irresistible to hypocrisy, by the theories which remained in the head and never reached the heart. A meeting was called at the school at which it was decided that, as the men of the village were all at the war, the cottagers' gardens should be dug and planted by pacifist members of the staff, 'for we realize', they said to the women who composed the audience, 'how much you depend on your gardens, and that the soil is too heavy for you to tackle'. The women clapped for the vote of thanks, but were not much impressed with the magnanimity of this offer, because being wiser than their betters they knew that if they did not dig their gardens themselves no one else would. And so indeed it turned out.

———

David had been in the army a year. He hated it all – the stupidity, the injustice, the red tape, and the conditions of camp life. But he worked hard to perfect himself in the job he had undertaken to become a proficient soldier, and it was with real pride that he brought home his first stripe for me to sew on his sleeve. He practised the Guards' smart salute, and was meticulously careful that his uniform was in order, with the buttons and buckles polished, and puttees wound in regulation style.

The map reading and the work with the prismatic compass he enjoyed; he also got a certain satisfaction from the route marches in Essex – a county he had not known before, which he found interesting and beautiful. His own inner life was submerged under these strange and difficult conditions, only coming to the surface in the odd moments when he could be alone, when he found infinite comfort and satisfaction in expressing himself in his poems. He offered some of these poems to various editors, but no one had any room for such quiet meditative verse, in which the profound love and knowledge of his country were too subtle in their patriotism for the nation's mood. This failure was a great disappointment to him, and it was difficult for him in the face of it and with his lack of self-confidence to believe the appreciative criticism he obtained from his friends . . .

. . . But his old periods of dark agony had gone for ever. The sensitive introspective quality of his nature remained, but the black despair had given way to calm acceptance. He was not resigned to the army life: he hated it, and saw clearly and without any illusion its cruelty, its madness, its inhuman mechanism, its cold cynicism; but having undertaken the job there was nothing that he shirked, and to the end his only fear was of being afraid . . .

———

. . . When David wrote to me that early in the new year he would be going to France, the fear and the icy chill took a closer grip, and the sense of statically existing – not living – grew more intense. Yet on the surface all was as usual – the housework done, the children played with, happy hours spent wooding in the snow-covered forest. My daily letters to David were written, and only then as I wrote to him did the chill melt away; thought and feeling returned, and words in which to utter them ran as swiftly ever from my pen . . .

. . . He wrote that his last leave was imminent, but would not include Christmas, which was now a few weeks distant. We each knew what we felt about this, and neither of us said a word. We had always made so much of festivals, but that we should not be together for this Christmas was all a part of that stoppage of living.

I remember the day this double news came. The children had been invited to a party at the house of a poet – a very dear friend. I had made Polly a pretty dress of some cheap but unusual material, and at the party several of the mothers came up to me and praised the child and the frock. But the sentence 'And Jenny, I can't get home for Christmas' thumped out a sort of tune in my head, and though with my ears I heard 'How lovely your baby looks,' 'How cleverly you have made the frock,' I listened with all my being to 'And Jenny, I can't get home for Christmas.' Our friends too were affected by the news, and during the gaiety of the party we comforted each other with unexpressed but none the less understood sympathy.

'Christmas must be prepared for, however,' I thought, and I became busy with cakes and puddings and what I could afford of Christmas fare, which was little enough. The children with me planned the box I should pack for David, with something of everything, including crackers and sweets, and they began to make their presents for him. Into these preparations which before had always gone with such happy zest the same feeling of unreality entered and my eagerness was assumed for the sake of the children. But they too found it difficult to anticipate with a joy Christmas so strange, and the activities fell flat. Outside circumstances mattered as never before – our poverty, the severity of the weather, the dreariness of the house – and over us all an indefinable shadow fell.

But a miracle happened. Suddenly this Christmas of all Christmasses became the most joyous; the snow-bound forest sparkled like Aladdin's Cave; the house was transformed into a festive bower of holly and ivy and fir boughs, and our listlessness was changed into animated happiness and excitement.

David after all *was* coming home for Christmas! . . .

———

. . . How we worked that day to get all ready! I snatched a couple of hours to go to London and do the shopping. I bought for David the best Jaeger sleeping-bag and thick gauntlet gloves and a volume of Shakespeare's sonnets, and for the children a real magic lantern with moving slides, and a special present for each one. I brought fruit and sweets and luxuries we had never tasted before, and wine as well. A frock of David's favourite red was my present to myself, and secretly for the baby the children and I dug a little Christmas tree out of the garden and loaded it with toys and trinkets, and candles ready to light.

Life was not paralysed now, but with new-found vigour sped along eager and joyous. Nor did time stand still. I was up half the night arranging the greenery that the children had ransacked the forest for during the day, and the finishing touches to all that was to make this Christmas of all Christmasses shine above its peers . . .

———

. . . The last two days of David's leave had come. Two days and two nights more we were to be together, and I prayed in my heart, 'Oh, let the snow melt and the sky be blue again!' so that the dread which was spoiling these precious hours would lift.

The first days had been busy with friends coming to say goodbye, all bringing presents for David to take out to the front – warm lined gloves, a fountain pen, a box of favourite sweets, books.

This was not a time when words of affection were bearable; so they heaped things that they thought he might need or would like. Everyone who came was full of fun and joking about his being an officer after having had, as it were, to go to school again and learn mathematics, which were so uncongenial to him, but which he had stuck to and mastered with that strange pertinacity that had made him stick to all sorts of unlikely and uncongenial things in his life. They joked about his short hair, and the little moustache he had grown, and about the way he had perfected the Guards' salute. We got large jugs of beer from the inn near by to drink his health in, and an end to the war. The hateful cottage became homely and comfortable under the influence of these friends, all so kind and cheerful.

Then in the evenings, when just outside the door the silence of the forest was like a pall covering too heavily the myriads of birds and little beasts that the frost had killed, we would sit by the fire with the children and read aloud to them, and they would sing songs that they had known since their babyhood, and David sang new ones he had learnt in the army – jolly songs with good choruses in which I, too, joined as I busied about getting the supper. Then, when the baby had gone to bed, Elizabeth would sit on his lap, content just to be there, while he and Philip worked out problems or studied maps. It was lovely to see those two so united over this common interest.

But he and I were separated by our dread, and we could not look each other in the eyes, nor dared we be left alone together . . .

———

. . . I sit and stare stupidly at his luggage by the wall, and his roll of bedding, kit-bag, and suitcase. He takes out his prismatic compass and explains it to me, but I cannot see, and when a tear drops on to it he just shuts it up and puts it away. Then he says, as he takes a book out of his pocket, 'You see, your Shakespeare's *Sonnets* is already where it will always be. Shall I read you some?' He reads one or two to me. His face is grey and his mouth trembles, but his voice is quiet and steady. And soon I slip to the floor and sit between his knees, and while he reads his hand falls over my shoulder and I hold it with mine.

'Shall I undress you by this lovely fire and carry you upstairs in my khaki overcoat?' So he undoes my things, and I slip out of them; then he takes the pins out of my hair, and we laugh at ourselves for behaving as we so often do, like young lovers. 'We have never become a proper Darby and Joan, have we?'

'I'll read to you till the fire burns low, and then we'll go to bed.' Holding the book in one hand, and bending over me to get the light of the fire on the book, he puts his other hand over my breast, and I cover his hand with mine, and he reads from *Antony and Cleopatra*. He cannot see my face, nor I his, but his low, tender voice trembles as he speaks the words so full for us of poignant meaning. That tremor is my undoing. 'Don't read any more. I can't bear it.' All my strength gives way. I hide my face on his knee, and all my tears so long kept back come convulsively. He raises my head and wipes my eyes and kisses them, and wrapping his greatcoat round me carries me to our bed in the great, bare ice-cold room. Soon he is with me, and we lie speechless and trembling in each other's arms. I cannot stop crying. My body is torn with terrible sobs. I am engulfed in this despair like a drowning man by the sea. My mind is incapable of thought. Only now and again, as they say drowning people do, I have visions of things that have been – the room where my son was born; a day, years after, when we were together walking before breakfast by a stream with hands full of bluebells; and in the kitchen of our honeymoon cottage, and I happy in his pride of me. David did not speak except now and then to say some tender word or name, and hold me tight to him. 'I've always been able to warm you, haven't I?' 'Yes, your lovely body never feels cold as mine does. How is it that I am so cold when my heart is so full of passion?' 'You must have Elizabeth to sleep with you while I am away. But you must not make my heart cold with your sadness, but keep it warm, for no one else but you has ever found my heart, and for you it was a poor thing after all.' 'No, no, no, your heart's love is all my life. I was nothing before you came, and would be nothing without your love.'

So we lay, all night, sometimes talking of our love and all that had been, and of the children, and what had been amiss and what right. We knew the best was that there had never been untruth between us. We knew all of each other, and it was right. So talking and crying and loving in each other's arms we fell asleep as the cold reflected light of the snow crept through the frost-covered windows.

David got up and made the fire and brought me some tea, and then got back into bed, and the children clambered in, too, and we sat in a row sipping our tea. I was not afraid of crying any more. My tears had been shed, my heart was empty, stricken with something that tears would not express or comfort. The gulf had been bridged. Each bore the other's suffering. We concealed nothing, for all was known between us. After breakfast, while he showed me where his account books were and what each was for, I listened calmly, and unbelievingly he kissed me when I said I, too, would keep accounts. 'And here are my poems. I've copied them all out in this book for you, and the last of all is for you. I wrote it last night, but don't read it now ... It's still freezing. The ground is like iron, and more snow has fallen. The children will come to the station with me; and now I must be off.'

We were alone in my room. He took me in his arms, holding me tightly to him, his face white, his eyes full of a fear I had never seen before. My arms were round his neck. 'Beloved, I love you,' was all I could say. 'Jenny, Jenny, Jenny,' he said, 'remember that, whatever happens, all is well between us for ever and ever.' And hand in hand we went downstairs and out to the children, who were playing in the snow.

A thick mist hung everywhere, and there was no sound except, far away in the valley, a train shunting. I stood at the gate watching him go; he turned back to wave until the mist and the hill hid him. I heard his old call coming up to me: 'Coo-ee!' he called. 'Coo-ee!' I answered, keeping my voice strong to call again. Again through the muffled air came his 'Coo-ee'. And again went my answer like an echo. 'Coo-ee' came fainter next time with the hill between us, but my 'Coo-ee' went out of my lungs strong to pierce to him as he strode away from me. 'Coo-ee!' So faint now, it might be only my own call flung back from the thick air and muffling snow. I put my hands up to my mouth to make a trumpet, but no sound came. Panic seized me, and I ran through the mist and the snow to the top of the hill, and stood there a moment dumbly, with straining eyes and ears.

There was nothing but the mist and the snow and the silence of death.

Then with leaden feet which stumbled in a sudden darkness that overwhelmed me I groped my way back to the empty house.

EDWARD THOMAS

Edward Thomas (1878–1917). Born of Welsh parents, in London. He was educated at St Paul's School and Oxford. He married Helen Thomas (*q.v.*) and before the war worked (often miserably) as a freelance writer. All his poetry, now highly regarded in England, was written during the war. He enlisted and served in the Artillery. He was killed in France at the battle of Arras, April 1917. His 'War Diary' was first published in the *Anglo-Welsh Review* (Autumn 1971) where it was introduced by one of Thomas's editors, R. George Thomas. There are several editions of Thomas's poetry, the most recent being that edited by R. George Thomas (1978). A fine appreciation of his poetry appears in F. R. Leavis's *New Bearings in English Poetry* (1932), an excerpt from which is included in this volume.

Source: Edward Thomas, 'War Diary', *Anglo-Welsh Review*, Autumn 1971.

January 1917

29. Up at 5. Very cold. Off at 6.30, men marching in frosty dark to station singing 'Pack up your troubles in your old kitbag'. The rotten song in the still dark brought one tear. No food or tea – freezing carriage. Southampton at 9.30, and there had to wait till dusk, walking up and down, watching ice-scattered water, gulls and dark wood beyond, or London Scottish playing improvised Rugger, or men dancing to concertina, in a great shed between railway and water. Smith and I got off for lunch after Horton and Capt. Lushington returned from theirs. Letter to Helen from 'South Western Hotel', where sea-captains were talking of the 'Black Adder' and of 'The Black Ball Line' that used to go to Australia. Hung about till dark – the seagulls as light failed nearly all floated instead of flying – then sailed at 7. Thorburn turned up. Now I'm in 2nd officer's cabin with Capt. and Horton, the men outside laughing and joking and saying fucking. Q.W.R.'s and Scottish and a Field Battery and 236 S.B., also on 'The Mona Queen'. Remember the entirely serious and decorous writing on urinal whitewash – name, address, unit, and date of sailing. A tumbling crossing but rested.

30. Arrived Havre 4 a.m. Light of stars and windows of tall pale houses and electric arcs on quay. March through bales of cotton in sun to camp. The snow first emptying its castor of finest white. Tents Mess full of subalterns censoring letters. Breakfast at 9.45 a.m. on arrival. Afternoon in Havre, which Thorburn likes because it is French. Mess unendurably hot and stuffy, tent unendurably cold till I got into my blankets. Slept well in fug. Snow at night.

31. Had to shift our lines in snow. 12 to a tent with 2 blankets each. Ankles bad. Nearly all water frozen in taps and basins. Mess crowded – some standing. Censoring letters about the crossing and the children and ailments etc. at home. Had to make a speech explaining that men need not be shy about writing familiar letters home. At 'Nouvel Hotel', Havre, while we had tea, waitress kissing a Capt. – and arranging for another visit. 4f. for 2 teas. Battery had to be specially warned against venereal in Havre. Read Sonnets in evening: to bed at 9 to escape hot stuffy room. Officers coming and going. Some faces you just see, remembering once and never again. More fine snow like sago.

February 1917

8. Weather as before. Physical drill, a hasty Welsh Rabbit with honey, and then off in lorries through Alaincourt, Barly, Fosseux, to Berneville – men billet in huge barn of a big uneven farmyard surrounded by spread arched stone barns and buildings with old pump at one side, kitchen at upper end. We forage. Enemy plane like pale moth beautiful among shrapnel bursts. A fine ride over high open snowy country with some woods. Rigging up table in mess and borrowing crockery. The battery is to split for the present: Rubin has taken guns to Saulty. We are for Dainville. A scramble dinner of half cold stuff, mostly standing. Taylor makes a table and says 'Very good, Sir' and 'It's the same for all. You gentlemen have to put up with the same as us'. Bed early. Rubin returns late. Heavy firing at night. Restless.

16th to do fire control on aeroplane shoot (only 10 rounds, observation being bad). Dull day. Left Thorburn on guns at 11.30. Bad temper. Afternoon up to O.P., but too hazy to observe. A mad Captain with several men driving partridges over the open and whistling and crying 'Mark over'. Kestrels in pairs. Four or five planes hovering and wheeling as kestrels used to over Mutton and Ludcombe. Women hanging clothes to dry on barbed entanglement across the road. Rain at last at 4.15. This morning the old Frenchman living in this ruin burst into our room while we were dressing to complain of our dirt and depredation, and when Rubin was rude in English, said he was a Frenchman and had been an officer. Nobody felt the slightest sympathy with his ravings, more than with the old white horse who works a mill walking up and up treadmill.

March 1917

4. Cold but bright clear and breezy. Nothing to do all morning but trace a map and its contours. Colonel and I went down to 244 before lunch to see the shell holes of last night and this morning. Hun planes over. More shells came in the afternoon. The fire is warm but the room cold. Tea with Lushington and Thorburn. Shelling at 5.30 – I don't like it. I wonder where I shall be hit as in bed I wonder if it is better to be on the window or outer side of room or on the chimney or inner side, whether better to be upstairs where you may fall or on the ground floor where you may be worse crushed. Birthday parcels from home.

7. A cold raw dull day with nothing to do except walk round to 244 to get a pair of socks. The wind made a noise in the house and trees and a dozen black crumpled sycamore leaves dance round and round on terrace. Wrote to Pearce and Irene. Rather cold and depressed and solitary.

11. Out at 8.30 to Ronville O.P. and studied the ground from Beaurains N. Larks singing over No Man's Land – trench mortars. We were bombarding their front line: they were shooting at Arras. R.F.A. officer with me who was quite concerned till he spotted a certain familiar Hun sentry in front line. A clear, cloudy day, mild and breezy. 8th shell carrying into Arras. Later Ronville heavily shelled and we retired to dugout. At 6.15 all quiet and heard blackbirds chinking. Scene peaceful, desolate like Dunwich moors except sprinkling of white chalk on the rough brown ground. Lines broken and linesmen out from 2.30 to 7 p.m. A little rain in the night; . . .

14. Ronville O.P. Looking out towards No Man's Land what I thought first was a piece of burnt paper or something turned out

to be a bat shaken at last by shells from one of the last sheds in Ronville. A dull cold morning, with some shelling of Arras and St. Sauveur and just 3 for us. Talking to Birt and Randall about Glostershire and Wiltshire, particularly Painswick and Marlborough. A still evening – blackbirds singing far off – a spatter of our machine guns – the spit of one enemy bullet – a little rain – no wind – only far-off artillery.

15. Huns strafe I-sector at 5.30. We reply and they retaliate on Arras and Ronville. Only tired 77s reach O.P. A sunny breezy morning. Tried to climb Arras chimney to observe, but funked. 4 shells nearly got me while I was going and coming. A rotten day. No letters for 5 days.

16. Larks and great tits. Ploughing field next to orchard in mist – horses and man go right up to crest in view of Hun at Beaurains. Cold and dull. Letters to Helen and Janet. In the battery for the day. Fired 100 rounds from 12–1.30. Sun shining but misty still. Letter from Bronwen. The first thrush I have heard in France sang as I returned to Mess at 6 p.m. Parcel from Mother – my old Artist boots. Wrote to Hodson. A horrible night of bombardment, and the only time I slept I dreamt I was at home and couldn't stay to tea . . .

17. . . . Then most glorious bright high clear morning. But even Horton, disturbed by 60-pounders behind his dugout, came in to breakfast saying: 'I am not going to stay in this — army; the day peace is declared I am out of it like a — rabbit'. A beautiful day, sunny with pale cloudless sky and W. wind, but cold in O.P. Clear nightfall with curled, cinereous cloud and then a cloudless night with pale stains in the sky over where Bosh is burning a village or something. Quiet till 3: then a Hun raid and our artillery over us to meet it: their shells into St. Sauveur, Ronville and Arras. Sound of fan in underground cave.

20th. Still deep mud all the way up and shelled as we started. Telegraph Hill as quiet as if only rabbits lived there. I took revolver and left this diary behind in case. For it is very exposed and only a few Cornwalls and MGC about. But Hun shelled chiefly over our heads into Beaurains all night – like starlings returning 20 or 30 a minute. Horrible flap of 5.9 a little along the trench. Rain and mud and I've to stay till I am relieved tomorrow. Had not brought warm clothes or enough food and had no shelter, nor had telephonists. Shelled all night. But the

M.G.C. boy gave me tea. I've no bed. I leant against wall of trench. I got up and looked over. I stamped up and down. I tried to see patrol out. Very light – the only sign of Hun on Telegraph Hill, though 2 appeared and were sniped at. A terribly long night and cold. Not relieved till 8. Telephonists out repairing line since 4 on the morning of the 21st.

23. Frosty clear. Ploughs going up over crest towards Beaurains. Rubin back from F.O.P. believes in God and tackles me about atheism – thinks marvellous escapes are ordained. But I say so are the marvellous escapes of certain telegraph posts, houses, etc. Sunny and cold – motored to Avesnes and Fosseux to buy luxuries and get letters. Crowded bad roads through beautiful hedgeless rolling chalk country with rows of trees, some along roads following curving ridges – villages on crests with church spires and trees. Troops, children holding hands, and dark skinned women, mud-walled ruined barns. Parcels from Mother and Helen, letters from Mother and J. Freeman.

27. Rain and sleet and sun, getting guns camouflaged, stealing a Decanville truck, laying out night lines. Letters from Hodson, Eleanor and Sgt. Pellissier. Still that aching below nape of my neck since my last O.P. day. Sat till 11 writing letters. As I was falling asleep great blasts shook the house and windows, whether from our own firing or enemy bursts near, I could not tell in my drowse, but I did not doubt my heart thumped so that if they had come closer together it might have stopped. Rubin and Smith dead tired after being up all the night before. Letters from Helen and Eleanor.

31. Up at 5 worn out and wretched. 5.9s flopping on Achicourt while I dressed. Up to Beaurains. There is a chalk-stone cellar with a dripping Bosh dugout far under and by the last layer of stones is the lilac bush, rather short. Nearby a graveyard for the 'tapferer franzos soldat' with crosses and Hun names. Blackbirds in the clear cold bright morning early in black Beaurains. Sparrows in the elder of the hedge I observe through – a cherry tree just this side of the hedge makes projection in trench with its roots. Beautiful clear evening everything dark and soft round Baiville Ulaise, after the rainbow there and the last shower. Night in lilac-bush cellar of stone like Berryfield. Letter to Helen. Machine gun bullets snaking along – hissing like little wormy serpents.

7. Up at 6 to O.P. A cold bright day of continuous shelling N. Vitasse and Telegraph Hill. Infantry all over the place in open preparing Prussian Way with boards for wounded. Hardly any shells into Beaurains. Larks, partridges, hedgesparrows, magpies by O.P. A great burst in red brick building in N. Vitasse stood up like a birch tree or a fountain. Back at 7.30 in peace. Then at 8.30 a continuous roar of artillery.

8. A bright warm Easter day but Achicourt shelled at 12.30 and then at 2.15 so that we all retired to cellar. I had to go over to battery at 3 for a practice barrage, skirting the danger zone, but we were twice interrupted. A 5.9 fell 2 yards from me as I stood by the f/C post. One burst down the back of the office and a piece of dust scratched my neck. No firing from 2–4. Rubin left for a course.

[On the last pages of diary are these notes:]

The light of the new moon and every star

And no more singing for the bird

ISABELLE RIMBAUD

Isabelle Rimbaud (1860–1917). Sister of the poet Arthur Rimbaud. She lived with her husband at Roche, near the Belgian border, in the path of the German invasion in August 1914. The first passages describe shutting up the family house and the last, 4 September, describes how they were caught by the invaders in Reims.

Source: Isabelle Rimbaud, *In the Whirlpool of War* (translated from *Dans les remous de la bataille*, Paris, Chapelot, 1917, by Archibald Williams), London, T. Fisher Unwin, 1918.

Wednesday, 26 August 1914

The people of Attigny are all in a flutter, standing in groups outside their houses, discussing things and deliberating what to do. I am astonished to see few or no soldiers in the square and streets, and am told that troops are stationed all round the town, which is in their care. A brave man who has won a reputation for his strong optimism comes up to me. He is pale and seems to have aged. I inquire anxiously after his health. 'I am unwell,' he replies; 'this bad news takes all the life out of me. Still, I keep hoping. Oh yes! we shall win right enough.'

I have a talk with the man who hires out cars. At first we arrange to depart on the following morning, without any luggage, just nightgear. The man then changes his mind, under pressure from another client, who no doubt offers better terms, and puts things off till Sunday.

On my return I tell my husband of the result of my journey, and he thinks that Sunday will be too late. 'But no doubt we are fated to suffer invasion,' he adds.

We now get busy on our preparations for the journey. I visit the deputy mayor to have the needful pass signed and stamped. Then I call Nelly.

'Are you still determined not to leave Roche?'

'I should be glad to leave, but how will my stepfather manage all by himself? There are cows to be milked and the harvest to finish; he wouldn't let me go.'

'I tell you again,' persists my husband, 'that the harvest will not be yours, and that you should think only of saving what you have already. Your stepfather doesn't understand the situation; and it would be a hard job to make him realize it. He should think first of getting your child into a safe place. You've got horses, a carriage, and a servant; why don't you have yourself driven to Reims, where, as you know, there is a lady who would gladly take you in and keep you with her while you see how things turn out?'

'I will look into it and speak to my stepfather.' But she will never dare to come to a decision, so I advise her further: 'If you stay and the Germans reach Roche, be careful; throw your house open to them and let them do what they like with it. Have as little to do with them as possible; don't laugh when talking to them; and see that your little girl, Hélène, doesn't try tricks or faces on them.'

A few days ago I recommended her to carry on her, in a bodice which she wears day and night, her bank-notes and gold – valuables which, in connivance with her stepfather, she had hidden with her jewels under a paving-stone in the stable.

'As for the jewels, they will be as safe in your cupboard as in the stable; leave the key in the cupboard to prevent the doors being broken open.'

Then follows the inevitable round of old treasures in the house. I have a ramble through the rooms and their contents. All of a sudden a host of objects of which I previously thought nothing become priceless in my eyes; yet I can't even think of taking anything large or heavy away with me. Most of these things are to me precious relics. Rather than they should run the risk of profanation, I am seized with the idea of collecting them and having an *auto-da-fé*; but I can't make up my mind to that – it would break my heart. So with the greatest possible care and with trembling hands I put the things back in place, saying farewell to them with eyes and lips, and becoming more and more sentimental as I look at the humblest of them, because of the events which they call to mind. In the double bottom of a chest I place my plate and some very precious papers. Everything else will stay in its usual place, and the keys will be left in doors and cupboards. Into the one small valise that I may take I cram a few knick-knacks which have a value for me alone: nothing on earth would make me part with *them*.

We collect the books scattered among the rooms and place them in the bookcases, and I put some on the deep shelf of an old cabinet. It is a pleasure – a sad pleasure, today – to run one's fingers over the bindings, peep into the volumes, smell the scent of the ink, and recall, as one takes each in hand, how it was acquired and what impressions were left by its perusal. So we must abandon all these books which were the delight and interest of our life! While I order the piles in the carved case I experience the feeling of protecting vainly the flower-decked grave of a child on a stormy day against the pitiless attacks of the furious elements.

Pierre is tired and goes to bed early. So as not to disturb him, I postpone till tomorrow the putting of clean sheets on the beds and clean covers on the dressing-tables. I shall lay a cloth and napkins on the big table in the dining-room, for French soldiers will certainly precede the German, and the first, our defenders and brothers, have a claim on everything we can provide . . .

Saturday, 29 August 1914

While I am making the last preparations for departure, outside, in the burning heat, I see a confused rushing to and fro of military material, amid which the tragic film of emigration unrolls itself without ceasing: people on foot, wagons and carts piled with heterogeneous articles on which are huddled old men and sick, sheltered by an awning stretched over poles made fast in the four corners of the vehicle. Cows, colts, calves are driven as best may be through the general confusion. The men are gloomy, all of them. Many of them have put on their best clothes, probably thinking that thus they will score off the enemy, and one has the sad and ridiculous spectacle of provincial and countrified women hobbling along on Louis XV heels, much damaged by walking, suffocating in small corsets and tight-fitting, rumpled, dirty skirts, wearing over their dejected faces hats trimmed with showy plumes, and displaying sunburnt throats through the scallop of their low-cut blouses. Police on foot, horseback, or cycle guide all these poor scared creatures like so much cattle and make them keep moving southwards; for if by any mischance the procession were to stop, the confusion would become hopeless. Among the fugitives we recognize some people from neighbouring villages. Their faces, but lately so jolly and kindly, now are drawn and pinched. We call to them: 'What, is it you? How are things going?' They turn their sad eyes to the sky and stammer words which are lost in the hubbub, while the police signal to them not to stop.

At noon there brushes past the half-closed shutters of the kitchen, in which I am busy, a procession the sight of which quite upsets me. In front walks a tall priest, his face dripping with sweat, leading by the bridle a horse drawing a cart in which are seated, each in an armchair, a man and a woman who seem to have reached the extreme limits of age and infirmity. Behind them comes a group of foot-passengers, among whom I recognize quite a number of people from Neuville and Day, villages lying four or five kilometres north of Roche. I go out to them. The curé of Neuville – it is he – explains to neighbours who have come up too that some French batteries have since morning been posted on the Neuville and Voncq heights, so he thought it his duty to remove his grandparents from among the dangers of the artillery engagement which seemed imminent. He is taking them southward, anywhither. He will not go farther today, but spend the night with his old relatives on a friendly farm at Roche. His parishioners, on the other hand, push on, and the human wave, kept to its course by the police, disappears in the distance. . .

The genuine peasant regards any one who doesn't work on the land as an idler. Yet these soldiers don't look lazy as they tramp along, pale-faced, worn out, covered with dust and sweat. There is not a single officer with them. Several are so exhausted that they sink down on the bank beside the road, declaring that they can't go a single step farther. Having nothing better, we carry them buckets of cold water, which they drain greedily. The non-coms., thoughtful men, advise them not to drink too much or they will do themselves harm. These are the survivors of a Breton regiment, now being taken ten kilometres behind the fighting line to get a short spell of rest. They may not stop in the village; those who are done up will be collected by the regimental vehicles. Where do they come from? What have they seen? We should greatly like to know, but they say nothing; perhaps they are under orders not to answer questions . . .

Five o'clock
The cannon's song is an effective lullaby. No longer harassed by the police, the emigrants fling themselves on the ground beside their packages, and make preparations for spending the night

there, without thought of eating, so great is the stupor of fatigue. The children, careless and bolder, roam through the village, and we give them what we have – alas, how little it is! – milk, soup, vegetables, fruit, the day's eggs.

Sunset
A thin, cold mist rises on the meadow . . .

Friday, 4 September 1914

My husband has gone ahead of us along the rue de Vesle. We catch him up. Ah! it would be difficult now to deny that the Prussians are in Reims. Their cars flash along the street in both directions at a giddy speed; splendid vehicles, in which happy-faced officers, whose triumphant look is quite indescribable, disport themselves. Some of them greet the crowd with forced and apparently ironical smiles; others blow kisses with their gloved hands to the young and pretty women seen at the windows. In each car, behind the officers, are four or six armed soldiers, standing or kneeling, facing the houses on both sides the street and ready to throw up their rifles. It looks as if the mayor's notice forbidding people to collect or stand about has been disregarded; for surely never did so many loafers line the street and exchange opinions . . . Now and then a municipal policeman tries to make people move on, but nobody heeds. I feel ashamed when I compare the stunted, stooping, puny men of Reims with the tall, straight, sturdy specimens of the German race now passing.

Our hostess knows every one here, and everybody knows her. She speaks to one, answers another, ventures on to the street in defiance of orders, keeps stopping. This gets on Pierre's nerves. 'I think,' says he, 'that we shouldn't stay here among all this crowd. It is unwise to do so. Let us go straight to the Royal Square, or go home again.' The words are hardly out of his mouth when a mighty explosion raises the echoes! Nobody takes any notice. We are abreast of St Jacques church when a second explosion occurs. That makes people turn round and ponder. 'There! they are celebrating their entry by blank fire.' But the haughty Prussian officers, who keep on passing, begin to frown and look astonished. We reach the theatre. A third explosion! This time loud cries are heard. Looking behind us, we see the lower end of the rue de Vesle filled with dust and smoke; the sunshine is dimmed by it. Everybody begins to run. From all sides people shout at us: 'They are bombarding us; take cover; get back home!' In the Royal Square the inquisitive people round the statue of Louis XV, who had climbed up on to the plinth, scatter in all directions, saying that the Germans have signalled them to get to cover. Mothers with babies rush off, uttering piercing cries; children sob and won't walk; men pommel and push the women riveted to the spot by fear. The streets are emptied in a twinkling, while the shells follow one another methodically and fall with a great uproar. We are much upset, my husband and I. As we don't know our way about Reims and cannot see any vehicle able to carry us, we instinctively take the first street to the right that we come to – the rue du Clôitre, which takes us to the apse of the Cathedral. Thence, by the rue Robert-de-Coucy, we head for the Parvis, hurrying along our friend, whose serenity seems as great as ever. 'Impossible, my dears,' she says; 'my heart trouble prevents me going fast. Go ahead without me.' We offer her our arms; but she refuses decidedly, pretending that it is too warm to hurry. We can't dream of leaving her, but how trying it is! I involuntarily quicken my pace and find myself a few yards ahead of the others. In the middle of the street, facing the gate of the Beau Dieu, two ecclesiastics in long cloaks, with still unmoved faces, have stopped and are coolly looking at the top of the north tower, partly hidden by a cloud of dust and screened by scaffolding, out of which fly a number of birds as large as pigeons. Strange objects, which at first I take to be bits of broken bottles, patter and jump on the pavement. I step forward to pick up one of these curious objects, and my hand has already been stretched out towards it when I realize its nature. It is death stalking about me. I feel afraid, and remain motionless, petrified, my eyes fixed mechanically on the sculptures of the lower part of the Cathedral, whose every detail now appears to me to stand out with extraordinary clearness. A short, haggard workman is dragging by the elbow a young woman who weeps and wraps her apron about a small child clasped in her arms. The man shouts at me: 'Get away! They're aiming at the Cathedral!'

My husband and Madame X catch me up. We want to retreat by the rue du Trésor. Somehow or other we have worked round in a circle, and a few moments later we find ourselves in the Parvis Square. The whining and bursting of the shells become worse, and we rush off through an adjacent street, which leads us to the colonnade of the theatre. We then feel that we are chasing our own tails, and we implore our hostess to take us home the shortest way possible. 'All right, my dears, that will be by the rue Libergier.' We go round the theatre and reach that street, a few yards from the Parvis Square. 'Look there!' cries our friend, stopping and gazing upwards. 'Look! A shell has fallen right on the Cathedral!' I can only see a cloud of dust or smoke, and the circling flight of the large birds; but the crash of shattered glass makes me shudder with fear. Madame X suggests entering the Café Saint-Denis close by.

While she stops to knock on the door of this establishment, whose shutters are closed, as were all the shops and house doors we passed, I set off running, or rather an invisible force seizes me by the arm and I am dragged from the rue Libergier and hurled into the rue Chanzy. A man hurrying past asks where I live; I tell him. He points the direction, and says something which the bursting of a shell prevents me from hearing. Madame X cries: 'Not that way! This way! This way!' I don't turn round. Pierre runs after me: 'Isabelle! Isabelle! where are you off to there?' Without stopping, I shout back to him over my shoulder: 'Quick! Quick!' No human argument would make me retrace my steps. The power which drags me forward dins into my ears: 'Hurry! Hurry! Don't give way. On with you.' I find myself in the rue Hincmar. My husband, following a long way behind, begs me not to go so fast, because of our friend. I answer fiercely and resolutely: 'Come! This is the way we should go!' Very fortunately Madame X has given up the rue Libergier and comes into sight eighty yards behind us. There is now not a living creature besides ourselves in the streets. Then begins for Pierre and me the most horrible torture.

ROGER MARTIN DU GARD

Roger Martin du Gard (1881–1958). His *roman-fleuve*, *Les Thibault*, was planned in 1920. In 1937, the year after *Summer 1914* appeared, Martin du Gard was awarded the Nobel Prize for Literature. In this passage from near the end of the novel Jacques Thibault is about to fly over the opposing armies scattering pacifist tracts. The plane crashes and Jacques is killed by a French policeman as a spy.

Source: Roger Martin du Gard, *The Thibaults* (*Summer 1914*) (translated from *L'Été 14*, Paris, Gallimard, 1936, by Stuart Gilbert), London, John Lane, 1940.

5–8 August [1914]

JACQUES'S SOJOURN AT BASEL

Sleep was impossible in the burning nights; every ten minutes he rose, dipped a towel in the water-jug and slaked his fevered limbs. Sometimes he lingered at his window, gazing out at what seemed like a glimpse of hell. Bathed in a livid sheen of arc-lamps, a horde of wraithlike forms scurried about the wharves, in an incessant din; further on, in the gloom of the coal-yards, drays and motor-lorries clattered to and fro, lights flashed out and sped in all directions. Still further on, again, along a glimmering network of rails, never-ending goods-trains shunted and whistled before plunging one after the other into the black night of Germany at war. Then he smiled. He alone *knew*. He alone knew that all this sound and fury was in vain. Deliverance was at hand. The pamphlet was finished. Kappel was going to make the German version of it, Plattner to print twelve hundred thousand copies. Meynestrel was making arrangements at Zurich for the plane. Only a few days more. 'Up tomorrow, all of you, with the first ray of dawn!'

After forty-eight hours' feverish work he felt the time had come to hand over his manuscript. 'Have everything ready for Saturday,' Meynestrel had told him.

He found Plattner at his shop, ensconced among bales of

paper, in the back-room; its double baize doors were closed, as were the windows, though the morning was well advanced. Plattner was an ugly, unhealthy-looking man in the forties; he had stomach-trouble and a bad breath. His thorax jutted out like a bird's breast, and his bald pate, scraggy neck and vast hook-nose brought to mind a vulture. The overhang of the enormous nose seemed to throw the whole body out of plumb, canting it forward, so that Plattner looked always on the point of falling headlong – which gave a feeling of discomfort to all who met him for the first time. But after the first shock caused by his grotesque appearance had worn off, no one could fail to be attracted by the frankness of his gaze, the geniality of his smile, and the gentleness of his rather sing-song voice, apt to wax emotional on any pretext and always vibrant with hearty affability. But Jacques had no need for new friends; from now on he stood alone.

Plattner was in low spirits. He had just received news that the Social Democrats in Germany had voted in favour of the War Levy.

'That the French socialists should have stood in with the Government when it came to a division was bad enough.' His voice shook with indignation. 'Still, after the murder of Jaurès, one rather expected something of the sort. But that the Germans, that our German Social Democrat Party, the greatest proletarian force in Europe, should behave like that – well, it's the hardest knock I've had in my whole career as a militant socialist. I'd refused to believe the government-inspired newspapers. I'd have laid any odds that the Social Democrats would grasp, to a man, this opportunity of inflicting a public rebuff on the Imperial Government. When I read the offical communiqués, I chuckled. "Tomorrow," I said to myself, "they'll have an eye-opener!" And then . . .! It's no good blinking the facts today. Those communiqués were true, damnably true. I haven't heard yet what went on behind the scenes. Likely as not we'll never know the truth. Rayer's story is that Behmann-Hollweg sent for Sudekum on the twenty-ninth to get him to arrange for the Social Democrat Party to withdraw its opposition.'

'The twenty-ninth!' Jacques exclaimed. 'But on the twenty-ninth at Brussels Haase made that speech . . . I heard him.'

'That's as may be. Anyhow Rayer asserts that when the German delegates got back to Berlin, a meeting of the central committee was called and they caved in all along the line. So the

Kaiser knew he could go ahead with mobilization, that there wouldn't be a rising or a general strike. I suspect the Party had a secret meeting before the Reichstag session – and a pretty stormy one it must have been! I still decline to lose faith in people like Liebknecht, Lederboer, Clara Zetkin and Rosa Luxemburg. Only, they must have been in a minority, they had to bow to the traitors. Still there's no getting behind it: they voted *with* the Government. Thirty years' hard work, thirty years of slow, painfully achieved progress – all wiped out! In one day Social Democracy has lost for ever the good opinion of the proletarian world. In the Duma, anyhow, the Russian socialists didn't kowtow to Tsarism. All of them voted against war. In Serbia, too. I've seen the copy of a letter from Duchan Popovitch; the socialist opposition in Serbia refuses to haul down its colours. Yet that's the one country where there would have been some excuse for taking a patriotic line, with the invader at their gates. Even in England socialism is putting up a stubborn fight; Keir Hardie won't let himself be beaten. I've read the latest declaration of the I L P. All that's encouraging, you can't deny. We mustn't lose heart. Little by little we'll get a hearing. They won't succeed in gagging all of us. Yes, our one hope is to stand firm, with all the world against us! International Socialism will come to life again one day. And that day it will call to account the men who had its trust and whom the imperialist governments have brought to heel so easily.'

Jacques let him ramble on, nodding approval more out of politeness than anything else; after what he had witnessed in Paris defections of this sort had lost the power of surprising him.

Some newspapers were lying on the table. Picking them up he glanced idly at the headlines.

A hundred thousand Germans marching on Liège. Britain mobilizing fleet and army. Grand Duke Nicholas appointed Commander-in-Chief of the Russian army. Italy officially announces her neutrality. Successful French offensive in Alsace.

Alsace! He put down the newspapers. So fighting had started in Alsace! 'Now you have sampled it, *their* war. You have heard the bullets whining past . . .' All that withdrew his thoughts from the high remoteness of his splendid dream had become odious to him, and now his one desire was to escape from the bookshop, out into the streets, as quickly as possible.

No sooner had Plattner taken over his manuscript and begun

the cast-off than he rose at once, and, brushing aside the printer's expostulations, hurried out.

Once in the street, he walked more slowly, at a saunterer's pace. Basel lay before him with its great squares and gardens and majestically rolling Rhine; with its abrupt contrasts of light and shade, of tropical heat and sudden coolness; with its many fountains, at one of which he washed his sweat-soiled hands. The city was ablaze with fervent sunlight; the air heavy with the pungent fumes of heated asphalt. As he climbed a narrow street leading to the cathedral close, a thought came to him of the Basel Congress of 1912. The Münsterplatz was empty; not a carriage, not a human being was in sight. The cathedral seemed to be shut up. Its red sandstone walls had weathered to the hue of ancient pottery; it brought to mind an old, discarded ter-racotta reliquary, forlorn in sunlight, huge and futile.

On the terrace overlooking the Rhine, under the chestnut trees, where the shadow of the apse and the swiftly flowing water below kept the air cool, Jacques was alone. Now and again the merry cries of a swimming party, hidden by the brushwood lining the river bank, were wafted up to him. For a while he watched the pigeons fluttering amongst the trees. Never since he came to Basel had he, the loneliest of men, felt himself so utterly alone as now. And this sense of utter isolation, of the dignity and power it conferred, filled him with rapture; it was a condition he would have abide with him from now on to the end. Suddenly an unlooked-for thought waylaid him. I'm acting as I'm doing only out of despair. To escape from myself. I shan't stop the war. I shan't save anyone – except myself. That's all; this act of self-fulfilment will save me, but me alone.' He sprang up, trying to drive away the hateful thought, clenching his fists. 'Ah, but it's something surely to defeat them, to have overcome the world. And find escape, in death.'

Beyond the red-stone parapet and the wide sweep of the river between two bridges, beyond the spires and factory chimneys of the outlying districts, lay fields and forests shimmering in the heat-mist. That was Germany, the Germany of today, a country under arms, already convulsed to its depths by the catastrophe of war. He had a sudden impulse to walk westwards, to the point where the frontier marches with the Rhine, where within a stone's throw from the Swiss bank of the river he could gaze at a foreshore and countryside that were German territory.

Through the St Alban district he made his way to the suburbs.

The sun was climbing zenithwards across a haze of dazzling light. The dapper little villas with their neatly clipped hedges, arbours, swings, white tables spread with flowered tablecloths, and green lawns with sprayers playing on them, bore witness that war's alarms had not disturbed the calm of this small oasis, set in the midst of storm-racked Europe. At Birsfelden, however, he saw a battalion of Swiss troops in field service uniform marching down, singing, from the Hard.

To his right was a wooded hillside. A long avenue, parallel with the river, ran through a grove of saplings; the signpost pointing up it was marked *Waldhaus*. On his left, between the tree-trunks, he had glimpses of green, sunlit meadows through which wound the Rhine. Jacques walked slowly, his mind void of thoughts. After his cloistered life of the last few days and, just now, his walk through sweltering city streets, he found a wonderful appeasement in the cool green shadows of the forest. Across a tracery of foliage, beyond a narrow valley, he saw white walls gleaming through the trees. 'That,' he thought, 'must be their *Waldhaus*.' A footpath leading down to the water's edge branched off the avenue. The nearness of the water made the air cooler still. A moment later he was standing on the river bank.

Yonder, separated from him only by that reach of limpid light, was Germany.

Germany was empty. On that morning not one fisherman was to be seen on the further bank; not a peasant in the apple orchards stretching from the riverside and the hamlet of red-roofed cottages nestling round a spire, up to the foot of the hills that compassed the horizon. But Jacques discerned hidden away near the water's edge amidst the brushwood of the shelving foreshore, the roof of a hut painted in stripes of three colours. What was it? he wondered. A sentry-box? A picquet-post? A customs-officer's look-out?

His eyes were held by this foreign countryside, rife with mysterious portents. His hands thrust deep into his pockets, his feet sinking into the waterlogged soil, he gazed long and earnestly at Germany – and Europe. Never before had he felt so calm, so lucid, so sure of himself as at this moment when, alone on the bank of the great river fraught with historic memories, he opened his eyes wide upon the world and his own destiny. A day will come, he thought, surely a day will come when at long last men's hearts will beat in unison, all will be equal in a world of dignity and justice. Perhaps it was needful for humanity to pass yet once again through a phase of hatred and brutality before winning through to universal brotherhood. But for me there's no more waiting possible; I've reached a stage when I can no longer postpone the surrender of my life wholly and finally. Have I ever given myself up wholly to anyone or anything? No, not even to the revolutionary cause. Not even to Jenny. Always I kept back something, some vital part of myself. I've gone through life as a dilettante, a man of half-measures, who grudgingly doles out only those portions of himself that he is willing to surrender. Only now I've come to know what it means, the utter self-immolation in which one's whole being is consumed.

Like a cleansing flame the vision of his sacrifice irradiated him. Gone was the time when despair hovered in the background of his thoughts, when he had to struggle daily against an impulse to give up the struggle. Death was no surrender, but the fulfilment of his destiny.

A sound of footsteps in the undergrowth behind him made him turn his head. He saw a man and a woman, woodcutters, both dressed in black. The man had a bill-hook slung on his belt, the woman a basket in each hand. They had the rather dour expression of most Swiss peasants, the frowning gaze and close-set lips that seem affirming life is no primrose path. Both shot a suspicious glance at the unknown young man they had came on loitering in the brushwood and watching so intently what was happening 'over there'.

Jacques realized he had been unwise to venture so near the frontier. Probably the river bank was being patrolled by customs-officers, if not by Swiss troops as well. Beating a hasty retreat, he cut across the bushes towards the highroad.

STEPHEN GRAHAM

Stephen Graham (1884–1975). Travel writer. Books about Russia before, during and after the war. His articles appeared in *The Times*. He was in the Altai Mountains when war was declared. His journey from this point on is described in *Russia and the World*. He later published an account of the earlier stages of this expedition in *Through Russian Central Asia* (1916). He translated a Russian account of the war by V. M. Doroshevich (*q.v.*).

Source: Stephen Graham, *Russia and the World*, London, Cassell, 1915.

HOW THE NEWS OF WAR CAME TO A VILLAGE ON THE CHINESE FRONTIER

I was staying in an Altai Cossack village on the frontier of Mongolia when the war broke out, 1,200 *versts*[1] south of the Siberian railway, a most verdant resting-place with majestic fir forests, snow-crowned mountains range behind range, green and purple valleys deep in larkspur and monkshood. All the young men and women of the village were out on the grassy hills with scythes; the children gathered currants in the wood each day, old folks sat at home and sewed furs together, the pitch-boilers and charcoal-burners worked at their black fires with barrels and scoops, and athwart it all came the message of war.

At 4 a.m. on 31 July the first telegram came through; an order to mobilize and be prepared for active service. I was awakened that morning by an unusual commotion, and, going into the village street, saw the soldier population collected in groups, talking excitedly. My peasant hostess cried out to me, 'Have you heard the news? There is war.' A young man on a fine horse came galloping down the street, a great red flag hanging from his shoulders and flapping in the wind, and as he went he called out the news to each and every one, 'War! War!'

Horses out, uniforms, swords! The village *feldscher* took his stand outside our one government building, the *volostnoe pravlenie*, and began to examine horses. The Tsar had called on the Cossacks; they gave up their work without a regret and burned to fight the enemy.

Who was the enemy? Nobody knew. The telegram contained no indications. All the village population knew was that the same telegram had come as came ten years ago, when they were called to fight the Japanese. Rumours abounded. All the morning it was persisted that the yellow peril had matured, and that the war was with China. Russia had pushed too far into Mongolia, and China had declared war.

The village priest, who spoke Esperanto and claimed that he had never met anyone else in the world who spoke the language, came to me and said:

'What think you of Kaiser William's picture?'

'What do you mean?' I asked.

'Why, the yellow peril!'

Then a rumour went round, 'It is with England, with England.' So far away these people lived they did not know that our old hostility had vanished. Only after four days did something like the truth come to us, and then nobody believed it.

'An immense war,' said a peasant to me. 'Thirteen powers engaged – England, France, Russia, Belgium, Bulgaria, Serbia, Montenegro, Albania, against Germany, Austria, Italy, Romania, Turkey.'

Two days after the first telegram a second came, and this one called up every man between the ages of eighteen and forty-three. Astonishing that Russia should at the very outset begin to mobilize its reservists 5,000 *versts* from the scene of hostilities!

Flying messengers arrived on horses, breathless and steaming, and delivered packets into the hands of the *Ataman*, the headman of the Cossacks – the secret instructions. Fresh horses were at once given them, and they were off again within five minutes of their arrival in the village. The great red flag was mounted on an immense pine-pole at the end of our one street, and at night it was taken down and a large red lantern was hung in its place. At the entrance of every village such a flag flew by day, such a lantern glowed by night.

The preparations for departure went on each day, and I spent much time watching the village vet certifying or rejecting mounts. A horse that could not go fifty miles a day was not passed. Each Cossack brought his horse up, plucked its lips apart to show the teeth, explained marks on the horse's body, mounted it bare-back and showed its paces. The examination was strict; the Cossacks had a thousand miles to go to get to the railway at Omsk. It was necessary to have strong horses.

On the Saturday night there was a melancholy service in the wooden village church. The priest, in a long sermon, looked back over the history of Holy Russia, dwelling chiefly on the occasion when Napoleon defiled the churches of 'Old Mother Moscow', and was punished by God. 'God is with us,' said the priest. 'Victory will be ours.'

Sunday was a holiday, and no preparations were made that day. On Monday the examination of horses went on. The Cossacks brought also their uniforms, swords, hats, half-*shubas*, overcoats, shirts, boots, belts – all that they were supposed to provide in the way of kit, and the *Ataman* checked and certified each soldier's portion.

On Thursday, the day of setting out, there came a third telegram from St Petersburg. The vodka shop, which had been locked and sealed during the great temperance struggle which had been in progress in Russia, might be opened for one day only – the day of mobilization. After that day, however, it was to be closed again and remain closed until further orders.

What scenes there were that day!

All the men of the village had become soldiers and pranced on their horses. At eight o'clock in the morning the holy-water basin was taken from the church and placed with triple candles on the open, sun-blazed mountain side. The Cossacks met there as at a rendezvous, and all their women-folk, in multifarious bright cotton dresses and tear-stained faces, walked out to say a last religious goodbye.

The bare-headed, long-haired priest came out in vestment of violent blue, and behind him came the old men of the village carrying the icons and banners of the church; after them the village choir, singing as they marched. A strange mingling of sobbing and singing went up to heaven from the crowd outside the wooden village, this vast irregular collection of women on foot clustered about a long double line of stalwart horsemen.

The consecration service took place, and only then did we learn the almost incredible fact that the war was with Germany. It made the hour and the act and the place even more poignant. I at least understood what it meant to go to war against Germany, and the destiny that was in store.

'God is with you,' said the priest in his sermon, the tears running down his face the while. 'God is with you; not a hair of your heads will be lost. Never turn your backs on the foe. Remember that if you do, you endanger the eternal welfare of your souls. Remember, too, that a letter, a postcard – one line – will be greedily read by all of us who remain behind . . . God bless His faithful slaves!'

1. A Russian measure, about two thirds of a mile.

STEPHEN GRAHAM

see also p. 73

Stephen Graham joined the Scots Guards and left for the front
on Good Friday, 1918. After some well-meaning but suspiciously
jolly descriptions of army life Graham writes of the scene after
he got to Arras with some horrific accuracy. Perhaps Paul
Fussell is being ironic when he describes Graham as 'hardly
educated at all' (in *The Great War and Modern Memory*, p. 155).

Source: Stephen Graham, *A Private in the Guards*, London, William
Heinemann, 1919; new edn, 'The Travellers' Library', 1928.

AS TOUCHING THE DEAD

'We were fighting in a rose-garden which was strewn with men
who had been dead for some days. The pink roses and the green
corpses were a strange combination,' said L., the young poet
who wrote charming lyrics and had such a taste in art. He was
fresh to the work and looked on the dead for the first time. The
memory was distasteful, and yet it inevitably recurred to his
mind. He strove to banish it as an elegant person in civil life
would naturally banish from the mind something evil and repulsive, such, as, for instance, say, some beggar woman's face
that his eyes by chance had seen. I met the same L. a month
later; we were discussing impressions of the war, and he confessed
that he felt no interest in the dead as such; they were just so
many old cases of what had once been men. He had seen so
many dead that already the instinctive horror had gone . . .

———

The fascination of going from dead to dead and looking at each,
and of going to every derelict tank, abandoned gun, and shattered aeroplane was so great that inevitably one went on further
and further from home, seeking and looking with a strange
intensity in the heart. I saw a great number of the dead, those
blue bundles and green bundles strewn far and wide over the

autumn fields. The story of each man's death was plainly shown in the circumstances in which he lay. The brave machine-gunners, with resolute look in shoulders and face, lay scarcely relaxed beside their oiled machines, which if you understood you could still use, and beside piles of littered brass, the empty cartridge-cases of hundreds of rounds which they had fired away before being bayonetted at their posts. Never to be forgotten was the sight of the dead defenders of Ecoust lying there with all their gear about them. On the other hand, facing those machine-gunners one saw how our men, rushing forward in extended formation, each man a good distance from his neighbour, had fallen, one here, another there, one directly he had started forward to the attack, and then others, one, two, three, four, five, all in a sort of sequence, here, here, here, here, here, one poor wretch had got far, but had got tangled in the wire, had pulled and pulled and·at last been shot to rags; another had got near enough to strike the foe and been shot with a revolver. Down at the bottom of deep trenches many dead men lay, flat in the mud, sprawling along the duck-boards or in the act of creeping cautiously out of holes in the side. In other parts of the field one saw the balance of battle and the Germans evidently attacking, not extended, but in groups, and now in groups together dead. One saw Germans taking cover and British taking cover in shell-holes inadequately deep, and now the men stiff as they crouched. I remember especially two of our fellows in a shell-hole, fear was in their faces, they were crouching un-naturally, and one had evidently been saying to the other, 'Keep your head down!' Now in both men's heads was a dent, the sort of dent that appears in the side of a rubber ball when not fully expanded by air. There were those who had thought their cover inadequate and had run for something better and been caught by a shell on the way – hideous butcheries of men; and there were men whose pink bodies lay stripped to the waist and some one had been endeavouring to save them and had ab-andoned them in death – men with all their kit about them, men without kit, men with their greatcoats on and men with-out greatcoats . . .

War robs the individual soldier of reverence, of care except for himself, of tenderness, of the hush of awe which should silence and restrain. War and the army have their own atmosphere, in which some one else being dead, as much as killing some one else, succeeds in being trivial and even upon occasion jocular. Two sergeants going out for a stroll came upon a German corpse with the steel helmet right down over the eyes. One of them lifted up the helmet in order to see the face properly. A saturnine gloom was on the lips and this had been intensified by the masking of the eyes. When the sergeant lifted the helmet it pulled up the flesh with it, and the upper lip rose from over the ivory teeth with a ghastly grin. 'Take that smile off your face,' said the sergeant, and let the helmet drop back over the eyes again. And they laughed. In these and in so many, imagination and sensitiveness were swallowed up by war. But another soldier, new to war's horrors, came upon a Royal Scot lying dead on a ridge. Beside the corpse was a packet of notepaper and envelopes, which some souvenir-hunter searching his kit had forgotten to take. The soldier was just in need of notepaper and envelopes to write home, and he took this packet away from that dead man.

All that night and for many days he seemed to hear the tiny, tiny voice of the corpse saying or rather whining in his ear, 'You've stolen my notepaper and envelopes,' grudging them and demanding them back – as if the dead were misers.

But the soldier did not return the stationery to the place where he found it, and after a while his mind seemed to harden and take on a sort of crust. He had been haunted by the faces of the dead, and then these faces ceased to haunt him, and he had obtained the soldier's peace of mind. The greatest and perhaps the only consoling truth which can be learned from the expression of the dead is that a corpse has very little to do with a living body. The dead body is sacred, but it is not the person who died. That person has mysteriously disappeared. The look of the dead body, its shrunken individuality as compared with that of a live man, must have partly caused the great vogue of spiritualism – that look might be taken as part of the evidence of immortality. That was the chief positive impression which I obtained. For the rest, the whole matter was infinitely pathetic. There were one or two of us who felt there would always, ever after, be a cast of sadness in us because of what we had seen. I felt how inhuman we had been to one another. How could we come at last to Our Father with all this brothers' blood upon our hands?

'Europe! Europe!' I thought; 'what a picture might be painted of Europe, the tragic woman, with bare breasts, anguished eyes, but no children. – *Oh, Europe, where are thy children?*'

STEPHEN GRAHAM

see also pp. 73 and 77

Stephen Graham was one of many writers who not only returned to the war in their writing but actually revisited the battlefields. *The Challenge of the Dead* is a strange mixture of acute observation and rather grandiose, sombre reflection. He described the book as 'A vision of the war and the life of the common soldier in France, seen two years afterwards between August and November, 1920'.

The following passage is both humorous and 'innocent'. Graham later continued his travels, writing about the poor and the immigrants to America. He 'tramped' with the poet Vachel Lindsay (see *Tramping with a Poet*, London, Macmillan, 1922). His autobiography, *Part of the Wonderful Scene*, London, Collins, appeared in 1964.

Source: Stephen Graham, *The Challenge of the Dead*, London, Cassell, 1921.

. . . Strolling along at dusk past the Cloth Hall tower a bright-eyed Belgian wolf asks you who you are. '*C'est triste, n'est ce pas?*' says he, pointing to the ruins. *Triste* is what they are not. The Belgian is from Poperinge. It is very dull there now. *Tous les soldats sont partis.* Also the mamzelles. Pas de jig-a-jig.

'Like a glass of beer?' asks the Belgian.

A spare woman of thirty serves two glasses of ale at a table outside a hotel. She seems to speak English for preference.

'You want someone to sleep with?' asks the man from Poperinge.

'No, I sleep with no man.'

'Not married?'

'No, and plenty time yet, and I shan't marry an English when I do. The English are all false.'

The man from Poperinge seems taken aback. At a further table a curious scene is being enacted. Here are sitting a pioneer corporal and a sergeant, both wearing the 1914 ribbon. They have their beer, and between them is an effervescent loose-mouthed Alsatian. The latter, like the man from Poperinge, stands treat.

'I vill take you, one minit, I vill take you,' says the Alsatian, kissing the tips of his fingers, 'just vait, not ten minits from 'ere.'

'Oh you go on, you bloomin' well shut up. I b'lieve you're agent for the girl or something,' says the sergeant.

'No, listen, I'll tell you vot it is . . . C'est *de gâteau*, got that, *gâteau*; naw need to drink any coffee, just ten minits, you see for yourself.'

The sergeant makes a mocking show of biffing him in the eye, and grins all over his weak sunburnt face. The shoeing corporal sips at his beer and smirks. The Alsatian on the tips of his toes, leaning forward on his chair which is tilted toward the table, gesticulates and slobbers –

'You wait till you see her, you'll felicitation yourself . . .'

And the sergeant is persuaded against his will and goes with him. Meanwhile dusk has grown to dark, and the ruined Cloth Hall tower on the other side of the way seems more gloomy, more moody and threatening, as if the war were not yet over.

This Ypres is a terrible place still. There is no life when night comes on but tavern life. Those who live and work here have lost their sense of proportion. They are out of focus somehow. 'You lookin' for dead soldiers,' says a Flemish woman to you with a glaring stare, wondering if you are one of the exhumers. Death and the ruins completely outweigh the living. One is tilted out of time by the huge weight on the other end of the plank, and it would be easy to imagine someone who had no insoluble ties killing himself here, drawn by the lodestone of death. There is a pull from the other world, a drag on the heart and spirit. One is ashamed to be alive. You try to sleep in a little bed in a cubicle with tiny doll's house window. You listen to a drunken company down below singing, 'Mademoiselle, have you got any rum?' A French couple enter the room next door, smacking one another's hips and confounding one another with coarse violent laughter – that is the light end of the plank. Then night ensues, the real night, breathless and sepulchral, the night which belongs to all lost hopes and ended lives and wearinesses.

You lie listless, sleepless, with Ypres on the heart, and then suddenly a grand tumult of explosion, a sound as of the tumbling of heavy masonry. You go to the little window, behold, the whole sky is crimson once more, and living streamers of flame ascend to the stars. An old dump has gone up at Langemark. Everyone in Ypres looks out and then returns to sleep – without excitement. The lurid glare dies down; stertorous night resumes her sway o'er the living and the dead. For a moment it was as if the old war had started again.

Day dawns in a mist. A veil hides the inner reality of Ypres, and as a visitor says – 'It looks more picturesque in the mist.' Ypres however is an altar to which the nation must return . . .

GUY CHAPMAN

Guy Chapman (1889–1972). Born in London. Educated at
Oxford. Called to the Bar in 1914. Served with the Royal
Fusiliers from 1914 to 1920. Later, Professor of Modern History
at the University of Leeds. Book on the Dreyfus affair. Edited
an important collection of prose from the war called *Vain Glory*
(1937). He returned to his wartime experiences in an autobiography, *A Kind of Survivor* (1975), which was edited by his
wife, the writer Storm Jameson. In the passage which follows
he describes an incident near Arras in 1917.

Source: Guy Chapman, *A Passionate Prodigality*, London, Ivor
Nicholson & Watson, 1933; 2nd edn, MacGibbon & Kee, 1965.

The attack was to be launched at streak of dawn, 4.25; and at
that moment a wild racket was once more loosed into the void.
Once more the curtain of darkness was changed to a whirling
screen in which flaming clusters, red, orange and gold, dropped
and died; and dun smoke, illuminated by explosions, drifted
away greyish white. Once more red and green rockets called
frantically for aid. Once more eyes stared into this impenetrable
cataract, vainly trying to pick out familiar outlines. The enemy's
barrage joined the din. Black columns of smoke stormed up in
the foreground. And through it all came wave on wave of the
malicious chitter of machine-guns.

Slowly the darkness grew to grey, to opal, to gold; and the
mist began to burn away. Shapes loomed up. Distances were
deceptive in the haze. The round top of Greenland Hill came
into outline. It was bare of life. A dark patch to the left became
Square Wood. A contact plane hovering in the centre fired
white Very-lights. Some red flares blossomed, like Chinese lan-
terns at a fête, on the edge of the chemical works.

As the day cleared, gunner officers and their linesmen began
to come into the trench. Our shelling died down, but the enemy
was shivering his old front line with vicious concentration. To
the north, we could see men coming up and down the road from
Gavrelle. Who they were no one could tell. We thought they

were both English and German, but which was escorting which?

The story of this attack will no doubt appear in the military history of the war, elucidated by diagrams. To the watchers on the hillside it was only a confused medley, in which English and Germans appeared most disconcertingly going to and fro, oblivious of each other. Even later it was only possible to glean that one brigade had lost direction, and coming up behind the flank of the other after the position had been taken, had swept on, carrying away with it the better part of two companies of the 13th; that some reached Square Wood, a mile past the objective, and that perhaps a dozen in all returned. This is part of history, but all we were able to see were some of the ingredients.

Questioning the countryside, I caught in my glass a grey ant crawling over the edge of the railway cutting, followed by another, and then more. They hurried into a road behind a shallow bank and lay down. The sun polished their steel helmets into a row of little shining discs. More and more were now coming out of the cutting. I pinched the elbow of the gunner beside me.

'See that? It's a counter-attack massing.'

'Not on my line,' he returned. 'Besides, they're out of range of field guns.'

I tumbled impetuously down the stairs and called division. A quiet voice in the distance assured me that the heavies would deal with what I had seen. When I looked again, the assembled ants had moved. They came crawling over the top of Greenland Hill in three lines, about six hundred strong. They were just starting down the forward slope when something flashed in front of them. A column of bright terracotta smoke was flung upwards so high, that there shot into my memory the pictures of the djinns in an old copy of the *Arabian Nights*, and I half expected a leering hook-nosed face to look down from its summit. Another and another rose until an arcade of smoking pillars seemed to move across the hillside. 'Six-inch How,' shouted my neighbour excitedly, 'firing one-o-six.'

Already the grey ants had thinned. The first line was hardly there. It merged with the second and mechanically the whole inclined southwards to avoid the shells. But the guns followed the movement and another line of smoking columns fountained into the air. At last, reduced to one line, the minute figures turned and stumbled back over the crest of the hill.

GORDON BOTTOMLEY
and
PAUL NASH

Gordon Bottomley (1874–1948). Born in Keighley, Yorkshire. Suffered from ill health. Started work in a bank at the age of 16. Wrote poetry and verse drama. Gained a wide audience with 'King Lear's Wife', which was included in Edward Marsh's *Georgian Poetry 1913–1915*. He was one of Rosenberg's editors. His correspondence with Paul Nash (see p. 370) lasted for many years and he donated a fine collection of Nash's work to the Carlisle Art Gallery. He enlisted on 10 September 1914.

Source: Poet and Painter: Being the Correspondence between Gordon Bottomley and Paul Nash 1910–1946, ed. Claude Colleer Abbott and Anthony Bertram, London, Oxford University Press, 1955.

Paul Nash to Gordon and Emily Bottomley
[*c.* mid August to early September 1914]

I am so sorry not to have written before but of course we have been rather disturbed [by] my War eventualities and I have not felt like writing letters. I hope you are not greatly upset at Silverdale & they wont regard your house as a temporary fort or watch tower or be taking it over as a hospital . . . here I was obliged to leave your letter and go off a harvesting: novel amusement for me and great fun – Jack & I have worked hard – tossing sheaves onto a cart and pitching 'em off in the yard to make a rick. Most farmers are short of hands by men enlisting or being otherwise called out so we are volunteering for all sorts of jobs and making ready for all emergencies. I am not keen to rush off and be a soldier. The whole damnable war is too horrible of course and I am all against killing anybody, speaking off hand, but beside all that I believe both Jack & I might be more useful as ambulance & red cross men and to that end we are training. There may be emergencies later & I mean to get some drilling locally & learn to fire a gun but I dont see the necessity for a gentleminded creature like myself to be rushed into some stuffy brutal barracks to spend the next few months practically doing nothing but swagger about di[s]guised as a soldier *in case* the Germans poor misguided fellows – should land. There is more to do at home attempting to relieve the sad wretches who are left hard up and miserable . . .

Paul Nash to Gordon Bottomley   [*c*. 27 September, 1914]
               Iver Heath, Bucks.

. . . it is so long ago since I first meant to write to you that I thought I had written. I am now an Artist in a wider sense! having joined the 'Artists' London Regiment of Territorials the old Corps which started with Rossetti[,] Leighton & Millais as members in 1860: Every man must do his bit in this horrible business so I have given up painting & bid it adieux for – who knows how long, to take up the queer business of soldiering. Every day I travel up to drill. There are many nice creatures in my company and I enjoy the burst of exercise – marching, drilling all day in the open air about the pleasant parts of Regents Park & Hampstead Heath. We are not camped any-where yet so live at home – later we may pig it at the Tower a dirty, haunted sort of a place I hear, but good in a way as it keeps me in London & near Bunty & my dear people.

Gordon Bottomley to Paul Nash   2 October 1914
               The Sheiling,
               Silverdale,
               Nr Carnforth

. . . I still dare not attempt a letter, but I could not rest until I had scrawled you this line to send you our benediction on your new enterprise. Having set out to do so worthy a share of our country's duty you will feel a contentment within yourself, both now and in times to come, that is better than anyone else's praises; so I will only say that we are happy in your choice. We love art and poetry better than war; but this is one of the times of the world when men must fight if they want to preserve the foundations on which art and poetry can alone be possible, and as I lie helpless I am bound to envy you your share. You do not say if your corps is for the front or for home defence; I hope you will not be called on to break the peace, but if you are I shall hope still more ardently for your safety, and for good days to come when you can bring a new world of experience to your art. And so say we both.

Rathbone never never brought me that BLAST until Tuesday of this very week. It looks amusingly stale and old-fashioned already, now. The text would be trite if it were not so very black, and the pictures look like theories that have gone cold too soon. The only pictures by the living men that appeal to me, and that seem to have an original feeling for beauty are the two (*Dancers* and *Religion*) by W. Roberts; as for the pictures by Lewis, Wadsworth et Cie, they would look far more convincing, reasonable, and valuable, if carried out by the yard in silk broché and made into opera cloaks.

Our remembrances to Ma'am'selle Bunty, please.

Gordon Bottomley to Paul Nash　　　　22 August 1918
　　　　　　　　　　　　　　　　　　The Sheiling,
　　　　　　　　　　　　　　　　　　Silverdale,
　　　　　　　　　　　　　　　　　　Nr Carnforth

. . . There is one aspect of the war which I do not as yet hear that you have treated, and which I should like to see you treat – and that is its effect on civilians. Why not make one of your large memorial paintings a shell-torn church still whole enough to shelter unhappy heaps of refugees at nightfall – dreadful huddled hunches of beings crouching about fires lit on the church pavement, monstrous tremendous shadows of them cast on the walls and vaulting by the smoky flare, other pale beings prostrate in the darker places. You should embody your knowledge of broken towns and villages in some such way . . .

RUDOLF BINDING

Rudolf Binding (1867–1938). Born in Basel. Studied medicine and law. Passion for horses. First military service in the Hussars. First stories published in 1909. In 1914, at the age of forty-six, accepted command of a squadron of dragoons. Served on the Western Front throughout the war apart from four months in Galicia in 1916. Never a member of the National Socialist Party but his relationship with it was ambivalent. His collected war poems, stories and recollections appeared in 1939 under the title *Dies war das Maß*. *A Fatalist at War* consists of unaltered diary entries and parts of letters written throughout the war. Seriously ill in 1918, when he wrote calmly but bitterly about the Work-men's and Soldiers' Councils. Ludwig Renn also described these; see the introductory note to the extract on p. 238 for an explanation of them.

Source: Rudolf Binding, *A Fatalist at War* (translated from *Aus dem Kriege*, Frankfurt, Rütten & Loening Verlag, 1927, by Ian F. D. Morrow), London, Allen & Unwin, 1929.

6 November 1914

. . . I also succeeded in negotiating a supply of milk with one of the inhabitants. A farm is burnt down; the cows are still there, but will not let themselves be caught for milking. That is, only one of them. The others were used to the sister. The sister was killed by a shell.

Coffee is coffee, the soldiers think. They mixed some fragrant coffee which arrived as a gift from home for the officers with some greasy looted stuff which tastes like cardboard. The card-board won. 'One makes an egg,' said Field-Marshal Von der Goltz, who came here from Brussels in a car for a short time yesterday, 'and one forces the enemy to surrender.' The ex-pression is cheering! The yoke of the egg is Ypres. We are at the pointed end; but the egg stoutly refuses to be surrounded.

We are still stuck here for perfectly good reasons; one might as well say for perfectly bad reasons.

Beginning of November 1914

What destinies must be buried here! I pass the ruins of a house every day in which I took shelter with a few men and horses during the first days of the attack. At that time it was evident that the inhabitants had just left the farm. Only two very old people who could not be brought away sat rigid and immovable on either side of the dying fire in the grate. The two sat there like fixtures of the house, like things that had always been there and always in the same place. Whether spoken to or not they did not utter a word. My men built up the fire and used the fireplace daily. They did not stir.

As we had enough to do to look after ourselves we forgot them entirely. I don't think that anyone gave them anything to eat or drink. On the third night I noticed a hunch-backed, stupid, and ill-formed young female in the darkness of the room, who stoked the embers carefully and furtively, and attended to the old people. I discovered that this creature belonged to the household and had fled to somewhere in the rear. She ventured to come only at night, looked after the two old people and, after making up the fire, left without a word. I never saw her in the daytime. A few mornings later the squadron moved billets, so I left this house. Although we came back in the evening to the same neighbourhood after a totally unsuccessful search, I did not occupy it again. The next day I went there on foot. The two old people sat motionless on their seats as before, the fire had burned down and was glimmering between them. A cricket which had taken shelter behind the warm hearth from the coming winter made childish, intimate music, as if to say it is good to be here. But it attracts no one. The next morning the house was burnt down, destroyed by enemy fire. The two old people disappeared. I do not know whether they are dead or alive or who might have brought them away. It is bright now over the dark hearth open to the sky. The cricket still chirps his carefree song among the warm stones of the hearth. But he, too, will be silent tomorrow.

War is a strange business. No one has really known it, and its methods of teaching are cruel, rough and primitive. Human methods seem foolish and clumsy – in fact, offensively theatrical compared with them. I can see in front of me the general who commands one of our brigades. He received a report that a small garrison was holding us up and firing busily from the white château – any old shed, the simplest kind of house, as long as it is not a peasant's habitation, is called a château here. He raised his arm with the gesture of a great commander and cried from his horse, pointing forward like a conqueror of the world, 'Lay fire to the castle!' which seemed to settle the matter as far as he was concerned. He behaved in the same sensible manner – and thought he was doing the right thing, I am sure – when he was snowed under with reports, when his troops were having the hottest time, when they were in the most dire need of calm, clear orders, when everything depended on his doing something decisive, and he cried to his brigade major in a state of terrific excitement, 'The horses, my dear L. Come, let us fling ourselves into the battle!'

Easter Letter   [1915]
                                             West Flanders

I have not written to you for a long time, but I have thought of you all the more as a silent creditor. But when one owes letters one suffers from them, so to speak, at the same time. It is, indeed, not so simple a matter to write from the war, really from the war; and what you read as Field Post letters in the papers usually have their origin in the lack of understanding that does not allow a man to get hold of the war, to breathe it in although he is living in the midst of it. Certainly it is a strange element for everyone; but I probably find it even stranger, and feel more like a fish out of water than many who write about it – because I try to understand it. The further I penetrate its true inwardness the more I see the hopelessness of making it comprehensible for those who only understand life in the terms of peacetime, and apply these same ideas to war in spite of themselves. They only think that they understand it. It is as if fishes living in the water would have a clear conception of what living in the air is like. When one is hauled out on to dry land and dies in the air, then he will know something about it.

So it is with the war. Feeling deeply about it, one becomes less able to talk about it every day. Not because one understands it less each day, but because one grasps it better. But it is a silent teacher, and he who learns becomes silent too.

The stagnation that this siege warfare has brought about gives a superficial observer the illusion of peace. One regulates intercourse with the local population as well as one can, one tries to arrange for the tillage of the land, one trains the men as well as possible in mud and filth, one visits the officers of neighbouring units, one spends hours in discussion. The war is ignored; for not everyone has the capacity or the habit to notice it in everything and everyone. Yet it is behind everything and everyone; that is the strange part of it! The starlings that winter hereabouts in hordes whistle like rifle-bullets; and as the bullets cannot have learnt to whistle from the starlings one may safely presume the opposite. And everything whistles its tune of the war – the houses, the fields, men, beasts, rivers, and even the sky. The very milk turns sour under the thunder of shell-fire.

You will think that I am romancing. But I am not. Only . . . the others do not notice this. They do not listen to the starlings; they hardly look at the fields; mankind has not changed since yesterday; and the milk has got sour through standing.

What exactly do they experience of the war? They know that the dug-outs in the line are comfortably fitted up, that they have brought up a mirror and a clock, that they have barbed wire in front of them, that the gunners hide their shells carefully, that troops are flung in here and there, that the Field Post functions, that there are brave men who have been rewarded with the Iron Cross.

Then again, they notice effects. They see the wounded, hear of the dead, hear of towns that have been taken, of positions lost or won. But that is not the melody of war. It is as if one were to describe and understand the being and the melody of the wind by saying that it chases dead leaves, that the weathercock creaks, and that the washing on the line dries. All that is not its melody; as the fitting out of a trench, the Iron Cross, and even the dead are only infinitesimal outward and recognizable signs of an unknown and hidden majesty, be it sublime or cruel.

Perhaps some poet has already seen this majesty unveiled – heard this melody, which may be nothing but a bellow, so that it can be reproduced. As for myself, the sounds increase, but the melody and rhythm remain obscure.

And if I could summon all the poets of past times to sing the war they might all remain silent – unless one should answer who has been through hell.

So you may appreciate how hard it is to write about the war. Its Being is veiled; and where the greatness is recognizable human speech has no expression to cope with it. What can you make of it when I tell you that I live in a house with no architectural style, windows that do not shut properly, and high rooms; that I have a bed; that two little old women wait on me and do my cooking; and that I curse the eternal rain that the sky of Flanders pours down upon us? All this seems to me so immeasurably dull compared with the war; just as one can only bear the insignificant things of life by not talking about them. I use the same soap as in peacetime; I have time to brush my teeth in the morning; I have a brown coffee-pot and a stove that does not heat well. Why should I tell you about them? The piping of the starlings, the aspect of the sickly fields, the thunderous air and the sour milk will tell you much more.

But in the midst of the monstrous event stands Man; the thousands and the hundreds of thousands, the combatants and the non-combatants; who all have one wish and one goal: to cast aside the war; to render its effect invisible so far as they can be understood; to let a well-earned Peace grow its grass over the victims and to carry on as before, broadly speaking. The times may be as big as they will; man remains small. Transformation and cleansing have nothing to do with him.

They say, they know, that we will win; what a wonderful thing it is to know this and to say it. But we shall not conquer ourselves. We will carry on as before and think what wonderful new things we have set up in place of the old. For many things that are ought to be scrapped; and many that are as yet undiscovered are worth bringing to life.

That sounds very hard, doesn't it? But it should at least be allowed to him who feels the hardness of the times to speak out his hard words. You will ask what I would put in the place of that which is past or what new things there are to be discovered.

I believe that it could be expressed thus – a religion of defensive power – for all peoples. There should be a belief in the right to be in a state of defence, to defend oneself; this and nothing more. This would give to us and to the world, which would adopt our religion, such immense strength – for religions outlast history, peoples and empires, civilization and philosophy, discoveries and the progress of man – so that no nation or concourse of nations would stand up to us. Defensive power would stand sanctified, with the weapons of defence in her hand, as with the products of toil in her arms; unattackable, uniting through the strength of the idea, resting on a joyous security of belief, inspiring piety because of man's belief in her. I would not challenge this time to bring forth a religion did I not know how great it is. It bears the child; we are but clumsy helpers in her heavy hour; and who shall deny either the immensity of the event or the helplessness of mankind – even for our people alone – to turn it into good?

An enormous longing arises in the world, not longing for strange countries, not for seas, fortresses, riches, and power – but for a gift of grace from these times that are worthy alike of themselves and of us.

ROBERT MUSIL

Robert Musil (1880–1942). Throughout his adult life Musil kept a series of notebooks or 'diaries' (many of which were undated). These provide a fascinating commentary on Musil's personal development and literary work, and are particularly valuable for an understanding of the elaboration of his great novel *The Man without Qualities*. The entries printed here are taken from the notebooks he kept during the war when he served as an officer in the Austrian army and fought on the Italian Front. He left Austria in 1938 for Switzerland and died in Geneva.

Source: Robert Musil, 'Diaries' (translated from *Tagebücher*, Reinbek bei Hamburg, Rowohlt Verlag, 1955, by David McDuff), Newcastle upon Tyne, *Stand*, Vol. 21, no. 2, 1980.

1914

Berlin, August, War

An atmosphere of night falling on all sides . . . The uprooted intellectuals.

The men who declare after a while that they have regained their equilibrium and do not need to alter their views in any way, e.g. [Oscar] Bie [publisher of the *New Review*].

Simultaneous with all the ecstasy, the ugly singing in the cafés. The nervous excitement that wants to fight its own little war for every copy of a newspaper. Men hurl themselves under trains because they are not required to fight. On the steps of the Commemorative Chapel laymen are beginning to preach while the services of Penitence and Supplication are going on inside.

Most of the last-minute weddings are taking place in the maternity hospitals.

Women are dressing more plainly.

I hang on to the roof of a fast-moving car is order to get a copy of the evening paper.

The call-up of the various professions: 'Apollo is silent and Mars rules the hour', concludes the message from the actors' union.

A single newspaper – the *Post* – is still campaigning against the Social Democrats, writing of 'the enemy within', of which one must not lose sight in the face of the enemy without. In the very first days of the war, when at evening everyone rushes through the streets in search of newspapers, the crowd grows madly fond of reading, forms a solid mass through which a tram attempts to move, very slowly. A big man in his late twenties begins to shout: 'Stand still, I tell you, stand still!' gesticulating wildly with his cane. His eyes have a lunatic expression. Psychotics are in their element, live out their psychoses.

1915

War. On a mountain-top. Valley peaceful as on a summer excursion. Behind the drag-chain of the sentries one walks like a tourist.

Far-off duel of heavy artillery. At intervals of twenty, thirty seconds and more. Reminiscent of boys hurling stones at one another over great distances. Without certainty of success they are for ever compelled to try one more shot.

Shells lunge into the ravine behind Vezzena. Ugly black smoke, as from a house on fire, settles for minutes on end.

Feeling for the poor, garlanded hill-district of Lavarone.

Far-off detonations of cannon: hard to say if it wasn't a door slamming shut somewhere, or a threshing-floor being beaten. Yet the pale impression of the sound is more closed, rounder, more gently defined. Unmistakable after a time.

The end of July. A fly is dying: world war. The gramophone has already worked its way through several hours of the evening. 'Rosa, we're going to Lodz, Lodz, Lodz'. And: 'Come into my arbour of love'. Sometimes, in between, Czech folksongs and Slezak or Caruso. Heads are clouded with melancholy and dancing. A fly has fallen from one of the many long flypapers that dangle from the ceiling. The fly is lying on its back. In a spot of light on the wax table-cloth. Near a tall vase of little roses. It is making efforts to get up. From time to time its six legs fold together, pointing acutely into the air. It is getting weaker. Dying all alone. Another fly comes near and flies away again.

Prisoners. With a little flourish they come round the corner, stand to, leaning their rifles against the wall, again with a little flourish, perhaps turning their faces away slightly as they do so. They are amiable and have their minds on the matter at hand. The officer greets them, they return the greeting.

They are dead tired. The officer throws himself on to the bed in the little room. I bring him cigarettes. He jumps up, smiles. It is as if I were in Italy.

Sentries posted everywhere. I constantly have the feeling that we have shut a bird inside the house.

14 August

'Fi - re' – Everyone runs for cover. Behind the house a rock is being blasted with explosives to provide building material for the command hut. Rain wipes its first strikes wetly over the grass. A fire is burning under a shrub on the other side of the brook. A young birch tree stands beside it like a spectator. A black pig is tied to this birch tree. One of the pig's legs is dangling in the air. The fire, the birch and the pig are alone. (And a lake of blood like a flag.)

3 September

What is left of the interim? The autumn evenings, which remind me of chinchilla fur. The rooms have such pleasant twilight. First Lieutenant Samsinger's hut with its large, right-angled window. [Sketch] Behind it the light grey mist. From there everything gradated so carefully up to light twilight. The short report of the mountain artillery. A hesitation in my step when I heard it after I had gone some way round a rock and thought that a shell had landed. The road from Portella down on the meadows. The shape of Randaschl lustrelessly black against a sky which still somehow manages to be light in places.

A night ride by Lago d'Ezze. Wonder, at the moment when one stoops into the cauldron of rocks and the black mountains tower into the black night. Dead man's landscape.

The horses lean more heavily into the bit on night rides in the mountains than at other times. Tired, slept three hours up there among the soldiers next to an old marksman. I was grateful for the warmth he afforded.

The combat actions, dead, etc., mostly in front of the emplacements, have so far not made any impression on me.

5 September

Snow on the Schrumspitze and the Schwarzkofel. Beneath them, in the sun, a field with bound sheaves of corn. And the sky white-blue.

22 September

The shrapnel fragment or flechette from Tenna (village on the ridge between Lake Caldonazzo and Lake Levico): you hear it a long time before it lands. A wind-like whistling or rushing sound. Growing louder and louder. Time seems very long. Suddenly it landed right beside me in the earth. As if the sound had been swallowed up. No memory of a shock-wave. No memory of suddenly swelling nearness. Must have been like that, though, for instinctively I wrenched the upper half of my body to one side and made a deep bow, my feet remaining where they were. Not a trace of fear, not even the simply nervous kind like palpitation, which also usually ensues without fear in cases of sudden shock. Afterwards, a pleasant feeling. Satisfaction at having survived. Pride, almost. Being accepted into a community, baptism.

10 October

The sound of the shell is a swelling and – if it goes past – once again fading whistle, in which an *ai* sound does not quite get formed. Large shells fired not too high over one's own position make a sound that swells to a rushing, even a droning of the air, with a metallic accompanying sound. So it was yesterday on Monte Carbonile when the Italians were shelling Pizzo di Vezzena from Cima Manderiolo, and the brigade on Panarotta were sending their shells above our heads at the Italian positions. The impression was one of some weird disturbance of nature. The rocks rustled and droned. Sense of a malevolent futility.

23 October

Patrol combat action. The dead man's few possessions lie wrapped in a shred of newspaper on our dining-table. A purse, the rose from his cap, a short, small pipe, two oval tin boxes containing ready-cut Toscani – cigar-like cigarettes – a small, round pocket mirror. From these objects streams a heavy sadness . . .

Italian picture postcards, taken from the prisoners. Not probable that this nation's desire for war is already exhausted. The cards show their soldiers in the favourite heroic poses; they are still nothing but a soldier's game. Particularly fetching is a card subtitled 'The Destruction of Austria's Frontiers'. An officer stands – quite small, his men behind him – on an upturned black and yellow frontier post. Approximately in the 'sortie' position. In his left hand the flag, in his right hand his *spadone*, lowered. He is shouting. Shouting into the void . . . Another sign of how much they still love war is reflected in the fact that the cards depict *la patria* and *l'Italia* in very erotic fashion: always as a young, tender, rather forlorn-looking girl, who does not really look very Italian. Here a feeling previously unknown breaks through to the surface.

1916–1918

Alarm in San Cristoforo al Mare, after a long period of quiet and peaceful acclimatization, like the blow of a fist. These curt orders. Battalion alarm, preparations for entrainment, etc. Nerves quiver, unaccustomed as yet. I was pale and agitated, with no reason for emotion.

Entrainment. During the long wait men start to disappear in dribs and drabs. By evening most of them are tipsy, some are completely drunk. The brigadier, with station staff, gives an address. A menagerie is lowing in the goods wagons. Normally well-mannered men are like animals. Friendly words and threats are of equally little avail. We close the sliding doors. Inside men beat on them with their fists. At some doors furtive resistance is offered. First Lieutenant von Hoffingott, who is supervising the closing of the doors, yells 'Hands off!', and for a moment slashes at the furtive hands with his cutlass . . . This motion of the cutlass was indescribable. Like an electric voltage unloading itself into a flash of lightning – but without flashing, glittering, or anything like that – something white and decisive . . .

Halt in Bolzano. Knowing that . . . Not being able to get in. Shameful powerlessness. Inward howling like a dog's.

Detrainment in Prvačina. Lively air action during the last part of the journey. Gunfire all round during detrainment. The horizon rumbles – long convoys of wounded in wagons and on foot. White bandages with patches of red. A vortex masters you, an excitement that sucks you inwards.

Cernizza, etc. For the first time, a house with a hearth. About 75cm above the floor, 4 to 2½ or 3 metres square. In the middle of it an open fire, with a cauldron hanging over it. Roofed, as by a hood, on top, like an ordinary fireplace. A red curtain borders the edges, about two yards wide. The hearth is built of Dutch bricks. Blue, green and yellow earthenware. The hearth is surrounded by a bench, and there are also some low chairs. A young woman is breast-feeding her child, a pretty girl is sitting next to her, a third woman is the landlady. All this at the far end of a longish room which one enters from the street. Nothing to eat. Wine that tastes like liquid manure.

Female type in the district: the face has something of both Raphael and the sow. Thick-set, athletic build and yet good figures. Stone-age women. The waist not drawn in towards the spine, but like a pure oval.

A certain human, natural friendliness.

There is an incessant rumbling in the north and the north-west.

Bombardment. Synopsis: Death is singing here. It sings above our heads, low, high. The batteries are distinguishable by their sound.

This singing and buzzing has something of the primeval jungle about it, one senses the fluttering of humming-birds and the leaping of great cats. Walking alone just for the sake of walking, e.g. in the morning when everyone is under cover. A certain mastery of the instincts at every step is then required. A shell comes screaming over about 100 metres away, and one is suffused with a feeling of happiness after it has passed. Death is something quite personal. One doesn't think about it, but for the first time one senses it. There is something slightly satisfying about this appearance of the willed action in war, as opposed to the passive receptivity of peacetime. (Will in peacetime mostly directed towards the impersonal, the expansive, money, study, etc. In war it is directed towards movements of the legs, decisions that are always intimately connected with oneself.)

Nurses. They discuss everything with one. Contagious diseases, urine tests, enemas. They dress and undress you and they would touch any part of your body. It as if they were immune to the sexual. Yet they remain women. Have favourite patients, walk up and down with the young gentlemen in the hallways, coo. The sort of sound you would expect to hear only in the hallways of young couples. Soldiers make obscene gestures. Lieutenants make grabs at the nurses' apron pockets.

Corpses: one lying completely hidden, or buried under earth and snow. You can see only its feet, only the nailed soles of its boots. From the soles of the boots you can see that it is a corpse. (Those most rigid of objects, steel nails, are somehow even more rigid than usual, and that scares you.)

WYNDHAM LEWIS

Percy Wyndham Lewis (1882–1957). Writer, critic, painter. Founded the Vorticist movement in 1914. Joined the artillery in 1916. Became an official war artist. Strongly anti-war although from a right-wing position. In 1932 described Sassoon's verse as 'very sentimental battle-doggerel', and held that Remarque indulged in 'the animalizing and caricaturing of the human being'. (See also *The Old Gang and the New Gang*, London, Desmond Harmsworth, 1932.) Some of the excerpts from his 'private history' *Blasting and Bombardiering* first appeared in the periodical *Blast*. Of 'Cantleman' Lewis wrote 'Need I repeat that this hero of mine is not to be identified with me? But to some extent, in the fragments I have quoted, you get the low-down on the editor of *Blast* . . . It was written on the spot . . . to report his sensations as soon as he got one.' 'Leo' was Ford Madox Ford.

Source: Wyndham Lewis, *Blasting and Bombardiering*, London, Eyre & Spottiswood, 1937; new edition with additions, London, Calder and Boyars, 1967.

PART II, CHAPTER II

MORPETH OLYMPIAD

(The account of the British mobilization from the pages of *Blast*)

MORPETH OLYMPIAD RECORD CROWD

. . . Eager for news, he went into a shop and got all the big popular London papers, *Mail*s and *Express*es, the loudest shouters of the lot. How they hollered 'War' to a thrilled universe! He found all his horizons, by the medium of this yellow journalism, turned into a sinister sulphur. He was as pleased as Punch.

Ah, the grand messengers of death, the three-inch capitals! With the words came a dark rush of hot humanity in his mind. An immense human gesture swept its shadows across him like a smoky cloud. 'Germany declares war on Russia' seemed a roar of guns. He saw active mephistophelian specks in Chancelleries – 'diplomats' like old Leo. He saw a rush of papers, a frowning race. He saw it with innate military exultation. His ancestor had stood beside Clive. His grandfather had served under Outram. The ground seemed to sway a little, as it would with the passage of a Juggernaut, or a proud and ponderous Express. He left the paper shop, gulping this big morsel down, with stony dignity.

The party at the golf links took his *News*, *Mail*s and *Mirror*s, as the run home started. Each manifested his gladness at the bad news in his own inimitable way, every shade of British restraint, *phlegm*, and matter-of-factness.

Would Old England declare War? Leo said *yes*, 'she' would. But Cantleman was all for 'her' not being a silly girl. She would keep out of it, as she always had, said he, the crafty old shop-keeping hussy! But the 'yeas' had it – if you counted in the back of the chauffeur. That back, with the melancholy wisdom of the working man, could only think one thing: namely that whatever was *bad* for the general run of men would probably be done. He knew 'England' better than the others – he had no illusions about 'her'. (He knew there was no 'her' at all, to start with.) His high-spirited masters would probably decide to blow his head off – he had learned that in a hard school. If it lay between letting him alone, and dragging him away to death in battle, almost certainly they would choose the latter course. They were like that. The silent back of the liveried servant said all and more than that. His lips were sealed, but his back was eloquent. . . .

———

PART II, CHAPTER III

JOURNEY DURING MOBILIZATION

. . . Mobilization was everywhere; the train was quite full. Ten people, chiefly women, slept upright against each other in one carriage. They revealed unexpected fashions in sleep. Their eyes seemed to be shut fast to enable them to examine some ludicrous fact within. It looked, from the corridor, like a séance of imbeciles . . .

He fell asleep. When he woke he was evidently upon a bridge. Newcastle on Tyne, he found it was. There were sentries on the bridge. It might be blown up otherwise – we were almost at war, and already spies were speeding towards all bridges with infernal machines ready for use. Stacks of rifles on the railway platform. More 'mobilization scenes', to delight the *Mail* or *Mirror* . . .

Newcastle woke them up with a banging of doors. They stared glassily at it, but without disturbing the symmetry of their *tableau vivant*. A squat seafaring figure in a stiff short coat got in. Cantleman made room for him. Six a side made a more massive effect than five, and no one was in a mood of aloofness at this juncture of Britain's history! The newcomer aimed his stern at the fissure between Cantleman's and the neighbouring body. He began a gradual sinking movement, towards the seat. He reached it a short time after the train had restarted.

This was not an attractive man. As he was on the way down to the seat he even showed a certain truculence. As it were defiantly, he announced that he was answering *a mobilization call*. The implication was that such a man had a right to be seated. He must have something to do with the navy's food, thought Cantleman.

'I'm not travelling for pleasure,' said the fellow later on, in a harsh and angry voice, looking at Cantleman with a bloodshot eye. 'No, I'm called up, I've been called up.'

'I guessed that,' said C.

'You did, did you! Yes, what are we going for – can you tell me that?' That Cantleman could not guess. He shook his head. 'Why, to take the place of other men, as soon as they're shot down!'

The trenchant hissing of the 'soon' and 'shot down' woke up one or two of the women, who looked at him resentfully out of one eye.

'The Kayser ought to be bloody well shot!' he went on.

'He's a bad emperor,' agreed Cantleman.

'Bad! He's worse than bad!'

'He's a wretched emperor,' said Cantleman, soothingly.

'He's bin getting ready for this 'ere for twenty years. Now he's going to have what he's bin askin' for. Hot and heavy – a-ah! Spendin' his private fortune on it, he has. For twenty years. He'll get it where the chicken got the chopper! Shootin's too good for his kind.'

'Who?' asked Cantleman.

'Why the Kayser,' the man roared out suspiciously. 'Who did you think I meant? Napoleon Boneypart!'

This fellow was round fifty, like a hard-featured Prussian. *Must* be connected with catering, to be so bellicose! thought Cantleman. A sea-grocer? The white apron of the German delicatessen-butcher fitted him, in the mind's eye. Did battleships have sausage-and-snack bars? Too noisy by far to be a fighting man. Near his pension perhaps. A very savage character . . .

THE WAR-CROWDS, 1914

THE CROWD
London, July 1914

Men drift in thrilling masses past the Admiralty, cold night tide. Their throng creeps round corners, breaks faintly here and there up against a railing barring from possible sights. Local ebullience and thickening: some madmen disturbing their depths with baffling and recondite noise.

The police with distant icy contempt herd London. They shift it in lumps, passim, touching and shaping it with heavy delicate professional fingers. Their attitude suggests that these universal crowds are out for some new vague Suffrage – which they may, but only after interminable battles, be accorded.

Is this opposition correct? In ponderous masses they prowl, with excited hearts. Are the Crowds then female? The police at all events handle them with a professional contempt of their excited violence, cold in their helmets. – Some tiny grain of suffrage will perhaps be thrown to the millions in the street. Or taken away.

The police are contemptuous, cold and disagreeable, however.

Already the newspapers smell carrion. They allow themselves the giant type reserved for great catastrophes. They know when they are on a good thing, and it is a good thing they are on.

Prussia should be the darling of the Press. The theatrical instinct of the New Germany has saved the Crowd from breaking up for a third of a century. It has kept men in crowds, enslaving them to the feminine entity of their meaningless numbers.

Bang! Bang!

Ultimatum to you!

Ultimatum to you!

Ultimatum to you!

ULTIMATUM!

From an evening paper: July —.

The outlook has become far more grave during the afternoon. Germany's attitude causes considerable uneasiness. She seems to be throwing obstacles in the way. – The German ambassador in Vienna has telegraphed to his government, etc.

Germany, the sinister brigand of latter-day Europe, *mauvais voisin* for the little French bourgeois-reservist, remains silent and ominously unhelpful in her armoured cave across the Rhine.

Do all these idiots really mean – ?! An *is it possible!* from Cantleman. To which there is only one answer. YES! . . .

Cantleman sees another analogy, to express the meaning of this Crowd. The Bachelor and the Husband Crowd. How about that? The married man as the symbol of the Crowd! – Is it not his function to bring one into being? To create one in the bowels of his wife? At the alter he embraces Death, just as the crowd does, who assembles to shout WAR!

―――

PART II, CHAPTER V

. . . You have read what Cantleman felt. Well, that is *pretty near* to what I felt. – *Great* interest. *Great* curiosity. But no identification of my personality with that collective Sensation. The war-crowds who roared approval of the declaration of war in 1914, were a jellyfish, in my judgement. For some they were a Great People in their wrath, roaring before the throne of the God of Justice, for the blood of the unrighteous. That was not my view of the matter.

This 'Cantleman' fragment (which as I started by saying appeared in *Blast*) was entitled '*The Crowd-Master*'. Deliberately autobiographical up to a point, it is the best possible material for an *Autobiography*: and what was meant by 'Crowdmaster' was that I was master of myself. Not of anybody else – that I have never wanted to be. I was master *in* the crowd, not master *of* the crowd. I moved freely and with satisfaction up and down its bloodstream, in strict, even arrogant, insulation from its demonic impulses.

This I regarded as, in some sort, a triumph of mind over matter. It was a triumph (as I saw it then) of the individualist principle. I believed a great deal in the individual. And I still prefer him to his collective counterpart, though recognizing his shortcomings.

Now you will probably see without my telling you what follows from all this. My attitude to War is complex. *Per se*, I neither hate it nor love it. War I only came to know gradually, it is true. War takes some getting to know. I know it intimately. And what's more, I know all about war's gestation and antecedents, and I have savoured its aftermaths. What I don't know about War is not worth knowing.

When first I met War face to face I brought no moral judgements with me at all. I have never been able to regard war – modern war – as good or bad. Only supremely stupid.

Certainly I understand that almost all wars are promoted and directed by knaves, for their own unpleasant ends, at the expense of fools, their cannonfodder. And certainly knaves are *bad men*, very bad men. But the greatest wickedness of all – if we much deal in moral values – is the perpetuation of foolishness which these carnivals of mass-murder involve.

But now I will take up the narrative in my own person again . . .

———

PART II, CHAPTER VIII

Before turning my back upon England, I will first refer to a few of the figures prominent in the literary world and in art, in 1914, who became soldiers. Principally two: namely T. E. Hulme and Gaudier-Brzeska. They were both killed, the former within a quarter of a mile of where I was standing. We were in neighbouring batteries.

I did not see him hit, but everything short of that, for we could see their earthworks, and there was nothing between to intercept the view. I watched, from ours, his battery being punched full of deep craters, with large naval shells: and from the black fountains of earth that spouted up, in breathless succession, occasional débris hurtled around us as we looked on. I remember a splintered balk of wood sailing over and striking the dug-out at my back . . .

———

PART III, CHAPTER II

. . . 'They've started shelling again!' he groaned in disgust, moving restlessly in his bed. 'This happens every night. They shelled us for an hour the night before last. They've spotted us, I think – they'll never let us alone now.'

No sooner had he uttered his complaint, than a second shell came over. As he heard the sound start, of its whooping approach, his bed gave a violent creak. I watched him heel over on one side. As the shell descended – with its strange parabolic whooping onrush – an anal whistle answered it, from the neighbouring bed. This response was forced out of him, by unrestrained dismay.

That was my first encounter with 'wind-up', as it was my first experience of shelling. In fact, it was the most perfect specimen of wind-up that it would be possible to find I think. And at each successive shell-swoop it was repeated. He raised himself slightly; and he answered the frightening onrush of the cylinder of metal with his humble gaseous discharge. He did not seem to mind at all my seeing this. I suppose he thought I would put it down to indigestion.

After a few shells had come over, we sat up in bed, and he gave me his opinion on the architecture of our dug-outs. I was glad, as it seemed to take his mind off the shells.

'This dug-out is a joke!' he told me. 'It wouldn't stop an india-rubber ball! These dug-outs are wash-outs.'

'Are they?' I said, glancing up with considerable uneasiness at the mud roof a foot or two away from my head.

Like most military novices I had innocently supposed that a dug-out – any dug-out – was there to keep out shell-fire, and was reasonably secure. I had felt as safe as houses in this earthen igloo. But he rapidly disabused me.

'A five-nine would go through this as if it was paper!' he assured me. 'If one of those shells happens to hit this dug-out – well, it's all up with us. We should both of us be dead within a second.'

As he spoke another shell plunged down outside, very much nearer this time. Indeed it seemed to me that it had come down a few feet off – for at first it is very difficult to judge the distance of a 'burst', from the sound, if you do not see it but only hear it.

'That was pretty near wasn't it?' I asked.

'No, they most of them fall in the next field. But it's quite near enough.'

'Quite,' I said. 'Oughtn't we to go out and see what's happening?'

'Nothing's happening,' he said. 'This goes on all the time. This might stop a splinter. But *a direct hit!* Then we're for it!'

I saw if we went outside we should be inviting a splinter. I supposed the chances of a direct hit were so much less that he was wise to stop where he was.

He went on instructing me in the futility of dug-outs, however

– especially *our* dug-outs. They were champion death-traps for unlucky subalterns.

'There's nothing on top here,' pointing up over his head, 'but a little loose earth. Just a few shovelsful of loose earth and a log or two.'

'Is that all?' I muttered indignantly.

'That's all. What's the use of that? There's a piece of corrugated iron!'

'Is there?' I asked, looking up with expectation.

'Somewhere I expect. A lot of use *that* is! The sandbags at the side are a foot thick if that. A shell goes through that like butter. It likes sandbags. Shells like making holes in sandbags.'

I tossed up my head, in scandalized silence.

'I don't know why they take the trouble to make them. They're useless. We might just as well be sleeping in a Nissen hut. It doesn't even keep the rain out. It drips on my face when it rains.

'I suppose,' I said for the sake of something to say, 'there is a slight chance. The logs might interfere with the burst.'

'Don't you believe it! It would come clean through and burst in our faces. We'd be full of splinters inside a second.'

I found subsequently that he was quite correct. As regards the surface dug-outs, of sandbags, balks, and earth, they were useless. Later on I was given a bedchamber of my own. It was a shack of corrugated iron, without any pretentions to being a parabellum.

———

PART III, CHAPTER IV

. . . This O C was more alive than most – a small commercial gent (perhaps a garage proprietor, I thought, or employee in a shipping office) blossomed suddenly into a major, R A. Slight in build, about thirty, lightly moustached, he was able and very collected when other people were the reverse. I concluded from what I saw of him that he had set his mind upon taking back a Military Cross to Balham. I was under the impression that he would deserve it, if he could extract it from the donors of such things . . .

Going through the lines of 'the Field' the shelling was heavy – though on the whole there was every evidence that the enemy were not replying with their customary aggressiveness. Their artillery was being moved back.

A Field Battery beside which we were making our way was

having a rough time, however. There were several casualties while we were passing its guns, but my little O C might have been taking a walk with his dog for all the notice he took. Good boy, I thought! He knew his stuff.

But at this point civilization ended. At least so far, we could be sure of our bearings. Beyond this battery was a short stretch of shell-pitted nothingness – for we had entered upon that arid and blistering vacuum; the lunar landscape, so often described in the war-novels and represented by dozens of painters and draughtsmen, myself among them, but the particular quality of which it is so difficult to convey. Those grinning skeletons in field-grey, the skull still protected by the metal helmet: those festoons of mud-caked wire, those miniature mountain-ranges of saffron earth, and trees like gibbets – these were the properties only of those titanic casts of dying . . .

––

. . . 'I'm going to Battalion Headquarters,' said the O C pointing towards the shell-burst, but every two seconds others were coming down in between. 'You stop here.'

I obeyed. There was nothing I wanted this dark game could give, but my O C had his plans. He was not a romantic person. What he did was methodic and in pursuance I am sure of business – plus patriotism, that is understood. Every step of that walk he took was a gamble with death, and he was a hardy gambler to whom I wished luck.

I call it a walk, but it was quite different to a walk. No sooner had he stepped on what was left of the road, than a shell rushed at him, and only just in time he flung himself upon his face. He got another two or three yards at most, and down crashed two more; and down he went for the count. But he was only lying low and resting. I would see his alert little figure rise from the dust of one shell burst, step briskly along and disappear in the spouting of the next. At last with a rush he made what was apparently the entrance to the subterranean headquarters of some invisible battalion.

He stayed down there a while. I sat drowsily nodding in the lee of the fragment of wall, only half-conscious of the whooping and thumping of the shells. The two men and myself became a waxwork trio in this wilderness. I suppose they continued to brew their infernal chicory, at my back. Suddenly I became aware of the imminence of my commanding officer's return. I stood up and after a half-dozen imperative prostrations, and as many headlong rushes, there he was before me, as cool and collected as ever, pointing back over his shoulder.

'As soon as they've got the front-line fixed, there's an old German dug-out there,' he pointed to the roadside, between us and Battalion Headquarters, 'which would make an excellent O. Pip. I'll come up tomorrow again with some signallers – there may be something better, but if not that will do.'

Our return journey was less peaceful. More German batteries were firing now, and a number of shells intercepted us. We met an infantry party coming up, about ten men, with earthen faces and heads bowed, their eyes turned inward as it seemed, to shut out this too-familiar scene. As a shell came rushing down beside them, they did not notice it. There was no sidestepping death if this was where you *lived*. It was worth *our* while to prostrate ourselves, when death came over-near. We might escape, *in spite of* death. But *they* were its servants. Death would not tolerate that optimistic obeisance from them! . . .

PART III, CHAPTER VI

. . . The gas-shells were small, came down with a soft sickly whistle, and struck the ground with a gentle *plock*. Their very sound was suggestive of *gas*. There was nothing to be afraid of unless they got a direct hit on your chest – except their gas. But in going to the lavatory they *were* liable to hit you. For some reason they fell, to start with, all round this place and on the pathway we had to take from the Mess.

In the morning the battery usually stank of sweet gas. Men were always going sick. A gunner who got down into a shell hole, where the gas clung for hours, was laid out. We kept them out of the holes if we could.

For weeks on end every man in the battery slept in his gas-mask. In lying down we fixed our gas-masks, with the tin teat just up against our lips. Before we were all asleep one of us – usually Boorfelt – would sit up, sniff, and say 'gas!' We would all sniff, and then said 'gas!' Then we stuck our tin teats in our mouths, and clipped the pincers upon our noses. So we would sleep for the rest of the night . . .

... Sixty per cent of the casualties on the Western Front were caused by shell-fire, forty per cent by bullets. (Bayonet wounds were so rare that they do not enter into the statistics.) Shell-fire is an interesting subject, therefore, for the soldier. And there is nothing I do not know about shell-fire. As a matter of fact our position by the side of an important road was peculiarly adapted to making one an expert in that subject.

Each 'burst' produces its spawn of 'splinters', which proceed to whizz in all directions till they lose momentum, and drop, or flop, on the ground. They were flopping the whole time round us, as well as buzzing past our shoulders. The force with which they arrived depended, naturally, upon the nearness of the burst. I was often spanked with a spent one – like being hit with a stone not thrown very hard ...

PART III, CHAPTER VIII

... The German front-line trench was almost immediately beneath us – the two front lines were so close together here that we could almost look into it. It was very thinly held at this time. I sometimes thought there were no Germans there at all.

On another occasion I was in this observation-post when a great barrage was laid upon the German trenches. A Field Artillery officer was up there with me and we waited down in the trench for the barrage zero hour. We got up just before the storm broke. Then, to the second, there was the muffled crash of massed artillery, and over came the barrage – every type of projectile, groaning, panting, bumbling, whistling and wheezing overhead. Down they plunged upon the German trench, a chain of every type of burst, and a screen of smoke and earth defined, as far as one could see on either hand, the German Line.

As we stood watching – there was no occasion to consider exposing ourselves to enemy fire, with such a tornado as this absorbing all his attention – the other officer clutched my arm and pointed his finger. 'See that!' he said. I looked where he pointed, and saw something dark fly into the air, in the midst of the smoke. My companion said it was the leg of a Bosche, but I thought, though it looked rather like a boot and half a thigh, that it was in fact some less sensational object. It may all the same have been a German limb: and if so it was probably my strong feeling that there were no Germans there that made me incredulous. – Also I did not care whether it was a leg or not, there is always that . . .

———

. . . A stunt had been announced. It was the morning of the attack. There had been a good deal of shelling. Menzies, in coming up with the relief, met in the support lines a figure being borne upon a stretcher. Its eye, as he passed, appeared aware of him; the head remained facing the sky. A solemn eye swept over him, as they passed, in placid recognition, nothing more. Menzies felt it was his O C, though he had not noticed the face as he passed him. He ran back.

'Are you hurt, sir?'

Polderdick's eye settled down in the corner of his head to observe his subaltern.

'My rheumatism's something cruel this morning. It's laid me out something proper. They're taking me back. – You carry on, my lad. Pass on! It's downed me this time properly.'

He spoke in the quiet voice of one in pain. Menzies got used, likewise, to this. Whenever a stunt was coming off, Polderdick disappeared, on a stretcher, if he could get one, to the rear, or he kept away till the worst was over.

Menzies and Marshall, the other subaltern of his section, talked over the situation. Marshall was resentful. He had been sent to Trench Mortars with death in his soul. A month of them had developed in him a hatred of everything in this inferno. Menzies did not entertain a severe view of Polderdick, however. He explained to the sullen Marshall the advantages, as he saw it, of the case. Also he excused him. He pointed out that Polderdick had been wounded in the temple. Before that – who could doubt, who had glanced casually at his left breast? – he had certainly been a very brave man. But also, of course (it was to be supposed) he had not then exclaimed 'Ha! Ha!' He had not prodded people in the stomach with his stick. – For Menzies there were two lives, where Polderdick was concerned. There had been one in which he had been a madly brave soldier in the ranks (look at his ribbons, consider his record!). There he got his crosses, his nickname, his prestige. Then there was the other one in which he was just *mad*, without however being brave. He was charming, but no longer brave.

Much of his *madness*, Menzies proceeded to argue – as they sat at the tin-table of the café in Bailleul where they had gone in a lorry for the afternoon to get tobacco and condensed milk for the officer's mess – much of his peculiar wildness, had gone into, had been absorbed by, his physical daring, about that there was little doubt. It had had to go somewhere. It had gone into that. Then the wound in the temple stopped that up, brusquely. You see? (Marshall did not see: he cursed the metaphysical Scot, he yawned, he stamped, he lit cigarettes, he glared). The wound, for whatever reason, prevented his madness from any longer flowing into the moulds of physical heroism. It found other outlets. He became a different man. He did not forget his past bravery, however. His new incarnation was its distorted child . . .

———

. . . This restless spirit of haunting adventure would sometimes make [Polderdick] mischievous. He would come up from the billet into a quiet world, a local truce reigning throughout the stagey ditches and melodramatic crypts and holes of the landscape, of which he was a notable faun. A few lonely shells sang or creaked along overhead, bursting in the remote distance, like the noisy closing of very far-off doors. Butterflies drifted here and there. German and English, Fritz and Tom, read the newspaper, slept, wrote to Gretchen or the lovely Minnie. – Polderdick would gaze round at this idyllic scene with a dissatisfied and restless eye.

On one of these occasions Marshall was on duty. He was sunning himself on a stretch of wet mud. One gunner was asleep, another writing a letter. Polderdick appeared and fixed his eye upon Marshall. Blankly with sudden unction he declared.

'Ha! *Ha*! Mr Marshall! An excellent opportunity for Trench Mortars! What do you think? Is that right?' He put up his periscope and peered into it. 'I see a Hun's back in what is evidently a post, an advanced post. They've got the cheek of the devil some of those Huns. The Fritzes in that sap to the left seem to have got it into their heads that this part of the line is a branch of the Millennium! Swelt my bob if I don't see two having a shave, the bastards, as large as life!'

As fast as they could be loaded, he sent his Flying Pig hurtling in all directions. All the peaceable warriors in the trenches were filled with amazement, which rapidly turned to fury when they realized what was happening. A raucous murmur, a tenuous hubbub of alarm and inquiry, floated across no man's land. This was quickly succeeded by a fusillade of every description of missile and projectile on which the enemy could lay his hands quickly. A black cloud of anger surged along our trench. Infantry officers rushed up to Polderdick, shaking their fists in his face. But flourishing his stick mysteriously, he hastily retired down the communication trench, and was seen no more till the next day.

Meantime the *riposte* had come and a furious bombardment had fallen on the trench. In the rear the Field started, the Heavies joined in, layer behind layer, until the enormous guns right back on the old ramparts of Ypres were shattering the air with their discharge, and for a short time all was confusion. On both sides everyone stood by, expecting an attack. Marshall was wounded in the lung, two gunners were killed. Menzies was telephoned for from the trench by the breathless telephonist, and as he was hurrying up he met his O C retiring hastily along the duckboard track.

'Is it an attack?' he asked.

'An attack? No-o, attack be buggered! It's as quiet as Heaven up there!'

'Marshall's wounded. Didn't you know?'

'Marshall wounded? Who said so?'

'The telephonist. They're probably attacking. Look at all this coming over!'

There was a line of black stumps on a low ridge to their left, and every few seconds an immense impressive chocolate black burst rose up and spent splinters flapped in the mud on either side of the duckboard track.

'Yes, it's not over healthy here, I agree,' Polderdick said, starting anxiously forward, his eye on a line of burst on the road ahead, that he would soon have to cross. 'I'm going to get back. My rheumatism's something awful today. But it's quiet enough up in the Line. I came away because there was nothing doing. You can go up there if you want a nap' . . .

———

. . . But his guns, although in position, and firmly cemented by written authority, were not so secure as they seemed. The infantry gathered for the attack. On a fine afternoon, when, in fact, Polderdick was on the point of exclaiming 'Ha! *Ha!* an excellent opportunity for Trench Mortars!' a suave, hirsute and old colonel arrived on the scene, and made straight for the Flying Pigs. Polderdick, with a dramatic leap, intercepted him, stick in hand, twirling and feinting. He appeared to take it for granted that this interloper had designs upon his fat little ordnance.

'Are these your guns?' The intercepted colonel fixed him severely with his veteran eye, that noted the ranker's ribbons, and sought to quell the life-long 'common soldier' beneath the new Sam Browne. Polderdick, on his side, saw nothing but a lieut-colonel in this hostile person.

'Yes. – Yes: yes. My guns. My pigs. My little pigs, sir.'

'I don't think that is a very good position for them.'

'No? No!'

'You must see that dug-out –'

'I see the dug-out. I've had my eye on it from the first. And if you know of a better hole, sir – well, you know what to do!'

'Yes, but that dug-out –'

'Yes sir, that dug-out – But you can't attack Fritz with a dug-out, sir. You fire nothing out of a dug-out, sir. You might fire Captain Nixon a hundred yards or so, with a big charge. But I'm accredited to these 9.45s, these "flying pigs" as they call them. I have no order, sir, as regards Captain Nixon –'

'Stop this tomfoolery please. Your guns are in the way where you have placed them. And they are not well-placed either –'

'I beg your pardon, sir?' Polderdick grew suddenly one harsh blotch of red, as though he had been slapped. 'Are you aware to whom you are speaking?' He drew himself up, and flung his chest out, the mad-soldier entering into him again for a moment following this direct affront to his professional pride. His voice too got its wild and shouting note. 'Do you know my name, sir? Captain Polderdick is my name, Polderdick. Burney Polderdick.'

He continued to glare at the colonel for a moment; but his eye gradually filled with the peculiar light of the transformed 'Burney', though more wild even than usual.

'*I am the* King of the Trenches!' he shouted. 'Didn't you know who I was? Yes! I am Burney Polderdick, the King of the Trenches! – Ha *Ha!*' He flourished his stick, twirled it lightly, lunged forward, and dug the colonel in the middle of the stomach . . .

... I, along with millions of others, was standing up to be killed. Very well: but *who* in fact was it, who was proposing to kill or maim me? I developed a certain inquisitiveness upon that point. I saw clearly that it was not my German opposite number. He, like myself, was an instrument. That we were all on a fool's errand had become plain to many of us, for, beyond a certain point, victory becomes at the best a Pyrrhic victory, and that point had been reached before Passchendaele started.

The scapegoat-on-the-spot did not appeal to me. So I had not even the consolation of 'blaming the Staff', after the manner of Mr Sassoon – of cursing the poor little general-officers.

> 'Good morning, good morning,' the General said,
> As we passed him one day as we went up the line.
> But the lads that he spoke to are most of them dead
> And we're cursing his staff for incompetent swine.
> 'He's a cheery old sport!' muttered Harry to Jack.
> But he's done for them both with his plan of attack.

That was too easy and obvious. It amazes me that so many people should accept that as satisfactory. The incompetent general was clearly such a very secondary thing compared with the incompetent, or unscrupulous, politician, that this conventional 'grouse' against the imperfect strategy of the military gentleman directing operations in the field seemed not only unintelligent but dangerously misleading. 'Harry and Jack' were killed, not by the general, but by the people, whoever they were, responsible for the war.

WYNDHAM LEWIS

see also p. 102

Reacting against, but influenced by, Marinetti and the Futurists, the first *Blast* was launched on 15 July 1914. Its major manifesto was signed, amongst others, by Richard Aldington, Ezra Pound, Gaudier-Brzeska, William Roberts, Edward Wadsworth and Wyndham Lewis himself. Lewis saw *Blast* as '. . . an art paper to advertise and popularize a movement in the visual arts which I had initiated'. The second, and last, issue came out a year later and was dominated by the war. It included poems by Pound, T. S. Eliot and Ford Madox Ford. Wyndham Lewis was a co-founder of *Blast*.

Source: Blast, War Number, July 1915 (reprinted by Black Sparrow Press, Santa Barbara, California, 1981).

THE SIX HUNDRED, VERESTCHAGIN AND UCCELLO

To the question 'why has not the present war produced fine poems, etc.?' you would reply, 'What fine poetry or literature did the Crimean War or the Franco-Prussian War produce?' Some clever stories by Guy de Maupassant, and Zola's *Débâcle* was about the only good literature 1870 has to show for itself. Tennyson's 'Cannon to the right of them, cannon to the left of them' is certainly not as good as Kipling's specializations in military matters, which came out of an Imperialistic period of Peace. Tolstoy's account of the Seige of Sebastopol is the sort of book of notes any War or similar adventure may be responsible for, if an observant person happens to be among those taking part in it. The Napoleonic Wars were different. The work of Stendhal, for instance, is a psychological monument of that epic, in that part of it which is the outcome of the hard and vulgar energies of his time. But at present Germany is the only country that harks back sufficiently to put up any show of analogy to those energies; and she is honeycombed with disintegration into another and more contemporary state of mind, which is her worst enemy – not England, as her journalists proclaim.

I have heard people say 'None of our great men have come up

to scratch. Not one has said anything adequate about the War.'
Shaw, Wells, etc., have seemingly all failed to come up to what
might be expected of the occasion. But when you consider that
none of them like the War at all, though all are more or less
agreed that England did right in fighting: that they are Socialists,
and do not wish to encourage and perpetuate War by saying
anything 'wonderful' about it, or flattering its importance; this is
not to be wondered at. There is one man in Europe who must be
in the seventh heaven: that is Marinetti. From every direction
come to him sound and rumours of conflict. He must be torn in
mind, as to which point of the compass to rush to and drink up
the booming and banging, lap up the blood! He must be a
radiant figure now!

Marinetti's one and only (but very fervent and literal) disciple
in this country, had seemingly not thought out, or carried to
their logical conclusion, all his master's precepts. For I hear that,
de retour du Front, this disciple's first action has been to write to
the compact Milanese volcano that he no longer shares, that he
REPUDIATES, all his (Marinetti's) utterances on the subject
of War, to which he formerly subscribed. Marinetti's solitary
English disciple has discovered that War is not *Magnifique*, or
that Marinetti's *Guerre* is not *la Guerre*.

Tant Mieux.

The dearth of 'War Verse' or good war literature has another
reason. The quality of uniqueness is absent from the present
rambling and universal campaign. There are so many actions
every day, necessarily of brilliant daring, that they become
impersonal. Like the multitudes of drab and colourless uniforms
– these in their turn covered with still more characterless mud –
there is no room, in praising the soldiers, for anything but an
abstract hymn. These battles are more like ant-fights than anything we have done in this way up to now. The Censor throws
further obstacles in the way of Minor and Major Verse.

Of similar interest to the question of War-Poetry is that of
War-Painting. To illuminate this point I will quote an article
called Historic Battle Pictures, in the *Daily News* of February 2nd.

One is already asking on the continent who will be the first to
immortalize on canvas or in marble the tremendous realities of
1914–15 – Every epoch has had its illustrious painters. Charlet
drew the old soldiers of the 'Grande Armée' and the bewhiskered
grenadiers; after the First Empire came the artillery officer

Penguilly l'Haridon, Boissard de Boisdenier, the friend of Delacroix and creator of the 'Retraite de Russie' in the Rouen gallery; Eugène Lami, Hippolyte Bellangé, Meissonier himself, Yvon, whose speciality was Zouaves, and Protais, the painter of the *chasseurs à pied*; and the names with which lovers of the priceless collection at Versailles are familiar.

Defeat inspired the historical painters in the seventies. Victory will be the new theme. The famous 'Les Voilà!' of Étienne Beaumetz adorns one of M. Millerand's rooms at the Ministry of War. It was Alphonse de Neuville who gave us most of the vivid details of the terrible year – the hand-to-hand encounters, the frenzied and bloody struggles of the dying, the calm portrayed on heroic countenances as death approaches, the flight and explosion of shrapnel. And after him Édouard Détaille, whose 'Défense de Champigny' is one of the greatest battle-pictures of any country or any age.

A NEW VERESTCHAGIN?

The campaign of last year and this! What masterpieces must be born!

It is useful to quote this article because, in its tone, it reproduces the attitude of the Public to War-Art. It also gives an eloquent list of names.

No critic of let us say a leading Daily Paper would pretend that the 'Meissonier himself' of this article, or 'Yvon whose speciality was Zouaves,' were very good painters; any more than today they would insist on the importance of Mr Leader or Mr Waterhouse. Édouard Détaille, whose ' "Défense de Champigny" is one of the greatest battle-pictures of any country or any age' is, in circles who discuss these matters with niceness and sympathy, considered, I believe, not so good as 'Meissonier himself'.

Shall we conclude from this that War-painting is in a category by itself, and distinctly inferior to several other kinds of painting? That is a vulgar modern absurdity: painting is divided up into categories, Portrait, Landscape, Genre, etc. Portrait being 'more difficult' than Landscape, and 'Battle Pictures' coming in a little warlike class of their own, and admittedly not such Very High Art as representations of Nude Ladies.

Soldiers and War are as good as anything else. The Japanese did not discriminate very much between a Warrior and a Buttercup. The flowering and distending of an angry face and the beauty of the soldier's arms and clothes, was a similar spur to creation to the grimace of a flower. Uccello in his picture at the National Gallery formularized the spears and aggressive prancing of the fighting men of his time till every drop of reality is frozen out of them. It is the politest possible encounter. Velasquez painted the formality of a great treaty in a canvas full of soldiers. And so on.

There is no reason why very fine representative paintings of the present War should not be done. Van Gogh would have done one, had he been there. But Derain, the finest painter to my knowledge at the front, will not paint one. Severini, on the other hand, if his lungs are better, and if Expressionism has not too far denaturalized his earlier Futurist work, should do a fine picture of a battle.

Gaudier-Brzeska, the sculptor, whose Vortex from the trenches makes his sentiments on the subject of War and Art quite clear, is fighting for France, but probably will not do statues afterwards of either Bosche or Piou-Piou; to judge from his treatment of the Prussian rifle-butt.

MARINETTI'S OCCUPATION

The War will take Marinetti's occupation of platform boomer away.

The War has exhausted interest for the moment in booming and banging. I am not indulging in a sensational prophecy of the disappearance of Marinetti. He is one of the most irrepressible figures of our time, he would take a great deal to discourage. Only he will have to abandon War-noise more or less definitely, and I feel this will be a great chagrin for him. If a human being was ever quite happy and in his element it was Marinetti imitating the guns of Adrianople at the Doré with occasional answering bangs on a big drum manipulated by his faithful English disciple, Mr Nevinson, behind the curtain in the passage. He will still be here with us. Only there will be a little something not quite the same about him. Those golden booming days between Lule Burgas and the Aisne will be over for ever. There is a Passéist Pathos about this thought. It has always been plain that as artists two or three of the Futurist Painters were of more importance than their poet-impresario. Balla and Severini would, under any circumstances, be two of the most amusing painters of our time. And regular military War was not their theme, as it was Marinetti's, but rather very intense and vertiginous Peace.

The great Poets and flashing cities will still be there as before the War. But in a couple of years the War will be behind us.

THE LONDON GROUP, 1915 (MARCH)

... As to Mr Nevinson's work, an artist can only receive fair treatment at the hands of one completely in sympathy with him. So it would not be fair for me to take Mr Nevinson's paintings for criticism, side by side with Wadsworth's, for instance. Nevertheless, I can say that his 'Marching Soldiers' have a hurried and harrassed melancholy and chilliness that is well seen. Also at the Alpine Club, Mr Nevinson's 'Searchlights', the best picture there, is perhaps too, the best he has painted ...

... Gaudier-Brzeska is not very well represented. He is busy elsewhere, and of the two statues here, one is two or three years old, I should think. As an archaism it has considerable beauty. The other little one in red stone has a great deal of the plastic character we associate with his work. It is admirably condensed, and heavily sinuous. There is a suave, thick, quite PERSONAL character about his best work. It is this, that makes his sculpture what we would principally turn to in England to show the new forces and future of this art. His beautiful drawing from the trenches of a bursting shell is not only a fine design, but a curiosity. It is surely a pretty satisfactory answer to those who would kill us with Prussian bullets: who say, in short, that Germany, in attacking Europe, has killed spiritually all the Cubists, Vorticists and Futurists in the world. Here is one, a great artist, who makes drawings of those shells as they come towards him, and which, thank God, have not killed him or changed him yet ...

... The critiques in the daily Press of this particular Exhibition have been much the same as usual. Two of them, however, may be answered. One of these, Mr Nevinson deals with elsewhere in this paper, in an open letter. There remains *The Times* notice on 'Junkerism in Art'.

Many people tell me that to call you a 'Prussian' at the present juncture is done with intent to harm, to cast a cloud over the movement, if possible, and moreover that it is actionable. But I do not mind being called a Prussian in the least. I am glad I am not one, however, and it may be worth while to show how, aesthetically, I am not one either. This critic relates the paintings by Mr Wadsworth, Mr Roberts and myself to Prussian Junkerism: he also says, 'Should the Junker happily take to painting, instead of disturbing the peace of Europe, he would paint pictures very similar to those of Mr Wadsworth, Mr Roberts, and Mr Wyndham Lewis.'

This last statement is a careless one: for the Junker, obviously, if he painted, would do florid and disreputable canvasses of nymphs and dryads, or very sentimental 'portraits of the Junker's mother'. But as to the more general statement, it crystallizes, topically, a usual error as to our aims. Because these paintings are rather strange at first sight, they are regarded as ferocious and unfriendly. They are neither, although they have no pretence to an excessive gentleness or especial love for the general public. We are not cannibals. Our rigid head-dresses and disciplined movements, which cause misgivings in the unobservant as to our intentions, are aesthetic phenomena: our goddess is Beauty, like any Royal Academician's though we have different ideas as to how she should be depicted or carved: and we eat beefsteaks, or what we can get (except human beings) like most people – As to goose-steps, (the critic compares 'rigidity' to 'goose-step') as an antidote to the slop of Cambridge Post Aestheticism (Post-Impressionism is an insult to Manet and Cézanne) or the Gypsy Botticellis of Mill Street, may not such 'rigidity' be welcomed? This rigidity, in the normal process of Nature, will flower like other things. THIS simple and massive trunk or stem may be watched. But we are not Hindu magicians to make our Mango tree grow in half an hour. It is too commonly suggested that rigidity cannot flower without 'renouncing' itself or may not in itself be beautiful. At the worst all the finest beauty is dependent on it for life.

HENRI GAUDIER-BRZESKA

Henri Gaudier-Brzeska (1891–1915). French sculptor, who studied in England and settled in London from 1911. In 1913 he was a founder member of the London Group and in 1914–15 of the Vorticists, contributing to *Blast* (see p. 118) and to the Vorticist exhibition of 1915. Vorticism was described variously and indirectly: 'With our Vortex the Present is the only active thing . . .' (Lewis); 'The Vorticist is not the slave of commotion but its master . . .' (Lewis); 'The vortex is the point of maximal energy . . . All the past that is vital, all the past that is capable of living into the future, is pregnant in the vortex . . .' (Pound); 'Will and consciousness are our VORTEX . . .' (Gaudier-Brzeska). The obituary immediately follows Gaudier-Brzeska's own piece in the original text.

Source: Blast, War Number, July 1915 (reprinted by Black Sparrow Press, Santa Barbara, California, 1981).

VORTEX GAUDIER-BRZESKA

(written from the trenches)

NOTE. The sculptor writes from the French trenches, having been in the firing line since early in the war.

In September he was one of a patrolling party of twelve, seven of his companions fell in the fight over a roadway.

In November he was nominated for sergeancy and has been since slightly wounded, but expects to return to the trenches.

He has been constantly employed in scouting and patrolling and in the construction of wire entanglements in close contact with the Boches.

I HAVE BEEN FIGHTING FOR TWO MONTHS and I can now gauge the intensity of Life.

HUMAN MASSES teem and move, are destroyed and crop up again.

HORSES are worn out in three weeks, die by the roadside.

DOGS wander, are destroyed, and others come along.

WITH ALL THE DESTRUCTION that works

around us NOTHING IS CHANGED, EVEN SUPER-FICIALLY. <u>LIFE IS THE SAME STRENGTH</u>, THE MOVING AGENT THAT PERMITS THE SMALL INDIVIDUAL TO ASSERT HIMSELF.

THE BURSTING SHELLS, the volleys, wire entangle-ments, projectors, motors, the chaos of battle DO NOT ALTER IN THE LEAST the outlines of the hill we are besieging. A company of PARTRIDGES scuttle along before our very trench.

IT WOULD BE FOLLY TO SEEK ARTISTIC EMOTIONS AMID THESE LITTLE WORKS OF OURS.

THIS PALTRY MECHANISM, WHICH SERVES AS A PURGE TO OVER-NUMEROUS HUMAN-ITY.

THIS WAR IS A GREAT REMEDY.

IN THE INDIVIDUAL IT KILLS ARROGANCE, SELF-ESTEEM, PRIDE.

IT TAKES AWAY FROM THE MASSES NUM-BERS UPON NUMBERS OF UNIMPORTANT UNITS, WHOSE ECONOMIC ACTIVITIES BECOME NOXIOUS AS THE RECENT TRADE CRISES HAVE SHOWN US.

<u>MY VIEWS ON SCULPTURE</u> REMAIN ABSO-LUTELY <u>THE SAME</u>, IT IS THE <u>VORTEX</u> OF WILL, OF DECISION, THAT BEGINS.

I SHALL DERIVE MY EMOTIONS SOLELY FROM THE <u>ARRANGEMENT OF SURFACES</u>, I shall present my emotions by the ARRANGEMENT OF MY SURFACES, THE PLANES AND LINES BY WHICH THEY ARE DEFINED.

Just as this hill where the Germans are solidly entrenched, gives me a nasty feeling, solely because its gentle slopes are broken up by earth-works, which throw long shadows at sunset. Just so shall I get feeling, of whatsoever definition, from a statue ACCORDING TO ITS SLOPES, varied to infinity.

I have made an experiment. Two days ago I pinched from an enemy a mauser rifle. Its heavy unwieldy shape swamped me with a powerful IMAGE of brutality.

I was in doubt for a long time whether it pleased or displeased me.

I found that I did not like it.

I broke the butt off and with my knife I carved in it a design, through which I tried to express a gentler order of feeling, which I preferred.

BUT I WILL EMPHASIZE that MY DESIGN got its effect (just as the gun had) FROM A VERY SIMPLE COMPOSITION OF LINES AND PLANES.

GAUDIER-BRZESKA

MORT POUR LA PATRIE.

Henri Gaudier-Brzeska: after months of fighting and two promotions for gallantry Henri Gaudier-Brzeska was killed in a charge at Neuville St Vaast, on 5th June, 1915.

OSKAR KOKOSCHKA

Oskar Kokoschka (1886–1980). Born in Austria and brought up in Vienna. Became an artist. Volunteered in 1914, taking his own horse with him into the cavalry. The passage below describes how he was severely wounded. After his recovery he returned to the Italian Front to escort journalists and war artists. He was shell-shocked. Travelled widely. Deprived of Austrian citizenship by the Nazis. Became a British citizen in 1947.

Source: Oskar Kokoschka, *My Life* (translated from *Oskar Kokoschka: Mein Leben*, Munich, Verlag F. Bruckmann KG, 1971, by David Britt), London, Thames & Hudson, 1974.

Since I had done no service previously, my training in the cavalry school at Wiener Neustadt lasted several months. The final theoretical and tactical exercises for all the regiments took place at Mährisch-Weisskirchen (now Hranice na Moravě). I had turned into a good horseman. However, my horse, though it did not balk at any obstacle in the open fields, refused every time it came to taking hurdles in the riding-school. My captain, a Swedish volunteer, could not believe this until he tried himself and failed. This last problem was solved by Prince Sapieha, who lent me one of his four horses for the final examination. On Sapieha's horse I sailed over the hurdles and passed with ease.

We made the endless journey to the Eastern Front in cattle trucks which also transported the horses. When we left Hungary, girls in colourful costumes brought us Tokay wine and cheered us; I lifted one girl on to my saddle. How proud I was to be on horseback! People in Galicia, the Austrian part of Poland, threw flowers and rejoiced in our coming; we were welcomed like liberators. Riding beside the commanding officer of my regiment, Brigadier von Bosch, who always rode at the head of his men, I was the first into Przemyśl, which had just been liberated from the Russians, and into Gorodok, Lvov and Vladimir-Volynskiy.

Beyond the Russian frontier the countryside was suddenly deserted. The Ukrainian population had been evacuated by the

Russians after the Galician offensive, for which the Austrians had already had to call in German reinforcements. Later we came upon groups of Russian prisoners, escorted by German military police, and saw hanging from the trees the bodies of those who had openly collaborated with the Germans. In the marshy woodland it was hard to get the horses through the mud. Our cavalry was protecting the flank of the infantry and artillery of the Austro-German army corps. I thought of Dürer's sombre picture 'Knight, Death and Devil'.

I had done all my examinations, but did not understand much about tactics, and I always volunteered to ride the advance patrol, with an experienced sergeant. I would never have lasted if I had stayed with the regimental staff; the gaps in my strategic knowledge would have shown up too obviously. So although I was the officer, my sergeant was in command of the patrol. At the beginning, we were not wearing field-grey. Our uniforms, red, blue and white, stood out only too well, and as I rode out, I felt spied upon by an unseen enemy in the dense, dark foliage of the forests.

The first dead that I encountered were young comrades-in-arms of my own, men with whom, only a few nights earlier, I had been sitting round the camp-fire in those Ukrainian forests, playing cards and joking. Not much more than boys they were, squatting there on the moss in their bright-coloured trousers, a group of them round a tree trunk. From a branch a few paces farther on a cap dangled, and on the next tree a dragoon's fur-lined blue cloak. He who had once worn these things himself hung naked, head downward, from a third tree. The horses lay in the forest with their hooves in the air, swollen-bellied, swarming with flies. At the sight of this huge dung-hill my own horse reared, so that I had to dismount in order to quiet her. My patrol had been sent out to relieve these friends, who now sat there together as peacefully as if they were picnicking. Only now they would never speak again, and when I thrust my hand into the hair of the youngest among them, his scalp slipped sideways and came off in my hand.

The next moment I was ambushed for the first time in the forest. My patrol had ridden on ahead. As in an old oleograph there was a flash of sulphur-yellow from the Russians' rifles. My horse reared and whirled round, and I could not help mentally comparing myself with the equestrian monument to that glorious King of Italy, Victor Emmanuel, which I had seen not so very long ago in Naples. Like him I flashed out my brand-new sword. What did not seem to belong to this picture at all was a wickerwork chair by a tree, on which the Russians had fixed up their field-telephone. I had no chance to get a closer look at this, for my Hungarian mount was already settling into a gallop, and she kept the lead in that race, leaving the little Russian horses simply nowhere. When I looked round and saw with relief that the distance between us was rapidly increasing, I expected to see the Cossacks at their equestrian acrobatics as in the circus. I was not yet ripe for war, though to be sure I was already crawling with lice . . .

———

Then it was war again. The cavalry was to cover the flank of the retreating army. Each of us tried to work out how to correct the strategic disaster of which we could speak only in whispers. If it came off, there was the order of Knighthood of Maria Theresa; if it didn't, court-martial for insubordination. Passing through abandoned villages, we saw swarms of bees in tree trunks, not in proper hives, as at home. In a clearing in the forest we spied a stray pig. Before the words 'Catch it!' had passed from man to man, the pig had breathed its last sigh and was chopped into as many slices as the troop had horsemen. Every trooper found room in his saddle-bag for his allotted portion. We were thirsty for fame, but we were hungry as well; all we got our fill of was rum. Once our field-kitchen ventured as far out as the forward patrols and even had an independent skirmish with the enemy.

In one of the hutments in the forest, in tumbledown thatched cottages, our cholera patients had been housed during the retreat and most of them died there too. We grew used to sleeping on the same straw palliasses from which we had just seen the dead being carted off. We were too tired to care. One night in an abandoned village, to which I had ridden over felled tree trunks instead of along a track – the place was so swampy – I was wakened by a sound. An old peasant with a long beard and the staring eyes of a madman was bending over me. The sound was a faint one, like that of a knife being whetted. His bleached hair lay like a thatched roof over his wrinkled forehead. The dirty coarse linen shirt he wore hung down over his trousers. 'You shan't slit my throat like a pig's!' I yelled, making a jump at him as he disappeared into the darkness, nimble and soundless on his bast-soled shoes. I managed to do no more than knock over the spinning-wheel, which looked like an old man in the light of the dying fire. Perhaps I'd been mistaken? Was it my own heart beating so loudly? After that I couldn't go to sleep again, so I looked round among the old-world domestic utensils by the light of a resin torch. Everything was made of wood, as in those villages built on stilts, except that here there was an ikon hanging under an oleograph of the Tsar in one corner of the room.

There was something stirring at the edge of the forest. Dismount! Lead horses! Our line was joined by volunteers, and we beat forward into the bushes as if we were going out to shoot pheasant. The enemy was withdrawing deeper into the forest, firing only sporadically. So we had to mount again, which was always the worst part, for since conscription had been introduced the requisitioned horses were as gun-shy as the reservists who had been called up were wretched horsemen. After all, most of them were used to sitting only on an office chair. In the forest suddenly we were met by a hail of bullets so near and so thick that one seemed to see each bullet flitting past; it was like a startled swarm of wasps. Charge! Now the great day had come, the day for which I too had been longing. I still had enough presence of mind to urge my mount forward and to one side, out of the throng of other horses that had now gone wild, as if chased by ghosts, the congestion being made worse by more coming up from the rear and galloping over the fallen men and beasts. I wanted to settle this thing on my own and to look the enemy straight in the face. A hero's death – fair enough! But I had no wish to be trampled to death like a worm. The Russians had lured us into a trap. I had actually set eyes on the Russian machine-gun before I felt a dull blow on my temple.

The sun and the moon were both shining at once and my head ached like mad. What on earth was I to do with this scent of flowers? Some flower – I couldn't remember its name however I racked my brains. And all that yelling round me and the moaning of the wounded, which seemed to fill the whole forest – that must have been what brought me round. Good lord, they must be in agony! Then I became absorbed by the fact that I couldn't control the cavalry boot with the leg in it, which was moving about too far away, although it belonged to me. I recognized the boot by the spur: contrary to regulations, my spurs had no sharp rowels. Over on the grass there were two captains in Russian uniform dancing a ballet, running up and kissing each other on the cheeks like two young girls. That would have been against regulations in our army. I had a tiny round hole in my head. My horse, lying on top of me, had lashed out one last time before dying, and that had brought me to my senses. I tried to say something, but my mouth was stiff with blood, which was beginning to congeal. The shadows all round me were growing huger and huger, and I wanted to ask how it was that the sun and moon were both shining at the same time. I wanted to point at the sky, but my arm wouldn't move. Perhaps I lay there unconscious for several days.

I returned to my senses only when enemy stretcher-bearers tipped me off their field-stretcher as a useless burden, beside a Russian with his belly torn open and an incredible mass of intestines oozing out. The stench was so frightful that I vomited, after which I regained full consciousness. Hadn't I promised my mother to be home by a certain date? Can't remember what date it is at all! I kept on trying to work it out – yes, well, it must be about the time. One, two, three, four, five I counted on my fingers, and there was that little round hole in my head. Was I actually still alive? Oh, definitely. After all, when I said goodbye to my mother I gave her a necklace of red glass beads to keep, which a certain lady had given me. Only I could know that. But what horrified me most was that I couldn't scream, I couldn't utter any sound at all, and that was far worse than suddenly seeing a man standing over me. I opened my eyes wide, which hurt, because they were all sticky, but I had to see what he was going to do to me. Actually all I could see of him was his head and shoulders, but that was enough: he was in Russian uniform, and hence my enemy. I watched him so long that I thought I should have to wait all eternity while he stood in the moonlight setting his glittering bayonet at my breast. In my right hand, the one that wasn't paralysed, I could feel my revolver, strapped to my wrist. The revolver was aimed straight at the man's breast. The man couldn't see that, because as he bent over me he was in his own shadow. My finger pressed the cock. I managed to do it lightly, and only I heard it, but the sound went right through me. In accordance with regulations, there was a bullet in the chamber. Then his bayonet pierced my jacket and I began sweating with pain. I thought I wouldn't be able to stand the pain, telling myself that it was only fear, while the bayonet came sliding through the stuff of the jacket. A slight pressure of my finger, just such as you, dear readers, exert in order to flick a little flame out of your cigarette-lighter, would have sufficed to bring me back alive to Vienna, home to mother. After all, it's our mothers who bring us into the world and not our fatherland. Now the point was beginning to pierce the skin, was searing into the flesh. My ribs were resisting, expanding, I couldn't breathe. My capacity for endurance was failing. It was unbearable. And still I went on telling myself, as I grew weaker and weaker: 'Just a second more! This ordinary Russian is only obeying orders!' Then suddenly I felt quite light and a wave of happiness – never since then in all my life have I felt it so physically – a sense of well-being positively flung me upward. I was buoyed up on the hot stream of blood from my lungs that was coming out of my mouth and nostrils and eyes and ears. I was floating in mid-air. So this was all there was to dying? I couldn't help laughing in the man's face before I breathed my last. And the ordeal was over. All I took with me to the other side was the sight of his astonished eyes. The enemy ran away, leaving his weapon sticking in my body. It fell out under its own weight.

What happened to me then I do not know. There are gaps in my memory. It seems that one, two, or more days later they lifted me into a railway wagon, and there was a Russian conscript who had lost both his feet who kept trying to push a withered apple into my mouth – but even a surgeon couldn't have opened it, my face was so swollen. Then they lifted me out, and Russian guards officers saluted, presumably mistaking the yellow cotton threads on my collar, the cadet's badge, for real gold. Yes, it was the scent of mimosa-pollen, that was what I hadn't been able to think of before. It was mimosa that I used to send to my lady-love in Nice every evening by express train from Vienna, so that she should have the scent of it before she encountered it in the flower markets there. And then I was required to write out my 'particulars' before I died – so one of these friendly people kept on insisting in broken German. He even guided my hand as I wrote, but the sheet of paper had not enough space for my name. Several times we poised the pencil, and I wrote right off the edge of the paper, as if into the sky. I might almost have ended as the Unknown Soldier of the First World War. Thanks to this medical orderly and another one who also came along, I was able to study the white shrapnel clouds mingling with the pink ones over the railway station, during the hours that the train stood there. On my promising to protect them, they stealthily lifted me out of the cattle-wagon and stayed by me that night, while the train travelled eastward. They were both Balts.

I would have promised anything to stop that rumbling of wheels going round in my head! As often as fur caps came bursting in, asking in menacing tones if there wasn't some damned German or Austrian there, I answered only with a smile, whereupon they too remained. After the thunder of the guns there was no rifle-fire to be heard. It was our troops coming closer. There was a bugle call! Then, in my own native language, an order to attack the station. The Russian orderlies raised me up so that I could be seen in the burnt-out window. They held my arm so that I could salute the lieutenant, saying: 'Cadet XY, reporting back for duty with eighteen prisoners.' For this my colonel pinned a medal to my breast, in front of the whole regiment. And there was a rose that someone had laid on the stretcher. Heaven alone knows where it had been picked.

JULES ROMAINS

Jules Romains (pen-name of Louis Farigoule, 1885–1972).
Teacher of philosophy. Did military service before the war and
was an auxiliary during it but did not see front-line fighting. *Les
Hommes de Bonne Volonté* appeared over fourteen years in twenty-
seven volumes. These, the concluding pages of *Verdun*, contrast
pointedly the moral world of the actual soldiers with those in
political and military charge of the operation. Mort-Homme
was a hill about eight miles north-west of Verdun itself.

Source: Jules Romains, *Verdun* (translated from *Les Hommes de
Bonne Volonté*, Books XV and XVI, Paris, Flammarion, 1938, by
Gerard Hopkins), London, Souvenir Press, 1962; Granada/May-
flower, 1973.

COUNTER-ATTACK AT MORT-HOMME

At 1 p.m. an encouraging rumour began to circulate among the
companies in reserve on the slope opposite Mort-Homme, to the
west of brigade headquarters:

'The Boche attack has failed.'

The bombardment had, in fact, ceased with dramatic sudden-
ness. There was no reason to suppose that this cessation was the
prelude to a fresh assault, since at midday, when the German
infantry had started to move forward, their guns, so far from
being silent, had worked up to a still greater degree of fury,
contenting themselves merely with lengthening their range.
Wazemmes, who since midnight had run the whole gamut of
emotions, was now conscious of an entirely new one. Its elements
were a sincere relief, which he did not allow to appear, and a
flicker of disappointment, of which he made considerable
parade.

'Damn nuisance,' he said to his young comrades of the '16
class. 'What's the matter with 'em?'

His disappointment was, in fact, perfectly genuine. Since,
obviously, something had got to happen sooner or later, the

sooner the better. Wazemmes felt that he was in just the right mood to face a crisis, worked up to a state of unprecedented excitement.

But what a day it had been! About midnight, just when they had all dropped into a sound sleep, had come the fall-in. 'It seems the Boches are going to attack tomorrow. Since we're in reserve, you can let your kids sleep a bit longer.' (The kids were the members of the '16 class who had been drafted into the regiment a few days earlier.) 'But see that they're all ready. The older men, and the NCOs of course, must take over sentry duties.' At 7 a.m., just when Wazemmes, his rifle between his legs, was snoozing against an angle of the trench wall, someone had shaken him by the shoulders.

'Hey! Wake up. The lieutenant's asking for you.'

The lieutenant commanding the company, who had joined the regiment a few days before Wazemmes, was a very young officer who, in the eyes of the latter, shone with all sorts of reflected glory. His name was Comte Voisenon de Pelleriès. He had been due to start his career at the Military College in 1914, but had been introduced to the school of war before he had known the discipline of that other, more normal school (he and his class-mates had not even had time to sit for their oral entrance examination). Among his companions had been many who had fallen in great numbers during that first winter 'advancing in dress uniform'. The Comte de Pelleriès was a slim, not very tall young man, who maintained a standard of quiet elegance even in the trenches. He had fine grey eyes, the hint of an auburn moustache, and spoke with so cordial a tone of friendliness that his voice at times took on a warm and tender timbre. Each one of his men felt that he was enveloped in an aura of confidence and affection. He had been wounded three times, once seriously. As a result of his last wound but one, he had been left with a slight limp – quite temporary, he maintained – which he disguised with easy grace.

'My dear Wazemmes,' he said, 'I understand that you were formerly a corporal. I am pleased to be able to tell you that, as the result of my personal representations, your stripes have been restored to you. Your squad will be composed entirely of young fellows of the '16 class. You will probably have to lead them forward under fire in the course of today. I know that you are brave enough to face any call upon your courage, and that you will give your men an admirable example.'

He held out his hand and shook Wazemmes's as though it had been that of an old friend.

At 8 a.m. – 'Boom, branranran, bang, bang ...' Wazemmes, drunk with sleep and with the prospect of glory, spent his time walking up and down among 'his men'.

'That was a 77 ... those greeny-yellowish bursts up there are 105 shrapnel ... That noise? That's probably trench-mortars firing on our front lines.'

The poor little devils were both delighted and appalled, now pink with emotion, now green with terror. Since the bombardment, violent though it was, was not falling on their position, they gradually grew in confidence, and more than one was heard to say that the guns' bark was worse than their bite. Without wishing to shatter their illusion on this point, the NCOs repeated various bits of advice about how they should behave in open ground in order to avoid unnecessary risks.

The information given by the Polish prisoners had turned out to be perfectly correct so far as it concerned the preliminary bombardment. It was felt, therefore, that it would probably be no less correct in its other details, and it was expected that the enemy assault would take place at midday.

About half-past eleven, the Comte de Pelleriès assembled his boys of the '16 class and, to the amazement of more than one of them, among whom Wazemmes was certainly numbered, made them a little speech in his kindly, cultivated voice, the gist of which was as follows: 'My dear friends, we are probably going to take part in the coming action. We shall not be called upon to receive the first waves of the German assault,' (he never let the word 'Boche' pass his lips), 'but since it is possible that our comrades in the front line may be forced to yield a little ground, we shall be called upon to bar the way to the attacking enemy, or perhaps to counter-attack with the purpose of recapturing the lost trenches. If we have to counter-attack, we shall carry out our duty bravely, shall we not, my friends? We are soldiers of the Republic. We are here to defend Verdun, because the fall of Verdun might mean the defeat of France. We do not want our country, which is a democracy, a republic of free men, to be conquered and enslaved by the men opposite, who are not free men, but live still in feudal conditions. Not far from here, at Valmy, a little over one hundred and twenty years ago, your ancestors drove back the foreigners who had come to crush the Great French Revolution. One of my ancestors, the Comte

Voisenon de Pelleriès, was present on that occasion too, with the rank of captain. He was not one of those who had emigrated . . . When, therefore, we move forward, I should like you, my friends, to shout with me: "*Vive la nation! Vive la République!*" as our ancestors shouted at Valmy, and then to advance on the enemy singing the "Marseillaise".'

In five minutes Wazemmes's political convictions had undergone a radical change. And since the portrait of Mlle Anne de Montbieuze had already been replaced on his heart by that of a charming typist of no marked political views, but probably sympathetic to the Left, whom he had met on the evening of 2 April, he had no difficulty in feeling now that he was a soldier of Valmy and a corporal of the Republic.

Suddenly, a rumour passed down the ranks.

'Seems we've got to counter-attack. The Boches have advanced again. They're going to come down this side of the Mort-Homme . . . The chasseurs have been driven from their trenches . . . We've got to retake them.'

There followed a period of intolerable waiting. The bombardment, which had started again, was spreading now on every side. Shells with all the names in the vocabulary, with all the magic, terrifying numbers which served to identify them, with their noises, none of which were really alike but which no ear could distinguish, so overwhelming was the uproar, with their bursts of smoke which looked like different species of poisonous fungus, with their smells which united into a single stench, gave the impression that they were all detonating at one and the same moment in the air, in the earth, in the interior of one's own stomach. The country which one could just glimpse through a breach in the parapet (strictly forbidden to show one's head) looked sad and comfortless. Though the sun was shining, a melancholy exuded from its bare, grey distances, which dwindled away towards the enemy lines in a series of slow undulations. The slope in front was the one to be climbed, there where each moment the earth was torn by some great shell. Smoke came from the ground as though a hook were drawing wool from a mattress with insistent regularity. The attacking line would have to move along the whole length of that slope so torn by shells, so witheringly swept by machine-gun fire. If only it needn't happen! If only the order to advance never came! Things do happen like that sometimes, luck does turn at the very last moment. Perhaps the Boches, too much exhausted by their own efforts, too badly mauled by our artillery (for our guns were hard at it, 75s, 155s, and all the rest) would retire of their own account. Perhaps the chasseurs might have sufficient self-pride to want to retake themselves the trenches they had lost. Perhaps, for some reason or other, the Staff might change its mind ... It was well known that Pétain did not like sacrificing men's lives.

Lieutenant Voisenon de Pelleriès could be seen putting on his gloves, smoothing his tiny moustache. He drew his sword (for, since this morning, he had taken to wearing it). In a voice of marked politeness he cried:

'My friends, it's our turn now!'

Then he clambered over the parapet, shouting:

'*Vive la nation! Vive la République!*'

The lads behind him shouted too, as men shout in dreams, without being quite sure whether their lips were uttering any audible sound. They leapt forward without, as yet, much difficulty, since the objective was still far away and the machine-guns were not, so far, concentrating on them. The lieutenant began to sing the 'Marseillaise'. They did their best to sing it too. From time to time, interrupting his singing, the lieutenant shouted to them:

'Do as I do! Lie down!'

But he only half lay down. He watched them from the corner of his eye. They flung themselves down at once.

A few of them began to fall. Sometimes their friends did not notice what had happened; sometimes they saw but could not believe their eyes. They took up a verse of the 'Marseillaise', shouting the first words that occurred to them. They had no idea whether it was the same verse as the one the lieutenant was singing, or their pals on either side.

'Careful, boys. We've got to get through an artillery barrage ... Do as I do ... Bend as low as you can, and jump to it ... Don't lie down again until you're fifty yards farther on.'

Wazemmes swallowed the scrap of the 'Marseillaise' which stuck in his throat, to pass the order back to 'his men':

'Do as I do ... Jump to it!'

He threw himself forward, bending his body as much as he could, and going as fast as he knew how. The noise was staggering.

'Ho!'

It was all over in a second. He had hardly time to realize that he had been hit, that the pain was hideous, that he was done for.

'There you are,' said Pétain to Geoffroy, holding out the sheet of manuscript which was still wet. 'Have it run off and distributed at once to all units ... I'd have liked to say something rather special about those lads of the '16 class, but I was afraid it might be too painful for their poor parents ... Do you know how many of them actually reached the trench lost by the chasseurs? Ten, out of a total of two companies engaged in the counter-attack? Ten, just think of it! I'm told that de Pelleriès was magnificent. He made those boys sing the 'Marseillaise'. He was killed half-way up the slope. I'm going to see that he gets a posthumous award of the Croix de Guerre.'

Geoffroy took the paper and read the general's rather large, angular script, to which the shaping of certain letters gave a curiously feminine quality (the ink of the last few lines was not yet dry):

To the Men of the IInd Army

The ninth of April is a glorious day in the annals of our military history.

The furious attacks delivered by the German soldiers under the command of the Crown Prince have been everywhere broken.

Infantry, artillery, engineers, and flying men of the IInd Army vied with one another in heroism.

Honour to them all!

The Germans will undoubtedly attack again. Let every man work and watch to the end that future successes may fall in no way short of yesterday's.

Courage ... We shall beat them yet!

Ph. Pétain

'Not bad, no , not at all bad,' said Geoffroy to himself as he took his way down the staircase. 'If only this could be the last order of the day to be issued in connection with the battle of Verdun!'

He crossed the vestibule and stepped out of the front door. There before him the road roared and rumbled, true to itself as ever, with its double line of trucks.

ROLAND DORGELÈS

Roland Dorgelès (pen name of Roland Lécavelé, 1886–1973). Trained as an architect. Enjoyed Paris café society. After a pacifist episode volunteered in 1914. After injury and convalescence became an army instructor in 1916. Began work on *Wooden Crosses*. 'Everything that I had stored up burst in an instant as if pierced with a scalpel.' (See John Flowers's essay on Dorgelès in *The First World War in Fiction*.) The following passages are self-explanatory.

Source: Roland Dorgelès, *Wooden Crosses* (translated from *Les Croix de bois*, Paris, Albin Michel, 1919), London, William Heinemann, 1920.

MOUNT CALVARY

. . . So the day passed, while we were bowed under the shells, scattering before the torpedoes.

Towards eleven o'clock, it all doubled in fury, and the party going for the soup hesitated a full minute before going off, more sheltered in the sap than in the trench, everywhere breached and broken. When they came back, half the wine was overturned and spilled, the macaroni full of earth, and Sulphart nearly choked insulting Lemoine, who was 'not even up to carrying a bottle'.

The stew eaten, we began to play cards and wait for night. Broucke had begun to snore; lying near him, Gilbert was trying to dream.

Suddenly he sat up and said to us, his voice dry and hard:

'They're digging underneath.'

Everyone turned about, letting the cards drop.

'Are you sure?'

He nodded his head for yes. Brutally I shook Broucke, who was still snoring, and Maroux, Bréval, Sulphart lay down in the gallery, their ears clapped to the ground. The rest of us looked at them, dumb, our hearts seemingly gripped in a vice. We had understood completely . . . a mine. Anxiously we listened, raging at the shells that shook the hill with their battering-ram. Bréval was the first to get up again.

'There is no possibility of a mistake,' said he in a half-whisper, 'they are digging.'

'There's only one of them at work, you can hear quite clearly,' said Maroux, giving it precision. 'They are not far off.'

We were all clustering together, motionless, lying on the hard earth. Someone had gone to fetch Sergeant Ricordeau. He arrived, listened for a moment, and said:

'Yes . . . We must tell the lieutenant.'

Each one in his turn lay down to listen, and rose up a trifle gloomier. In the trench the news had already spread like wild-fire, and between each shell the watchers listened to the alarming mattock that went on digging, digging, digging . . .

Sous-Lieutenant Berthier came along at night with the soup party. He listened for a considerable time, wagged his head, and straightway was fain to reassure us.

'Pooh! . . . It may be pioneers digging a trench, and quite a long way off, too . . . It's most deceptive, you know, a noise like that . . . I'm going to ask somebody in the engineers . . . But don't you be getting rattled, it's certainly a long way off still; there's no danger . . .'

We took the watch. The shells were still falling, but they did not frighten us so much just now. We were listening to that pickaxe.

Our two hours over, we went back into the grotto. Broucke listened and said:

'He's a reasonable chap, he's not going too hard at it.'

And placidly he went to sleep.

We were on the point of blowing out the candle when Lieutenant Berthier came back, accompanied by an adjutant of engineers. Everybody got up again and crowded into the gallery. The first word we caught was:

'We suspected that.'

Fouillard had a spasm that puckered up his eye.

The adjutant had lain down, his ear against the earth, and was listening with closed eyes. Our very silence was intently listening with him. He rose up, brushed the chalk from his whitened coat with a slap, and went off again with Berthier without saying anything to us, not a single word.

'That means there's no danger yet,' surmised Lemoine.

'It means we're going to be sent up,' predicted Sulphart.

All the same, we lay down, and we went to sleep. Berthier

came back at early dawn; he had an air of gloom, an air of profound concern that we did not recognize in him and which all at once made us uneasy. What did he know? He listened to the pickaxe that still went on digging, without gluing his ear to the ground, for the blows were now coming to us more distinct and clear. We felt ourselves troubled by a vague presentiment, an obscure mixed fear. Berthier came again.

'Bréval's squad, fall in.'

He eyed us all, with the deep look of a brave man; then, letting his eyes rest only on Bréval, who since he had the chip knocked out of him wore a dressing about his neck like a linen collar, he said to him:

'As you had guessed, the Germans are digging a mine. The engineers perhaps will come along to open a sap, but theirs had to be very far advanced for us to be able to cut it. And so . . . you see . . . it's unnecessary for everybody to stay here . . . You understand that clearly, of course . . . And so . . . it is your squad, Bréval, that is to remain; it has been drawn by lot. The two sections are to be relieved, and you are to stay here with your squad and the machine-gunners . . . It's not much, but the colonel has every confidence in you; you are well known to be brave fellows . . . And then there is no attack to be feared, since they are still actually digging . . . Anyway, their mine is not yet nearly finished; you needn't be afraid . . . There's no danger, no danger whatever at all . . . It's just simply a measure of precaution.'

He was beginning to stammer, his throat was dry and contracted. His eyes wandered once more around the whole squad, seeking all our eyes in turn. Nobody said a word; only Fouillard sputtered out:

'We can go, anyhow, to fetch the soup.'

'It will be sent up to you.'

The others remained silent – a little pale, that was all. Courage? No, discipline . . . Our turn had come . . .

'We're for it,' said Vieublé simply.

'No, no, you're crazy!' broke in the lieutenant quickly. 'Don't get that into your head . . . Look here' – and he dropped his eyes in embarrassment – 'I would have liked very much to stay with you. It was my place. The colonel refused. Come, good luck to you!'

His lower lip was trembling, and under his glasses a film of moisture dimmed his eyes. With a brusque movement, he shook hands with each one of us and went off, with his teeth clenched and a pale face.

Already our comrades were going, pushing and scrambling, as if they were afraid that death might lay hold of them. They eyed us with queer looks as they passed before us, and the last of them bade us 'good luck'. The light little clink of the chains on their mess-tins died away, the clatter of the empty cans, the sound of pebbles rolling under their feet, their voices ... We remained alone. The machine-gunners sat down to their weapon. Three of the squad went down into the trench, and we went back again into the mine.

'There's nothing to be done now but wait,' said Demachy, exaggerating his air of aloof indifference.

Wait for what? All of us sitting on the edge of our beds, we kept staring at the ground, as a despairing man might stare at the dark, melancholy water running by before his last leap. It seemed to us that the pickaxe was striking harder now, as hard as our beating hearts. Despite ourselves, we lay down full-length to listen yet again.

Fouillard had gone to bed in a corner, his head under the blanket so as not to go on hearing, to see nothing more. Bréval said in a hesitating voice:

'After all, it's not settled that we're going to be blown up ... A mine isn't made just as easy as all that.'

'Especially through rock.'

'You might think it's quite near, and yet there might be enough work in it to keep them at it a week.'

They were all talking at once, just now; they were all making up lies to put heart in themselves, to go on hoping in spite of everything. There was a loud argument for a minute, in which everyone had his own story of mines to tell, and when they listened again it seemed to them that the blows were not falling so loud. Mechanically they unrolled their blankets and went to rest.

'Talk about waking up with a jump!' grumbled Vieublé as he took off his boots.

Where was the earth going to yawn and split in two? Shutting your eyes, you could imagine you saw those horrible photographs reproduced in the illustrated papers; those gaping funnel-shaped holes with stakes and bits of old iron and fragments of men sticking out through the surface, half buried.

Lying there with our heads resting on our packs, we no longer heard anything but the terrible pick, as regular as the ticking of a clock, that was digging our grave for us.

'That'll make something like a noise,' murmured Belin. 'Talk about the sort of charge it'll need to rip up a hill like that!'

'There are three days still before we get out of it.'

'No, not more than two and a half: we ought to be relieved on Wednesday night.'

Bréval was writing on his knees, completely absorbed, using his pack as a writing-desk.

'You're doing the emotional stunt at your old woman,' chaffed Lemoine. 'Are you telling her that we're going up?'

The shells were falling less thick this night. The short aurora of the rockets sprang to life and died on the tent canvas. The night was almost calm. Only that muffled sound of the mattock, lulling us to sleep . . .

———

Tock . . . tock . . . tock . . . It was still digging away . . . Tock, tock . . . Then it stopped. We listened then, straining, more agonized. No. Tock . . . tock . . . tock . . .

That went on for two days more and one night. Forty hours that we counted, that we tore off in patches of minutes. Two days and one night to listen, our mouths dried with fever. The last evening it was impossible to keep Vieublé back: he set off with four grenades in his wallet, and at the end of an hour we heard four sharp barking bursts, one after another, then cries of distress howled out in the fringes of the wood. He had well and duly distributed his 'sodas'.

As he was getting back into the trench Lieutenant Berthier arrived, preceding the relief. We were already putting our packs up on our shoulders, ready to start.

'Ah,' he said to us. 'I am glad . . . You see, you must never lose heart. It's all over.'

'We've not got away yet,' trembled Fouillard.

'To be sent up now, that really would be anything but luck,' remarked Lemoine with complete gravity.

The regular strokes were still coming to us, reassuring in spite of everything. But it was no longer only the pickaxe we were watching for now, it was the relief. A dull murmur told us they were at hand.

'The relief . . . Go into the grotto to hand over. I will look after the orders,' Berthier said to us.

We looked at men of a regiment we did not know as they passed. There were ten of them only, and four machine-gunners. The last man stopped, having guessed at us as we stood in the shadow of the gallery.

'So, then, they're digging a mine underneath? . . . We're certain to be sent up. What do *you* think! – four days of it . . .'

All speaking at once, we endeavoured to reassure them.

'No reason why you should . . . Look at us, we've jolly well stayed in it . . . It takes long, that kind of stunt . . . You mustn't get worried . . .'

But over his pack we were closely keeping a watch on the lieutenant, with quaking in our knees, so hot we were to be gone. Fouillard, nobody knows how or when, had already disappeared. Berthier at last came back.

'*En route!* . . . Good luck, my lads!'

And turning towards, Demachy, he added quite below his breath:

'Poor fellows! I am afraid for them . . .'

But for the lieutenant, who was going at our head at a good round pace, we might perhaps have broken into a run. We were afraid of that sinister, wan Calvary, which every now and then the rockets showed up in all its nakedness – fear of that danger that we always felt behind us, always very near.

We slipped into the chalky road, quickly we crossed the footbridge over the river, and there only did we venture to turn ourselves about. The Calvary stood out terrible, a dreadful thing against the green night, with its battered stumps of trees like the uprights of a cross.

We had our food at the exit from the trenches. The cooks had made gravy and we ate voraciously, not feeling now in our entrails those crooked fingers that clutched and worked inside you. We drank wine in full cups: the buckets had to be emptied before we went. Bragging and boasting, Sulphart was pitching yarns to the boys of the company:

'And I say, how we made them yelp, the Boches, with that lad Vieublé! . . .

Every man of the squad had his own group round him and was holding forth. Vieublé, whose lazy voice with its rolling r's, the typical voice of a town loafer, was notable among the others, was telling about his patrol.

'You may say they did howl! . . . I had stood up, and I was

holding one of the posts of their barbed wire in my left hand, and whizz, bang, in on top of them ... I never even got a touch of a bullet ... And twig the topping field-glass I took off a Boche stiff, an officer ...'

The company was following the canal in a long, rambling, disjointed file. From the gunners' dug-outs, burrowed into the steep bank, a mist was rising, and we envied their damp dens: 'To see the war out in there, well, you might call that a streak of luck!'

The black water mirrored nothing but the night, and was without life except for a light lapping ripple. We crossed the river on a heaving bridge made out of boats and casks. The canal once passed, we entered into the woods, and the coolness fell on your shoulders like a damp cloak. It smelled of drenching springtime. Somewhere a bird was singing, not realizing that it was wartime.

Behind us the rockets marked out the infinite, endless line of the trenches. Soon the trees hid them out of sight, and the tall forests stifled the raging voice of the guns. We were moving away from death.

As we entered into the first village, the leading squad started to hum softly, and mechanically we all began a march in step to the rhythm:

> *C'est aujourd'hui marche de nuit*
> *Au lieu d'roupiller, on s'promène...*

Then suddenly, from afar, a heavy dull noise shattered and shook the night: a thundering noise of cataclysm, that the echoes repeated long and long. The mine had gone up.

The column had halted as though at the word of command. Not a voice was heard now ... We were still listening, our hearts contracted, as if we had been able from the banks on which we were standing to hear the cries. The guns, too, had held their tongues in order to listen.

But no, nothing more; it was all over.

'How many were there?' asked a choking voice from the ranks.

'Ten ...' somebody answered. 'And four machine-gunners.'

WILLIAM FITZWATER WRAY

William Fitzwater Wray (1867–1938). An illustrator and 'cycling correspondent' with the *Daily Herald* and *Daily News*. With the outbreak of war he found himself out of work, since newspapers had no space for news unconnected with the 'savour of cordite'. He set out on his bicycle to describe not 'wartime in France . . . but France in wartime'. While this passage gives little hint of his extraordinary gifts as a translator (Barbusse's *Under Fire* and *The Brother*), it is not without poignant observation.

Source: W. Fitzwater Wray, *Across France in War Time*, London, Dent, 1916.

. . . I had to ride hard then to get to Arcis before dark. The road entered the town over a railway crossing, and a hundred people had gathered there to watch the slow passage of a military train of interminable length. A gentleman came up and asked me for an English souvenir, and I parted with one of my *Punch* cartoons. The sentries here were highly pleased with the portentous size and decoration of my Foreign Office passport – 'It is almost a diploma,' said one.

Very kindly, and without hesitation, they received me at the Hôtel du Mulet. The landlady was a woman of superior intelligence with several charming little girls. There were boarders in this hotel. Two of them were man and wife from a town in the French Ardennes, where they had a printing business and ran a local newspaper. Madame spoke the most beautifully articulated French I have ever heard, so that it was easy and pleasant to listen to her story. They had fled to Arcis when the Germans first swept through the Ardennes. Then, during a temporary withdrawal of the enemy, the printer and his wife returned to find that German officers had lived in their house, and, of course, made free with everything. 'Do you know,' said Madame, with a comical grimace, 'they had even worn all my chemises!'

But they had to become refugees again, and had now not seen their home for a month, nor knew even if it still stood.

One of the little girls of the household told me with wide-open eyes of the hard fighting there had been just to the north of the town, and of the dreadful jetsam of war; but now, she added reassuringly, '*Tout est enterré.*' Look up your dictionary if you stick at the terse and dread significance of the phrase. But she was wrong.

At this most excellent inn I paid 7 francs 80 centimes for dinner, bed, breakfast, and extras. After breakfast (which would have been a heavy meal could I have seen ahead), I watched a strange procession. From the yard of the hotel, where they had stood for several weeks, three or four big farm carts were being led out; overloaded and top-heavy with an amazing medley of household effects, furniture, bedding, clothing, domestic utensils, and each with a bicycle or two slung behind. They belonged to three French peasant families who had just received the news that at last the enemy had been driven back from their far-off village, and that their little homes were still intact.

In front of one cart sat a woman and three little children, with a lurid bed-quilt serving as apron for the lot. The early morning air was damp and chilly. As papa led the horse carefully through the archway into the road – it was a close fit, and he feared that some of the load might be swept off – he caught my eye, and said, 'This is misery.'

'On the contrary,' I replied, 'you are going home, and it is happiness.'

He dropped the reins suddenly, turned and grasped both my hands in his, and there were tears in his eyes.

DAVID JONES

David Jones (1895–1974). Born in Kent and studied at the Camberwell and Westminster Schools of Art. He served as an infantryman in the war but did not publish *In Parenthesis*, his work of prose and verse that records his response to the war, until 1937. In his Preface Jones wrote: 'I have only tried to make a shape in words, using as data the complex of sights, sounds, fears, hopes, apprehensions, smells, things exterior and interior, the landscape and paraphernalia of that singular time and of those particular men.'

Source: David Jones, *In Parenthesis*, London, Faber, 1937.

John Ball heard the noise of the carpenters where he squatted to clean his rifle. Which hammering brought him disquiet more than the foreboding gun-fire which gathered intensity with each half-hour. He wished they'd stop that hollow tap-tapping. He'd take a walk. He'd go and find his friend with the Lewis guns. And perhaps Olivier would be there. No orders were out yet, and tea would not yet be up.

These three seldom met except for very brief periods out of the line – at brigade rest perhaps – or if some accident of billeting threw them near together. These three loved each other, but the routine of their lives made chances of foregathering rare. These two with linked arms walked together in a sequestered place above the company lines and found a grassy slope to sit down on. And Signaller Olivier came soon and sat with them. And you feel a bit less windy.

They talked of ordinary things. Of each one's friends at home; those friends unknown to either of the other two. Of the possible duration of the war. Of how they would meet and in what good places afterwards. Of the dissimilar merits of Welshmen and Cockneys. Of the diverse virtues of Regular and Temporary Officers. Of if you'd ever read the books of Mr Wells. Of the poetry of Rupert Brooke. Of how you really couldn't very well carry more than one book at a time in your pack. Of the losses of the Battalion since they'd come to France. Of the hateful discomfort of having no greatcoats with fighting-order, of how bad this was. Of how everybody ought rightly to have Burberry's, like officers. Of how German knee boots were more proper to trench war than puttees. Of how privileged Olivier was because he could manage to secrete a few personal belongings along with the signaller's impedimenta. Of how he was known to be a favourite with the Regimental and how he'd feel the draught if he were back with his platoon. Of whether they three would be together for the Duration, and how you hoped so very much indeed. Of captains of thousands and of hundreds, of corporals, of many things. Of the Lloyd George administration, of the Greek, Venizelos, who Olivier said was important, of whom John Ball had never previously heard. Of the neutrality of Spain. Of whether the French nation was nice or nasty. Of whether anyone would ever get leave and what it would be like if you did. Of how stripes, stars, chevrons, specializations, jobs away from the battalion, and all distinguishing marks were better resisted for as long as possible. Of how it were best to take no particular notice, to let the stuff go over you, how it were wise to lie doggo and to wait the end.

And watched the concentration in the valley.

Where the road switch-backed the nearer slope, tilted, piled-to-overloading limbers, their checking brakes jammed down, and pack-beasts splayed their nervous fore-legs – stiffened to the incline. And where it cut the further hill a mechanized ambulance climbed up and over, and another came toward.

Every few minutes thinned-out smoke wreaths spread up from beyond, to signify the norm of his withdrawing range and the reluctant ebb of his fire. But now and then a more presuming burst would seem to overreach its mark and plunge up white rubble this side; for although the tide be most certainly outbound, yet will some local flow, swell in with make-believe recovery, to flood again the drying shingle and mock with saucy spray the accuracy of their tide-charts; make brats too venturesome flop back with belly-full and guardian nurse girls squeal.

> Amelia's second-best parasol
> > sails the raging main;
> her fine fancy's properly split
> > she won't see that ever

they cut it a bit too fine . . .

HENRY WILLIAMSON

Henry Williamson (1895–1977). Born in Parkstone, Dorset.
Served as an infantry officer. Recalls talking to the German
soldiers during the 1914 Christmas truce. The realization that
'they believed they were fighting for the same causes and ideals
as we were' brought him 'startled dismay and then happiness'.
The Patriot's Progress is the first of his novels about the war,
which is important in many of his other works, including *The
Pathway* (1931). Williamson's text was the concrete poured
between the 'shuttering' of William Kermode's linocuts.

Source: Henry Williamson, *The Patriot's Progress*, London, Geoffrey Bles, 1930 (reprinted Macdonald & Jane's, 1968; Sphere,
1978).

... He was terrified of the idea of going over the top. Every time
the brutal droning of shells increased into the deep, savage,
sudden buzzing which told they were going to burst near, he
crouched and sweated and cringed. He had spent a month at
Étaples with trench fever, which some said was caused by the
bite of lice: these chaps said they hadn't loused themselves,
hoping to get the fever. His half-sleeping was sharp and jagged
with fearful dreams; he chewed cordite, as recommended by an
old sweat swinging the lead in the ward, got from a cartridge
when the bullet had been worked out. It gave him a headache,
but would it increase his temperature? Fear of being rumbled
had made him chuck his little store into the latrine. Then had
come the mutiny at the Old Tipperary Camp, the boys being
fed up with all the bloody slaughter going on up in the salient,
battalions going in seven hundred strong and coming out seventy
after a few hours, and being made up to strength and going in
again, and nothing doing except a fresh layer of stiffs and
wounded on top of the others. The mutiny had begun with the
organized defiance of orders at the Bull Ring; the streaming
back of thousands of men singing and cheering; the shooting
of the sergeant of the Gordon Highlanders by an NCO of
the Military Field Police, a bloody great hulking swine of an

ex-champion heavyweight boxer dodging the column at the base, who used to twist the arms and legs of the insubordinate Australian soldiers doing Field Punishment No. I. He ran like hell, and hid in the RTO's office. John Bullock had seen the APM, who was said to have been a North West Mounted Policeman in Canada before the war, rolled in the road. The general had tried to address them – 'Are you Englishmen, or are you blackguards?' – and had been told to put a sock in it. 'See here, general, you've been doing all the talking so far, and now it's the turn of the Poor Bloody Private Soldier.' Then the hunt of the red-caps through Etapps; the looting of the estaminets; the Australians sent down from the line to stop the mutiny of more than 100,000 men; the Aussies joining in. 'War's over, Jerry's fed up, so are we. Jerry didn't want the war, nor did we. It's only the bloody profiteers who want it to go on. They are the enemies of the masses.' Some said that junior officers had been disguised as private soldiers in order to get into the estaminets and spot the organizers of the mutiny; after them had come the break-up patrols armed with entrenching tool handles, laying out the leaders when found. A posh battalion of territorials from GHQ; machine-guns on the bridge over the river; no food; the end of the wild hopes of going home and seeing wives and kids and mothers and girls again. Dozens of poor sods handcuffed wrist to wrist, two by two, outside the commandant's office, awaiting court martial and the firing-squad. That was the end of that! And the war went on as usual, and the Bloody Butcher sending in the division again and again and getting them —d up to hell. Thus our hero's thoughts as he carried what, many times during the many times he rested beside it on the duckboard track, he swore at as a sodding great lump of firewood. The bloke following him was fed up too: he shouted out as he let his load slide off his shoulders, 'Let the bleedun brass hats come and carry their — matchsticks!' . . .

He lumbered on, reached the dump, and hurried back after the others to the dump beyond Bridge No. 4. Wipers, with the sun on it, looked like the long white jaw-bone of a mule, with its teeth chipped and splintered, its jaw-bone cracked and shot away . . .

———

. . . Others sitting at tables, hats on backs of heads, smoking and laughing, glasses before them. They ignored his entry. An interior door opened and a broad, almost harsh, woman's voice shouted out a word that he couldn't catch. A man jumped up, grabbed his hat, and went out of the door, leaving them grinning at each other. Then the pontoon players picked up more cards, and the group round the crown-and-anchor board went on placing their money on the crown-and-anchor board. This was a worn folding square of cloth marked with six sections, corresponding to Heart, Crown, Diamond, Spade, Anchor and Club; called Heart, Major (sergeant-major), Dinkie, Curse, Mud-hook and Shamrock. 'Lay your money single and pick up double. You lay and we pay, the good old Sweaty Sox, out since Mons, often bent but never broke, the rough and tough, the old and bold. If you don't speculate you can't accumulate. Come along, gentlemen, you are not on parade. Who fancies the lucky old Major? Copper, silver and gold. You come in rags and ride away in motor-cars. Back your judgement, gentlemen. The Mud-hook, the Curse, the Heart, the Major. Now then, up she comes!' A pile of torn and dirty paper notes and silver lay within the crook of the banker's left arm on the table. As it grew it was crammed into his pockets. He was an ASC driver, rumoured to be worth a hundred thousand francs. One after another a man got up from a chair or left the crowd around the board, pinched out his fag and stuck it behind his ear, and went out of the door after the deep 'Next' of madame. She served the drinks, grumbling at the tattered, dirty notes offered her. The only dirt she recognized was on paper money. John Bullock was the eighteenth. He had entered the place at 16 hours; his turn came just before 17 hours 30 minutes. That old woman led him upstairs. She wore a leather pouch like a tram driver. It jingled with money. Beyond the open door he saw a fattish half-undressed woman. He could not look at her, after the first glance. She had thick ankles and legs in coarse black stockings. The room smelt musty. He wished he hadn't come. 'Fife!' said Madame in her fat double-chinned voice. 'Fife,' holding up five fingers. He gave her a note. 'Champagne,' he said recklessly, and gave her three five-franc notes. She smiled, 'Now spik to Suzanne. She spik English. Quite clean girl. She make you much happiness.' Suzanne dangled a hand towards him. He went forward. The door was shut. She looked up and smiled. He tried to overcome his reluctance, increased by the sight of spittle on the floor. 'Don't be shy, old soldier,' she said. 'Non,' he said, and waited. 'Poor, bloody Tommee,' she

153

smiled sidelong at him. 'This bloody war no bloody good, eh?' He began to feel better and dared to stroke her head. She caught his hand and put one of his fingers in her mouth, then pulled him down on the couch beside her, and began to mess him about. Then the booze came. He swallowed a couple of glasses, and convinced himself, supporting her heavy bulk on his knees, that he was beginning to feel as he should have felt. He grew rough as he overcame his unmanly shame, and she swiped him across the ear, and cursed him in a hard, deadly voice, mixing English and Flemish words and phrases, from which he flinched as from a machine gun burst in No man's land at night. She told him to – off out of here, the – smeerlop, the dirty Ingleesh stoomer-kloit, etc. Then, seeing his eyes, she twined her arms round his neck and fastened her mouth hard against his mouth and pulled him down on the couch. His mind and senses could not fuse into oneness and abandon. Trying to ward off his reluctance he strove to feel as he imagined he ought to feel, lest she become impatient and despise him as an ungrown-up weakling. Only when, in desperation at the raps of the old woman on the door, he thought himself into the physical likeness of Nobby Clark, did he get rid of himself and achieve some sort of freedom. Afterwards he put on his coat and belt and cap and went out without a word, unable to look at her. He slipped out of the estaminet, a part of England that has sought, in vain, to find its inner sun. He went back to the estaminet where he had had a few drinks before . . .

———

. . . Half the sky leapt alight behind them, there were shouts and cries, a cascade of sound slipped solidly upon them, seeming to John Bullock to swell and converge upon the place where his now very trembling body was large and alone. He saw a long pale shadow before him an instant before it vagged and vanished in the shock of the earth rushing up in fire before him. He was aware of men going forward, himself with them, of the unreality of all movement, of the barrage which was all-weight and all-sound, so that he was carried forward effortlessly over a land freed from the force of gravity and matter. As in a nightmare of rising green and white showers of light about the rending fire he shouted without sound in a silent world, his senses fused into a glassy delirium which lasted until he realized that of the figures on either side of him some were slowly going down on their knees, their chins on their box-respirators, their rifles loosening from their hands. He was hot and swearing, and his throat was dried up. That sissing noise and far-away racketting must be emma-gees. Now the fire wall was going down under his nose and streaking sparks were over and he was lying on his back watching a great torn umbrella of mud, while his head was drawn down into his belly . . .

(The vacuum of a dud shell falling just behind him.) He retched for breath. His ears screamed in his head. He crawled to his knees and looked to see what had happened. Chaps going on forward. He was on his feet in the sissing criss-cross and stinking of smoking earth gaping – hullo, hullo, new shell-holes, this must be near the first objective. They had come three hundred yards already! Cushy! Nothing in going over the top! Then his heart instead of finishing its beat and pausing to beat again swelled out its beat into an ear-bursting agony and great lurid light that leapt out of his broken-apart body with a spinning shriek

and the earth was in his eyes and up his nostrils and going away smaller and smaller

into blackness

and   tiny   far   away

   Rough and smooth. Rough was wide and large and tilting with sickness. He struggled and struggled to clutch smooth, and it slid away. Rough came back and washed harshly over him. He cried out between the receding of rough and the coming of smooth white, then rough and smooth receded . . .

EDMUND BLUNDEN

Edmund Blunden (1896–1974). Born in Yalding, Kent. Educated at Christ's Hospital, the school attended by Coleridge, Lamb, Leigh Hunt, and the Second World War poet Keith Douglas. A fine appreciation of Blunden's 'war' poetry by F. R. Leavis is included in this volume (p. 166). Joined the Royal Sussex Regiment and served in England, Ireland and on the Western Front between 1915 and 1919. See also *The Mind's Eye* (1934) and 'Fall In, Ghosts', in Edmund Blunden, *A Selection of his Poetry and Prose*, (edited by K. Hopkins, 1950). Blunden's first prose account of the war, *De Bello Germanico*, was written in 1918. He described it, in the 'Preliminary' to *Undertones of War*, as 'in its details not much affected by the perplexities of distancing memory', but 'noisy with a depressing forced gaiety then very much the rage'. This early work was, in effect, privately printed.

Source: Edmund Blunden, *De Bello Germanico: a Fragment of Trench History*, Hawstead, G. A. Blunden, 1930 (250 copies and 25 signed).

... We took the air. With awe and his conversational laugh, which we later on found was successfully imitated by half the battalion, the padre pointed out a litter of rusting ironware in a ditch, and informed us that these were old German bombs. This seemed a point of the first interest, but the interest evaporated when he told us in gruesome tones that two transport men had been examining them last week when somehow one went off, seriously wounding both. We now thought these bombs should be interred, and criticized anonymous authorities for having failed to do it. Evidently a very slack war ...

——

... We leant our shoulders to a ration truck and started afresh. The simple-sounding matter of pushing a truck along a trench tramway is rather complex on a dark and/or dirty night. Special adroitness is necessary, and an instinct for varying the length of one's pace, to keep stepping on the metal sleepers and to avoid the chasms between. This cat-like tread, too frequently rewarded with a barked shin, or bootful of icy slime, must be combined with frantic energy in propelling the truck, particularly on wooden rails. Add to this, the probability of a sudden visitation of bullets or five-nines: which you are pensively brooding on when your trolley jolts off the track or disappears into a yawning pit in front, scattering its cargo. With indescribable labour and language this is remedied and you move on, when sudden looming figures with long strides and short tempers begin to scuffle past and grimly remark that the rest of the battalion's coming on behind. These have barely passed, you are just congratulating yourself, when an interminable stream of displeased and ejaculatory Jocks repeat the act – coming off working party. There are also people pushing trucks down the track . . . Yet even evil journeys of this type have an end, and at last we came to the tramhead. The rationeers shouldered their loads, overturned their trucks beside the track, and vanished through the dark in different directions . . .

———

. . . The hot gold sun was already drowsy in the blue, and the war seemed to have slunk into a corner and fallen asleep. Old friends seemed to be all round; a skylark was floating and climbing steep above us, like his cousins over Sussex lands, with his fine melody let fall in prodigal enchantments. There was the growing drone of summer in the grassfields and orchards behind, and on the broken hawthorn tree the blackbird was asking what war was; and did not see the sparrowhawk hanging bloodthirstily over the stubbles. A tabby cat came sleekly round a traverse and purred peace and goodwill. My own idea of war improved wonderfully, till presently a sickly breeze came by with history of the great and murderous battle here a year ago, and L. pointed me out the skulls, jagging bones, and wooden crosses with their weather-worn 'TO AN UNKNOWN BRITISH SOLDIER' and 'RIP', on the side of the trench. Of these there was no lack, and out in the open L. said there were still unburied skeletons in rotted uniforms . . .

———

. . . Meanwhile, I was beginning to know and be known in the company, though terrified of nearly everyone outside it, whether general or serjeant-major. I well remember the concerned expressions of two officers, later on well-known to me, to whose dug-out I was sent on some duty which compelled me to wait there. 'Have a drink?' 'No thanks, I don't drink.' 'Have a cigarette?' 'No thanks I don't smoke.' 'Play bridge?' 'Sorry, I don't play cards.' 'Well, what the hell *do* you do?' No known heading apparently applied to me. Nevertheless, my knowledge of Sussex appealed to the men, as also my efforts on their behalf to persuade vacant R E officers of the merits of piece work. This zeal often saw us finish a job in two or three hours and file down the trench for 'home', where the plan of four hours' digging would have meant finicky work and ill temper. Sometimes I would come from these working parties the sadder and quieter for a casualty or two: and Death is so whimsical in war that we have in 'quiet sectors' lost perhaps a dozen men by occasional sniping or wild firing, whereas in a morass of still-multiplying shell-holes and under daily and nightly barrages we have escaped with less mortality . . .

. . . Towards Cuinchy village there was evidence of a vigorous and quite recent war – shell-holes, telegraph-wires in hanks, rusty ruins of factories, gunpits, a forbidding loneliness, the canal like green glue, stagnant and stinking. The effect of this surprising, unreal deformity, glowering through the blue burning haze at the canal's seeming end, was to make me feel like the victim of a trick. A control sentry directed us down 'Harley Street' to our battalion headquarters. The scarecrow houses leaned to watch us on both sides, silent as the grave . . .

. . . None of us knew the way, but we found where the wounded mostly were, after scrambling through the most awkward trenches and somehow dodging quite a deluge of five-nines. It was my first wild night. One of the wounded was in a very bad case, and over him hung his brother half frantic, himself wounded. Brothers in the same battalion – there were several pairs in this – give rise perhaps to the sharpest griefs of all in war. Meanwhile, L.'s men were digging out the dead and only just alive in the front line. In spite of the tremendous noise and confusion, the Germans made no infantry attack, and towards daybreak, the shelling died down.

After this episode I was pleased to be presented with a shrapnel helmet, which had been, with so many other desirable things, 'on indent'. In the middle of the battle, the unfortunate Adjutant at 'Kingsclere' was trying to cope with the situation, and frantically canvassing front companies for news, by phone and runner. He was disturbed – a call from brigade – perhaps there was urgent information from flank battalions? Perhaps not! At this critical moment his straining ear discerned the still small voice of the staff captain, solemnly pronouncing these relevant words: 'The baths at Z 25 c 4.9 are allotted to you this morning' –

About this time magnificent rumours of a victory by the British fleet, and several dozen German ships scuppered, began to masquerade. A sound of cheering farther up the line was our first intimation. I once more began to think of the war as temporary. The same night came Pessimists, who substituted German for British and vice versa in the first bulletins. To this day, I don't know anything more definite about Jutland than I then did.

The company now moved into the front line. We were now proudly – but with chattering teeth – defending the ill-famed Brickstacks. Of all battlefields this was perhaps the most grotesque and gripping. Brute, squat and monstrous, out of a flat wilderness queasy with gamboge darnel and festering heliotrope poppies and waled with dirty white trench outlines, upstood a score or so of brickstacks. In the dim and distant past of the war, already almost traditional, these obvious forts had been fought for with a sort of mania; in the present impasse, the Germans and ourselves shared them almost equally, but far from equably. These maltreated masses of red brick covered a multitude of people and things. Each had its number, but one adjective did duty for all. Inside, stifling creep-holes twisted up to 'secret' machine-guns and look-outs, with painted instruction-boards against the day of attack: below, muddy staircases opened into tunnellers' and infantry's dug-outs, telephone centres and trench stores. From these nerve centres with more or less effrontery led forward or backward a series of boyaux, alleys half choked with glutiness pudder of a filthy grey, crumbling, aromatic, tangled with signallers' wires. The front line itself was a mere ditch; with defects. Of the German trenches our notion was a shadow; though everyone knew that the carcass of a train on their end of the railway hid a Teutonic sniper – a thing so likely as to be unlikely.

An intolerable landscape, sickly yellow and sallow, upheaved and brutalized, scrawled with leprous white, and smutched with cinder-black – and, as though the bricks were still burning, heat-fumes of blue shrouding the few acres visible. Behind us cowered the rubble-heaps marked Cuinchy on the map, but high over a communication trench a white, beautiful calvary defied flying death. In front, like the waste of dreadful days to come, stretched no man's land, a blur, a curse to the eyes, gouged into great craters and innumerable shell-holes, strewn with the apparatus of wire entanglements . . .

———

. . . A memorable message came down to company headquarters from the Sussex cricketer C., who happened to be the officer on trench duty. It ran, I think: '*Huns have just thrown 6 bombs into Jerusalem Crater. Shall we throw any back?*'

———

Wherever we might be going, the inhabitants seemed utterly uninterested. Goings-out for them were immediately followed by comings-in; *c'était la guerre*; regiments were all one to folks surrounded with soldiery all day and every day. There was one, however, who betrayed feelings of sorrow at our departure. This was an undergrown, odoriferous mongrel who existed on a chain in the corner of the courtyard. Marie, the linguist, asked when he was last let run, had ventured a hazy recollection that it was about August 1914. This naïve confession depressed our warm-hearted men. Silent friends had released the decrepit little dog and taken him for runs beyond his wildest dreams, the last two nights. But now these things were at an end. He saw, with remorse at the fickleness of man, the friends departing bag and baggage. Feebly oscillating his tail in an effort to persuade himself that this was only play, but fearing more and more the dreadful truth, he stood with lack-lustre eye among his festering hunks of bully, the very image of misery.

EDMUND BLUNDEN
see also p. 156

Blunden, like many other war writers, found himself impelled to 'go over the ground again'. *Undertones of War* was developed from *De Bello Germanico* and also included a selection of his poetry. 'A voice, perhaps not my own, answers within me. You will be going over the ground again, it says, until that hour when agony's clawed face softens into the smilingness of a young spring day . . .' He wrote this in Tokyo in 1924 and *Undertones of War* was first published in 1928.

Source: Edmund Blunden, *Undertones of War*, London, Richard Cobden-Sanderson, 1928; Penguin Books, 1936.

. . . Was it on this visit to Étaples that some of us explored the church – a fishing-village church – and took tea comfortably in an inn? Those tendernesses ought not to come, however dimly, in my notions of Étaples. I associate it, as millions do, with 'The Bull-Ring', that thirsty, savage, interminable training-ground. Marching up to it, in the tail of a long column, I was surprised by shouts from another long column dustily marching the other way: and there, sad-smiling, waving hands and welcoming, were two or three of the convalescent squad who had been so briefly mine on the April slopes opposite Lancing. I never saw them again; they were hurried once more, fast as corks on a millstream, without complaint into the bondservice of destruction. Thinking of them, and the pleasant chance of their calling to me, and the evil quickness with which their wounds had been made no defence against a new immolation, I found myself on the sandy, tented training-ground. The machine-guns there thudded at their targets, for the benefit of those who had advanced through wire entanglements against such furies equally with beginners like myself. And then the sunny morning was darkly interrupted. Rifle-grenade instruction began. A Highland sergeant-major stood magnificently before us, with the brass brutality called a Hales rifle-grenade in his hand. He explained the piece, fingering the wind-vane with easy assurance; then stooping to the fixed rifle, he prepared to shoot the grenade by way of demonstration. According to my unsoldierlike habit, I had let the other students press near the instructor, and was listlessly standing on the skirts of the meeting, thinking of something else when, the sergeant-major having just said 'I've been down here since 1914, and never had an accident', there was a strange hideous clang. Several voices cried out; I found myself stretched on the floor, looking upwards in the delusion that the grenade had been fired straight above and was about to fall among us. It had indeed been fired, but by some error had burst at the muzzle of the rifle: the instructor was lying with mangled head, dead, and others lay near him, also blood-masked, dead and alive. So ended that morning's work on the Bull-Ring.

This particular shock, together with the general dreariness of the great camp, produced in me (in spite of the fear with which I had come into France) a wish to be sent quickly to the line. The wish was answered the next afternoon or thereabouts . . .

===

. . . Our men lived in the 'keeps' which guarded the village line. East Keep in particular was a murky sandbagged cellar and emplacement smelling of wet socks and boots. To go from keep to keep alone in the hour before dawn, by way of supervising the 'stand to arms', was an eccentric journey. Then, the white mist (with the wafting perfume of cankering funeral wreaths) was moving with slow, cold currents above the pale grass; the frogs in their fens were uttering their long-drawn *co-aash, co-aash;* and from the line the popping of rifles grew more and more threatening, and more and more bullets flew past the white summer path. Festubert was a great place for bullets. They made a peculiar anthem, some swinging past with a full cry, some cracking loudly like a child's burst bag, some in ricochet from the wire or the edge of ruins groaning as in agony or whizzing like gnats. Giving such things their full value, I took my road with no little pride of fear; one morning I feared very sharply, as I saw what looked like a rising shroud over a wooden cross in the clustering mist. Horror! but on a closer study I realized that the apparition was only a flannel gas helmet spread out over the memorial . . .

===

There was enough to occupy a commanding officer in the Cuinchy trenches, without lightning raids. It was as dirty, bloodthirsty and wearisome a place as could well be found in ordinary warfare; many mines had been exploded there, and tunnelling was still going on. We had scarcely found out the names of the many trenches, boyaux and saps when midnight was suddenly maddened with the thump and roar of a new mine blown under our front companies. The shock was like a blow on the heart; our dug-out swayed, there were startled eyes and voices. I was sent up, as soon as it appeared that this disaster was on our front, with some stretcher-bearers, and as we hurried along the puzzling communication trenches I began to understand the drift of the war; for a deluge of heavy shells was rushing into the ground all round, baffling any choice of movement, and the blackness billowed with blasts of crashing sound and flame. Rain (for Nature came to join the dance) glistened in the shocks of dizzy light on the trench bags and woodwork, and bewilderment was upon my small party, who stoopingly hurried onward; we endured a barrage, but we were not wanted after all.

Brothers should not join the same battalion. When we were at the place where some of the wounded had been collected under the best shelter to be found, I was struck deep by the misery of a boy, whom I knew and liked well; he was half-crying, half-exhorting over a stretcher whence came the clear but weakened voice of his brother, wounded almost to death, waiting his turn to be carried down. Not much can be said at such times; but a known voice perhaps conveyed some comfort in the inhuman night which covered us. In this battalion, brothers had frequently enlisted together; the effect was too surely a culmination of suffering; I shall hint at this again . . .

———

Who that had been there for but a few hours could ever forget the sullen sorcery and mad lineaments of Cuinchy? A mining sector, as this was, never wholly lost the sense of hovering horror. That day I arrived in it the shimmering arising heat blurred the scene, but a trouble was at once discernible, if indescribable, also rising from the ground. Over Coldstream Lane, the chief communication trench, deep red poppies, blue and white cornflowers and darnel thronged the way to destruction; the yellow cabbage-flowers thickened here and there in sickening brilliance. Giant teazels made a thicket beyond. Then the ground became torn and vile, the poisonous breath of fresh explosions skulked all about, and the mud which choked the narrow passages stank as one pulled through it, and through the twisted, disused wires running mysteriously onward, in such festooning complexity that we even suspected some of them ran into the Germans' line and were used to betray us. Much lime was wanted at Cuinchy, and that had its ill savour, and often its horrible meaning. There were many spots mouldering on, like those legendary blood-stains in castle floors which will not be washed away . . .

———

By good luck, I escaped a piece of trouble in this sector. Had I come on trench watch two hours later, not young C. but myself would have been puzzled by the appearance of a German officer and perhaps twenty of his men, who, with friendly cries of 'Good morning, Tommy, have you any biscuits?' and the like, got out of their trench and invited our men to do the same. What their object was, beyond simple fraternizing, I cannot guess; it was afterwards argued that they wished to obtain an identification of the unit opposite them. And yet I heard they had already addressed us as the 'bastard Sussek'. In any case, our men were told not to fire upon them, both by C. and the other company's officer on watch; there was some exchange of shouted remarks, and after a time both sides returned to the secrecy of their parapets. When this affair was reported to more senior members of the battalion, it took on rather a gloomy aspect; it appeared that the bounden duty of C. and R. had been to open fire on the enemy, and one hoped that the business might be kept from the ears of the brigade commander. Such hopes were, of course, nothing to the purpose; the story was out and growing, the unfortunate subalterns were reproved, and, what is more, placed under arrest.

Under arrest they marched towards the Somme battle of 1916. When we left Givenchy, it was known that we were at length 'going south', and, curious as it may seem, the change produced a kind of holiday feeling among us. For some time to come, it was clear, we should be out of the trenches, and on our travels among unbroken houses, streets of life, and peaceful people; hitherto there had been very little but relieving here, and being relieved, and almost at once relieving there, a sand-bag rotation. While the battalion was romantically lodged in ancient Béthune, it fell to me to haunt the sandbags a little longer.

The British barrage struck. The air gushed in hot surges along that river valley, and uproar never imagined by me swung from The British barrage struck. The air gushed in hot surges along that river valley, and uproar never imagined by me swung from ridge to ridge. The east was scarlet with dawn and the flickering gunflashes; I thanked God I was not in the assault, and joined the subdued carriers nervously lighting cigarettes in one of the cellars, sitting there on the steps, studying my watch. The ruins of Hamel were soon crashing chaotically with German shells, and jags of iron and broken wood and brick whizzed past the cellar mouth. When I gave the word to move, it was obeyed with no pretence of enthusiasm. I was forced to shout and swear, and the carrying party, some with shoulders hunched, as if in a snowstorm, dully picked up their bomb buckets and went ahead. The wreckage around seemed leaping with flame. Never had we smelt high explosive so thick and foul, and there was no distinguishing one shell-burst from another, save by the black or tawny smoke that suddenly shaped in the general miasma. We walked along the river road, passed the sandbag dressing-station that had been rigged up only a night or two earlier where the front line ('Shankill Terrace') crossed the road, and had already been battered in; we entered no man's land, past the trifling British wire on its knife-rests, but we could make very little sense of ourselves or the battle. There were wounded Black Watch trailing down the road. They had been wading the marshes of the Ancre, trying to take a machine-gun post called Summer House. A few yards ahead, on the rising ground, the German front line could not be clearly seen, the water-mist and the smoke veiling it; and this was lucky for the carrying party. Halfway between the trenches, I wished them good luck, and pointing out the place where they should, according to plan, hand over the bombs, I left them in charge of their own officer, returning myself, as my orders were, to my colonel. I passed good men of ours, in our front line, staring like persons in a trance across no man's land, their powers of action apparently suspended.

F. R. LEAVIS

Frank Raymond Leavis (1895–1978). Served as a stretcher-
bearer with the Friends' Ambulance Unit. Suffered from gas
and shell-shock. The following passage comes from Chapter 11,
'The Situation at the End of World War 1'.

Source: F. R. Leavis, *New Bearings in English Poetry*, London,
Chatto & Windus, 1932, Penguin Books, 1963.

. . . He [Brooke] was in the first days of his fame notorious for his
'unpleasantness', his 'realism'.

> I'm (of course) unrepentant about the 'unpleasant' poems. I don't
> claim great credit for the *Channel Passage*: but the point of it was
> (or should have been!) 'serious'. There are common and sordid
> things – situations or details – that may suddenly bring all tragedy,
> or at least the brutality of actual emotions, to you. I rather grasp
> relievedly at them, after I've beaten vain hands in the rosy mists of
> poets' experiences.[1]

– But he was always, as he reveals here, poetical at heart: the
last sentence is especially betraying.

A grasping in a like spirit at common and sordid things was
frequent among Georgian poets: there was a determination to
modernize poetry and bring it closer to life . . .

—

. . . Then there is the central group of Georgian poets who
specialize in country sentiment and the pursuit of Beauty in her
more chaste and subtle guises. Mr Middleton Murry has dealt
with them adequately in the article already mentioned, and
there is no need to enumerate them here. But two poets
commonly included deserve to be distinguished from the group:
Mr Edmund Blunden, because he has some genuine talent and is
an interesting case, and Edward Thomas, an original poet of
rare quality, who has been associated with the Georgians by mischance.

The Shepherd, Mr Blunden's first mature book of verse, marked him out from the crowd as a poet who, though he wrote about the country, drew neither upon the *Shropshire Lad* nor upon the common stock of Georgian country sentiment. There was also in his poems, for all the rich rusticity, the home-spun texture that is their warrant, a frank literary quality: Mr Blunden was concerned with art; he was making something. And – what gives them their interest for us – corresponding to this quality in the form there appeared to be something in the intention behind: out of the traditional life of the English countryside, especially as relived in memories of childhood, Mr Blunden was creating a world – a world in which to find refuge from adult distresses; above all, one guessed, from memories of the war.

The later volumes, *English Poems, Retreat,* and *Near and Far,* confirm this conjecture. The peculiar poise that constituted Mr Blunden's distinction has proved difficult to maintain. On the one hand, the stress behind the pastoral quiet becomes explicit in poems dealing with mental conflict, hallucination, and war-experience; on the other, the literary quality becomes, in other poems, more pronounced and takes the form of frank eighteenth-century echoes, imitations, and reminiscences:

> From *Grongar Hill* the thrush and flute awoke,
> And Green's mild sibyl chanted from her oak,
> Along the vale sang Collins' hamlet bell.

Mr Blunden's retreat is to an Arcadia that is rural England seen, not only through memories of childhood, but through poetry and art (see *A Favourite Scene recalled on looking at Birket Foster's Landscapes*). Eighteenth-century meditative pastoral is especially congenial to him; he takes over even the nymphs and their attendant classicalities. On the other hand, he attempts psychological subtleties, and deals directly with his unease, his inner tensions, instead of implying them, as before, in the solidity of his created world. And it becomes plain that he is attempting something beyond him. The earlier method suited his powers and enabled him better to harmonize his various interests. There was something satisfying about the dense richness of his pastoral world, with its giant puff-balls and other evocations of animistic fancy instead of nymphs and naiads. But in the later volumes there is a serious instability in Mr Blunden's art. The visionary gleam, the vanished glory, the transcendental suggestion remain too often vague, the rhythms stumble, and the characteristic packed effects are apt to degenerate into cluttered obscurity.

The development, however, it seems reasonable to suppose, was inevitable. A poet serious enough to impose his pastoral world on us at all could hardly rest in it. Indeed, it was interesting very largely for the same reasons that his tenure of it was precarious. The achievement in any case is a very limited one, but a limited achievement of that kind is notable today. Mr Blunden's best poetry, with its simple movements, its conventional decorum, and its frank literary quality, is the poetry of simple pieties (even if the undertones that accompany the use-hallowed mannerisms and the weathered gravity are not so simple). He was able to be, to some purpose, conservative in technique, and to draw upon the eighteenth century, because the immemorial rural order that is doomed was real to him. It is not likely that a serious poet will be traditional in that way again. Mr Blunden is at any rate significant enough to show up the crowd of Georgian pastoralists.

Only a very superficial classification could associate Edward Thomas with Mr Blunden, or with the Georgians at all. He was a very original poet who devoted great technical subtlety to the expression of a distinctively modern sensibility. His art offers an extreme contrast with Mr Blunden's. Mr Blunden's poems are frankly 'composed', but Edward Thomas's seem to happen. It is only when the complete effect has been registered in the reader's mind that the inevitability and the exquisite economy become apparent. A characteristic poem of his has the air of being a random jotting down of chance impressions and sensations, the record of a moment of relaxed and undirected consciousness. The diction and movement are those of quiet, ruminative speech. But the unobtrusive signs accumulate, and finally one is aware that the outward scene is accessory to an inner theatre. Edward Thomas is concerned with the finer texture of living, the here and now, the ordinary moments, in which for him the 'meaning' (if any) resides. It is as if he were trying to catch some shy intuition on the edge of consciousness that would disappear if looked at directly. Hence, too, the quietness of the movement, the absence of any strong accent or gesture.

October, for instance, opens with the autumn scene:

> The green elm with the one great bough of gold
> Lets leaves into the grass slip, one by one, –
> The short hill grass, the mushrooms small milk-white,
> Harebell and scabious and tormentil,

That blackberry and gorse, in dew and sun,
Bow down to; and the wind travels too light
To shake the fallen birch leaves from the fern;
The gossamers wander at their own will.

The exquisite particularity of this distinguishes it from Georgian
'nature poetry'. But the end of the poem is not description;
Edward Thomas's concern with the outer scene is akin to Mrs
Woolf's: unobtrusively the focus shifts and we become aware of
the inner life which the sensory impressions are notation for.

> ... and now I might
> As happy be as earth is beautiful,
> Were I some other or with earth could turn
> In alternation of violet and rose,
> Harebell and snowdrop, at their season due,
> And gorse that has no time not to be gay.
> But if this be not happiness, – who knows?
> Some day I shall think this a happy day ...

A whole habit of sensibility is revealed at a delicate touch ...

————

Edward Thomas died in the war. The war, besides killing poets,
was supposed at the time to have occasioned a great deal of
poetry; but the names of very few 'war-poets' are still remembered. Among them the most current (if we exclude
Brooke's) is Siegfried Sassoon's. But though his verse made a
wholesome immediate impact it hardly calls for much attention
here. Wilfred Owen was really a remarkable poet, and his verse
is technically interesting. His reputation is becoming well established. Isaac Rosenberg was equally remarkable, and even
more interesting technically, and he is hardly known. But
Edward Thomas, Owen, and Rosenberg together, even if they
had been properly recognized at once, could hardly have constituted a challenge to the ruling poetic fashions.

1. Brooke, quoted in Sir Edward Marsh's 'Memoir', prefixed to *The Collected
Poems of Rupert Brooke*, London, Sidgwick & Jackson, 1918, p. lxvii.

ENID BAGNOLD

Enid Bagnold (1889–1981). Educated at Godalming in Surrey, and on the Continent. She studied art until she became a nurse during the war but displeased the hospital authorities by basing her *Diary Without Dates* (1918) upon her VAD experiences. Later, she joined the First Aid Nursing Yeomanry, serving in France as a driver. The *Diary*, from which the excerpts below are taken, was her first work.

Source: Enid Bagnold, *A Diary Without Dates*, London, William Heinemann, 1918.

... The new sister has come. That should mean a lot. What about one's habits of life ...?

The new sister has come, and at present she is absolutely without personality, beyond her medal. She appears to be deaf.

I went along tonight to see and ask after the man who has his nose blown off.

After the long walk down the corridor in almost total darkness, the vapour of the rain floating through every open door and window, the sudden brilliancy of the ward was like a haven.

The man lay on my right on entering – the screen removed from him.

Far up the ward the sister was working by a bed. Ryan, the man with his nose gone, was lying high on five or six pillows, slung in his position by tapes and webbing passed under his arms and attached to the bedposts. He lay with his profile to me – only he has no profile, as we know a man's. Like an ape, he has only his bumpy forehead and his protruding lips – the nose, the left eye, gone.

He was breathing heavily. They don't know yet whether he will live.

When a man dies they fetch him with a stretcher, just as he came in; only he enters with a blanket over him, and a flag covers him as he goes out. When he came in he was one of a convoy, but every man who can stand rises to his feet as he goes out. Then they play him to his funeral, to a grass mound at the back of the hospital . . .

———

Pain . . .

To stand up straight on one's feet, strong, easy, without the surging of any physical sensation, by a bedside whose coverings are flung here and there by the quivering nerves beneath it . . . there is a sort of shame in such strength.

'What can I do for you?' my eyes cry dumbly into his clouded brown pupils.

I was told to carry trays from a ward where I had never been before – just to carry trays, orderly's work, no more.

No. 22 was lying flat on his back, his knees drawn up under him, the sheets up to his chin; his flat, chalk-white face tilted at the ceiling. As I bent over to get his untouched tray his tortured brown eyes fell on me.

'I'm in pain, sister,' he said.

No one has ever said that to me before in that tone.

He gave me the look that a dog gives, and his words had the character of an unformed cry.

He was quite alone at the end of the ward. The sister was in her bunk. My white cap attracted his desperate senses.

As he spoke his knees shot out from under him with his restless pain. His right arm was stretched from the bed in a narrow iron frame, reminding me of a hand laid along a harp to play the chords, the fingers with their swollen green flesh extended across the strings; but of this harp his fingers were the slave, not the master.

'Shall I call your sister?' I whispered to him.

He shook his head. 'She can't do anything. I must just stick it out. They're going to operate on the elbow, but they must wait three days first.'

His head turned from side to side, but his eyes never left my face. I stood by him, helpless, overwhelmed by his horrible loneliness.

Then I carried his tray down the long ward and past the sister's bunk. Within, by the fire, she was laughing with the MO and drinking a cup of tea – a harmless amusement . . .

———

'I couldn't make a friend of that man!' the youngest sister loves to add to her criticism of a patient.

It isn't my part as a VAD to cry, 'Who wants you to?'

'I couldn't trust that man!' the youngest sister will say equally often.

This goes deeper . . .

But whom need one trust? Brother, lover, friend . . . no more. Why wish to trust all the world? . . .

'They are not real men,' she says, 'not men through and through.'

That's where she goes wrong; they are men through and through – patchy, ordinary, human. She means they are not men after her pattern.

Something will happen in the ward. Once I have touched this bedrock in her I shall be for ever touching it till it gets sore!

One should seek for no response. They are not elastic, these nuns . . .

In all honesty the hospital is a convent, and the men in it my brothers.

This for months on end . . .

For all that, now and then someone raises his eyes and looks at me; one day follows another and the glance deepens.

'*Charme de l'amour qui pourrait vous peindre!*'

Women are left behind when one goes into hospital. Such women as are in a hospital should be cool, gentle; anything else becomes a torment to the 'prisoner'.

For me, too, it is bad; it brings the world back into my eyes; duties are neglected, discomforts unobserved.

But there are things one doesn't fight.

'*Charme de l'amour* . . .' The ward is changed! The eldest sister and the youngest sister are my enemies; the patients are my enemies – even Mr Wicks, who lies on his back with his large head turned fixedly my way to see how often I stop at the bed whose number is 11.

Last night he dared to say, 'It's not like you, nurse, staying so much with that rowdy crew . . .' The gallants . . . I know! But one among them has grown quieter, and his bed is No. 11.

Even Mr Wicks is my enemy.

He watches and guards. Who knows what he might say to the eldest sister? He has nothing to do all day but watch and guard.

In the bunk at tea I sit among thoughts of my own. The sisters are my enemies . . .

I am alive, delirious, but not happy.

I am at anyone's mercy; I have lost thirty friends in a day. The thirty-first is in bed No. 11.

This is bad: hospital cannot shelter this life we lead, No. 11 and I. He is a prisoner, and I have my honour, my responsibility towards him; he has come into this room to be cured, not tormented.

Even my hand must not meet his – no, not even in a careless touch, not even in its 'duty'; or, if it does, what risk!

I am conspired against: it is not I who make his bed, hand him what he wishes; some accident defeats me every time . . .

———

Later, I stood down by the hatch waiting for the tray of fish, and as I stood there, the youngest sister beside me, he came down, for he was up and dressed yesterday, and offered to carry the tray. For he is reckless, too . . .

She told him to go back, and said to me, looking from her young, condemning eyes, 'I suppose he thinks he can make up for being the cause of all the lateness tonight.'

'Sister . . .' and then I stopped short. I hated her. Were we late? I looked at the other trays. We were not late; it was untrue. She had said that because she had had to wrap her barb in something and hadn't the courage to reprove me officially. I resented that and her air of equality. Since I am under her authority and agree to it, why dare she not use it?

As for me, I dared not speak to her all the evening. She would have no weapons against me. If I am to remember she is my sister I must hold my hand over my mouth.

She would not speak to me, either. That was wrong of her: she is in authority, not I.

It is difficult for her because she is so young; but I have no room for sympathy.

At moments I forget her position and, burning with resentment, I reflect, '. . . this schoolgirl . . .'

———

. . . One has illuminations all the time!

There is an old lady who visits in our ward, at whom, for one or two unimportant reasons, it is the custom to laugh. The men, who fall in with our moods with a docility which I am beginning to suspect is a mask, admit too that she is comic.

This afternoon, when she was sitting by Corrigan's bed and talking to him I saw where her treatment of him differed from ours. She treats him as though he were an individual; but there is more in it than that . . . She treats him as though he had a wife and children, a house and a back garden and responsibilities: in some manner she treats him as though he had dignity.

I thought of yesterday's injection. That is the difference: that is what the sisters mean when they say 'the boys' . . .

The story of Rees is not yet ended in either of the two ways in which stories end in a hospital. His arm does not get worse, but his courage is ebbing. This morning I wheeled him out to the awful sleep again – for the third time.

They will take nearly anything from each other. The only thing that cheered Rees up as he was wheeled away was the voice of Pinker crying, 'Jer want white flowers on yer coffin? We'll see to the brass 'andles!'

From Pinker, a little boy from the Mile End Road, they will stand anything. He is the servant of the ward (he says), partly through his good nature and a little because he has two good arms and legs. 'I ain't no skivvy,' he protests all the time, but every little odd job gets done.

Rees, when he wakes, wakes sobbing and says, 'Don' go away, nurse . . .' He holds my hand in a fierce clutch, then releases it to point in the air, crying, 'There's the pain!' as though the pain filled the air and rose to the rafters . . .

———

Patches of the corridor are thick with soapsuds; patches are dry. The art of walking the corridor in the morning can be learnt, and for a year and five months I have done it with no more than a slip and a slide.

But yesterday I stepped on a charwoman's hand. It was worse than stepping on a puppy; one knows that sickening lift of the heart, as though the will could undo the weight of the foot . . .

The stagger, the sense of one's unpardonable heaviness . . . I slipped on her hand as on a piece of orange-peel, and, jumping like a chamois, sent the next pail all over the heels of the front rank.

It was the sort of situation with which one can do nothing.

I met a friend yesterday, one of the old Chelsea people. He has followed his natural development. Although he talks war, war, war, it is from his old angle, it wears the old hall-mark.

He belongs to a movement which believes it 'feels the war'. Personal injury or personal loss does not enter the question; the heart of this movement of his bleeds perpetually, but impersonally. He claims for it that this heart is able to bleed more profusely than any other heart. Individual or collective, in . . . let us limit it to England!

In fact it is the only blood he has noticed.

When the taxes go up he says, 'Well, now perhaps it will make people feel the war!' For he longs that every one should lose their money so that at last they may 'feel the war,' 'stop the war' (interchangeable!).

He forgets that even in England a great many quite stupid people would rather lose their money than their sons.

How strange that these people should still picture the minds of soldiers as filled with the glitter of bright bayonets and the glory of war! They think we need a vision of blood and ravage and death to turn us from our bright thoughts, to still the noise of the drum in our ears. The drums don't beat, the flags don't fly . . .

He should come down the left-hand side of the ward and hear what the dairyman says.

'I 'ates it, nurse; I 'ates it. Them 'orses'll kill me; them drills . . . It's no life for a man, nurse' . . .

———

. . . There are men and men. Scutts has eleven wounds, but he doesn't 'mind' the war. God made many brands of men, that is all; one must accept them.

But war finds few excuses; and there are strange minnows in the fishing-net. Sometimes, looking into the TB ward, I think: 'It almost comes to this: one must spit blood or fight . . .'

VERA BRITTAIN

Vera Brittain (1896–1970). Born in Newcastle under Lyme and educated at Kingswood and Oxford. She served as a nurse in the war, and her experience during that period forms the bulk of her *Testament of Youth* (1933). Her 'War Diary, 1913–17', *Chronicle of Youth*, which forms the basis of some of the *Testament*, was published by Gollancz in 1981. This excerpt from the *Testament* describes life in No. 24 General Hospital, Étaples, in 1917. Edward was her brother. He was killed in action in Italy in June 1918.

Source: Vera Brittain, *Testament of Youth*, London, Gollancz, 1933; Fontana, in association with Virago, 1978.

... One tall, bearded captain would invariably stand to attention when I had re-bandaged his arm, click his spurred heels together, and bow with ceremonious gravity. Another badly wounded boy – a Prussian lieutenant who was being transferred to England – held out an emaciated hand to me as he lay on the stretcher waiting to go, and murmured: 'I tank you, Sister.' After barely a second's hesitation I took the pale fingers in mine, thinking how ridiculous it was that I should be holding this man's hand in friendship when perhaps, only a week or two earlier, Edward up at Ypres had been doing his best to kill him. The world was mad and we were all victims; that was the only way to look at it. These shattered, dying boys and I were paying alike for a situation that none of us had desired or done anything to bring about. Somewhere, I remembered, I had seen a poem called 'To Germany', which put into words this struggling new idea; it was written, I discovered afterwards, by Charles Hamilton Sorley, who was killed in action in 1915:

> You only saw your future bigly planned,
> And we, the tapering paths of our own mind,
> And in each other's dearest ways we stand,
> And hiss and hate. And the blind fight the blind.

'It is very strange that you should be nursing Hun prisoners,' wrote Edward from the uproar in the Salient, 'and it does show how absurd the whole thing is; I am afraid leave is out of the question for the present; I am going to be very busy as I shall almost certainly have to command the coy. in the next show . . . Belgium is a beastly country, at least this part of it is; it seems to breathe little-mindedness, and all the people are on the make or else spies. I will do my best to write you a decent letter soon if possible; I know I haven't done so yet since I came out – but I am feeling rather worried because I hate the thought of shoulder-ing big responsibilities with the doubtful assistance of ex-NCO subalterns. Things are much more difficult than they used to be, because nowadays you never know where you are in the line and it is neither open warfare nor trench warfare.'

A few days afterwards he was promoted, as he had expected, to be acting captain, and a letter at the end of August told me that he had just completed his course of instruction for the forthcoming 'strafe'.

'Captain B.,' he concluded, 'is now in a small dug-out with our old friend Wipers on the left front, and though he has got the wind up because he is in command of the company and may have to go up the line at any moment, all is well for the present.'

In the German ward we knew only too certainly when 'the next show' began. With September the 'Fall In' resumed its embarrass-ing habit of repetition, and when we had no more beds available for prisoners, stretchers holding angry-eyed men in filthy brown blankets occupied an inconvenient proportion of the floor. Many of our patients arrived within twenty-four hours of being wounded; it seemed strange to be talking amicably to a German officer about the '*Putsch*' he had been in the previous morning on the opposite side to our own.

Nearly all the prisoners bore their dreadful dressings with stoical fortitude, and one or two waited phlegmatically for death. A doomed twenty-year-old boy, beautiful as the young Hyacinth in spite of the flush on his concave cheeks and the restless, agonized biting of his lips, asked me one evening in a courteous whisper how long he had to wait before he died. It was not very long; the screens were round his bed by the next afternoon.

Although this almost unbearable stoicism seemed to be an understood discipline which the men imposed upon themselves, the ward atmosphere was anything but peaceful. The cries of the many delirious patients combined with the ravings of the five or six that we always had coming round from an anaesthetic to turn the hut into pandemonium; cries of '*Schwester!*' and '*Kamerad!*' sounded all day. But only one prisoner – a nineteen-year-old Saxon boy with saucer-like blue eyes and a pink-and-white complexion, whose name I never knew because everybody called him 'the Fish' – demanded constant attention. He was, he took care to tell us, '*ein einziger Knabe*'. Being a case of acute empyema as the result of a penetrating chest wound, he was only allowed a milk diet, but continually besieged the orderlies for '*Fleisch, viel Brot, Kartoffeln!*'

'*Nicht so viel schreien, Fisch!*' I scolded him. '*Die anderen sind auch krank, nicht Sie allein!*'

But I felt quite melancholy when I came on duty one morning to learn that he had died in the night.

OLIVE SCHREINER

Olive Schreiner (1855–1920). Born in Wittebergen near the border with Basutoland, South Africa. She was staying with Count and Countess von Moltke (he was Chief of the German General Staff) when war broke out. Von Moltke enabled her to reach Holland and she left Amsterdam on the last train out. Arrived in England on 3 August 1914. She is best known for *The Story of an African Farm* (1883), a work which had a profound influence on Vera Brittain (*q.v.*).

Source: Olive Schreiner, *The Letters of Olive Schreiner 1876–1920*, ed. S. C. Cronwright-Schreiner, London, T. Fisher Unwin, 1924.

To Havelock Ellis   Kensington, 3 August

Arrived at midnight last night after a most awful journey of fifteen hours from Amsterdam. It was the last train taking foreigners, thousands of men, women and children on the boat fleeing – people just lay about on the deck in the wet when there was no more room in the cabins and saloons. The sea was wild and the spray poured over the deck. I shall never forget it. Then there was a wild fight for seats in the trains! Goodbye, dear you and Edith. I long to see you.

Germany is determined to fight. It is *she* who is the cause of all. In Holland they are expecting the Prussians there tomorrow, to take the Hague and the ports. All the soldiers are mobilized, but of course they can do nothing. *War is Hell*. They will fight in Africa, too.

To Havelock Ellis   Kensington, 21 August

I'm still here as I've not been able to find a quiet place. I am troubled with the worst insomnia I have had for twenty years. To me this is the most sordid war in which England has ever engaged. She is backing Russia, not because she loves Russia but because millions of her money are invested there, and millions more in France, whose money system will break if the Russian autocracy falls. She fights Germany, not to set the Germans free from military rule, but because she is her trade rival whom she must crush. I am trying to write something on the war, but I doubt whether it will be taken.

To Havelock Ellis   Hythe, 5 October

I don't know how long I shall be able to stand this mist and fog . . . Just now the landlady came up to say all the curtains must be closed and blinds pulled down as there was an order this evening all lights were to be put out. All the lamps are out and even the big lighthouse at Dungeness. I can still see the few lights at Folkestone and Sandgate. I suppose they think there are German men of war near here. But I'm sure the Germans would not be so mad as to come into the narrow part of this channel.

There are no English here, only swarms of Belgians. They, especially the men, are the ugliest mongrel-looking folk I've ever seen. A. S. said long ago that when she went from Holland into Belgium she was struck by the ugly inharmonious faces. I suppose they are a mixed breed?

Your *Impressions and Comments* is very interesting, so far as I've got – written in a nice simple style, not so much 'damned fine horse'.

I shall be so thankful if I can get that little flat at Chelsea. If a person can't climb stairs and can't go to boarding houses because you can't eat the food, it's awfully hard to find a place in London when your purse is short. I suppose it will be in England as in Africa, where there were many real cases of insanity caused by the war.

I have not had any news from the Cape for weeks. The strain is considerable. I hardly know what I shall do if I get no letter from Cron this week. All letters are opened and read and marked by the censors. I have a feeling there have been awful losses in South Africa where the Union is attacking German West Africa. The papers report fifteen killed and forty-one wounded and some missing, but that may not be a third of the number, or a tenth. My body is here but my thoughts are always in De Aar. I seem to see it before my eyes all the time. Are you back in London? Where is Edith?

To Havelock Ellis   London, 8 October

I am ill. But I think London is best . . . Goodbye, dear. The world has never seemed so blank to me. I suppose my spiritual eyes are dim, therefore I cannot see light. Only death gives an end to it.

To Havelock Ellis   London, 13 October
I am going tomorrow to Durrants Hotel, Manchester Square. I hope I shall get better there as it's very dry. Do come and see me soon. I long to see you. How scared people are about the Zeppelins? If you have lived through a war and had your house burnt and all you prized taken from you, you learn to take these things as all in the day's work. War *is* Hell. Though people like the English who have always made it in other peoples' countries have never realized [it]. It's when it comes to your own land that its full horror bursts on you. Did I tell you Oliver has joined his regiment and may be sent to the front any hour? And the diplomatists who for ten years have been bringing things into this state will live on. Our beautiful innocent ones, of all nations, must die. Goodbye, dear.

To Havelock Ellis   Kensington Palace Mansions, 16 October
Yesterday at Durrants Hotel a boy brought a note. It ran: 'Madam, When Mrs Smith took the room for you she did not mention that your name was *Schreiner*. As we find that is either an Austrian or a German name you will please leave our Hotel at once.' Of course I took a taxi and my things and left at once. I have fortunately found this place. It's much more expensive. I can't stay but I must rest here as I'm worn out. [She stayed for ten months.] The great use of not being very poor is that it helps one to health.

To Edward Carpenter   London, October
I think so much of your tired face as you went away. You know, Edward, we can live through all this, but it's simply crushing us, who had such hopes for the future twenty years ago . . . I wish I could feel with you that this war is going to bring the Kingdom of Heaven. I feel it is the beginning of half a century of the most awful wars the world has seen. First this then another war probably of England and Germany against Russia, then as the years pass, with India, Japan and China and the Native Races of Africa. While the desire to dominate and rule and possess Empire is in the hearts of men, there will always be war.

... Again and again when I tried to get rooms they wouldn't let me have them on account of my name. Just before I left I found very nice cheap rooms in Chelsea, there was a sweet refined looking little woman who let them; I told her I would take them, and come the next day. When I told her my name she turned and *glared* at me. I inquired what was the matter. She asked me if my name was not German. I said it was, but I was a British subject born in South Africa, that my husband was a British subject of pure British descent, and my mother was English, that my father who left Germany eighty years ago, was a naturalized British subject, and had been dead nearly fifty years. She turned round and stormed at me, all her seemingly gentle face contorted with rage and hate. She said that if my ancestors came from Germany 'three hundred years ago' it would make no difference, no one with a German name should come into her house, and poured forth a stream of abuse that was almost inconceivable. The worst was, that I was feeling so ill and worn out, that I dropped into a chair and burst out crying. It's the only time I've cried in two years. It seemed so contemptibly weak of me; but you know how you feel when you are utterly worn out mentally and physically! I could only say, 'It isn't because you are so unkind to me, it's because all the world's so wicked.'

Oh Emily the worst of war is not the death on the battle fields; it is the meanness, the cowardice, the hatred it awakens. Where is the free England of our dreams, in which every British subject, whether Dutch, English, French or German in extraction, had an equal right and freedom? I wouldn't have come here if I had not thought one would be free here from these petty attacks. What this war has shown me is not so much the wickedness as the meanness of human nature. War draws out all that is basest in the human heart. Perhaps I shall be able to get up to London before you leave.

ROSA LUXEMBURG

Rosa Luxemburg (1870–1918). Born in Poland, she settled in Germany *c.* 1895 and acquired German nationality by marriage. During the 1914–18 war she cooperated with Liebknecht in anti-war propaganda and in founding the Spartacus League. She was imprisoned and wrote a series of prison letters. Released in November 1918, she was murdered together with Liebknecht. The letters below are addressed to Sophie Liebknecht, Karl Liebknecht's wife. They have been specially translated by Cecil Davies.

Source: Rosa Luxemburg, *Briefe aus dem Gefängnis*, Berlin, Verlag Junge Garde, Verlag Klaus Guhl, 1920.

To Sophie Liebknecht   15 January 1917
                                          Wronke

... Ah, there was a moment today that I felt bitterly. The whistle of the 3.19 train told me Mathilde was steaming off, and straight away I ran to and fro along the usual 'walk' by my wall like a caged animal, and my heart shrank with pain, because I can't get away from here, too – just away from here! But that doesn't matter – my heart got a smack directly afterwards and had to submit – it's already used to obeying – like a well-trained dog. Don't let's talk about me.

Sonitschka, do you remember what we've planned to do when the war is over? A journey south together. And we'll do it! I know you dream of going with me to Italy – Italy is the most sublime thing for you. But on the other hand I'm planning to drag you to Corsica. That is something even more than Italy. There you forget Europe – modern Europe at least. Imagine a broad, heroic landscape with sharp contours of mountains and valleys – up above, nothing but bare masses of noble, grey rock – down below, luxuriant olives, cherry laurels and ancient chestnut trees. And over everything a primeval stillness – no human voice, no bird-call, only a streamlet slips somewhere between stones, or the wind in high places whispers between rocky cliffs – still the same wind that filled Odysseus' sails. And what you see of people harmonizes exactly with the landscape. For instance, round a bend in the mountain path a caravan suddenly appears – the Corsicans always walk behind each other in long caravans, not in groups like our peasants. Usually a dog is running in front, then maybe a goat stalking along or a little donkey laden with sacks full of chestnuts, then follows a great mule on which sits a woman, sideways on to the animal with her legs hanging straight down, a child in her arms. She sits erect, high and slim like a cypress, motionless; at her side strides a bearded man with quiet, firm carriage, both are silent. You would swear it is the Holy Family. And you meet such scenes there at every step. I was so touched each time that I wanted instinctively to go down on my knees, as I always must before consummate beauty. The Bible and the Ancient World are still alive there. We must go – just as I did: cross the whole island on foot, sleep every night in a different place, greet every sunrise when already walking. Does that attract you? I'd be happy to show you that world . . .

Read a lot, you must progress spiritually, too – and you can do that – you are still young and pliant. And now I must close. Be cheerful and quiet on this day.

Your
Rosa

To Sophie Liebknecht

2 May 1917
Wronke

. . . But naturally it does indeed pain me that everything shatters me so deeply now. Do you know – I often have the feeling that I'm not a proper human being but some bird or other animal in human form. Inwardly I feel myself much more at home in a little scrap of garden, as here, or in the open country among bumble-bees and grass, than – at a party conference. Perhaps I can actually say all this to you: you won't straightway start suspecting me of betraying socialism. But my innermost ego belongs rather to my great tits than to the 'Comrades'. And not because, like so many inwardly bankrupt politicians, I find a refuge or rest in Nature. On the contrary, I also find everywhere in nature so much that is cruel that I suffer a great deal. Consider, for instance, that I can't get the following little experience out of my mind. Last spring I was walking home from a country stroll along the silent, empty street, when a dark little spot on the ground attracted my attention. I bent down and saw a silent tragedy: a big dung-beetle was lying on its back helplessly defending itself with its legs, while a whole crowd of tiny ants swarmed around on it and – ate its living body! It made me shudder; I got out my handkerchief and began to drive the cruel beasts away. But they were so impudent and obstinate that I had to have a long struggle with them, and when I'd freed the poor, silent sufferer at last and laid it a long way off on the grass, two of its legs had already been eaten away . . . I walked on with the tormenting feeling that in the end I'd done the beetle a very dubious good turn.

To Sophie Liebknecht   End of May, 1917
                                                 Wronke

Sonjuscha, do you know where I am, where I'm writing this letter to you? In the garden! I've dragged my little table out here and now I'm sitting hidden among green shrubs. On my right the yellow flowering currant which smells like aromatic pinks, on the left a privet bush, over me a Norway maple and a slim young chestnut tree hold out their broad green hands to each other, and in front of me the big, solemn and gentle white poplar slowly rustles its white leaves. On the paper on which I'm writing dance light shadows of the leaves with bright rings of sunlight, and now and then a drop falls on my face and hands from the rain-moistened foliage. In the prison church the service is on; the muffled sound of the organ penetrates indistinctly out here, submerged under the rustling of the trees and the clear choir of birds, who are all lively today; from the distance the cuckoo calls. How lovely it is, how lucky I am, you almost feel in midsummer mood – the full, voluptuous ripeness of summer and ecstasy of living; do you know the scene in Wagner's Master-singers, the folk-scene, where a lively crowd clap their hands: Midsummer Day! Midsummer Day! – and everyone suddenly begins to dance an early Victorian waltz? You could get into that mood in these days. What happened to me, of all things, yesterday! I must tell you. During the morning I found a big peacock butterfly on the window in the bathroom. It had probably been there a few days already and had fluttered itself to death by exhaustion on the hard pane; by now it only gave weak signs of life with its wings. When I saw it, I got dressed again, trembling with impatience, climbed up to the window and took it carefully in my hands: it didn't resist any longer and I thought it was probably dead already. I put it near me on the window-ledge, so that it might come to itself, and then the little flame of life roused itself feebly again, but it stayed sitting still. Then I put a few open flowers in front of its antennae, so that it might have something to eat; just outside the window a garden warbler was singing brightly and wantonly, so that it resounded. Involuntarily I said aloud: Listen, how the little bird is singing happily – so a bit of life must come back to you! I had to laugh myself over this speech to the half-dead peacock butterfly, and I thought to myself: Lost words! But no – no, after half an hour the little creature recovered, slipped a bit here and there at first and finally flew slowly away. How I rejoiced over this rescue! That was an experience! . . .

Always your
Rosa

To Sophie Liebknecht   Middle of December, 1917
                                        Breslau

. . . Karl [Liebknecht] has been imprisoned in Luckau for a year now. I've thought about it often this month, and exactly a year ago you visited me in Wronke, and you gave me that lovely Christmas tree . . . This year I've ordered one here, but they brought me quite a mangy one, with branches missing – no comparison with last year's. I don't know how I'll fix on the eight little candles I've bought. It's my third Christmas in gaol, but don't take it tragically. I'm as peaceful and cheerful as ever. Yesterday I lay awake for a long time – I can never get to sleep now before one, but I have to go to bed as early as ten – then I dream about all sorts of things in the dark. So yesterday I thought: how remarkable it is that I live regularly in a joyful ecstasy – without any special reason. For instance, I'm lying here in the dark cell on a mattress as hard as rock, around me in the house the usual churchyard silence reigns, you feel as if you're in the grave; from the window the reflection of the lamp that is burning the whole night outside the prison is pictured on the ceiling. From time to time you hear very faintly the distant rattle of a railway train going by, or quite near under the windows the sentry clearing his throat as he takes a few steps slowly in his heavy boots to move his stiff legs. The sand grates so hopelessly under these footsteps that the whole emptiness and ineluctability of existence rings out of it in the damp, dark night. There I lie alone and still, swathed in these manifold black blankets of the dark, of boredom, lack of liberty, of winter, – and at the same time my heart beats from an inconceivable, obscure inner joy, as if I were walking on a flowery meadow in radiant sunshine. And I smile at life in the darkness, as if I knew some magic secret that gives the lie to everything evil and sorrowful and turns it into open brightness and happiness. And at that, I myself look for a cause of this joy, find nothing, and have to smile at myself again. I believe the secret is nothing else but life itself; the deep darkness of night is as beautiful and soft as velvet, if you only look at it aright. And the grating sound of the damp sand under the slow, heavy footsteps of the sentry also sings a beautiful little song of life – if you only listen aright. In such moments I think of you and want so much to share this magic key with you, so that you perceive the beauty and joy of life always and in all situations, so that you also live in ecstasy and walk as if over a gaily coloured meadow. Indeed I don't intend to put you off with asceticism, with imaginary joys. I am bestowing on you all the real joys of the senses. In addition I only want to give you my inexhaustible inner happiness, so that I may be tranquil concerning you, so that you go through life in a coat embroidered with stars, which protects you against everything small, trivial and worrying . . .

. . . Ah, Sonitschka, I've felt sharp pain here; in the courtyard where I take my exercise wagons often come from the military fully loaded with sacks of old soldier's jackets and shirts, often with blood-stains . . . they're unloaded here, distributed in the cells, patched, then loaded up again and delivered to the military. Recently a wagon like this came with buffaloes instead of horses harnessed to it. I saw the animals close to for the first time. They are built more strongly and broadly than our cattle, with flat heads and horns bent low, so that their skulls are more like our sheep, quite black with big, gentle eyes. They come from Romania and are trophies of war . . . The soldiers who drive the wagons say it was very laborious to catch these wild animals and even harder to make use of them as draught beasts, accustomed as they were to freedom. They were fearfully beaten, so much so that the phrase *vae victis* could be applied to them . . . There are said to be a hundred of these animals in Breslau alone; moreover, having been used to lush Romanian pasture, they get miserable and meagre fodder. They are ruthlessly exploited in hauling all manner of heavy wagons and soon die as a result. – Some days ago a wagon came driven in like this whose load was stacked up so high that the buffaloes couldn't get it over the threshold at the entrance-gate. The soldier who was with them, a brutal fellow, began to go for the animals with the thick end of his whip-handle, so violently that the wardress asked him indignantly if he had no pity for the beasts! 'No one has pity for us humans either,' he answered with an evil smile, and pitched in more strongly . . . The animals got moving at last and came up the hill, but one was bleeding . . . Sonitschka, buffalo-skin is proverbial for its thickness and toughness, and it was in shreds. As the wagon was being unloaded the animals stood quite still and exhausted, and one of them – the one that was bleeding – looked around with an expression in its black face and gentle black eyes like a child with a tear-stained face. It was exactly the expression of a child who has been severely punished and doesn't know why or wherefore, doesn't know how to escape from the torment and brute force . . . I stood in front of the animal and it looked at me: the tears ran down my face – they were *its* tears: you can't flinch more painfully for your dearest brother than I in my helplessness flinched for this silent suffering. How far, how unattainably lost were the open lush green meadows of Romania! How differently the sun shone and the wind blew there, how different were the beautiful sounds of the birds or the tuneful call of the herdsmen. And here – this dreadful foreign town, the stifling byre, the nauseating musty hay mixed with rotten straw, the fearful foreign people, and – the blows, the blood that runs out of the fresh wounds. O my poor buffalo, my poor, beloved brother, we both stand here so helpless and spiritless, united only in pain, helplessness and longing. Meanwhile the prisoners hurried busily around the wagon, unloaded the heavy sacks and dragged them into the house. But the soldier stuck both hands in his trouser pockets, wandered about the courtyard with big strides, smiled and softly whistled a popular song. And the whole glorious war filed past me . . .

> Write soon. I embrace you, Sonitschka,
> Your
> Rosa

Sonjuscha, Dearest, be calm and cheerful in spite of everything. That's life and we must take it as it is – bravely, undaunted and smiling – in spite of everything.

HENRI BARBUSSE

Henri Barbusse (1873–1935). Born in Paris. Already forty-one in 1914 and with a history of poor health, Barbusse volunteered at the start of the Great War. A socialist and pacifist, he hoped that the war would mark a step forward for socialism. He died in Moscow. These passages from the 'War Diaries' interestingly mix realism and expressionism, fact and fiction. They appeared in France only in 1965 and excerpts here are translated for the first time by Janet Whitehouse.

Source: Henri Barbusse, 'War Diary', first published in 1965 edition of *Le Feu*, Paris, Flammarion, 1965.

WAR DIARY

14 October 1915

We're in one of the dug-outs on the Béthune road. Momial and I set off at half-past nine this morning, under cover of the thick fog which lay over the plain this morning, to try to reach Souchez. We climbed up on to the road. The bodies which were lined up had been removed. They had looked awful, pitiful. There was one whose face was completely black, with mournful, swollen lips and mutilated hands, a sort of little, child's hand with the palm mutilated; it was monstrous, horrifying. The others, shapeless, filthy bundles, with vague objects protruding from them; around them fluttered letters which had dropped out of their pockets while they'd been being laid out, elbows to the ground. One of these letters: My dear Henri, the weather's fine on your saint's-day, etc. Further on, they'd moved a body in such a state that they'd had to wrap it in wire netting and tent-canvas, holding the whole lot together with rope fixed to a tent-peg. Foul stench. Piles of tent canvas and stained tattered greatcoats, stiffened by the dried blood.

We went down the Béthune road. On either side, shattered trees, embankments ploughed up by shells, heaps of rubbish, refuse, debris of all sorts. All along, trenches, saps, various flags. A track to the left. The whole plain is criss-crossed with 'tracks', with saps, and, since the taking of the positions which had dominated us, they've built a narrow-gauge railway.

The Cabaret Rouge. Nothing left of it. We're shown a bit of floor left intact, like a curiosity [. . .] the rubble heaped up there is reddish, like the brick the house had been built of, when there had been a house.

We reached the other front-line German trench which runs more or less alongside the road. In places, black and sooty, it has been completely opened up by the ravages of the shells, each shell crater touching the next. We saw German and French corpses which had been there for a fortnight, perhaps a month, which they hadn't been able to bury as long as the firing line was there.

Photographed five Germans, crushed, decomposed, black and crawling with vermin, on the other side of the trench taken during the attack of 25–28 September. Photographed the German trench too. I chose a spot which seemed particularly torn apart and shattered. But it's impossible to choose, really; it's all been churned up, full of rotting remains and debris. It stinks of cataclysm. [. . .] We went on further, and came to Souchez; flattened, completely flattened. The village has returned to the plain, with piles of ruins, of beams. Here and there, shell craters [. . .] Smell of the charnel-house. You walk on shrapnel, broken weapons; everywhere are unexploded shells, tattered equipment, suspicious heaps of clothing, sticky with a brownish mud. A few corpses. One is still fresh. A cook with his string of loaves. His comrades' water-bottles round his body. He must have been killed last night; shrapnel in the back. The Germans have been bombarding Souchez heavily these last few days. From a distance we could see great billows of smoke from the 150s or 210s rising, with a deafening metallic crash as the shells burst, from the hollow where we are at present. Obviously it wasn't a very safe place and we were lucky not to get knocked out! We went as far as the end of the village – if that's what you can call it – towards the only dwelling with its foundations intact (through a hole we saw a blood-soaked bedstead in the courtyard). Then we returned.

Never have I seen such total devastation of a village. Ablain-Saint-Nazaire and Carency were still recognizable as places, with their houses torn apart and courtyards choked up with rubble.

Here, nothing with any shape left, not even a stretch of wall, a railing, a doorway left standing. It might have been a dirty, boggy wasteland near a town whose inhabitants had, through the years, been tipping on it their debris, rubbish, rubble from demolished buildings and scrap iron. In the foreground, the fog, the unearthly scene of massacred trees.

Few corpses; a few holes containing decomposing horses. Others containing what were men, now disfigured remains, deformed by their injuries. Under the shelling the water-mill had been cut off from things to such an extent that it had diverted the stream on a haphazard course, forming a pond on a little square.

15 October

I went with the fifth battalion to the slope held by the Zouaves. This slope was taken during our attack of the 28th, and reached by the Zouaves and Moroccans in the attack of the 7th. The attackers, who had run to that point from la Croix de Berthonval and who had entrenched themselves as best they could at the foot of the hillock in fox-holes, making a sort of beehive out of the place, had been taken from the side by the machine-guns and massacred. The gully and the embankments which stretch over a length of several kilometres are now no more than a vast necropolis. Everywhere mummified, skeletal corpses, reduced to the state of little heaps mixed with reddish mud. Or you might see a sole sticking out; sometimes a foot here and there, or a scrap of cloth protruding from the earth, showing the position of a body. There were great numbers of corpses that the Germans, while they were occupying the positions, had left to rot. You see a face like that of Rameses II emerging from a minced-up bag, huddled under it, shin-bones, thigh-bones, bones of hands and feet packed like knuckle-bones round suspicious bulges. From bits of tattered, tar-smeared cloth, emerges a fragment of back-bone. These are no longer bodies, but heaps of dried-up refuse which seem to have been abandoned along with discarded equipment, beakers, water-bottles, rubbish-bins. Without counting the innumerable bits of rubbish, the scattered tin cans dropped by the soldiers who had lived there and left to pile up around the billets.

As for the dead from the attacks of the 28th, they're carried away every day, and every day they're buried. We've got a row of them at the foot of the Zouaves' Honeycomb. They are like those that I saw the day before yesterday and yesterday, lined up on the Béthune road, full of mud, hideously mutilated and disfigured, the faces swollen and black as a Negro's, the flesh bloated and full of insects and worms collected into heaps. The rifles were lined up.

———

ON THE CAUSES OF WAR

Without going into details, it is obviously somewhat naïve to attribute all the blame to Germany and to claim that before the war the whole of Germany was bellicose and the whole of France pacifist. In reality there were war-mongering and pacifist elements on both sides; but in Germany the militarist elements were in control and all-powerful, and from this point of view carried the rest with them.

There was in France a very active faction for revenge, whose influence on public opinion was noticeable, and throughout more or less the whole country there was a bitter memory of the military humiliation of 1870, a glorious hope of victories in keeping with the character of many Frenchmen.

It was not the necessary army that was being attacked. It was not the three-year law which was conceived as a weapon. It was a state of mind, the simple desire to dominate by strength in order to regain the lost provinces and to impose a need for national glory outside national affairs.

———

Short-sighted view. The man who forms a definitive opinion on a doctrine because of a fact of detail or a presumption.

Short-sighted view. Those who content themselves with the formula of dogma: religious dogma, which in the end crystallized.

The flag-idol.

The ancient idols are resurrected in that idol.

The flag, my friends, an idol. In raising it, in striving to destroy it, I am doing the same thing as those who, through deeper and higher moral ideas, attacked idols of stone.

'The flag isn't the same thing.'

'It doesn't appear to be the same thing, but for posterity it will appear the same thing and even worse.'

Keep in mind the idea of the multiplication, of the continuity of misery.

Peace straight away. It's the end of the war. Later, it's perhaps the end of all war.

——

STATISTICS

Cocon explains to me that we've slept in thirty towns, that the regiment has been replenished three times, that we once stayed in the trains for sixteen days, that we've had three rest-periods. Each man has worn out two rifles, four greatcoats, two pairs of trousers, six pairs of boots.

Final words of a soldier, showing that people don't realize this effort.

He had a very small head, but a very ugly one. He had a huge body, but not spread out, and on his square torso a minute head, so tiny you'd have thought it the head of a carved duck.

In his flat face, his little nose which he works with his finger and constantly wriggles, stands up straight like a cork.

You might have said a snail walking with his hands.

Fouillade, an admirable soldier. The heroic act which he performed. At the beginning he is the bearer of his citation.

In the troubles, they talk about Landrin, a fast-living young man of some means, who achieved his aim of being accepted as a roadmender in the army. Tirette tells me, 'Once you're in, you're a long time in.'

The lover (the praying mantis = Madame X)[1]

The count complained = (Count X)

In Babylon, at the time of Queen Seminariste.

We saw some English officers pass by, in very fine, close-fitting leather. We called them 'les sanglés'.[2]

Oaths: Evil of our bones. May Satan rise up. Hell hole. Satan burn me. Five hundred blasphemies, Satan and his Lady. May the cholera purge me. Satan and his cooking pot. One hundred sorcerers.

The bird that sings. He's the one who's right.

I'm trying to give you what hope I can. We talk of the definite defeat of Germany before the winter. They talk about the possibility of predicting the future. They ask my advice. They trust me. I say straight out: most certainly. Predictions of this sort have come about, that's a promise.

Men scattered in the distance, like swarms of lice.

POLEMIC

They're good, your articles. Passed for press, yes.[3]

SUBJECT FOR SHORT STORY

Propenson is a braggart. He also got the Croix de Guerre with two palms, and the Military Medal. The wretched Beot, good-for-nothing gallows bird, moving over the battlefield, sniffing like a jackal, believes him dead. He steals his papers. From then on, he will be Propenson. He is taken prisoner. After the war, he finds the police after him. Propenson had in fact been the worst of rogues. He had behaved courageously, but his previous crimes were still outstanding [. . .] The identity-thief is sentenced to death. He tries in vain to explain that he is not Propenson but Beot; they don't believe him. He had got himself too well entangled and surrounded with a solid network of precautions. Moreover, those who had known him had disappeared at Mort Homme.[4]

———

Duty is danger.

The abuse, the sophism of the 'moaners'. I'll be of more use in a safe, sheltered post. Or even staying at home, because of my intellectual and artistic resources that I shall thus be safeguarding for my country. So let the others go where you really get killed.

She could be seen in the shaft of light, straight and tender like a curtain of sun, coming in through the window. Her cheek drew close to the cheek of a rose.

War exists only through the unseen work of these infinitely small men.

Each soldier is, because of the multitude, invisible and silent.

Truth. The battlefield. The depths of night. Man-worm. Men-worms. All this moves in the invisible fire of fever. In the early morning, they smoke like rubble, calling; one moves, falls lower down. Are they the source of the fog?

V's anger about danger: those who bear on their collars the stigmata of officers.

At the point where the ring is put on, they feel like saying to Blaire: 'Why are you so dirty? D'you think it's pleasant for your wife to have a filthy pig like you close to her?' But they don't dare.

The eel. Chapter in the Balzac fashion.

Jesus Christ was a poor, pure-souled chap; he didn't deserve all the harm his ideas have done.

Tenderness: something on animals and pity, something on tenderness.

The magnificent hatred you have, which serves only to do harm.

The Motor Department. Dodges not to be put in the infantry. The MD has never let a man go, if it could help it. Men have even refused, on principle, enlistment in the infantry. You could hear drivers say, 'I wanted to join up; they wouldn't have me.' It wasn't true, but it was a bit of Jesuitry. That driver would be dismissed and put back in the middle of the squad like a prisoner.

To Monsieur F. de C. Those who in peacetime were so clever at getting themselves talked about, in war so clever at getting themselves forgotten.
    ... The case of B., C. of those for whom they managed to contrive, from two days out of two years of ambush, one circumstance to win them the Croix de Guerre.

I want to be judged by my peers,[5] and not by the Ascensionist Fathers of the rue Bayard or the rue François Ier.

———

Nationalism; like the man who smokes because he thinks it clever, throws his matches in his straw, fights the flames and thinks up sophisticated pump systems to put out the fires which break out in his home from time to time.

Men seen from afar: little black beads which serve to make flowers of beads and wire that are hung on tombs.

Return to the sources. Attack established things, accepted ideas, prescribed theories.

The contract signed by God the Father affirms without question that man must stay in the past . . . An odd doctrine, where making progress lies in marking time.

This is the freedom, the light which is called progress.

This idea is greater than the idea of individual egoism or even collective egoism. Social progress depends on the Internationale.

You are fighting for something.

For something great, important, sublime.

For something simple. You must be told quite clearly and quite loudly so that everyone hears. In reply to the . . . of the dead and even to the cries of the wounded, can be seen the profound and grandiose framework of things human.

Great cries, human words have rung out, lighting up the stages of progress present and future. It is for one of these great things that you are fighting, for the greatest of all, for justice and the equality of man.

IDEA FOR A SHORT STORY

The Emperor. There is something which frightens me: pictures. There were at the court some of Philip IV, terrible and sombre; in the palace the size of a town (there were two thousand windows) amongst the jesters and the chamberlains, was a character given responsibility by royal favour for vague ceremonial duties, such as supervising processions and sorting out the positions of the nobles. His name was Don Diego Rodríguez de Silva y Velasquez. You might have lived at the Escorial and not remember him, but his paintings were there. Philip IV is dead. Reigns have gone by. Generations have gone by, through war and peace. Those pictures are still alive. They are fantastic things, with their everlasting presence which wipes out everything. They wipe out Philip IV, and war, and splendour. And further back even Charles V and Charlemagne. They will wipe out Spain with their inexhaustible immortality. They are capable of surviving Europe one day. I am disturbed by great paintings, those things which no longer move in the palaces – and the monuments themselves are fragile these days.

YESTERDAY AND TOMORROW

1. The dream.

Intoxication of the hearts. Intoxication of hope. The madness of obscurity and short-sighted views, everything compact, indelible, systematized by the ignorant and the semi-learned.

2. The drama, then the nightmare.

THE STORM

3. Truth, Light.

Malady of simplicity and light, of tearing, wrenching away.

Simplicity, opportunity to go back to the sources, to the causes, to make a general criticism.

I return flayed, sensitive . . .

Grudges; I've got some that I didn't have before; I've no more than I used to have.

7. Enchantment.

To condense into a hundred and fifty pages as it were a romantic novel, to note all the details necessary to the conclusions; especially action. No exposition: reflections themselves. Traits of character or of drama.

SHORT STORY

Nurse in the hospital ward. He loves her and, once better, takes her away. Then things no longer go well, and she goes back to nursing and returns to the hospital. He goes back (not as a patient). The same settings as before, and, despite themselves, despite the experience of their trial, they try to start up the idyll once again. They begin to make the same promises as before.

The man who doesn't see far ahead; he does however always look ahead, he seems to look in front of him, but his eyes are empty.

You can count on him to say something inadequate, something unfinished.

He is the man with a goose's head and a hoarse voice.

There are two short-sighted types: the smug and the 'good chap'.

The explosive and brittle.

Astral transfiguration.

The charred skeletons of the trees.

The old lady with her black cape and her lampshade.

The hands with their armour of chilblains.

The pool under the agony of the oaks; the shadowy church with its crystal paving-stones.

Dawn creates patches of crystal on the stretch of water.

The Nightmare.

This must be the shortest part. Fifty pages.

1:150. 2:50. 3:100.

It's my whole time in the trenches: a fortnight.

I arrive at the depot for the battles.

The men bathing: you can see their wounds, their gashes, their scars, their patches: even those who have apparently remained intact.

The arrival at the depot. It isn't raining, it's very cold. It's sad, sad. The whole plain, all is dismal. Only glory is radiant.

1. The pun here, lost in English, is on *l'amante* = lover, and *la mante* = praying mantis.

2. The pun is on *'les Anglais'* = the English, and *'les sanglés'* = people 'strapped up' or 'straight-laced'.

3. The pun is on *'bons à tirer'* = 'fit for shooting' as well as 'ready for the press'.

4. Mort Homme: a hill, the scene of fierce fighting near Verdun.

5. There is a pun here on the French word *'pairs'*, which means 'peers', and sounds like *'pères'*, which means 'fathers'.

HENRI BARBUSSE

see also p. 189

Barbusse served in the front line in Artois and Picardy from 1914 till the first weeks of 1916. *Le Feu* grew out of the 'Diaries' in 1915 and was written in about six months in hospitals in Chartres and Plombières. It was awarded the Prix Goncourt in 1917. This translation appeared in June 1917 and influenced Sassoon and Owen. (See also Fitzwater Wray's own *Across France in War Time*, p. 147.) Action Française accused Barbusse of being a German agent. However, *Le Feu* was banned in Germany. The opening 'Vision' seems to lie behind Owen's 'The Show' (see Jon Stallworthy, *Wilfred Owen, A Biography*, Oxford, Oxford University Press, 1974). 'The Vision' and 'In the Earth' form the opening of the book; the later extracts are from the key chapter, 'Under Fire'.

Source: Henri Barbusse, *Under Fire* (translated from *Le Feu*, Paris, Flammarion, 1916, by W. Fitzwater Wray), London, Dent, 1917; Everyman edn, 1926.

THE VISION

Mont Blanc, the Dent du Midi, and the Aiguille Verte look across at the bloodless faces that show above the blankets along the gallery of the sanatorium. This roofed-in gallery of rustic woodwork on the first floor of the palatial hospital is isolated in Space and overlooks the world. The blankets of fine wool – red, green, brown, or white – from which those wasted cheeks and shining eyes protrude are quite still. No sound comes from the long couches except when some one coughs, or that of the pages of a book turned over at long and regular intervals, or the undertone of question and quiet answer between neighbours, or now and again the crescendo disturbance of a daring crow, escaped to the balcony from those flocks that seem threaded across the immense transparency like chaplets of black pearls.

Silence is obligatory. Besides, the rich and high-placed who have come here from all the ends of the earth, smitten by the same evil, have lost the habit of talking. They have withdrawn into themselves, to think of their life and of their death.

A servant appears in the balcony, dressed in white and walking softly. She brings newspapers and hands them about.

'It's decided,' says the first to unfold his paper. 'War is declared.'

Expected as the news is, its effect is almost dazing, for the audience feels that its portent is without measure or limit. These men of culture and intelligence, detached from the affairs of the world and almost from the world itself, whose faculties are deepened by suffering and meditation, as far remote from their fellow men as if they were already of the Future — these men look deeply into the distance, towards the unknowable land of the living and the insane.

'Austria's act is a crime,' says the Austrian.

'France must win,' says the Englishman.

'I hope Germany will be beaten,' says the German.

They settle down again under the blankets and on the pillows, looking to heaven and the high peaks. But in spite of that vast purity, the silence is filled with the dire disclosure of a moment before.

War!

Some of the invalids break the silence, and say the word again under their breath, reflecting that this is the greatest happening of the age, and perhaps of all ages. Even on the lucid landscape at which they gaze the news casts something like a vague and sombre mirage.

The tranquil expanses of the valley, adorned with soft and smooth pastures and hamlets rosy as the rose, with the sable shadow-stains of the majestic mountains and the black lace and white of pines and eternal snow, become alive with the movements of men, whose multitudes swarm in distinct masses. Attacks develop, wave by wave, across the fields and then stand still. Houses are eviscerated like human beings and towns like houses. Villages appear in crumpled whiteness as though fallen from heaven to earth. The very shape of the plain is changed by the frightful heaps of wounded and slain.

Each country whose frontiers are consumed by carnage is seen tearing from its heart ever more warriors of full blood and force. One's eyes follow the flow of these living tributaries to the River of Death. To north and south and west afar there are battles on every side. Turn where you will, there is war in every corner of that vastness.

One of the pale-faced clairvoyants lifts himself on his elbow, reckons and numbers the fighters present and to come — thirty millions of soldiers. Another stammers, his eyes full of slaughter, 'Two armies at death-grips — that is one great army committing suicide.'

'It should not have been,' says the deep and hollow voice of the first in the line. But another says, 'It is the French Revolution beginning again.'

'Let thrones beware!' says another's undertone.

The third adds, 'Perhaps it is the last war of all.' A silence follows, then some heads are shaken in dissent whose faces have been blanched anew

by the stale tragedy of sleepless night —'Stop war? Stop war? Impossible!
There is no cure for the world's disease.'

Some one coughs, and then the Vision is swallowed up in the huge sunlit
peace of the lush meadows. In the rich colours of the glowing kine, the
black forests, the green fields and the blue distance, dies the reflection of
the fire where the old world burns and breaks. Infinite silence engulfs the
uproar of hate and pain from the dark swarmings of mankind. They who
have spoken retire one by one within themselves, absorbed once more in their
own mysterious malady.

But when evening is ready to descend within the valley, a storm breaks
over the mass of Mont Blanc. One may not go forth in such peril, for the
last waves of the storm-wind roll even to the great veranda, to that harbour
where they have taken refuge; and these victims of a great internal wound
encompass with their gaze the elemental convulsion.

They watch how the explosions of thunder on the mountain upheave the
level clouds like a stormy sea, how each one hurls a shaft of fire and a
column of cloud together into the twilight; and they turn their wan and
sunken faces to follow the flight of the eagles that wheel in the sky and
look from their supreme height down through the wreathing mists, down to
earth.

'Put an end to war?' say the watchers. —'Forbid the Storm!'

Cleansed from the passions of party and faction, liberated from prejudice
and infatuation and the tyranny of tradition, these watchers on the
threshold of another world are vaguely conscious of the simplicity of the
present and the yawning possibilities of the future.

The man at the end of the rank cries, 'I can see crawling things down
there' — 'Yes, as though they were alive' — 'Some sort of plant, perhaps' —
'Some kind of men' —

And there amid the baleful glimmers of the storm, below the dark
disorder of the clouds that extend and unfurl over the earth like evil spirits,
they seem to see a great livid plain unrolled, which to their seeing is made
of mud and water, while figures appear and fast fix themselves to the
surface of it, all blinded and borne down with filth, like the dreadful
castaways of shipwreck. And it seems to them that these are soldiers.

The streaming plain, seamed and seared with long parallel canals and
scooped into water-holes, is an immensity, and these castaways who strive
to exhume themselves from it are legion. But the thirty million slaves,
hurled upon one another in the mud of war by guilt and error, uplift their
human faces and reveal at last a bourgeoning Will. The future is in the
hands of these slaves, and it is clearly certain that the alliance to be
cemented some day by those whose number and whose misery alike are
infinite will transform the old world.

IN THE EARTH

The great pale sky is alive with thunderclaps. Each detonation reveals together a shaft of red falling fire in what is left of the night, and a column of smoke in what has dawned of the day. Up there – so high and so far that they are heard unseen – a flight of dreadful birds goes circling up with strong and palpitating cries to look down upon the earth.

The earth! It is a vast and water-logged desert that begins to take shape under the long-drawn desolation of daybreak. There are pools and gullies where the bitter breath of earliest morning nips the water and sets it a-shiver; tracks traced by the troops and the convoys of the night in these barren fields, the lines of ruts that glisten in the weak light like steel rails, mud-masses with broken stakes protruding from them, ruined trestles, and bushes of wire in tangled coils. With its slime-beds and puddles, the plain might be an endless grey sheet that floats on the sea and has here and there gone under. Though no rain is falling, all is drenched, oozing, washed out and drowned, and even the wan light seems to flow.

Now you can make out a network of long ditches where the lave of the night still lingers. It is the trench. It is carpeted at bottom with a layer of slime that liberates the foot at each step with a sticky sound; and by each dug-out it smells of the night's excretions. The holes themselves, as you stoop to peer in, are foul of breath.

I see shadows coming from these sidelong pits and moving about, huge and misshapen lumps, bear-like, that flounder and growl. They are 'us'. We are muffled like Eskimos. Fleeces and blankets and sacking wrap us up, weigh us down, magnify us strangely. Some stretch themselves, yawning profoundly. Faces appear, ruddy or leaden, dirt-disfigured, pierced by the little lamps of dull and heavy-lidded eyes, matted with uncut beards and foul with forgotten hair.

Crack! Crack! Boom! – rifle fire and cannonade. Above us and all around, it crackles and rolls, in long gusts or separate explosions. The flaming and melancholy storm never, never ends. For more than fifteen months, for five hundred days in this part of the world where we are, the rifles and the big guns have gone on from morning to night and from night to morning. We are buried deep in an everlasting battlefield; but like the ticking of the clocks at home in the days gone by – in the now almost legendary Past – you only hear the noise when you listen . . .

———

We watch the shadows of the passersby and of those who are seated, outlined in inky blots, bowed and bent in diverse attitudes under the grey sky, all along the ruined parapet. Dwarfed to the size of insects and worms, they make a queer dark stirring among these shadow-hidden and Death-pacified lands where for two years war has caused cities of soldiers to wander or stagnate over deep and boundless cemeteries.

Two obscure forms pass in the dark, several paces from us; they are talking together in low voices – 'You bet, old chap, instead of listening to him, I shoved my bayonet into his belly so that I couldn't haul it out.'

'There were four in the bottom of the hole. I called 'em to come out, and as soon as one came out I stuck him. Blood ran down me up to the elbow and stuck up my sleeves.'

'Ah!' the first speaker went on, 'when we are telling all about it later, if we get back, to the other people at home, by the stove and the candle, who's going to believe it? It's a pity, isn't it?'

'I don't care a damn about that, as long as we do get back,' said the other; 'I want the end quickly, and only that.'

Bertrand was used to speak very little ordinarily, and never of himself. But he said, 'I've got three of them on my hands. I struck like a madman. Ah, we were all like beasts when we got here!'

He raised his voice and there was a restrained tremor in it: 'It was necessary,' he said, 'it was necessary, for the future's sake.'

He crossed his arms and tossed his head: 'The future!' he cried all at once as a prophet might. 'How will they regard this slaughter, they who'll live after us, to whom progress – which comes as sure as fate – will at last restore the poise of their conscience? How will they regard these exploits which even we who perform them don't know whether one should compare them with those of Plutarch's and Corneille's heroes or with those of hooligans and apaches?

'And for all that, mind you,' Bertrand went on, 'there is one figure that has risen above the war and will blaze with the beauty and strength of his courage –'

I listened, leaning on a stick and towards him, drinking in the voice that came in the twilight silence from the lips that so rarely spoke. He cried with a clear voice – '*Liebknecht*!'

He stood up with his arms still crossed. His face as profoundly serious as a statue's, drooped upon his chest. But he emerged once again from his marble muteness to repeat, 'The future, the future! The work of the future will be to wipe out the present, to wipe it out more than we can imagine, to wipe it out like something abominable and shameful. And yet – this present – it had to be, it had to be! Shame on military glory, shame on armies, shame on the soldier's calling, that changes men by turns into stupid victims or ignoble brutes. Yes, shame. That's the true word, but it's *too* true; it's true in eternity, but it's not yet true for us. It will be true when there is a Bible that is entirely true, when it is found written among the other truths that a purified mind will at the same time let us understand. We are still lost, still exiled far from that time. In our time of today, in *these* moments, this truth is hardly more than a fallacy, this sacred saying is only blasphemy!'

A kind of laugh came from him, full of echoing dreams – 'To think I once told them I believed in prophecies, just to kid them!'

I sat down by Bertrand's side. This soldier who had always done more than was required of him and survived notwithstanding, stood at that moment in my eyes for those who incarnate a lofty moral conception, who have the strength to detach themselves from the hustle of circumstances, and who are destined, however little their path may run through a splendour of events, to dominate their time.

'I have always thought all those things,' I murmured.

'Ah!' said Bertrand. We looked at each other without a word, with a little surprised self-communion. After this full silence he spoke again. 'It's time to start duty; take your rifle and come.'

From our listening-post we see towards the east a light spreading like a conflagration, but bluer and sadder than buildings on fire. It streaks the sky above a long black cloud which extends suspended like the smoke of an extinguished fire, like an immense stain on the world. It is the returning morning.

It is so cold that we cannot stand still in spite of our fettering fatigue. We tremble and shiver and shed tears, and our teeth chatter. Little by little, with dispiriting tardiness, day escapes from the sky into the slender framework of the black clouds. All is frozen, colourless and empty; a deathly silence reigns everywhere. There is rime and snow under a burden of mist. Everything is white. Paradis moves – a heavy pallid ghost, for we two also are all white. I had placed my knapsack on the other side of the parapet, and it looks as if wrapped in paper. In the bottom of the hole a little snow floats, fretted and grey in the black foot-bath. Outside the hole, on the piled-up things, in the excavations, upon the crowded dead, snow rests like muslin . . .

———

. . . The extreme end of our lines was then on Berthonval Wood, five or six kilometres from here. In that attack, which was one of the most terrible of the war or of any war, those men got here in a single rush. They thus formed a point too far advanced in the wave of attack, and were caught on the flanks between the machine-guns posted to right and to left on the lines they had overshot. It is some months now since death hollowed their eyes and consumed their cheeks, but even in those storm-scattered and dissolving remains one can identify the havoc of the machine-guns that destroyed them, piercing their backs and loins and severing them in the middle. By the side of heads black and waxen as Egyptian mummies, clotted with grubs and the wreckage of insects, where white teeth still gleam in some cavities, by the side of poor darkening stumps that abound like a field of old roots laid bare, one discovers naked yellow skulls wearing the red cloth fez, whose grey cover has crumbled like paper. Some thigh-bones protrude from the heaps of rags stuck together with reddish mud; and from the holes filled with clothes shredded and daubed with a sort of tar, a spinal fragment emerges. Some ribs are scattered on the soil like old cages broken; and close by, blackened leathers are afloat, with water-bottles and drinking-cups pierced and flattened. About a cloven knapsack, on the top of some bones and a cluster of bits of cloth and accoutrements, some white points are evenly scattered; by stooping one can see that they are the finger and toe constructions of what was once a corpse.

Sometimes only a rag emerges from long mounds to indicate that some human being was there destroyed, for all these unburied dead end by entering the soil . . .

GEORGES DUHAMEL

Georges Duhamel (1884–1966). Associated with Jules Romains. (Both were poets of the Unanimist group interested in expressing collective experience.) Duhamel was trained in medicine and served as an army surgeon during the war. Brief encounters with the wounded and dying result in a vision both angry and horrified, and yet not without humour and affection for those in his care. Best known in England for his *roman-fleuve Les Pasquier* (1933–41).

Source: Georges Duhamel, *The New Book of Martyrs* (translated from *Vie des martyrs*, Paris, Mercure de France, 1917, by Florence Simmonds), London, William Heinemann, 1918.

February–April 1916
Verdun

We were going northward by forced marches, through a France that was like a mournful garden planted with crosses. We were no longer in doubt as to our appointed destination; every day since we had disembarked at B— our orders had enjoined us to hasten our advance to the fighting units of the Army Corps. This Army Corps was contracting, and drawing itself together hurriedly, its head already in the thick of the fray, its tail still winding along the roads, across the battlefield of the Marne.

February was closing in, damp and icy, with squalls of sleet, under a sullen, hideous sky, lowering furiously down to the level of the ground. Everywhere there were graves, uniformly decent, or rather according to pattern, showing a shield of tricolour or black and white, and figures. Suddenly, we came upon immense flats, whence the crosses stretched out their arms between the poplars like men struggling to save themselves from being engulfed. Many ancient villages, humble, irremediable ruins. And yet here and there, perched upon these, frail cabins of planks and tiles, sending forth thin threads of smoke, and emitting a timid light, in an attempt to begin life again as before, on the same spot as before. Now and again we chanced upon a hamlet which the hurricane had passed by almost completely, full to overflowing with the afflux of neighbouring populations.

Beyond P—, our advance, though it continued to be rapid, became very difficult, owing to the confluence of convoys and troops. The main roads, reserved for the military masses which were under the necessity of moving rapidly, arriving early, and striking suddenly, were barred to us. From every point of the horizon disciplined multitudes converged, with their arsenal of formidable implements, rolling along in an atmosphere of benzine and hot oil. Through this ordered mass, our convoys threaded their way tenaciously and advanced. We could see on the hillsides, crawling like a clan of migrating ants, stretcher-bearers and their dogs drawing handcarts for the wounded, then the columns of orderlies, muddy and exhausted, then the ambulances, which every week of war loads a little more heavily, dragged along by horses in a steam of sweat.

From time to time, the whole train halted at some crossroad, and the ambulances allowed more urgent things to pass in front of them – things designed to kill, sturdy grey mortars borne along post-haste in a metallic rumble.

A halt, a draught of wine mingled with rain, a few minutes to choke over a mouthful of stale bread, and we were off again, longing for the next halt, for a dry shelter, for an hour of real sleep.

Soon after leaving C— we began to meet fugitives. This complicated matters very much, and the spectacle began to show an odious likeness to the scenes of the beginning of the war, the scenes of the great retreat.

Keeping along the roadsides, the by-roads, the field paths, they were fleeing from the Verdun district, whence they had been evacuated by order. They were urging on miserable old horses, drawing frail carts, their wheels sunk in the ruts up to the nave, loaded with mattresses and eiderdowns, with appliances for eating and sleeping, and sometimes, too, with cages in which birds were twittering. On they went, from village to village, seeking an undiscoverable lodging, but not complaining, saying merely:

'You are going to Verdun? We have just come from X—. We were ordered to leave. It is very difficult to find a place to settle down in.'

Women passed. Two of them were dragging a little baby-carriage in which an infant lay asleep. One of them was quite young, the other old. They held up their skirts out of the mud. They were wearing little town shoes, and every minute they sank into the slime like ourselves, sometimes above their ankles.

All day long we encountered similar processions. I do not remember seeing one of these women weep; but they seemed terrified, and mortally tired.

Meanwhile, the sound of the guns became fuller and more regular. All the roads we caught sight of in the country seemed to be bearing their load of men and of machines. Here and there a horse which had succumbed at its task lay rotting at the foot of a hillock. A subdued roar rose to the ear, made up of trampling hoofs, of grinding wheels, of the buzz of motors, and of a multitude talking and eating on the march.

Suddenly we debouched at the edge of a wood upon a height whence we could see the whole battlefield. It was a vast expanse of plains and slopes, studded with the grey woods of winter. Long trails of smoke from burning buildings settled upon the landscape. And other trails, minute and multicoloured, rose from the ground wherever projectiles were raining. Nothing more: wisps of smoke, brief flashes visible even in broad daylight, and a string of captive balloons, motionless and observant witnesses of all.

But we were already descending the incline and the various planes of the landscape melted one after the other. As we were passing over a bridge, I saw in a group of soldiers a friend I had not met since the beginning of the war. We could not stop, so he walked along with me for a while, and we spent these few minutes recalling the things of the past. Then as he left me we embraced, though we had never done so in times of peace.

Night was falling. Knowing that we were now at our last long lap, we encouraged the worn-out men. At R— I lost touch with my formation. I halted on the roadside, calling aloud into the darkness. An artillery train passed, covering me with mud to my eyes. Finally, I picked up my friends, and we marched on through villages illumined by the camp-fires which were flickering under a driving rain, through a murky country which the flash of cannon suddenly showed to be covered with a multitude of men, of horses, and of martial objects.

It was 27 February. Between ten and eleven at night we arrived at a hospital installed in some wooden sheds, and feverishly busy. We were at B—, a miserable village on which next day the Germans launched some thirty monster shells, yet failed to kill so much as a mouse.

The night was spent on straw, to the stentorian snores of fifty men overcome by fatigue. Then reveille, and again, liquid mud over the ankles. As the main road was forbidden to our ambulances there was an excited discussion as a result of which we separated: the vehicles to go in search of a byway, and we, the pedestrians, to skirt the roads on which long lines of motor lorries, coming and going, passed each other in haste like the carriages of an immense train.

We had known since midnight where we were to take up our quarters; the suburb of G— was only an hour's march farther on. In the fields, right and left, were bivouacs of colonial troops with muddy helmets; they had come back from the firing-line, and seemed strangely quiet. In front of us lay the town, half hidden, full of crackling sounds and echoes. Beyond, the hills of the Meuse, on which we could distinguish the houses of the villages, and the continuous rain of machine-gun bullets. We skirted a meadow strewn with forsaken furniture, beds, chests, a whole fortune which looked like the litter of a hospital. At last we arrived at the first houses, and we were shown the place where we were expected.

GEORGES DUHAMEL

see also p. 206

Duhamel's second book about the war was *Civilisation*. It reflects a greater sense of the absurdity of war and the individual's place in it than *The New Book of Martyrs*. 'Civilisation', with its unforgettable images of an efficient hospital as part of the industrialized war-machine, is the concluding chapter. Henry Williamson ranked *Civilisation* with Barbusse's *Under Fire*, far above Remarque's *All Quiet on the Western Front*. Middleton Murry also refers to it in his review of Sassoon's poems (*q.v.*). 'ACA' is an abbreviation for Ambulance du Corps d'Armée.

Source: Georges Duhamel, *Civilisation* (translated from *Civilisation*, Paris, Mercure de France, 1918, by T. P. Conwil-Evans), London, Swarthmore Press, 1919.

CIVILIZATION

... 'You, sergeant,' said one officer to me —'you will remain at the hospital and take charge of the ACA section. I'll send a number of men to help you' ...

From Saturday onwards the wounded arrived in batches of a hundred. I got them arranged as methodically as I could in the wards of the ACA.

But the work was not going on at all well. My absurd stretcher-bearers, unable to fall in with each other's movements, stumbled like broken-kneed, miserable nags, causing the wounded to scream with pain. In a nibbling, haphazard sort of way, they tried to deal with the waiting masses of the injured, and the whole ACA seemed to stamp with impatience. The effect was rather like a human meat factory which has its machinery going at full strength without being fed with oil and materials.

I must really describe the ACA to you. In war slang it means an automatic hospital ('autochir') – the latest thing in surgical invention. It's the last word in science, just like our 400 mm calibre guns which run on metal rails: it follows the armies with motors, steam-driven machinery, microscopes, laboratories, the complete equipment of a modern hospital. It is the first great repair depot which the wounded man enters on coming out of the destructive, grinding mill on the extreme front. Here are brought the parts of the military machine that are most spoiled. Skilled workmen take them in hand at once, loosen them quickly, and with a practised eye examine them, as one would a hydro-pneumatic break, an ignition chamber or a collimator. If the part is seriously damaged, it goes through the usual routine of being scrapped; but if the 'human material' is not irretrievably ruined, it is patched up ready to be used again at the first opportunity, and that is called 'preserving the effectives' . . .

My stretcher-bearers, with the jolting clumsiness of drunken dockers, were bringing to the ACA a few of the injured, who were at once swallowed up and eliminated. And the factory continued to growl, like some Moloch whose appetite has been whetted by the fumes of the first sacrifice.

I had picked up a stretcher. Helped by a gunner who had been wounded in the neck, and whose only desire was to be of some use while awaiting his operation, I led my crew in amongst the heap of men that lay on the ground. It was then that I saw some one passing along wearing a high-grade officer's hat – a sensible sort of man who smiled in spite of his solicitous bearing.

'There is something wrong with your ambulance work,' he said. 'I'll send you eight negroes. They are excellent stretcher men, these fellows from Madagascar.'

Ten minutes afterwards the negroes had come.

To be exact, they were not all natives of Madagascar: they were types selected from the 1st Colonial Corps which was at that very moment strenuously fighting before Laffaux. There were a few natives of the Sudan, whose age was difficult to tell, sombre and wrinkled, and concealing under their regimental tunics charms that were coated with dirt, and smelling with leather, sweat and exotic oils. The negroes of Madagascar were of medium height, looking like embryos, very dark and silent.

They slipped on the straps, and at my command began carrying the wounded with quiet unconcern, as if they were unloading bales of cotton at the docks.

I was content, or rather reassured. The ACA, surfeited at last, worked at high pressure, and hummed like well-tended machines that drip with oil, shining and flashing from every point.

Flash! The word is not too strong. I was dazzled on entering the operating hut. Night had just fallen – one of those warm beautiful nights of this brutal spring. The gunfire came and went in short spasms, like a sick giant. The wards of the hospital overflowed with a heaving mass of pain, and death was trying to restore order there. I breathed in deeply the night air of the garden and, as I was saying, I entered the operating hut.

It had been partitioned off into several rooms. The one I suddenly stepped into made a bulge in the side of the building. It was as hot as a puddling-oven. Men were cleaning, scrubbing, and polishing, with scrupulous care, a mass of shining instruments, while others were stoking fires which gave out the white heat of soldering lamps. With never a pause, orderlies were coming and going, carrying trays held out rather stiffly at arm's length, like hotel-keepers devoted to the ceremonious rites of the table.

'It's warm here,' I murmured, in order to say something.

'Come over here: you'll find it all right,' said a grinning little chap as hairy as a kobold.

I lifted a lid, feeling I was opening the breast of some monster. In front of me steps led to a kind of throne on which, seated like a king, the heart of the thing was to be found. It was a sterilizer – an immense pot in which a calf could easily have been cooked whole. It lay on its stomach and emitted a jet of steam that stupefied one, and its weary monotony made one hardly conscious of time and space. But suddenly the infernal noise stopped, and it was like the end of eternity. On the back of the machine a load of kettles continued to spit and gurgle. A man looking like a ship's pilot was turning a large heavy wheel, and the lid of the cauldron, suddenly unbolted, rose, exposing to view its red-hot bowels, from which all sorts of boxes and packages were taken out. The heat of the furnace had given way to the damp, crushing atmosphere of a drying-stove.

'But where do they operate on the wounded?' I asked a boy who was washing a pair of rubber gloves in a big copper tub.

'Over there, in the operating-room, of course. But don't go in that way.'

I went out again into the freshness of the night, and proceeded to the waiting-room to find my stretcher-bearers.

At that moment it was the turn of the cuirassiers to be brought in. A division of 'foot cavalry' had been fighting since morning. Hundreds of the finest men in France had fallen, and they waited there like broken statues which are still beautiful in their ruins. Their limbs were so strong, and their chests so solid, that they could not believe in death, and as they felt their rich healthy blood dripping from their wounds, they held at bay, with curses and laughter, the weakness of their broken flesh.

'They can do what they like with this flesh of mine,' said one of the two; ' but to make me unconscious, damn me! I'm not having any.'

'Yes, whatever they like,' said another, 'but not amputation! I want my paw; even done to the world, I want it!'

These two men were coming out of the X-ray ward. They lay naked under a sheet, and carried, pinned to their bandages, papers of different sizes and shapes, rough sketches, formulae, and something like an algebraical statement of their wounds, the expression in numbers of their misery and disordered organs.

They spoke of this their first visit to the laboratory like clever children who realize that the modern world would not know how to live or die without the meticulous discipline of the sciences.

'What did he say, the X-rays major?'

'He said it was an antero-posterior axis.'

'Just what I feared.'

'It's in my belly. I heard him say *abdomen*. But I am sure it's in my belly. Ah, damn it! but I'm not going to be put to sleep. That I won't stand!'

The door of the operating-theatre opened at this point, and the waiting-room was flooded with light. A voice cried:

'The next lot! And the belly chap first!'

The black bearers adjusted their straps, and the two talkers were carried off. I followed the stretchers.

Imagine a shining rectangular block set in sheer night like a jewel in coal. The door closed again, and I found myself imprisoned in that light, which was reflected from the spotless canvas of the ceiling. The floor, level and springy, was strewn with red soaked linen which the orderlies picked up quickly with forceps. Between the floor and the ceiling, four strange forms that were men. They were dressed completely in white, their faces hidden behind masks which, like those of Tuareg, only admit the eyes to view. Like Chinese dancers, they held in the air their hands covered with rubber, and the perspiration streamed from their brows.

You could hear the muffled vibrations of the motor which generated the light. Filled up again to overflowing, the sterilizer disturbed the world with its piercing lament. Small radiators were snorting like animals when they are stroked the wrong way. It all made a savage, flamboyant music, and the men who were moving about seemed to perform rhythmically a religious dance – a kind of austere and mysterious ballet.

The stretchers glided in between the tables like canoes in an archipelago. The instruments were set out on spotless linen and sparkled like jewels in glass cases; and the little Madagascar negroes, alert and obedient, took great care in handling their burden. They stopped on the word of command, and waited. Their dark slender necks yoked with the straps, and their fingers clutching the handles of the stretchers, reminded one of sacred apes trained to carry idols. The heads and feet of the two wan and enormous cuirassiers stuck out beyond the limits of the stretchers.

A few gestures that were almost ritualistic, and the wounded men were placed on the operating-tables.

At that moment I caught the eye of one of the negroes, and I experienced a feeling of extreme discomfort. It was the calm deep look of a child or a young dog. The savage was slowly turning his head from left to right and looked at the extraordinary men and the extraordinary things all around him. His dark eyes stopped lightly on all the wonderful parts of this workshop devoted to repairing the human machine. And those eyes, which betrayed no thought, were on that account even more disquieting. For one second I was fool enough to think 'How astonished he must be!' But the absurd thought soon left me, and I was overwhelmed with unutterable shame.

The four negroes left the room. That afforded me a little comfort. The wounded looked dazed and bewildered. The ambulance men hastened to bind their hands and feet and rub them with alcohol. The masked men were giving orders and moving about the tables with the deliberate gestures of officiating priests.

'Who is the head here?' I whispered to some one.

He was pointed out to me. He was a man of medium height and was sitting down, with his gloved hands held up, dictating something to a clerk.

Fatigue, the blinding light, the booming of the guns, the rumble of the machinery acted as a sort of lucid drug on my brain. I remained fixed where I was, in a veritable whirl of thought. Everything here worked for one's good ... it was civilization finding within itself the supreme reply, the corrective to its destructive excesses; nothing less than this complex organism would suffice to reduce by the smallest degree the immense evil creation of the machine age. I thought again of the indecipherable look of the savage, and my emotion was a mixture of pity, anger and loathing . . .

The man who, as I had learnt, was in charge of the operating-theatre had finished dictating. He remained fixed in the position of a heraldic messenger and seemed to be absorbed in thought. I noticed that behind his spectacles gleamed a look that was solemn, tranquil and sad, though full of purpose. Scarcely anything of his face was visible, the mask hiding his mouth and beard; but on his temples could be seen a few fresh grey hairs, and a large swollen vein marked his forehead, betraying the strained efforts of a tense will.

'The man's unconscious,' said someone.

The surgeon approached the table. The man had indeed lost consciousness; and I saw it was the very one who swore he would not take the anaesthetic. The poor man had not dared even to make a protest. Caught, as it were, in the cogs of the wheel, he was at once overpowered, and he delivered himself up to the hungry machine, like pig-iron devoured by the rolling-mills. And then, too, he must have known it was for his good, because this is all the good that is left to us in these days.

'Sergeant,' some one remarked, 'you are not allowed to remain in the operating-theatre without a cap.'

On going out, I looked once again at the surgeon. He hung over his work with an assiduity in which, despite his overalls, his mask and his gloves, a feeling of tenderness was plainly marked.

I thought with conviction: 'No! No! He, at least, has no illusions!'

And I found myself once more in the waiting-room, that smelt of blood, like a wild beast's lair.

A dim light came from a veiled lamp. Some wounded were moaning; others chatted in low voices.

'Who said tank?' said one of them. 'Why, I was wounded in a tank.'

There was silence, brief and respectful. The man, who was buried in bandages, added: 'Our petrol-tank burst: my legs are broken and I am burnt in the face. Oh! I know all about tanks!'

He said that with a queer emphasis in which I recognized the age-long torment of humanity – pride.

I went out into the night to enjoy a smoke. The world seemed to be dazed, bewildered, tragic; and I think that in reality . . .

Believe me, sir, when I speak of civilization and regret it, I quite know what I am saying; and it is not wireless telegraphy that will alter my opinion. It is all the more tragic because we are helpless; we cannot reverse the course which the world is taking. And yet!

Civilization – the true civilization – exists. I think often of it. In my mind it is the harmony of a choir chanting a hymn; it is a marble statue on an arid, burnt-up hillside; it is the Man who said, 'Love one another,' or 'Return good for evil.' But for two thousand years these phrases have been merely repeated, and the chief priests have too much vested interest in temporal things to conceive anything of the kind.

We are mistaken about happiness and about good. The noblest natures have also been mistaken, for silence and solitude are too often denied them. I have seen the monstrous sterilizer on its throne. I tell you, of a truth, civilization is not to be found there any more than in the shining forceps of the surgeon. Civilization is not in this terrible trumpery; and if it is not in the heart of man, then it exists nowhere.

ERNST GLAESER

Ernst Glaeser (1902-62). Born in Butzbach, Hesse. Became a journalist. Left Germany when Hitler came to power but returned to edit a soldiers' paper in 1939. *Class 1902* concerns a group of schoolboys growing to maturity during the war. Like many works of the period the novel is constructed as a group of semi-autonomous short stories. The passages from 'The Funeral' relate the children's perception of the outbreak of the war. Those from 'Homer and Anna' take us to early 1918. The narrator is still supposed to be receiving a rigorous classical education while German society crumbles around him. Too hungry to learn his Greek in class, he nevertheless shares his knowledge of Greek heroes with the young train guard Anna. They later share a smuggled goose. They live within earshot of the guns at Verdun and Anna is herself the victim of an air-raid. This book, and those of Remarque, Zweig, Renn and 'Schlump' (*qq.v.*) were all published within a few months in England.

Source: Ernst Glaeser, *Class 1902* (translated from *Jahrgang 1902*, Berlin, Gustav Kiepenheuer Verlag AG, 1928, by Willa and Edwin Muir), London, Martin Secker, 1929.

THE FUNERAL

The English declaration of war had come as a complete surprise. Nobody in our town had expected it. My father had declared that the English were really Germans, and I recollected as well a pronouncement of the famous professor in the waiting-room at Basel, according to which the English as representatives of the blond race were our natural allies; in them too existed the Siegfried spirit; and if they betrayed it, there was always Japan, who would straightway, with its army officered by Germans, attack the English in India.

I found this pronouncement very puzzling at the time – for what had Japan to do with Siegfried?

But the professor was a famous man; he must know.

I was walking with Ferd through the town. The flags hung

limp. The air was sultry and as if stagnant. In the western sky towered thunder-clouds.

Ferd smiled. 'It is all coming out as my father said. We'll lose the war.'

I was so horrified that I stood still. 'It's a lie,' I cried, 'for then all this would have happened for nothing.'

'That's just what my father says, all this will lead to nothing . . .'

'England has betrayed us,' said I, to comfort myself, 'it will be punished for that.'

'How stupid you are,' Ferd replied. 'England has never lost a war yet.'

I walked beside him and noticed that I was gradually beginning to hate him. Again he wanted to forbid me something. My faith in Germany, my faith in the new purified world of the grown-ups. For without victory what sense had all this brotherhood, all this unity? And was not God on our side? Had Liège not fallen? Could God lie? . . . Yes, earlier, while the grown-ups were still bad, I had believed the Red Major; but now when even Kremmelbein had shaken hands with Dr Persius, now that the war had revealed itself as the great unifier and regenerator of mankind, I was bound to praise and love it.

Everything in me rose in resistance to Ferd, and as I slowly drew back from him, as if he were carrying a dangerous pestilence about with him, I spat at him: 'You yourself are half English . . .'

Ferd did not say a word. He only bowed his head. Then, after a horrible pause, I heard him saying: 'My father reports to his regiment this evening.' We walked on in silence. I did not understand why he was crying. I would have been proud if my father could have helped, as a major, to beat the enemy. My father was only a sergeant in the Landsturm . . . Really *I* should have been the one to cry.

On a red-carpeted balcony in front of the town hall the pastor S. was standing giving an address. He was known as a fiery orator. His voice had an astounding resonance. After every sentence the people even in the farthest outskirts of the crowd cheered.

'England has betrayed us!' he bellowed, swinging his arms as if he wanted to buffet the clouds: 'Down with England!'

From the market-place rose a single shout: 'Down with England!'

218

The pastor drew a deep breath, his right hand clenched itself, and while he brought it down with a thunderous blow, from his mouth came in a bellow the mighty words: 'God, who sees all sins, the Avenger and Ruler – *God punish England!*'

In a harsh and resolute chorus the crowd repeated his words. I saw women praying; the men raised their hands and swore; above stood the stalwart form of the pastor giving us his blessing. We all took off our hats, the soldiers raised their helmets. Ferd had disappeared.

August had climbed on to a lamp-post. When he saw me he slid down. 'I say, my father has gone to D— to the barracks there. In a fortnight he'll be on active service. He must drill recruits first; he's a sergeant. And who do you think is in his section as a private? Galopp, the judge.' August's face was radiant. 'The war!' he cried 'the war's making everything right again!'

As we were making our way with great difficulty through the excited crowd, I saw my father coming out of a public-house with J. the apothecary. They were carrying rifles and had white bands with badges round their arms. 'We've registered as special constables,' said my father, showing his rifle proudly. 'We're going to post ourselves on the outskirts and hold up all the cars with civilians in them. For there's news come that the French are trying to smuggle millions of gold through to Russia in motor cars. Besides, the whole neighbourhood's swarming with spies. We've power to arrest anybody that looks suspicious, and shoot if they don't stop after we've called "Halt!" three times. You go home and ask mother to tell Kathinka to bring me some coffee about midnight; we'll be stationed at the bridge with the poplars until sunrise.'

'Father!' I cried, 'Father, I'll bring the coffee at midnight!'

And August begged to be allowed to come too.

'Good,' said my father, visibly moved, patting our heads, 'good, my lads – the password is "Count Haeseler".'

Then they shouldered their rifles and marched towards the outskirts of the town. In the middle of the street, not on the pavement. As if they were vehicles.

I invited August to supper.

As we neared the park behind which my parents' house lay, we saw a band of boys jumping excitedly round a tree to which they had bound somebody. August, who had keen sight, suddenly cried out: 'They've got hold of Ferd!' And at once he set off at a run. I ran after him. All my anger against Ferd vanished before the fact that they had set on him. He stood alone against a superior force of enemies. That turned the scale. 'Of course Haugwitz and the whole of his precious crew!' cried August, gaining three yards on me. We took a short cut, leapt over the rose-beds and flung ourselves with wild howls among the enemy, who were just then taking council what they should do to Ferd. They had bound him to an ash with their book-straps and left two 'men' to guard him. The Kalmuck was just proposing: 'Each of us will walk up to him and give him one on the ear, and spit in his face,' when with a noiseless spring August was among them, dealt the Kalmuck a kick in the belly, so that he rolled on the ground with his face turning green, and seized young Haugwitz by his tartan scarf, shook him three times backwards and forwards, and then gave him a buffet on the nose, so that the blood streamed.

'You swine!' he cried, and his eyes were blood-shot with rage, 'ten against one!' Then he rushed almost howling to the tree and with his pocket-knife cut the straps and set Ferd free. Meantime I had settled the guard and landed a blow on the bread-basket of a third. 'Captain!' cried August, standing beside the ash wiping Ferd's bloody face with his handkerchief. Then he rubbed Ferd's wrists, which were blue and swollen.

Then Haugwitz, his nose still running blood, stepped forward and said to August: 'We didn't set on him because he's your captain. But because he said that Germany would lose the war . . .'

'Yes,' cried another, 'he did say it. We offered him friendship first because there's a war, and we all want to be allies. But he laughed at us and then said that the English, the traitors, would win. He's a spy!'

'Yes,' they screamed in chorus, gaining courage again, 'his mother was English, and that's why he wants the English to win.'

Ferd stood beside August and wiped the mud from his shoes with wisps of grass. His face was scornful. He behaved as if all this had nothing to do with him. 'You set of liars!' cried August, flourishing his pocket-knife, 'Ferd never said that!'

—'Then ask him yourself!' jeered the others. And the Kalmuck sprang forward, seized Ferd by the wrist and demanded: 'What did you say?' Ferd shook him off, then he lifted his small head and said into the fading dusk: 'Yes, Germany will lose the war . . .'

We were all struck dumb. I too felt as if someone had knocked me on the head, although I was hearing the words for the second time. 'Spy!' screamed the boys. Then August went up to Ferd, gripped him by the shoulders, and while he kept on shaking him as if he were trying to waken him he cried, 'Captain! Captain!' He was crying.

'I believe my father,' replied Ferd, and with a proud step walked past us towards the street. August broke into loud sobbing. 'He's betrayed us,' he said to me. 'He's English.' I felt as sad as August.

Then behind a bush we saw the Kalmuck lifting a stone and throwing it at Ferd. It hit him. Ferd tottered. Then he fell in a heap on a pile of sand which lay by the side of the road. We ran to him, even young Haugwitz ran. Ferd was bleeding from the back of his head. In soft runnels the blood flowed down to the nape of his neck. August supported him. Young Haugwitz said: 'Even if he is English, that was a rotten thing to do.' We bound Ferd's head with our handkerchiefs. The wound was not danger-ous, for the Kalmuck had happened to lift a blunt stone. 'I want to go home,' murmured Ferd, and began to walk on alone. August held him fast. 'We'll go with you.' We led him. When we reached the last houses, the Kalmuck sprang from behind some bushes and shouted 'Spy!'

I thought, why isn't the Kalmuck English?

We made for the farm. August spoke to Ferd coaxingly; he must come to his senses, Germany couldn't possibly lose the war, all the comrades were of the same opinion – but if in spite of everything he didn't believe it, then he should only talk about it to us two, and not to the others. August said it would be a hard job always having to rescue him again.

Ferd only smiled. Then he was sick. We carried him for a bit. He vomited. I could not help thinking of Leo, and that time when we had led him home from the school. Suddenly Ferd asked what time it was. 'Five minutes to eight,' August answered proudly. His father had given him a nickel watch as a parting present. 'My father is leaving for his regiment at nine,' said Ferd. He laid his arms over our shoulders. We went on at a run. 'For his regiment?' said August. 'Then he *does* believe that we'll win.'

'No, he's only doing his duty as an officer.' Then August was piqued.

'Our fathers are doing their duty too!'

'But they don't know that it's no use.'

'He must be ill, that's it,' whispered August to me. I nodded. It seemed the likeliest explanation to me.

We were nearing the farm. From the town the bugles sounded the evening roll call. Thunder crashed . . .

———

HOMER AND ANNA

It was the end of July, and the offensive had come to a deadlock. 'Oh God,' said my mother, 'still another winter!' In our town the church bells were taken away. Even the parson shed tears. The Kalmuck had to join up; he had hidden himself in the ice-house when they came for him. Dysentery was rampant in D—. The first air raids were made, and we had to go into the cellar whenever the alarm was sounded in the school. That made the teachers furious, for it meant interrupting the class lessons. August wrote home to me that his father, who had got leave at last, had refused to go back to the front; 'Yesterday they arrested him, thank God for that,' wrote August. That was the time when my father sent us a goose from Russia.

My mother had gone off to the neighbouring big town where the man on furlough was staying who had brought the goose with him. She left a note for me telling me that she was coming by the last train, and that I was to wait for her in M—. Just before entering the station she would fling the parcel down the embankment, and I was to be there to catch it. She would get out at M— and wait for me at the station exit, and then we would smuggle the goose home together through the woods.

These measures were necessary, for there were double patrols of gendarmes standing in the station of our town.

In the evening I got ready and took the train to M—, a little village of working-men which lay in voluntary darkness because in the last air raid a bomb had fallen on its outskirts and killed three children at play.

I crawled up to the embankment and hid myself in an empty potato-pit in a neighbouring field, which was warm enough because there was straw in it. There I lay for an hour.

When I saw the dimmed headlights of the train I threw myself flat against the embankment. It had a burnt smell; the grass was singed.

I felt the ground grow uneasy, tremble, rock and thunder

beneath me, and suddenly a jet of steam was let off over my head. It blinded my eyes and muffled my ears – and just at that moment, about two yards on my left, a parcel swished through the air and fell whack on the ground. I lay close to the earth listening keenly, but there was nobody near. Slowly the last red lights of the train vanished into the station.

I jumped up, grabbed the parcel in the dark and ran on tiptoe in a detour through the field towards the end of the village. There I hid behind a small bridge and waited for my mother.

When she came up we neither of us spoke a word. We avoided the main road and took a little path through the woods. The pine needles deadened our steps. Once my mother bent to me and whispered: 'It weighs twelve pounds.'

We quickened our pace.

We could hear the hooting of the owls, the cooing of the wild pigeons, the working of the sap in the trees, and the crackling of the brushwood which snapped under our shoes. We held our breath.

Just before the town I made another detour so as to slip in unnoticed by a side street on the north side. My mother took the direct way; she wanted meanwhile to light a fire in the house, for we had decided to roast the goose that very night.

When I got into the kitchen my mother embraced me. Then she stuffed up the windows with tow to keep the neighbours from smelling anything. I went into the garden and cut some heads of lettuce. My mother stood before the stove, where a great hissing and sputtering was going on; the air of the little kitchen was soon rich with the smell of melting fat.

When my mother began to cut up the goose I uncorked our last bottle of wine with a joyous pop. We had really been keeping it for my father's triumphant return home. It still had some genuine tinfoil on it.

Then we ate.

An hour later my mother groaned: 'I can't do any more ...' Then she turned sick. I took her upstairs to her room; we were so full that we forgot to wish each other good-night.

When I got into bed, my head heavy with the fat savour of the unaccustomed food, I could not help thinking suddenly of Anna. I had a vision of her sitting asleep in the train, leaning her pale face against the wall and scarcely breathing.

Soon I was out of bed and sneaking down to the kitchen with wonderful sureness. I found the goose in the darkness, and ripped the last meat from its bones. I even found a drumstick left. I tore out some of the bones from which I could not prise the flesh.

My fingers were bleeding as I packed it all in a paper bag and sneaked back to my room.

'Anna,' I thought, 'Anna . . .' Then I stuck the package into my school-bag between Homer and my grammar, making them both greasy.

Then I fell asleep. It was already light. Anna kissed me in my dreams.

Next morning I raced to the station, and got there a quarter of an hour too soon. When the train ran in I waved to Anna. I climbed in, and when we were at last under way I opened my bag and showed her the package. Tenderly I unfolded the paper bag and drew her attention to the fragrant meat. 'Where did you get that?' Her voice was very excited.

'Take it, do,' I cajoled her, 'it's for you!'

'Where did you get it?' cried Anna, seizing me by the shoulders.

'What does that matter?' I stuttered, 'it doesn't matter at all.'

'No!' she shouted, so that even the sleeping guard was disturbed, 'no, I must know.' With that she held my face firmly with her two hands and looked into it.

'Oh, Anna,' said I, weakening under the power of her gaze, 'oh, Anna – I stole it from my mother.'

Then she gave a shrill cry and threw her arms round me and kissed me passionately and tenderly on the lips. 'You do love me, you do love me,' she cried, 'oh, you do care for me . . .'

ERICH MARIA REMARQUE

Erich Maria Remarque (1898–1970). Born Erich Paul Remark, Osnabrück, and died in Locarno. Called up in 1916 with school friends portrayed in *All Quiet on the Western Front*. He did not take part in front-line fighting but he was injured during a surprise British raid while carrying a wounded soldier out of the action. His mother was ill throughout this period and he had frequent leave to visit her. She died in 1917. He returned to school after the war and then became a teacher. *All Quiet* was written quickly in 1927 and Brian A. Rowley estimates that $3\frac{1}{2}$ million copies were sold in Germany and in translation within fifteen months (*The First World War in Fiction*). In the first of these extracts the hero, Paul Bäumer, has leave to visit home. In the second, he is guarding Russian prisoners, 'these enemies of ours'.

Source: Erich Maria Remarque, *All Quiet on the Western Front* (translated from *Im Westen Nichts Neues*, Berlin, Propyläen, January 1929, by A. M. Wheen), London, Putnam, 1929.

In my room behind the table stands a brown leather sofa. I sit down on it.

On the walls are pinned countless pictures that I once used to cut out of the newspapers. In between are drawings and post-cards that have pleased me. In the corner is a small iron stove. Against the wall opposite stand the book-shelves with my books.

I used to live in this room before I was a soldier. The books I bought gradually with the money I earned by coaching. Many of them are second-hand, all the classics for example, one volume in blue cloth boards cost one mark twenty pfennig. I bought them complete because I was thoroughgoing, I did not trust the editors of selections to choose all the best. So I purchased only 'collected works'. I read most of them with laudable zeal, but few of them really appealed to me. I preferred the other books, the moderns, which were of course much dearer. A few I came by not quite honestly, I borrowed and did not return them because I did not want to part with them.

One shelf is filled with school books. They are not so well cared for, they are badly thumbed, and pages have been torn out for certain purposes. Then below are periodicals, papers, and letters all jammed in together with drawings and rough sketches.

I want to think myself back into that time. It is still in the room, I feel it at once, the walls have preserved it. My hands rest on the arms of the sofa; now I make myself at home and draw up my legs so that I sit comfortably in the corner, in the arms of the sofa. The little window is open, through it I see the familiar picture of the street with the rising spire of the church at the end. There are a couple of flowers on the table. Pen-holders, a shell as a paperweight, the ink-well – here nothing is changed.

It will be like this too, if I am lucky, when the war is over and I come back here for good. I will sit here just like this and look at my room and wait.

I feel excited; but I do not want to be, for that is not right. I want that quiet rapture again. I want to feel the same powerful, nameless urge that I used to feel when I turned to my books. The breath of desire that then arose from the coloured backs of the books, shall fill me again, melt the heavy, dead lump of lead that lies somewhere in me and waken again the impatience of the future, the quick joy in the world of thought, it shall bring back again the lost eagerness of my youth. I sit and wait.

It occurs to me that I must go and see Kemmerich's mother; – I might visit Mittelstaedt too, he should be at the barracks. I look out of the window; – beyond the picture of the sunlit street appears a range of hills, distant and light; it changes to a clear day in autumn, and I sit by the fire with Kat and Albert and eat potatoes baked in their skins.

But I do not want to think of that, I sweep it away. The room shall speak, it must catch me up and hold me, I want to feel that I belong here, I want to hearken and know when I go back to the front that the war will sink down, be drowned utterly in the great home-coming tide, know that it will then be past for ever, and not gnaw us continually, that it will have none but an outward power over us.

The backs of the books stand in rows. I know them all still, I remember arranging them in order. I implore them with my eyes: Speak to me – take me up – take me, Life of my Youth – you who are carefree, beautiful – receive me again –

I wait, I wait.

Images float through my mind, but they do not grip me, they are mere shadows and memories.

Nothing – nothing –

My disquietude grows.

A terrible feeling of foreignness suddenly rises up in me. I cannot find my way back, I am shut out though I entreat earnestly and put forth all my strength.

Nothing stirs; listless and wretched, like a condemned man, I sit there and the past withdraws itself. And at the same time I fear to importune it too much, because I do not know what might happen then. I am a soldier, I must cling to that.

Wearily I stand up and look out of the window. Then I take one of the books, intending to read, and turn over the leaves. But I put it away and take out another. There are passages in it that have been marked. I look, turn over the pages, take up fresh books. Already they are piled up beside me. Speedily more join the heap, papers, magazines, letters.

I stand there dumb. As before a judge.

Dejected.

Words, Words, Words – they do not reach me.

Slowly I place the books back in the shelves.

Nevermore.

Quietly, I go out of the room

——

. . . I am often on guard over the Russians. In the darkness one sees their forms move like sick storks, like great birds. They come close up to the wire fence and lean their faces against it; their fingers hook round the mesh. Often many stand side by side, and breathe the wind that comes down from the moors and the forest.

They rarely speak and then only a few words. They are more human and more brotherly towards one another, it seems to me, than we are. But perhaps that is merely because they feel themselves to be more unfortunate than us. Anyway the war is over so far as they are concerned. But to wait for dysentery is not much of a life either.

The Territorials who are in charge of them say that they were much more lively at first. They used to have intrigues among themselves, as always happens, and it would often come to blows and knives. But now they are quite apathetic and listless; most of them do not masturbate any more, they are so feeble, though otherwise things come to such a pass that whole huts full of them do it.

They stand at the wire fence; sometimes one goes away and then another at once takes his place in the line. Most of them are silent; occasionally one begs a cigarette butt.

I see their dark forms, their beards move in the wind. I know nothing of them except that they are prisoners; and that is exactly what troubles me. Their life is obscure and guiltless; – if I could know more of them, what their names are, how they live, what they are waiting for, what are their burdens, then my emotion would have an object and might become sympathy. But as it is I perceive behind them only the suffering of the creature, the awful melancholy of life and the pitilessness of men.

A word of command has made these silent figures our enemies; a word of command might transform them into our friends. At some table a document is signed by some persons whom none of us knows, and then for years together that very crime on which formerly the world's condemnation and severest penalty fall, becomes our highest aim. But who can draw such a distinction when he looks at these quiet men with their childlike faces and apostles' beards. Any non-commissioned officer is more of an enemy to a recruit, any schoolmaster to a pupil, than they are to us. And yet we would shoot at them again and they at us if they were free.

I am frightened: I dare think this way no more. This way lies the abyss. It is not now the time but I will not lose these thoughts, I will keep them, shut them away until the war is ended. My heart beats fast: this is the aim, the great, the sole aim, that I have thought of in the trenches; that I have looked for as the only possibility of existence after this annihilation of all human feeling; this is a task that will make life afterward worthy of these hideous years.

I take out my cigarettes, break each one in half and give them to the Russians. They bow to me and then light the cigarettes. Now red points glow in every face. They comfort me; it looks as though there were little windows in dark village cottages saying that behind them are rooms full of peace . . .

ERICH MARIA REMARQUE

see also p. 225.

Remarque started *The Road Back* in 1928. He completed it in 1930 while living in Osnabrück after leaving Berlin to escape from the controversy caused by *All Quiet on the Western Front.* He was being attacked by the National Socialists led by Goebbels, and had to leave for Switzerland in 1931. Goebbels tried to persuade him to return, pointing out that he had benefited financially from the attacks which, he claimed, had increased the book's sales! Remarque was not convinced. Both *All Quiet* and *The Road Back* were banned and burned in 1933. *The Road Back* concerns a group of ex-soldiers trying to live in defeated Germany. The excerpt, from Part VI, describes a demonstration in which old comrades find themselves on opposite sides of the fence.

Source: Erich Maria Remarque, *The Road Back* (translated from *Der Weg zurück*, Berlin, Propyläen, 1931, by A. M. Wheen), London, Putnam, 1931.

The later it gets the more disturbed the city becomes. I go with Albert through the streets. Men are standing in groups at every corner. Rumours are flying. It is said that the military have already fired on a procession of demonstrating workers.

From the neighbourhood of St Mary's church comes suddenly the sound of rifle shots, at first singly, then a whole volley. Albert and I look at each other; without a word we set off in the direction of the shots.

Ever more and more people come running toward us. 'Bring rifles! the bastards are shooting!' they shout. We quicken our pace. We wind in and out of the groups, we shove our way through, we are running already – a grim, perilous excitement impels us forward. We are gasping. The racket of rifle-fire increases. 'Ludwig!' I shout.

He is running beside us. His lips are pressed tight, the jaw bones stand out, his eyes are cold and tense – once more he has the face of the trenches. Albert too. I also. We run towards the rifle shots, as if it were some mysterious, imperative summons.

The crowd, still shouting, gives way before us. We plough our way through. Women hold their aprons over their faces and go stumbling away. A roar of fury goes up. A wounded man is being carried off.

We reach the Market Square. There the Reichwehr has taken up a position in front of the Town Hall. The steel helmets gleam palely. On the steps is a machine-gun ready for action. The square is empty; only the streets that lead into it are jammed with people. It would be madness to go farther – the machine-gun is covering the square.

But one man is going out, all alone! Behind him the seething crowd surges on down the conduits of the streets; it boils out about the houses and gathers together in black clots.

But the man is far in advance. In the middle of the square he steps out from the shadow thrown by the church and stands in the moonlight – 'Back!' calls a clear, sharp voice.

The man is lifting his hands. So bright is the moonlight that when he starts to speak his teeth show white and gleaming in the dark hole of his mouth. 'Comrades –' All is silence.

His voice is alone between the church, the great block of the Town Hall and the shadow. It is alone on the square, a fluttering dove. 'Comrades, put up your weapons! Would you shoot at your brothers? Put up your weapons and come over to us.'

Never was the moon so bright. The uniforms on the town hall steps are like chalk. The windows glisten. The moonlit half of the church tower is a mirror of green silk. With gleaming helmets and visors the stone knights by the doorway spring forward from the wall of shadow.

'Back! or we fire!' comes the command coldly. I look round at Ludwig and Albert. It was our company commander! That was Heel's voice. A choking tension grips me, as if I must now look on at an execution. Heel will fire – I know.

The dark mass of people moves within the shadow of the houses, it sways and murmurs. An eternity goes by. Two soldiers with rifles detach themselves from the steps and make towards the solitary man in the midst of the square. It seems endlessly long before they reach him – as though they marked time in some grey morass, glittering, tinselled rag puppets with loaded, lowered rifles. The man awaits them quietly. 'Comrades –' he says again as they come up.

They grab him by the arms and drag him forward. The man does not defend himself. They run him along so fast that he stumbles. Cries break out behind us. The mob is beginning to move, an entire street moving slowly, irregularly forward. The clear voice commands: 'Quick! back with him! I fire!'

A warning volley crackles out upon the air. Suddenly the man wrenches himself free. But no, he is not saving himself! he is running toward the machine-gun! 'Don't shoot, Comrades!'

Still nothing has happened. But when the mob sees the unarmed man run forward, it advances too. In a thin stream it trickles along the side of the church. The next instant a command resounds over the square. Thundering the tick-tack of the machine-gun shatters into a thousand echoes from the houses, and the bullets, whistling and splintering, strike on the pavement.

Quick as lightning we have flung ourselves behind a jutting corner of the houses. In the first moment a paralysing, cur-like fear seized me, quite different from any that ever I felt at the front. Then it changes into rage. I have seen the solitary figure, how he spun round and fell forward. Cautiously I peer round the corner. He is trying to rise again, but he cannot. He only props on his arms, lifts up his pale face and groans. Slowly the arms bend, the head sinks, and, as though exceeding weary, his body sags down upon the pavement – Then the lump loosens in my throat – 'No!' I cry, 'No!' The cry goes up shrill between the walls of the houses.

I feel myself pushed aside. Ludwig Breyer stands up and goes out over the square towards the dark lump of death.

'Ludwig!' I shout.

But he still goes on – on – I stare after him in horror.

'Back!' comes the command once again from the Town Hall steps.

For a moment Ludwig stands still. 'Fire away, Lieutenant Heel!' he calls back to the Town Hall. Then he goes forward and stoops down to the thing lying there on the ground.

We see an officer come down the steps. Without knowing quite how, we are suddenly all standing there beside Ludwig, awaiting the coming figure that for a weapon carries only a walking-stick. He does not hesitate an instant, though there are now three of us, and we could drag him off if we wanted to – his soldiers would not dare to shoot for fear of hitting him.

Ludwig straightens up. 'I congratulate you, Lieutenant Heel. The man is dead.'

A stream of blood is running from under the dead man's tunic and trickling into the cracks between the cobble-stones. Near his right hand that has thrust forward, thin and yellow, out of the sleeve, it is gathering to a pool of blood that reflects black in the moonlight.

'Breyer,' says Heel.

'Do you know who it is?' asks Ludwig.

Heel looks at him and shakes his head.

'Max Weil.'

'I wanted to let him get away,' says Heel after a time, almost pensively.

'He is dead,' answers Ludwig.

Heel shrugs his shoulders.

'He was our comrade,' Ludwig goes on.

Heel does not answer.

Ludwig looks at him coldly. 'A nice piece of work!'

Then Heel stirs. 'That does not enter into it,' he says calmly. 'Only the purpose – law and order.'

'Purpose –' replies Ludwig contemptuously. 'Since when do you offer excuse for yourself? Purpose! Occupation – that is all that you ask. Withdraw your men, so that there shall be no more shooting!'

Heel makes a gesture of impatience. 'My men stay where they are! If they withdrew they would be attacked tomorrow by a mob ten times as big – You know that yourself. In five minutes I occupy all the road heads. I give you till then to take off this dead man.'

'Set to it,' says Ludwig to us. Then he turns to Heel once again. 'If you withdraw now, no one will attack you. If you stay more will be killed. And through you! Do you realize that?'

'I realize it,' answers Heel coldly.

For a second longer we stand face to face. Heel looks at the row of us. It is a strange moment. Then something snaps.

We take up the limp body of Max Weil and bear him away. The streets are again filled with people. A wide passage opens before us as we come. Cries go up. 'Noske bloodhounds!' 'Police thugs!' 'Murderers!' From Max Weil's back the blood drips.

We take him to the nearest house. It is the restaurant, the Holländische Diele. A couple of ambulance men are already there binding up two people who lie on the dance floor. A woman with a blood-stained apron is groaning and keeps asking to go home. With difficulty they detain her till a stretcher is brought and a doctor arrives. She has a wound in the stomach. Beside her lies a man still wearing his old army tunic. Both his knees have been shot through. His wife is kneeling beside him moaning: 'He didn't do anything! He was only walking by. I was just bringing his supper –' She points to a grey enamel billy-can. 'Just his supper –'

The women dancers are huddled together in a corner. The manager is running to and fro excitedly, asking if the wounded cannot be taken elsewhere. – His business will be ruined, if it gets about. No guest will want to dance there again. – Anton Demuth in his gilded porter's uniform has fetched a bottle of brandy and is holding it to the wounded man's lips. The manager looks on in horror and makes signs to him, but Anton takes no notice. 'Do you think I'll lose my legs?' the wounded man asks. 'I'm a chauffeur.'

The stretchers come. Again shots are heard outside. We spring up. Hoots, screams, and a clatter of broken glass. We run out. 'Rip up the pavement,' shouts someone, driving a pick into the cobbles. Mattresses are being thrown down from the houses, chairs, a perambulator. Shots flash out from the square, and now are answered from the roofs.

'Lights out!' A man springs forward and throws a brick. Immediately it is dark. 'Kosole!' shouts Albert. It is he. Valentin is beside him. Like a whirlpool the shots have drawn everyone in. 'Into 'em Ernst! Ludwig! Albert!' roars Kosole. 'The swine are shooting at women!'

We crouch in the doors of the houses, bullets lashing, men shouting; we are submerged, swept away, devastated, raging with hate; blood is spurting on the pavement, we are soldiers once more – it has us again, crashing and raging war roars above us, between us, within us – it is finished, comradeship riddled by machine-guns, soldiers shooting at soldiers, comrades at comrades, ended, it is finished –

ARNOLD ZWEIG

Arnold Zweig (1887–1965). Produced nationalistic war stories until 1916. Served at Verdun and at the German Army Head-quarters in the east. Began to read anti-war literature, including Barbusse's *Under Fire*. Zweig left Germany in 1933 because of the persecution of the Jews. After a period in Palestine he lived in the GDR. *Sergeant Grischa* is based on an actual case. The Russian sergeant escapes from the Germans, is caught, tried and executed as a German deserter. This is the opening of the novel. (Barbusse outlines the plot for a story with similar problems of mistaken identity in his 'Diaries', *q.v.*)

Source: Arnold Zweig, *The Case of Sergeant Grischa* (translated from *Der Streitum den Sergeanten Grischa*, Potsdam, 1928, by E. Sutton), London, Martin Secker, 1928; Hutchinson, 1947.

THE PLIERS

This earth of ours, the little planet Tellus, was whirling busily through pitch-black airless icy space that is for ever swept by myriad waves, vibrations, and motions of the uncharted Ether; which, from the shock of contact with a solid thing, flash up in Light or Electricty, in strange unknown influences, baleful or benignant. Earth, swathed in her thick woolly veils of air, had now outrun the stage in her elliptical race, which keeps her north-westerly parts furthest from their life-spring in the Sun; and she was turning them again towards him in the ceaseless revolutions of her course. Now the rays of the great fiery ball beat more exultantly upon the face of Europe. The atmosphere began to seethe, and everywhere fierce winds rushed from the Arctic wastes to the warmer regions, where, lured by the magic of reviving light, all things awoke and blossomed. In the Northern lands life's wave was slowly rising and to her peoples came bewildering changes with the changing year.

A man was standing in the thick snow, at the foot of a bare and blackened tree, that rose up slantwise in the charred forest, black against the trampled white expanse. Encased in many coverings, the man plunged his hands into the pockets of the outermost of these, and stared before him, thinking. 'Butter,' he thought, 'a pound and a half, two and a half pounds of meal from a farm, a loaf that I can put by, and some peas. Yes, that'll do. She can carry on for a bit with that. I'll give it to Fritzke to take with him tomorrow when he goes on leave. Perhaps I can swop my tobacco for a bit of dripping; if I throw in a mark from my pay, cookie will hand it out. Butter,' he thought, 'a pound and a half . . .' And so once more in his heavy, deliberate mind he spread out the contents of a parcel which he was planning to send to his wife, wondering whether he could not find room for yet something more.

Somewhere down in the vague depths of his inner consciousness he felt he would have liked to rub his feet together, for they were rather cold, but they were enveloped in thick boots, and wrapped round with rags and the lower part of his trousers, so he let them be. His legs were embedded in the deep snow, side by side like the hind feet of an elephant. He was wearing an iron-grey cloak, with absurd red squares on the collar under his chin, and a strip of blue cloth with a number on each shoulder. And tucked closely under his arm, while he stood thinking of peas and dripping, was a long heavy cudgel-like object of wood, affixed to an odd-looking iron contrivance, the whole being called a rifle; with this he was able to produce cunningly directed explosions, and by their means to kill or maim other men far away from him. This man, whose ears were hidden under soft black flaps, and in whose mouth was a small pipe adapted for smoking dried leaves – a German working man – was not standing under this tree in the burnt forest for his pleasure. His thoughts were continuously driving westward, where in two or three cubical rooms in a walled house his wife and child awaited him. Here he stood, while they lay huddled in a far-off room. He yearned for them, but something had come between them, unseen but very strong: an Order: the order to watch other men. The time is winter 1917, and, more exactly, the middle of March. The inhabitants of Europe were engaged in a war which had for some time been pursued with no small determination. In the midst of a forest in these eastern marches, wrested for the time being from those white men called Russians, stood this German soldier musing, Lance-Corporal Birkholz from Eberswalde, guarding prisoners, soldiers of these same Russians who must now labour for the Germans.

A good seventy yards away from him, on a railway line, the huge red-brown and grey-green goods trucks were being loaded up with timber. Two men were handling each truck. Others dragged up on their shoulders heavy, carefully graded beams and planks, which others again, a few days before, had hewn from the dead pines, whose once green and reddish-brown expanses had been eaten away in many directions by the hatchets and saws of the prisoners.

Much further than the eye could reach between the tree-trunks, a day's ride in each direction, the black pillars of this corpse of a forest stood out stark against the snow and the sky – fifty thousand acres of it. Incendiary bombs from aeroplanes, shells from field-guns, had each in their own time during the past summer done their work upon it faithfully. Pines and firs, birches and beeches, all alike: burnt and singed, or withered and choked from afar by the fumes of battle – all perished, and now their corpses were made to serve their turn. There was still a reek of burning from the scaling bark.

In the last truck two Russians were speaking in their own language about a pair of pliers.

'Impossible,' said the slighter of the two. 'How can I get you such a thing? I'll have no hand in such foolery, Grischa.'

The other, turning upon his friend two strangely powerful grey-blue eyes, laughed shortly.

'I've as good as got them in my pocket already, Aljoscha.'

And they went on piling up the yellowish white props, that were to serve as supports for those human caves called dug-outs and communication trenches, in a certain order in the truck, the front of which hung down from its hinges. Grischa worked above and superintended the stacking of the planks; below was Aljoscha, who kept passing up to him the fragrant bolts of wood. They were a little shorter than a man, fully one and a half inches thick, and so grooved that they could be neatly fitted into each other.

'All I want now is a pair of pliers,' persisted Grischa.

Five prisoners in a row, each with four of these props on his shoulder; they flung them down in front of the truck, with the hollow clatter of dead wood, then all seven of them stood up for a moment in a group. They said nothing. Those who had carried the planks let their arms fall by their sides, and looked at the huge heap of timber.

'That'll do,' said Grischa. 'Go and warm yourselves, boys; time's up.'

'Right you are, Grischa,' answered one of them. 'We'll take your word for it,' and they nodded to him and went off. Further up, between the rails of the two lines that met at this point, a small field railway track and the main line, a large fragrant fire was burning. Beside it, standing or sitting on sleepers, planks or stumps, were the guards and the Russian labourers with their German foreman, men of the Landsturm Army Service Corps. Iron cauldrons of coffee were hanging over the flames, and here and there a man was toasting bread on a green twig. The mighty element devoured the resinous wood with spurts and hisses and crackling leaps of flame. In front of the railway the forest fell back to left and right. Like rusted ghosts of the living, the great trunks towered above the snow, the thick powdery frozen March snow of western Russia on which the sun flings blue and golden lights and shadows, seamed by the tracks of heavily nailed boots. From the loaded white branches moisture dripped at the contact with the sun, and froze in the circles of shadow. The remote deep blue sky drew the men's glances upwards. 'Spring's coming,' said Grischa, meaningly.

LUDWIG RENN

Ludwig Renn (pen-name of Arnold Friedrich Vieth von Gols-
senau, 1889–1979). A career officer. After the war became a
communist. Imprisoned 1933–5. Fought in the Spanish Civil
War, about which he published a book in 1955. The opening
and closing passages of *War* have been chosen and they cover
the beginning and end of the war itself. The Muir translation is
successfully idiomatic. Renn describes the 'order' to nominate
platoon representatives which was part of the widespread establishment of Soldiers' and Workers' Councils in the closing days
of October 1918 following the Kiel naval mutiny. As German
institutions became supervised by revolutionary councils the
concept of officer command in the army became highly questionable. Retreating soldiers were sometimes, understandably, perplexed.

Source: Ludwig Renn, *War* (translated from *Krieg*, Frankfurt,
Frankfurtfurter Societäts-Druckerei, 1929, by Willa and Edwin
Muir), London, Martin Secker, 1929.

PREPARATIONS

When the day of mobilization came I was a lance-corporal. I
could not get away to say goodbye to my mother, so I sent her a
parting letter. I got her reply on the day that we left:

> My dear boy, – Be true and play the man; that is all I can write
> you. We shall have our hands full here. Your brother is called up
> too, and we two women will have to manage by ourselves. The
> grandchildren are not much use yet. I am sending you a pair of
> warm socks with this. Farewell!   Your Mother.

I stuck the letter in my pocket-book and went to the canteen
to get some more letter-paper. People were rushing about the
passages. In the canteen they were standing before the counter.

'Hello, Ludwig!' Ziesche pushed a glass of schnapps before me,
grinning. 'Here's to the first Russian.'

I clinked with Ziesche.

Max Domsky, the 'Pearl', sat on a table swinging his legs. He was looking at all of us, one after the other, and smiling.

In the background a stocky, bearded lance-corporal was holding forth: 'They'll see what German steel is like, the dogs!' He became scornful. 'I know that crowd. I've not been in Paris for three years for nothing! As soon as they see a German militiaman coming, they'll take to their heels.'

I bought my letter-paper and went out.

'The Pearl' came running after me. I did not even glance at him.

'Aren't you glad?' he asked.

'Of course,' I replied distantly.

'Then why didn't you stay with the crowd?'

'I can't stand that kind of talk.'

He said nothing. But I saw that he wanted to tell me something.

When we were in our room I sat down on a stool and asked: 'Well, what is it?'

He sat on the table and looked at me expectantly. My question apparently did not strike him as a question at all.

'Are you afraid of the war?' I asked.

'Well, the others are all so delighted.'

I thought it over. It could only be something connected with the war and the risk of being killed which was bothering him.

'Ludwig!'

I was startled. He had never called me Ludwig before.

'I haven't a father.' He said this as if he were presenting me with an opening. What was I to do? Grasp his hand? But the Pearl was not in the least sentimental.

'Well, Max,' I said, 'you have a brother.' I felt ashamed.

He gazed at me quite calmly. He had understood me! And yet often he did not understand the simplest things.

He showed no sign of elation. He did not even reply, but got his things ready. I fixed the heavy haversack on my shoulders. I did not expect him to say anything more either. A few soldiers came rushing in. I went once more to the latrine, and then downstairs to fall in. I had the feeling that my eyes were taking everything in quite independently, while I myself was completely withdrawn inside myself. My legs kept moving, the haversack was heavy, but that had nothing to do with me . . .

COLLAPSE

We marched the whole night through and in the grey dawn came to a closely built little town with dismal houses. My platoon was quartered in the back garden of a villa in which stood a few flowerpots with straggling plants. We slept till midday.

In the afternoon we stood about the street.

Mehling came laughing. 'There have been prisoners here, several companies of them. They were set free by their guards. And the prisoners have flung themselves on a food train that was standing in the station and sold all the provisions to the inhabitants. A company of our regiment has had to interfere.'

'There's nothing to laugh about in that!'

I jumped round. It was the company sergeant-major, and his eyes were blazing as he looked at Mehling.

'The provisions that they sold were intended for us, and were supposed to keep us going for several weeks – or longer!'

'But how does it come that the train is still standing here although we're the last troops to retire?' I asked.

'The mutineers have disbanded our bakers' column and sent them home.'

'What? Then where are we to get bread from?' asked Höhle.

'We'll have to bake it ourselves. And that's why the General Command instructed the train to wait for us here with meal and sugar and the other provisions.'

'But how are we to bake on the march?'

'You'd better ask that from the crowd that have disbanded our bakers' column!' returned the sergeant-major.

'I would like to have one of those rotters here,' growled Höhle. 'These swine at the base stuffed themselves while we were being shot down, and now they must strike us a blow in the back as well!'

The company commander came out of a house. We stood at attention.

'Have you got any bread?' he asked the sergeant-major.

'No, sir. We must bake on the march.'

'But we can't do that!'

'I think it might be done, sir, if you will put all the bakers in the company at my disposal – there are five. Two of them must bake the whole night through, and the next night the others must take their turn.'

'Well, it's to be hoped the bread will be good!' said Schubring, and went away.

I lost my temper. Couldn't he have said something else to a good suggestion?

'But, sergeant-major, where are you to get the flour?' asked Mehling.

'I've secured some in time. – The only thing we'll be rather short of is sugar.'

In the course of the afternoon all the remaining troops marched out of the town. We were to remain there by ourselves as a rearguard.

The feeling in the company became more and more bitter against the crowd behind the front, above all when the news came that in Brussels the shirkers had crept out of the holes and corners where they had been kept hidden by the natives. And these men had torn the shoulder straps from the officers' shoulders. The ringleader of the band, it was said, was a Jewish doctor, Dr Freund – or something like that. At that the inhabitants of Brussels had risen. The staff officers and the German civil authorities had escaped with the greatest difficulty.

IX

The following afternoon we marched out of the quiet town as the last to go, and after about an hour came up with the rest of the regiment. The fifth company was amalgamated with ours as a new first platoon under Lieutenant Ssymank. Hanfstengel's and Höhle's platoons were thrown into one. The officers had long discussions. Then the company commander came and called the company round him:

'I have to let you know that revolution has broken out in Germany. His Majesty the Kaiser has fled to Holland, and the Crown Prince as well. – The division has ordered that every company is to choose three representatives. By tomorrow the platoons must nominate one each. I may say further that these representatives are not soldiers' delegates, as in Russia, but that they are intended purely to consolidate the confidence between officer and man still more strongly.'

Lieutenant Ssymank stood in front of his platoon with knitted brows. He raised his hand to his steel helmet, which he still had on after the marching. 'May I ask what you mean? Each platoon is to nominate one representative. Does my company count as three platoons or as one?'

241

'Well, we can't allow a representative to be chosen for every little private interest!'

'One platoon, then,' said Ssymank coldly and clearly.

'I have nothing further to communicate,' said Schubring.

We went away.

The representatives were chosen without any disorder: in my platoon Mehling, in Hanfstengel's Höhle, and in Ssymank's Lance-Corporal Hermann, a man in the forties with a surly expression.

x

We went on marching. Our bakers had used up more than half of our supply of flour in one night's baking. But the bread was so doughy that we could hardly eat any of it. Schubring cursed the bakers and the sergeant-major.

'That might happen with the best baker, sir, when using an oven that he doesn't know,' said the latter.

'But now we've no more flour!'

'I'll see that I get hold of some more, sir.'

Next day appeared a two-wheeled waggon drawn by oxen and loaded with sacks of flour.

Schubring looked impressed. 'Has that been got by proper means?'

'Certainly, sir. The quartermaster gave a receipt for it.'

After a long march I had to set up a double post on a bridge over a canal during the night. I myself with my platoon was stationed as an outpost in a house close beside the canal. The moon was shining. I went along the embankment to the left and found the next post some little distance away. I had sent a patrol to the right. It did not come back for a considerable time.

'We went first to the next bridge. There was nobody there. So we went on to the next again. There's a main road there that crosses the canal. And there was nobody there either.'

Next morning I sent a patrol over there again. It came back in twenty minutes.

'There are Belgian sentries standing on the bridges now.'

I wrote a report on the business at once to the company commander, sent it off and sat there in uncertainty. But I got no answer.

XI

Next morning we moved off. It had grown cold, but the sun shone. The wide road ran straight through a flat landscape that looked cheerful. But as the day went on it became unfriendly. The trees looked grey to me, and the place we marched into looked inhospitable. Against the walls of a dismal church leaned a number of machine-guns. Artillery of all descriptions was standing in the churchyard.

One of our machine-gun companies had halted before it and were flinging their guns inside. These were weapons which had to be surrendered to the enemy after the armistice. They would let them stand in the rain, and soon they would all be old iron.

We marched for fully two weeks through the Flemish part of Belgium and came at last to the French-speaking part. As permanent rearguard we marched always a day's march ahead of the pursuing enemy. Before the houses stood civilians who looked at us with hatred and cursed.

Again we were to have received flour and sugar, and again the troops in front of us had sold the whole of it to the natives for a song. The feeling against the revolutionaries grew bitterer than ever, and Höhle and Lance-Corporal Mann kept stirring it up, while Hermann, the social democrat, tried to soothe it down. This Hermann with his perpetual surly expression had the soul of a petty official and was against any decisive step.

XII

In the neighbourhood of Lüttich we were given a day's rest. Mehling went in to Lüttich with some of the other men. I took a walk to a fortress near by and had a look at the deep fosse and the broken concrete defences.

In front of a big farm several men from our regiment were arguing with a Belgian.

'Sergeant' – one of them turned to me – 'we have a requisition form for straw from our quartermaster, but this man here won't part with any.'

'And why won't he?'

'He says he won't have enough left for himself. But he has a whole barn full.'

'Then you must go to an officer about it. If I say anything to the farmer it'll have no effect.'

Mehling did not come back from Lüttich until late; he related that the whole town was beflagged. French, English and Belgian soldiers were there already. They sat in the cafés. They were playing the 'Marseillaise' and shouting hurrah. Mehling was still full of happiness and elation from having seen it. But I felt sad. The damned old Fatherland was still dear to me!

XIII

Next morning we went over the Maas by a long bridge; the river here is really a majestic sight. Then we wound hour after hour up the heights on the other side.

When it was growing dark we marched into a little village with a church and lying in a valley. It was cold. We halted on a bridge under which a stream babbled. The billeting officers came.

'How is it here?'

'Good quarters,' they cried.

We scattered. I suddenly noticed that I had a pain in my right foot, where my wound had been. It was not like the pain from a blister, but a sort of dull internal pain.

We went across a steep grassy slope with fruit trees and came to a wooden house standing by itself. The wooden stair inside shone as if it were polished, and the landing on the first floor was panelled in plain dark wood without embellishment. A few chests, a few wooden stools and a tall clock stood against the walls.

Out of a door came a young man with his wife and invited us with a friendly look into a big room, where mattresses and blankets were lying on the floor.

I pulled off my boot at once and felt my foot. The scar on the ball of my foot was sensitive. We had been marching now for three weeks. I went to the kitchen and asked for warm water.

'*Blessé?*' asked the man, pointing to my foot.

'*Oui, monsieur.*'

He got up at once. His wife brought a bucket and a chair, so that I might sit with them and put my foot in the water at once. There I sat on my chair with them before the hearth. Outside the moon shone coldly on the sloping meadow. Perhaps it was freezing again. The man and his wife looked healthy. They sat in contented silence. Why should one trouble, anyway, to put into words what the other knew?

I was happy in that house.

XIV

While we fell in next morning Ssymank and Hanfstengel were cursing the awful people who stayed in this village. They had been billeted on the priest, and he had refused them water to wash in and anything else that he could. When they took him to task for this, he had spoken of barbarians and 'Boches', who should be beaten to death. Ssymank had become so furious that he had wanted to lay hands on the priest. But Hanfstengel had held him back.

Thereupon Ssymank had turned to the priest in a fury, shouted 'You're a swine!' and marched out.

We marched gaily throughout the day, which was overcast. My foot was all right again. Today we should cross the German frontier.

Early in the afternoon began a series of halts. We kept pushing our way up a valley a few steps at a time towards a village in front.

The men were in good spirits.

'Another little yard and another little yard and a – yupp!' they shouted in chorus. Then some of them began to sing:

> 'For this 'ere *cam*paign
> Ain't no express train.
> So take some sandpaper,
> And wipe your tears away.'

In two or three hours we reached the village and a crossroads. From the left came the marching column of a division we did not know, and our column issuing from the valley had to take the same road. Our regimental commander pulled up his horse and tried to get his regiment forward. There was a general with the other division. He stood near his car, which was drawn up in the square before a café. Men from all ranks of the service were standing there, or sitting on chairs or on the kerb blowing on coffee, which in their tin mugs had to cool first before one could put one's lips to it.

Others were flinging down tots of brandy. Mehling had already pushed his way through the crowd into the café. I knew we had still more than six miles to the frontier, and would certainly have to march a good bit beyond that. I sat down by the kerb to rest my foot.

It was not until dusk that our column got going again. We were tired with hanging about. When after an hour and a half the column began to stick again, there was a fresh roar of 'Another little yard, and another little yard, and a – yupp!' Then they sang:

>'In Hamburg I've been often seen,
> In silks and satins like a queen;
> But don't you ask my name, sonny,
> For I'm a girl that's out for money.'

They sang it in a sentimental yearning drawl into the night. Some had sat down in the road. A corporal of artillery came riding along. 'Make way!' They scrambled up cursing.

A motor car slid past with the general.

'He can leg it like us ones!'

The march got going again.

Another car overtook us. 'Make way!' There were four airmen in it, with cocked bonnets.

'What are they swanking for in a car?'

'Footpads!' cried one of the men in the car jeeringly.

'Turn them out, they're swine from the base!'

Several men made a rush at the car, but it accelerated recklessly right into the middle of the men in front of us. They jumped to the side. 'Heave 'em out!' cried one man, but no longer playfully. The car vanished.

We were continually blocked. The cry 'Heave 'em out!' grew more and more frequent.

We were approaching a rumbling noise of heavy lorries.

'That's the frontier road we're coming to,' said Hanfstengel.

'How far off is it, sir?'

'I make it another hour and a half, if we can keep moving.'

'I'm not able to do it, sir,' grumbled a corporal.

'We can do without you,' laughed Mehling. 'Just make yourself comfortable in the ditch. Meanwhile we'll look for a better hole.'

Somebody laughed. The corporal muttered away to himself.

The rumbling noise was now quite near. I could discern the road, which came at right angles towards ours. From the right two parallel lines of heavy guns were rolling past.

We got very slowly on to the road. 'Lieutenant!' cried someone, who could not be identified in the darkness and the hubbub of men, horses and lorries, 'the major says the companies are to play follow-my leader along the ditch!'

Now we had to go in single file, sometimes at a crawl, sometimes half running, along the uneven surface of the ditch. My foot began to ache. I tried to set it down firmly with an even balance, but that only wearied my ankle.

About eleven o'clock, while the lorries and gun carriages were still rumbling along on our right, the dark outlines of some factories rose to the left of the road. We halted.

'Why can't we get on? We want our billets!'

Lieutenant Schubring stood there as stiff as a poker, watching the clattering lorries roll by.

'We can get along well enough without any officers!'

'Shut your mouths!' cried Höhle. 'The lieutenant can't conjure the billeting officers here! Have you any notion where to go?'

We had to go on waiting. Even Hanfstengel, who was so popular, was abused by his men.

Mehling said to me privately, 'If you'll take my rifle I'll go and look for the billeting officers. They're sure to be somewhere on the road, and all I need to do is to yell for them every few paces.'

I went over to my platoon and told them Mehling was on the hunt.

'What a bloody mess!'

'The war might have taught you where to find a billeting officer, surely.'

'When are we going to be demobilized, sergeant?' asked a reedy voice.

'That I can't tell you,' said I.

'You won't be demobbed at all. This bloody mess is going on for ever. We'll have to leg it ourselves!'

It grew pretty cold.

At long last, after an hour and a half, Schubring had found the billeting officers. He had abused them, and they had yelled at him. 'If you will muck your men about like that!'

Mehling was missing.

We marched in the moonlight down a by-road, which we had to ourselves. The fields on either side looked black. To be marching on a firm surface again did me good. But my foot was aching a lot.

After midnight we reached a small village. An enormous building towered there; its door opened, letting out a reddish light. A man was standing in the door.

'Where do we bunk?' asked one man in a surly voice.

All at once Mehling appeared. 'Behave yourselves decently. The miller here has had coffee made, and we're to have a warm room.'

'Just come in,' said the man in a friendly way. 'Up the stairs! I can't do it so quickly as you.'

247

Upstairs in the room there lay sacks of straw. The miller went round asking if we had enough water, and: 'There's the closet, just outside to the right.'

'Let's play squat!' suggested a young lad.

'You've gone dotty! I've had enough and to spare from the march.'

xv

Our field-kitchens and the other lorries did not arrive until noon. They took the covers off at once and handed out coffee.

'Going strong, aren't you?' said Höhle.

'Well, at least we're not like the rabble in the other lorries, that never have been at the front and are blowing now all over the place!'

'Are they giving themselves airs?'

'Not half,' said the other cook. 'And they've no business to poke in their noses at all; a crowd of half-men, half-blind or half-deaf or groggy in the heart. Not that I believe a word of it. They only didn't want to be sent to the front.'

'They're all shits!' said the driver, leading his heavy horses into the stable.

'If they get too cocky,' said Höhle, 'just you tell us. We'll lead them a fine dance!'

'Don't you bother,' laughed the smaller of the two cooks. 'I could take them all on myself. And as for Max here, he was the pet of the athletic club in Dessau!'

In the afternoon we marched off and reached Aix-la-Chapelle at dusk. All the houses were beflagged. Our band played up for a while in front of us, and the drums echoed from the houses, from which people were gazing out. A crowd accompanied us as we marched.

We were the last German troops in front of the advancing French and Belgians.

Next day we moved to the station and waited in pouring rain for our train. It was well on in the night before it arrived. There were only cattle-trucks with sliding doors. We did not know where we were going to, except that it was not yet straight to our homes.

ADOLF ANDREAS LATZKÓ

Adolf Andreas Latzkó (1876–1943). Born in Budapest. After his military service was completed in 1898 he started writing (in Hungarian). Travelled widely. Returned to Europe in 1914. Shell-shocked on the Austrian Front in 1917, he went to Switzerland. *Men in Battle* was suppressed (not only in Germany), and Latzkó was reduced to the ranks and condemned to death in his absence. He saved himself by staying in Switzerland. Died in Holland. *Men in Battle* was attacked again during the Second World War when Archibald MacLeish (poet and Librarian of Congress) asserted that writers of the First World War such as Latzkó, Remarque, Hemingway and Dos Passos had effectively helped the rise of fascism. They were defended by Edmund Wilson (*q.v.*). In 'The Victor', General X has taken over a town and runs it as a happy and prosperous base camp sixty miles behind the lines. He is visited by a journalist who receives reassurance about the progress of the war. However, the intrusion of an injured man sours the interview and the journalist departs to visit the front where the enemy is about to break through. The translation is by Adele Seltzer, friend of D. H. Lawrence. Her husband was Lawrence's publisher in America.

Source: Adolf Andreas Latzkó, *Men in Battle* (translated from *Menschen in Krieg*, Zurich; Max Rascher Verlag, 1918, by Adele Seltzer), London, Cassell, 1918.

THE VICTOR

. . . His adjutant got up from the table next to his, approached hesitatingly, and whispered a few words in His Excellency's ear.

The great man shook his head, waving the adjutant off.

'It is an important foreign newspaper, Your Excellency,' the adjutant urged; and when his commander still waved him aside, he added significantly: 'The gentleman has brought a letter of recommendation from headquarters, Your Excellency.'

At this the general finally gave in, arose with a sigh, and said, half in jest, half in annoyance to the lady beside him:

'A drumfire would be more welcome!' Then he followed his adjutant and shook hands jovially with the bald civilian, who popped up from his seat and bent at the middle like a penknife snapping shut. His Excellency invited him to be seated.

The war correspondent stammered a few words of admiration, and opened his notebook expectantly, a whole string of questions on his lips. But His Excellency did not let him speak. In the course of time he had constructed for occasions like this a speech in which every point was well thought out and which made a simple impression. He delivered it now, speaking with emphasis and pausing occasionally to recall what came next.

To begin with, he spoke of his brave soldiers, praising their courage, their contempt of death, their wonderful deeds of valour. Then he expressed regret at the impossibility of rewarding each soldier according to his merits, and – this in a raised voice – invoked the Fatherland's eternal gratitude for such loyalty and self-abnegation even unto death. Pointing to the heavy crop of medals on his chest, he explained that the distinctions awarded him were really an honour done to his men. Finally he wove in a few well-chosen remarks complimenting the enemy's fighting ability and cautious leadership, and concluded with an expression of his unshakeable confidence in ultimate victory.

The newspaper man listened respectfully, and occasionally jotted down a note. The main thing, of course, was to observe the Great One's appearance, his manner of speech, his gestures, and to sum up his personality in a few striking phrases.

His Excellency now discarded his military rôle, and changed himself from the Victor of — into the man of the world.

'You are going to the front now?' he asked with a courteous smile, and responded to the correspondent's enthusiastic 'Yes' with a deep, melancholy sigh.

'How fortunate you are! I envy you. You see, the tragedy in the life of the general of today is that he cannot lead his men personally into the fray. He spends his whole life preparing for war, he is a soldier in body and soul, and yet he knows the excitement of battle only from hearsay.'

The correspondent was delighted with this subjective utterance which he had managed to evoke. Now he could show the commander in the sympathetic role of one who renounces, one who cannot always do as he would. He bent over his notebook for an instant. When he looked up again he found to his astonishment that His Excellency's face had completely changed. His brow was furrowed, his eyes stared wide-open with an anxiously expectant look in them at something behind the correspondent.

The correspondent turned and saw a pale, emaciated infantry captain making straight towards His Excellency. The man was grinning, and he had a peculiar shambling walk. He came closer and closer, and stared with glassy, glaring eyes, and laughed an ugly, idiotic laugh. The adjutant started up from his seat frightened. The veins on His Excellency's forehead swelled up like ropes. The correspondent saw an assassination coming and turned pale. The uncanny captain swayed to within a foot or two of the general and his adjutant, then stood still, giggled foolishly, and snatched at the orders on His Excellency's chest like a child snatching at a beam of light.

'Beautiful – shines beautifully –' he gurgled in a thick voice. Then he pointed his frightfully thin, trembling forefinger up at the sun and shrieked, 'Sun!' Next he snatched at the medals again and said, 'Shines beautifully.' And all the while his restless glance wandered hither and thither as if looking for something, and his ugly, bestial laugh repeated itself after each word.

His Excellency's right fist was up in the air ready for a blow at the fellow's chest for approaching him so disrespectfully, but, instead, he laid his hand soothingly on the poor idiot's shoulder.

'I suppose you have come from the hospital to listen to the music, Captain?' he said, winking to his adjutant. 'It's a long ride to the hospital in the tram-car. Take my automobile. It's quicker.'

'Auto – quicker,' echoed the lunatic with his hideous laugh. He patiently let himself be taken by the arm and led away. He turned round once with a grin at the glittering medals, but the adjutant pulled him along.

The general followed them with his eyes until they entered the car. The 'storm-signal' was hoisted ominously between his eyebrows. He was boiling with rage at such carelessness in allowing a creature like that to walk abroad freely. But in the nick of time he remembered the civilian at his side, and controlling himself, said with a shrug of the shoulders:

'Yes, these are some of the sad aspects of the war. You see, it is just because of such things that the leader must stay behind, where nothing appeals to his heart. No general could ever summon the necessary severity to direct a war if he had to witness all the misery at the front.'

'Very interesting,' the correspondent breathed gratefully, and closed his book. 'I fear I have already taken up too much of Your Excellency's valuable time, but may I be permitted one more question? When does Your Excellency hope for peace?'

The general started, bit his under lip, and glanced aside with a look that would have made every staff officer of the —th Army shake in his boots. With a visible effort he put on his polite smile and pointed across the square to the open portals of the old cathedral.

'The only advice I can give is for you to go over there and ask our Heavenly Father. He is the only one who can answer that question.'

A friendly nod, a hearty handshake, then His Excellency strode to his office across the square amid the respectful salutations of the crowd.

When he entered the building the dreaded furrow cleaving his brow was deeper than ever. An orderly tremblingly conducted him to the office of the head army physician. For several minutes the entire house held its breath while the voice of the Mighty One thundered through the corridors. He ordered the fine old physician to come to his table as if he were his secretary, and dictated a decree forbidding all the inmates of the hospitals, without distinction or exception, whether sick or wounded, to leave the hospital premises. 'For' – the decree concluded – 'if a man is ill, his place is in bed; and if he feels strong enough to go to town and sit in the coffee-house, he should report at the front, where his duty calls him.'

This pacing to and fro with clinking spurs and this thundering at the cowering old doctor calmed his anger. The storm had about blown over when unfortunately the general's notice was drawn to the report from the brigade that was being most heavily beset by the enemy and had suffered desperate losses, and was holding its position only in order to make the enterprise as costly as possible to the advancing foe. Behind it the mines had already been laid, and a whole new division was already in wait in subterranean hiding ready to prepare a little suprise for the enemy after the doomed brigade had gone to its destruction. Of course, the general had not considered it necessary to inform the brigadier that he was holding a lost position, and all he was to do was to sell his hide as dearly as possible. The longer the struggle raged the better! And men fight so much more stubbornly if they hope for relief until the very last moment . . .

JAROSLAV HAŠEK

Jaroslav Hašek (1883–1923). Called up in 1915 and fought for
the German side on the Eastern Front. 'Taken prisoner' by the
Russians, he joined the Czechs living in Russia and encouraged
them to fight the Germans. Later joined the Bolsheviks and did
not return to Prague till 1920. It is particularly difficult to select
representative passages from this enormous, episodic work. The
following extract shows Švejk in conflict with the 'law'. Hašek
himself had dubious dealings with dogs (see Sir Cecil Parrott,
The Bad Bohemian, London, Bodley Head, 1978).

Source: Jaroslav Hašek, *The Good Soldier Švejk* (translated from
Osudy dobrého uojàka Švejkaza světové války, 1921–3, by Cecil Par-
rott), London, William Heinemann in association with Penguin
Books, 1973.

'Did you not read the advertisement in *Bohemie* and in the
Tagblatt about the loss of my stable pinscher? You didn't read
the advertisement which your superior officer put into the newspaper?'

The colonel clapped his hands.

'Really, these young officers! Where has discipline gone? The
colonel puts in advertisements and the lieutenant doesn't read
them.'

'If only I could give you a few across the jaw, you bloody old
dotard,' Lieutenant Lukáš thought to himself, looking at the
colonel's side whiskers which were reminiscent of an orang-utan.

'Come with me for a moment,' said the colonel. And so they
walked along and had a very pleasant conversation:

'At the front, lieutenant, a thing like this cannot happen to
you again. Promenading with stolen dogs behind the lines is
certainly very agreeable. Yes, walking about with your superior
officer's dog at a time when every day we are losing a hundred
officers on the battlefield. And advertisements are not read! For
a hundred years I could insert notices that my dog is lost. Two
hundred years! Three hundred years!'

The colonel blew his nose noisily, which with him was always a sign of great fury, and said: 'You can go on with your walk.' Then he turned round and went away, angrily striking with his riding whip across the ends of his officer's greatcoat.

Lieutenant Lukáš crossed to the opposite pavement and heard once more: 'Halt!' The colonel had just stopped an unfortunate infantryman in the reserve, who was thinking about his mother at home and had not noticed him.

The colonel took him in person to the barracks for punishment and swore at him for being a swine and bastard.

'What shall I do with Švejk,' thought the lieutenant. 'I'll smash his jaw, but that's not enough. Even tearing his skin from his body in little strips would be too good treatment for that blackguard.' Disregarding the fact that he was due to meet a lady, he set off home in a fury.

'I'll kill him, the dirty hound,' he said to himself as he got into the tram.

Meanwhile the good soldier Švejk was deep in conversation with an orderly from the barracks. The soldier had brought the lieutenant some documents to sign and was now waiting.

Švejk treated him to coffee and they discussed together how Austria would be smashed.

They carried on this conversation as though it could be taken for granted. There was an endless series of utterances which would certainly have been defined in the court as treasonable and for which both of them would have been hanged.

'His Imperial Majesty must be completely off his rocker by this time,' declared Švejk. 'He was never bright, but this war'll certainly finish him.'

'Of course he's off his rocker,' the soldier from the barracks asserted with conviction. 'He's so gaga he probably doesn't know there's a war on. Perhaps they're ashamed of telling him. If his signature's on the manifesto to his peoples, then it's a fraud. They must have had it printed without his knowledge, because he's not capable of thinking about anything at all.'

'He's finished,' added Švejk knowingly. 'He wets himself and they have to feed him like a little baby. Recently a chap at the pub told us that His Imperial Majesty has two wet nurses and is breast-fed three times a day.'

'If only it was all over,' sighed the soldier from the barracks, 'and they knocked us out, so that Austria at last had peace!'

And both continued the conversation until finally Švejk condemned Austria for ever with the words: 'A monarchy as idiotic as this ought not to exist at all,' whereupon the other, to complete his utterance by adding something of a practical kind, said: 'When I get to the front I'll hop it pretty quick.'

And when both continued to interpret the views of the average Czech about the war, the soldier from the barracks repeated what he had heard that day in Prague, that guns could be heard at Náchod and that the Tsar of Russia would soon be in Cracow.

Then they related how our corn was being carted away to Germany and how German soldiers were getting cigarettes and chocolate.

Then they remembered the times of the old wars, and Švejk solemnly argued that when in the olden days they threw stink-pots into a beleaguered castle it was no picnic to have to fight in such a stink. He had read that they had besieged a castle somewhere for three years and the enemy did nothing else except amuse themselves every day in this way with the beleaguered inside.

He would certainly have added something else interesting and informative if their conversation had not been interrupted by the return of Lieutenant Lukáš.

Casting at Švejk a fearful, crushing glance, he signed the documents and after dismissing the soldier motioned Švejk to follow him into his sitting-room.

Frightful lightning shafts darted from the lieutenant's eyes. Sitting on the chair he looked at Švejk and pondered how he should start the massacre.

'First I'll give him a few across the jaw,' he thought. 'Then I'll break his nose and tear off his ears. And after that we'll see.'

But he was confronted by the honest and kindly gaze of the good and innocent eyes of Švejk who dared to interrupt the calm before the storm with the words: 'Humbly report, sir, you've lost your cat. She ate up the boot polish and permitted herself to pass out. I threw her into the cellar – but next door. You won't find again such a good and beautiful Angora cat.'

'What shall I do with him?' flashed through the lieutenant's mind. 'For Christ's sake, what an idiotic expression he has.'

And the kindly innocent eyes of Švejk continued to glow with gentleness and tenderness, combined with an expression of complete composure; everything was in order and nothing had happened, and if something had happened, it was again quite in order that anything at all was happening.

Lieutenant Lukáš jumped up, but did not hit Švejk as he had originally intended to do. He brandished his fist under his nose and roared out.'Švejk, you *stole* the dog!'

'Humbly report, sir, I know of no such case recently and I would like to observe, sir, that you yourself took Max this afternoon out for a walk and so I couldn't have stolen it. I saw at once when you came back without the dog that something must have happened. That's called a situation. In Spálená Street there is a bag-maker named Kuneš and he couldn't take a dog out for a walk without losing it. Usually he left it somewhere at a pub or someone stole it from him or borrowed it and never returned it . . .'

'Švejk, you bastard, you, Himmellaudon, hold your tongue! Either you're a cunning blackguard or else you're a camel and a fat-headed idiot. You're a real object lesson, but I tell you you'd better not try anything on me! Where did you get that dog from? How did you get hold of it? Do you know that it belongs to our colonel, who took it off with him when we happened to meet? Do you realize that this is a colossal world scandal? So speak the truth now! Did you steal it or not?'

'Humbly report, sir, I didn't steal it.'

'Did you know that it was a stolen dog?'

'Humbly report, sir, I knew it was stolen.'

'Švejk, Jesus Mary, Himmelherrgott, I'll have you shot, you bastard, you cattle, you oaf, you pig. Are you really such a half-wit?'

'Humbly report, sir, I am.'

'Why did you bring me a stolen dog? Why did you put that beast into my apartment?'

'To give you a little pleasure, sir.'

And Švejk's eyes looked kindly and tenderly into the face of the lieutenant, who sat down and sighed: 'Why did God punish me with this bastard?'

The lieutenant sat on the chair in quiet resignation and felt he had not the strength even to roll a cigarette, let alone give Švejk one or two across the jaw, and he had no idea why he sent Švejk to get *Bohemie* and *Tagblatt* so that Švejk could read the colonel's advertisement about the stolen dog.

With the newspaper open on the advertisement pages Švejk returned. He beamed and proclaimed joyfully: 'It's there, sir. The colonel describes that stolen stable pinscher so beautifully that it's a pure joy, and into the bargain he offers the finder of it a hundred crowns. That's quite a handsome reward. Generally they only give fifty. A chap called Božetěch from Košíře made a business just out of this. He always stole dogs, then looked in the advertisements to see whether one had run away and at once went there. On one occasion he stole a beautiful black pom, and because the owner didn't advertise it in the newspapers, he tried to put an advertisement in himself. He spent ten crowns on advertisements until finally a gentleman announced that it was his dog, that he had lost it and that he had thought that it would be useless to try and look for it, as he didn't believe any longer in people's honesty. But now he saw that all the same there were honest people to be found, and this gave him tremendous pleasure. He said he was opposed on principle to rewarding honesty, but as a souvenir he would give him his book on indoor and outdoor plant cultivation. The good Božetěch took that black pom by its back legs and hit the gentleman over the head with it and from that time he swore he wouldn't put in any more advertisements. He'd rather sell a dog to a kennel, if no one wanted to advertise for it.'

'Go to bed, Švejk,' the lieutenant ordered. 'You are capable of drivelling on like this till tomorrow morning.' And he went to bed too. In the night he dreamt of Švejk, how Švejk had also stolen the horse of the Heir to the Throne and brought it to him, and how the Heir to the Throne had recognized the horse at a review, when the unfortunate Lieutenant Lukáš rode on it at the head of his company.

In the morning the lieutenant felt as if he had gone through a night of debauch during which he had been knocked many times over the head. An unusually oppressive nightmare clung to him. Exhausted by the frightful dream he fell asleep towards the morning, only to be woken by a knocking on the door. The kindly face of Švejk appeared and asked when he should wake the lieutenant.

The lieutenant groaned in bed: 'Get out, you monster, this is sheer hell!'

But when he was already up and Švejk brought him his breakfast, the lieutenant was surprised by a new question from Švejk: 'Humbly report, sir, would you wish me to look for another nice doggie for you?'

'You know, Švejk, that I feel like having you court-martialled,' said the lieutenant with a sigh, 'but they'd only acquit you, because they'd never have seen anything so colossally idiotic in all their lives. Do look at yourself in the mirror. Doesn't it make you sick to see your own drivelling expression? You're the most idiotic freak of nature that I've ever seen. Now, tell me the truth, Švejk, do you really like yourself?'

'Humbly report, sir, I don't. In this mirror I am somehow lopsided or something. But the glass is not properly cut. At the Chinaman, Staněk's, they once had a convex mirror and when anybody looked at himself in it he wanted to spew. A mug like this, a head like a slop-pail, a belly like a sozzled canon, in short a complete scarecrow. Then the Governor of Bohemia passed by and saw himself in it and the mirror had to be removed at once.'

The lieutenant turned away, sighed and thought it right to pay attention to his coffee rather than to Švejk.

Švejk was already pottering about in the kitchen, and Lieutenant Lukáš heard him singing:

> 'Grenevil is marching through the Powder Gate.
> Swords are flashing, pretty girls are weeping . . .'

And then there came from the kitchen another song:

> 'We're the boys who make the noise,
> Win the hearts of all the tarts,
> Draw our pay and then make hay.'

'You certainly make hay, you bastard,' the lieutenant thought to himself and spat.

Švejk's head appeared in the doorway: 'Humbly report, sir, they've come here for you from the barracks. You're to go at once to the colonel. His orderly officer is here.'

And he added confidentially: 'Perhaps it's because of that dog.'

'I've already heard,' said the lieutenant, when the orderly officer wanted to report to him in the hall.

He said this dejectedly and went out casting an annihilating glance at Švejk.

This was not regimental report. It was something worse. When the lieutenant stepped into his office the colonel sat in his chair frowning frightfully.

'Two years ago, lieutenant,' said the colonel, 'you asked to be transferred to the 91st regiment in Budějovice. Do you know where Budějovice is? It's on the Vltava, yes, on the Vltava, where the Ohře or something like that flows into it. The town is big, so to speak, and friendly, and if I'm not mistaken it has an embankment. Do you know what an embankment is? It is a wall built over the water. Yes. However, this is not relevant here. We had manoeuvres there.'

The colonel was silent, and looking at the ink pot passed quickly to another subject: 'My dog's ruined after having been with you. He won't eat anything. Look, there's a fly in the ink pot. It's very strange that flies should fall into the ink pot in winter. That's disorderly.'

'Well, say your say, you bloody old dodderer,' thought the lieutenant to himself.

The colonel got up and walked once or twice up and down the office.

'I've thought for a long time, lieutenant, what I ought to do with you to prevent this *recurring*, and I remembered that you wanted to be transferred to the 91st regiment. The high command recently informed us that there is a great shortage of officers in the 91st regiment because they have all been *killed by the Serbs*. I give you my word of honour that within three days you will be in the 91st regiment in Budějovice, where they are forming *march battalions for the front*. You don't need to thank me. The army requires officers who . . .'

And not knowing what else to say he looked at his watch and pronounced: 'It's half-past ten and high time to go to regimental report.'

And with this the agreeable conversation came to an end, and the lieutenant felt very relieved when he left the office and went to the volunteers' school, where he announced that very soon he would be going to the front and was therefore organizing a farewell evening party in Nekázanka.

Returning home he said significantly to Švejk: 'Do you know, Švejk, what a march battalion is?'

'Humbly report, sir, a march battalion is a *maršbaťák* and a march company is a *marškumpačka*. We always use abbreviations.'

'Very well then, Švejk,' said the lieutenant in a solemn voice. 'I wish to tell you that you are going with me on the *maršbaťák*, if you like such abbreviations. But don't think that at the front you'll be able to drop such bloody awful clangers as you've done here. Are you happy?'

'Humbly report, sir, I'm awfully happy,' replied the good soldier Švejk. 'It'll be really marvellous when we both fall dead together for His Imperial Majesty and the Royal Family . . .'

ANONYMOUS

Schlump was published anonymously in Munich in 1928 and
made an immediate impact both in Germany and in England
when it was translated in 1929. It ran to five impressions
between September 1929 and February 1930. 'Schlump (Emil
Schulz) was just sixteen years old when, in 1914, the war broke
out.' The first passage describes an attack in which Schlump is
wounded. The later episode concerns Schlump's Švejk-like
'business' after he returns to Maubeuge (near Charleroi) to
work in the local Occupation Headquarters early in 1918.

Source: Anonymous, *Schlump: The Story of a Unknown Soldier*
(translated from *Schlump: Geschichten und Abenteuer aus dem Leben
des unbekannten Musketiers Emil Schulz, genannt 'Schlump'; von ihm
selbst erzählt*, Munich, Kurt Wolf Verlag, 1928, by Maurice
Samuel), London, Martin Secker, 1929.

BOOK TWO

. . . In front of them stood the Tommies, about twenty of them,
absolutely motionless. They were blind drunk. They continued
to throw their hand-grenades without intermission, but in that
pandemonium the explosions were absolutely inaudible.
Suddenly Schlump collapsed; he felt pain – he could not tell
where, but he could not get on to his feet again. Michel continued
to charge – no bullet touched him. Now he was on the Tommies:
with a skilful blow he struck the weapon from the grip of one of
them.

And now something strange happens. He flings his own rifle
away and grabs the Tommy with both arms, as though he wants
to wrestle with him. The Tommy is taller than Michel by a
head, and of tremendous width. They remain locked in the
struggle, while the others charge on. Michel's strength must be
superhuman. He holds the Tommy in a tight grip against
himself, with his right arm. He has managed to free his left. He
tears a hand-grenade out of his pouch and shoves it between
himself and his enemy. He presses the other still closer to himself.
With his teeth he tears the white cap from the grenade. Now –

now – the two of them are torn into tatters. There, where they just stood, locked in combat, rolls Michel's head. It rolls and rolls till it stops, right side up, and looks over at Schlump, the eyes open wide, looking as though it is trying to laugh.

Schlump lay among the dead on the battlefield, unconscious, surrounded by blood, blood, bloody tatters, human limbs, uniforms and equipment stained dark with blood.

It was morning when he came to. The Tommies had lifted the barrage again over to the third lines, near the second position. But they kept sweeping the field with shell and shrapnel. Schlump felt an agonizing pain in his left shoulder. He could not move his arm. His limbs had slid down into a hole which led into a collapsed dug-out. He could feel the blood trickling down his back. His right thigh was swollen, but he could discover no wound. Perhaps an exhausted splinter of shell had bruised him. Suddenly something landed close by: the stones flew past his head. He started up, terrified, and stumbled away. Near the ruins of a cemented dug-out he collapsed. But he regained mastery of himself swiftly; the bombardment became livelier. Suffering indescribable agonies he rose to his feet again, and looked round for a stretcher-bearer. He was mad with thirst. But there was nothing to be seen. No soldier, no stretcher-bearer, no Tommies. Only the dead lay around; blood had painted the sods red and black, and the shells landing around him exploded with terrific detonations . . .

BOOK THREE

. . . It was not long before Schlump too began to do business. He had struck up with a Frenchman who sold him bed sheets. The good man went round telling his countrymen that the Germans were on the point of requisitioning all bedclothes because they were building new hospitals, and the poor people sold him their last possessions for a song. He brought the sheets to Schlump by the dozen, and Schlump passed them on to the head waiter of the dining-car on the train which ran daily between headquarters and Cologne. They were heavy sheets specially woven for the French beds, in which no one ever sleeps alone. First of all they had to be washed. The head waiter gave Schlump eight marks for every sheet, and then also had to tip the railway official who was go-between. The latter hid the sheets under the seats in the first and second class, where the officers sat in their red striped trousers, and afterwards passed them on to the big German supply houses. There the sheets were dyed and made into dresses, and our pretty girls ran proudly around in their new colours, never suspecting how much the dresses they wore had already seen of love.

Schlump also dealt in whisky, which he got out of the canteen in the barracks and which the civilians paid high prices for. The whisky was brought to him in the evening, against cash payment, and the next morning it was called for, also against cash payment. Thus he gradually piled up some money and lived a jolly life. He bought flour and sugar and butter and every week sent home a package. But one day the big chance came – he was on the point of becoming a rich man with a single deal.

During this time Schlump had been transferred to Haumont, where he took charge of the exchange office. One day a soldier came in who had just left the trenches. He unstrapped his pack and brought out a thick, heavy bundle. Carefully and with much ado, he undid it and laid on the table a number of neat, pretty packages, each of which contained a pile of brand-new notes – the paper money of French cities. He looked straight into Schlump's eyes, hit himself on the thigh, and with a loud triumphant laugh said: 'I found that. Give me half a million German marks for it and you can have it.' Schlump was rigid with amazement. He looked at the notes: they were actually absolutely new municipal notes such as the French cities issued for the payment of workers and purchase of supplies. Schlump took up one of the notes – it represented five francs – and tested it. There wasn't the slightest doubt about it – it was genuine paper money. But he suddenly laid the money down again and said, 'You can take the whole bunch back: you won't get a mark for it.'

'Are you mad?' cried the other. 'Why won't they give me a mark for it?'

'Because,' said Schlump, 'they don't carry the signature of the mayor and the stamp of the mayoral office. Perhaps they forgot this paper when they had to leave the city. The stuff is worth nothing – you can give it to the dustman.' The soldier picked up a note, looked at it closely, and threw it down. Then he picked up his pack, hitched it on, and went out. But at the door he turned for an instant and shouted, 'You're nothing but a gang of thieves!'

Schlump picked up the notes, packed all together, and carried everything into his room. He began to think the whole thing over. There was surely something in it all the same. As a matter of fact there was lots of paper money in circulation from cities which had long since been wiped out. Schlump thought and thought and thought. In the evening he went over to his friend who in civilian life had been an architect, and who was now in charge of the civilian labourers who were laying down the new track.

And in the night they set to work feverishly. His friend cut out a stamp and Schlump worked on the facsimile of the mayor's signature. They tried it a hundred times and at last they got it right.

The next night they sat stamping notes until the perspiration streamed from them.

The half million was all stamped and provided with a signature.

But how were they to put the money into circulation? Schlump was to call as much German money into his exchange office as possible and spend French money but he would keep the counterfeit money.

It would have been dangerous to spend half a million in false money and new notes at that. His friend had an idea. Every week he had to pay the workers who were employed on the railway. The payments were made in municipal money. In the past he had come more than once to Schlump's office with German money and exchanged it against local municipal money. Well, Schlump was to give him the counterfeit money, and he would bring good German marks for it.

At first the plan worked to schedule. They repeated the trick a couple of times – until one day an order appeared at headquarters, stating that there was a lot of false money in circulation; the paper was authentic, but the signature had been forged.

Thereupon the two of them became frightened. They destroyed the rest of the money and kept quiet.

A couple of days later an MP turned up, searched the place thoroughly, and found nothing. He accepted a drink from Schlump and disappeared.

Then the matter was forgotten. Each of them now had ten thousand marks in his pocket. Schlump put a couple of hundred-mark notes in a letter and sent them home. The rest he sewed into his coat.

ERNST TOLLER

Ernst Toller (1893–1939). Eagerly volunteered in 1914. Went to
the Western Front in early 1915. Discharged after thirteen
months as unfit for further service. Important dramatist. Imprisoned for his political views in 1919. Left Germany in 1932.
Committed suicide in 1939. The following passages include
much of his description of his thirteen months at the front.

Source: Ernst Toller, *I was a German* (translated from *Eine Jugend
in Deutschland*, Amsterdam, Querido Verlag, 1933, by Edward
Crankshaw), London, John Lane, The Bodley Head, 1934.

. . . The observation post was situated in a little pocket just
under the peak of the hill. With the aid of glasses I could make
out the French trenches and behind them the devastated town of
Pont à Mousson and the Moselle winding its sluggish course
through the early spring landscape. Gradually I became aware
of details: a company of French soldiers was marching through
the streets of the town. They broke formation, and went in
single file along the communication trench leading to the front
line. Another group followed them.

A subaltern was watching through his glasses.

'See those Frenchies?' he asked.

'Yes, sir.'

'Let's tickle 'em up! Range twenty-two hundred,' he cried to
the telephonist.

And 'Twenty-two hundred,' echoed the telephonist.

I kept my eyes glued to the glasses. My head was in a whirl,
and I was trembling with excitement, surrendered to the passion
of the moment like a gambler, like a hunter. My hands shook
and my heart pounded wildly. The air was filled with a sudden
high-pitched whine, and a brown cloud of dust dimmed my field
of vision.

The French soldiers scattered, rushed for shelter; but not all of
them. Some lay dead or wounded.

'Direct hit!' cried the subaltern.

The telephonist cheered.

I cheered . . .

———

. . . The French inhabitants who lingered on in their villages in the fighting zone lived wretchedly in cellars and barns, in odd little rooms or kitchen cupboards, like shipwrecked sailors clinging to bits of wreckage, only to be swept off into eternity by a sudden storm. Impotent witness of its own downfall, the village in which parents and grandparents still lived was blown to bits, its fields ploughed by guns and sown with shells instead of seed; and the fruit of the seed was death and destruction.

The French got enough from the Germans to save them from starvation; but many a woman sold herself for a loaf or a chunk of sausage. Soldiers and peasants lived together on friendly terms; they knew each other and their everyday routines, and trusted each other; they shook their heads together over the war and grumbled together at idiotic orders and swore when the women were forced to do dirty work.

We need not have been afraid that there would not be anything for us to do at the front. There was no sign of the war finishing; the armies had dug themselves into the soil of France, Poland, Russia and Asia, and our men began to sing:

> 'This campaign
> Is a damn slow train;
> I'll be late for my wedding if I don't look out.'

Our battery commander was a medical student who had once been a cadet but had been expelled from the regiment and deprived of his stripes; when the war came, however, he had been made acting first lieutenant. His vanity, stupidity, and arrogance were the bane of our lives.

Once I failed to salute him with the requisite smartness, and next day the sergeant-major read out the following order:

'Private Toller will report to the observation post in full marching order at 11.15 each day until further orders.'

At 11.15 I was at the observation post. Lieutenant Siegel was sitting at the table, reading. I reported to Lance-Corporal Sedlmeier, and he looked through my pack.

'Your socks are not properly packed.'

'Go back and put 'em right. Then report to me again,' said Lieutenant Siegel softly.

I ran back down the slope, which at that time of day was

always swept by shrapnel. Sweating all over I ran to earth in the dug-out, rearranged my pack and tore back to the observation post.

'Where's your field dressing?'

'I must have left it behind.'

'Go back and get it!' spat Lieutenant Siegel.

Sedlmeier clicked his heels and laughed ingratiatingly.

Once more I ran back to the dugout, and once more back to the observation post. I was trembling with rage.

This farce continued for three days.

I sat sleeplessly in my corner staring in front of me.

'I'll blow the blackguard's head off if it goes on much longer,' I said aloud.

'What's he got his knife into you for?' asked Franz.

'Ask me another!'

'I know why it is. You're educated, you are; and he's afraid of you. It's always like that.'

Early next morning I reported to the major of the Bavarian troops to which our battery was attached.

'Private Toller, sir.'

The major, an energetic officer from Karlsruhe with a genial, drink-sodden face, looked at me in astonishment. I had broken all regulations in applying direct to him, and he would have to give me field punishment. I told him my trouble, and he was silent. I knew very well that he couldn't stand the pseudo-lieutenant either.

'Sit down,' he said, 'and have a glass of schnaps. What do you expect me to do about it?'

'I'd like a transfer, sir.'

'Where to?'

'To the infantry, if possible.'

'But why the infantry? What's wrong with the artillery?'

'Well, sir, we shoot, and don't know who we're shooting at, and the others shoot back, and don't know who they're shooting at either. I'd like to see what I'm up against.'

'You're a poet?' said the major.

'Yes, sir.'

'Free verse, what? So you want a little romantic war all on your own? – Your health!'

'Your health, sir.'

'Have you anything particular in mind?'

'I was thinking of the machine-gun section at Bois-le-Prêtre.'

'Just as you like. If you ever come through you must send me your new poems.'

'Thank you, sir.'

Two hours later the sergeant-major gave me formal notice of my transfer. I packed my kit, mixed the things up in a hopeless mess, and reported to Lieutenant Siegel, who received me with an oily smile.

'Shall we let bygones be bygones?' he said, and offered me his hand.

I turned abruptly.

'Halt!' he cried.

I turned round and faced him.

'Didn't you see my hand?'

'Yes, sir.'

'What's the matter, then?'

'If it's an order, sir,' I said, and held my hand stiffly out. His face turned dull red.

'Go to hell!'

'Thank you, sir.'

A devastated wood; miserable words. A tree is like a human being. The sun shines on it. It has roots, and the roots thrust down into the earth; the rain waters it, and the wind stirs its branches. It grows, and it dies. And we know little about its growth and still less about its death. It bows to the autumn gales, but it is not death that comes then; only the reviving sleep of winter.

A forest is like a people. A devastated forest is like a massacred people. The limbless trunks stare blankly at the day; even merciful night cannot veil them; even the wind is cold and alien.

Through one of those devastated woods which crept like a fester across Europe ran the French and German trenches. We lay so close to one another that if we had stuck our heads over the parapet we could have talked to each other without raising our voices.

We slept huddled together in sodden dug-outs, where the water trickled down the walls and the rats gnawed at our bread, and our sleep was troubled with dreams of home and war. One day there would be ten of us, the next only eight. We did not bury our dead. We pushed them into the little niches in the wall of the trench cut as resting places for ourselves. When I went slipping and slithering down the trench, with my head bent low,

I did not know whether the men I passed were dead or alive; in that place the dead and the living had the same yellow-grey faces.

Not that we always had to find a dumping place for the dead.

Often the bodies were blown to pieces, so that only a shred of flesh sticking to a tree stump told where a man had died.

Or they rotted away in the barbed wire between the trenches.

Or if a mine blew up a section of the trench the earth was its own grave-digger.

Three hundred yards to the right of us, in that witches' cauldron, was a blockhouse which had been occupied twenty times by the Germans and twenty times by the French. The bodies of the dead soldiers were heaped together in one vast embrace. An appalling stench hung over them and they had been covered with a thin layer of white quicklime.

The machine-gunners were to be withdrawn, and I was transferred to a battery east of Verdun. The green shade of ancient beeches protected us from spying aircraft; we shot and were shot at, and on the whole led a peaceful, monotonous life. The only cause for complaint was the bad food. The range-finder and the NCOs had grilled steak, and filled their bellies every day. That made for bad blood. Added to that was the fact that the officers at the base had had a new mess built, while our dug-outs let in water for lack of duckboards and revetting material. Also near our battery there was a new concrete dug-out for the staff, complete with every comfort. 'That cost twenty thousand marks,' one of the builders said. 'A lot of money like that ought to last more than one winter.'

Latrine rumours were passing from mouth to mouth. Soldiers had mutinied in such-and-such a place, in so-and-so they had been fraternizing with the French; here they'd poured the coffee on the ground in front of a general, and there a soldier had shot an officer in the line.

The Kaiser was coming to visit the trenches, and we had to parade; the CO picked out the men with the cleanest uniforms for the inspection, and finally it was a little band of cooks, clerks, and so on who paraded before the Kaiser and were decorated with Iron Crosses. Front-hogs need not apply! said the men; and the news that all guns must be unloaded and all bayonets handed in before the Kaiser appeared was received with howls of laughter.

We used to get on best with the officers who concerned themselves only with facts and necessities; but we had a bad time with the petty-minded reserve-officers who used to fuss about and take every opportunity of spying on the men, as though they felt it incumbent upon them to prove themselves lords of creation.

Once Franz's people sent him a light waterproof, and a young reserve-officer asked him who the hell he thought he was, going about in a thing like that? It was the soldier's job not to mind a bit of rain and mud; the war wasn't a joke! And anyway, if common soldiers went about in waterproofs today, tomorrow they would be parading in officers' caps!

'The officers can die like us,' said Franz, 'but they certainly can't live like us.'

All we knew of the war was what was going on in our own little sector; for news of the other fronts we had to rely on the newspapers. Many of us indeed had no clear notion of what we ourselves had done until the papers came, when our own confused ideas were modified and often proved all wrong.

According to the newspaper *feuilletons* the French were a crowd of degenerates, the English a cowardly lot of shopkeepers, the Russians swine. This mania for disparaging, abusing, and calumniating the enemy was so disgusting that I sent a paragraph to the *Kunstwart* deprecating an attitude which could only reflect badly on ourselves. But the editor returned it with a letter that made me despair. One had to bear in mind public opinion, he said. And thus was that public opinion bred which the men at the front came in time to spit upon.

The village A had to be evacuated. The order came through at seven in the morning, and at seven-thirty the last inhabitant had left. When I walked through the silent streets half an hour later and wandered into houses through the open doors where there was nobody to turn me away and nobody to invite me in, I was not alone. In passage and room the air was still full of human warmth, still warm with the life of the people who had lived there until so recently. Even the lifeless objects seemed in some way still attached to their owners. Hands seemed only just raised from knob and latch; the solicitous glance of the housewife seemed still to linger on china and saucepan; cupboards and chests of drawers still sheltered clothes and precious possessions;

the odour of everyday life and happy hours still hung about them. The things of man part from man less readily than man parts from his things; and even when a man has long been dead his possessions remain inscrutably his.

Here the people had only left their homes because the war had driven them away; they could take no more with them than they could carry in their arms, and every room told of some painful choice. In one a woman had bundled all her bed-linen together, and then left it lying. In another a dress had been torn from the wardrobe only to be finally discarded. In another the mother or the child had collected a heap of toys and tied them up, only to abandon them at the last minute.

In the silence of this forsaken village there was nobody to question me, as I said out loud, as if one of those poor people had stood there:

'This had to be.'

I hurried away. There was no one in sight; from whom was I escaping?

I was promoted to corporal. Every night I was on duty with the infantry in the trenches; we had to time the French artillery, the time between flash and detonation gave the exact distance of the battery. We worked in three shifts: the first came on at eight in the evening, the second at midnight, the third at four in the morning. After a few hours' sleep we left our dug-out by the battery and silently plodded down the waterlogged road to the wood which lay behind the third line of trenches. Around us fell the enemy shells, moaning and roaring and echoing through the night. We stumbled over tree-stumps, jumped from shell hole to shell hole, fell into deep pools and bogged ourselves in the mud. The shattered wood was so lit up by the bombardment that there was no knowing whether the stars were shining or whether the night was black as soot. At last we would find the communication trench, and need no longer keep our eyes glued to the ground before us.

We would shelter behind the wall of the trench and watch. Bullets sprayed up the earth into a rain of fire, ricochets screamed over our heads, Very lights hissed quietly up and cast their pallid glare over the barbed wire of no man's land; the sounds of war mingled with the voices of the night. Far away in the distance flames would dart from the muzzles of the French artillery, and we would count the seconds that elapsed before we heard the muffled thud of the detonation. But for all these horrors the night soothed our hearts; earth and all her creatures lay under a vast and solemn veil, and our breathing was easier, our pulse quieter, as, resistlessly, we were drawn into the silent stream of immutable law.

One night we heard a cry, the cry of one in excruciating pain; then all was quiet again. Someone in his death agony, we thought. But an hour later the cry came again. It never ceased the whole night. Nor the following night. Naked and inarticulate the cry persisted. We could not tell whether it came from the throat of German or Frenchman. It existed in its own right, an agonized indictment of heaven and earth. We thrust our fingers into our ears to stop its moan; but it was no good: the cry cut like a drill into our heads, dragging minutes into hours, hours into years. We withered and grew old between those cries.

Later we learned that it was one of our own men hanging on the wire. Nobody could do anything for him; two men had already tried to save him, only to be shot themselves. We prayed desperately for his death. He took so long about it, and if he went on much longer we should go mad. But on the third day his cries were stopped by death.

I saw the dead without really seeing them. As a boy I used to go to the Chamber of Horrors at the annual fair, to look at the wax figures of emperors and kings, of heroes and murderers of the day. The dead now had that same unreality, which shocks without arousing pity.

I stood in the trench cutting into the earth with my pick. The point got stuck, and I heaved and pulled it out with a jerk. With it came a slimy, shapeless bundle, and when I bent down to look I saw that wound round my pick were human entrails. A dead man was buried there.

A – dead – man.

What made me pause then? Why did those three words so startle me? They closed upon my brain like a vice; they choked my throat and chilled my heart. Three words, like any other three words.

A dead man – I tried to thrust the words out of my mind; what was there about them that they should so overwhelm me?

A – dead – man –

And suddenly, like light in darkness, the real truth broke in upon me; the simple fact of Man, which I had forgotten, which had lain deep buried and out of sight; the idea of community, of unity.

A dead man.

Not a dead Frenchman.

Not a dead German.

A dead man.

All these corpses had been men; all these corpses had breathed as I breathed; had had a father, a mother, a woman whom they loved, a piece of land which was theirs, faces which expressed their joys and their sufferings, eyes which had known the light of day and the colour of the sky. At that moment of realization I knew that I had been blind because I had wished not to see; it was only then that I realized, at last, that all these dead men, Frenchmen and Germans, were brothers, and I was the brother of them all.

After that I could never pass a dead man without stopping to gaze on his face, stripped by death of that earthly patina which masks the living soul. And I would ask, who were you? Where was your home? Who is mourning for you now? But I never asked who was to blame. Each had defended his own country; the Germans Germany, the Frenchmen France; they had done their duty ...

———

... Behind our line a French aeroplane was brought down in flames. The machine was completely shattered, the pilot burnt to a cinder; only his boots of yellow Russian leather came through unscathed. They were immediately appropriated by a corporal from the second battery, and he showed them off to the French girls in the village. 'Commes elles sont chics!' the girls laughed. 'Real French!' grinned the corporal; and he related their history. The girls cast down their eyes, mutely and fearfully.

'Airman *kaput, la France kaput!*' said the corporal.

'*Jamais!*' one of the girls retorted hotly.

'I and you *amour,*' said the corporal.

I was at the front for thirteen months, and by the end of that time the sharpest perceptions had become dulled, the greatest words mean. The war had become an everyday affair; life in the line a matter of routine; instead of heroes there were only victims; conscripts instead of volunteers; life had become hell, death a bagatelle; we were all of us cogs in a great machine which sometimes rolled forward, nobody knew where, sometimes backwards, nobody knew why. We had lost our enthusiasm, our courage, the very sense of our identity; there was no rhyme or reason in all this slaughtering and devastation; pain itself had lost its meaning; the earth was a barren waste.

We used to hack away the copper guiding-rings of unexploded shells out of sheer perversity; only the other day one had exploded and blown up two men – but what did that matter?

I applied for a transfer to the Air Force, not from any heroic motive, or for love of adventure, but simply to get away from the mass, from mass-living and mass-dying.

But before my transfer came through I fell ill. Heart and stomach both broke down, and I was sent back to hospital in Strassburg. In a quiet Franciscan monastery kind and silent monks looked after me. After many weeks I was discharged. Unfit for further service.

LEONHARD FRANK

Leonhard Frank (1882–1961). Born in Wurzburg. Working-class background. Various jobs, then trained as an artist. A pacifist, he left Berlin for Switzerland in 1915. Returned in 1918 but left again for Switzerland, France, Portugal and the US. Returned to Munich in 1950. *Carl and Anna* was published in Berlin in 1927 and was dramatized and filmed. Carl and Richard have been prisoners of the Russians since 1914. Richard tells Carl all about his wife, Anna, whom he has not seen for four years. Carl becomes infatuated with the idea of Anna so he escapes, finds her and poses as Richard. The first passage (Chapter IV) describes life in Anna's tenement block with her new 'husband'. Does she believe Carl? Even if she does not, does she love him? The second passage (Chapter VI), after the Armistice, describes Richard's journey home. Anna is pregnant by Carl. Later, Carl and Anna leave Richard accompanied by the jeers of the other tenement dwellers.

Source: Leonhard Frank, *Carl and Anna* (translated from *Karl und Anna*, Berlin, 1927, by Cyrus Brooks), London, Peter Davies, 1929; Penguin Books, 1938.

CHAPTER IV

Anna's friend, Marie, lived with her sister, and had a fourth-floor room overlooking the second of the three courtyards. The room was the same length as the narrow iron bed which occupied every inch of space between the inner wall and the window.

By the window the room broadened a little. An iron frame stood there, with three curved legs and wash-basin. There was no space for chair or table. When Marie washed in the morning, she had to kneel on the bed and thence plunge her face into the water.

One Sunday afternoon Anna was sitting on the foot of the bed, and Marie was standing on it quite naked, preparing to dress for a walk.

In the larger room next door, the man who lived with Marie's sister – whose husband was at the war – lay sleeping on the rust-brown settee. The sister's two sons, aged eight and nine, stood deep in thought before an old perambulator, in which their six-month-old brother – the son of the sleeping man – lay with both little fists pressed into his cheeks. They were discussing how they could provide themselves with a truck for the afternoon.

'We'll just take off the body,' said the elder, who had a screwdriver in his hand; 'then we can use the chassis.'

'But do it quietly or he'll start yelling.'

They took out the eight screws, lifted the upper part, with the awakening infant inside it, on to the floor, and crept out of the room with the framework and wheels. 'We'll put the body on again tonight . . . There, he's beginning to howl!'

The man awoke also – he was a motor-mechanic – and looked round at once for the perambulator. The place where it had stood was vacant. Yet, beyond all doubt, there was a baby crying in the room. He rubbed his eyes and stared down, perplexed and half awake, at his son. A few seconds later he was smilingly carrying him up and down the room.

It had come about of itself, the result of circumstances. He had rented a place to sleep in – the bed of the husband who was at the war. At first the table had stood between the two beds, to mark the frontier. During the first week, the light was turned out when they went to bed. For the money he would have had to spend on inferior meals in a cheap restaurant, the woman fed the whole family, which had been left unprovided for. The two beds stood side by side again.

The woman appeared in the doorway, her apron wet from washing and a scrubbing-brush in her hand. 'Has he been crying?' Her face was grey, the skin flaccid. But the red-brown lips were smooth and firm and full of blood, and, being open, matched her wide-open, questioning eyes. She was older than the motor-mechanic.

'Look at that!' he cried, his face, brightening again, and pointing.

'That's what the two rascals were talking about in bed last night.' She gave the baby her breast, which was surprisingly youthful, white, not large, and with sky-blue veins.

The mechanic looked on, his hands in his trouser-pockets, watching with close attention his son's sucking lips and greedy gulpings.

In a few days' time the husband was expected home on leave.

The little room next door echoed with Marie's laughter. She was still standing on the bed, trying on, with Anna's help and criticism, a short chemise which she had made herself during the morning.

Still standing, she pulled on her stocking. Her leg, from the small foot to the knee, was slender, girlish, and beautiful. Above the deep mark of the garter, the woman began: the body swelled outwards in soft, rolling curves; the skin was darkly discoloured and in places rough.

The band of her knickers, which were trimmed with open-work machine-embroidery of a coarse pattern, sank into her waist, and immediately above rose the slender, exceedingly delicate, inexperienced back of a child.

Anna handed her a cotton frock with blue spots. Even when her head and arms had vanished under the frock, she went on telling Anna all that had happened in the tenement since they had last met.

First appeared the short, outspread fingers with their short, broad nails, then the firm, very narrow head, the face with its uniform warm tint as of some rare wood, the fine eyes. The brows and curling lashes were much darker than her fragrant, fair hair. She had dimples that came and went in the firm smoothness of her cheeks, coming always with living charm at the bidding of her little mouth.

She let herself fall backwards, stiffly, at full length, and in an access of high spirits turned on her side as the mattress rebounded, and put her head in Anna's lap. Anna clasped her hands round the girl's glowing cheeks.

The noise of some one bawling with all the force of powerful lungs came from a ground-floor dwelling. The sound crashed against the walls, and was hurled echoing up the narrow court, past the fourth-floor windows, towards the sky. Another outbreak, lasting the length of a breath. Then a woman's shrill, rising voice.

'There, he's beating her again.' Marie had started up. 'They quarrel every day, and yet they won't separate.'

The woman who was being thrashed had taken up with another man while her husband was at the war. Many women did it. And no one could keep a secret. Marie could talk for hours of the hate and misery, the disease and guilt, the undeserved suffering and also the devotion and loving care, which the tenement housed.

It would be just the same with me, thought Anna: You take another man, because your husband isn't there or has left you. It happens every day.

On the second floor, Carl was standing behind the closed window, immobile as a prisoner who is learning how to wait.

'And when your husband comes home and sees what we've been doing, suppose he smashes everything up?' said the motor-mechanic in the next room.

A crowd had collected in a corner of the court: half-naked children, pale and consumptive, women in rags, men in shirt-sleeves. Livid faces. They had carried out into the air an old man, weak with hunger, who had had a fainting fit.

A powerful young labourer was standing in the centre of the court in the pose of an archer, with his body thrown backwards almost at a right angle. He drew his bow, a strip of thin, flat steel, five feet long and almost straight, with all his strength, bending it to a semicircle. The long arrow of nickelled steel tubing, thin as a reed, whizzed up vertically into the freedom of the summer sky, made a slow, gleaming turn, and dropped back into the narrow, gloomy court. A dangerous missile in strong, unsteady hands, which as it falls may wound even the archer himself.

He shot again and again. All looked up, huddled together in the corner: a grey, shadowy group. Even the old man who was weak with hunger looked up.

The bicycle-bell summoned Elfi to the window. 'Frau Anna's got a visitor. He's standing down there . . . Had a good dinner?'

'Yes; carrots.'

'Oh, carrots?'

Soon after, dressed up in their coloured finery, they were tripping arm in arm down the road up which Carl had trudged weeks before. Both had long legs, without calves and as thin as sticks, and wore gaudy green ribbons in their hair: two water-wag-tails.

Marie also had looked down. Carl was still standing motionless at the window. 'I say, who's your visitor? . . . Tell me, who is he?'

Anna's silence lengthened into a confession. She was grave and agitated. And thus she went out of the room.

There would be some one there, when she went down. Not merely a casual acquaintance. Such an hour as that on their first morning brings people near together. Very near. It binds them together. Some one would be there when she went in. And that would be welcome. The room would not be so – so orderly and empty as it used to be . . . Was her husband still alive? *He* claimed that he was her husband, and in a way that almost compelled belief. She must break him of that habit, that foolish habit. She must make him give it up. She must outwit him.

Yes, but supposing her husband was still alive. What then? What if he were still living? ... Then the whole thing became impossible. One couldn't just leave one's husband without more ado and go to another man. It was not so simple as all that ... She had only to think of his eyes, the way he used to look at her. And of his big, honest hand. Yes, and of the complete trust she had had in him. With him she had been sheltered and safe. That was true. Safe, absolutely safe!

'We could go for a walk, if you'd like to.'

'Yes,' said Carl slowly, and looked down at his clothes.

'You can put on one of my husband's white collars if you like.'

'I want nothing at all. Not a thing!'

Only me. He'll take nothing from him but me. 'You say he's still alive, and yet you want me to be your wife!'

'That would make no difference to me,' he said, with a black look. And suddenly, without leading up to it, and in such a tone that she knew he had been thinking of it while she was away, and had made up his mind to say it: 'The salesman that recommended those curtains to us had a very small, black moustache – no bigger than that! – and he had two pimples on his forehead, if you want to know. I pointed them out to you at the time.'

A movement of angry impatience ran through her. 'I don't know where you got hold of all that. I'm angry with you! It's hateful, what you're doing – hateful!'

His face stiffened with a despairing impotence, such as a man feels only when the gravest wrong has been done him.

The faces of many of the passers-by, dull with the boredom of their Sunday afternoon walk, were touched for a few seconds with life, as they caught sight of these two: Anna so smart, so mild and strong, striding so lightly from her tall hips, and, at her side, the dark, unkempt man, without a collar, glowing as a live coal glows through a thin coating of ash.

They were walking towards the town. It was the first time they had been out together. What fulfilment for him, who had tramped on foot for three months, across frontiers and through forests, to get to her! Now he was walking by her side.

He dropped back a few paces to see how she walked, and the vision he had had of her, away there in the steppe, came back to him. She had appeared to him in a tight dress of smooth, brownish stuff, like a dead woman coming back to her lover, wandering without substance down a familiar path under the trees. He paled before the immediate onslaught of his feeling.

I'll wait years if necessary, he thought, and was unwilling to wait a minute.

As she turned round, ingenuous wisdom in her face, and in her glance a wise temperance and inner richness, she experienced suddenly the sky-blue sense of having turned to him once before in exactly the same emotional situation. 'Is it possible –'

He guessed her meaning. For his will and emotions circled unceasingly round the same point. 'It is so.'

'– that I've been here with you before?'

They turned into an avenue of trees that connected the suburb with the town: the avenue of his vision. 'You were here once before, under the trees: it was evening and you were waiting for me.'

Richard had never told him that. But he knew it was true. He had seen Anna walking and waiting. The truth was in him, and he had spoken it.

Down the whole of her left side, which was next to him, Anna felt a melting warmth. Reality, with its hindrances, vanished. Innermost feelings burst forth into life. Their hearts streamed together.

Anna did not think. She believed what she felt. And to taste the final sweetness, she had to give words to her feeling, she had to say the name. And she said it: 'Richard.'

He closed the magical circle: he said simply: 'I love you.' Thus they went.

'And the child? Now do you want it? Now do you want one?'

As her lips opened to him, her eyelids drooped and closed. Yet she was a woman slow to move.

He asked again with his lips against hers. With the deep comfort of her unspoken answer in his heart, he entered the inn-garden with his tall wife.

Had he not been there once before, as a child? And the landlord's daughter, yes, Anna, with her arm round his neck, had pushed the glass of milk towards him.

Seated under a tree in an almost deserted corner of the garden, they were for a time very close to each other, as though life had never led Anna and Richard together, as though chance with its millionfold activities, which opens the door to lifelong errors and decides whole destinies, had been utterly overcome by the force and desire of two hearts, hearkening fresh and strong to each other's beat, as though it had been thus from the beginning.

A workman's family arrived at the next table. Before she sat down, the woman hurriedly unpacked the sandwiches she had brought, and the four children, their noses scarcely above the table-edge, began to clamour like a greedy brood when the mother-bird alights on the edge of the nest. And so the outside world arose afresh.

Anna began to think again. But the lot that falls to one among thousands had fallen to her: she loved. She was in the power of that absolute necessity, whose source is unfathomable, which is independent of the circumstances, the appearance, the character, the particular qualities of the loved one; which is there or is not there; which is heavy as lead and insubstantial as an odour; smaller than an atom and as great as the earth, which lifts a man into bliss or sinks him into such misery that he envies a rat. The inscrutable mystery had unfolded itself within her.

The brass band began at eight. The garden was already full. The patrons were punctual. Carl noticed the glances of the people sitting round. But the relation between Anna and himself had already reached the stage of profound and mutual sympathy. Carl had passed over all the preliminary stages, even that of being proud of showing himself with a desirable woman. The outside world in all its manifestations could no longer affect them. Surrounded by the tumult of life, they were absorbed in the fight against and for each other, in which wounds were inflicted and healed again with a look.

A little old man, bent almost double with age, floated from table to table under his red, blue, and green cloud of balloons, like the small, black car of an airship.

They went back through the avenue, where their late experience still lurked. Both thought of it. They walked slowly and in silence: two persons who belonged to each other.

Anna resisted. It had come upon her too quickly. And nothing had yet been cleared up. This obscurity was repugnant to her. But she was suddenly assaulted, with irresistible and stinging force, by a temporary but passionate readiness to blot out all that had gone before and believe Carl in everything.

As they went through the main door, the two wagtails put their heads together and whispered. Their faces and arms were burnt by the sun. Elfi was wearing the yellow now, and Alma the blue. They had exchanged frocks by the lake.

'You're a lucky one, Frau Anna; I must congratulate you,' said a man on the staircase, and went on downstairs. 'It does happen now and then that a man comes home after he's been reported dead. But it's pretty seldom.'

'We heard about it last night,' cried Elfi loudly.

'Who from?' asked the man, who was now in the next floor below, and Anna heard the answer: 'From Frau Bösch.'

She was an old woman who knew all that happened in the tenement, and gossiped about it with anyone who would listen.

And what now? thought Anna. And suddenly she was in the arms of her friend, and felt the tears on Marie's cheeks. 'Why didn't you tell me about it? The whole house knew it but me! You are a one for keeping secrets! I want to see him ... Herr Richard. I must see you at once.' It was dark on the staircase.

'Well, and what now?'

'How glad I am!'

Anna was glad too. What a load of happiness, she thought. A load of happiness! Full of the sense of it, she went to the door, opened it, and lighted the lamp.

She could have said that Carl was not her husband, that she had a lover. There was nothing in that to make a secret of. It was a matter of course for the dwellers in the tenement that women whose husbands were in the field should have relations openly with other men.

And she could have said, without fear of being convicted of a lie, that Carl was her husband. For in those eight days – from their arrival in the city till the outbreak of war – Richard had made the acquaintance of no one, had not even spoken to their neighbours. And four years had passed since then.

But it was not those considerations, though they flashed through her mind with the quickness of thought, that decided her, but her own wish and what she had just experienced with Carl.

The question of whether he was Richard had become a matter of no importance. She knew that he was not lying. And her own emotion and experience was not a lie. It was happiness, real and true. Let them all think he was her husband, if he and their good fortune willed it so. And she, did not she wish it?

There he stood and gave Marie his hand, quite unperturbed. Stood there quite unperturbed, with his shining face.

Oh, she wished it too! She wished it! She wished it! ... This wild fellow, who could be as still as the geranium plant there on the sill. Just because he too was happy and no longer alone ... No longer alone! How good that was! How good, how good! ... Marie's radiant face. She was actually laughing and crying with pleasure at the same time. Life was beautiful after all. Only it had passed her by for so long.

Instead of the many-voiced quarrelling of the afternoon, peaceful silence rose up to them out of the court. Strange notes began to sound, thin and fragile. Two tenement musicians were tuning up their home-made instruments: a piano – a macaroni-box of deal, one-foot-eight in length with black-and-white painted keys – and a fiddle made from an old cigar-box.

One lifted the frail little piano on to a bench they had brought with them, and carefully adjusted its position, so that it should stand firmly, and not fall to pieces; the other turned his fiddle slowly round – it had a neck like a cello – and rested the neck cautiously against the bench. The music sounded equally cautious.

The great, workman's hands and thick fingers of the pianist could hardly find room on the keyboard. Both musicians had to restrain their natural vigour, lest their fragile little instruments should go to pieces while they played. So they were compelled to make good music. They sang the tunes. A hundred dwellers in the tenement listened. Not a sound. Even the babies had been silenced. The three friends in Anna's room listened also. The tones were sweet.

When they had finished, the fair-haired, four-year-old boy began to bawl his song: '*Mariechen's got a baby –*' He could not help it. The music had taken hold of him. He shouted to heaven with all the strength of his lungs. He knew no better. He waved his arms and legs in his enthusiasm. '*She doesn't know its dad.*'

CHAPTER VI

... When at last the train rolled into the station and came to a stop, Richard took leave of his companions with the stolid, powerful composure which was as much a part of him as his own head, and strode, at the hour when Anna was spreading the table for herself and Carl, who was now leaving his distant factory, alone and limping across the station-square, his grey bundle under his arm. Even his joy and eagerness could not drive him to a quicker pace. For four years he had been yearning for Anna, and in that time he had learnt to wait. Now he was as good as with her. He had reached his goal. The actual meeting could not add perceptibly to what he felt already.

Only a quite unwonted gaiety, fluctuating, intangible, and light as down, fluttered round his massive certainty, like a butterfly round an elephant.

It was a long way. No trams were running in those days. Carl's way from the factory to the tenement was about a third longer. But he strode out sharply and had sound legs.

Anna had laid the table for the meal, and went down to get some bread. Towards evening, when she knew that Carl would soon be home, she always grew calmer.

An empty dray overtook Richard, drawn by two powerful horses, and open at the back. The driver stopped and asked the limping home-comer if he would like a lift. Richard scrambled in backwards. The horses fell into a slow trot.

He had to walk the last bit of the way. At the street-door, the motor-mechanic was standing with Marie. Richard studied the building attentively. Four years ago it had been new; now the façade was neglected and decayed.

'Are you looking for some one in the house?' asked the motor-mechanic, and Anna's excitable friend glanced nervously at the dishevelled soldier, who looked as hard as iron and overflowing with strength, and yet bore traces of the immense burden of the war years.

His unwonted gaiety made him say: 'Yes, yes, my wife.' And he mentioned her name. 'She still lives here, doesn't she?'

'Yes, but –' began Marie, in confusion, and did not know how to go on.

'– but Frau Anna can only be married to one man and not to two at a time,' said a young workman with a cheerful grin, completing her sentence. He was standing in the doorway, and Richard had already passed him.

As he went limping on, in his long coat that brushed the stairs, tired, crusted with filth, somewhat bent, it was as though he had been wandering alone on foot for four years, through loneliness and horror, misery and anguish of heart, and had just reached that spot.

Anna heard his heavy, limping tread, which sounded as though two men were dragging a load up the stairs. She looked so fair and radiant, as women sometimes do before their confinement.

He had not knocked. The door was open. A black, strange man was standing in the doorway . . .

HERBERT READ

Herbert Read (1893–1968). Born in Yorkshire and educated at Halifax and at the University of Leeds. Served as an infantryman on the Western Front. He remains an underrated poet. Yeats thought his long poem 'The End of a War', 1933, the best poem to come out of the Great War and published it (and not Owen and Rosenberg, for instance) in *The Oxford Book of Modern Verse*, 1936. Read published his prose 'autobiographies', *The Contrary Experience*, in 1963.

Source: Herbert Read, *The Contrary Experience*, London, Faber, 1963.

WAR DIARY

... The young man whose diary of the First World War is now resuscitated many years after the event had not had the time to polish any of his ideas.

———

... The young man we meet at the opening of the Diary, in January 1915, had recently attained the age of twenty-one, and more recently still had been commissioned as a second-lieutenant in the infantry.

12.iv.17

Three weary days have passed, waiting rather impatiently for orders to proceed up to the line. I was inoculated this morning – and now umpteen million germs are disporting themselves in my blood, making me somewhat stiff – and cross.

But I really feel extraordinarily calm and happy – very different sensations from those that accompanied my former 'coming out'. Then I felt reckless with the rest – and rather bacchanalian. Didn't care a hang what happened. And, in a way, I don't care a hang this time, but it's a different way, a glad way. And it rather troubles my soul to know why? Because, as you may know, I'm not exactly a warrior by instinct – I don't glory in fighting for fighting's sake. Nor can I say that I'm wildly enthusiastic for 'the Cause'. Its ideals are a bit too commercial and imperialistic for my liking. And I don't really hate the Hun – the commonest inspiration among my comrades. I know there are a lot of nasty Huns – but what a lot of nasty Englishmen there are too. But I think my gladness may be akin to that Rupert Brooke expressed in one of his sonnets:

> Now God be thanked who has match'd us with His hour
>   And caught our youth, and wakened us from sleeping,
> With hand made sure, clear eye, and sharpen'd power,
>   To turn, as swimmers into cleanness leaping,
> Glad from a world grown old and cold and weary,
>   Leave the sick hearts that honour could not move,
> And half-men, and their dirty songs and dreary,
>   And all the little emptiness of love.

Though I must say I'm not yet so 'fed up' with the world as the sonnet implies. I haven't yet proved 'the little emptiness of love'. The half-men I still have with me in goodly numbers. And I've still faith that there are hearts that can be moved by honour and ideals. But England of these last few years has been rather cold and weary, and one finds little left standing amid the wreckage of one's hopes. So one is glad to leap into the clean sea of danger and self-sacrifice. But don't think that I am laying claim to a halo. I don't want to die for my king and country. If I do die, it's for the salvation of my own soul, cleansing it of all its little egotisms by one last supreme egotistic act . . .

9.v.17

One thing troubles me: that you don't understand why I am out here: I thought I had made that clear. I've no doubt about my position. If I were free today, I'm almost sure I should be compelled by every impulse within me to join this adventure. For I regard it as an adventure and it is as an adventure that it appeals to me. I'll fight for Socialism when the day comes, and fight all the better for being an 'old soldier'. It is my desire to disassociate myself from the red, white and blue patriot that makes me 'growl'. Why a person like myself *can* fight with a good heart in a war like this, I have tried to express in the enclosed unfinished article. I have one or two good friends who are active conscientious objectors (one of them in prison) and they fail to see why I should be so militant in what they regard as an extraneous cause. I've always *felt* that I was in the right and now I am trying to express my feelings.

Your criticism of Hardy and James is *shallow* (I hope I don't offend). It fails to realize the nobility of suffering – the greatness of man in tragedy. 'Untrue to the facts of life' – look around you! When will we aspire to nobility of character, instead of maudlin happiness?

1.viii.17

Well, the 'stunt' is over, so now I can tell you something about it. I, along with another officer, was detailed to get as many volunteers as we could from our company and, on a certain dark and dirty night, to raid the enemy's trenches, kill as many as possible and bring back at least one prisoner for identification purposes. Out of a possible sixty we got forty-seven volunteers ... That was a jolly good start. We had about a fortnight to make our plans and rehearse. This we set about with enthusiasm – everybody was keen. Our plans were made with all the low villainous cunning we were capable of. When the battalion went into the front line we were left behind to train and take things easy. We two officers had to do a good amount of patrolling and observation. We had to discover the weak points in the enemy's wire, the best routes thither and as much of the enemy's habits as we could ... This went on until the fateful night arrived. Picture us about midnight: our faces were blackened with burnt cork, everything that might rattle was taken off or tied up. We armed ourselves with daggers and bombs and various murderous devices to blow up the enemy's wire and dug-outs – and, of course, our rifles or revolvers. The raid was to be a stealth raid and depended for its success on surprise effect. So out thro' our own wire we crept – our hearts thumping but our wills determined. We had 540 yards to traverse to the objective. The first half were simple enough. Then we began to crouch and then to crawl – about a yard a minute. Suddenly, about 150 yards from the German trenches, we saw and heard men approaching us. We were following one another in Indian file. They seemed scattered to the right and left as far as we could see. In a moment all our carefully prepared plans were thrown to the winds. New plans had to be made on the spur of the moment. Our position was tactically very weak. My fellow-officer began to crawl carefully back to reorganize the men into a defensive position, leaving me in front to deal with the situation if necessary. I could now see what was happening. The Huns were coming out to wire (had already started as a matter of fact) and were sending out a strong covering party to protect the wirers from surprise. This party halted and took up a line in shell-holes about twenty yards from us. Then some of them began to come forward to reconnoitre. We lay still, looking as much like clods of earth as we possibly could. Two Boche were getting very near me. I thought we had better surprise them before they saw us. So up I get and run to them pointing my revolver and shouting '*Hände hoch*' (hands up), followed by my trusty sergeant and others. Perhaps the Boche didn't understand my newly acquired German. At any rate they fired on me – and missed. I replied with my revolver and my sergeant with his gun. One was hit and shrieked out. Then I was on the other fellow who was now properly scared and fell flat in a shell-hole. '*Je suis officer!*' he cried in French. By this time there was a general fight going on, fire being opened on all sides. In a minute or two the guns were on and for five minutes it was inferno. The real object of the raid was achieved – a prisoner and a valuable one at that had been captured. So I began to make my way back with him whilst the other officer organized covering fire. In another five minutes we were back in our own trenches, and, all things considered, very glad to get there. Our casualties were only one missing and two slightly wounded. We must have inflicted twenty on the enemy, for, besides our rifle fire and bombs, we drove him back into a barrage put up by our trench mortars.

I took the prisoner along to Headquarters. He spoke a little French, so on the way we carried on a broken conversation. He told me his name, age, that he was married and where he came from. When we got to HQ there was an officer who spoke German and then the prisoner began to talk twenty to the dozen. We gave him a drink, cigarette, etc. He turned out to be an ex-schoolmaster of some sort and a very intelligent fellow. We got any amount of useful information from him. He was very interesting on things in general. Does not think we shall ever win this war, but neither will they. Says the new man, Michaelis, is a people's man and will gradually democratize the German government. But the Kaiser is still the people's hero and we must not expect the German nation to consent to his dethronement in the terms of peace. He says there is no chance of a revolution in Germany. Did not think much of the French, but was almost enthusiastic in his praise of the English. Said it was a mistaken idea to think the Germans hated the English. That was only an idea propagated by the German militarists and our own Press. We were of the same racial stock – should be allies – not enemies – etc., etc.

He himself won the Iron Cross at Verdun where he took eighty-five French prisoners.

We had to take him down to Brigade – an hour's walk. It was a beautiful early morning and everything was peaceful and the larks were singing. In our broken French we talked of music. He played both the violin and the piano and we found common enthusiasms in Beethoven and Chopin. He even admired Nietzsche and thenceforth we were sworn friends. He wrote his name and address in my pocket-book and I promised to visit him after the war if I ever came to Germany. By the time I handed him over to the authorities at the Brigade we were sorry to part with each other. And a few hours previously we had done our best to kill each other. *C'est la guerre* – and what a damnable irony of existence . . . at any rate a curious revelation of our common humanity.

I've got a beautiful automatic revolver as a souvenir.

In my next letter I'll answer the futile attack on *Art and Letters* in this week's *New Age*.

26.x.17

Your letter was waiting for me when we came out of the line . . . nothing better could have greeted me. We have had a terrible time – the worst I have ever experienced (and I'm getting quite an old soldier now). Life has never seemed quite so cheap nor nature so mutilated. I won't paint the horrors to you. Some day I think I will, generally and for the public benefit. I was thoroughly 'fed up' with the attitude of most of the people I met on leave – especially the Londoners. They simply have no conception whatever of what war really is like and don't seem concerned about it at all. They are much more troubled about a few paltry air raids. They raise a sentimental scream about one or two babies killed when every day out here hundreds of the very finest manhood 'go west'. Of course, everyday events are apt to become rather monotonous . . . but if the daily horror might accumulate we should have such a fund of revulsion as would make the world cry 'enough!' So sometimes I wonder if it is a sacred duty after all 'to paint the horrors'. This reminds me of a poem I'll quote – by one of our moderns and a woman at that.

> Another life holds what this lacks,
> a sea unmoving, quiet –
> not forcing our strength
> to rise to it, beat on beat –
> a stretch of sand,
> no garden beyond, strangling
> with its myrrhlilies –
> a hill not set with black violets,
> but stones, stones, bare rocks,
> dwarf trees, twisted, no beauty
> to distract – to crowd
> madness upon madness.
>
> Only a still place
> and perhaps some outer horror,
> some hideousness to stamp beauty
> a mark
> on our hearts.

H.D.

10.i.18

. . . I also managed to write a short article and send it on to the *New Age*. I don't really expect them to accept it, as it is very much against their point of view. I called it 'Our Point of View' and my chief points were:

(*a*) That the means of war had become more portentous than the aim – i.e. that the game is not worth the candle.

(*b*) That this had been realized by the fighting soldier and on that account there has been, out here, an immense growth of pacifist opinion.

Of course, it might offend the censor. But it is the truth. I know my men and the sincerity of their opinions. They know the impossibilty of a knock-out blow and don't quite see the use of another long year of agony. We could make terms now that would clear the way for the future. If, after all that Europe has endured, her people can't realize their most intense ideal (Good-will) – then Humanity should be despaired of – should regard self-extinction as their only salvation. But I for one have faith, and faith born in the experience of war.

––

27.ii.18

... I've finished the final proof of 'Kneeshaw' – the realistic war poem I told you of, and sent it off to Rutter for No. 4 *Art and Letters*. It is to form the nucleus of a small volume of its kind, which I hope to get published in autumn – if I can overcome the paper scarcity. I've already got nearly as many poems as I want – about twenty. I want to write a preface and design a frontispiece and then I shall be ready. It isn't exactly a joyful book: it is a protest against all the glory camouflage that is written about the war: It means I have to be brutal and even ugly. But the truth should be told, and though I'm not quite conceited enough to imagine that I can do it finally, I think my voice might get a hearing. But I'd rather write one 'pastoral' than a book of this realism. My heart is not in it: it is too objective.

17.iii.18

... I have started *Walden* and find it full of wisdom, especially as to the use to be made of life.

9.v.18

... How sick I am of the whole business. Most of the prisoners we took were boys under twenty. Our own recent reinforcements were all boys. Apart from uniforms, German and English are as like as two peas: beautiful fresh children. And they are massacred in inconceivable torment. This is the irony of this war: in-dividually we are the one as good as the other: you can't hate these innocent children simply because they dress in grey uni-forms. And they are all magnificently brave, English and German alike. But simply because we are united into a callous inhuman association called a State, and because a State is ruled by politicians whose aim (and under the circumstances their duty) is to support and maintain the life and sovereignty of this monster, life and hope are denied and sacrificed. And look at their values. On the one hand national well-being and vanity, commercial expansion, power: on the other love, joy, hope – all that makes life worth living – all that persuades one to consent to live among so much that is barbarous and negative. So perhaps you will begin to see the connection between 'the German push, Thoreau and anarchy'. And perhaps you will get 'a glimpse of how, in my heart of hearts, I regard my whole connection with the Army and its work'. I could make my connection with it something of a success *if I had the will. Without* the will I have not done so badly. I like its manliness, the courage it demands, the fellowship it gives. These are infinitely precious things. But I hate the machine – the thing as a whole and its duty (to kill), its very existence. My will is to destroy it and my energies must be devoted to that end. Is this the glimpse you wanted? . . .

10.ix.18

. . . Today I have written to the War Office cancelling my application for a regular commission. The war, I am glad to say, is over – much to some people's disappointment. I have been fairly disgusted these last few weeks. I do not think the national temper is anything to be proud of. Christian sentiments being out of fashion or obsolete, I thought we might at any rate have exercised the Englishman's renowned sense of fair play – of not hitting a man when he is down, etc. No. That is another damned hypocrisy exposed. We only do that when it pays. At present it will pay most of us to leave Germany incapacitated for foreign trade, etc., for a century. League of Nations? 'Damned idealistic rot. Can't imagine why we let a dreamy bloke like Wilson dictate to us. What I say is: Give 'em a taste of what they gave Little Belgium. Burn their villages, stick their babies, and rape their women. And now for a strong Army & Navy and keep the old flag flying.'

Do you realize that that is the way the average Englishman is talking just now? I'll soon be out of all this, by fair means or foul. At present I am gagged, bound hand and foot, mutely to listen to such rot. If it is not demoralizing, it is enough to drive me mad.

At present I am wondering by what conceivable chain of circumstance, of flattery, promise of ease, blindness to reality, I came seriously to consider staying in the Army.

FREDERIC MANNING

Frederic Manning (1887–1935). Born in Sydney, Australia, son
of William Manning, mayor of that city. Frederic Manning
came to England in 1902 and was educated privately. Knew
Pound. Published *Poems* (1910). He joined the Shropshire Light
Infantry and served on the Somme from August to December
1916. *Her Privates We* first appeared under the authorship of
'Private 19022' – Manning's actual number. Bourne, the main
character's name, was the name of the town where Manning
lived after the war. After service in France and Ireland he left
the army before the war ended. Interestingly, he chose to let
Bourne die, as Remarque did Paul Bäumer. Some of the language, toned down in the original publication, has been restored
to what it was in the private edition of 1929, *The Middle Post of
Fortune*. We have retained the later, better known title.

Source: Frederic Manning, *Her Privates We*, London, Peter Davies,
1930; 2nd edn, 1964.

... 'A lot o' them are new to it, yet,' said Williams, tolerantly.
'You might take a drop o' tea up to the corporal, will you? 'e's a
nice chap, Corporal 'amley. I gave 'im some o' your toffees last
night, an' we was talkin' about you. I'll fill it, in case you feel
like some more.'

Bourne took it, thanking him, and lounged off. There was now
a little more movement in the camp, and when he got back to
his own tent he found all the occupants awake, enjoying a
moment of indecision before they elected to dress. He poured
some tea into Corporal Hamley's tin, and then gave some to
Martlow and there was about a third left.

'Who wants tea?' he said.

'I do,' said Weeper Smart, and in his blue shirt with cuffs
unbuttoned and white legs sprawled out behind him, he lunged
awkwardly across the tent, holding out his dixie with one hand.
Smart was an extraordinary individual, with the clumsy agility
of one of the greater apes; though the carriage of his head rather
suggested the vulture, for the neck projected from wide, sloping
shoulders, rounded to a stoop; the narrow forehead, above

arched eyebrows, and the chin, under loose pendulous lips, both receded abruptly, and the large, fleshy beak, jutting forward between protruding blue eyes, seemed to weigh down the whole face. His skin was an unhealthy white, except at the top of the nose and about the nostrils, where it had a shiny redness, as though he suffered from an incurable cold: it was rather pimply. An almost complete beardlessness made the lack of pigmentation more marked, and even the fine, sandy hair of his head grew thinly. It would have been the face of an imbecile, but for the expression of unmitigated misery in it, or it would have been a tragic face if it had possessed any element of nobility; but it was merely abject, a mask of passive suffering, at once pitiful and repulsive. It was inevitable that men, living day by day with such a spectacle of woe, should learn in self-defence to deride it; and it was this sheer necessity which had impelled some cruel wit of the camp to fling at him the name of Weeper, and make that forlorn and cadaverous figure the butt of an endless jest. He gulped his tea, and his watery eyes turned towards Bourne with a cunning malevolence.

'What I say is, that if any o' us'ns tried scrounging round the cookers, we'd be for it.'

Bourne looked at him with a slightly contemptuous tolerance, gathered his shaving-tackle together, flung his dirty towel over his shoulder, and set off again in the direction of the cookers to scrounge for some hot water. He could do without the necessaries of life more easily than without some small comforts . . .

——

'. . . men are strictly forbidden to stop for the purpose of assisting wounded . . .'

The slight stiffening of their muscles may have been imperceptible, for the monotonous inflexion did not vary as the reader delivered a passage, in which it was stated that the staff considered they had made all the arrangements necessary to effect this humanitarian, but somewhat irrelevant, object.

'. . . you may be interested to know,' and this was slightly stressed, as though to overbear a doubt, 'that it is estimated we shall have one big gun – I suppose that means hows. and heavies – for every hundred square yards of ground we are attacking.'

An attack delivered on a front of twenty miles, if completely successful, would mean penetrating to a depth of from six to seven miles, and the men seemed to be impressed by the weight of metal with which it was intended to support them. Then the officer came to the concluding paragraph of the instructional letter.

'It is not expected that the enemy will offer any very serious resistance at this point . . .'

There came a whisper scarcely louder than a sigh.

'What fuckin' 'opes we've got!'

The still small voice was that of Weeper Smart, clearly audible to the rest of the section, and its effect was immediate. The nervous tension, which had gripped every man, was suddenly snapped, and the swift relief brought with it an almost hysterical desire to laugh, which it was difficult to suppress. Whether Captain Thompson also heard the voice of the Weeper, and what construction he may have placed on the sudden access of emotion in the ranks, it was impossible to say. Abruptly, he called them to attention, and after a few seconds, during which he stared at them impersonally, but with great severity, the men were dismissed. As they moved off, Captain Thompson called Corporal Hamley to him.

'Where will some of us poor buggers be come next Thursday?' demanded Weeper of the crowded tent, as he collapsed into his place; and looking at that caricature of grief, their laughter, high-pitched and sardonic, which had been stifled on parade, found vent.

'Laugh, you silly fuckers!' he cried in vehement rage. 'Yes, you laugh now! You'll be laughing the other side o' your bloody mouths when you 'ear all Krupp's fuckin' iron-foundry comin' over! Laugh! One big gun to every bloody 'undred yards, an' don't expect any serious resistance from the enemy! Take us for a lot o' bloody kids, they do! 'aven't we been up the line and . . .'

'You shut your blasted mouth, see!' said the exasperated Corporal Hamley, stooping as he entered the tent, the lift of his head, with chin thrust forward as he stooped, giving him a more desperately aggressive appearance. 'An' you let me 'ear you talkin' on parade again with an officer present and you'll be on the bloody mat, quick. See? You miserable bugger, you! A bloody cow like you's sufficient to demoralize a whole fuckin' army corps. Got it? Get those buzzers out, and do some bloody work, for a change' . . .

———

. . . It's no manner o' use us sittin' 'ere pityin' ourselves, an' blaming God for our own faults. I've got nowt to say again Mr

Rhys. 'e talks about liberty, an' fightin' for your country, an' posterity, an' so on; but what I want to know is what all us'ns are fightin' for . . .'

'We're fightin' for all we've bloody got,' said Madeley, bluntly.

'An' that's sweet fuck all,' said Weeper Smart. 'A tell thee, that all a want to do is to save me own bloody skin. An' the first thing a do, when a go into t'line, is to find out where t'bloody dressing-stations are; an' if a can get a nice blighty, chaps, when once me face is turned towards home, I'm laughing. You won't see me bloody arse for dust. A'm not proud. A tell thee straight. Them as thinks different can 'ave all the bloody war they want, and me own share of it, too.'

'Well, what the 'ell did you come out for?' asked Madeley.

Weeper lifted up a large, spade-like hand with the solemnity of one making an affirmation.

'That's where th'ast got me beat, lad,' he admitted. 'When a saw all them as didn't know any better'n we did joinin' up, an' a went walkin' out wi' me girl on Sundays, as usual, a just felt ashamed. An' a put it away, an' a put it away, until in th' end it got me down. I knew what it'd be, but it got the better o' me, an' then, like a bloody fool, a went an' joined up too. A were ashamed to be seen walkin' in the streets, a were. But a tell thee, now, that if a were once out o' these togs and in civvies again, a wouldn't mind all the shame in the world; no, not if I'ad to slink through all the back streets, an' didn't dare put my nose in t'Old Vaults again. A've no pride left in me now, chaps, an' that's the plain truth a'm tellin'. Let them as made the war come an' fight it, that's what a say' . . .

———

. . . 'They're all in it wi' us, now, an' one man's no better nor another,' said Weeper, when Humphreys said something about Mr Rhys being a bit rattled. 'They can do nowt wi'out us'ns; an', gentle-folk an' all, we all stan' the same chance now.'

The thought of that equality seemed to console him. The change in him was perhaps more apparent than real; all his pessimism and melancholy remained, but now his determination emerged from it. Looking at that lean, ungainly, but extraordinarily powerful figure, with the abnormally long arms and huge hands, one realized that he might be a very useful man in a fight. And yet there was nothing of cruelty in him. The unbounded pity he felt for himself did, in spite of his envious and embittered nature, extend to others. Glazier was the kind of person who killed automatically, without either premeditation or remorse, but Weeper was a very different type. He dreaded the thought of killing, and was haunted by the memory of it; and yet there was a kind of fatalism in him now, as though he were the instrument of justice, prepared for any gruesome business confronting him.

———

... One of the fugitives charged down on Jakes, and that short but stocky fighter smashed the butt of his rifle into the man's jaw, and sent him sprawling. Bourne had a vision of Sergeant-Major Glasspool.

'You take your fuckin' orders from Fritz!' he shouted as a triumphant frenzy thrust him forward.

For a moment they might have broken and run themselves, and for a moment they might have fought men of their own blood, but they struggled on as Sergeant Tozer yelled at them to leave that bloody tripe alone and get on with it. Bourne, floundering in the viscous mud, was at once the most abject and the most exalted of God's creatures. The effort and rage in him, the sense that others had left them to it, made him pant and sob, but there was some strange intoxication of joy in it, and again all his mind seemed focused into one hard, bright point of action. The extremities of pain and pleasure had met and coincided too.

He knew, they all did, that the barrage had moved too quickly for them, but they knew nothing of what was happening about them. In any attack, even under favourable conditions, the attackers are soon blinded; but here they had lost touch almost from the start. They paused for a brief moment, and Bourne saw that Mr Finch was with them, and Shem was not. Minton told him Shem had been hit in the foot. Bourne moved closer to Martlow. Their casualties, as far as he could judge, had not been heavy. They got going again, and, almost before they saw it, were on the wire. The stakes had been uprooted, and it was smashed and tangled, but had not been well cut. Jakes ran along it a little way, there was some firing, and bombs were hurled at them from the almost obliterated trench, and they answered by lobbing a few bombs over, and then plunging desperately among the steel briars, which tore at their puttees and trousers. The last strand of it was cut or beaten down, some more bombs came at them, and in the last infuriated rush Bourne was knocked off his feet and went practically headlong into the trench; getting up, another man jumped on his shoulders, and they both fell together, yelling with rage at each other. They heard a few squeals of agony, and he saw a dead German, still kicking his heels on the broken boards of the trench at his feet. He yelled for the man who had knocked him down to come on, and followed the others. The trench was almost obliterated: it was nothing but a wreckage of boards and posts, piled confusedly in what had become a broad channel for the oozing mud. They heard some more bombing a few bays farther on, and then were turned back. They met two prisoners, their hands up, and almost unable to stand from fear, while two of the men threatened them with a deliberate, slow cruelty.

'Give 'em a chance! Send 'em through their own bloody barrage!' Bourne shouted, and they were practically driven out of the trench and sent across no man's land.

On the other flank they found nothing; except for the handful of men they had encountered at first, the trench was empty. Where they had entered the trench, the three first lines converged rather closely, and they thought they were too far right. In spite of the party of Germans they had met, they assumed that the other waves of the assaulting troops were ahead of them, and decided to push on immediately, but with some misgivings. They were now about twenty-four men. In the light, the fog was coppery and charged with fumes. They heard in front of them the terrific battering of their own barrage and the drumming of the German guns. They had only moved a couple of yards from the trench, when there was a crackle of musketry. Martlow was perhaps a couple of yards in front of Bourne, when he swayed a little, his knees collapsed under him, and he pitched forward on to his face, his feet kicking and his whole body convulsive for a moment. Bourne flung himself down beside him, and, putting his arms round his body, lifted him, calling him.

'Kid! You're all right, kid?' he cried eagerly.

He was all right. As Bourne lifted the limp body, the boy's hat came off, showing half the back of his skull shattered where the bullet had come through it; and a little blood welled out on to Bourne's sleeve and the knee of his trousers. He was all right; and Bourne let him settle to earth again, lifting himself up almost indifferently, unable to realize what had happened, filled with a kind of tenderness that ached in him, and yet

298

extraordinarily still, extraordinarily cold. He had to hurry, or he would be alone in the fog. Again he heard some rifle-fire, some bombing, and, stooping, he ran towards the sound, and was by Minton's side again, when three men ran towards them, holding their hands up and screaming; and he lifted his rifle to his shoulder and fired; and the ache in him became a consuming hate that filled him with exultant cruelty, and he fired again, and again. The last man was closest to him, but as drunk and staggering with terror. He had scarcely fallen, when Bourne came up to him and saw that his head was shattered, as he turned it over with his boot. Minton looking at him with a curious anxiety, saw Bourne's teeth clenched and bared, the lips snarling back from them in exultation.

'Come on. Get into it,' Minton cried in his anxiety.

And Bourne struggled forward again, panting, and muttering in a suffocated voice.

'Kill the buggers . . .! Kill the bloody fucking swine! Kill them!'

All the filth and ordure he had ever heard came from between his clenched teeth; but his speech was thick and difficult. In a scuffle immediately afterwards a Hun went for Minton, and Bourne got him with the bayonet, under the ribs near the liver, and then, unable to wrench the bayonet out again, pulled the trigger, and it came away easily enough.

'Kill the bastards!' he muttered thickly.

He ran against Sergeant Tozer in the trench.

'Steady, ol' son! Steady. 'ave you been 'it? You're all over blood.'

'They killed the kid,' said Bourne, speaking with sudden clearness, though his chest heaved enormously. 'They killed him. I'll kill every bugger I see.'

'Steady. You stay by me. I want you. Mr Finch 'as been 'it, see? You two come as well. Where's that bloody bomber?' . . .

—

. . . Weeper was ahead when he and Bourne reached the gap in the wire. Star-shell after star-shell was going up now, and the whole line had woken up. Machine-guns were talking; but there was one that would not talk. The rattle of musketry continued, but the mist was kindly to them, and had thickened again. As they got beyond the trammelling, clutching wire, Bourne saw Weeper a couple of paces ahead of him, and what he thought was the last of their party disappearing into the mist about twenty yards away. He was glad to be clear of the wire. Another star-shell went up, and they both froze into stillness under its glare. Then they moved again, hurrying for all they were worth. Bourne felt a sense of triumph and escape thrill in him. Anyway the Hun couldn't see them now. Something kicked him, in the upper part of the chest, rending its way through him, and his agonized cry was scarcely audible in the rush of blood from his mouth, as he collapsed and fell.

Weeper turned his head over his shoulder, listened, stopped, and went back. He found Bourne trying to lift himself; and Bourne spoke, gasping, suffocating.

'Go on. I'm scuppered.'

'A'll not leave thee,' said Weeper.

He stooped and lifted the other in his huge, ungainly arms, carrying him as tenderly as though he were a child. Bourne struggled wearily to speak, and the blood, filling his mouth, prevented him. Sometimes his head fell on Weeper's shoulder. At last, barely articulate, a few words came.

'I'm finished. Le' me in peace, for God's sake. You can't . . .'

'A'll not leave thee,' said Weeper in an infuriate rage.

He felt Bourne stretch himself in a convulsive shudder, and relax, becoming suddenly heavier in his arms. He struggled on, stumbling over the shell-ploughed ground through that fantastic mist, which moved like an army of wraiths, hurrying away from him. Then he stopped, and taking the body by the waist with his left arm, flung it over his shoulder, steadying it with his right. He could see their wire now, and presently he was challenged, and replied. He found the way through the wire, and staggered into the trench with his burden. Then he turned down the short stretch of Delaunay to Monk Trench, and came on the rest of the party outside A Company's dug-out.

'A've brought 'im back,' he cried desperately, and collapsed with the body on the duckboards. Picking himself up again, he told his story incoherently, mixed with raving curses.

'What are you gibbering about?' said Sergeant Morgan. ''aven't you ever seen a dead man before?'

Sergeant-Major Tozer, who was standing outside the dug-out, looked at Morgan with a dangerous eye. Then he put a hand on Weeper's shoulder.

'Go down an' get some 'ot tea and rum, ol' man. That'll do you good. I'd like to 'ave a talk with you when you're feelin' better.'

'We had better move on, Sergeant,' said Mr Cross, quietly.

'Very good, sir.'

The party moved off, and for a moment Sergeant-Major Tozer was alone in the trench with Sergeant Morgan.

'I saw him this side of their wire, Sergeant-Major, and thought everything would be all right. 'pon my word, I would 'ave gone back for 'im myself, if I'd known.'

'It was hard luck,' said Sergeant-Major Tozer with a quiet fatalism.

Sergeant Morgan left him; and the sergeant-major looked at the dead body propped against the side of the trench. He would have to have it moved; it wasn't a pleasant sight, and he bared his teeth in the pitiful repulsion with which it filled him. Bourne was sitting: his head back, his face plastered with mud, and blood drying thickly about his mouth and chin, while the glazed eyes stared up at the moon. Tozer moved away, with a quiet acceptance of the fact. It was finished. He was sorry about Bourne, he thought, more sorry than he could say. He was a queer chap, he said to himself, as he felt for the dug-out steps. There was a bit of a mystery about him; but then, when you come to think of it, there's a bit of a mystery about all of us.

FRANK RICHARDS

Frank Richards (1883–1961). He was a private in the Royal Welch Fusiliers, and *Old Soldiers Never Die* contains references to both Graves and Sassoon, with whom he served. Holger Klein considers Richards's war 'flat and "unreal"', because of his lack of literary skill (*The First World War and Fiction*). On the other hand, Bernard Bergonzi sees the book as 'colloquial, salty, sardonic ... Richards's tough and comic narrative recalls the long-suffering humour of Shakespeare's humble soldiers' (*Heroes' Twilight*). After regular army service in India, Richards was a private at the front for most of the First World War.

Source: Frank Richards, *Old Soldiers Never Die*, with an introduction by Robert Graves, London, Faber, 1933 (reprinted 1970).

... One of our chaps who spoke a little French told the landlord what Billy required. The wine was brought but we did not care for it very much, so we left for another café. I remonstrated with Billy and told him we could not treat the French who were our allies the same as we treated the eastern races. He said: 'Look here, Dick, there is only one way to treat foreigners from Hong Kong to France, and that is to knock hell out of them.' Billy and I spent a very enjoyable evening and the two young ladies who we picked up with proved true daughters of France. Billy said that Rouen was a damned fine place and he hoped that we would be stationed there until the war finished. I went out by myself the following evening, Billy being on guard. Going by the cathedral I struck up an acquaintance with a young English lady who informed me that she was an English governess to a well-to-do French family in Rouen. She took me around Rouen, showing me the places of interest and informed me that the opinion of the upper and middle classes of Rouen was that Great Britain had only come into the war for what she could make out if it, and that if she could see there was nothing to be gained she would soon withdraw her army that she was now sending over ...

. . . In those early days British soldiers could get anything they wanted and were welcomed everywhere, but as the war progressed they were only welcomed if they had plenty of money to spend, and even then they were made to pay through the nose for everything they bought.

———

. . . We could now see the effects of our night's work: a lot of the enemy dead lay out in front. One of the men in our left platoon threw his equipment off, jumped on the parapet with his hands above his head and then pointed to a wounded German who was trying to crawl to our lines. He then went forward, got hold of the wounded man and carried him in, the enemy clapping their hands and cheering until he had disappeared into our trench . . .

———

. . . Many a day-sentry had been drilled through the head before periscopes had been introduced. One morning Stevens and I were watching a man fixing a hand-pump; the trench at this point took a sharp turn to our right front and we were on the corner. It was Berry, the man who had that bullet in his haversack on the Marne. He had his boots, socks and puttees off, with his trousers rolled up above his knees, and his language was delightful to listen to. Soon he slipped on his back in the water and we burst out laughing. Then suddenly Stevens too dropped down in a sitting position with his back against the back of the trench; but this was no laughing matter. A sniper on our right front had got him right through the head. No man ever spoke who was shot clean through the brain: some lived a few seconds and others longer. Stevens lived about fifteen minutes. We buried him that night in Bois Grenier cemetery. He was a married man with children and one of the cleanest white men I ever met. He was different to the majority of us, and during the time he was in France never looked at another woman and he could have had plenty of them in some of the places we were in, especially during our first fortnight in France . . .

———

There were no hard and fast rules as regards sniping, and although we had one recognized company sniper any man could go sniping if he wished to. I felt very sore after Stevens and for a number of days I spent many hours in that sniping-post. A man needed plenty of patience when sniping and might wait hours before he could see a man to fire at. I was very fortunate on two days and felt that I had amply revenged Stevens. We could always tell when a man had been hit by an expanding bullet, which caused a frightful wound. Whenever one of our men got shot by one of those bullets, some of us would cut off the tips of our own bullets which made them expanding and then go on sniping with them. It would be very difficult to decide which side used those bullets first, but one man of ours whom I knew very well never went sniping unless he had cut the tips of his bullets off . . .

We were all coughing and sneezing and some of my company were soon gas cases. One of my old platoon, Private Dale, was coughing very badly and also vomiting: a man by the name of Morris was ordered to assist him down to the casualty clearing station. Two months later Dale rejoined the battalion and told me that when they arrived at the casualty clearing station Morris dug up a cough from somewhere that would take some beating and the doctor, who was very busy, evacuated the both of them as gas cases. Travelling down to one of the base hospitals Morris told Dale that he was not gassed but he was going to try and work it to get home. On arrival at the base hospital Morris dug up a series of coughs that were as loud as high shrapnel exploding, and also commenced retching. In less than twenty-four hours he was in England as a bad gas case. Dale himself had not been further than the base hospital and the base camp before being sent up the line again. Four months later he was severely wounded at Givenchy . . .

During the whole of that night the company were employed bringing in the wounded and dead and the enemy didn't fire a shot during the whole of the night. The dead that were too far out were left. Young Mr Graves worked like a Trojan in this work and when I saw him late in the night he looked thoroughly exhausted. He was helping to get a stretcher down in the trench when a sentry near him forgot orders and fired a round. Mr Graves called him a damned fool and wanted to know why he was starting the bloody war again. He told a few of us outside the signallers' dug-out in the trench how bravely Major Samson had died. He had found him with his two thumbs in his mouth which he had very nearly bitten through to save himself crying out in his agony, and also not to attract enemy fire on some of the lightly wounded men that were laying around him. Some of the men as they died had stiffened in different attitudes. One was on his knees in a boxing attitude and another had died with his right hand pointing straight in front of him. (I remember a man on the Arras front in 1917 who was down on one knee with his rifle at his shoulder as if he was about to fire. He must have died at that moment and stiffened in that position . . .)

———

It was a glorious summer morning the next day and anyone who had visited this part of the front would have thought it was the most peaceful spot in France. No shells coming over, no reports of rifles, and the larks were up singing beautifully. It was generally like this after a show. A staff colonel from the corps visited the front line to see the crater, and a few old soldiers put the dead German officer on a fire-step, fixing a lighted candle in one of his hands and a small pocket Bible in the other. Just as the staff officer approached them they fixed a lighted cigarette in his mouth. The staff officer didn't stay long in that part of the trench. This was done out of no disrespect to the dead German officer, but just to give the staff officer a shock; who I don't expect would have come up to the front line if the enemy had been shelling it. We all hated the sight of staff officers and the only damned thing the majority seemed to be any good at was to check men who were out of action for not saluting them properly. The big mine-crater was afterwards called Red Dragon Crater, after our regimental badge. A prisoner told one of our chaps that the German officer was the bravest and most popular officer in the whole of the Jaeger Battalion to which he belonged. The same chaps that had propped him up on the fire-step also gave him a decent burial about thirty yards behind the back of the trench . . .

———

The following morning one hundred bombers of the battalion under the command of Mr Sassoon were sent to the Cameronians to assist in a bombing attack on the Hindenburg Trench on our right. A considerable part of it was captured but was lost again during the day when the enemy made a counter-attack. During the operations Mr Sassoon was shot through the top of the shoulder. Late in the day I was conversing with an old soldier and one of the few survivors of old B Company who had taken part in the bombing raid. He said, 'God strike me pink, Dick, it would have done your eyes good to have seen young Sassoon in that bombing stunt. He put me in mind of Mr Fletcher. It was a bloody treat to see the way he took the lead. He was the best officer I have seen in the line or out since Mr Fletcher, and it's wicked how the good officers get killed or wounded and the rotten ones are still left crawling about. If he don't get the Victoria Cross for this stunt I'm a bloody Dutchman; he thoroughly earned it this morning.' This was the universal opinion of everyone who had taken part in the stunt, but the only decoration Mr Sassoon received was a decorated shoulder where the bullet went through. He hadn't been long with the battalion, but long enough to win the respect of every man that knew him . . .

———

Our new Church of England chaplain was in the sunken road to see what he could do for the wounded. He was a powerfully built man and looked strong enough to carry a Lewis gun in each hand as easily as an ordinary man could carry a rifle. If he had said to one of the weaklings in the battalion, 'Here, son, give me your rifle and equipment: you are weaker than I and I will take your place in the attack,' no doubt the One above would have considered it a very Christian act and would have amply rewarded him if he had gone west. But he never said anything of that order at all. The clergy on both sides were a funny crowd: they prayed for victory and thundered from the pulpits for the enemy to be smitten hip and thigh, but did not believe in doing any of the smiting themselves. They were all non-combatants with the exception of the Catholic priests who were forced to serve in the French Army the same as anybody else . . .

———

I found the frail Wesleyan minister I have mentioned with this company. I liked him very much, although he had chastized me several times for my language. I told him the attack would start in about five minutes and he told me that he was going over with the first wave of attacking troops, so that he could attend the wounded as soon as they were hit. I told him that he was different from all the chaplains of my experience and that I admired his pluck but not his sense. It would be far better if he waited a few minutes until after the first wave had gone over; then he would be able to go forward and attend the wounded. But if he went over with the first wave it was quite possible he would get knocked out himself and would not be able to attend anyone. He would not take my advice and went over with the first wave, dropping dead before he had run ten paces. This company lost a third of their men by machine-gun fire before they entered the village.

ROBERT GRAVES

Robert Graves (1895–1985). Born in London. Educated at
Charterhouse and St John's College, Oxford. Served with the
Royal Welch Fusiliers in the war. His war experiences were
recorded in *Goodbye to All That: An Autobiography* (1929), from
which the excerpt below is taken. The interested reader may
compare Graves's account (here) of Sassoon's protest against
the war with Sassoon's own account (see below).

Source: Robert Graves, *Goodbye to All That*, London, Jonathan
Cape, 1929; revised edn Cassell, 1957; Penguin Books, 1960.

[1915]

. . . Going towards company headquarters to wake the officers I
saw a man lying on his face in a machine-gun shelter. I stopped
and said: 'Stand to, there!' I flashed my torch on him and saw
that one of his feet was bare.

The machine-gunner beside him said: 'No good talking to
him, sir.'

I asked: 'What's wrong? Why has he taken his boot and sock
off?'

'Look for yourself, sir!'

I shook the sleeper by the arm and noticed suddenly the hole
in the back of his head. He had taken off the boot and sock to
pull the trigger of his rifle with one toe; the muzzle was in his
mouth.

'Why did he do it?' I asked.

'He went through the last push, sir, and that sent him a bit
queer; on top of that he got bad news from Limerick about his
girl and another chap' . . .

———

. . . A corpse is lying on the fire-step waiting to be taken down to
the graveyard tonight: a sanitary-man, killed last night in the
open while burying lavatory stuff between our front and support
lines. His arm was stretched out stiff when they carried him in

and laid him on the fire-step; it stretched right across the trench. His comrades joke as they push it out of the way to get by. 'Out of the light, you old bastard! Do you own this bloody trench?' Or else they shake hands with him familiarly. 'Put it there, Billy Boy.' Of course, they're miners, and accustomed to death. They have a very limited morality, but they keep to it. It's moral, for instance, to rob anyone of anything, except a man in their own platoon. They treat every stranger as an enemy until he proves himself their friend, and then there's nothing they won't do for him. They are lecherous, the young ones at least, but without the false shame of the English lecher. I had a letter to censor the other day, written by a lance-corporal to his wife. He said that the French girls were nice to sleep with, so she mustn't worry on his account, but that he far preferred sleeping with her and missed her a great deal . . .

———

9 June

I am beginning to realize how lucky I was in my gentle introduction to the Cambrin trenches. We are now in a nasty salient, a little to the south of the brick-stacks, where casualties are always heavy. The company had seventeen casualties yesterday from bombs and grenades. The front trench averages thirty yards from the Germans. Today, at one part, which is only twenty yards away from an occupied German sap, I went along whistling 'The Farmer's Boy', to keep up my spirits, when suddenly I saw a group bending over a man lying at the bottom of the trench. He was making a snoring noise mixed with animal groans. At my feet lay the cap he had worn, splashed with his brains. I had never seen human brains before; I somehow regarded them as a poetical figment. One can joke with a badly-wounded man and congratulate him on being out of it. One can disregard a dead man. But even a miner can't make a joke that sounds like a joke over a man who takes three hours to die, after the top part of his head has been taken off by a bullet fired at twenty yards' range . . .

———

Like everyone else, I had a carefully worked out formula for taking risks. In principle, we would all take any risk, even the certainty of death, to save life or to maintain an important position. To take life we would run, say, a one-in-five risk, particularly if there was some wider object than merely reducing the enemy's manpower; for instance, picking off a well-known sniper, or getting fire ascendancy in trenches where the lines came dangerously close. I only once refrained from shooting a German I saw, and that was at Cuinchy, some three weeks after this. While sniping from a knoll in the support line, where we had a concealed loop-hole, I saw a German, perhaps seven hundred yards away, through my telescopic sights. He was taking a bath in the German third line. I disliked the idea of shooting a naked man, so I handed the rifle to the sergeant with me. 'Here, take this. You're a better shot than I am.' He got him; but I had not stayed to watch . . .

———

At this point the Royal Welch Fusiliers came up Maison Rouge Alley. The Germans were shelling it with five-nines (called 'Jack Johnsons' because of their black smoke) and lachrymatory shells. This caused a continual scramble backwards and forwards, to cries of: 'Come on!' 'Get back you bastards!' 'Gas turning on us!' 'Keep your heads, you men!' 'Back like hell, boys!' 'Whose orders?' 'What's happening?' 'Gas!' 'Back!' 'Come on!' 'Gas!' 'Back!' Wounded men and stretcher-bearers kept trying to squeeze past. We were alternately putting on and taking off our gas-helmets, which made things worse. In many places the trench had caved in, obliging us to scramble over the top. Childe-Freeman reached the front line with only fifty men of B Company; the rest had lost their way in some abandoned trenches half-way up.

The adjutant met him in the support line. 'Ready to go over, Freeman?' he asked.

Freeman had to admit that he had lost most of his company. He felt this disgrace keenly; it was the first time that he had commanded a company in battle. Deciding to go over with his fifty men in support of the Middlesex, he blew his whistle and the company charged. They were stopped by machine-gun fire before they had got through our own entanglements. Freeman himself died – oddly enough, of heart-failure – as he stood on the parapet.

A few minutes later, Captain Samson, with C Company and the remainder of B, reached our front line. Finding the gas-cylinders still whistling and the trench full of dying men, he decided to go over too – he could not have it said that the Royal

Welch had let down the Middlesex. A strong, comradely feeling bound the Middlesex and the Royal Welch, intensified by the accident that the other three battalions in the brigade were Scottish, and that our Scottish brigadier was, unjustly no doubt, accused of favouring them. Our adjutant voiced the extreme non-Scottish view 'The Jocks are all the same; both the trousered kind and the bare-arsed kind: they're dirty in trenches, they skite too much, and they charge like hell – both ways.' The First Middlesex, who were the original 'Diehards', had more than once, with the Royal Welch, considered themselves let down by the Jocks. So Samson charged with C and the remainder of B Company.

One of C officers told me later what happened. It had been agreed to advance by platoon rushes with supporting fire. When his platoon had gone about twenty yards, he signalled them to lie down and open covering fire. The din was tremendous. He saw the platoon on his left flopping down too, so he whistled the advance again. Nobody seemed to hear. He jumped up from his shell-hole, waved, and signalled 'Forward!'

Nobody stirred.

He shouted: 'You bloody cowards, are you leaving me to go on alone?'

His platoon-sergeant, groaning with a broken shoulder, gasped: 'Not cowards, sir. Willing enough. But they're all f—ing dead.' The Pope's Nose machine-gun, traversing, had caught them as they rose to the whistle.

A Company, too, had become separated by the shelling. I was with the leading platoon. The Surrey man got a touch of gas and went coughing back. The Actor accused him of scrimshanking. This I thought unfair; the Surrey man looked properly sick. I don't know what happened to him, but I heard that the gas-poisoning was not serious and that he managed, a few months later, to get back to his own regiment in France. I found myself with The Actor in a narrow communication trench between the front and support lines. This trench had not been built wide enough for a stretcher to pass the bends. We came on The Boy lying on his stretcher, wounded in the lungs and stomach. Jamaica was standing over him in tears, blubbering: 'Poor old Boy, poor old Boy, he's going to die; I'm sure he is. He's the only one who treated me decently.'

The Actor, finding that we could not get by, said to Jamaica: 'Take that poor sod out of the way, will you? I've got to get my company up. Put him into a dug-out, or somewhere.'

Jamaica made no answer; he seemed paralysed by the horror

of the occasion and kept repeating: 'Poor old Boy, poor old Boy!'

'Look here,' said The Actor, 'if you can't shift him into a dug-out we'll have to lift him on top of the trench. He can't live now, and we're late getting up.'

'No, no,' Jamaica shouted wildly.

The Actor lost his temper and shook Jamaica roughly by the shoulders. 'You're the bloody trench-mortar wallah, aren't you?' he shouted.

Jamaica nodded miserably.

'Well, your battery is a hundred yards from here. Why the hell aren't you using your gas-pipes to some purpose? Buzz off back to them!' And he kicked him down the trench. Then he called over his shoulder: 'Sergeant Rose and Corporal Jennings! Lift this stretcher up across the top of the trench. We've got to pass.'

Jamaica leaned against a traverse. 'I do think you're the most heartless beast I've ever met,' he said weakly . . .

———

. . . On the morning of the 27th a cry arose from no man's land. A wounded soldier of the Middlesex had recovered consciousness after two days. He lay close to the German wire. Our men heard it and looked at each other. We had a tender-hearted lance-corporal named Baxter. He was the man to boil up a special dixie for the sentries of his section when they came off duty. As soon as he heard the wounded Middlesex man, he ran along the trench calling for a volunteer to help fetch him in. Of course, no one would go; it was death to put one's head over the parapet. When he came running to ask me I excused myself as being the only officer in the company. I would come out with him at dusk, I said – not now. So he went alone. He jumped quickly over the parapet, then strolled across no man's land, waving a handkerchief; the Germans fired to frighten him, but since he persisted they let him come up close. Baxter continued towards them and, when he got to the Middlesex man, stopped and pointed to show the Germans what he was at. Then he dressed the man's wounds, gave him drink of rum and some biscuit that he had with him, and promised to be back again at nightfall. He did come back, with a stretcher-party, and the man eventually recovered. I recommended Baxter for the Victoria Cross, being the only officer who had witnessed the action, but the authorities thought it worth no more than a Distinguished Conduct Medal . . .

———

Siegfried Sassoon had, at the time, published only a few privately printed pastoral pieces of eighteen-ninetyish flavour, and a satire on Masefield which, half-way through, had forgotten to be a satire and turned into rather good Masefield. We went to the cake shop and ate cream buns. At this time I was getting my first book of poems, *Over the Brazier*, ready for the press; I had one or two drafts in my pocket-book and showed them to Siegfried. He frowned and said that war should not be written about in such a realistic way. In return, he showed me some of his own poems. One of them began:

> Return to greet me, colours that were my joy,
> Not in the woeful crimson of men slain . . .

Siegfried had not yet been in the trenches. I told him, in my old-soldier manner, that he would soon change his style . . .

———

[1916]

. . . Propaganda reports of atrocities were, it was agreed, ridiculous. We remembered that while the Germans *could* commit atrocities against enemy civilians, Germany itself, except for an early Russian cavalry raid, had never had the enemy on her soil. We no longer believed the highly coloured accounts of German atrocities in Belgium; knowing the Belgians now at first-hand. By atrocities we meant, specifically, rape, mutilation, and torture – not summary shootings of suspected spies, harbourers of spies, *francs-tireurs*, or disobedient local officials. If the atrocity-list had to include the accidental-on-purpose bombing or machine-gunning of civilians from the air, the Allies were now committing as many atrocities as the Germans. French and Belgian civilians had often tried to win our sympathy by exhibiting mutilations of children – stumps of hands and feet, for instance – representing them as deliberate, fiendish atrocities when, as likely as not, they were merely the results of shell-fire. We did not believe rape to be any more common on the German side of the line than on the Allied side. And since a bully-beef diet, fear of death, and absence of wives made ample provision of women necessary in the occupied areas, no doubt the German army authorities provided brothels in the principal French towns behind the line, as the French did on the Allied side. We did not believe stories of women's forcible enlistment in these establishments. 'What's wrong with the voluntary system?' we asked cynically.

As for atrocities against soldiers – where should one draw the line? The British soldier, at first, regarded as atrocious the use of bowie-knives by German patrols. After a time, he learned to use them himself; they were cleaner killing weapons than revolvers or bombs. The Germans regarded as equally atrocious the British Mark VII rifle bullet, which was more apt to turn on striking than the German bullet. For true atrocities, meaning personal rather than military violations of the code of war, few opportunities occurred – except in the interval between the surrender of prisoners and their arrival (or non-arrival) at headquarters. Advantage was only too often taken of this opportunity. Nearly every instructor in the mess could quote specific instances of prisoners having been murdered on the way back. The commonest motives were, it seems, revenge for the death of friends or relatives, jealousy of the prisoner's trip to a comfortable prison camp in England, military enthusiasm, fear of being suddenly overpowered by the prisoners, or, more simply, impatience with the escorting job. In any of these cases the conductors would report on arrival at headquarters that a German shell had killed the prisoners; and no questions would be asked. We had every reason to believe that the same thing happened on the German side, where prisoners, as useless mouths to feed in a country already short of rations, would be even less welcome. None of us had heard of German prisoners being more than threatened at headquarters to get military information from them. The sort that they could give was not of sufficient importance to make torture worth while; and anyhow, it had been found that, when treated kindly, prisoners were anxious in gratitude to tell as much as they knew. German intelligence officers had probably discovered that too.

The troops with the worst reputation for acts of violence against prisoners were the Canadians (and later the Australians). The Canadians' motive was said to be revenge for a Canadian found crucified with bayonets through his hands and feet in a German trench. This atrocity had never been substantiated; nor did we believe the story, freely circulated, that the Canadians crucified a German officer in revenge shortly afterwards. How far this reputation for atrocities was deserved, and how far it could be ascribed to the overseas habit of bragging and leg-pulling, we could not decide. At all events, most overseas men, and some British troops, made atrocities against prisoners a boast, not a confession.

Later in the war, I heard two first-hand accounts.

A Canadian-Scot: 'They sent me back with three bloody prisoners, you see, and one started limping and groaning, so I had to keep on kicking the sod down the trench. He was an officer. It was getting dark and I felt fed up, so I thought: "I'll have a bit of a game." I had them covered with the officer's revolver and made 'em open their pockets without turning round. Then I dropped a Mills bomb in each, with the pin out, and ducked behind a traverse. Bang, bang, bang! No more bloody prisoners. No good Fritzes but dead 'uns.'

An Australian: 'Well, the biggest lark I had was at Morlancourt, when we took it the first time. There were a lot of Jerries in a cellar, and I said to 'em: "Come out, you Camarades!" So out they came, a dozen of 'em, with their hands up. "Turn out your pockets," I told 'em. They turned 'em out. Watches and gold and stuff, all dinkum. Then I said: "Now back to your cellar, you sons of bitches!" For I couldn't be bothered with 'em. When they were all safely down I threw half a dozen Mills bombs in after 'em. I'd got the stuff all right, and we weren't taking prisoners that day' . . .

———

Siegfried wrote of his joy to hear I was alive again.[1] He had been sent back to England with suspected lung trouble and felt nine parts dead from the horror of the Somme fighting. We agreed to take our leave together at Harlech when I got well enough to travel. I was able to travel in September. We met on Paddington Station. Siegfried bought a copy of *The Times* at the book-stall. As usual, we turned to the casualty list first; and found there the names of practically every officer in the First Battalion, listed as either killed or wounded. Edmund Dadd, killed; his brother Julian, in Siegfried's Company, wounded – shot through the throat, as we learned later, only able to talk in a whisper, and for months utterly prostrated. It had happened at Ale Alley near Ginchy, on 3 September. A dud show, with the battalion outflanked by a counter-attack. News like this in England was far more upsetting than in France. Still feeling very weak, I could not help crying all the way up to Wales. Siegfried complained bitterly: 'Well, old Stockpot got his CB at any rate!'

England looked strange to us returned soldiers. We could not understand the war-madness that ran wild everywhere, looking for a pseudo-military outlet. The civilians talked a foreign language; and it was newspaper language. I found serious conversation with my parents all but impossible. Quotations from a single typical document of this time will be enough to show what we were facing:

A MOTHER'S ANSWER TO 'A COMMON SOLDIER'

By A Little Mother

A Message to the Pacifists.   *A Message to the Bereaved.*

A Message to the Trenches.

Owing to the immense demand from home and from the trenches for this letter, which appeared in *The Morning Post*, the Editor found it necessary to place it in the hands of London publishers to be reprinted in pamphlet form, seventy-five thousand copies of which were sold in less than a week direct from the publishers.

Extract from a letter from Her Majesty

The Queen was deeply touched at the 'Little Mother's' beautiful letter, and Her Majesty fully realizes what her words must mean to our soldiers in the trenches and in hospitals.

To the Editor of 'The Morning Post'

Sir, – As a mother of an only child – a son who was early and eager to do his duty – may I be permitted to reply to Tommy Atkins, whose letter appeared in your issue of the 9th inst.? Perhaps he will kindly convey to his friends in the trenches, not what the government thinks, not what the pacifists think, but what the mothers of the British race think of our fighting men. It is a voice which demands to be heard, seeing that we play the most important part in the history of the world, for it is we who 'mother the men' who have to uphold the honour and traditions not only of our Empire but of the whole civilized world.

To the man who pathetically calls himself a 'common soldier', may I say that we women, who demand to be heard, will tolerate no such cry as 'Peace! Peace!' where there is no peace. The corn that will wave over land watered by the blood of our brave lads shall testify to the future that their blood was not spilt in vain. We need no marble monuments to remind us. We only need that force of character behind all motives to see this monstrous world tragedy brought to a victorious ending. The blood of the dead and the dying, the blood of the 'common soldier' from his 'slight wounds' will not cry to us in vain. They have all done their share, and we, as women, will do ours without murmuring and without complaint. Send the pacifists to us and we shall very soon show them, and show the world, that in our homes at least there shall be no 'sitting at home warm and cosy in the winter, cool and "comfy" in the summer'. There is only one temperature for the women of the British race, and that is white heat. With those who disgrace their sacred trust of motherhood we have nothing in common. Our ears are not deaf to the cry that is ever ascending from the battlefield from men of flesh and blood whose indomitable courage is borne to us, so to speak, on every blast of the wind. We women pass on the human ammunition of 'only sons' to fill up the gaps, so that when the 'common soldier' looks back before going 'over the top' he may see the women of the British race at his heels, reliable, dependent, uncomplaining.

The reinforcements of women are, therefore, behind the 'common soldier'. We gentle-nurtured, timid sex did not want the war. It is no pleasure to us to have our homes made desolate and the apple of our eye taken away. We would sooner our lovable, promising, rollicking boy stayed at school. We would have much preferred to have gone on in a light-hearted way with our amusements and our hobbies. But the bugle call came, and we have hung up the tennis racquet, we've fetched our laddie from school, we've put his cap away, and we have glanced lovingly over his last report which said 'Excellent' – we've wrapped them all in a Union Jack and locked them up, to be taken out only after the war to be looked at. A 'common soldier', perhaps, did not count on the women, but they have their part to play, and *we* have risen to our responsibility. We are proud of our men, and they in turn have to be proud of us. If the men fail, Tommy Atkins, the women won't.

> Tommy Atkins to the front,
> He has gone to bear the brunt.
> Shall 'stay-at-homes' do naught but snivel and but sigh?
> No, while your eyes are filling
> We are up and doing, willing
> To face the music with you – or to die!

Women are created for the purpose of giving life, and men to take it. Now we are giving it in a double sense. It's not likely we are going to fail Tommy. We shall not flinch one iota, but when the war is over he must not grudge us, when we hear the bugle call of 'Lights out', a brief, very brief, space of time to withdraw into our secret chambers and share, with Rachel the Silent, the lonely anguish of a bereft heart, and to look once more on the college cap, before we emerge stronger women to carry on the glorious work our men's memories have handed down to us for now and all eternity.

Yours, etc.,
A Little Mother

———

... In November, Siegfried and I rejoined the battalion at Litherland, and shared a hut. We decided not to make any public protest against war. Siegfried said that we must 'keep up the good reputation of the poets' – as men of courage, he meant. Our best place would be back in France, away from the more shameless madness of home-service. There, our function would not be to kill Germans, though that might happen, but to make things easier for the men under our command. For them, the difference between being commanded by someone whom they could count as a friend – someone who protected them as much as he could from the grosser indignities of the military system – and having to study the whims of any petty tyrant in an officer's tunic, made all the difference in the world. By this time, the ranks of both line battalions were filled with men who had enlisted for patriotic reasons and resented the professional-soldier tradition ... Siegfried had already shown what he meant. The Fricourt attack was rehearsed over dummy trenches in the back areas until the whole performance, having reached perfection, began to grow stale. Siegfried, ordered to rehearse once more on the day before the attack, led his platoon into a wood and instead read to them – nothing military or literary, just the *London Mail*. Though the *London Mail*, a daring new popular weekly, was hardly in his line, Siegfried thought that the men would enjoy the '*Things We Want To Know*' column.

Officers of the Royal Welch were honorary members of the Formby Golf Club. Siegfried and I went there often. He played golf seriously, while I hit a ball alongside him. I had once played at Harlech as a junior member of the Royal St David's, but resigned when I found it bad for my temper. Afraid of taking the game up again seriously, I now limited myself to a single iron. My mis-hits did not matter. I played the fool and purposely put Siegfried off his game. This was a time of great food shortage; German submarines sank about every fourth food ship, and strict meat, butter, and sugar ration had been imposed. But the war had not reached the links. The leading Liverpool business-men were members of the club, and did not mean to go short while there was any food at all coming in at the docks. Siegfried and I went to the clubhouse for lunch on the day before Christmas, and found a cold-buffet in the club dining-room, offering hams, barons of beef, jellied tongues, cold roast turkey, and chicken. A large, meaty-faced waiter presided. Siegfried asked him sarcastically: 'Is this all? There doesn't seem to be quite such a good spread as in previous years.' The waiter blushed. 'No, sir, this isn't quite up to the usual mark, sir, but we are expecting a more satisfactory consignment of meat on Boxing Day.' The dining-room at the clubhouse was always full, the links practically deserted . . .

. . . At the Bull Ring, the instructors were full of bullet-and-bayonet enthusiasm, with which they tried to infect the drafts. The drafts consisted, for the most part, either of forcibly enlisted men, or wounded men returning; and at this dead season of the year could hardly be expected to feel enthusiastic on their arrival. The training principles had recently been revised. *Infantry Train-ing, 1914*, laid it down politely that the soldier's ultimate aim was to put out of action or render ineffective the armed forces of the enemy. The War Office no longer considered this statement direct enough for a war of attrition. Troops learned instead that they must HATE the Germans, and KILL as many of them as possible. In bayonet-practice, the men had to make horrible grimaces and utter blood-curdling yells as they charged. The in-structors' faces were set in a permanent ghastly grin. 'Hurt him, now! In at the belly! Tear his guts out!' they would scream, as the men charged the dummies. 'Now that upper swing at his privates with the butt. Ruin his chances for life! No more little Fritzes! . . . Naaoh! Anyone would think that you *loved* the bloody swine' . . .

[1917]

. . . Siegfried's platoon went to support the Cameronians, and when these were driven out of some trenches they had won, he regained the position with a bombing-party of six men. Though

319

shot through the throat, he continued bombing until he collapsed. The Cameronians rallied and returned, and the brigadier sent Siegfried's name in for a Victoria Cross – a recommendation refused, however, on the ground that the operations had been unsuccessful; for the Cameronians were later driven out again by a bombing-party under some German Siegfried.

Back in London now, and very ill, he wrote that often when he went for a walk he saw corpses lying about on the pavements. In April, Yates had sent him a note saying that four officers were killed and seven wounded in a show at Fontaine-les-Croiselles – a 'perfectly bloody battle'. But the battalion advanced nearly half a mile which, to Siegfried, seemed some consolation. Yet in the very next sentence he wrote how mad it made him to think of the countless good men being slaughtered that summer, and all for nothing. The bloody politicians and ditto generals with their cursed incompetent blundering and callous ideas would go on until they tired of it or had got as much kudos as they wanted. He wished he could do something in protest, but even if he were to shoot the Premier or Sir Douglas Haig, they would only shut him up in a madhouse like Richard Dadd of glorious memory. (I recognized the allusion. Dadd, a brilliant nineteenth-century painter, and incidentally a great-uncle of Edmund and Julian, had made out a list of people who deserved to be killed. The first on the list was his father. Dadd picked him up one day in Hyde Park and carried him on his shoulders for nearly half a mile before publicly drowning him in the Serpentine.) Siegfried went on to say that if, as a protest, he refused to go out again, they would only accuse him of being afraid of shells. He asked me whether I thought we should be any better off by the end of that summer of carnage. We would never break the German line by hammering at it. So far our losses were heavier than the Germans'. The Canadians at Vimy had suffered appallingly, yet the official *communiqués* told unblushing lies about the casualties. Julian Dadd had visited him in hospital and, like everyone else, urged him to take a safe job at home – but he knew that this could only be a beautiful dream: he would be morally compelled to go on until he got killed. The thought of going back now was agony, just when he had come out into the light again – 'Oh, life, oh, sun!' (A quotation from a poem of mine about my return from the grave.) His wound was nearly healed, and he expected to be sent for three weeks to a convalescent home. He didn't like the idea, but *anywhere* would be good enough if he could only be quiet and see no one, simply watch the trees dressing up in green and feel the same himself. He was beastly weak and in a rotten state of nerves. A gramophone in the ward plagued him beyond endurance. *The Old Huntsman* had come out that spring after all, and for a joke he would send a copy to Sir Douglas Haig. He couldn't be prevented from doing *that* anyhow.

In June, he had visited the Morrells at Oxford, not knowing that I was still there, but wrote that perhaps it was as well we didn't meet, neither of us being at our best; at least one of us should be in a normal frame of mind when we were together. Five poems of his had appeared in *The Cambridge Magazine* (one of the few aggressively pacifist journals published in England at the time, the offices of which were later sacked by Flying Corps cadets). None of them, he admitted, was much good except as a dig at the complacent and perfectly unspeakable people who thought the war ought to go on indefinitely until everyone got killed but themselves. The pacifists were now urging him to produce something red hot in the style of Barbusse's *Under Fire*, but he couldn't do it. He had other things in his head, *not poems*. (I didn't know what he meant by this, but hoped that it was not a Richard Dadd assassination programme.) The thought of France nearly drove him dotty sometimes. Down in Kent he could hear the guns thudding ceaselessly across the Channel, on and on, until he didn't know whether he wanted to rush back and die with the First Battalion, or stay in England and do what he could to prevent the war going on. But both courses were hopeless. To go back and get killed would be only playing to the gallery – the wrong gallery – and he could think of no means of doing any effective preventive work at home. His name had gone in for an officer-cadet battalion appointment in England, which would keep him safe if he pleased; but it seemed a dishonourable way out.

At the end of July, another letter from Siegfried reached me at Osborne. It felt rather thin. I sat down to read it on the bench dedicated by Queen Victoria to John Brown ('A truer and more faithful heart never burned within human breast.'). As I opened the envelope, a newspaper cutting fluttered out, marked in ink: '*Bradford Pioneer*, Friday, 27 July 1917'. I read the wrong side first:

The conscientious objector is a brave man. He will be remembered as one of the few noble actors in this world drama when the impartial historian of the future sums up the history of this awful war.

The CO is putting down militarism. He is fighting for freedom and liberty. He is making a mighty onslaught upon despotism. And, above all, he is preparing the way for the final abolition of war.

But thanks to the lying, corrupt, and dastardly capitalist Press these facts are not known to the general public, who have been taught to look upon the conscientious objectors as skunks, cowards, and shirkers.

Lately a renewed persecution of COs has taken place. In spite of the promises of 'truthful' Cabinet Ministers, some COs have been sent to France, and there sentenced to death – a sentence afterwards transferred to one of 'crucifixion' or five or ten years' hard labour. But even when allowed to remain in this country we have to chronicle the most scandalous treatment of these men – the salt of the earth. Saintly individuals like Clifford Allen, Scott Duckers, and thousands of others, no less splendid enthusiasts in the cause of anti-militarism, are in prison for no other reason than because they refuse to take life; and because they will not throw away their manhood by becoming slaves to the military machine. These men MUST BE FREED.

The political 'offenders' of Ireland ...

Then I turned over and read:

FINISHED WITH THE WAR
A Soldier's Declaration

(This statement was made to his commanding officer by Second-Lieutenant S. L. Sassoon, Military Cross, recommended for DSO, Third Battalion Royal Welch Fusiliers, as explaining his grounds for refusing to serve further in the army. He enlisted on 3 August 1914, showed distinguished valour in France, was badly wounded and would have been kept on home service if he had stayed in the army.) [2]

This filled me with anxiety and unhappiness. I entirely agreed with Siegfried about the 'political errors and insincerities' and thought his action magnificently courageous. But more things had to be considered than the strength of our case against the politicians. In the first place, he was in no proper physical condition to suffer the penalty which the letter invited: namely to be court-martialled, cashiered, and imprisoned. I found myself most bitter with the pacifists who had encouraged him to make this gesture. I felt that, not being soldiers, they could not understand what it cost Siegfried emotionally. It was wicked that he should have to face the consequences of his letter on top of those Quadrangle and Fontaine-les-Croiselles experiences. I also realized the inadequacy of such a gesture. Nobody would follow his example, either in England or in Germany. The war would inevitably go on and on until one side or the other cracked.

I at once applied to appear before a medical board that sat next day; and asked the doctors to pass me fit for home service. I was not fit, and they knew it, but I asked it as a favour. I had to get out of Osborne and attend to this Siegfried business. Next, I wrote to the Hon. Evan Morgan, with whom I had canoed at Oxford a month or two previously, the private secretary to one of the Coalition Ministers. I asked him to do everything possible to prevent republication of, or comment on, the letter; and arrange that a suitable answer should be given to Mr Lees-Smith, the leading pacifist Member of Parliament, when he asked a question about it in the House. I explained to Evan that I was on Siegfried's side really, but that he should not be allowed to become a martyr to a hopeless cause in his present physical condition. Finally, I wrote to the Third Battalion. I knew that Colonel Jones-Williams was narrowly patriotic, had never been to France, and could not be expected to take a sympathetic view. But the second-in-command, Major Macartney-Filgate, was humane; so I pleaded with him to make the colonel see the affair in a reasonable light. I told him of Siegfried's recent experiences in France and suggested that he should be medically boarded and given indefinite leave.

Presently, Siegfried wrote from the Exchange Hotel, Liverpool, that no doubt I was worrying about him. He had come up to Liverpool a day or two before and walked into the Third Battalion orderly room at Litherland, feeling like nothing on earth, but probably looking fairly self-possessed. Major Macartney-Filgate, whom he found in command, the colonel being away on holiday, had been unimaginably decent, making him feel an utter brute, and had consulted the general commanding the Mersey Defences. Now the general was 'consulting God, or someone like that'. Meanwhile, I could write to him at the hotel, because he had promised not to run away to the Caucasus. He hoped, in time, to persuade them to be nasty – they probably didn't realize that his performance would soon be given great publicity. Though he hated the whole business more than ever, he knew more than ever that he was right and would never repent of what he had done. He added that things were looking better in Germany, but that Lloyd George would probably call it a 'plot'. The politicians seemed to him incapable of behaving like human beings.

The general consulted not God but the War Office; and Evan's Minister persuaded the War Office not to press the matter as a disciplinary case, but to give Siegfried a medical board. Evan had done his part well. I next set myself somehow to get Siegfried in front of the medical board. I rejoined the battalion and met him at Liverpool. He looked very ill; he told me that he had just been down to the Formby links and thrown his Military Cross into the sea. We discussed the political situation; I took the line that everyone was mad except ourselves and one or two others, and that no good could come of offering common sense to the insane. Our only possible course would be to keep on going out until we got killed. I expected myself to go back soon, for the fourth time. Besides, what would the First and Second Battalions think of him? How could they be expected to understand his point of view? They would accuse him of ratting, having cold feet, and letting the regiment down. How would Old Joe, even, the most understanding man in the regiment, understand it? To whom was his letter addressed? The army could, I repeated, only read it as cowardice, or at the best as a lapse from good form. The civilians would take an even unkinder view, especially when they found out that 'S.' stood for 'Siegfried'.

He refused to agree with me, but I made it plain that his letter had not been given, and would not be given, the publicity he intended. At last, unable to deny how ill he was, Siegfried consented to appear before the medical board.

So far, so good. Next, I had to rig the medical board. I applied for permission to give evidence as a friend of the patient. There were three doctors on the board – a regular RAMC colonel and major, and a 'duration of the war' captain. I very soon realized that the colonel was patriotic and unsympathetic;

but ignorant; and the captain a competent nerve-specialist, right-minded, and my only hope. I had to go through the whole story again, treating the colonel and major with the utmost deference, but using the captain as an ally to break down their scruples. Much against my will, I had to appear in the rôle of a patriot distressed by the mental collapse of a brother-in-arms – a collapse directly due to his magnificent exploits in the trenches. I mentioned Siegfried's 'hallucinations' of corpses strewn along on Piccadilly. The irony of having to argue to these mad old men that Siegfried was not sane! Though conscious of a betrayal of truth, I acted jesuitically. Being in nearly as bad a state of nerves as Siegfried myself, I burst into tears three times during my statement. Captain McDowell, who proved to be a well-known Harley Street psychologist, played up well. As I went out, he said to me: 'Young man, you ought to be before this board yourself.' I prayed that when Siegfried came into the boardroom after me he would not undo my work by appearing too sane. But McDowell argued his seniors over to my view.

Macartney-Filgate detailed me as Siegfried's escort to a convalescent home for neurasthenics at Craiglockhart, near Edinburgh. Siegfried and I both thought this a great joke, especially when I missed the train and he reported to 'Dottyville', as he called it, without me. At Craiglockhart, Siegfried came under the care of Professor W. H. R. Rivers, whom we now met for the first time, though we already knew him as a leading Cambridge neurologist, ethnologist, and psychologist . . .

1. Graves had been mistakenly reported killed in July 1916.
2. See Sassoon, *Memoirs of an Infantry Officer*, below, p. 331.

SIEGFRIED SASSOON

Siegfried Sassoon (1886–1967). Born in London; educated at Marlborough, the school which Charles Hamilton Sorley also attended, and Cambridge. He served in France from the beginning of the war in the Royal Welch Fusiliers (see also Frank Richards). Before the end of the war he had published a volume of anti-war poems, *Counter-Attack* (1918). His protest against the war is charted in the account below, which is taken from *Memoirs of an Infantry Officer* (1930). This was to become the second volume of the trilogy *The Complete Memoirs of George Sherston* (1937). Sassoon's account of his protest and defection from the army may be compared with Graves's taken from *Goodbye to All That* (1929) on p. 322. Sassoon died in Wiltshire in 1967. 'George Sherston' is Sassoon himself. The 'editor of the *Unconservative Weekly*' is H. J. Massingham (1888–1952) editor of *The Nation*. 'Tyrrell' is Bertrand Russell and 'Cromlech' is Robert Graves.

Source: Siegfried Sassoon, *Memoirs of an Infantry Officer*, London, Faber, 1930; reprinted in *The Complete Memoirs of George Sherston*, London, Faber, 1937.

... It was a case of direct inspiration; I had, so to speak, received the call, and the editor of the *Unconservative Weekly* seemed the most likely man to put me on the shortest road to martyrdom. It really felt very fine, and as long as I was alone my feelings carried me along on a torrent of prophetic phrases. But when I was inside Markington's office (he sitting with fingers pressed together and regarding me with alertly mournful curiosity) my internal eloquence dried up and I began abruptly. 'I say, I've been thinking it all over, and I've made up my mind that I ought to do something about it.' He pushed his spectacles up on to his forehead and leant back in his chair. 'You want to do something?' 'About the war, I mean. I just can't sit still and do nothing. You said the other day that you couldn't print anything really outspoken, but I don't see why I shouldn't make some sort of statement – about how we ought to publish our War Aims and all that and the troops not knowing what they're fighting about. It might do quite a lot of good, mightn't it?' He got up and went to the window. A secretarial typewriter tick-tacked in the next room. While he stood with his back to me I could see the tiny traffic creeping to and fro on Charing Cross Bridge and a barge going down the river in the sunshine. My heart was beating violently. I knew that I couldn't turn back now. Those few moments seemed to last a long time; I was conscious of the stream of life going on its way, happy and untroubled, while I had just blurted out something which alienated me from its acceptance of a fine day in the third June of the Great War. Returning to his chair, he said, 'I suppose you've realized what the results of such an action would be, as regards yourself?' I replied that I didn't care two damns what they did to me as long as I got the thing off my chest. He laughed, looking at me with a gleam of his essential kindness. 'As far as I am aware, you'd be the first soldier to take such a step, which would, of course, be welcomed by the extreme pacifists. Your service at the front would differentiate you from the conscientious objectors. But you must on no account make this gesture – a very fine one if you are really in earnest about it – unless you can carry it through effectively. Such an action would require to be carefully thought out, and for the present I advise you to be extremely cautious in what you say and do.' His words caused me an uncomfortable feeling that perhaps I was only making a fool of myself; but this was soon mitigated by a glowing sense of martyrdom. I saw myself 'attired with sudden brightness, like a man inspired', and while Markington continued his counsels of prudence my resolve strengthened toward its ultimate obstinacy. After further reflection he said that the best man for me to consult was Thornton Tyrrell. 'You know him by name, I suppose?' I was compelled to admit that I didn't. Markington handed me *Who's Who* and began to write a letter while I made myself acquainted with the details of Tyrrell's biographical abridgement, which indicated that he was a pretty tough proposition . . .

—

. . . Tyrrell said very little, his object being to size me up. Having got my mind warmed up, I began to give him a few of my notions about the larger aspects of the war. But he interrupted my 'and after what Markington told me the other day, I must say', with, 'Never mind about what Markington told you. It amounts to this, doesn't it – that you have ceased to believe what you are told about the objects for which you supposed yourself to be fighting?' I replied that it did boil down to something like that, and it seemed to me a bloody shame, the troops getting killed all the time while people at home humbugged themselves into believing that everyone in the trenches enjoyed it. Tyrrell poured me out a second cup of tea and suggested that I should write out a short personal statement based on my conviction that the war was being unnecessarily prolonged by the refusal of the Allies to publish their war aims. When I had done this we could discuss the next step to be taken. 'Naturally I should help you in every way possible,' he said. 'I have always regarded all wars as acts of criminal folly, and my hatred of this one has often made life seem almost unendurable. But hatred makes one vital, and without it one loses energy. "Keep vital" is a more important axiom than "love your neighbour". This act of yours, if you stick to it, will probably land you in prison. Don't let that discourage you. You will be more alive in prison than you would be in the trenches.' Mistaking this last remark for a joke, I laughed, rather half-heartedly. 'No; I mean that seriously,' he said. 'By thinking independently and acting fearlessly on your moral convictions you are serving the world better than you would do by marching with the unthinking majority who are suffering and dying at the front because they believe what they have been told to believe. Now that you have lost your faith in what you enlisted for, I am certain that you should go on and let the consequences take care of themselves. Of course your action would be welcomed by people like myself who are violently opposed to the war. We should print and circulate as many copies of your statement as possible ... But I hadn't intended to speak as definitely as this. You must decide by your own feeling and not by what anyone else says.' I promised to send him my statement when it was written and walked home with my head full of exalted and disorderly thoughts. I had taken a strong liking for Tyrrell, who probably smiled rather grimly while he was reading a few more pages of Kropotkin's *Conquest of Bread* before going upstairs to his philosophic slumbers.

Although Tyrrell had told me that my statement needn't be more than two hundred words long, it took me several days to formulate. At first I felt that I had so much to say that I didn't know where to begin. But after several verbose failures it seemed as though the essence of my manifesto could be stated in a single sentence: 'I say this war ought to stop.' During the struggle to put my unfusilierish opinions into some sort of shape, my confidence often diminished. But there was no relaxation of my inmost resolve, since I was in the throes of a species of conversion which made the prospect of persecution stimulating and almost enjoyable . . .

What could I do if Tyrrell decided to discourage my candidature for a court martial? Chuck up the whole idea and go out again and get myself killed as quick as possible? 'Yes,' I thought, working myself up into a tantrum, 'I'd get killed just to show them all I don't care a damn.' (I didn't stop to specify the identity of 'them all'; such details could be dispensed with when one had lost one's temper with the Great War.) But common sense warned me that getting sent back was a slow business, and getting killed on purpose an irrelevant gesture for a platoon commander. One couldn't choose one's own conditions out in France . . . Tyrrell had talked about 'serving the world by thinking independently'. I must hang on to that idea and remember the men for whom I believed myself to be interceding. I tried to think internationally; the poor old Boches must be hating it just as much as we did; but I couldn't propel my sympathy as far as the Balkan States, Turks, Italians, and all the rest of them; and somehow or other the French were just the French and too busy fighting and selling things to the troops to need my intervention. So I got back to thinking about 'all the good chaps who'd been killed with the First and Second Battalions since I left them' . . . Ormand, dying miserably out in a shell-hole . . . I remembered his exact tone of voice when saying that if his children ever asked what he did in the Great War, his answer would be, 'No bullet ever went quick enough to catch me'; and how he used to sing 'Rock of ages cleft for me, let me hide myself in thee,' when we were being badly shelled. I thought of the typical Flintshire Fusilier at his best, and the vast anonymity of courage and cheerfulness which he represented as he sat in a frontline trench cleaning his mess-tin. How could one connect him with the gross profiteer whom I'd overheard in a railway carriage remarking to an equally repulsive companion that if the war lasted another eighteen months he'd be able to retire from business? . . . How could I coordinate such diversion of human behaviour, or believe that heroism was its own reward? Something must be put on paper, however, and I re-scrutinized the rough notes I'd been making: *Fighting men are victims of conspiracy among (a) politicians; (b) military caste; (c) people who are making money out of the war.* Under this I had scribbled, *Also personal effort to dissociate myself from intolerant prejudice and conventional complacence of those willing to watch sacrifices of others while they sit safely at home.* This was followed by an indignant afterthought. *I believe that by taking this action I am helping to destroy the system of deception, etc., which prevents people from facing the truth and demanding some guarantee that the torture of humanity shall not be prolonged unnecessarily through the arrogance and incompetence of* . . . Here it broke off, and I wondered how many c's there were in 'unnecessarily'. *I am not a conscientious objector. I am a soldier who believes he is acting on behalf of soldiers.* How inflated and unconvincing it all looked! If I wasn't careful I should be yelling like some crank on a barrel in Hyde Park. Well, there was nothing for it but to begin all over again. I couldn't ask Tyrrell to give me a few hints. He'd insisted that I must be independent-minded, and had since written to remind me that I must decide my course of action for myself and not be prompted by anything he'd said to me.

Sitting there with my elbows on the table I stared at the dingy red wallpaper in an unseeing effort at mental concentration. If I stared hard enough and straight enough, it seemed, I should see through the wall. Truth would be revealed, and my brain would become articulate. *I am making this statement as an act of wilful defiance of military authority because I believe that the War is being deliberately prolonged by those who have the power to end it.* That would be all right as a kick-off, anyhow . . .

———

. . . July was now a week old. I had overstayed my leave several days and was waiting until I heard from the Depot. My mental condition was a mixture of procrastination and suspense, but the suspense was beginning to get the upper hand of the procrastination, since it was just possible that the adjutant at Clitherland was assuming that I'd gone straight to Cambridge.

Next morning the conundrum was solved by a telegram, *Report how situated.* There was nothing for it but to obey the terse instructions, so I composed a letter (brief, courteous, and regretful) to the colonel, enclosing a typewritten copy of my statement, apologizing for the trouble I was causing him, and promising to return as soon as I heard from him. I also sent a copy to Dottrell, with a letter in which I hoped that my action would not be entirely disapproved of by the First Battalion. Who else was there, I wondered, feeling rather rattled and confused.

There was Durley, of course, and Cromlech also – fancy my forgetting him! I could rely on Durley to be sensible and sympathetic; and David was in a convalescent hospital in the Isle of Wight, so there was no likelihood of his exerting himself with efforts to dissuade me. I didn't want anyone to begin interfering on my behalf. At least I hoped that I didn't; though there were weak moments later on when I wished they would. I read my statement through once more (though I could have recited it only too easily) in a desperate effort to calculate its effect on the colonel. '*I am making this statement as an act of wilful defiance of military authority, because I believe that the War is being deliberately prolonged by those who have the power to end it. I am a soldier, convinced that I am acting on behalf of soldiers. I believe that this War, upon which I entered as a war of defence and liberation, has now become a war of aggression and conquest. I believe that the purposes for which I and my fellow soldiers entered upon this War should have been so clearly stated as to have made it impossible to change them, and that, had this been done, the objects which actuated us would now be attainable by negotiation. I have seen and endured the sufferings of the troops, and I can no longer be a party to prolong these sufferings for ends which I believe to be evil and unjust. I am not protesting against the conduct of the War, but against the political errors and insincerities for which the fighting men are being sacrificed. On behalf of those who are suffering now I make this protest against the deception which is being practised on them; also I believe that I may help to destroy the callous complacency with which the majority of those at home regard the continuance of agonies which they do not share, and which they have not sufficient imagination to realize.*' It certainly sounds a bit pompous, I thought, and God only knows what the colonel will think of it.

Thus ended a most miserable morning's work. After lunch I walked down the hill to the pillar-box and posted my letters with a feeling of stupefied finality. I then realized that I had a headache and Captain Huxtable was coming to tea. Lying on my bed with the window curtains drawn, I compared the prospect of being in a prison cell with the prosy serenity of this buzzing summer afternoon. I could hear the cooing of the white pigeons and the soft clatter of their wings as they fluttered down to the little bird-bath on the lawn. My sense of the life-learned house and garden enveloped me as though all the summers I had ever known were returning in a single thought. I had felt the same a year ago, but going back to the war next day hadn't been as bad as this . . .

... I had to wait until Thursday before a second Clitherland telegram put me out of my misery. Delivered early in the afternoon and containing only two words, *Report immediately* ...

... Alone in that first-class compartment, I shut my eyes and asked myself out loud what this thing was which I was doing; and my mutinous act suddenly seemed outrageous and incredible. For a few minutes I completely lost my nerve. But the express train was carrying me along; I couldn't stop it, any more than I could cancel my statement. And when the train pulled up at Liverpool I was merely a harassed automaton whose movements were being manipulated by a typewritten manifesto. To put it plainly, I felt 'like nothing on earth' while I was being bumped and jolted out to the camp in a ramshackle taxi ...

After the glaring sunlight, the room seemed almost dark. When I raised my eyes it was not the colonel who was sitting at the table, but Major Macartney. At another table, ostensibly busy with army forms and papers, was the deputy-assistant-adjutant (a good friend of mine who had lost a leg in Gallipoli). I stood there, incapable of expectation. Then, to my astonishment, the major rose, leant across the table, and shook hands with me.

'How are you, Sherston? I'm glad to see you back again.' His deep voice had its usual kindly tone, but his manner betrayed acute embarrassment. No one could have been less glad to see me back again than he was. But he at once picked up his cap and asked me to come with him to his room, which was only a few steps away. Silently we entered the hut, our feet clumping along the boards of the passage. Speechless and respectful, I accepted the chair which he offered me. There we were, in the comfortless little room which had been his local habitation for the past twenty-seven months. There we were; and the unfortunate major hadn't a ghost of an idea what to say.

He was a man of great delicacy of feeling. I have seldom known as fine a gentleman. For him the interview must have been as agonizing as it was for me. I wanted to make things easier for him; but what could I say? And what could he do for me, except, perhaps, offer me a cigar? He did so. I can honestly say that I have never refused a cigar with anything like so much regret. To have accepted it would have been a sign of surrender. It would have meant that the major and myself could have puffed our cigars and debated – with all requisite seriousness, of course – the best way of extricating me from my dilemma. How blissful that would have been! For my indiscretion might positively have been 'laughed off' (as a temporary aberration brought on, perhaps, by an overdose of solitude after coming out of hospital). No such agreeable solution being possible, the major began by explaining that the colonel was away on leave. 'He is deeply concerned about you, and fully prepared to overlook the' – here he hesitated – 'the paper which you sent him. He has asked me to urge you most earnestly to – er – dismiss the whole matter from your mind.' Nothing could have been more earnest than the way he looked at me when he stopped speaking. I replied that I was deeply grateful but I couldn't change my mind. In the ensuing silence I felt that I was committing a breach, not so much of discipline as of decorum.

The disappointed major made a renewed effort. 'But, Sherston, isn't it *possible* for you to reconsider your – er – ultimatum?' This was the first time I'd heard it called an ultimatum, and the locution epitomized the major's inability to find words to fit the situation. I embarked on a floundering explanation of my mental attitude with regard to the war; but I couldn't make it sound convincing, and at the back of my mind was a misgiving that I must seem to him rather crazy. To be telling the acting-colonel of my regimental training depot that I had come to the conclusion that England ought to make peace with Germany – was this altogether in focus with rightmindedness? No; it was useless to expect him to take me seriously as an ultimatumist. So I gazed fixedly at the floor and said, 'Hadn't you better have me put under arrest at once?' – thereby causing poor Major Macartney additional discomfort. My remark recoiled on me, almost as if I'd uttered something unmentionable. 'I'd rather die than do such a thing!' he exclaimed. He was a reticent man, and that was his way of expressing his feeling about those whom he had watched, month after month, going out to the trenches, as he would have gone himself had he been a younger man.

At this point it was obviously his duty to remonstrate with me severely and to assert his authority. But what fulminations could be effective against one whose only object was to be put under arrest? ... 'As long as he doesn't really think I'm dotty!' I thought. But he showed no symptom of that, as far as I was aware; and he was a man who made one feel that he trusted one's integrity, however much he might disagree with one's opinions.

No solution having been arrived at for the present, he now suggested – in confidential tones which somehow implied sympathetic understanding of my predicament – that I should go to the Exchange Hotel in Liverpool and there await further instructions . . .

———

. . . During the next two days my mind groped and worried around the same purgatorial limbo so incessantly that the whole business began to seem unreal and distorted. Sometimes the wording of my thoughts became incoherent and even nonsensical. At other times I saw everything with the haggard clarity of insomnia.

So on Saturday afternoon I decided that I really must go and get some fresh air, and I took the electric train to Formby. How much longer would this ghastly show go on, I wondered, as the train pulled up at Clitherland Station. All I wanted now was that the thing should be taken out of my own control, as well as the colonel's. I didn't care how they treated me as long as I wasn't forced to argue about it any more. At Formby I avoided the golf course (remembering, with a gleam of woeful humour, how Aunt Evelyn had urged me to bring my 'golf sticks', as she called them). Wandering along the sand dunes I felt outlawed, bitter, and baited. I wanted something to smash and trample on, and in a paroxysm of exasperation I performed the time-honoured gesture of shaking my clenched fists at the sky. Feeling no better for that, I ripped the M C ribbon off my tunic and threw it into the mouth of the Mersey . . .

———

Next morning I was sitting in the hotel smoking-room in a state of stubborn apathy. I had got just about to the end of my tether. Since it was Sunday and my eighth day in Liverpool I might have chosen this moment for reviewing the past week, though I had nothing to congratulate myself on except the fact that I'd survived seven days without hauling down my flag. It is possible that I meditated some desperate counter-attack which might compel the authorities to treat me harshly, but I had no idea how do do it. 'Damn it all, I've half a mind to go to church,' I thought, although as far as I could see there was more real religion to be found in the *Golden Treasury* than in a church which only approved of military-aged men when they were in khaki. Sitting in a sacred edifice wouldn't help me, I decided. And then I was taken completely by surprise; for there was David Cromlech, knobby-faced and gawky as ever, advancing across the room. His arrival brought instantaneous relief, which I expressed by exclaiming: 'Thank God you've come!'

He sat down without saying anything. He, too, was pleased to see me, but retained that air of anxious concern with which his eyes had first encountered mine. As usual he looked as if he'd slept in his uniform. Something had snapped inside me and I felt rather silly and hysterical. 'David, you've got an enormous black smudge on your forehead,' I remarked. Obediently he moistened his handkerchief with his tongue and proceeded to rub the smudge off, tentatively following my instructions as to its where-abouts. During this operation his face was vacant and childish, suggesting an earlier time when his nurse had performed a similar service for him. 'How on earth did you manage to roll up from the Isle of Wight like this?' I inquired. He smiled in a knowing way. Already he was beginning to look less as though he were visiting an invalid; but I'd been so much locked up with my own thoughts lately that for the next few minutes I talked nineteen to the dozen, telling him what a hellish time I'd had, how terribly kind the depot officers had been to me, and so on. 'When I started this anti-war stunt I never dreamt it would be such a long job, getting myself run in for a court martial,' I concluded, laughing with somewhat hollow gaiety.

In the meantime David sat moody and silent, his face twitching nervously and his fingers twiddling one of his tunic buttons. 'Look here, George,' he said, abruptly, scrutinizing the button as though he'd never seen such a thing before, 'I've come to tell you that you've got to drop this anti-war business.' This was a new idea, for I wasn't yet beyond my sense of relief at seeing him. 'But I can't drop it,' I exclaimed. 'Don't you realize that I'm a man with a message? I thought you'd come to see me through the court martial as "prisoner's friend".' We then settled down to an earnest discussion about the 'political errors and insincerities for which the fighting men were being sacrificed'. He did most of the talking, while I disagreed defensively. But even if our conversation could be reported in full, I am afraid that the verdict of posterity would be against us. We agreed that the world had gone mad; but neither of us could see beyond his own experience, and we weren't life-learned enough to share the patient selfless stoicism through which men of maturer age were acquiring anonymous glory. Neither of us had the haziest idea of what the politicians were really up to (though it is possible that the politicians were only feeling their way and trusting in providence and the output of munitions to solve their problems). Nevertheless we argued as though the secret confabulations of cabinet ministers in various countries were clear as daylight to us, and our assumption was that they were all wrong, while we, who had been in the trenches, were far-seeing and infallible. But when I said that the war ought to be stopped and it was my duty to do my little bit to stop it, David replied that the war was bound to go on till one side or the other collapsed, and the Pacifists were only meddling with what they didn't understand. 'At any rate Thornton Tyrrell's a jolly fine man and knows a bloody sight more about everything than you do,' I exclaimed. 'Tyrrell's only a doctrinaire,' replied David, 'though I grant you he's a courageous one.' Before I had time to ask what the hell he knew about doctrinaires, he continued, 'No one except people who've been in the real fighting have any right to interfere about the war; and even they can't get anything done about it. All they can do is to remain loyal to one another. And you know perfectly well that most of the conscientious objectors are nothing but skrimshankers.' I retorted that I knew nothing of the sort, and mentioned a young doctor who'd played rugby football for Scotland and was now in prison although he could have been doing hospital work if he'd wanted to. David then announced that he'd been doing a bit of wire-pulling on my behalf and that I should soon find that my pacifist M P wouldn't do me as much good as I expected. This put my back up. David had no right to come butting in about my private affairs. 'If you've really been trying to persuade the authorities not to do anything nasty to me,' I remarked, 'that's about the hopefullest thing I've heard. Go on doing it and exercise your usual tact, and you'll get me two years' hard labour for certain, and with any luck they'll decide to shoot me as a sort of deserter.' He looked so aggrieved at this that I relented and suggested that we'd better have some lunch. But David was always an absent-minded eater, and on this occasion he prodded disapprovingly at his food and then bolted it down as if it were medicine.

A couple of hours later we were wandering aimlessly along the shore at Formby, and still jabbering for all we were worth. I refused to accept his well-meaning assertion that no one at the front would understand my point of view and that they would only say that I'd got cold feet. 'And even if they do say that,' I argued, 'the main point is that by backing out of my statement I shall be betraying my real convictions and the people who are supporting me. Isn't that worse cowardice than being thought cold-footed by officers who refuse to think about anything except the gentlemanly traditions of the regiment? I'm not doing it for fun, am I? Can't you understand that this is the most difficult thing I've ever done in my life? I'm not going to be talked out of it just when I'm forcing them to make a martyr of me.' 'They won't make a martyr of you,' he replied. 'How do you know that?' I asked. He said that the colonel at Clitherland had told him to tell me that if I continued to refuse to be 'medically boarded' they would shut me up in a lunatic asylum for the rest of the war. Nothing would induce them to court martial me. It had all been arranged with some big bug at the War Office in the last day or two. 'Why didn't you tell me before?' I asked. 'I kept it as a last resort because I was afraid it might upset you,' he replied, tracing a pattern on the sand with his stick. 'I wouldn't believe this from anyone but you. Will you swear on the Bible that you're telling the truth?' He swore on an imaginary Bible that nothing would induce them to court martial me and that I should be treated as insane. 'All right, then, I'll give way.' As soon as the words were out of my mouth I sat down on an old wooden breakwater.

So that was the end of my grand gesture. I ought to have known that the blighters would do me down somehow, I thought, scowling heavily at the sea. It was appropriate that I should behave in a glumly dignified manner, but already I was aware that an enormous load had been lifted from my mind. In the train David was discreetly silent. He got out at Clitherland. 'Then I'll tell Orderly Room they can fix up a Board for you tomorrow,' he remarked, unable to conceal his elation. 'You can tell them anything you bloody well please!' I answered ungratefully. But as soon as I was alone I sat back and closed my eyes with a sense of exquisite relief. I was unaware that David had, probably, saved me from being sent to prison by telling me a very successful lie. No doubt I should have done the same for him if our positions had been reversed.

SIEGFRIED SASSOON

see also p. 326

In *Siegfried's Journey, 1916–1920*, Sassoon uses real names to tell parts of the story not covered in the Sherston books. He met Wilfred Owen (*q.v.*) at Craiglockhart, a hospital for shell-shocked cases in Edinburgh where he had been sent after his protest. Here Sassoon, and probably Owen, read Barbusse (*q.v.*). There is some controversy as to how much influence Sassoon actually had on Owen and on the nature of their attitudes to each other. (See, e.g., Dennis Welland, *Wilfred Owen*, London, Chatto & Windus, 2nd edn, 1978, p. 182).

In this extract Sassoon refers to Edmund Blunden's 'Memoir' on Owen, which appeared in his edition of Owen's *Poems* (published by Chatto & Windus in 1931).

Source: Siegfried Sassoon, *Siegfried's Journey, 1916–1920*, London, Faber, 1945.

One morning at the beginning of August, when I had been at Craiglockhart War Hospital about a fortnight, there was a gentle knock on the door of my room and a young officer entered. Short, dark-haired, and shyly hesitant, he stood for a moment before coming across to the window, where I was sitting on my bed cleaning my golf clubs. A favourable first impression was made by the fact that he had under his arm several copies of *The Old Huntsman*. He had come, he said, hoping that I would be so gracious as to inscribe them for himself and some of his friends. He spoke with a slight stammer, which was no unusual thing in that neurosis-pervaded hospital. My leisurely, commentative method of inscribing the books enabled him to feel more at home with me. He had a charming honest smile, and his manners – he stood at my elbow rather as though conferring with a superior officer – were modest and ingratiating. He gave me the names of his friends first. When it came to his own I found myself writing one that has since gained a notable place on the roll of English poets –Wilfred Owen. I had taken an instinctive liking to him, and felt that I could talk freely. During the next half-hour or more I must have spoken mainly about my book and its interpretations of the war. He listened eagerly, questioning me with reticent intelligence. It was only when he was departing that he confessed to being a writer of poetry himself, though none of it had yet appeared in print.

It amuses me to remember that, when I had resumed my ruminative club-polishing, I wondered whether his poems were any good! He had seemed an interesting little chap but had not struck me as remarkable. In fact my first view of him was as a rather ordinary young man, perceptibly provincial, though un-obtrusively ardent in his responses to my lordly dictums about poetry. Owing to my habit of avoiding people's faces while talking, I had not observed him closely. Anyhow, it was pleasant to have discovered that there was another poet in the hospital and that he happened to be an admirer of my work. For him on the other hand, the visit to my room – as he subsequently assured me – had been momentous. It had taken him two whole weeks, he said, to muster up enough courage to approach me with his request. I must add that, in a letter to his mother – shown me many years afterwards – he reported me as talking badly. 'He accords a slurred suggestion of words only ... The last thing he said to me was "Sweat your guts out writing poetry". He also warned me against early publishing. He is himself thirty. Looks under twenty-five.' This must have been written a few days later, after he had diffidently shown me a selection of his verse, for he describes me – I am thankful to say – as 'applauding some of it long and fervently' and pronouncing one of his recent lyrics ('Song of Songs') 'perfect work, absolutely charming', and asking him to copy it for me. I record my thankfulness, because I have an uncomfortable suspicion that I was a bit slow in recognizing the exceptional quality of his poetic gift. Manuscript poems can be deceptive when handed to one like school exercises to be blue-pencilled, especially when one has played thirty-six holes of golf and consumed a stodgy hospital dinner. I was sometimes a little severe on what he showed me, censuring the over-luscious writing in his immature pieces, and putting my finger on 'She dreams of golden gardens and sweet glooms' as an example. But it was the emotional element, even more than its verbal expression, which seemed to need refine-ment. There was an almost embarrassing sweetness in the senti-ment of some of his work, though it showed skill in rich and melodious combinations of words. This weakness, as hardly requires pointing out, he was progressively discarding during the last year of his life. In his masterpiece *Strange Meeting* he left us the finest elegy written by a soldier of that period, and the conclusive testimony of his power and originality. It was, however, not until some time in October, when he brought me his splendidly constructed sonnet *Anthem for Doomed Youth*, that it dawned on me that my little friend was much more than the promising minor poet I had hitherto adjudged him to be. I now realized that his verse, with its sumptuous epithets and large-scale imagery, its noble naturalness and depth of meaning, had impressive affinities with Keats, whom he took as his supreme exemplar. This new sonnet was a revelation. I suggested one or two slight alterations; but it confronted me with classic and imaginative serenity. After assuring him of its excellence I told him that I would do my best to get it published in *The Nation*. This gratified him greatly. Neither of us could have been expected to foresee that it would some day be added to *Palgrave's Golden Treasury*.

It has been loosely assumed and stated that Wilfred modelled his war poetry on mine. My only claimable influence was that I stimulated him towards writing with compassionate and challenging realism. His printed letters are evidence that the impulse was already strong in him before he had met me. The manuscript of one of his most dynamically descriptive war poems, *Exposure*, is dated February 1917, and proves that he had already found an authentic utterance of his own. (For some reason, he withheld this poem from me while we were together.) Up to a point my admonitions were helpful. My encouragement was opportune, and I can claim to have given him a lively incentive during his rapid advance to self-revelation. Meanwhile I seem to hear him laughingly implore me to chuck these expository generalizations and recover some of the luminous animation of our intimacy. How about my indirect influence on him? he inquires in his calm velvety voice. Have I forgotten our eager discussions of contemporary poets and the technical dodges which we were ourselves devising? Have I forgotten the simplifying suggestions which emanated from my unsophisticated poetic method? (For my technique was almost elementary compared with his innovating experiments.) Wasn't it after he got to know me that he first began to risk using the colloquialisms which were at that time so frequent in my verses? And didn't I lend him Barbusse's *Le Feu*, which set him alight as no other war book had done? It was indeed one of those situations where imperceptible effects are obtained by people mingling their minds at a favourable

340

moment. Turning the pages of Wilfred's *Poems*, I am glad to think that there may have been occasions when some freely improvised remark of mine sent him away with a fruitful idea. And my humanized reportings of front-line episodes may have contributed something to his controlled vision of what he had seen for himself. Of his own period of active service he seldom spoke. I was careful to avoid questioning him about the experiences which had caused his nervous breakdown, and was only vaguely aware of what he had been through in the St Quentin sector and elsewhere. Fourteen years later, when reading the letters quoted by Edmund Blunden in his finally authoritative Memoir, I discovered that Wilfred had endured worse things than I had realized from the little he told me. On arriving at the Western Front he had immediately encountered abominable conditions of winter weather and attrition warfare. But of this he merely remarked to me that he wished he'd had my luck in being inured to the beastly business by gradual stages. His thick dark hair was already touched with white above the ears.

As I remember him during those three months we spent together at Craiglockhart he was consistently cheerful. Dr Brock, who was in charge of his case, had been completely successful in restoring the balance of his nerves. He seemed contented and had found plenty to occupy him. He edited *The Hydra*, the fortnightly hospital magazine, and was an active member of the Field Club. In a number of *The Hydra*, the proceedings of the Field Club include the following unexpected item: 'An interesting paper on the classification of soils, soil air, soil water, root absorption and fertility was given by Mr Owen on 1 October.' My sonnet *Dreamers* made its first appearance in the magazine, thus inconspicuously inaugurating a career of frequent quotation and reprinting. It is also worth noting that it was only through my urgent instigation that he printed a short poem of his own. This was in accordance with his essential unassumingness. Though not clearly conscious of it at the time, I now realize that in a young man of twenty-four his selflessness was extraordinary. The clue to his poetic genius was sympathy, not only in his detached outlook upon humanity but in all his actions and responses towards individuals. I can remember nothing in my observations of his character which showed any sign of egotism or desire for self-advancement. When contrasting the two of us, I find that – highly strung and emotional though he was – his whole personality was far more compact and coherent than mine. He readily recognized and appreciated this contrast, and I remember with affection his amused acceptance of my exclamatory enthusiasms and intolerances. Most unfairly to himself, he even likened us to Don Quixote and Sancho Panza! I have already mentioned the velvety quality of his voice, which suggested the Keatsian richness of his artistry with words. It wasn't a vibrating voice. It had the fluid texture of soft consonants and murmurous music. Hearing him read poetry aloud in his modest unemphatic way, one realized at once that he had an exceptionally sensitive ear. One of his poems begins 'All sounds have been as music to my listening', and his sense of colour was correspondingly absorbent. Sounds and colours, in his verse, were mulled and modulated to a subdued magnificence of sensuous harmonies, and this was noticeable even in his everyday speaking. His temperament, as I apprehend it, was unhurrying, though never languid. Only now and then was he urgently quickened by the mysterious prompting and potency of his imagination. His manuscripts show that he seldom brought his poems to their final form without considerable recasting and revision. There was a slowness and sobriety in his method, which was, I think, monodramatic and elegiac rather than leapingly lyrical. I do not doubt that, had he lived longer, he would have produced poems of sustained grandeur and ample design. It can be observed that his work is prevalently deliberate in movement. Stately and processional, it has the rhythm of emotional depth and directness and the verbal resonance of one who felt in glowing primary colours and wrote with solemn melodies in his mind. It can be taken for granted that there were aspects of him which I never saw. To others he may have revealed much that I missed, since he had the adaptability of a beautifully sympathetic nature. But I like to believe that when with me he was at his best, and I can remember no shadow of unhappiness or misunderstanding between us.

As a letter writer he was – like most of us in our youth – a shade self-conscious and liable to indulge in fine phrases. But if any proof were needed of his physical toughness and intellectual determination it can be found in the wonderful pages sent to his mother from the front. And he always communicated vividly what was uppermost in his thoughts at the moment.

Wilfred's face will be known to posterity by a photograph taken in uniform, and to some extent disguised by the animal health of army life. It shows him very much as he was when I was with him. He wasn't a fine-drawn type. There was a full-blooded robustness about him which implied reserves of mental energy and solid ability. Under ordinary conditions it wasn't a spiritual face. It was of the mould which either coarsens or refines itself in later life. I cannot say that I ever saw what is called 'a look of genius' in it. His mouth was resolute and humorous, his eyes long and heavy-lidded, quiescent rather than penetrating. They were somewhat sleepy eyes, kind, shrewd, and seldom lit up from within. They seemed, like much else in his personality, to be instinctively guarding the secret sources of his inward power and integrity. His face – what would it have become? While calling him back in memory I have been haunted by the idea of the unalterable features of those who have died in youth. Borne away from them by the years, we – with our time-troubled looks and diminished alertness – have submitted to many a gradual detriment of change. But the young poet of twenty-five years ago remains his world-discovering self. His futureless eyes encounter ours from the faintly smiling portrait, unconscious of the privilege and deprivation of never growing old, unconscious of the dramatic illusion of completeness that he is destined to create . . .

JOHN MIDDLETON MURRY

John Middleton Murry (1889–1957). Born in London. Critic, editor and author. Leading figure in the London literary world. Married Katherine Mansfield in 1918. During the war worked in the political intelligence department of the War Office. Finds Sassoon's work 'not poetry' and generally lacking in intellectual distance compared with Duhamel (*q.v.*). However, this review is not without distinction and it touches some interesting raw nerves. It appeared unsigned.

Source: The Nation, 13 July 1918.

MR SASSOON'S WAR VERSES

Counter-Attack, and Other Poems
by Siegfried Sassoon (Heinemann. 2s. 6d. net)

It is the fact, not the poetry, of Mr Sassoon, that is important. When a man is in torment and cries aloud, his cry is incoherent. It has neither weight nor meaning of its own. It is inhuman, and its very inhumanity strikes to the nerve of our hearts. We long to silence the cry, whether by succour and sympathy, or by hiding ourselves from it. That it should somehow stop or be stopped, and by ceasing trouble our hearts no more, is our chief desire; for it is ugly and painful, and it rasps at the cords of nature.

Mr Sassoon's verses – they are not poetry – are such a cry. They touch not our imagination, but our sense. We feel not as we do with true poetry or true art that something is, after all, right, but that something is intolerably and irremediably wrong. And, God knows, something is wrong – wrong with Mr Sassoon, wrong with the world that has made of him the instrument of a discord so jangling. Why should one of the creatures of the earth be made to suffer a pain so brutal that he can give it no expression, that even this most human and mighty relief is denied him?

For these verses express nothing, save in so far as a cry expresses pain. Their effect is exhausted when the immediate impression dies away. Some of them are, by intention, realistic pictures of battle experience, and indeed one does not doubt their truth. The language is overwrought, dense and turgid, as a man's mind must be under the stress and obsession of a chaos beyond all comprehension.

> The place was rotten with dead; green clumsy legs
> High-booted, sprawled and grovelled along the saps;
> And trunks, face downward, in the sucking mud,
> Wallowed like trodden sand-bags loosely filled;
> And naked sodden buttocks, mats of hair,
> Bulged, clotted heads slept in the plastering slime.
> And then the rain began – the jolly old rain!

That is horrible, but it does not produce the impression of horror. It numbs, not terrifies, the mind. Each separate reality and succeeding vision is, as it were, driven upon us by a hammer, but one hammer-beat is like another. Each adds to the sum more numbness and more pain, but the separateness and particularity of each is lost.

> Bullets spat
> And he remembered his rifle . . . rapid fire . . .
> And started blazing wildly . . . then a bang
> Crumpled and spun him sideways, knocked him out
> To grunt and wriggle: none heeded him: he choked
> And fought the flapping veils of smothering gloom,
> Lost in a blurred confusion of yells and groans . . .

We are given the blurred confusion, and just because this is the truth of the matter exactly rendered we cannot apprehend it any more than the soldier who endures it can. We, like him, are 'crumpled and spun sideways'!

There is a value in the plain, unvarnished truth; but there is another truth more valuable still. One may convey the chaos of immediate sensation by a chaotic expression, as does Mr Sassoon. But the unforgettable horror of an inhuman experience can only be rightly rendered by rendering also its relation to the harmony and calm of the soul which it shatters. In this context alone can it appear with that sudden shock to the imagination which is overwhelming. The faintest discord in a harmony has within it an infinity of disaster, which no confusion of notes, however wild and various and loud, can possibly suggest. It is in this that the wise saying that poetry is emotion recollected in tranquillity, is so firmly based, for the quality of an experience can only be given by reference to the ideal condition of the human consciousness which it disturbs with pleasure or with pain. But in Mr Sassoon's verses it is we who are left to create for ourselves the harmony of which he gives us only the moment of its annihilation. It is we who must be the poets and the artists if anything enduring is to be made of his work. He gives us only the data. There is, perhaps, little enough harm in this, and probably there would be none at all if Mr Sassoon had not chosen a poetic form in which to cast the record of his experience, and deliberately given the name of poems to his verses. Thereby he is misleading himself most grievously, and he may easily end by wrecking the real poetic gift which at rare intervals peeps out in a line.

> The land where all
> Is ruin and nothing blossoms but the sky.

The last five words are beautiful because they do convey horror to the imagination, and do not bludgeon the senses. They manage to convey horror to the imagination precisely because they contain, as it were, a full octave of emotional experience, and the compass ranges from serenity to desolation, not merely of the earth, but of the mind. The horror is in relation; it is placed, and therefore created. But in the following lines there is no trace of creation or significance:

> A yawning soldier knelt against the bank
> Staring across the morning blear with fog;
> He wondered when the Allemands would get busy;
> And then, of course, they started with five-nines
> Traversing, sure as fate, and never a dud.

We choose these lines because they make a tolerable, if not a very lively, prose. Those which follow them in the piece which gives the book its name are more extravagant journalese. But why on earth should such middling prose be ironed out into nominal blank verse lines, unless Mr Sassoon somehow imagined that he was, in fact, writing poetry? What he was doing was to make a barely sufficient entry in a log-book. That he should for one moment imagine he was doing anything else is almost incomprehensible. If the lines of the whole piece were transposed into the prose form for which they clamour, they would then, surely, appear to be the rough notes (perhaps for a novel, much less probably for a poem) which they are.

Mr Sassoon is evidently in some sense aware that an element of creation, or of art, is lacking to his work. Perhaps, on reading some of his own lines, he may have felt that they were not, after all, a new kind of poetry; and he may have been sensible of some inexplicable difference between his own verses and those of Mr Thomas Hardy, which are a new kind of poetry. For we think we can detect a certain straining after pregnancy, due to the attempt to catch the method of Mr Hardy. The overloading of epithet and verb in such a line as –

> He winked his prying torch with patching glare,

imitates the mere accidents of a poetic method, of which the real strength and newness consists exactly in the element which has no place at all in Mr Sassoon's mental composition. Against the permanence of the philosophic background in Mr Hardy's work, each delicate shade of direct emotion is conveyed with all the force that comes of complete differentiation. With Mr Sassoon there is no background, no differentiation; he has no calm, therefore he conveys no terror; he has no harmony, therefore he cannot pierce us with the anguish of discord.

The one artistic method which he employs is the irony of epigram. On these occasions alone does he appeal to a time beyond the immediate present of sensation. There is an effort at comparison and relation, or, in other words, an effort to grapple with his own experience and comprehend it. Certainly, the effort and the comprehension do not go very far, and they achieve rather a device of technique than a method of real expression; but the device is effective enough.

> 'Good morning; good morning!' the General said,
>   When we met him last week on our way to the line.
> Now the soldiers he smiled at are most of 'em dead,
>   And we're cursing his staff for incompetent swine.
> 'He's a cheery old card,' grunted Harry to Jack,
> As they slogged up to Arras with rifle and pack.
>
> But he did for them both by his plan of attack.

The comprehension does not go far enough, however. The experiences of battle, awful, inhuman, and intolerable as they are, are only experiences for the mind which is capable of bringing their horror and their inhumanity home to the imagination of others. Without the perspective that comes from intellectual remoteness there can be no order and no art. Intellectual remoteness is not cold or callous; it is the condition in which a mind works as a mind, and a man is fully active as a man. Because this is wanting in Mr Sassoon we are a prey to uneasiness when confronted with his work. We have a feeling of guilt, as though we were prying into secrets which were better hid. We have read, for instance, in the pages of M. Duhamel, far more terrible things than any Mr Sassoon has to tell, but they were made terrible by the calm of the recording mind. Mr Sassoon's mind is a chaos. It is as though he had no memory, and the thing itself returned as it was. That is why the fact, or the spectacle, or Mr Sassoon, is so much more impressive than his verses. That one who asked for perfect happiness, so little of life, as the writer of 'Break of Day' –

> Unlatch the gate
> And set Golumpus going on the grass

should be reduced to the condition in which he cannot surmount the disaster of his own experience –

> Thud, thud, thud – quite soft . . . they never cease
> Those whispering guns – O Christ! I want to go out
> And screech at them to stop – I'm going crazy,
> I'm going stark, staring mad because of the guns.

– that is awful and inhuman and intolerable. And to that it makes no difference that it is Mr Sassoon who is the martyr, and we ourselves who are the poets.

RANDOLPH BOURNE

Randolph Bourne (1896–1918). Bourne studied at Columbia University. He was a perceptive, left-wing, social critic. He was also an extremely sympathetic spokesman for the young people of his generation. A tribute to Bourne's courage and pertinacity appears in John Dos Passos's *1919* (*q.v.*). His pacifist articles were posthumously collected as *Untimely Papers* (1919), and his philosophical and critical views are summed up in *The History of a Literary Radical* (1920), edited by Van Wyck Brooks.

Source: 'The War and the Intellectuals', *The Seven Arts*, II, June, 1917, and 'The Collapse of American Strategy', *The Seven Arts*, II, August, 1917, reprinted in *The World of Randolph Bourne*, ed. Lilian Schlissel, New York, Dutton, 1965.

From
THE WAR AND THE INTELLECTUALS

To those of us who still retain an irreconcilable animus against war, it has been a bitter experience to see the unanimity with which the American intellectuals have thrown their support to the use of war technique in the crisis in which America found herself. Socialists, college professors, publicists, new-republicans, practitioners of literature, have vied with each other in confirming with their intellectual faith the collapse of neutrality and the riveting of the war mind on a hundred million more of the world's people. And the intellectuals are not content with confirming our belligerent gesture. They are now complacently asserting that it was they who effectively willed it, against the hesitation and dim perceptions of the American democratic masses. A war made deliberately by the intellectuals! A calm moral verdict, arrived at after a penetrating study of inexorable facts! Sluggish masses, too remote from the world conflict to be stirred, too lacking in intellect to perceive their danger! An alert intellectual class saving the people in spite of themselves, biding their time with Fabian strategy until the nation could be moved into war without serious resistance! An intellectual class gently guiding a nation through sheer force of ideas into what the other nations entered only through predatory craft or popular hysteria or militarist madness! A war free from any taint of self-seeking, a war that will secure the triumph of democracy and internationalize the world! This is the picture which the more self-conscious intellectuals have formed of themselves, and which they are slowly impressing upon a population which is being led no one knows whither by an indubitably intellectualized President. And they are right, in that the war certainly did not spring from either the ideals or the prejudices, from the national ambitions or hysterias, of the American people, however acquiescent the masses prove to be, and however clearly the intellectuals prove their putative intuition . . .

———

Our intellectual class might have been occupied, during the last two years of war, in studying and clarifying the ideals and aspirations of the American democracy, in discovering a true Americanism which would not have been merely nebulous but might have federated the different ethnic groups and traditions. They might have spent the time in endeavoring to clear the public mind of the cant of war, to get rid of old mystical notions that clog our thinking. We might have used the time for a great wave of education, for setting our house in spiritual order. We could at least have set the problem before ourselves. If our intellectuals were going to lead the administration, they might conceivably have tried to find some way of securing peace by making neutrality effective. They might have turned their intellectual energy not to the problem of jockeying the nation into war, but to the problem of using our vast neutral power to attain democratic ends for the rest of the world and ourselves without the use of the malevolent technique of war. They might have failed. The point is that they scarcely tried. The time was spent not in clarification and education, but in a mulling over of nebulous ideals of democracy and liberalism and civilization which had never meant anything fruitful to those ruling classes who now so glibly used them, and in giving free rein to the elementary instinct of self-defense. The whole era has been spiritually wasted. The outstanding feature has been not its Americanism but its intense colonialism. The offense of our intellectuals was not so much that they were colonial – for what could we expect of a nation composed of so many national elements? – but that it was so one-sidedly and partisanly colonial. The official, reputable expression of the intellectual class has been that of the English colonial. Certain portions of it have been even more loyalist than the king, more British even than Australia. Other colonial attitudes have been vulgar. The colonialism of the other American stocks was denied a hearing from the start. America might have been made a meeting ground for the different national attitudes. An intellectual class, cultural colonists of the different European nations, might have threshed out the issues here as they could not be threshed out in Europe. Instead of this, the English colonials in university and press took command at the start, and we became an intellectual Hungary where thought was subject to an effective process of Magyarization. The reputable opinion of the American intellectuals became more and more either what could be read pleasantly in London, or what was written in an earnest effort to put Englishmen straight on their war aims and war technique. This Magyarization of thought produced as a counterreaction a peculiarly offensive and inept German apologetic, and the two partisans divided the field between them. The great masses, the other ethnic groups, were inarticulate. American public opinion was almost as little prepared for war in 1917 as it was in 1914 . . .

———

It is depressing to think that the prospect of a world so strong that none dare challenge it should be the immediate ideal of the American intellectual. If the League is only a makeshift, a coalition into which we enter to restore order, then it is only a description of existing fact, and the idea should be treated as such. But if it is an actually prospective outcome of the settlement, the keystone of American policy, it is neither realizable nor desirable. For the program of such a League contains no provision for dynamic national growth or for international economic justice. In a world which requires recognition of economic internationalism far more than of political internationalism, an idea is reactionary which proposes to petrify and federate the nations as political and economic units. Such a scheme for international order is a dubious justification for American policy. And if American policy had been sincere in its belief that our participation would achieve international beatitude, would we not have made our entrance into the war conditional upon a solemn general agreement to respect in the final settlement these principles of international order? Could we have afforded, if our war was to end war by the establishment of a league of honor, to risk the defeat of our vision and our betrayal in the settlement? Yet we are in the war, and no such solemn agreement was made, nor has it ever been suggested.

The case of the intellectuals seems, therefore, only very speciously rational. They could have used their energy to force a just peace or at least to devise other means than war for carrying through American policy. They could have used their intellectual energy to ensure that our participation in the war meant the international order which they wish. Intellect was not so used. It was used to lead an apathetic nation into an irresponsible war, without guarantees from those belligerents whose cause we were saving. The American intellectual, therefore, has been rational neither in his hindsight nor his foresight. To explain him we must look beneath the intellectual reasons to the emotional disposition. It is not so much what they thought as how they felt that explains our intellectual class. Allowing for colonial sympathy, there was still the personal shock in a world war which outraged all our preconceived notions of the way the world was tending. It reduced to rubbish most of the humanitarian internationalism and democratic nationalism which had been the emotional thread of our intellectuals' life . . .

Never having felt responsiblity for labor wars and oppressed masses and excluded races at home, they had a large fund of idle emotional capital to invest in the oppressed nationalities and ravaged villages of Europe. Hearts that had felt only ugly contempt for democratic strivings at home beat in tune with the struggle for freedom abroad. All this was natural, but it tended to over-emphasize our responsibility. And it threw our thinking out of gear. The task of making our own country detailedly fit for peace was abandoned in favor of a feverish concern for the management of the war, advice to the fighting governments on all matters, military, social, and political, and a gradual working up of the conviction that we were ordained as a nation to lead all erring brothers toward the light of liberty and democracy. The failure of the American intellectual class to erect a creative attitude toward the war can be explained by these sterile mental conflicts which the shock to our ideals sent raging through us.

Mental conflicts end either in a new and higher synthesis or

352

adjustment, or else in a reversion to more primitive ideas which have been outgrown but to which we drop when jolted out of our attained position. The war caused in America a recrudescence of nebulous ideals which a younger generation was fast outgrowing because it had passed the wistful stage and was discovering concrete ways of getting them incarnated in actual institutions. The shock of the war threw us back from this pragmatic work into an emotional bath of these old ideals. There was even a somewhat rarefied revival of our primitive Yankee boastfulness, the reversion of senility to that republican childhood when we expected the whole world to copy our republican institutions. We amusingly ignored the fact that it was just that Imperial German régime, to whom we are to teach the art of self-government, which our own federal structure, with its executive irresponsible in foreign policy and with its absence of parliamentary control, most resembles. And we are missing the exquisite irony of the unaffected homage paid by the American democratic intellectuals to the last and most detested of Britain's Tory premiers as the representative of a 'liberal' ally, as well as the irony of the selection of the best hated of America's bourbon 'old guard' as the missionary of American democracy to Russia . . .[1]

Is there no place left, then, for the intellectual who cannot yet crystallize, who does not dread suspense, and is not yet drugged with fatigue? The American intellectuals, in their preoccupation with reality, seem to have forgotten that the real enemy is War rather than Imperial Germany. There is work to be done to prevent this war of ours from passing into popular mythology as a holy crusade. What shall we do with leaders who tell us that we go to war in moral spotlessness, or who make 'democracy' synonymous with a republican form of government? There is work to be done in still shouting that all the revolutionary by-products will not justify the war, or make war anything else than the most noxious complex of all the evils that afflict men. There must be some to find no consolation whatever, and some to sneer at those who buy the cheap emotion of sacrifice. There must be some irreconcilables left who will not even accept the war with walrus tears. There must be some to call unceasingly for peace, and some to insist that the terms of settlement shall be not only liberal but democratic. There must be some intellectuals who are not willing to use the old discredited counters again and to support a peace which would leave all the old inflammable materials of armament lying about the world. There must still be opposition to any contemplated 'liberal' world order founded on military coalitions. The 'irreconcilable' need not be disloyal. He need not even be 'impossibilist'. His apathy toward war should take the form of a heightened energy and enthusiasm for the education, the art, the interpretation that make for life in the midst of the world of death. The intellectual who retains his animus against war will push out more boldly than ever to make his case solid against it. The old ideals crumble; new ideals must be forged. His mind will continue to roam widely and ceaselessly. The thing he will fear most is premature crystallization.

From
THE COLLAPSE OF AMERICAN STRATEGY[2]

... From the present submission of the German people to the war régime nothing can be deduced as to their subserviency after the war. Prodigious slaughter will effect profound social changes. There may be going on a progressive selection in favor of democratic elements. The Russian army was transformed into a democratic instrument by the wiping out in battle of the upper-class officers. Men of democratic and revolutionary sympathies took their places. A similar process may happen in the German army. The end of the war may leave the German 'army of the people' a genuine popular army intent upon securing control of the civil government. Furthermore, the continuance of Pan-German predatory imperialism depends on a younger generation of Junkers to replace the veterans now in control. The most daring of those aristocrats will almost certainly have been destroyed in battle. The mortality in upper-class leadership will certainly have proved far larger than the mortality in lower-class leadership. The maturing of these tendencies is the hope of German democracy. A speedy ending of the war, before the country is exhausted and the popular morale destroyed, is likely best to mature these tendencies. In this light it is almost immaterial what terms are made. Winning or losing, Germany cannot replace her younger generation of the ruling class. And without a ruling class to continue the imperial tradition, democracy could scarcely be delayed. An enfeebled ruling class could neither hold a vast world military empire together nor resist the revolutionary elements at home. The prolongation of the war delays democracy in Germany by convincing the German people that they are fighting for their very existence and thereby forcing them to cling even more desperately to their military leaders. In announcing an American strategy of 'conquer or submit', the President virtually urges the German people to prolong the war. And not only are the German people, at the apparent price of their existence, tacitly urged to continue the fight to the uttermost, but the Allied governments are tacitly urged to wield the 'knockout blow'. All those reactionary elements in England, France, and Italy, whose spirits drooped at the President's original bid for a negotiated peace, now take heart again at this apparent countersigning of their most extreme programs . . .

1. Arthur Balfour (1848–1930), British Foreign Secretary 1915–16; head of the War Commission sent to Washington in 1917 to purchase war materials and secure commitment of American troops to European battlefields. Elihu Root (1845–1937), Wilson's special envoy to Russia in 1917 to determine Russian ability to continue the war after the March revolution. [LS]

2. In December 1916, Wilson called on the belligerents to state their terms for peace. In January 1917, he addressed the United States Senate, and declared that America sought to effect a 'peace without victory'. On 2 April 1917, Wilson delivered his War Message, but repeated that this country had no territorial ambitions and went to war to 'make the world safe for democracy'. [LS]

E. E. CUMMINGS

Edward Estlin Cummings (1894–1962). Born in Cambridge, Mass., and educated at Harvard. He served as a volunteer ambulance driver in France during the war, and, for his pains, was imprisoned by the French authorities on a 'mistaken' charge of treason. The letters below describe his duties and his arrest. He was later to develop his account of La Ferté Macé into *The Enormous Room*.

Source: E. E. Cummings, *Selected Letters of E. E. Cummings*, ed. F. W. Dupee and George Stade, London, André Deutsch, 1972.

To his father   [20 July 1917
                                 Camp at Ham, Noyon sector]

Dear Dad –

It was very good to hear from you – even though mother has kept you well under espionage judging from frequent reports received via mail. It seems that your sermons are getting more and more (if possible) patriotic, that Lowell (who previously talked only with the Creator) has come down off his high horse and is asking all sorts of favors of you, that Taft, Roosevelt, McKinley, and Admiral Dewey call on you hourly, and that Wilson keeps the wires in a continual state of apoplexy whenever you arrive chez-vous from your almost nightly diplomatic visits to Lisbon, Bruxelles, Westminster Abbey, and New South Greenland (Arkansaw). All I have to say is: keep them waiting. Some days since I received a telegraphic sans fil from Tokio, forwarded from Africa, in a code which I managed to intercept as follows: 'Rev. C. busy bee crowned heads of Urope afraid of he.' I repeat, it's necessary that you keep your feet in this mêlé. I suggest an hourly discipline on the Ford, drinking plenty of orangeade, and a frequent application of spirits of ammonia. Be careful that your stenographer doesn't overhear anything unimportant, and don't, <u>please</u> don't trust Pershing * * *

Just to give you air, D. D., I'll tell you all the news from Nowhere in France. First I have writ some member of family about weekly. If letters do not arrive, blame ye not this dusky earth-worm. Second, having had nothing to do since I joined 'my section', save carry 'malades', who (according to camp humorist) have mumps – certainly nothing worse – I am now in répos in a neighboring town, expecting daily to leave for another larger town, where it is said that 'we' will rest for perhaps a year, doing absolutely nothing, seeing no service, anchored to our Fords or Fiats, and generally miserable. In all of which the little finger of God the lord may be plainly seen with the aid of an 8 billion sun-power telescope. Same humorist says we are 'sleeping for France'. It's a lie. The 'comrades' snore too much for me, at any rate. We are, however, eating for France, eating much of 3rd class food.

I will recount the sole piece of 'service' I have seen. It will probably be my last. A man from Minnesota named O'Sullivan and I were in a Ford sleeping at a 'post'. 11.30 p.m. 6 obus dropped by Bosch all around us, sans warning. In stocking feet (I haven't undressed for weeks) with our casques on our heads, we lit in a little hole, one on top of other, while no. 2 landed, just 53 metres away, making (as we saw next day) a hole 5 feet deep, 12 feet long, 6 feet wide. We cranked up, & as we turned around, no. 3 burst hard by, which hastened our speed. The others pursued us down the road. After a few minutes we came back and I slept very well the rest of the night at the same 'post'; in fact, I never awaked when a second fusillade came off at 3 a.m.

I will send a snap of me in uniform as soon as I can. The casque is very becoming to anybody.

To his mother   [2 August 1917
                                 Camp at Ham, Noyon sector]

Dear Mother –

Your letter dated '13 July, 1917' reporting the receipt of my letter of 18 June 'from the Front' is 'at hand', as they might say at 'Colliers the Nat'l Weakly'. The tooth-kit will be welcome, as also the handkefs, of which I have only 4 dozen left, I believe or perhaps 8, I forget which. As I have already tried to indicate in foregoing letter, I have received 3 socks & their contents.

Since that letter, I have moved three times, and am now in répos not far from the 'base' you hypotheticize. My car was taken away from me the other day, and Brown (who was on it with me) was put on a Fiat with a crank ex-chauffeur, while I drew the place of aid on a Fiat with a 'typical' American. As it happened, I drew the better place, for the only time Mr Typical went out, he was in a hurry to get back here before moon-set, and an interesting trip resulted, as follows: I drove for $\frac{1}{2}$ hour at average of 35 miles, thru villages, round corners, over holes, perspiration dripping from my hands, capless, intent – splended picture? – then Mr T. took the wheel, putting my driving in the shade, averaging about 40, corners, turns, etc. – this being perfectly all right till we arrived at a bridge leading into the aforesaid 'base', when a faint light (no lantern allowed), set on a pole, abruptly indicated Eternity. With a fine presence of mind, Mr T. A. swerved, took off part of central island (of wood) which halves these little wooden affairs, also his entire tool box, hit other side of bridge & lost his other box, and on we went for 500 feet. When we got out to look at the Fiat, the rear axle looked like a mosquito's beak, and there were 2 shoes blown, plus a ruined carrossière and total lack of tools etc. As there is no water in the river, the latter were found later under the bridge. The car was abandoned there, and we drove home on luxurious cushions in the lieutenant's Renault, which, by a peculiar coincidence, met us just after the accident. Of course Mr T. A. being a true T. A. (at least true to type hereabouts) announced himself as a martyr to the negligence of the French gov't which failed to put any light on the bridge! Very very droll.

Do you wonder at my love for Americans? Please, please, PLEASE don't get the idea that I am ever in danger of my life, or that I ever carry wounded soldiers, or that I am ever anything but grateful for the little incidents which serve to puncture the desperate situation of being quartered in the Divine Country with a bunch of —s, [sic] incapable of escape, action or anything else.

I wrote father an account of a polite conversation with an obus. Not nearly as exciting, perhaps, as the accident above-told. The only other amusing thing happened at what might truly be called a Juicy place, whence we arrived here. Id est: the Bosch daily used to drop obus into an ex-aviation field an eighth of a mile away. Very droll to see the dirt fly and the poilus beat it. Of course the shell-song sounds right in line with your nose. Cheer up! They say after 2 weeks here in répos we may follow the division of the French army (to which we were attached at first) to the great ex-battlefield of the north, or the Road of Sweet Ladies. I hope, God knows, we get some excitement.

I received a letter from Sib [James Sibley Watson], who is in Paris, waiting to be signed up, waiting because, as he says, 'all the organizations are changing hands' – that's as much as I know, save that 'tis reported Richard N. is hanging on by his eye teeth. God keep us from being taken over by the American Army!!!!!! I shall not come back after my 6 months is up under any circumstances. I wear a khaki uniform like this: with a nice fleecy-insided over-coat, which makes you very abstract [sketch] indeed. The sweater of Nana's will be fine. I am glad A.W. got his commission, but can't say I'm thunderstruck! He's a great boy.

The belt and pseudo-leather puttees cost me a pretty penny – the latter were supposed to be furnished with the uniform, but Brown & I never got them owing to the fine system at the tailors, 'Messrs Sleater & Carter, Avenue de l'Opera, Paris', Leather here is immensely dear. The cloth puttees, which at this moment I wear, & which I also bought, look like this. [sketch] The uniform material is very heavy and well-wearing.

Hope Dad ne s'en fache pas with my 4th of July-ish Declaration of Undipendence! Give him my best love, and keep some for Yourself.

For your schedule, would state my different locations as follows:
1 Paris – 1 month (May 8, on)
2 'Front' (a place hardly germain to my malcontent nature) – Letter of June 18th.
3 'Semi-Répos' (a place SO quiet that Dickens' 'little Nell' might well be read as daily work)
4 'Front', really almost interesting (the juicy place aforesaid)
5 'Répos' pure and (very) simple (from which I write you this)

Au revoir!

Will try to get photos to send you, but have had hard luck in that respect so far.
P. S. the quiet life here has already driven 2 'comrades' home to the militant U S with shattered spleens.

To his mother   [1 October 1917
                                 La Ferté Macé, Orne, France]

Dearest of Mothers!
   At 11 a.m. Monsieur le Ministre de Sûreté plus 2 or 3

gendarmes convoyed my friend and me in separate voitures to his abode in N. [Noyon] Here we dined, each with his gendarme, still apart, and later were examined. Then removed to separate cells where we spent the night. My friend must have left the following day: I spent another night in my cell (sans sortir) having enjoyed a piece of bread, a piece of chocolate (thanks to friend) a small pail (or marmite) of grease-meat soup, more bread, ditto of beans, ditto soup & bread. This sounds like a lot. At 10 a.m. I left in the company of 2 gendarmes for the station of N. A distance of almost ½ mile. Had some trouble with a gendarme, who told me if I didn't want to carry my bagge I could leave it (I had a duffle-bag, chuck full, a long ambulance coat, a fur coat, a bed-roll, & blankets, total – 150 lbs) by the wayside – which I naturally refused to do. We finally compromised by my hiring a sweet kid to lug the bed-roll (which he did with greatest difficulty). Chemin-de-fer till 5 o'clock when landed at G. where supped on grease-meat-soup in a better cell, and slept on planks in blankets (other baggage forbidden) till 4 a.m., when another pair of gendarmes took me to the station of G. (I with baggage) where we boarded c. de f. for Paris, arriving at 6 a.m. Wait till 12 noon. In interval coffee & newspapers. At 1 train left for B., where we arrived at 9.30 p.m. I having dined on bread. All this time, my friend was 1 day ahead of me. Arrived at B., we checked big duffle bag & roll in gare, and set off on foot for La Ferté Macé, I carrying this time merely a small bag of letters, n. books, & souvenirs, which a gendarme had always carried hitherto. Douze kilomètres. Arrived midnight. Given straw pallet & slept on floor sans blankets. In morning found self in hugely long room with my long-lost friend and about 30 others as I guess – very cosmopolite group.

The following program is ours now till 15 October, when a commission comes to examine us for pacifism or something of the sort: 6-up. Coffee. 7 down to yard. 9.30 up. 10 down to salle à manger. 10.30–3.45 yard. 3.45 up. 4 down to salle à manger. 4.30–7 yard. 7 up. 9-lights out. I am having the time of my life. Never so healthy. Our meals are both soup, but we are allowed a spoon, which is better than eating with fingers, as we did in prison. By the way, a gendarme assured me this is not prison.

By the time this reaches you I shall have been out for some time. It's been a great experience. Monsieur le Surveillant is a fine man. We (my friend & I) have instituted '3 Old Cat' which we all play in the yard when it's fair. I couldn't possibly want anything better in the way of keep, tho' you have to get used to the snores, and they don't allow you a knife, so you can't cut the air at night which is pretty thick, all windows being shut.

Elos's letter I got before leaving the 'front' and please thank her & give her my much love, as to all.

You can't imagine, Mother mine, how interesting a time I'm having. Not for anything in the world would I change it! It's like working – you must experience it to comprendre – but how infinitely superior to Colliers! If I thought you would excite yourself I wouldn't write from this place, but I know you will believe me when I reiterate that I am having <u>the time of my life!</u>

PS. My bagge has been given back. I have my bed and am finely off! No more floor-sleeping.
PPS. arrested a week ago today.

E. E. CUMMINGS

see also p. 356

The Enormous Room, 1922, was Cummings's first book. It charts the experience of his 'trial' and subsequent imprisonment. His modernist techniques did not go down well with his English readers and his 'enjoyment' of life with his fellow inmates, such as Jean Le Nègre, was seen as perverse: 'Those whose standards are so far from the normal as his are not ideal fillers of the quadruple role of witness, prosecuting counsel, jury and judge' – Cyril Falls in *The Times Literary Supplement*, 26 July 1928.

Source: E. E. Cummings, *The Enormous Room*, New York, Boni & Liveright, 1922; Penguin Books, 1971.

I BEGIN A PILGRIMAGE

... Monsieur le Ministre may have felt that he was losing his case, for he played his trump card immediately: 'You are aware that your friend has written to friends in America and to his family very bad letters.' 'I am not,' I said.

In a flash I understood the motivation of Monsieur's visit to *Vingt-et-Un:* the French censor had intercepted some of B.'s letters, and had notified Mr A. and Mr A.'s translator, both of whom had thankfully testified to the bad character of B. and (wishing very naturally to get rid of both of us at once) had further averred that we were always together and that consequently I might properly be regarded as a suspicious character. Whereupon they had received instructions to hold us at the section until Noyon could arrive and take charge – hence our failure to obtain our long-overdue permission.

'Your friend,' said Monsieur in English, 'is here a short while ago. I ask him if he is up in the aeroplane flying over Germans will he drop the bombs on Germans and he say no, he will not drop any bombs on Germans.'

By this falsehood (such it happened to be) I confess that I was nonplussed. In the first place, I was at the time innocent of third-degree methods. Secondly, I remembered that, a week or so since, B., myself and another American in the section had written a letter – which, on the advice of the *sous-lieutenant* who accompanied *Vingt-et-Un* as translator, we had addressed to the Under-Secretary of State in French Aviation – asking that inasmuch as the American Government was about to take over the Red Cross (which meant that all the Sanitary Sections would be affiliated with the American, and no longer with the French, Army) we three at any rate might be allowed to continue our association with the French by enlisting in l'Esquadrille Lafayette. One of the 'dirty Frenchmen' had written the letter for us in the finest language imaginable, from data supplied by ourselves.

'You write a letter, your friend and you, for French aviation?'

Here I corrected him: there were three of us; and why didn't he have the third culprit arrested, might I ask? But he ignored this little digression, and wanted to know: Why not American aviation? – to which I answered: 'Ah, but as my friend has so often said to me, the French are after all the finest people in the world.'

This double-blow stopped Noyon dead, but only for a second.

'Did your friend write this letter?' – 'No,' I answered truthfully. – 'Who did write it?' – 'One of the Frenchmen attached to the section.' – 'What is his name?' – 'I'm sure I don't know,' I answered; mentally swearing that, whatever might happen to me the scribe should not suffer. 'At my urgent request,' I added . . .

———

. . . Following up this *sortie*, I addressed the mustache: 'Write this down in the testimony – that I, here present, refuse utterly to believe that my friend is not as sincere a lover of France and the French people as any man living! – Tell him to write it,' I commanded Noyon stonily. But Noyon shook his head, saying: 'We have the very best reason for supposing your friend to be no friend of France.' I answered: 'That is not my affair. I want my opinion of my friend written in; do you see?' 'That's reasonable,' the rosette murmured; and the mustache wrote it down.

'Why do you think we volunteered?' I asked sarcastically, when the testimony was complete.

Monsieur le Ministre was evidently rather uncomfortable. He writhed a little in his chair, and tweaked his chin three or four times. The rosette and the mustache were exchanging animated phrases. At last Noyon, motioning for silence and speaking in an almost desperate tone, demanded:

'*Est-ce-que vous détestez les boches?*'

I had won my own case. The question was purely perfunctory. To walk out of the room a free man I had merely to say yes. My

examiners were sure of my answer. The rosette was leaning
forward and smiling encouragingly. The mustache was making
little *ouis* in the air with his pen. And Noyon had given up all
hope of making me out a criminal. I might be rash, but I was
innocent; the dupe of a superior and malign intelligence. I
would probably be admonished to choose my friends more
carefully next time and that would be all . . .

Deliberately, I framed the answer:

'*Non. J'aime beaucoup les français.*'

Agile as a weasel, Monsieur le Ministre was on top of me: 'It is
impossible to love Frenchmen and not to hate Germans.'

I did not mind his triumph in the least. The discomfiture of
the rosette merely amused me. The surprise of the mustache I
found very pleasant.

Poor rosette! He kept murmuring desperately: 'Fond of his
friend, quite right. Mistaken of course, too bad, meant well.'

With a supremely disagreeable expression on his immaculate
face the victorious minister of security pressed his victim with
regained assurance: 'But you are doubtless aware of the atrocities
committed by the boches?'

'I have read about them,' I replied very cheerfully.

'You do not believe?'

'*Ça ce peut.*'

'And if they are so, which of course they are' (tone of profound
conviction) 'you do not detest the Germans?'

'Oh, in that case, of course anyone must detest them,' I
averred with perfect politeness.

And my case was lost, forever lost. I breathed freely once
more. All my nervousness was gone. The attempt of the three
gentlemen sitting before me to endow my friend and myself with
different fates had irrevocably failed.

At the conclusion of a short conference I was told by Monsieur:

'I am sorry for you, but due to your friend you will be
detained a little while' . . .

———

APOLLYON

. . . Also I recollected glancing through on open door into the
women's quarters, at the risk of being noticed by the *planton* in
whose charge I was at the time (who, fortunately, was stupid even
for a *planton*, else I should have been well punished for my curiosity)

and beholding *paillasses* identical in all respects with ours reposing on the floor; and I thought, if it is marvellous that old men and sick men can stand this and not die, it is certainly miraculous that girls of eleven and fifteen, and the baby which I saw once being caressed out in the women's *cour* with unspeakable gentleness by a little *putain* whose name I do not know, and the dozen or so oldish females whom I have often seen on promenade – can stand this and not die. These things I mention not to excite the reader's pity nor yet his indignation; I mention them because I do not know of any other way to indicate – it is no more than indicating – the significance of the torture perpetrated under the Directeur's direction in the case of the girl Lena. If incidentally it throws light on the personality of the torturer I shall be gratified.

Lena's confinement in the *cabinot* – which dungeon I have already attempted to describe but to whose filth and slime no words can begin to do justice – was in this case solitary . . .

———

. . . But the experience *à propos les femmes*, which meant and will always mean more to me than any other, the scene which is a little more unbelievable than perhaps any scene that it has ever been my privilege to witness, the incident which (possibly more than any other) revealed to me those unspeakable foundations upon which are builded with infinite care such at once ornate and comfortable structures as *La Gloire* and *Le Patriotisme* – occurred in this wise.

The men, myself among them, were leaving *le cour* for The Enormous Room under the watchful eye (as always) of a *planton*. As we defiled through the little gate in the barbed wire fence we heard, apparently just inside the building whither we were proceeding on our way to The Great Upstairs, a tremendous sound of mingled screams, curses and crashings. The *planton* of the day was not only stupid – he was a little deaf; to his ears this hideous racket had not, as nearly as one could see, penetrated. At all events he marched us along toward the door with utmost plantonic satisfaction and composure. I managed to insert myself in the fore of the procession, being eager to witness the scene within; and reached the door almost simultaneously with Fritz, Harree and two or three others. I forget which of us opened it. I will never forget what I saw as I crossed the threshold.

The hall was filled with stifling smoke; the smoke which straw makes when it is set on fire, a peculiarly nauseous choking, whitish-blue smoke. This smoke was so dense that only after some moments could I make out, with bleeding eyes and wounded lungs, anything whatever. What I saw was this: five or six *plantons* were engaged in carrying out of the nearest *cabinot* two girls, who looked perfectly dead. Their bodies were absolutely limp. Their hands dragged foolishly along the floor as they were carried. Their upward white faces dangled loosely upon their necks. Their crumpled fingers sagged in the *plantons'* arms. I recognized Lily and Renée. Lena I made out at a little distance tottering against the door of the kitchen opposite the *cabinot*, her haycolored head drooping and swaying slowly upon the open breast of her shirt-waist, her legs far apart and propping with difficulty her hinging body, her hands spasmodically searching for the knob of the door. The smoke proceeded from the open *cabinot* in great ponderous murdering clouds. In one of these clouds, erect and tense and beautiful as an angel – her wildly shouting face framed in its huge night of dishevelled hair, her deep sexual voice, hoarsely strident above the din and smoke, shouting fiercely through the darkness – stood, triumphantly and colossally young, Celina. Facing her, its clenched, pinkish fists raised high above its savagely bristling head in a big, brutal gesture of impotence and rage and anguish – the Fiend Himself paused quivering. Through the smoke, the great bright voice of Celina rose at him, hoarse and rich and sudden and intensely luxurious, a quick, throaty, accurate, slaying deepness:

SHIEZ, SI VOUS VOULEZ, SHIEZ,

and over and beneath and around the voice I saw frightened faces of women hanging in the smoke, some screaming with their lips apart and their eyes closed, some staring with wide eyes; and among the women's faces I discovered the large placid interested expression of the Gestionnaire and the nervous clicking eyes of the Surveillant. And there was a shout – it was the Black Holster shouting at us as we stood transfixed –

'Who the devil brought the men in here? Get up with you where you belong, you . . .'

– And he made a rush at us, and we dodged in the smoke and passed slowly up the hall, looking behind us, speechless to a man with the admiration of Terror till we reached the further flight of stairs; and mounted slowly, with the din falling below us, ringing in our ears, beating upon our brains – mounted slowly with quickened blood and pale faces – to the peace of The Enormous Room.

I spoke with both *balayeurs* that night. They told me, independently, the same story: the four incorrigibles had been locked in the *cabinot ensemble*. They made so much noise, particularly Lily, that the *plantons* were afraid the Directeur would be disturbed. Accordingly the *plantons* got together and stuffed the contents of a *paillasse* in the cracks around the door, and particularly in the crack under the door wherein cigarettes were commonly inserted by friends of the entombed. This process made the *cabinot* airtight. But the *plantons* were not taking any chances on disturbing Monsieu le Directeur. They carefully lighted the *paillasse* at a number of points and stood back to see the results of their efforts. So soon as the smoke found its way inward the singing was supplanted by coughing; then the coughing stopped. Then nothing was heard. Then Celina began crying out within – 'Open the door, Lily and Renée are dead' – and the *plantons* were frightened. After some debate they decided to open the door – out poured the smoke, and in it Celina, whose voice in a fraction of a second roused everyone in the building. The Black Holster wrestled with her and tried to knock her down by a blow on the mouth; but she escaped, bleeding a little, to the foot of the stairs – simultaneously with the advent of the Directeur who for once had found someone beyond the power of his weapon, Fear, someone in contact with whose indescribable Youth the puny threats of death withered between his lips, someone finally completely and unutterably Alive whom the Lie upon his slavering tongue could not heal . . .

———

JEAN LE NÈGRE

. . . There was another game – a pure child's game – which Jean played. It was the name game. He amused himself for hours together by lying on his *paillasse*, tilting his head back, rolling up his eyes, and crying in a high quavering voice – 'J A W-neeeeeee.' After a repetition or two of his own name in English, he would demand sharply '*Qui m'appelle?* Mexique? *Est-ce que tu m'appelle*, Mexique?' and if Mexique happened to be asleep, Jean would rush over and cry in his ear shaking him thoroughly – '*Est-ce tu m'appelle, toi?*' Or it might be Barbu, or Pete the Hollander, or B. or myself, of whom he sternly asked the question – which was always followed by quantities of laughter on Jean's part. He was never perfectly happy unless exercising his inexhaustible imagination . . .

Of all Jean's extraordinary selves, the moral one was at once the most rare and most unreasonable. In the matter of *les femmes* he could hardly have been accused by his bitterest enemy of being a Puritan. Yet the Puritan streak came out one day, in a discussion which lasted for several hours. Jean, as in the case of France, spoke in dogma. His contention was very simple: '*La femme qui fume n'est pas une femme.*' He defended it hotly against the attacks of all the nations represented; in vain did Belgian and Hollander, Russian and Pole, Spaniard and Alsatian, charge and counter-charge – Jean remained unshaken. A woman could do anything but smoke – if she smoked she ceased automatically to be a woman and became something unspeakable. As Jean was at this time sitting alternately on B.'s bed and mine, and as the alternations became increasingly frequent as the discussion waxed hotter, we were not sorry when the *planton's* shout, '*A la promenade les hommes!*' scattered the opposing warriors. Then up leaped Jean (who had almost come to blows innumerable times) and rushed laughing to the door, having already forgotten the whole thing.

Now we come to the story of Jean's undoing, and may the gods which made Jean Le Nègre give me grace to tell it as it was.

The trouble started with Lulu. One afternoon, shortly after the telephoning, Jean was sick at heart and couldn't be induced either to leave his couch or to utter a word. Every one guessed the reason – Lulu had left for another camp that morning. The *planton* told Jean to come down with the rest and get *soupe*. No answer. Was Jean sick? '*Oui*, me seek.' And steadfastly he refused to eat, till the disgusted *planton* gave it up and locked Jean in alone. When we ascended after *la soupe* we found Jean as we had left him, stretched on his couch, big tears on his cheeks. I asked him if I could do anything for him; he shook his head. We offered him cigarettes – no, he did not wish to smoke. As B. and I went away we heard him moaning to himself, 'Jawnee no see Loo-Loo no more.' With the exception of ourselves, the inhabitants of La Ferté Macé took Jean's desolation as a great joke. Shouts of Lulu! rent the welkin on all sides. Jean stood it for an hour; then he leaped up, furious; and demanded (confronting the man from whose lips the cry had last issued) – 'Feeneesh Loo-Loo?' The latter coolly referred him to the man next to him; he in turn to some one else; and round and round the room Jean stalked, seeking the offender, followed by louder and louder shouts of Lulu! and Jawnee! the authors of which (so soon as he challenged them) denied with innocent faces their guilt and recommended that Jean look closer next time. At last Jean took to his couch in

368

utter misery and disgust. – The rest of *les hommes* descended as usual for the promenade – not so Jean. He ate nothing for supper. That evening not a sound issued from his bed.

Next morning he awoke with a broad grin, and to the salutations of Lulu! replied, laughing heartily at himself 'FEEN-EESH Loo-Loo.' Upon which the tormentors (finding in him no longer a victim) desisted; and things resumed their normal course. If an occasional Lulu! upraised itself, Jean merely laughed and repeated (with a wave of his arm) 'FEENEESH'. Finished Lulu seemed to be . . .

———

. . . Now the *Surveillant* returned and made a speech, to the effect that he had received independently of each other the stories of four men, that by all counts *le nègre* was absolutely to blame, that *le nègre* had caused an inexcusable trouble to the authorities and to his fellow-prisoners by this wholly unjustified conflict, and that as a punishment the *nègre* would now suffer the consequences of his guilt in the *cabinot*. – Jean had dropped his arms to his sides. His face was twisted with anguish. He made a child's gesture, a pitiful hopeless movement with his slender hands. Sobbing, he protested: '*C'est pas ma faute, monsieur le surveillant! Ils m'attaquaient! J'ai rien fait! Ils voulaient me tuer! Demandez à lui*' – he pointed to me desperately. Before I could utter a syllable the *Surveillant* raised his hand for silence: *le nègre* had done wrong. He should be placed in the *cabinot*.

– Like a flash, with a horrible tearing sob, Jean leaped from the surrounding *plantons* and rushed for the coat which lay on his bed screaming – 'AHHHHH – *mon couteau!*' – 'Look out or he'll get his knife and kill himself!' some one yelled; and the four *plantons* seized Jean by both arms just as he made a grab for his jacket. Thwarted in this hope and burning with the ignominy of his situation, Jean cast his enormous eyes up at the nearest pillar, crying hysterically: '*Tout le monde me fout au cabinot parce que je suis noir.*' – In a second, by a single movement of his arms, he sent the four *plantons* reeling to a distance of ten feet; leaped at the pillar: seized it in both hands like a Samson, and (gazing for another second with a smile of absolute beatitude at its length) dashed his head against it. Once, twice, thrice he smote himself, before the *plantons* seized him – and suddenly his whole strength wilted; he allowed himself to be overpowered by them and stood with bowed head, tears streaming from his eyes – while the smallest pointed a revolver at his heart . . .

PAUL NASH

Paul Nash (1889–1946) Born in London and educated at St Paul's School, and, like Bomberg, Rosenberg and Stanley Spencer, at the Slade School of Fine Art. He enlisted in the Artists' Rifles in 1914, and served on the Western Front. He is generally regarded as one of the finest painters to respond to the war (along with Spencer) and some of his finest work was produced out of this experience. He was one of the official War Artists on the Western Front during the autumn of 1917. *Outline* was published posthumously in 1949, and contains letters from Nash, who was then on the Western Front, to his wife. Excerpts from these letters appear below. Nash died in 1946.

Source: Paul Nash, *Outline, An Autobiography and Other Writings*, London, Faber, 1949.

> 4 April 1917
> Front Line Trench,
> St Eloi, Ypres Salient

. . . Since I came into camp again, I have received and executed a strange commission. Our peculiar CO requested a life-size figure of a man scratching himself to describe an anti-bug powder he is interested in, so I have painted a colossal figure on wood planks with very crude paints, and today the CO happened to come along and is mightily pleased with it. Good news, too, for you. I have been detailed to go with Coleman on a month's course at the Divisional School, which means I lose the line next time, and when I get out the battalion will probably be out at rest for about three weeks. So God knows when I shall see the jolly old trenches again. Still, for your sake, I am glad, you can rest peacefully and with any decent luck I shall also get time to work on some of the drawings and get permission to send them home.

> 6 April,
> Good Friday, 1917

The last week has been one so full that I have literally been unable to write. My inner excitement and exultation was so great that I have lived in a cloud of thought these last days. This combined with a certain physical strain has hindered and chained me from quiet continuous writing. Oh, these wonderful trenches at night, at dawn, at sundown! Shall I ever lose the picture they have made in my mind. Imagine a wide landscape flat and scantily wooded and what trees remain blasted and torn, naked and scarred and riddled. The ground for miles around furrowed into trenches, pitted with yawning holes in which the water lies still and cold or heaped with mounds of earth, tangles of rusty wire, tin plates, stakes, sandbags and all the refuse of war. In the distance runs a stream where the stringy poplars and alders lean about dejectedly, while farther a slope rises to a scarred bluff the foot of which is scattered with headless trees standing white and withered, hopeless, without any leaves, done, dead. As shells fall in the bluff, huge spouts of black, brown and orange mould burst into the air amid a volume of white smoke, flinging wide incredible débris, while the crack and roar of the explosion reverberates in the valley. In the midst of this strange country, where such things happen, men are living in their narrow ditches, hidden from view by every cunning device, waiting and always on the watch, yet at the same time, easy, careless, well fed, wrapped up in warm clothes, talking, perpetually smoking, and indifferent to anything that occurs. Unless a shell falls into the trench there is no excitement, and even this provokes the minimum of disturbance. All day long, with only a few intervals, the shells pass overhead, always the same sound as of a body leaving the sky like canvas, and so loud and so easy to follow in imagination that it seems ridiculous that you can never see them. Of course the heavy trench mortars throw over shells that can be plainly seen heaving through the air tumbling over and over until they fall, and then a second's pause and then a bang. The earth rises in a complicated eruption of smoke, and bits begin to fall for yards wide splashing into the pools, flinging up the water, rattling on the iron sheets, spattering us and the ground near by. As night falls the monstrous land takes on a strange aspect. The sun sinks in a clear evening and smoke hangs in narrow bars of violet and dark. In the clear light the shapes of the trench stand massy and cold, the mud gleams whitely, the sandbags have a hard, rocky look, the works of men look a freak of nature, rather, the landscape is so distorted from its own gentle forms, nothing seems to bear the imprint of God's hand, the whole might be a terrific creation of some malign fiend working a crooked will on the innocent countryside. Twilight quivers above, shrinking into night, and a perfect crescent moon sails uncannily below pale stars. As the dark gathers, the horizon brightens and again vanishes as the Very lights rise and fall, shedding their weird greenish glare over the land, and acute contrast to their lazy silent flight breaks out the agitated knocking of the machine-guns as they sweep the parapets. So night falls gradually becoming greater as the hours increase, the great quiet of Nature's sleep only broken by occasional shots from snipers, or distant booming when some 'strafe' is in progress toward the north, and when the restless Maxim shatters silence and again silence – it only closes in profounder, stiller, after the echoes have died away . . .

I am writing this impression of the front line which you shall have later; maybe you can feel something of the weird beauty from this little letter . . .

18 April 1917

I have been a good deal worried over the papers lately, for, in spite of your brave efforts at stoicism, we can see things are in a bad way. It is fearfully difficult here to realize there is such a great shortage of food as there would seem to be in the country, and it is more than damnable to know this while we are overfed here. Something must be shamefully crooked in the works in England. We read about profiteers, we see cartoons depicting them as monsters eating the people's food – but why are they allowed to live? No one in our country ever seems to have the simplest notion of grappling with things – we are a shilly-shally-ing people unable to deal with decision. Determination is our strength – sticking it; we shall starve splendidly, it will bring out all the national grit – in the bread. But apart from any bitter thoughts one may have on the subject, we are all uneasy out here. The letters of 'Eve' drivel on each week and a new batch of snaky actresses crop up in *The Tatler* and *Sketch* – personally I like reading Eve's nonsense and looking at the legs of the pretty actresses, if I am not thinking of anything at all, but sometimes I sit up with a start and wonder if we are all mad. As for the newspapers, I don't know why, but out here they are more maddening than ever. As I read, it just seems as if I heard all the pap being made and dripping, dripping into the foolish blubber mouth of the people which greedily laps it up, loving it so – the great brain fodder, the food of the little gods. I seem to see the label on the bottle, 'specially prepared for His Majesty and all His people by Northcliffe and Co. and the damned almighty Press'. It is intolerable – I cannot read the papers – it's just humbug from beginning to end. We need a spirit to stamp out cant and lies from England, a race of men and women in England to supersede a brood of efts and leeches. You speak of a revolution that will come at home if war grinds us to famine; it would be a pity to nurse your sorrows and your wrongs until the men return, that is when revolution would come. Out here men have been thinking, living so near to silence and death, their thoughts have been furious, keen, and living has been alive. Hammering in their minds are a hundred questions, festering in their hearts a thousand wrongs. The most insistent question is 'Why am I here?' The greatest wrong 'I am still here'; but an end will come one day and the next will be a day of reckoning. Everyone knows that out here – do they know it at home, I wonder – they will. Strange for me to burst into a tirade! . . .

2 May 1917

. . . We are a very long way from the line among rolling hills of pasture land and quiet hamlets. Three days we were on the march and not one man fell out. The men are magnificent, all war-worn and ruddy with health. You would admire them no end if you could be by the roadside and see a battalion go by. There is a quiet confident strength, an easy carriage and rough beauty about these men which would make your heart jump and give you a lumpy throat with pride. The other day as I watched them I felt near tears somehow. Poor little lonely creatures in this great waste . . . I can't write of Billy, I haven't realized it yet; when these things happen I am always strangely unemotional. At first I feel a sort of clutch at my heart, then nothing but vague, dull thoughts. Billy, he was such a dear fellow. I will try and write to his people. Thomas (Edward Thomas) is dead, the same way. I brood on it dully. Sometimes I am almost afraid, I know not of what, but it will not be so very long before we are in the fight. I shall not fear then. I only pray I don't think of you when the moment comes – only of my men. But if I am hit, then it does not matter, and I can think of you at the last and for ever after till we meet again. Do not fear, I am not morbid, and you will never hear me speak of death again; but you have spoken of it, and I may as well just say so much of my many thoughts . . .

5 November 1917
(Intelligence HQ, France)

. . . Today I have seen one of the latest and most terrible battlefields of Flanders, where I return tomorrow to do more drawings. It is indescribable. So soon as I have a minute's rest I will write you a decent letter. This one is done in the car while we dodge in and out of the traffic. I've been painfully writing it all day. I have an excellent driver who does the most amazing things. He also has a reputation of being able to show one almost every pretty girl in this part of France. So I'm alright, I think. The French are robbers and annoy me terribly by their cupidity. Masterman won't like the bill. How is everybody at home?

13 November 1917

I am settled here for a week, so very soon expect letters will come through to me as I have wired GHQ my address. Yesterday I made twelve drawings, nine of different aspects of one of the most famous battlefields in the war (Passchendaele); I just missed the battle. The day was freshening cold, but wonderfully changeable in colour and light, so I was able to get some useful looking sketches . . .

Three days later

I have had to postpone this letter, it is even more difficult than it was when I was out last. I start off directly after breakfast and do not get home till dinner-time, and after that I work on my drawings until about eleven o'clock at night, when I feel very sleepy and go to bed. Today, Sunday, has been more or less a holiday, so I motored down to take the old man out. We spent a great day and I have just got back (9 p.m.). The prevailing idea that he is depressed and hopeless is entirely wrong, he says he has never been so, and he seems to have got an enormous lot out of life over here. He is a real good soldier and very proud of it. Of course, he is dying to get home for a bit, and very keen now on getting a commission and wearing decent clothes again, but I assure you he has borne all the rough times magnificently, and he has really had it very rough. He is simply splendid and never stops talking of the good friends he has made and how they make the best of things and stick it out together. The whole thing has done him the world of good and as for wit it sparkles brighter than ever ... I have just returned, last night, from a visit to Brigade Headquarters up the line, and I shall not forget it as long as I live. I have seen the most frightful nightmare of a country more conceived by Dante or Poe than by nature, unspeakable, utterly indescribable. In the fifteen drawings I have made I may give you some vague idea of its horror, but only being in it and of it can ever make you sensible of its dreadful nature and of what our men in France have to face. We all have a vague notion of the terrors of a battle, and can conjure up with the aid of some of the more inspired war correspondents and the pictures in the *Daily Mirror* some vision of a battlefield; but no pen or drawing can convey this country – the normal setting of the battles taking place day and night, month after month. Evil and the incarnate fiend alone can be master of this war, and no glimmer of God's hand is seen anywhere. Sunset and sunrise are blasphemous, they are mockeries to man, only the black rain out of the bruised and swollen clouds all through the bitter black of night is fit atmosphere in such a land. The rain drives on, the stinking mud becomes more evilly yellow, the shell holes fill up with green-white water, the roads and tracks are covered in inches of slime, the black dying trees ooze and sweat and the shells never cease. They alone plunge overhead, tearing away the rotting tree stumps, breaking the plank roads, striking down horses and mules, annihilating, maiming, maddening, they plunge into the grave which is this land; one huge grave, and cast up on it the poor dead. It is unspeakable, godless, hopeless. I am no longer an artist interested and curious, I am a messenger who will bring back word from the men who are fighting to those who want the war to go on for ever. Feeble, inarticulate, will be my message, but it will have a bitter truth, and may it burn their lousy souls. –

ISAAC ROSENBERG

Isaac Rosenberg (1890–1918). Born in Bristol of Jewish parents. When he was seven the family moved to the Jewish ghetto of East London. He started his artistic life, at least in the eyes of the world, as a painter, and became a student at the Slade School of Fine Art in London – through the generosity of three Jewish women. He was friendly with the painter David Bomberg, who also studied at the Slade School (as did Stanley Spencer). Rosenberg's most recent *Collected Works*, edited by Ian Parsons (with substantial assistance from Richard Anderson), was published in 1979; this is the edition from which the letters below are drawn. Rosenberg was killed in action on the Western Front, 1 April 1918.

Source: Isaac Rosenberg, *The Collected Works of Isaac Rosenberg*, ed. Ian Parsons, London, Chatto & Windus, 1979.

[Apparently unfinished letter to Ezra Pound, 1915]

87 Dempsey Street
Stepney E

Dear Mr Pound

Thank you very much for sending my things to America. As to your suggestion about the army I think the world has been terribly damaged by certain poets (in fact any poet) being sacrificed in this stupid business. There is certainly a strong temptation to join when you are making no money.

[Late April 1915]
87 Dempsey Street
Stepney E

My Dear Marsh

I am so sorry – what else can I say?

But he himself[1] has said 'What is more safe than death?' For us is the hurt who feel about English literature, and for you who knew him and feel his irreparable loss.

Yours sincerely
Isaac Rosenberg

Dear Marsh

I am very sorry to have had to disturb you at such a time with pictures. But when one's only choice is between horrible things you choose the least horrible. First I think of enlisting and trying to get my head blown off, then of getting some manual labour to do – anything – but it seems I'm not fit for anything. Then I took these things to you. You would forgive me if you knew how wretched I was. I am sorry I can give you no more comfort in your own trial but I am going through it too.

Thank you for your cheque[;] it will do for paints and I will try and do something you'll like.

Yours sincerely
Isaac Rosenberg

Dear Mr Schiff

... I am thinking of enlisting if they will have me, though it is against all my principles of justice – though I would be doing the most criminal thing a man can do – I am so sure my mother would not stand the shock that I don't know what to do.

Yours sincerely
Isaac Rosenberg

Dear Mr Schiff

... Painting was once an honest trade, now the painter is either a gentleman, or must subsist on patronage – anyway I won't let painting interfere with my peace of mind[.] If later on I haven't forgotten it I may yet do something. Forgive this private cry but even the enormity of what is going on all

through Europe always seems less to an individual than his own
struggle.

> Yours sincerely
> Isaac Rosenberg

The drawings will follow

> [October 1915]
> 87 Dempsey Street
> Stepney E

Dear Mr Schiff

Thank you for the cheque which is as much to me now as all
the money in America would be to the Allies. When I am settled
I hope you will allow me to return it either in drawings or
money. I expect to know enough for my purpose in 2 months,
and I will let you know how I get on. As to what you say about
my being luckier than other victims I can only say that one's
individual situation is more real and important to oneself than
the devastation of fates [2] and empires especially when they do
not vitally affect oneself. I can only give my personal and if you
like selfish point of view that I[,] feeling myself in the prime and
vigour of my powers (whatever they may be) have no more free
will than a tree; seeing with helpless clear eyes the utter destruction of the railways and avenues of approaches to outer communication cut off. Being by the nature of my upbringing, all
my energies having been directed to one channel of activity,
crippled from other activities and made helpless even to live. It
is true I have not been killed or crippled, been a loser in the
stocks, or had to forswear my fatherland, but I have not quite
gone free and have a right to say something.

Forgive all this bluster but – salts for constipation – moral of
course.

> Yours sincerely
> Isaac Rosenberg

> [1915 ?October]
> 87 Dempsey Street
> Stepney E

Dear Mr Schiff

... I have changed my mind again about joining the army. I

feel about it that more men means more war, – besides the immorality of joining with no patriotic convictions.

Thank you very much for your cheque.

Yours sincerely
Isaac Rosenberg

On Y M C A notepaper, headed 'H M Forces on Active Service'

[October 1915]
Priv. I. Rosenberg
Bat. Bantam, Regt. 12th Suffolk,
New Depot, Bury St Edmunds

Dear Mr Schiff,

I could not get the work I thought I might so I have joined this Bantam Battalion (as I was too short for any other) which seems to be the most rascally affair in the world. I have to eat out of a basin together with some horribly smelling scavenger who spits and sneezes into it etc. It is most revolting, at least up to now – I don't mind the hard sleeping the stiff marches etc but this is unbearable. Besides my being a Jew makes it bad amongst these wretches. I am looking forward to having a bad time altogether. I am sending some old things to the New English and if they get in you may see them there. I may be stationed here some time or be drafted off somewhere else; if you write I will be glad to hear[.]

Yours sincerely
I. Rosenberg

[October 1915]
12th Suffolks
Bantam Bat.
New Offices Recruiting Depot
Bury St Edmunds

Dear Marsh

I have just joined the Bantams and am down here amongst a horrible rabble – Falstaff's scarecrows were nothing to these. Three out of every 4 have been scavengers[,] the fourth is a ticket of leave . . .

379

Dear Mr Schiff

... I wanted to join the R A M C [3] as the idea of killing upsets me a bit, but I was too small. The only regiment my build allowed was the Bantams.

Yours sincerely
I. Rosenberg

[November 1915]
Priv. I. Rosenberg
12th Suffolk Bantams
Military Hospital, Depot,
Bury St Edmunds
Tuesday night

Dear Mr Schiff

... I hope you are happy with your work. Any kind of work if one [can] only be doing something is what one wants now. I feel very grateful at your appreciation of my position, it keeps the clockwork going. To me this is not a result but one motion of the intricate series of activities that all combine to make a result. One might succumb[,] be destroyed – but one might also (and the chances are even greater for it) be renewed, ...

[Early December 1915]
22648
Company C, Bat. Bantam,
Regt. 12th Suffolks,
Bury St Edmunds

Dear Mr Schiff

... The money you sent me I was forced to buy boots with as the military boots rubbed all the skin off my feet and I've been marching in terrible agony. The kind of life does not bother me much. I sleep soundly on boards in the cold; the drills I find fairly interesting, but up till now these accidents have bothered me and I am still suffering with them. My hands are not better and my feet are hell. We have pups for officers – at least one –

who seems to dislike me – and you know his position gives him power to make me feel it without me being able to resist. When my feet and hands are better I will slip into the work but as I am it is awkward. The doctor here too, Major Devoral, is a ridiculous bullying brute and I have marked him for special treatment when I come to write about the army . . .

[December 1915]
Pte I. Rosenberg
No 22648
Platoon No 3
12th Suffolks. Hut No 2
Depot. Bury St Edmunds

My Dear Marsh

I have devoured your chocolates with the help of some comrades and am now out of the hospital. I have been kept very busy and I find that the actual duties though they are difficult at first and require all one's sticking power are not in themselves unpleasant, it is the brutal militaristic bullying meanness of the way they're served out to us. You're always being threatened with 'clink' . . .

[Late December 1915]
87 Dempsey Street
Stepney London E
Thursday

Dear Mr Schiff

I shall be home for 4 days from tomorrow, Fri, as you asked me to let you know. I must be looking smart, for I was offered a stripe which I declined. I have some more pictures at home if you care to see, though I, since I have joined[,] have hardly given poetry or painting a thought. I feel as if I were casting my coat, I mean, like a snake or butterfly. Here's another one of myself, not much like a poet – I'm afraid.

Yours sincerely
Isaac Rosenberg

My Dear Marsh

I have sent on the poems to L.A. I sent this one as well which I like.[4] But it is something else I want to write about. I never joined the army from patriotic reasons. Nothing can justify war. I suppose we must all fight to get the trouble over. Anyhow before the war I helped at home when I could and I did other things which helped to keep things going. I thought if I'd join there would be the separation allowance for my mother. At Whitehall it was fixed up that 16/6 would be given including the 3/6 a week deducted from my 7/-. Its now between 2 and 3 months since I joined; my 3/6 is deducted right enough, but my mother hasn't received a farthing. The paymaster at barracks of course is no use in this matter. I wonder if you know how these things are managed and what I might do.

Yours sincerely
Isaac Rosenberg

[Postmarked 29 January 1916]
24520
A Coy, 12th South Lancs
Alma Bks, Blackdown Camp
Farnborough, Hants

My Dear Marsh

I don't remember whether I told you I'd got transferred to this lot and am now near Aldershot. We are having pretty rigourous training down here and the talk is we are going out the middle of next month. Except for the starvation rations and headachy moments I get its not so bad down here . . .

To Lascelles Abercrombie

11 March 1916
24520
A Coy, 12th South Lancs
Alma Bks, Blackdown Camp
Farnborough

Dear Sir

Your letter was sent to me from home and it gave me a lot of pleasure. I really wonder whether my things are worth the trouble you have taken in analysing them, but if you think they are, and from your letter, you do, of course I should feel encouraged. I send you here my two latest poems, which I have managed to write, though in the utmost distress of mind, or perhaps because of it. Believe me the army is the most detestable invention on this earth and nobody but a private in the army knows what it is to be a slave.

I wonder whether your muse has been sniffing gunpowder.

Thank you for your good wishes.

Yours sincerely
Isaac Rosenberg

[1916, ?March]
24520
A Coy, 12th South Lancs
Alma Bks, Blackdown Camp
Farnborough, Hants

Dear Mr Schiff

I have been in this reg about 2 months now and have been kept going all the time. Except that the food is unspeakable, and perhaps luckily, scanty, the rest is pretty tolerable. I have food sent up from home and that keeps me alive, but as for the others, there is talk of mutiny every day. One reg close by did break out and some men got bayoneted. I don't know when we are going out but the talk is very shortly . . .

[No date]
22311 A Coy 3 platoon
11th K.O.R.L. B.E.F.

Dear Mrs Cohen

We are on a long march and I'm writing this on the chance of getting it off; so you should know I received your papers and also your letter. The notice in the Times of your book is true – especially about your handling of metre. It is an interesting number. The Poetry Review you sent is good – the articles are too breathless, and want more packing, I think. The poems by

383

the soldier are vigorous but, I feel a bit common-place. I did not
like Rupert Brooke's begloried sonnets for the same reason.
What I mean is second hand phrases 'lambent fires' etc takes
from its reality and strength. It should be approached in a
colder way, more abstract, with less of the million feelings
everybody feels; or all these should be concentrated in one
distinguished emotion. Walt Whitman in 'Beat, drums, beat',
has said the noblest thing on war . . .

> 4 August [1916]
> c/o 40th Divisional Coy Officer
> B.E.F. Pte I. Rosenberg 22311

My Dear Marsh
   . . . I work more and more as I write into more depth and
lucidity, I am sure. I have a fine idea for a most gorgeous play,
Adam and Lilith. If I could get a few months after the war to
work and absorb myself completely into the thing, I'd write a
great thing . . .
   I am enclosing a poem[5] I wrote in the trenches, which is
surely as simple as ordinary talk. You might object to the second
line as vague, but that was the best way I could express the sense
of dawn . . .

> [August 1916]
> 22311
> A Coy 3 Platoon
> 11th K.O.R.L. B.E.F.

My Dear Marsh
   . . . I have been forbidden to send poems home, as the censor
won't be bothered with going through such rubbish, or I would
have sent you one I wrote about our armies, which I am rather
bucked about. I have asked the 'Nation' to print it, if they do,
you will see it there . . .

To Laurence Binyon   [Autumn 1916]
It is far, very far, to the British Museum from here (situated as I
am, Siberia is no further and certainly no colder), but not too
far for that tiny mite of myself, my letter, to reach there. Winter
has found its way into the trenches at last, but I will assure you,

and leave to your imagination, the transport of delight with which we welcomed its coming. Winter is not the least of the horrors of war. I am determined that this war, with all its powers for devastation, shall not master my poeting; that is, if I am lucky enough to come through all right. I will not leave a corner of my consciousness covered up, but saturate myself with the strange and extraordinary new conditions of this life, and it will all refine itself into poetry later on. I have thoughts of a play round our Jewish hero, Judas Maccabeus. I have much real material here, and also there is some parallel in the savagery of the invaders then to this war . . .

[Postmarked 18 January 1917]
[Address given below]

My Dear Marsh

My sister wrote me she would be writing to you. She'd got the idea of my being in vile health from your letter addressed to Dempsey Street, and naturally they at home exaggerated things in their minds. Perhaps though it is not so exaggerated. That my health is undermined I feel sure of; but I have only lately been medically examined, and absolute fitness was the verdict. My being transfer[r]ed may be the consequence of my reporting sick, or not; I don't know for certain. But though this work does not entail half the hardships of the trenches, the winter and the conditions naturally tells on me, having once suffered from weak lungs, as you know. I have been in the trenches most of the 8 months I've been here, and the continual damp and exposure is whispering to my old friend consumption, and he may hear the words they say in time. I have nothing outwardly to show yet, but I feel it inwardly. I don't know what you could do in a case like this; perhaps I could be made use of as a draughtsman at home; or something else in my own line, or perhaps on munitions. My new address is

> Pte I. R. 22311
> 7 Platoon F. Coy
> 40th Division
> Works Battalion
> B.E.F . . .

[Postmarked 30 July 1917]
Pte I. R. 22311
11th K.O.R.L.
Attached 229 Field Coy R.E.s.
B.E.F.

My Dear Marsh

I think with you that poetry should be definite thought and clear expression, however subtle; I don't think there should be any vagueness at all; but a sense of something hidden and felt to be there; Now when my things fail to be clear I am sure it is because of the luckless choice of a word or the failure to introduce a word that would flash my idea plain, as it is to my own mind. I believe my Amazon poem [6] to be my best poem. If there is any difficulty it must be in words here and there[,] the changing or elimination of which may make the poem clear. It has taken me about a year to write; for I have changed and rechanged it and thought hard over that poem and striven to get that sense of inexorableness the human (or inhuman) side of this war has. It even penetrates behind human life for the 'Amazon' who speaks in the second part of the poem is imagined to be without her lover yet, while all her sisters have theirs, the released spirits of the slain earth men; her lover yet remains to be released. I hope however to be home on leave, and talk it over, some time this side of the year. In my next letter I will try and send an idea of 'The Unicorn'.

If you are too busy don't bother about answering;

Yours sincerely
Isaac Rosenberg

To Miss Seaton   [Dated 14 February 1918]

We had a rough time in the trenches with the mud, but now we're out for a bit of a rest, and I will try and write longer letters. You must know by now what a rest behind the line means. I can call the evenings – that is, from tea to lights out – my own; but there is no chance whatever for seclusion or any hope of writing poetry now. Sometimes I give way and am appalled at the devastation this life seems to have made in my nature. It seems to have blunted me. I seem to be powerless to compel my will to any direction, and all I do is without energy and interest.

[?23 February 1918]
22311 Pte I. R.
8 Platoon, B Coy. 1st K.O.R.L
B.E.F.

Dear Rodker
... I suppose I could write a bit if I tried to work at a letter as
an idea – but sitting down to it here after a day's dull stupefying
labour – I feel stupefied. When will we go on with the things
that endure?

Yours sincerely
Isaac Rosenberg

To Gordon Bottomley   [Postmarked 26 February 1918]
I wanted to send some bits I wrote for the 'Unicorn' while I was
in hospital, and if I find them I'll enclose them. I tried to work
on your suggestion and divided it into four acts, but since I left
the hospital all the poetry has gone quite out of me. I seem even
to forget words, and I believe if I met anybody with ideas I'd be
dumb. No drug could be more stupefying than our work (to me
anyway), and this goes on like that old torture of water trickling,
drop by drop unendingly, on one's helplessness.

To Gordon Bottomley   [Dated 7 March 1918]
I believe our interlude is nearly over, and we may go up the line
any moment now, so I answer your letter straightaway. If only
this war were over our eyes would not be on death so much: it
seems to underlie even our underthoughts. Yet when I have
been so near to it as anybody could be, the idea has never
crossed my mind, certainly not so much as when some lying
doctor told me I had consumption. I like to think of myself as a
poet; so what you say, though I know it to be extravagant, gives
me immense pleasure.

To Miss Seaton   [8 March 1918]
... Did I send you a little poem, 'The Burning of the Temple'? I
thought it was poor, or rather, difficult in expression, but G.
Bottomley thinks it fine. Was it clear to you? If I am lucky, and
come off undamaged, I mean to put all my innermost experiences
into the 'Unicorn'. I want it to symbolize the war and all the

devastating forces let loose by an ambitious and unscrupulous will. Last summer I wrote pieces for it and had the whole of it planned out, but since then I've had no chance of working on it and it may have gone quite out of my mind.

1. Rupert Brooke (1887–1915) poet and close friend of Marsh, had died of blood-poisoning on his way to the Dardanelles with the Naval Division on 23 April, and was buried on the island of Skyros. Rosenberg did not admire Brooke's 1914 sonnets. [IP]
2. R clearly wrote 'fates' but this was presumably a slip of the pen for 'states'. [IP]
3. Royal Army Medical Corps.
4. 'Marching – as seen from the left file'. [IP]
5. 'Break of Day in the Trenches', although 'A Worm Fed on the Heart of Corinth' appears to have been enclosed in the same letter. [IP]
6. 'Daughters of War'.

WILFRED OWEN

Wilfred Owen (1893–1918). Born in Plas Wilmot, Oswestry, Shropshire. Educated at the Birkenhead Institute and Shrewsbury Technical School. Served in the Manchester Regiment in the war and was killed in action while trying to get his men across the Sambre Canal on 4 November 1918 (one week before the Armistice). The 'Preface' was written for the collection of poems he was planning to publish – poems mainly written in response to his experience of war on the Western Front. The collection was published posthumously. The most recent editions have been edited by Edmund Blunden (*q.v.*), C. Day Lewis, Dominic Hibberd, Jon Stallworthy and Jon Silkin. The letters included below were written when he was living in France as a teacher at the outbreak of the war; at various points in his army life; from Scotland and England when he was suffering from shell-shock; and again from France just before his death. The *Letters* were edited by his brother, Harold Owen, and John Bell, and were published in 1967.

Source: 'Preface', in Wilfred Owen, *The Collected Poems of Wilfred Owen*, London, Chatto & Windus, 1963; *Wilfred Owen: Collected Letters*, ed. H. Owen and J. Bell, London, Oxford University Press, 1967.

FROM OWEN'S PROPOSED VOLUME OF POEMS

PREFACE

This book is not about heroes. English poetry is not yet fit to speak of them.

Nor is it about deeds, or lands, nor anything about glory, honour, might, majesty, dominion, or power, except War.

Above all I am not concerned with Poetry.

My subject is War, and the pity of War.

The Poetry is in the pity.

Yet these elegies are to this generation in no sense consolatory. They may be to the next. All a poet can do today is warn. That is why the true Poets must be truthful.

(If I thought the letter of this book would last, I might have used proper names; but if the spirit of it survives – survives Prussia – my ambition and those names will have achieved themselves fresher fields than Flanders . . .)

From
WILFRED OWEN: COLLECTED LETTERS

To Harold Owen

23 September 1914
12 rue Blanc Dutrouilh
Bordeaux

. . . I went with my friend the Doctor Sauvaître to one of the large hospitals one day last week, where he is operating on the wounded. The hospital is in the buildings of the Boys' *Lycée* and appliances are altogether crude. First I saw a bullet, like this  cut out of a Zouave's[1] leg. Then we did the round of the wards; and saw some fifty German wretches: all more seriously wounded than the French. The Doctor picked out those needing surgical attention; and these were brought on stretchers to the Operating Room; formerly a Class room, with the familiar ink-stains on floor, walls, and ceiling; now a chamber of horrors with blood where the ink was. Think of it: there were eight men in the room at once, Germans being treated without the slightest distinction from the French: one scarcely knew which was which. Considering the lack of appliances – there was only one water-tap in the room – and the crowding – and the fact that the doctors were working for nothing – and on Germans too – really good work was done. Only there were no anaesthetics – no time – no money – no staff for that. So after that scene I need not fear to see the creepiest operations. One poor devil had his shin-bone crushed by a gun-carriage-wheel, and the doctor had to twist it about and push it like a piston to get out the pus. Another had a hole right through the knee; and the doctor passed a bandage thus:

Another had a head into which a ball had entered and come out

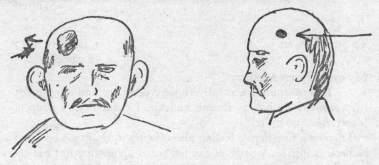

again. This is how the bullet lay in the Zouave. Sometimes the feet were covered with a brown, scaly, crust – dried blood.

covered
with dirt
- blood

I deliberately tell you all this to educate you to the actualities of the war.[2]

To Susan Owen   Saturday 18 March [1916]
                                 Y.M.C.A.
                                 [Romford]

... We are learning far more in a week here than a month of camp. The only nuisance is the Sergeant Major, Coldstream Guard, a consummate bully, amusing enough in *Punch*, but not viewed from the ranks.

The Army as a life is a curious anomaly; here we are prepared – or preparing – to lay down our lives for another, the highest moral act possible, according to the Highest Judge, and nothing of this is apparent between the jostle of discipline and jest. Again, we turn from the meanest of jobs scrubbing floors, to do delicate mapping, and while staying in for being naughty, we study the abstractions of Military Law.

On the whole, I am fortunate to be where I am, and happy sometimes, as when I think it is a life pleasing to you & Father and the Fatherland.

All the love of the whole heart of your

Wilfred

To Susan Owen 1 January 1917
[France]

My own dearest Mother,

... This morning I was hit! We were bombing and a fragment from somewhere hit my thumb knuckle. I coaxed out 1 drop of blood. Alas! no more!!

There is a fine heroic feeling about being in France, and I am in perfect spirits. A tinge of excitement is about me, but excitement is always necessary to my happiness.

I don't think it is the real front I'm going to.

If on my Field Post Card I cross out 'I am being sent down to the base' with a double line ========== then I shall actually be at the Front.

Can't believe it.

Nor must you.

Now I must pack. Your own Wilfred xx

To Susan Owen 4 January 1917
2nd Manchester Regt. B.E.F.

My own dear Mother,

... On all the officers' faces there is a harassed look that I have never seen before, and which in England, never will be seen – out of jails. The men are just as Bairnsfather [3] has them – expressionless lumps.

We feel the weight of them hanging on us. I have found not a few of the old Fleetwood Musketry party here. They seemed glad to see me, as far as the set doggedness of their features would admit.

I censored hundreds of letters yesterday, and the hope of peace was in every one ...

To Susan Owen Tuesday, 16 January 1917
[2nd Manchester Regt, B.E.F.]

My own sweet Mother,

... I can see no excuse for deceiving you about these last 4 days. I have suffered seventh hell.

I have not been at the front.

I have been in front of it.

I held an advanced post, that is, a 'dug-out' in the middle of No Man's Land.

We had a march of 3 miles over shelled road then nearly 3 along a flooded trench. After that we came to where the trenches had been blown flat out and had to go over the top. It was of course dark, too dark, and the ground was not mud, not sloppy mud, but an octopus of sucking clay, 3, 4, and 5 feet deep, relieved only by craters full of water. Men have been known to drown in them. Many stuck in the mud & only got on by leaving their waders, equipment, and in some cases their clothes.

High explosives were dropping all around us, and machine-guns spluttered every few minutes. But it was so dark that even the German flares did not reveal us.

Three quarters dead, I mean each of us $\frac{3}{4}$ dead, we reached the dug-out, and relieved the wretches therein. I then had to go forth and find another dug-out for a still more advanced post where I left 18 bombers. I was responsible for other posts on the left but there was a junior officer in charge.

My dug-out held 25 men tight packed. Water filled it to a depth of 1 or 2 feet, leaving say 4 feet of air.

One entrance had been blown in & blocked.

So far, the other remained.

The Germans knew we were staying there and decided we shouldn't.

Those fifty hours were the agony of my happy life.

Every ten minutes on Sunday afternoon seemed an hour.

I nearly broke down and let myself drown in the water that was now slowly rising over my knees.

Towards 6 o'clock, when, I suppose, you would be going to church, the shelling grew less intense and less accurate: so that I was mercifully helped to do my duty and crawl, wade, climb and flounder over No Man's Land to visit my other post. It took me half an hour to move about 150 yards.

I was chiefly annoyed by our own machine-guns from behind. The seeng-seeng-seeng of the bullets reminded me of Mary's canary. On the whole I can support the canary better.

In the Platoon on my left the sentries over the dug-out were blown to nothing. One of these poor fellows was my first servant whom I rejected. If I had kept him he would have lived, for servants don't do Sentry Duty. I kept my own sentries half way down the stairs during the more terrific bombardment. In spite of this one lad was blown down and, I am afraid, blinded.[4]

This was my only casualty.

The officer of the left Platoon has come out completely prostrated and is in hospital.

I am now as well, I suppose, as ever.

I allow myself to tell you all these things because I am never going back to this awful post. It is the worst the Manchesters have ever held; and we are going back for a rest.

I hear that the officer who relieved me left his 3 Lewis Guns behind when he came out. (He had only 24 hours in). He will be court-martialled.

In conclusion, I must say that if there is any power whom the Soldiery execrate more than another it is that of our distinguished countryman.[5] You may pass it on via Owen, Owen.

To Susan Owen   Friday, 19 January 1917
                                 [2nd Manchester Regt, B.E.F]

... They want to call No Man's Land 'England' because we keep supremacy there.

It is like the eternal place of gnashing of teeth; the Slough of Despond could be contained in one of its crater-holes; the fires of Sodom and Gomorrah could not light a candle to it – to find the way to Babylon the Fallen.

It is pock-marked like a body of foulest disease and its odour is the breath of cancer.[6]

I have not seen any dead. I have done worse. In the dank air I have perceived it, and in the darkness, felt. Those 'Somme Pictures' are the laughing stock of the army – like the trenches on exhibition in Kensington.

No Man's Land under snow is like the face of the moon chaotic, crater-ridden, uninhabitable, awful, the abode of madness.

To call it 'England'!

I would as soon call my House (!) Krupp Villa, or my child Chlorina-Phosgena.

Now I have let myself tell you more facts than I should, in the exuberance of having already done 'a Bit.' It is done, and we are all going still farther back for a long time. A long time. The people of England needn't hope. They must agitate. But they are not yet agitated even. Let them imagine 50 strong men trembling as with ague for 50 hours!

Dearer & stronger love than ever W.E.O.

To Susan Owen   Sunday, 4 February 1917
                       [Advanced Horse Transport Depot]

My own dear Mother,

. . . The marvel is that we did not all die of cold.[7] As a matter of fact, only one of my party actually froze to death before he could be got back, but I am not able to tell how many have ended in hospital. I had no real casualties from shelling, though for 10 minutes every hour whizz-bangs fell a few yards short of us. Showers of soil rained on us, but no fragments of shell could find us.

I had lost my gloves in a dug-out, but I found 1 mitten on the Field; I had my Trench Coat (without lining but with a Jerkin underneath.) My feet ached until they could ache no more, and so they temporarily died. I was kept warm by the ardour of Life within me. I forgot hunger in the hunger for Life. The intensity of your Love reached me and kept me living. I thought of you and Mary without a break all the time. I cannot say I felt any fear. We were all half-crazed by the buffetting of the High Explosives. I think the most unpleasant reflection that weighed on me was the impossibility of getting back any wounded, a total impossibility all day, and frightfully difficult by night.

We were marooned on a frozen desert.

There is not a sign of life on the horizon and a thousand signs of death.

Not a blade of grass, not an insect; once or twice a day the shadow of big hawk, scenting carrion.

By degrees, day by day, we worked back through the reserve, & support lines to the crazy village where the Battalion takes breath . . . Auntie Emma fairly hit it when she 'perceived the awful distaste underlying' my accounts. Dear Aunt was ever a shrewd Doogie.

I suppose I can endure cold, and fatigue, and the face-to-face death, as well as another; but extra for me there is the universal pervasion of Ugliness. Hideous landscapes, vile noises, foul language and nothing but foul, even from one's own mouth (for all are devil ridden), everything unnatural, broken, blasted; the distortion of the dead, whose unburiable bodies sit outside the dug-outs all day, all night, the most execrable sights on earth. In poetry we call them the most glorious. But to sit with them all day, all night ... and a week later to come back and find them still sitting there in motionless groups, THAT is what saps the 'soldierly spirit' ...

To Susan Owen   25 April 1917
                                                 A. Coy., My Cellar

My own dearest Mother,
   ... I think the worst incident was one wet night when we lay up against a railway embankment. A big shell lit on the top of the bank, just 2 yards from my head. Before I awoke, I was blown in the air right away from the bank! I passed most of the following days in a railway Cutting, in a hole just big enough to lie in, and covered with corrugated iron. My brother officer of B Coy. 2/Lt Gaukroger lay opposite in a similar hole. But he was covered with earth, and no relief will ever relieve him, nor will his Rest will be a 9 days-Rest. I think that the terribly long time we stayed unrelieved was unavoidable; yet it makes us feel bitterly towards those in England who might relieve us, and will not ...

To Susan Owen   2 May 1917
                                                 13th Casualty Clearing Station

Dearest Mother,
   Here again! The Doctor suddenly was moved to forbid me to go into action next time the Battalion go, which will be in a day or two. I did not go sick or anything, but he is nervous about my nerves, and sent me down yesterday – labelled Neurasthenia. I still of course suffer from the headaches traceable to my concussion. This will mean that I shall stay here and miss the next Action Tour of Front Line; or even it may mean that I go further down & be employed for a more considerable time on Base Duty or something of the sort. I shall now try and make my French of some avail ... having satisfied myself that, though in Action I bear a charmed life, and none of woman born can hurt me, as regards flesh and bone, yet my nerves have not come out without a scratch. Do not for a moment suppose I have had a 'breakdown'. I am simply avoiding one ...

To Susan Owen   [16? May 1917]
                                                 41st Stationary Hospital

My own dear Mother,

. . . Incidentally, I think the big number of texts which jogged
up in my mind in half-an-hour bears witness to a goodly store of
them in my being. It is indeed so; and I am more and more
Christian as I walk the unchristian ways of Christendom. Already
I have comprehended a light which never will filter into the
dogma of any national church: namely that one of Christ's
essential commands was: Passivity at any price! Suffer dishonour
and disgrace; but never resort to arms. Be bullied, be outraged,
be killed; but do not kill. It may be a chimerical and an
ignominious principle, but there it is. It can only be ignored:
and I think pulpit professionals are ignoring it very skilfully and
successfully indeed.

Have you seen what ridiculous figures Frederick & Arthur
Wood are cutting? If they made the Great Objection, I should
admire them. They have not the courage.

To begin with I think it was puny of Fritz to deny his name.
They are now getting up a petition, mentioning their 'unique
powers' 'invaluable work' and so on, and wish to carry on their
work from 82 Mortimer St. W. as usual. I do not recollect
Christ's office address in Jerusalem, but in any case I don't think
He spent much time there.

St Paul's business premises, if I remember, were somewhat
cramped, not to say confined.

But I must not malign these Brethren because I do not know
their exact Apologia.

And am I not myself a conscientious objector with a very
seared conscience?

The evangelicals have fled from a few Candles, discreet incense, serene altars, mysterious music, harmonious ritual to
powerful electric-lighting, overheated atmosphere, palm-tree
platforms, grand pianos, loud and animated music, extempore
ritual; but I cannot see that they are any nearer to the
Kingdom.

Christ is literally in no man's land. There men often hear His
voice: Greater love hath no man than this, that a man lay down
his life – for a friend.

Is it spoken in English only and French?
I do not believe so.

Thus you see how pure Christianity will not fit in with pure patriotism.

To Susan Owen   Tuesday night [8 August 1917]
                                 Craiglockhart

Dearest of Mothers,
... The other day I read a Biography of Tennyson, which says he was unhappy, even in the midst of his fame, wealth, and domestic serenity. Divine discontent! I can quite believe he never knew happiness for one moment such as I have – for one or two moments. But as for misery, was he ever frozen alive, with dead men for comforters. Did he hear the moaning at the bar, not at twilight and the evening bell only, but at dawn, noon, and night, eating and sleeping, walking and working, always the close moaning of the Bar; the thunder, the hissing and the whining of the Bar?

———

Tennyson, it seems, was always a great child.
So should I have been, but for Beaumont Hamel.
(Not before January 1917 did I write the only lines of mine that carry the stamp of maturity: these:

But the old happiness is unreturning.
Boys have no grief so grievous as youth's yearning;
Boys have no sadness sadder than our hope.) ...

To Susan Owen   Friday night [13 August 1917]
                                 [Craiglockhart]

My own dear Mother,
... I laughed at your hoping I should learn German during my stay in Edinburgh. It's a vile language to learn. I'm overjoyed that you think of making bandages for the wounded. Leave Black Sambo ignorant of Heaven. White men are in Hell. Aye, leave him ignorant of the civilization that sends us there, and the religious men that say it is good to be in that Hell. (Continued, because important) Send an English Testament to his Grace of Canterbury, and let it consist of that one sentence, at which he winks his eyes:

'Ye have heard that it <u>hath</u> been said: An eye for an eye, and a tooth for a tooth:

But I say that ye resist not evil, but whosoever shall smite thee on thy right cheek, turn to him the other also.'

And if his reply be 'Most unsuitable for the present distressing moment, my dear lady! But I trust that in God's good time . . . etc.' – <u>then there is only one possible conclusion</u>, that there are no more Christians at the present moment than there were at the end of the first century.

While I wear my star and eat my rations, I continue to take care of my Other Cheek; and, thinking of the eyes I have seen made sightless, and the bleeding lad's cheeks I have wiped, I say: Vengeance is mine, I, Owen, will repay.

Let my lords turn to the people when they say 'I believe in . . . Jesus Christ', and we shall see as dishonest a face as ever turned to the East, bowing, over the Block at Tyburn.

I fear I've written like a converted Horatio Bottomley.

And to you who need no such words.

That is why I want you not to destroy them; for I write so because I see clear at this moment. In my eye there is no mote nor beam, when I look through you across the world.

There is a mote in many eyes, often no other than a tear. It is this: That men are laying down their lives for a friend. I say it is a mote; a distorted view to hold in a general way.

For that reason, if no other, I won't publish in any way the 'Kings and Christs.' . . .

To Susan Owen   15 August 1917
                  Scottish Conservative Club, Edinburgh

Dearest Mother,

. . . I have just been reading Siegfried Sassoon, and am feeling at a very high pitch of emotion. Nothing like his trench life sketches has ever been written or ever will be written. Shakespere reads vapid after these. Not of course because Sassoon is a greater artist, but because of the subjects, I mean. I think if I had the choice of making friends with Tennyson or with Sassoon I should go to Sassoon.

That is why I have not yet dared to go up to him and parley in a casual way. He is here you know because he wrote a letter to the Higher Command which was too plain-spoken. They promptly sent him over here! I will send you his book, one day, and tell you what sort of pow-wow we've had.

Your own W.E.O. x

Friday aft. Just had yours. Haven't given it close attention yet.

To Siegfried Sassoon   5 November 1917
                                  Mahim, Monkmoor Road
                                  Shrewsbury

My dear Sassoon,

. . . Know that since mid-September, when you still regarded me as a tiresome little knocker on your door, I held you as Keats + Christ + Elijah + my Colonel + my father-confessor + Amenophis IV in profile.

What's that mathematically?

In effect it is this: that I love you, dispassionately, so much, so very much, dear Fellow, that the blasting little smile you wear on reading this can't hurt me in the least.

If you consider what the above Names have severally done for me, you will know what you are doing. And you have fixed my Life – however short. You did not light me: I was always a mad comet; but you have fixed me. I spun round you a satellite for a month, but I shall swing out soon, a dark star in the orbit where you will blaze. It is some consolation to know that Jupiter himself sometimes swims out of Ken! . . .

To Susan Owen   31 December 1917
                                  Scarborough

My own dear Mother,

I am not dissatisfied with my years. Everything has been done in bouts:

Bouts of awful labour at Shrewsbury & Bordeaux; bouts of amazing pleasure in the Pyrenees, and play at Craiglockhart; bouts of religion at Dunsden; bouts of horrible danger on the Somme; bouts of poetry always; of your affection always; of sympathy for the oppressed always.

I go out of this year a Poet, my dear Mother, as which I did not enter it. I am held peer by the Georgians; I am a poet's poet.

I am started. The tugs have left me; I feel the great swelling of the open sea taking my galleon.

Last year, at this time, (it is just midnight, and now is the intolerable instant of the Change) last year I lay awake in a windy tent in the middle of a vast, dreadful encampment. It seemed neither France nor England, but a kind of paddock where the beasts are kept a few days before the shambles. I heard the revelling of the Scotch troops, who are now dead, and who knew they would be dead. I thought of this present night, and whether I should indeed – whether we should indeed – whether you would indeed – but I thought neither long nor deeply, for I am a master of elision.

But chiefly I thought of the very strange look on all faces in that camp; an incomprehensible look, which a man will never see in England, though wars should be in England; nor can it be seen in any battle. But only in Étaples.

It was not despair, or terror, it was more terrible than terror, for it was a blindfold look, and without expression, like a dead rabbit's.

It will never be painted, and no actor will ever seize it. And to describe it, I think I must go back and be with them.

We are sending seven officers straight out tomorrow.

I have not said what I am thinking this night, but next December I will surely do so.

I know what you are thinking, and you know me.

Wilfred.

To Osbert Sitwell   July 1918
                                                    [Scarborough]

Dear Osbert Sitwell,

... For 14 hours yesterday I was at work – teaching Christ to lift his cross by numbers, and how to adjust his crown; and not to imagine he thirst till after the last halt; I attended his Supper to see that there were no complaints; and inspected his feet to see that they should be worthy of the nails. I see to it that he is dumb and stands to attention before his accusers. With a piece of silver I buy him every day, and with maps I make him familiar with the topography of Golgotha ...

To Susan Owen   Saturday [10 August 1918]
                                                    Scarborough

Dearest Mother,

Tomorrow I am for a medical inspection with 21 others, to be declared fit for draft. This means we may be sent on draft leave tomorrow, & I may reach you even before this letter! I know not. I am glad. That is I am much gladder to be going out again than afraid. I shall be better able to cry my outcry, playing my part.

The secondary annoyances & discomforts of France behind the line can be no worse than this Battalion. On Friday we were called up at 3 a.m. and had the usual day's work. The Adjutant is ill, & Stiebel is ill. I did Stiebel's job on the Stunt, & am still doing it.

These are only mock alarms of course. But this morning at 8.20 we heard a boat torpedoed in the bay about a mile out, they say who saw it. I think only 10 lives were saved. I wish the Bosche would have the pluck to come right in & make a clean sweep of the Pleasure Boats, and the promenaders on the Spa, and all the stinking Leeds & Bradford War-profiteers now reading *John Bull* on Scarborough Sands . . .

To Susan Owen   Saturday, 31 August 1918
                                 E.F.C., Officers Rest House and Mess

[half page missing] Arriving at Victoria. I had to wheel my own baggage down the platform & through the streets to the Hotel, which was full. But I got a bed (as I [half page missing] My last hours in England were brightened by a bathe in the fair green Channel, in company of the best piece of Nation left in England – a Harrow boy, of superb intellect & refinement, intellect because he detests war more than Germans, and refinement because of the way he spoke of my going away; and the way he spoke of the Sun; and of the Sea, and the Air; and everything. In fact the way he spoke.

And now I go among cattle to be a cattle-driver . . .

I am now fairly and reasonably tired & must go to my tent, without saying the things which you will better understand unsaid . . .

To Siegfried Sassoon   22 September 1918
                                  D Coy. 2nd Manchester Regt.

My dear Siegfried,
    Here are a few poems to tempt you to a letter. I begin to think your correspondence must be intercepted somewhere. So I will state merely

I have had no letter from you $\begin{cases} \text{lately} \\ \text{for a long time,} \end{cases}$
and say nothing of my situation, tactical or personal.

You said it would be a good thing for my poetry if I went back.

That is my consolation for feeling a fool. This is what shells scream at me every time: Haven't you got the wits to keep out of this?

———

Did you see what the Minister of Labour said in the *Mail* the other day? 'The first instincts of the men after the cessation of hostilities will be to return home.' And again –
'All classes acknowledge their indebtedness to the soldiers & sailors . . .'

About the same day, Clemenceau is reported by the *Times* as saying: 'All are worthy . . . yet we should be untrue to ourselves if we forgot that the greatest glory will be to the splendid poilus, who, etc.'[8]

I began a Postcript to these Confessions, but hope you will already have lashed yourself, (lashed yourself!) into something . . .

———

O Siegfried, make them Stop![9]

W.E.O.

To Susan Owen   4 (or 5) October 1918
                              In the Field

Strictly private

My darling Mother,

As you must have known both by my silence and from the newspapers which mention this Division – and perhaps by other means & senses – I have been in action for some days.

I can find no word to qualify my experiences except the word SHEER. (Curiously enough I find the papers talk about sheer fighting!) It passed the limits of my Abhorrence. I lost all my earthly faculties, and fought like an angel.

If I started into detail of our engagement I should disturb the censor and my own Rest.

You will guess what has happened when I say I am now

Commanding the Company, and in the line had a boy lance-corporal as my Sergeant-Major.

With this corporal who stuck to me and shadowed me like your prayers I captured a German Machine Gun and scores of prisoners.

I'll tell you exactly how another time. I only shot one man with my revolver (at about 30 yards!); The rest I took with a smile. The same thing happened with other parties all along the line we entered.

I have been recommended for the Military Cross; and have recommended every single N.C.O. who was with me!

My nerves are in perfect order.

I came out in order to help these boys – directly by leading them as well as an officer can; indirectly, by watching their sufferings that I may speak of them as well as a pleader can. I have done the first.

Of whose blood lies yet crimson on my shoulder where his head was – and where so lately yours was – I must not now write.

It is all over for a long time. We are marching steadily <u>back</u>.

Moreover

The War is nearing an end.

Still,

Wilfred and more than Wilfred

To Siegfried Sassoon   10 October 1918
                                              [2nd Manchester Regt.]

Very dear Siegfried,

Your letter reached me at the exact moment it was most needed – when we had come far enough out of the line to feel the misery of billets; and I had been seized with writer's cramp after making out my casualty reports. (I'm O.C. D Coy).

The Batt. had a sheer time last week. I can find no better epithet: because I cannot say I suffered anything; having let my brain grow dull: That is to say my nerves are in perfect order.

It is a strange truth: that your *Counter-Attack* frightened me much more than the real one: though the boy by my side, shot through the head, lay on top of me, soaking my shoulder, for half an hour.

Catalogue? Photograph? Can you photograph the crimson-hot iron as it cools from the smelting? That is what Jones's blood looked like, and felt like. My senses are charred.

I shall feel again as soon as I dare, but now I must not. I don't take the cigarette out of my mouth when I write Deceased over their letters . . .

1. Member of French light-infantry corps, originally formed of Algerians and retaining their uniform. [HO, JB]
2. HO was sailing in submarine waters at this time. [HO, JB]
3. Bruce Bairnsfather (1888–1959), artist and journalist, whose war cartoons were famous. They were published in *Fragments from France*, *The Better 'Ole*, *Bullets and Billets*, *From Mud to Mufti*, etc. [HO, JB]
4. This incident became the subject of 'The Sentry'. [HO, JB]
5. David Lloyd George of Dwyfor, 1st Earl (1863–1945), Minister for War before becoming Prime Minister 1916–22. [HO, JB]
6. C. Day Lewis points out that 'The Show' (*Poems*, pp. 50–51), probably written in November 1917, is foreshadowed in this letter. [HO, JB]
7. 'Exposure' (*Poems*, p. 48) is dated February 1916, an evident slip, as EB points out, for February 1917. It must have been written at Abbeville. [HO, JB]
8. Cf Owen's poem 'Smile, Smile, Smile'.
9. The last words of [Sassoon's] 'Attack' (*Counter-Attack*) are: 'O Jesus, make it stop!' [HO, JB]

REBECCA WEST

Rebecca West (pen name of Cicily Isabel Fairfield, 1892–1983).
Born in London. Journalism, politics and criticism from 1911.
Feminist and active suffragist. Wrote on Pound and Imagism in
The New Freewoman. *The Return of the Soldier* was her first novel.
Chris returns from the war, his memory impaired. Unable to
relate to his wife, Kitty, he can only recall an early love affair
with a woman, Margaret, now married and of a different class.
In his shell-shocked state his emotional life, and that of many
others, is in ruins; but he is safely unfit for service. If he is cured
he will go back to Flanders. The appalling decision as to how he
should be treated rests with the women.

Source: Rebecca West, *The Return of the Soldier*, London, Nisbet,
1918; reprinted Virago, 1980.

'A complete case of amnesia,' he was saying, as Margaret, white-
lipped yet less shy than I had ever seen her, went to a seat by the
window and I sank down on the sofa. 'His unconscious self is
refusing to let him resume his relations with his normal life, and
so we get this loss of memory.'

'I've always said,' declared Kitty, with an air of good sense,
'that if he would make an effort . . .'

'Effort!' He jerked his round head about. 'The mental life that
can be controlled by effort isn't the mental life that matters.
You've been stuffed up when you were young with talk about a
thing called self-control – a sort of barmaid of the soul that says,
"Time's up, gentlemen," and "Here, you've had enough." There's
no such thing. There's a deep self in one, the essential self, that
has its wishes. And if those wishes are suppressed by the superficial self – the self that makes, as you say, efforts and usually
makes them with the sole idea of putting up a good show before
the neighbours – it takes its revenge. Into the house of conduct
erected by the superficial self it sends an obsession. Which
doesn't, owing to a twist that the superficial self, which isn't
candid, gives it, seem to bear any relation to the suppressed
wish. A man who really wants to leave his wife develops a hatred

406

for pickled cabbage which may find vent in performances that lead straight to the asylum. But that's all technical!' he finished bluffly. 'My business to understand it, not yours. The point is, Mr Baldry's obsession is that he can't remember the latter years of his life. Well –' his winking blue eyes drew us all into a community we hardly felt – 'what's the suppressed wish of which it's the manifestation?'

'He wished for nothing,' said Kitty. 'He was fond of us, and he had a lot of money.'

'Ah, but he did!' countered the doctor gleefully. He seemed to be enjoying it all. 'Quite obviously he has forgotten his life here because he is discontented with it. What clearer proof could you need than the fact you were just telling me when these ladies came in – that the reason the War Office didn't wire to you when he was wounded was that he had forgotten to register his address? Don't you see what that means?'

'Forgetfulness,' shrugged Kitty, 'he isn't business-like.' She had always nourished a doubt as to whether Chris was really, as she put it, practical; his income and his international reputation weighed as nothing against his so evident inability to pick up the pieces at sales.

'One forgets only those things that one wants to forget. It's our business to find out why he wanted to forget this life.'

'He can remember quite well when he is hypnotized,' she said obstructively. She had quite ceased to glow.

'Oh, hypnotism's a silly trick. It releases the memory of a dissociated personality which can't be related – not possibly in such an obstinate case as this – to the waking personality. I'll do it by talking to him. Getting him to tell his dreams.' He beamed at the prospect. 'But you – it would be such a help if you could give me any clue to this discontent.'

'I tell you,' said Kitty, 'he was not discontented till he went mad.'

He caught at last the glint of her rising temper. 'Ah,' he said, 'madness is an indictment not of the people one lives with, only of the high gods! If there was anything it's evident that it was not your fault –' A smile sugared it, and knowing that where he had to flatter his dissecting hand had not an easy task he turned to me, whose general appearance suggests that flattery is not part of my daily diet. 'You, Miss Baldry, you've known him the longest . . .'

'Nothing and everything was wrong,' I said at last. 'I've always felt it . . .' A sharp movement of Kitty's body confirmed my deep, old suspicion that she hated me.

He went back further than I thought he would. 'His relations with his father and mother, now?'

'His father was old when he was born, and always was a little jealous of him. His mother was not his sort. She wanted a stupid son, who would have been satisfied with shooting.'

He laid down a remark very softly, like a hunter setting a snare.

'He turned, then, to sex with a peculiar need.'

It was Margaret who spoke, shuffling her feet under her chair.

'Yes, he was always very dependent.' We gaped at her, who said this of our splendid Chris, and I saw that she was not as she had been. There was a directness of speech, a straight stare, that was for her a frenzy. 'Doctor,' she said, her mild voice roughened, 'what's the use of talking? You can't cure him.' She caught her lower lip with her teeth and fought back from the brink of tears. 'Make him happy, I mean. All you can do is to make him ordinary.'

'I grant you that's all I do,' he said. It queerly seemed as though he was experiencing the relief one feels on meeting an intellectual equal. 'It's my profession to bring people from various outlying districts of the mind to the normal. There seems to be a general feeling it's the place where they ought to be. Sometimes I don't see the urgency myself.'

She continued without joy. 'I know how you could bring him back. A memory so strong that it would recall everything else – in spite of his discontent.'

The little man had lost in a moment his glib assurance, his knowingness about the pathways of the soul. 'Well, I'm willing to learn.'

'Remind him of the boy,' said Margaret.

The doctor ceased suddenly to balance on the balls of his feet. 'What boy?'

'They had a boy.'

He looked at Kitty. 'You told me nothing of this!'

'I didn't think it mattered,' she answered, and shivered and looked cold as she always did at the memory of her unique contact with death. 'He died five years ago.'

He dropped his head back, stared at the cornice, and said with the soft malignity of a clever person dealing with the slow-witted, 'These subtle discontents are often the most difficult to deal with.' Sharply he turned to Margaret. 'How would you remind him?'

'Take him something the boy wore, some toy they used to play with.'

Their eyes met wisely. 'It would have to be you that did it.'

Her face assented.

Kitty said, 'I don't understand. Why does it matter so much?' She repeated it twice before she broke the silence that Margaret's wisdom had brought down on us. Then Dr Anderson, rattling the keys in his trouser pockets and swelling red and perturbed, answered, 'I don't know why. But it does' . . .

———

. . . I knew that one must know the truth. I knew quite well that when one is adult one must raise to one's lips the wine of truth, heedless that it is not sweet like milk but draws the mouth with its strength, and celebrate communion with reality, or else walk for ever queer and small like a dwarf. Thirst for this sacrament had made Chris strike away the cup of lies about life that Kitty's white hands held to him, and turn to Margaret with this vast trustful gesture of his loss of memory. And helped by me she had forgotten that it is the first concern of love to safeguard the dignity of the beloved, so that neither God in his skies nor the boy peering through the hedge should find in all time one possibility for contempt, and had handed him the trivial toy of happiness. We had been utterly negligent of his future, blasphemously careless of the divine essential of his soul. For if we left him in his magic circle there would come a time when his delusion turned to a senile idiocy; when his joy at the sight of Margaret disgusted the flesh, because his smiling mouth was slack with age; when one's eyes no longer followed him caressingly as he went down to look for the first primroses in the wood, but flitted here and there defensively to see that nobody was noticing the doddering old man. Gamekeepers would chat kindly with him and tap their foreheads as he passed through the copse, callers would be tactful and dangle bright talk before him. He who was as a flag flying from our tower would become a queer-shaped patch of eccentricity on the countryside, the stately music of his being would become a witless piping in the bushes. He would not be quite a man.

I did not know how I could pierce Margaret's simplicity with this last cruel subtlety, and turned to her stammering. But she said, 'Give me the jersey and the ball.'

The rebellion had gone from her eyes and they were again the seat of all gentle wisdom.

'The truth's the truth,' she said, 'and he must know it.'

I looked up at her, gasping yet not truly amazed, for I had always known she could not leave her throne of righteousness for long, and she repeated, 'The truth's the truth,' smiling sadly at the strange order of this earth.

We kissed, not as women, but as lovers do; I think we each embraced that part of Chris the other had absorbed by her love. She took the jersey and the ball and clasped them as though they were a child. When she got to the door she stopped and leaned against the lintel. Her head fell back, her eyes closed, her mouth was contorted as though she swallowed bitter drink.

———

There had fallen a twilight which was a wistfulness of the earth. Under the cedar boughs I dimly saw a figure mothering something in her arms. Almost had she dissolved into the shadows; in another moment the night would have her. With his back turned on this fading happiness Chris walked across the lawn. He was looking up under his brows at the over-arching house as though it were a hated place to which, against all his hopes, business had forced him to return. He stepped aside to avoid a patch of brightness cast by a lighted window on the grass; lights in our house were worse than darkness, affection worse than hate elsewhere. He wore a dreadful decent smile; I knew how his voice would resolutely lift in greeting us. He walked not loose limbed like a boy, as he had done that very afternoon, but with the soldier's hard tread upon the heel. It recalled to me that, bad as we were, we were yet not the worst circumstance of his return. When we had lifted the yoke of our embraces from his shoulders he would go back to that flooded trench in Flanders under that sky more full of flying death than clouds, to that no man's land where bullets fall like rain on the rotting faces of the dead . . .

'Jenny, aren't they there?'

'They're both there.'

'Is he coming back?'

'He's coming back.'

'Jenny, Jenny! How does he look?'

'Oh . . .' How could I say it? 'Every inch a soldier.'

She crept behind me to the window, peered over my shoulder and saw.

I heard her suck her breath with satisfaction. 'He's cured!' she whispered slowly. 'He's cured!'

IVOR GURNEY

Ivor Gurney (1890–1937). Born in Gloucester and educated at King's School and Royal College of Music. Served as infantryman, in the ranks, with the Gloucesters in the war and suffered a mental collapse in 1918, from which he intermittently made brief temporary recoveries. He died in the City of London Mental Hospital in 1937. His *Collected Poems* were published in 1982, and a selection of his wartime letters published under the title *War Letters* was edited by R. K. R. Thornton and published in 1983. Thornton has provided dates where possible: (P) indicates that the date is derived from a postmark, (E) indicates a date assigned by a recipient or earlier editor.

Source: Ivor Gurney, *War Letters*, edited by R. K. R. Thornton, Ashington, Mid-Northumberland Arts Group, Manchester, Carcanet, 1983.

To F. W. Harvey

February 1915 (?)
19 Barton Street,
Gloucester

Dear Willy:

Well, here I am, and a soldier, in your own regiment's 2nd reserve – to go to Northampton on Monday for the first Reserve.

I am glad you are pretty well now, a week should put you right, and make you happy. Tonight I have been reading the Georgian Poetry Book, and it is this that has made me write to you. Our young poets think very much as we, or rather as we shall when body and mind are tranquil. Masefields feeling of beauty and its meaning strike chords very responsive in ourselves. I found myself remembering old things, old times together as I read 'Biography', and it brought you very near. May 1925 see us both happy and revered by the few who count and know the good when they see it.

Meanwhile there is a most bloody and damnable war to go through. Let's hope it'll do the trick for both of us, and make us so strong, so happy, so sure of ourselves, so crowded with fruitful memories of joy that we may be able to live in towns or earn our living at some drudgery and yet create whole and pure joy for others. It is a far cry for me, but who knows what a year may do? And I mean to touch music no more till I must . . .

To F. W. Harvey   February 1915 (?)
                                                   2nd 5th Glosters
                                                   [tomorrow to be]
                                                   Chelmsford, Essex

. . . The Sonnet of R.B. you sent me, I do not like. It seems to me that Rupert Brooke would not have improved with age, would not have broadened; his manner has become a mannerism, both in rythm and diction. I do not like it. This is the kind of work which his older lesser inspiration would have produced. Great poets, great creators are not much influenced by immediate events; those must sink in to the very foundations and be absorbed. Rupert Brooke soaked it in quickly and gave it out with as great ease. For all that we have very much to be grateful for; but what of 1920? What of the counterpart to 'The Dynasts' which may still lie within another Hardy's brain a hundred years today? . . .

To Herbert Howells   September/October 1915
                                                   2/5 Glosters
                                                   Chelmsford

. . . You can imagine, too, what the hope of being able to praise England and make things to honour her is in me, as in yourself. You can imagine too what a conflict there is between that idea and warfare . . . If only I could be convinced that there was nothing unique, nothing that was not easily paralleled in me, I would not care. But to be neurasthenic – to wonder what my capabilities are –to have patience only because, someday, there may come something to give joy to men and especially Englishmen . . . to suffer all this in the thought-vacuum in which the Army lives, moves and has its being, is a hard thing. The hardest thought of all is that I am deceiving myself, that nothing especially worthy is in me; and that I should take a commission at once . . .

To Marion Scott   17 May 1916 (P)
[*to Miss Scott but with no address or perhaps even first page. Postmarked from Park House Camp*]

... On Saturday the gods gave me a brief respite from servitude, and I snatched a space at High Wycombe, after great gulfs of wasted time at Andover, Basingstoke and Maidenhead and Reading. From Basingstoke to Reading I travelled with a corporal of the Coldstreams, who had been out since Mons. He was the kind of man who would make an efficient and self-effacing member of a Church Council. Quiet voiced and quiet-eyed he exhorted us never to spare any Germans, never to take prisoners; and backed it up with some effective evidence. It would have been the queerest thing, before the war, to have seen this quiet man uttering the most bloodthirsty wisdom. He did not hate, bore no malice apparently, but merely was determined to kill every German he might lay hands on. One thing he told us was that the Prussian Guard at Loos was a very mixed lot and very inferior to the original ...

To Mrs Voynich   June 1916

... Well as the whole world sees, we can behave well enough; and the account of Beatty's squadron fighting against so great a superiority should stir us to all nobility, act word thought and appearance.

    Let's do it after the high Roman fashion,
    And make death proud to take us'.

This is a queer war though. Guns are going in the distance, and every moment there is the chance of a strafe (we have had one, not a bad one) yet the note of the whole affair is boredom. The Army is an awful life for an artist, even if he has such experiences as we had with the Welsh. Either it is slogging along uselessly with a pack or doing nothing but hang about after – or boredom or hell in the trenches. Very little between ...

To Marion Scott   5 July 1916

... Our sergeant-major has softened to all the world, and that includes even me, who went to him and asked him where the biscuits and cheese were; in a strafe; his mind being then set on less mundane matters. And so, in the trenches, I never shave, wash late in the day if I please, and wear horrid looking sandbags round my legs because of the mud. When the S.M. tackled me about looking so like a scarecrow – or rather ... 'Come, come, Gurney, look more like a soldier for the Lords

413

sake'. 'Well, He doesnt seem to be doing much for *my* sake, and anyway I'm not a soldier. I'm a *dirty civilian*'. He has taken to being more pious and is careful of the words he utters. Whereas I delight in expressing contumelious opinions of the Lord Almighty, and outlining the lecture which I have prepared against the Last Day. He is surprised that the 'coal box' did not fall in *my* bay, but I reassured him that there was a worse thing laid up for me, and left him somewhat cheered.

But, in the name of the Pleiades what *has* a neurasthenic musician to do with all this? ...

To Marion Scott   7 August 1916

... It is difficult in these letters to interest you, and yet avoid trouble with the Censor. I would like to tell you where we are and when we managed to get more than a general mention in 'the rest of the front', but it cant be. And on the other hand, humour and things humorous are either impossible to show in a letter or too long to write of. But there *is* fun, occasionally. What there is to see, and see with joy – is, men behaving coolly with white lips, or even unaltered faces. Men behaving kindly to one another. Strained eyes and white faces yet able to smile. The absence of swank of any sort – among the men. The English virtues displayed at their best and least demonstrative, and musical taste at its lowest, worst, I would not have missed it for anything, and wait for my Nice Blighty with satisfaction, pride, and trepidation, lest the Almighty may have misunderstood my wishes in the matter. They talk about a Trade War after this. Will not the fact that so many Englishmen have become masters of Life have a bearing on this, in spite of the calculations of our Economic Experts? ...

To Herbert Howells   August 1916 (?)

... You will be pleased to hear the Glosters continue to do well, and are taking honours and getting commended more than any other battallion in the division. The note of our men is not cheeriness. It is ordinarily a spirit of comradeship, sustained and real. Not much laughter, but many smiles. A hunger for the news of the end of the war, and an unflinching determination to stick it until Our Peace is obtained. No kind of hate of the Germans, but a kind of pity and wonder mixt – on account of the terrible power of our explosives, and their detestation of the German mind. A fixed grey-coloured nobility of mind that will last longer than hate and fury, for it is subject to no after effects of exhaustion or lethargy of spent force.

To Marion Scott   3 February 1917

... But O, cleaning up! I suppose I get as much Hell as any one in the army; and although I give the same time to rubbing and polishing as any of the others, the results – I will freely confess it – are not all they might be. Today there was an inspection by the Colonel. I waited trembling, knowing that there was six weeks of hospital and soft-job dirt and rust not yet all off; no, not by a long way. I stood there, a sheep among the goats (no, vice versa) and waited the bolt and thunder. Round came He-Who-Must-Be-Obeyed. Looked at me, hesitated, looked again, hesitated, and was called off by the R.S.M. who was afterwards heard telling the Colonel (a few paces away from me) 'A Good man, sir, quite all right. Quite a good man, sir, but he's a musician, and doesn't seem able to get himself clean.' When the aforesaid R S M came round for a back view, he chuckled, and said 'Ah Gurney, I am afraid we shall never make a soldier of you.'

It is a good thing they are being converted to this way of thought at last; it has taken a long time. Anyway the R.S.M. is a brick, and deserves a Triolet ...

To Marion Scott   14 February 1917

... These Sonnetts. For England. Pain. Homesickness. Servitude, and one other; are intended to be a sort of counterblast against 'Sonnetts 1914', which were written before the grind of the war and by an officer (or one who would have been an officer). They are the protest of the physical against the exalted spiritual; of the cumulative weight of small facts against the one large. Of informed opinion against uninformed (to put it coarsely and unfairly) and fill a place. Old ladies wont like them, but soldiers may, and these things are written either for soldiers or civilians as well informed as the French what 'a young fresh war' means. (Or was it 'frische (joyful) Krieg'. I cant remember, but something like it was written by the tame Germans in 1914.) I know perfectly well how my attitude will appear, but – They will be called 'Sonnetts 1917.' ...

To Marion Scott   14 April 1917
My Dear Friend:

Well, I am wounded; but not badly; perhaps not badly
enough; as although kind people told me it meant Blighty for
me, yet here I am at Rouen marked 'Tents'. I do not yet give up
hopes, but very few boats have been running lately; none at all
for some days; and the serious cases go first of course. It was
during an attack on Good Friday night that a bullet hit me and
went clean through the right arm just underneath the shoulder –
the muscles opposite the biceps, to describe them more or less
accurately. It hurt badly for half an hour, but now hurts not at
all; I am writing in bed with the arm resting on the clothes
merely. Well, I suppose your letters will be lost to me for a little;
please send them to me when you receive them . . .

To Marion Scott   Late June/early July 1917 (?)
My Dear Friend:

Here am I, sheltered from the sun by the parados of a trench
behind a blockhouse; reading 'The Bible in Spain.' That's
finished now, and 'Robinson Crusoe' need not be begun for we
are being relieved tonight, and O! the relief! 'Robinson' may
follow; we shall have tomorrow off anyway. What a life! What a
life! My memories of this week will be, – Blockhouse; an archway
there through which a sniper used his skill on us as we emerged
from the rooms at the side; cold; stuffy heat; Brent Young;
Smashed or stuck Tanks; A gas and smoke barrage put up by us,
a glorious but terrifying sight; Fritzes shells; One sunset; two
sunrises; 'Bible in Spain'; The tale of the cutting up of the
KRRs in 1914 ; of Colonel Elkington; of the first gas attacks
also; of the Brigade Orderly; and of the man who walked in his
sleep to Fritz, slept well, woke, realised, and bolted; Thirst; Gas;
Shrapnel; *Very* H.E.; Our liquid fire; A first sight of an aeroplane
map . . . Does it sound interesting? May God forgive me if I ever
come to cheat myself into thinking that it was, and lie later to
younger men of the Great Days. It was damnable; and what in
relation to what might have happened? Nothing at all! We have
been lucky, but it is not fit for men to be here – in this tormented
dry-fevered marsh, where men die and are left to rot because of
snipers and the callousness that War breeds. 'It might be me
tomorrow. Who cares? Yet still, hang on for a Blighty.'

Why does this war of spirit take on such dread forms of

ugliness, and why should a high triumph be signified by a body shattered, black, stinking; avoided by day, stumbled over by night, an offence to the hardest? No doubt there is consolation in the fact that men contemplate such things, such possible endings; and are yet undismayed, yet persistent; do not lose laughter nor the common kindliness that makes life sweet – And yet seem such boys – Yet what consolation can be given me as I look upon and endure it? Any? Sufficient? The 'End of War'? Who knows, for the thing for which so great a price is paid is yet doubtful and obscure; and our reward most sweet would seem to depend on what we make of ourselves and give ourselves; for clearer eyes and more contented minds; more contented because of comparisons ironically to be made . . . and yet

etc (Not quite correct)

Forgive all this; and accept it as a sincere reflection; a piece of technique; only one side of the picture; trench-weariness; thoughts of a not too courageous, not too well-balanced mind. Like Malvolio, I think nobly of man's soul, and am distressed. God should have done better for us than this; Could He not have found some better milder way of changing the Prussian (whom he made) than by the breaking of such beautiful souls? Now *that* is what one should write poetry upon. Someday I will say it in Music, after a while . . .

Now I must go into the Blockhouse, may get a Blighty doing so . . . and O if it were but a small hole in the leg! . . .

To Marion Scott   4 October 1917
. . . I am likely to be here another fortnight, for on the colonel's inspection I was one of the very few not marked Con: Camp.

'Why?' 'Accompaniments, my dear'. For once, I saw the Army winking its eye at me, and wunk back.

I hope that what comes from an Italian source as to America's Peace offer is correct. These are none so bad. And, barring an absolutely complete military victory, as good as we can get. Of course, the terms are too generous for Germany, but without generosity I cannot see how she is ever to assert herself against the Junkers. So much priceless blood has been spilt, the organisation has been so perfected, that, right or wrong, a commercial blockade for 25 years would mean an eating cancer in the heart of Europe. We have to encourage democracy, in this case by discrediting a ruling caste. I dont believe a commercial blockade would do more than pull Germany together under the old rule and keep Europe safe – granted! But there is a better way. To crush Germany more than is needed of effort. France cannot ever be hopeless again. So much we have gained. To sum up – It is a great pity that Europe cannot gain the same unconditional surrender of Germany as a parent may exact of a child, but if things are properly managed, *in the event of German accepting the proposals of USA of course*, then the price is too great to pay any longer. It is time we left off, with a Faith in God, and an International agreement which would make agression hopeless for any country.

Lastly, a complete military victory will not guarantee South Eastern Europe for long, if Russia will not see reason. This arrangement is far more likely to keep peace and to make reason a moving force in International communication. A military victory will not guarantee peace, neither will this; but it has more promise as a birth or potential force of peace, because further conflict will leave Germany weaker than ever. It is more unwise to weaken her, than to trust that her people have learnt a lesson; because in the essential things of self-government we cannot interfere.

Excuse this long, long dissertation . . .

To Marion Scott   3 November 1917 (P)
My Dear Friend:
    . . . There's a bit of luck; owing to slight indigestion (presumably due to gas; wink, wink!) I am to go to Command Depot for two months – a sort of Con: Camp in Khaki. I hope they *will* keep me for two months, and then of course, if the indigestion isn't cured . . .

To Marion Scott   21 November 1917 (P)
                                                  Pte Gurney 241281,
                                                  B Co 4th Reserve Batt:
                                                  Gloucester Regt,
                                                  Seaton Delaval,
                                                  Northumberland.

My Dear Friend:
   ... By the way, some time ago Sassoon walked up to his
colonel, and said he would fight no more. Flashes, of course: and
blue fire. There were questions in the House, and a general dust-
up; but at last they solved it in a becoming official fashion, and
declared him mad, and put him in a lunatic-asylum; from which
there will soon come a second book, and that it will be interesting
to see ...

To Herbert Howells   January 1918 (?)
                                              [*Mouse-eaten and incomplete*]

My Dear Howells:
   ... Here is a new, more orthodox, song. Please send it on to
Miss Scott when digested. It is beautiful, isnt it.
You know why ...
[   ] she could hear it.
[   ] Nelson Drummond is older than I thought –
born sooner I mean. She is 30 years old and most perfectly
enchanting. She has a pretty figure, pretty hair, fine eyes, pretty
hands and arms *and* walk. A charming voice, pretty ears, a
resolute little mouth. With a great love in her she is glad to give
when the time comes. In Hospital, the first thing that would
strike you is 'her guarded flame'. There was a mask on her face
more impenetrable than on any other woman I have ever seen.
(But that has gone for me.) In fact (at a guess) I think it will
disappear now she has found someone whom she thinks worthy.

   A not unimportant fact was revealed by one of the patients at
hospital – a fine chap – I believe she has money. Just think of it!
Pure good luck, if it is true (as I believe it is). But she is more
charming and tender and deep than you will believe till you see
her.

   O Erbert, O Erbert ...

To Marion Scott   28 March 1918 (E)
R. K. R. Thornton, the editor of Gurney's *War Letters* writes

'I have not been successful in unearthing this letter from the Gurney archive but it seems important enough to reproduce portions printed in Michael Hurd, *The Ordeal of Ivor Gurney*, Oxford, OUP, 1979.']

Yesterday I felt and talked to (I am serious) the spirit of Beethoven.

No, there is no exclamation mark behind that, because such a statement is past ordinary ways of expressing surprise. But you know how sceptical I was of any such thing before.

It means that I have reached higher than ever before – in spite of the dirt and coarseness and selfishness of so much of me. Something happened the day before which considerably lessened and lightened my gloom. What it was I shall not tell you, but it was the strangest and most terrible spiritual adventure. The next day while I was playing the slow movement of the D major [sonata] I felt the presence of a wise and friendly spirit; it was old Ludwig van all right. When I had finished he said 'Yes, but there's a better thing than that' and turned me to the 1st movement of the latest E flat Sonata – a beauty (I did not know it before). There was a lot more; Bach was there but does not care for me. Schumann also, but my love for him is not so great. Beethoven said among other things that he was fond of me and that in nature I was like himself as a young man. That I should probably not write anything really big and good; for I had started much too late and had much to do with myself spiritually and much to learn. Still he said that he himself was not much more developed at my age, and at the end – when I had shown my willingness to be resigned to God's will and try first of all to do my best, he allowed me (somehow) to hope more, much more. It depends on the degree of spiritual height I can attain – so I was led somehow to gather.

There! What would the doctors say to *that*? A Ticket certainly, for insanity. No, it is the beginning of a new life, a new vision . . .

I could not get much about Howells off L van B: (the memory is faint) he was reluctant to speak; whether Howells is to die or not to develop I could not gather.

How I would like to see your face! No, you'll take it seriously, and decide I am not unbalanced or overstrung. This letter is quite sane, n'est ce pas?

To Marion Scott   19 June 1918 (P)

[R. K. R. Thornton writes: This letter is sent, unlike others from England and Scotland, without a stamp but with the words 'Wounded Soldiers Letter' on the envelope where the letters from France had borne the words 'On Active Service' instead of a stamp.]

The Soldiers' Home, Bold Street, Warrington.

My Dear Friend:

This is a good-bye letter, and written because I am afraid of slipping down and becoming a mere wreck – and I know you would rather know me dead than mad, and my only regret is that my Father will lose my allotment.

Thank you most gratefully for all your kindness, dear Miss Scott. Your book is in my kit bag which will be sent home, and thank you so much for it – at Brancepeth I read it a lot.

Goodbye with best wishes from one who owes you a lot.

May God reward you and forgive me.

Ivor Gurney

To Marion Scott   20 June 1918 (?)
                                   6A West Ward,
                                   Lord Derbys War Hospital,
                                   Warrington, Lancs.

Dear Miss Scott

Please forgive my letter of yesterday. I meant to do that I spoke of, but lost courage. Will you please let Sir Hubert know?

I B Gurney

STANLEY SPENCER

Stanley Spencer (1891–1959). Born Cookham, Berkshire, and studied at the Slade School of Fine Art 1909–12. From 1915–17 he was in the Royal Army Medical Corps, and then in the infantry – the Royal Berkshire Regiment. Part of Spencer's war was in Macedonia, and the account of his experiences there as well as the excerpts from Spencer's letters from this period are included in a biography by Richard Carline. Carline first met Spencer in 1915 and his sister became Spencer's wife. The biography is presented through Spencer's letters, notebooks and autobiographical writings. Richard Carline (1896–1980) was himself an artist. During the Great War he was employed on camouflage design and was an official War Artist in Europe and the Middle East. Those interested in Spencer, and his response to the war, will want to see his murals for the War Memorial Chapel at Burghclere in Hampshire (1926–34). Carline started to write about the murals at Spencer's request in 1928 and *Stanley Spencer at War* is, in part, a fulfilment of that request. The following extracts from a letter to Carline in 1929, and 'subsequent reminiscences', describe his duty in a dug-out near Bulgarian outposts.

Source: Richard Carline, *Stanley Spencer at War*, London, Faber, 1978.

. . . My feelings about the Bulgars were acted upon in a very remarkable way, owing to the simple fact that I *never* saw them, and yet they were only a few yards away. I felt that if I did see one, it would be more extraordinary than seeing a ghost; and can you imagine under such circumstances how fascinating it was to hear the sound of the gravel crunching . . . made by the wheels of their wagons?

Of course, it is very difficult to express all the many wonderful feelings I had about the Bulgars, a number of these wonderful feelings resulting from the fact that they were the enemy. First, the 'enemy' element gave me this feeling of remoteness from them – a feeling that they belonged to another planet. Also, it gave me the feeling I used to have about places, where the wall was so high that I could not see over into them. Secondly, there was the fact that we only went into 'no-man's land' in the night, so that I never saw what that land looked like in the daylight. Everything had to be done in dead silence, and can you imagine the mystery when, on some pale Macedonian moonlight night, we were told to go into this unknown land, and we go and with all the feeling and wonder that one might experience in entering a jungle full of wild beasts?

We, at length, arrive at a ravine which is full of flowers and ferns, not that one can see the flowers, but I could smell them. And all these scents and the just discernible shapes of the ferns and undergrowth, all somehow suggesting the presence of this fearful, yet wonderful mystery – the enemy.

To call a big fat Bulgarian – a very homely sort of man – a wonderful mystery, is not what I do here. What is a 'wonderful mystery' is that quality which a hill or a man or an animal or a ravine gets when it is to be feared. Who does not long to see a tiger in a jungle and not in a cage? ... Is there not something that adds, imperceptibly, a feeling of mystery to the tiger, owing to the fact that one must not approach it? It therefore becomes remote. In this same sense a Bulgar became remote ... When you see some bird or animal ... and are told that that bird or animal is extremely rare, it gives you a feeling that you are looking at one of the innermost secrets of nature. So with the Bulgar. The fact that he was only a few yards away and the fact that he was never to be seen gave him this feeling of 'rareness' and the feeling of being a wild secret of nature.

... As the only contact with the Bulgars was during the night, I got the impression of their being a kind of beings which came from an essential and permanent night, and that each night, we, as midnight drew near, approached their dark abode and, as the morning came, descended and came away from it. I never felt that they like us, descended to their day as we descended to ours, but that somewhere further up in time in a place more midnight than midnight, they were in some way away in my mind still existing. Some nights it was extraordinary to me to hear the ground crunching under the wheels of some cart when I was told it was the Bulgars' ration carts coming up, just as ours brought ours up. No 'Looking-glass' world was ever as intangible as that seemed to me.

It seemed to me a queer arrangement that our activities consisted of outpost duty and patrolling the wire at night and in the daytime just doing odd fatigues, just outside our dug-outs . . . We formed up, in the evening just before sunset, outside the dug-outs . . . taking two bombs each from a box as we did so. It was always suspected by the Bulgars as being the time to start a barrage . . . The shells dropped uncomfortably near and I was glad when . . . getting to the outposts, we were able to take cover in a communication trench.

JOSEPH CONRAD

Joseph Conrad (1857–1924). On 25 July 1914, Conrad, his wife, Jessie, and sons, Borys and John, left their home in Kent to stay on an estate in Poland. They travelled via Hamburg and Berlin to Cracow. He shows the town to Borys and remembers his own father's funeral. The description of the outbreak of war and of his own condition is more restrained here than in his letters and in the accounts given by Borys and Jessie.

Source: Joseph Conrad, *Notes on Life and Letters*, London, Dent, 1921 (edn of 1965) ('Poland Revisited' was first published in the *Daily News*, 29 and 31 March, 6 and 7 April, 1915.)

We arrived in Cracow late at night. After a scrambly supper, I said to my eldest boy, 'I can't go to bed. I am going out for a look round. Coming?'

He was ready enough. For him, all this was part of the interesting adventure of the whole journey. We stepped out of the portal of the hotel into an empty street, very silent, and bright with moonlight. I was, indeed, revisiting the glimpses of the moon. I felt so much like a ghost that the discovery that I could remember such material things as the right turn to take and the general direction of the street gave me a moment of wistful surprise.

The street, straight and narrow, ran into the great Market Square of the town, the centre of its affairs and of the lighter side of its life. We could see at the far end of the street a promising widening of space. At the corner an unassuming (but armed) policeman, wearing ceremoniously at midnight a pair of white gloves which made his big hands extremely noticeable, turned his head to look at the grizzled foreigner holding forth in a strange tongue to a youth on whose arm he leaned.

The Square, immense in its solitude, was full to the brim of moonlight. The garland of lights at the foot of the houses seemed to burn at the bottom of a bluish pool. I noticed with infinite satisfaction that the unnecessary trees the Municipality insisted upon sticking between the stones had been steadily refusing to grow. They were not a bit bigger than the poor victims I could remember. Also, the paving operations seemed to be exactly at the same point at which I left them forty years before. There were the dull, torn-up patches on that bright expanse, the piles of paving material looking ominously black, like heads of rocks on a silvery sea. Who was it that said that Time works wonders? What an exploded superstition! As far as these trees and these paving stones were concerned, it had worked nothing. The suspicion of the unchangeableness of things already vaguely suggested to my senses by our rapid drive from the railway station, was agreeably strengthened within me . . .

———

In the moonlight-flooded silence of the old town of glorious tombs and tragic memories, I could see again the small boy of that day following a hearse; a space kept clear in which I walked alone, conscious of an enormous following, the clumsy swaying of the tall black machine, the chanting of the surpliced clergy at the head, the flames of tapers passing under the low archway of the gate, the rows of bared heads on the pavements with fixed, serious eyes. Half the population had turned out on that fine May afternoon. They had not come to honour a great achievement, or even some splendid failure. The dead and they were victims alike of an unrelenting destiny which cut them off from every path of merit and glory. They had come only to render homage to the ardent fidelity of the man whose life had been a fearless confession in word and deed of a creed which the simplest heart in that crowd could feel and understand.

It seemed to me that if I remained longer there in that narrow street I should become the helpless prey of the Shadows I had called up. They were crowding upon me, enigmatic and insistent, in their clinging air of the grave that tasted of dust and of the bitter vanity of old hopes.

'Let's go back to the hotel, my boy,' I said. 'It's getting late.'

It will be easily understood that I neither thought nor dreamt that night of a possible war. For the next two days I went about amongst my fellow men, who welcomed me with the utmost consideration and friendliness, but unanimously derided my fears of a war. They would not believe in it. It was impossible. On the evening of the second day I was in the hotel's smoking room, an irrationally private apartment, a sanctuary for a few choice minds of the town, always pervaded by a dim religious light, and more hushed than any club reading-room I've ever been in. Gathered into a small knot, we were discussing the situation in subdued tones suitable to the genius of the place.

A gentleman with a fine head of white hair suddenly pointed an impatient finger in my direction and apostrophized me.

'What I want to know is whether, should there be war, England would come in.'

The time to draw a breath, and I spoke out for the Cabinet without faltering.

'Most assuredly. I should think all Europe knows that by this time.'

He took hold of the lapel of my coat, and, giving it a slight jerk for greater emphasis, said forcibly:

'Then, if England will, as you say, and all the world knows it, there can be no war. Germany won't be so mad as that.'

On the morrow by noon we read of the German ultimatum. The day after came the declaration of war, and the Austrian mobilization order. We were fairly caught. All that remained for me to do was to get my party out of the way of eventual shells. The best move which occurred to me was to snatch them up instantly into the mountains to a Polish health resort of great repute – which I did (at the rate of one hundred miles in eleven hours) by the last civilian train permitted to leave Cracow for the next three weeks.

And there we remained amongst the Poles from all parts of Poland, not officially interned, but simply unable to obtain the permission to travel by train, or road. It was a wonderful, a poignant two months. This is not the time, and, perhaps, not the place, to enlarge upon the tragic character of the situation; a whole people seeing the culmination of its misfortunes in a final catastrophe, unable to trust any one, to appeal to any one, to look for help from any quarter; deprived of all hope and even of its last illusions, and unable, in the trouble of minds and the unrest of consciences, to take refuge in stoical acceptance. I have seen all this. And I am glad I have not so many years left me to remember that appalling feeling of inexorable fate, tangible, palpable, come after so many cruel years, a figure of dread, murmuring with iron lips the final words: Ruin – and Extinction.

But enough of this. For our little band there was the awful anguish of incertitude as to the real nature of events in the West. It is difficult to give an idea how ugly and dangerous things looked to us over there. Belgium knocked down and trampled out of existence, France giving in under repeated blows, a military collapse like that of 1870, and England involved in that disastrous alliance, her army sacrificed, her people in a panic! Polish papers, of course, had no other but German sources of information. Naturally we did not believe all we read, but it was sometimes excessively difficult to react with sufficient firmness. We used to shut our door, and there, away from everybody, we sat weighing the news, hunting up discrepancies, scenting lies, finding reasons for hopefulness, and generally cheering each other up. But it was a beastly time. People used to come to me with very serious news and ask, 'What do you think of it?' And my invariable answer was, 'Whatever has happened, or is going to happen, whoever wants to make peace, you may be certain that England will not make it, not for ten years, if necessary.'

But enough of this, too. Through the unremitting efforts of Polish friends we obtained at last the permission to travel to Vienna. Once there, the wing of the American Eagle was extended over our uneasy heads. We cannot be sufficiently grateful to the American ambassador (who, all along, interested himself in our fate) for his exertions on our behalf, his invaluable assistance and the real friendliness of his reception in Vienna. Owing to Mr Penfield's action we obtained the permission to leave Austria. And it was a near thing, for His Excellency has informed my American publishers since that a week later orders were issued to have us detained till the end of the war. However, we effected our hair's-breadth escape into Italy; and, reaching Genoa, took passage in a Dutch mail steamer, homeward-bound from Java with London as a port of call.

On that sea-route I might have picked up a memory at every mile if the past had not been eclipsed by the tremendous actuality. We saw the signs of it in the emptiness of the Mediterranean, the aspect of Gibraltar, the misty glimpse in the Bay of Biscay of an outward-bound convoy of transports, in the presence of British submarines in the Channel. Innumerable drifters flying the naval flag dotted the narrow waters and two naval officers coming on board off the South Foreland, piloted the ship through the Downs.

The Downs! There they were, thick with the memories of my sea-life. But what were to me now the futilities of an individual past? As our ship's head swung into the estuary of the Thames, a deep, yet faint, concussion passed through the air, a shock rather than a sound, which missing my ear found its way straight into my heart. Turning instinctively to look at my boys, I happened to meet my wife's eyes. She also had felt profoundly, coming from far away across the grey distances of the sea, the faint boom of the big guns at work on the coast of Flanders – shaping the future.

JOSEPH CONRAD

see also p. 425

Joseph Conrad describes in his letters to the Galsworthys the problems of being caught between Russia and Germany at the outbreak of war. His real name was Konrad Korzeniowski. Joseph and Tola Retinger had invited the Conrads to stay in Poland. Capel House was the Conrads' home in Kent. This account of the sea voyage home is rather different in emphasis from that of Borys and from his own account in 'Poland Revisited'. Joseph Retinger's account of his own escape can be read in Joseph Retinger, *Joseph Retinger, Memoirs of an Eminence Grise*, Brighton, Sussex University Press, 1972.

Source: Joseph Conrad, 'Two Letters to John Galsworthy', in Joseph Conrad, *Life and Letters of Joseph Conrad*, G. Jean-Aubry, London, William Heinemann, 1927.

To John Galsworthy

1st August 1914
Grand Hôtel. Cracovie
Galicie (Autriche).
Cracow.

Dearest Jack

I don't know when this letter will reach you, – or even if it will reach you: but I must tell you what is happening to us.

This mobilization has caught us here. The trains will run for the civil population for three days more: but with Jessie as crippled as she is and Jack not at all well (temperature) I simply dare not venture on the horrors of a war-exodus. So urged and advised, and after long meditation (24 hours), I have decided to take myself and all the unlucky tribe to Zakopane (in the mountains, about 4 hours [by] rail from here) out of the way of all possible military operations. I had rather be stranded here, where I have friends, than try to get away and be caught perhaps in some small German town in the midst of the armies.

But if the war takes on a European character, I shall be cut off from home for many months perhaps. I have about £70 with me at this moment and have just written Pinker to send me a hundred in banknotes. I wish now I had asked for more. Anyhow the sum won't last for ever, though the war may be a comparatively short one. If England finds itself at war with Austria I entreat you, my dear fellow, to try to open communications with me through the Foreign Office and through such ambassador or envoy of some neutral power who will be charged with the interests of such British subjects as may be left in Austria. It will possibly be the Swiss envoy, – or the Spanish minister. Here the wildest rumours are flying about, but there is no news of any kind. The town is in a state of siege, telegraph and 'phones closed and papers censored. The army magnificent and the mildest behaved.

I have seen not enthusiasm, perhaps, but the greatest desire to be done with a state of suspense which had lasted nearly three years prevails in the population. Yet till two days ago nobody believed in a great war. Now everybody does. Write to me (if possible) to this hotel in the name of Konrad Korzeniowski in accordance with my passport. If, eventually, you have to go to our officials and they are annoyed as to the trouble, I think that the crippled state of wife and illness of child will explain sufficiently why I must remain here. The Austrians won't worry me, – and as to that I can get protection anyhow; but they don't expel people with Polish names and I'll be out of the way too. Communication could be also opened with me through Count Ladislas Zamoyski, who has a country house near Zakopane.

Our dear love to you and Ada.

Retinger is determined to get back to England, and if he succeeds, he will explain all about my position to you. He asks me to ask you to give him a hearing.

To Mr and Mrs Galsworthy   15 Nov. '14
                                             Capel House

My Dearest Jack and Ada,

I was really too ill to write before. You must know that I started on our journey from Austria with an already gouty knee. It was a propitious moment which I dared not miss; the great rush of German and Austrian re-inforcing troops was over for a time and the Russians were falling back after their first advance. So we started suddenly, at one in the morning, on the 7th Oct. in a snowstorm in an open conveyance of sorts to drive 30 miles to a small railway station where there was a chance of finding something better than a horse-truck to travel in with *ma petite famille*. From there to Cracow, some fifty miles, we sat 18 hours in a train smelling of disinfectants and resounding with groans. In Cracow we spent untold hours sitting in the restaurant by the railway station, waiting for room in some train bound to Vienna. All the time I suffered exquisite tortures – Ada will understand. We managed to get away at last and our journey to Vienna was at comparatively lightning speed; 26 hours for a distance which in normal conditions is done in five hours and a half. But in Vienna I had to go to bed for five days. Directly I could put foot to the ground again we made a fresh start, making for Italy, which we entered through Cormona, the better Pontebba route being closed.

Borys was very good, showing himself vigorous and active in looking after his crippled parents and his small brother. Jessie went through it all with her usual serenity. During the sea-passage from Genoa to Gravesend (in a Dutch mailboat) I managed to hobble about the decks but felt beastly ill all the time. In London I felt even worse. On reaching home I just rolled into bed and remained there till yesterday, in a good deal of pain but mostly suffering from a sort of sick-apathy which I am trying now to shake off.

I won't try to write more just now. Perhaps we'll see each other before long. As to what you call 'this hell,' it is fiendish enough in all conscience: but it may be more in the nature of a Purgatory if only in this respect that it won't last for ever. It's the price nations have to pay for many sins geographical and historical, of commission and of omission, – but the door of Mercy is not closed: neither can it kill the hopes of better things. At least, one would fain believe so: but it is a bitter weariness to think endlessly about it. So no more at present. Our dear love to you both.

JOSEPH CONRAD

see also pp. 425 and 430

Conrad's 'The Tale' was first mentioned in a letter of 31 October 1916, though Cunningham Graham says it was written in 1917 (Preface to *Tales of Hearsay*). A man is telling a tale to a woman concerning 'duty' and 'absolution'. In the tale a naval commanding officer has come across a supposedly neutral ship in British waters. He suspects the Northman, master of the neutral ship, of supplying German submarines. The British and neutral ships are anchored in a remote cove waiting for thick fog to lift. The commanding officer, who turns out to be the narrator of the tale, decides to investigate and to test the Northman's credibility. Conrad wrote little fiction about the Great War. In October and November 1916 he joined various naval patrol ships at the invitation of the Admiralty.

Source: Joseph Conrad, 'The Tale', *Tales of Hearsay and Last Essays*, London, Dent, 1928.

... '"I dare say," he began, suddenly, "you are wondering at my proceedings, though I am not detaining you, am I? You wouldn't dare to move in this fog?"

'"I don't know where I am," the Northman ejaculated, earnestly. "I really don't."

'He looked around as if the very chart-room fittings were strange to him. The commanding officer asked him whether he had not seen any unusual objects floating about while he was at sea.

'"Objects! What objects? We were groping blind in the fog for days."

'"We had a few clear intervals," said the commanding officer. "And I'll tell you what we have seen and the conclusion I've come to about it."

'He told him in a few words. He heard the sound of a sharp breath indrawn through closed teeth. The Northman with his hand on the table stood absolutely motionless and dumb. He stood as if thunderstruck. Then he produced a fatuous smile.

'Or at least so it appeared to the commanding officer. Was

this significant, or of no meaning whatever? He didn't know, he couldn't tell. All the truth had departed out of the world as if drawn in, absorbed in this monstrous villainy this man was – or was not – guilty of.

'"Shooting's too good for people that conceive neutrality in this pretty way," remarked the commanding officer, after a silence.

'"Yes, yes, yes," the Northman assented, hurriedly – then added an unexpected and dreamy-voiced "Perhaps."

'Was he pretending to be drunk, or only trying to appear sober? His glance was straight, but it was somewhat glazed. His lips outlined themselves firmly under his yellow moustache. But they twitched. Did they twitch? And why was he drooping like this in his attitude?

'"There's no perhaps about it," pronounced the commanding officer sternly.

'The Northman had straightened himself. And unexpectedly he looked stern, too.

'"No. But what about the tempters? Better kill that lot off. There's about four, five, six million of them," he said, grimly; but in a moment changed into a whining key. "But I had better hold my tongue. You have some suspicions."

'"No, I've no suspicions," declared the commanding officer.

'He never faltered. At that moment he had the certitude. The air of the chart-room was thick with guilt and falsehood braving the discovery, defying simple right, common decency, all humanity of feeling, every scruple of conduct.

'The Northman drew a long breath. "Well, we know that you English are gentlemen. But let us speak the truth. Why should we love you so very much? You haven't done anything to be loved. We don't love the other people, of course. They haven't done anything for that either. A fellow comes along with a bag of gold . . . I haven't been in Rotterdam my last voyage for nothing."

'"You may be able to tell something interesting, then, to our people when you come into port," interjected the officer.

'"I might. But you keep some people in your pay at Rotterdam. Let them report. I am a neutral – am I not? . . . Have you ever seen a poor man on one side and a bag of gold on the other? Of course, I couldn't be tempted. I haven't the nerve for it. Really I haven't. It's nothing to me. I am just talking openly for once."

'"Yes. And I am listening to you," said the commanding officer, quietly.

'The Northman leaned forward over the table. "Now that I know you have no suspicions, I talk. You don't know what a poor man is. I do. I am poor myself. This old ship, she isn't much, and she is mortgaged, too. Bare living, no more. Of course, I wouldn't have the nerve. But a man who has nerve! See. The stuff he takes aboard looks like any other cargo – packages, barrels, tins, copper tubes – what not. He doesn't see it work. It isn't real to him. But he sees the gold. That's real. Of course, nothing could induce me. I suffer from an internal disease. I would either go crazy from anxiety – or – or – take to drink or something. The risk is too great. Why – ruin!"

'"It should be death." The commanding officer got up, after this curt declaration, which the other received with a hard stare oddly combined with an uncertain smile. The officer's gorge rose at the atmosphere of murderous complicity which surrounded him, denser, more impenetrable, more acrid than the fog outside.

'"It's nothing to me," murmured the Northman, swaying visibly.

'"Of course not," assented the commanding officer, with a great effort to keep his voice calm and low. The certitude was strong within him. "But I am going to clear all you fellows off this coast at once. And I will begin with you. You must leave in half an hour."

'By that time the officer was walking along the deck with the Northman at his elbow.

'"What! In this fog?" the latter cried out, huskily.

'"Yes, you will have to go in this fog."

'"But I don't know where I am. I really don't."

'The commanding officer turned round. A sort of fury possessed him. The eyes of the two men met. Those of the Northman expressed a profound amazement.

'"Oh, you don't know how to get out." The commanding officer spoke with composure, but his heart was beating with anger and dread. "I will give you your course. Steer south-by-east-half-east for about four miles and then you will be clear to haul to the eastward for your port. The weather will clear up before very long."

'"Must I? What could induce me? I haven't the nerve."

'"And yet you must go. Unless you want to –"

'"I don't want to," panted the Northman. "I've enough of it."

435

'The commanding officer got over the side. The Northman remained still as if rooted to the deck. Before his boat reached his ship the commanding officer heard the steamer beginning to pick up her anchor. Then, shadowy in the fog, she steamed out on the given course.

'"Yes," he said to his officers, "I let him go."'

The narrator bent forward towards the couch, where no movement betrayed the presence of a living person.

'Listen,' he said, forcibly. 'That course would lead the Northman straight on a deadly ledge of rock. And the commanding officer gave it to him. He steamed out – ran on it – and went down. So he had spoken the truth. He did not know where he was. But it proves nothing. Nothing either way. It may have been the only truth in all his story. And yet . . . He seems to have been driven out by a menacing stare – nothing more.'

He abandoned all pretence.

'Yes, I gave that course to him. It seemed to me a supreme test. I believe – no, I don't believe. I don't know. At the time I was certain. They all went down; and I don't know whether I have done stern retribution – or murder; whether I have added to the corpses that litter the bed of the unreadable sea the bodies of men completely innocent or basely guilty. I don't know. I shall never know.'

He rose. The woman on the couch got up and threw her arms round his neck. Her eyes put two gleams in the deep shadow of the room. She knew his passion for truth, his horror of deceit, his humanity.

'Oh, my poor, poor –'

'I shall never know,' he repeated, sternly, disengaged himself, pressed her hands to his lips, and went out.

JESSIE CONRAD

Jessie Conrad (1873–1936). Jessie Conrad writes of the family's return from Zakopane to Cracow and thence to Vienna and Italy. In this, as in other passages from the Conrads' work, one gets a clear sense of the European obsession with 'papers' and national identity.

Source: Jessie Conrad, *Joseph Conrad as I Knew Him*, London, William Heinemann, 1926.

... I shall never forget the hours we spent in Cracow. We had no permission to leave the station, and had to sit eleven hours on hard wooden chairs. Numerous trains thundered through, stopping to discharge their varied loads of anxious travellers, wounded soldiers, and one or two prisoners. One of these, a tall Russian general, sat stiffly between his two Austrian captors, glancing superciliously around the big refreshment-room, without taking the least notice of anything going on around him. One of the Austrians, a plump little officer, was exhibiting a bullet hole in his grey-blue cap to a table full of VAD nurses, who were talking excitedly together. We were the only English-speaking people and we seemed to interest the occupants of the room not a little. I was most sorry for John, who was too young to understand anxiety and too young to take much interest in human nature. I managed at last to make one of the officials understand that I wanted to wash my little boy's hands. The man eyed me up and down and shrugged his shoulders. He then called two very slatternly girls across to him, and gave them some brief directions and the key of the door at the end of the long room. I followed them, with my hand on John's shoulder and leaning on my stick. We passed through long, narrow passages reeking of blood and fennel, past long rows of blood-stained figures seated against the wall, some with their eyes closed; others were evidently trying to endure pain in silence, and sat wringing their hands and swaying slightly to and fro. The railway station was also a dressing-station. Suddenly I caught sight of a huge pail full of human scraps, and I hurriedly covered my boy's eyes with my hand.

When we got back to the refreshment-room our friend had returned and was imparting some news of moment to my husband. They were speaking Polish, but from their anxious glances in our direction I guessed that the news, whatever it might be, concerned us. The last hour and a half of weary waiting seemed more trying than all the preceding ones. John had exhausted his interest in the little piece of paper, which was all I had to give him, and, poor child, he was very tired. Our train was due to leave at eleven. At last it thundered into the station, and we started on another phase of our too eventful journey. Always at the back of all our minds was the fear that we might be stopped and held up in some remote place away from our Polish friends. Every now and then my husband would ask, 'Do you still wish to go on?' The decision always rested with me, and sometimes, waking at night, I was panic-stricken and almost decided to say so, but with the daylight my courage invariably came back. I held my tongue and we travelled on.

———

. . . By the morning the gout had got a firm grip of my husband, and I had no medicine left. As soon as it was light, we went out into the town to seek a chemist who could speak English. One and all had removed the notice from their window, 'English spoken here', and we were unsuccessful for some time. At last the expression on the face of one assistant led me to believe that he could perfectly well understand what I said, and I was thankful to find him human enough to give me what I needed, though he carefully refrained from uttering a word. We glanced at many of the shop windows on our way back to the hotel, and we were disturbed to see windows full of maps of England.

The next day we came across an old man, a facsimile of Don Q., immortalized by Captain Kettle, with pointed face, round hat, and the black cloak. This queer individual spoke quite decent English, and undertook to act as guide and interpreter. We started in a taxi to make the round of all the railway stations, trying to recover our lost luggage. Don Q. insisted on sharing my seat in the taxi, and we made the round of the stations with the persistence of despair. At last (so my husband says) I made myself so objectionable to the officials that they threw open the double doors of a large kind of shed and gruffly directed us to 'look for ourselves'. On the very top of the pile, which must have been over forty feet high, we caught sight of our lost property. Those trunks which happened to be at the bottom were crushed as flat as newspapers. I had the list of the contents written in German, and as soon as the officials were satisfied that we had claims, they handed it over for nine marks. This was the one we had lost on 2 August. It speaks well for their organization that we should have recovered it intact as late as 14 October, and so far from the place where we had lost it. By the time we reached the hotel, we found that Cook's had recovered the other. This we took as a good augury, and we revelled in our good luck. All this time there was the haunting dread that we should not be able to proceed any farther on our travels. As soon as Conrad could put his foot to the ground, he paid a visit to the American ambassador (the late Mr Penfield), who proved himself a true friend in need. He managed to get us permission to proceed to the Italian frontier. It was only a verbal permission, and no one could give us more. Never shall I forget standing in the rain when we reached the frontier and watching Conrad's face. He was positively ashen; then he suddenly launched out into German – a language he had not spoken since he was a tiny boy. The official, who obviously was quite ignorant of what he was looking at, fingered our papers, adopting a knowing air, and, blessed relief, allowed us to go. He gruffly warned us that the Italians might make trouble as we had come from the district where there had been some cholera.

After this we reached Milan with comparatively little trouble, and our minds were set more at ease by the knowledge that England was still holding her own and not doing it too badly. We stayed a week in Milan, and from there we journeyed to Genoa. Here we were fortunate enough to get a passage in a Dutch steamer, and we reached England on 3 November. A chill feeling of dismay came over me at Fenchurch Street Station on seeing the taxis with their grim behests to all to join up. We had crossed the Italian frontier only one short week before orders were received from Germany to hold us back till the end of the war. We had had a narrow escape.

BORYS CONRAD

Borys Conrad (1898–1978). Joseph Conrad's elder son accompanied his parents on their trip to Poland. In this passage he describes their stay in Vienna and journey home. Borys later served on the Western Front and was badly gassed.

Source: Borys Conrad, *My Father: Joseph Conrad*, London, Calder & Boyars, 1970.

... My Father and I went about together a lot as usual, and one day as we wandered through the streets, he suggested we should patronize a shooting gallery which seemed to be attracting a lot of customers. When we got inside, however, we were shocked at finding that this was no ordinary shooting gallery; it appeared to be a sort of war propaganda entertainment. Instead of conventional targets there were cinema screens on which were being shown a film of kilted Scottish infantry charging with fixed bayonets, and the marksmen had to fire at the figures as they ran across the screens. When a hit was made the film stopped and the marksman was invited to choose a prize from the trays of junk displayed. My Father paused and uttered a startled exclamation when he saw what we had walked into, and then gripped my arm and urged me forward saying: 'We have to go through with it Boy, to retract now would draw too much attention, but take care you don't hit any of those fellows.' This admonition was accompanied by one of his most virulent glares. When our turn came he purchased the minimum amount of ammunition – five rounds each – and we took the rifles handed to us. I took a deep breath, hoped for a lot of luck, and concentrated on missing those running figures. My relief at seeing them still running after firing my last shot was abruptly dissipated by my Father who handed me his five cartridges growling: 'You had better use these as well.' I realized that this action on his part was no gesture of paternal affection – he just felt he dare not fire them himself – so I took another deep breath, and, I am thankful to say, succeeded in 'missing' five more times. He would have been terribly distressed if I had hit one of those running figures.

As the days passed, it became clear that he was feeling the strain of waiting and hoping for a permit to leave the country, and Mother, although as always she gave no outward sign of anxiety, told me that she feared an attack of gout was imminent. I had also been expecting something of the sort, and we were greatly relieved when at last a message came asking my Father to call at the US Embassy. Although I went with him, I was not actually present during his interview with the ambassador. All I know is that a document was provided which was to enable us to travel to Udine, on the Italian frontier.

Before setting out on this stage of the journey which, although long and tedious, was without incident, our water bottles had been refilled and a supply of food packed for us by the hotel. So far as I remember it was early morning when the train eventually reached the frontier and my Father at once alighted and went to present his papers at the Austrian frontier post, taking me with him. We found that the Austrian troops had been withdrawn from duty and replaced by Germans. This, as we heard later, had been done on direct orders from the Kaiser's headquarters with the object of tightening up the restrictions against people trying to leave the country. A Prussian non-commissioned officer took our papers and, after a casual glance, handed them back with a contemptuous gesture which clearly indicated that he considered them unacceptable.

My Father had always insisted that he could only speak a few words of German, however, in this emergency, it seemed to me that he spoke at considerable length and with great fluency, but the only effect this had on the Prussian was to cause him to lose his temper and start shouting at us.

My Father eventually shrugged his shoulders and turned away with a gesture of despair, saying 'It's "no go" Boy.' Then he stopped abruptly, put his hand into the breast pocket of his coat and pulled out our British passport which he opened at the page bearing the German visa that had been necessary to enable us to travel through Germany on the outward journey. He turned back and thrust it under the Prussian's nose. The result was remarkable – the fellow examined the visa and then clicked his heels smartly and assumed an expression which might conceivably be described as friendly as he handed the passport back to my Father and waved us to our compartment. When discus-

sing his action later we concluded that he must have accepted
the visa solely because it was written in German, and overlooked
the fact that it was in a British passport. We were very lucky –
far more so than we realized at the time, because after we got
back to England, we heard through US diplomatic channels,
that soon after we left Vienna, orders came from Berlin to detain
Joseph Conrad and his family.

JOHN CONRAD

John Conrad (1906–1982). Has produced the most recent account of the Conrads' visit to Poland. This extract describing his father's enjoyment of trips with the navy in 1916 is in marked contrast to the sombre, enigmatic quality of 'The Tale' which was written at the time.

Source: John Conrad, *Joseph Conrad: Times Remembered*, Cambridge, Cambridge University Press, 1981.

... The war dragged on but it did not have any impact to speak of on me as my parents did not discuss it when I was about. If I asked a question about the war my father answered it briefly, but my mother would either ignore the question or say that it did not concern me. For most of the time I was at preparatory school but on several occasions I was called home to keep my mother company if JC had to be away, and so it was in early November of 1916 that I returned home to be with my mother.

My father had been asked by the Admiralty to visit some units of the Royal Navy so his wish to do something to help was at last fulfilled. He had said, very often, that he wished he could do something, however insignificant, so it gave him considerable pleasure when the letter arrived. He tried not to show his eagerness as my mother was more than a little anxious about this trip. There had been quite animated conversation between them that I had not followed, and after I had helped my mother with the washing-up she went into the drawing-room and continued the conversation. I stayed up quite late that evening after returning from school, I remember, and had not gone to sleep when they came upstairs. Usually I had dropped off by the time my mother came up, after listening to the murmur of voices in the drawing-room below. My father used to work late into the night or more correctly into the early morning, coming to bed about half-past two or three o'clock. I heard them talking through the open doorway between our rooms while my mother did the packing for JC. There was a pause and then my mother said, 'Boy, don't go – you know I wish you weren't going! What shall I do if anything happens?'

'Come, come, Jess, I can't back out now even if I wanted to. You must realize that and besides you know and have known all along that I have set my heart on this trip or something like it. I'll be alright, you'll see. There is nothing to worry about and you have Jackilo to keep you company. He'll see you are alright. You just carry on till I come aboard again.'

The day arrived when he was due to leave and as he put his coat on he turned to me and said, 'Oh, lend me that gold pencil please, the one given you recently. I must have something to write with.' I rushed off to get it. It had not yet become a precious possession and I was very pleased that my father should have asked me to lend him something of mine. We saw him out to the taxi and, after he had kissed my mother goodbye, she said with a very straight face: 'Mind you don't get your feet wet!' My father turned back and said with equal seriousness: 'Seagulls always do when they alight on the sea!' We were all in a state of tension but my parents felt more than I did. Although I was aware of my mother's anxiety I was also conscious of a feeling of pride at, and a sympathy for, my father's eagerness to be off and away. We stood and watched the taxi go down the drive and disappear behind the hedge and as we waved the tension evaporated to be replaced by a feeling of loneliness which all the efforts of Nellie Lyons, our maid, could do nothing to dispel.

With my father away Capel seemed to become very empty and my mother found the solitude too much of a burden with only the household and a small boy to talk to, so she decided to go to Folkestone and stay at the Royal Pavilion Hotel down by the harbour. We managed to get rooms on the first floor in the eastern corner overlooking the quays and the channel. My recollections of this period are very vague, except for the tedious walks along the Leas or the shore with Nellie Lyons while my mother talked with the other people staying in the hotel. After what seemed to me to be a long time we heard from my father and returned to Capel House to wait for him.

I remember being wakened late in the night, or perhaps, the early hours of the morning, by J C bending over my bed to greet me, his shadow, cast by the light of a candle, seemed immense and grotesque as it passed over the ceiling. The excitement of the trip and the long journey home from the north had made him rather tired and it was some days before we heard the salient points. I had the impression that he spoke more from a desire to 'fill the silence', as my mother did not seem to have any interest in his adventure, than to tell us what had happened.

He was most apologetic for having dropped my pencil overboard into the North Sea when he was taken for a flight in a Short seaplane but said he would get another like it when he went to town. Gradually we heard more about his adventures but what pleased him above everything else was the kindness and appreciation shown him by the officers and men of the Royal Navy.

He had been to sea in a 'Q' ship for about ten days, hunting for German submarines, which he thoroughly enjoyed as the sea air and excitement made him feel much fitter. Later on he explained to me with the help of sketches, how the dummy deck cargoes folded down to expose the guns with which the ships were armed. After a number of explanations he asked me to build him a model, complete with dummy cargoes and guns, out of Meccano. This time I took care to sheet over the metal structure with cardboard, remembering the doubts he expressed previously about the seaworthiness of ships built of metal strips with holes in! He was delighted when I carried the model into his room and showed him how it operated, and it stayed on a table in his room when I returned to school. In the holidays he would ask me to 'Send an artificer to adjust the catches' or carry out other minor repairs. It never occurred to me that some people might think that he was selfish in retaining the model; in fact I was rather flattered and proud that I had created something that gave him so much pleasure. I had plenty of other toys and occupations to keep me busy.

One evening the postman arrived in a great splutter asking if we had seen the German aircraft which he thought had been bombing the railway workshops at Ashford. We all trooped out into the garden and there, far above us, were six or seven Taubes, like little white 'bow-ties' coming from the direction of the town. I believe this was the first air raid of the First World War but I do not remember seeing any other enemy aircraft though we saw several Zeppelins caught in the searchlights later on.

ILYA EHRENBURG

Ilya Ehrenburg (1891–1967). Born in Kiev. Jewish. Lived mainly in Paris between 1908 and 1917. Tried to join the Foreign Legion but was rejected on medical grounds. Controversial figure in later Soviet life.

Source: Ilya Ehrenburg, *People and Life: Memoirs of 1891–1921*, translated by Anna Bostock and Yvonne Kapp, London, MacGibbon & Kee, 1961; NY, Alfred Knopf, 1962.

... The war became a war of position. Shivering soldiers in the trenches hunted for lice in their shirts. Typhoid fever set in. There were attacks and counter-attacks for the possession of the notorious ferryman's house. Sappers laid mines in the forest of Argonne. Communiqués were short, but thousands of men died each day.

Letters came from Tikhon. We learned that the Russian volunteers had been posted to the Foreign Legion. Brutal non-commissioned officers called the Russians *métèques*, saying that the *métèques* were 'eating the bread of Frenchmen'. (As though the Champagne front were a restaurant!)

The story of the volunteers who went off with flags and songs to defend France is a tragic one. Until the war the Foreign Legion had consisted of criminals of every nationality who changed their names and, on completing their period of service, became French citizens enjoying full rights. Generally the *légionnaires* were sent to the colonies to put down rebellions. Nothing more need be said to indicate the customs that prevailed in the Legion. The Russians (consisting for the most part of political émigrés, Jews who had left the Jewish Pale after pogroms, and students) insisted on being posted to regular French regiments, but no one listened to them. The persecutions continued. On 22 June 1915, the volunteers rioted and beat up a few particularly detestable non-commissioned officers. A court martial at Carency sentenced nine Russians to be shot. A. A. Ignatyev, the military attaché at the Russian embassy, horrified by this injustice, managed to get the sentence rescinded, but he was too late. The Russians died with the cry: '*Vive la France.*'

———

. . . A particularly harsh fate befell the Russian brigades which the Tsarist government had sent to France in 1916. The Russian soldiers' lot had been a tragic one from the start. General Lokhvitsky and his officers were in the habit of flogging any soldier who committed the slightest offence. The French found this out and began treating the Russians with pity and contempt. When Russian troops arrived in a village for a rest, the town crier, on the orders of the Russian command, announced to the accompaniment of a drum that it was strictly forbidden to sell grape wine to Russian soldiers. In France wine is given to children. The peasants were afraid to look out of their windows: the newcomers who could not be given wine must be savages, drunk before they had had a drink.

The first mutiny of Russian soldiers took place in June 1916. They killed an officer known for his outstanding cruelty. Nine ringleaders were shot.

For a year the Russians and the French took each other's measure. I kept a note of some comments by Russian soldiers on the French, both critical and favourable.

'They say "*camarade*". But what kind of comrades are they? They don't know what it means. Here, everyone's out for himself.'

'They say we're dirty, but just look at them! They've got pomade on their hair, but you can bet it's a year since any one of them had a bath. They don't wash their dirt off, they rub it in.'

'A courteous people. You go into a shop and it's *monsieur* and *merci*.'

'With us, they knock you about just as soon as look at you. But I've seen one of them standing there, reporting to a general just as if he were talking to his equal. I've seen a French soldier sitting in a café; a colonel came in and he didn't bat an eye.'

'Call this an *izba*? Why, it isn't every gentleman at home that lives like this.'

I remember a comical argument in which the Russians came out on top. The French do not eat buckwheat porridge (during the last war they tried giving it to the Normandie airmen,[1] but they wouldn't touch it). And so the French started jeering at the

Russian soldiers: 'You know, we feed cattle that stuff.' The Russians retorted: 'What about you? You eat snails and frogs. Our cattle at home wouldn't look at that.'

However, until the summer of 1917 relations between the Russian soldiers and the population were peaceful.

In April 1917 the French command attempted to carry out an offensive in the area of Reims. Two Russian brigades took part in the fighting. Shortly before, General Nivelle received some foreign journalists. After praising the fighting spirit of the French, he turned to me and said with unconcealed irony: 'I hope that the air of France has immunized your fellow countrymen against the bleating of demagogues.' The Russian brigades fought well and occupied a position on which the fate of Reims depended; but support from other units was not forthcoming and they were obliged to withdraw. Losses were heavy.

On 1 May the Russian troops were resting. A big meeting was held. The band played the 'Marseillaise', then the 'Internationale'. The peasants were amazed. One of them said to me: 'I can understand their mutinying. Everyone's sick of the war; our fellows are mutinying, too. But why are there officers among them? And why do they sing the "Marseillaise"? What a funny lot you are!'

The Russian soldiers demanded only one thing: to be sent back to Russia. The tragedy took place later. Just before my departure, I learned that the Russian brigades were being held at the La Courtine camp as prisoners of war; the intention was to send them to Africa.

I suddenly received an invitation from the British command to visit an Anzac sector. It turned out that, under the law, Australian soldiers were required to take part in parliamentary elections; ballot boxes were brought up to the front line. The commanding officer explained to me that it would doubtless be of value for a Russian to study the technique of front-line voting.

Various people began to take an interest in me, not, of course, as the author of *Poems About the Eves*, but as the correspondent of a Petrograd newspaper. Marx's grandson, the Socialist Jean Longuet, talked to me at great length about the conflict between anti-imperialism and the need to save France. Then he suddenly laughed ruefully and said: 'I can't remember who it was, Nietzsche I think, who said that it is foolish to lecture an earthquake.' At a foreign-press luncheon the Minister of War,

Painlevé, spoke to me of his love for Tolstoy, Chekhov, and Gorky. He had good, intelligent eyes. He was a gifted mathematician; I do not know what made him choose a statesman's career.

At the Maison de la Presse they told me with great indignation that Senegalese soldiers at Saint-Raphäel were mutinying and demanding 'soviets' for the soldiers. It soon turned out that what the Senegalese wanted was leave; but the newspapers insisted that the Russians were trying to 'undermine the morale of our brave colonial troops'.

A wave of strikes began in Paris. The first to come out were the midinettes – dressmakers, seamstresses, and milliners. Young girls marched down the streets singing an audacious little tune with an entirely harmless content: they wanted the 'English week', that is, a half-day on Saturdays, and more pay. Soldiers on leave joined the demonstrations. They liked the girls, and at the same time they took the opportunity to acquaint the Parisians with a different and more serious tune: 'Down with the war!'

Soldiers began to mutiny. A man on leave came to the Rotonde and told us that his friend, a young sculptor, had been shot.

——

... I remember my last night in Paris. I walked with Chantal along the banks of the Seine, looking about me yet seeing nothing. I was no longer in Paris and not yet in Moscow; I believe I was nowhere at all. I told her the truth: I was happy and unhappy. My life in Paris had been dreadful, and yet I loved Paris. I had come there as a mere boy, but I knew what I must do and where I must go. Now I was twenty-six. I had learned a great deal, but I understood very little any more. Perhaps I had lost my way?

She tried to comfort me and said: '*Au revoir.*' I felt like answering: 'Farewell.'

The French wrote slogans on the walls: 'Be careful, enemy ears are listening.' Everybody talked about vigilance. Once I went from Paris to Épernay. My pass bore stamps from five different authorities: the Ministry of Foreign Affairs, the Ministry of War, military headquarters, the Bureau of Movements in the Military Zone, and the Aliens Control Office. I had spent five days in five different offices; I cherished the document obtained with such effort, but no one ever asked to see it.

The English wrote nothing on their walls, and my passport

was stamped with only one British visa. But I discovered what vigilance really was. I have been searched many times in my life, but no one ever did it with such artistry as the English. They made me take off my shoes and carted them off somewhere. They examined all the seams of my coat and trousers. They took away my notebook, Max Jacob's poems, and after long arguments, agreed to give me back Chantal's photograph. The Englishman who did all this had such a pleasant smile that it was impossible to be angry with him.

In London we were told that it was not known when we should continue on our way and from what port we should sail: it was a military secret. An Estonian called Ruddi, whom I knew from the Rotonde, was travelling with me. We set out for a walk through the big, completely strange city. Everything was far quieter than in Paris – perhaps because the war was farther away, perhaps because the English do not like to get excited. London seemed to me beautiful, majestic, and dreary. I thought that here Modigliani would be put in a lunatic asylum.

We spent two or three days in London. They took us to the station; our destination was still a secret. There were many of us, political émigrés and Russian soldiers who had escaped from German prisoner-of-war camps. All the carriages were overcrowded. The émigrés, of course, began arguing at once; some were *oborontsy*, others supported Lenin. In one of the compartments they almost came to blows,

We were taken to the north of Scotland. I left the compartment to stand on the platform that connected the carriages, telling Ruddi that I wanted some fresh air. In reality I felt that I was breathing peace. Here one did not have any sense of the presence of history. Scattered cottages, hills covered with purple heather, flocks of sheep, the pink, unreal light of a northern white night. Nature can teach a man many things, but that summer I had no time for wisdom. I stood a while, breathed a while, and returned to the smoke-filled carriage, where someone was shouting hoarsely: 'In what way is your Plekhanov different from Guchkov, just tell me that?'

At Aberdeen we were put on a troopship . . .

1. A volunteer squadron of the Free French which served with the Soviet army during the First World War. [AB,YK]

ARTHUR RANSOME

Arthur Ransome (1884–1967). Born in Leeds, Yorkshire. Ransome first visited Russia in 1913 and went in 1915 to Petrograd as correspondent to the *Daily News*. The incidents described took place in 1916. A minor literary figure in London before the war (he was a friend of Edward Thomas) he was one of the few English people in Russia during the Revolution. He knew Lenin and Trotsky, whose secretary, Evgenia, he married. Famous now for *Swallows and Amazons*, etc., and *Rod and Line*. General Brusilov's 'breakthrough in the west' was the ill-fated 'advance' described by Florence Farmborough (*q.v.*)

Source: Arthur Ransome, *The Autobiography of Arthur Ransome*, ed. Rupert Hart-Davis, London, Jonathan Cape, 1976.

It was March 1916 before I was given my first limited permission to visit the Russian front as a war correspondent. I believe that in the 1939–45 war correspondents were encouraged and given every opportunity of seeing the war it was their business to describe. In 1916, on the Russian front, they had a struggle to see anything at all. We were fully persuaded that the enemy knew more about the position of the Russian armies than Russia's allies were allowed to know. Further, most of the foreign correspondents knew no Russian, or very little, and so needed interpreters and constant shepherding by some Russian officer detailed for that purpose.

When with another correspondent I got down to Galicia the gratitude of the officer in charge of us on finding that we could sometimes do without him was almost touching. We went to Kiev and thence to the South Western Army Headquarters at Berditchev, where we met for the first time General Brusilov, the smartest-uniformed and most elegant of all Russian generals, later to be famous for his breakthrough in the west, and for the disasters his armies suffered in retreat. We spent about a month in that strange rolling country that was so unlike Russia. The peasants working on the land were very unwilling to identify themselves as belonging to any one of the warring nations. Again and again, on asking a peasant to what nationality he belonged,

Russian, Little-Russian or Polish, I heard the reply 'Orthodox', and when the man was pressed to say to what actual race he belonged I heard him answer safely 'We're local.'

I remember little of what we saw, except the things that no serious reader would think worth remembering, such as an observation post designed by some Russian who had not forgotten the stories told him as a child. It was disguised as a muckheap in a huge area of ploughed land where there were at least fifty muckheaps all alike. And of course I remember that other night when, on a quiet sector, I was walking with a Russian officer who mistook his direction and we were suddenly brought up short by hearing German spoken a few yards ahead of us. I still have the little luminous phosphorescent compass by which we found our way back. This was a sector where the enemy forces were Austrian, the trenches were very near together, and a Russian raiding-party, pushing deep into the Austrian lines, found an unguarded waggon of comforts for the troops, mainly musical instruments. These were distributed and I still have the *czakan*, a sort of Hungarian flageolet, that fell undeserved to my share. I remember, too, on one of these expeditions, an Easter Eve service in a tent, with the candle flames shivering in the wind, and rockets in the sky over no man's land to announce that Christ was risen.

I remember interminable driving in vehicles of all kinds along roads that war had widened from narrow cart-tracks to broad highways half a mile wide. Drivers had moved out of the original road to ground on either side of it not yet churned to mud. As each new strip turned to bog the drivers steered just outside it, so that in many places two carts meeting each other and going in opposite directions would be out of shouting distance. I remember Tarnopol and Trembovlya, where the railway staff used to leave the railway station at five minutes to eight every morning and the hotel staff left it to the Germans to call their guests for them, since station-master and hotel-keeper alike could count on a German aeroplane dropping a bomb on or near the station at eight o'clock precisely. Was it at Tarnopol that I tried to teach Hamilton Fyfe to fish for tench in a horse-pond? Was it here or at Berditchev that he was so angry with me for rousing unjustified ambition in bootblacks? We had an appointment some distance away in local headquarters, and I was slow with my breakfast and came down to find Fyfe outside the hotel with one of his boots already cleaned and a bootboy setting to work on the other. 'You are going to make us both late,' said Fyfe, as another bootboy started on mine. I bent down and told my bootboy he should have a rouble if my boots were cleaned before Fyfe's. The boy's brushes fairly whirled, and I gave him his rouble and set off down the street just as Fyfe's boy was finishing. But my boy could not resist gloating, with the result that Fyfe's boy refused the usual twenty kopecks and demanded a rouble for himself also and with outstretched hand and complaining voice kept pace with the unyielding Fyfe all the way down the street.

But why pile these trivialities together? Looking back now I seem to have seen nothing, but I did in fact see a great deal of that long-drawn-out front and of the men who, ill-armed, ill-supplied, were holding it against an enemy who, even if his anxiety to fight was no greater than the Russian's, was infinitely better equipped. I came back to Petrograd full of admiration for the Russian soldiers who were holding the front without enough weapons to go round. I was much better able to understand the grimness with which those of my friends who knew Russia best were looking into the future. I came back also to find myself telegraphing, sometimes twice and three times in a day. It often happened that the news editor would cable telling me not to send so much. These cables I always disregarded and always, a few days later, he would cable again asking for more . . .

———

. . . In August, during a visit to the front, Berenger sent a well-meant but silly telegram to England in which he mentioned (most unnecessarily) that the correspondent of the *Daily News* when flying in a Russian aeroplane had come under fire. The truth was that I had indeed flown along the front in one of the old two-seated Voisin machines in which the passenger sat as if in an open canoe with a foot on each side of the pilot, in whose stupidity he had the utmost confidence. It was cold in the air and I well remember beating my hand against the outside of the canoe to get my fingers warm enough to take a photograph. There had been a little shooting over the actual front and the pilot had praised the deafening noise of the engine so very close to our heads, pointing out that even when the puff of smoke flowered quite close to us we could not hear the explosion, and that once we saw that puff we could be sure we had been missed. Our real trouble, such as it was, began when just before dusk we flew back to the place from which we had started. We began to spiral down and instantly there appeared puff after puff of smoke from shells sent up to meet us. The pilot suddenly turned the nose of the machine up, pointing with a grin to a small new tear in one wing. Presently he spiralled down again and again was greeted with shells from below. Once more we sheered off, this time with curses, and on coming back yet again we were, at last, recognized as friends and allowed to land. I dined that night with the battery that had done the shooting, and sat next to the officer in charge. I complained that I did not think he had given me a very hospitable reception. 'Perhaps not,' he replied. 'I'm very sorry, my dear chap, to have kept you waiting on the doorstep, so to speak, but really you ought to count yourself lucky, for usually when we fire at our own machine we hit it.' In case I had not understood, he explained that their aeroplanes had been given to the Russian army because they were not good enough for the French. They were very slow and therefore easy targets . . .

JOHN REED

John Reed (1887–1920). Born in Portland, Oregon. He graduated from Harvard in the same class as T. S. Eliot. There is an interesting portrait of him in Dos Passos's *U.S.A.* He died in Russia. Best known for *Ten Days that Shook the World*, London, 1926 (recently filmed). Reported on the war in the east between April and October 1915 for the *Metropolitan Magazine*. Crossed into Russia at the river Prut at the frontiers of Romanian Moldavia, Austrian Bucovina and Russian Bessarabia. He went north as far as Moscow and Petrograd and left via Romania and Bulgaria. Many of the places he mentions were visited by Ransome and also by Farmborough (*qq.v.*). The use of the ellipsis (. . .) is part of Reed's style and does not, in this case, indicate abbreviation by the editors.

Source: John Reed, *The War in Eastern Europe*, New York, Charles Scribner's Sons, 1916.

Early the next morning we came out of our lodgings to the shrill sound of Yiddish blessings and reproaches mixed, and found the Jew smirking and rubbing his hands.

'Where's the carriage?' I asked, suspecting further extortion. The Jew pointed to a temporary scaffolding such as is used for digging artesian wells, upon which sat an incredibly discouraged-looking moujik. On closer inspection we discovered wheels, fastened to arbitrary places with bits of wire and rope; and apparently unattached to the structure, two aged and disillusioned horses leaned against each other.

'B-r-r-r-r-r!' said the moujik to these animals, implying that they would run away if he didn't. 'B-r-r-r-r!'

We mounted, while the Jew abusively impressed upon his driver that we were to be taken to Zalezchik, through Boyan and Zastevna; he also told him to get whatever money he could out of us . . . At the end of this tirade, the peasant rose and stolidly beat the horses with a long string fastened to a stick, shouting hoarsely: 'Ugh! Eeagh! Augh!' The horses awoke, sighed, and moved experimentally – by some mechanical miracle the wheels turned, a shudder ran along our keel, and we were off!

Across the bridge into Austrian Novo Sielitza we rattled, and out upon the hard road that led frontward, slowly gaining upon and passing a long train of ox-carts driven by soldiers and loaded with cases of ammunition. Now we were in Bucovina. On the left, low fields green with young crops stretched flatly to the trees along the Prut, beyond which rose the rich hills of Romania; to the right the valley extended miles to cultivated rolling country. Already the June sun poured down windless, moist heat. The driver slumped gradually into his spine, the horses' pace diminished to a merely arithmetical progression, and we crawled in a baking pall of dust like Zeus hidden in his cloud.

'Hey!' We beat upon his back. 'Shake a leg, Dave!'

He turned upon us a dirty, snub-nosed face, and eyes peering through matted hair, and his mouth cracked slowly in an appalling, familiar grin – with the intelligent expression of a loaf of bread. We christened him immediately Ivan the Horrible . . .

'Ooch!' he cried with simulated ferocity, waving the string. 'Aich! Augh!'

The horses pretended to be impressed, and broke into a shuffle; but ten minutes later Ivan was again rapt in contemplation of the infinite, the horses almost stationary, and we moved in white dust . . .

Slowly we drew near the leisurely sound of the cannon, that defined itself sharply out of the all-echoing thunder audible at Novo Sielitza. And topping a steep hill crowned with a straggling thatched village, we came in sight of the batteries. They lay on the hither side of an immense rolling hill, where a red gash in the fields dribbled along for miles. At intervals of half a minute a gun spat heavily; but you could see neither smoke nor flame – only minute figures running about, stiffening, and again springing to life. A twanging drone as the shell soared – and then on the leafy hills across the river puffs of smoke unfolding. Over there were the towers of white Czernowitz, dazzling in the sun. The village through which we passed was populous with great brown soldiers, who eyed us sullenly and suspiciously. Over a gateway hung a Red Cross flag, and along the road trickled a thin, steady stream of wounded – some leaning on their comrades, others bandaged around the head, or with their arms in slings; and peasant carts jolted by with faintly groaning heaps of arms and legs . . .

The road slanted down until we were close to the crashing

batteries. For hours we drove along behind a desultory but gigantic artillery battle. Gun after gun after gun, each in its raw pit, covered with brush to shield it from aeroplanes. Sweating men staggered under the weight of shells, moving about the shining caissons; methodically the breech snapped home and the pointer singsonged his range; a firer jerked the lanyard – furious haze belched out, gun recoiled, shell screamed – miles and miles of great cannon in lordly syncopation.

In the very field of the artillery, peasants were calmly ploughing with oxen, and in front of the roaring guns a boy in white linen drove cattle over the hill toward the pastures along the river. We met long-haired farmers, with orange poppies in their hats, unconcernedly driving to town. Eastward the world rolled up in another slow hill that bore curved fields of young wheat, running in great waves before the wind. Its crest was torn and scarred with mighty excavations, where multitudinous tiny men swarmed over new trenches and barbed-wire tangles. This was the second-line position preparing for a retreat that was sure to come . . .

We swung northward, away from the artillery, over the bald shoulder of a powerful hill. Here the earth mounted in magnificent waves, patterned with narrow green, brown, and yellow fields that shimmered under the wind. Through valleys whose sides fell like a bird's swoop were vistas of checkered slopes and copses soft with distance. Far to the west the faint blue crinkly line of the Carpathians marched across the horizon. Tree-smothered villages huddled in the immense folds of the land – villages of clay houses unevenly and beautifully moulded by hand, painted spotless white with a bright blue stripe around the bottom, and elaborately thatched. Many were deserted, smashed, and black with fire – especially those where Jews had lived. They bore marks of wanton pillage – for there had been no battle here – doors beaten in, windows torn out, and lying all about the wreckage of mean furniture, rent clothing. Since the beginning of the war the Austrians had not come here. It was Russian work . . .

Peasants smiling their soft, friendly smile took off their hats as we went by. A gaunt man with a thin baby in his arms ran forward and kissed my hand when I gave him a piece of chocolate. Along the roadside stood hoary stone crosses inscribed with sacred verses in the old Slavonic, before which the peasants uncovered and crossed themselves devoutly. And there were rude wooden crosses, as in Mexico, to mark the spots where men had been assassinated . . .

———

It was on the other side of Zastevna, where we stopped beside some ruined houses for a drink, that we saw the Austrian prisoners. They came limping along the road in the hot sun, about thirty of them, escorted by two Don Cossacks on horseback; gray uniforms white with dust, bristly faces drawn with fatigue. One man had the upper left-hand part of his face bound up, and the blood had soaked through; another's hand was bandaged, and some jerked along on improvised crutches. At a sign from the Cossacks, who dismounted, they reeled and stumbled to the side of the road, and sullenly threw themselves down in the shade. Two dark-faced men snarled at each other like beasts. The man with the wounded head groaned. He with the bandaged hand began tremblingly to unwrap the gauze. The Cossacks good-naturedly waved us permission to talk with them, and we went over with handfuls of cigarettes. They snatched at them with the avidity of smokers long deprived of tobacco – all except one haughty-faced youth, who produced a handsome case crammed with gold-tipped cigarettes, declined ours frigidly, and took one of his own, without offering any to the others.

'He is a count,' explained a simple, peasant-faced boy with awe.

The man with the wounded hand had got his bandage off at last, and was staring at his bloody palm with a sort of fascination.

'I think this had better be dressed again,' said he at last, glancing diffidently at a stout, sulky-looking person who wore a Red Cross arm-band. The latter looked across with lazy contempt and shrugged his shoulders.

'We've got some bandages,' I began, producing one. But one of the Cossacks came over, scowling and shaking his head at me. He kicked the Red Cross man with a look of disgust, and pointed to the other. Muttering something, the stout man fumbled angrily in his case, jerked out a bandage, and slouched across.

There were thirty of them, and among that thirty-five races were represented: Czechs, Croats, Magyars, Poles, and Austrians. One Croat, two Magyars, three Czechs could speak absolutely not a word of any language but their own, and, of course, none of the Austrians knew a single word of Bohemian, Croatian, Hungarian, or Polish. Among the Austrians were Tyroleans,

Viennese, and a half-Italian from Pola. The Croats hated the Magyars, and the Magyars hated the Austrians – and as for the Czechs, no one would speak to them. Besides, they were all divided up into sharply defined social grades, each of which snubbed its inferiors ... As a sample of Franz Joseph's army the group was most illuminating.

They had been taken in a night attack along the Prut, and marched more than twenty miles in two days. But they were all enthusiastic in praise of their Cossack guards.

'They are very considerate and kind,' said one man. 'When we stop for the night the Cossacks personally go around to each man, and see that he is comfortable. And they let us rest often . . .'

'The Cossacks are fine soldiers,' another broke in; 'I have fought with them, and they are very brave. I wish we had cavalry like them!'

A young volunteer of the Polish legion asked eagerly if Romania was coming in. We replied that it seemed like it, and suddenly he burst out, quivering:

'My God! My God! What can we do? How long can this awful war last? All we want is peace and quiet and rest! We are beaten – we are honorably beaten. England, France, Russia, Italy, the whole world is against us. We can lay down our arms with honor now! Why should this useless butchery go on?'

And the rest sat there, gloomily listening to him, without a word . . .

Toward evening we were rattling down a steep gully between high cliffs. A stream plunged down beside the road, turning a hundred water-wheels whose mills lay shattered by artillery fire; shacks in partial ruin shouldered each other along the gully, and on top of the eastern cliff we could see disembowelled trenches and an inferno of twisted, snarled barbed wire, where the Russians had bombarded and stormed the Austrian defenses a month before. Hundreds of men were at work up there clearing away the wreckage and building new works. We rounded a corner suddenly and came out upon the bank of the Dnestr, just below where the tall railroad bridge plunged into the water its tangle of dynamited girders and cables. Here the river made a huge bend, beneath earthen cliffs a hundred feet high, and across a pontoon bridge choked with artillery the once lovely town of Zalezchik lay bowered in trees. As we crossed, naked Cossacks

459

were swimming their horses in the current, shouting and splashing, their powerful white bodies drenched with golden light . . .

Zalezchik had been captured, burned, and looted three times by two armies, shelled for fifteen days, and the major portion of its population wiped out by both sides because it had given aid and comfort to the enemy. Night was falling when we drove into the market-place, surrounded with the shocking debris of tall houses. A sort of feeble market was going on there under miserable tilted shacks, where sad-eyed peasant women spread their scanty vegetables and loaves of bread, the centre of a mob of soldiers. A few Jews slunk about the corners. Ivan demanded a hotel, but the man smiled and pointed to a tall crumbling brick wall with 'Grand Hotel' painted boldly across it – all that remained. Where could we get something to eat?

'Something to eat? There is not enough food in this town to feed my wife and children.'

An atmosphere of terror hung over the place – we could feel it in the air. It was in the crouching figures of the Jews, stealing furtively along the tottering walls; in the peasants as they got out of the way of our carriage, doffing their hats; in the faces of cringing children, as soldiers went by. It got dark, and we sat in the carriage, debating what to do.

An *Apteka* – apothecary shop – stood on the corner, comparatively undamaged, with a light inside. I found the druggist alone, a Jew who spoke German.

'What are you?' he asked suspiciously, peering at me.

'An American.'

'There is no hotel here,' he burst out suddenly. 'There is no place to stay and nothing to eat. A month ago the Russians came in here – they slaughtered the Jews, and drove the women and children out there.' He pointed west. 'There is no place here –'

'Then,' I said, 'the military commandant must take care of us. Where can I find him?'

'I will send my assistant with you,' he answered. His face stiffened with fear. 'You will not say to them what I have told, noble *Herr*? You will not –'

The entry of two Russian soldiers interrupted him, and he rose, addressing me insolently for their benefit:

'I can't drive you out of the shop. It's a public shop. But remember, I assume no responsibility for you. I didn't ask you to come here. I don't know you.' For, after all, we might be undesirable people.

We bestowed upon Ivan a two-rouble piece, which, after biting, he put away in his pocket with hoarse sounds betokening gratitude. And we left him sitting on his vehicle in the middle of the square, gazing at nothing. When we came out of the *Apteka* he was still there, hunched over in the same position, and an hour later, when we issued from the colonel's headquarters, he had not moved, though it was quite dark. What was passing in that swampy mind? Perhaps he was trying to remember the name of Novo Sielitza, his home – perhaps he was merely wondering how to get there . . .

We sat long over dinner with the genial colonel and his staff, chattering politics and gossip in intensely fragmentary German. Among other officers were a young Finnish lieutenant and an old Cossack major with a wrinkled Mongolian face like the pictures of Li Hung Chang, who were very much excited over the sinking of the *Lusitania*, and sure that America would go to war.

'What can we do for you?' asked the colonel.

We said that we would like to visit this part of the front, if there were any fighting going on.

'That, I am afraid, is impossible from here,' he regretted. 'But if you will go to Tarnopol, the general commanding this army will surely give you permission. Then you must return here, and I shall be glad to accompany you myself. A train for Tarnopol leaves tonight at eleven.'

Could he give us any idea what was happening along the front?

'With pleasure,' said he eagerly, telling an orderly to bring the maps. He spread them out on the table. 'Now here, near Zadagora, we have ten big guns placed in these positions, to stop the Austrian flanking column that is rolling up from the Prut. Over here, near Kaluz, the Austrians imagine that we have nothing but cavalry, but in about three days we'll throw three regiments across this little stream at this point –'

I remarked that all those maps seemed to be German or Austrian maps.

'Oh, yes,' he replied. 'At the beginning of the war we had no maps at all of Bucovina or Galicia. We didn't even know the lay of the land until we had captured some . . .'

—

We changed trains at Rovno, where there was a wait of nine hours. There we ran into Miroshnikov, the English-speaking subofficer who had looked after us in Tarnopol, now bound north on official business.

'Let's walk around,' he proposed. 'I want to show you a typical Jewish town of the Pale.'

As we went along, I asked the meaning of the red, white, and blue cord that edged his shoulder-straps.

'That means I am a volunteer – exempt from compulsory service. The Russian word for "volunteer,"' he answered the question with a grin, 'is "*Volnoopredielyayoustchemusia*."'

We gave up all hopes of learning the language . . .

I can never forget Rovno, the Jewish town of the Pale of Settlement. It was Russian in its shabby largeness, wide streets half paved with cobbles, dilapidated sidewalks, rambling wooden houses ornamented with scroll-saw trimmings painted bright green, and the swarming uniforms of its minor officialdom. Tiny-wheeled cabs abounded, with their heavy Russian yoke, driven by hairy degenerates who wore tattered velveteen robes and bell-top hats of outrageous shape. But all the rest was Jewish . . . The street was heaped with evil-smelling rubbish, amid slimy puddles splashed up by every passing conveyance. Clouds of bloated flies buzzed about. On both sides a multitude of little shops strangled each other, and their glaring signs, daubed with portraits of the articles for sale, made a crazy-quilt up and down as far as one could see. The greasy proprietors stood in their reeking doorways, each one bawling to us to buy from *him*, and not from his cheating competitor across the way. Too many shops, too many cab-drivers, barbers, tailors, herded into this narrow world where alone Jews are allowed to live in Russia; and periodically augmented with the miserable throngs cleared out from the forbidden cities, where they have bribed the police to stay. In the Pale a Jew gasps for breath indeed.

How different these were from even the poorest, meanest Jews in Galician cities. Here they were a pale, stooping, inbred race, refined to the point of idiocy. Cringing men with their 'sacred fringes' showing under their long coats – it was at Rovno that we first noticed the little peaked caps worn by Polish Jews – faintly bearded boys with unhealthy faces, girls prematurely aged with bitter work and eternal humiliation, grown women wrinkled and bent, in wigs and slovenly mother hubbards. People who smiled deprecatingly and hatefully when you looked at them, who stepped into the street to let Gentiles pass. And in the very centre of it all, a Russian church with blue incense pouring out the open door, a glitter of gold, jewels, and candle-lighted icons within, priests in stoles heavy with woven gold threads, atremble with slow, noble chanting.

For a thousand years the Russians and their Church have done their best to exterminate the Jews and their religion. With what success? Here in Rovno were thousands of Jews shut in an impregnable world of their own, scrupulously observing a religion incessantly purified, practising their own customs, speaking their own language, with two codes of morals – one for each other and the other for the Gentiles. Persecution has only engendered a poison and a running sore in the body of the Russian people. It is true what Miroshnikov said, as we drank kvass in a little Jewish bar – that all Jews were traitors to Russia. Of course they are.

An officer whom we had met on the train came in. He sniffed the air, bowed to us, and staring malevolently at the frightened girls who served, said distinctly: 'The dirty Jews! I detest them!' and walked out . . .

V. M. DOROSHEVICH

Vlas Mikhailovich Doroshevich (1864–1922). Popular with liberal readers, he was a journalist, writer and theatre critic. Defended the interests of the landowners in the war. The strong Christian element in *The Way of the Cross* appealed to Stephen Graham (*q.v.*), who introduced, and presumably translated, the English version. Doroshevich visited and described for his own paper, *The Russian Word*, the refugees escaping from the German invasion of August–September 1915. Graham thought that these accounts were 'probably the first Russian war literature translated into English'.

Source: Vlas Mikhailovich Doroshevich, *The Way of the Cross*, London, Constable, 1916.

IN THE FOREST

It is getting colder and colder.

The golden and rose and flame colours of sunset have played themselves out on the cloudless pale green sky.

On the left, over the forest, like a phantom, is seen the pale fine sickle of the new moon.

From the marsh and from the little river over which we pass comes an icy breath.

There are mists in the low-lying places.

Everywhere it becomes darker and darker.

The moon's sickle is getting all yellow, all clear, more and more full of light.

Stars are scattered about in the sky as on a winter night – so many there are.

In their light the sky appears darkly, darkly, blue.

And, as if enchanted, the dark black forest comes to life.

On the right, on the left, there, here, near at hand, in the depths, through the thicket of fine black branches gleams the red of large fires.

Pillars of sparks arise and float above.

It is as if fireworks were being let off in the forest.

The sweet scent of burning wood is in the air.

The farther we go into the forest the stronger is this scent, the oftener do we meet the fires.

And it seems as if we are not in the forest at all – but as if a kind of illuminated endless town were stretching itself out upon the road.

We stop the car – the forest is full of rustlings and noises.

Human sounds are heard – here and there an axe resounds, bonfires crackle.

I stop for a little and go into the forest.

I make my way through the branches – there is a hewn glade around which the thicket stands like a wall.

A covered cart, a camp-fire; all is quiet.

Nothing is heard save the champing of the horses, munching hay.

Around the fire in silence sits a family.

The first thing that meets the eye is the bare feet of the children almost into the fire.

'Good evening, good people!'

The appearance of a man at night in the forest, coming from no one knows where, causes no surprise, no curiosity, does not even appear strange.

They don't even look round.

'What's this man come for?'

They answer kindly and civilly:

'Good evening, sir!'

'What are you doing in the forest? Why didn't you stay near the "point"?'

'It's exposed there, sir, it's cold. It's warmer in the forest. Look at the children.'

'Are they very ill?'

'They get wet and cold, and then they die.'

'The ground is as cold as iron. And they're barefoot.'

The children of the refugees are their most precious possession. They grieve most of all for the children. But the children are almost without clothing.

The peasant men are warmly clad. Almost every one has a warm coat.

The women are all right. They're muffled up somehow.

But the children . . .

For the children evidently there had been no previous provision.

At home, children are part of the general surroundings – something like dear domestic animals. And one thinks about them as much as one would about a cat.

'Why should one trouble about a child?'

For the children nothing is made.

And the refugees' children die like flies.

'They lie with their stomachs to the fire, and their backs are as cold as ice. They turn their backs to the fire and their stomachs freeze.'

And they die.

And the children sit there in silence, sticking out their little red hands and dirty bare legs almost into the fire, and listen to what is said about them.

'Inevitable death.'

On the fire some food is being cooked in saucepans.

On the bonfire.

The saucepans are not made to hang over the fire.

They are the ordinary pots for cooking on a stove.

Not suitable for a nomad life!

Now we've got to the reason why dysentery is raging.

In order to cook potatoes, cabbage, porridge – they place the pot near the fire, turning first one side and then the other.

The food cannot get cooked through.

It is burnt at the sides, in the middle it remains raw.

They eat this mixture of half-burnt, half-raw food – and thence arises this terrible dysentery.

The woman picks up what looks like a bundle of rags lying near the fire, and from it comes suddenly a little whine.

'I suppose you haven't a little powder with you, sir? The baby is ill. It's taken a chill, and is ill.'

'Did you show it to the people at the "point"?'

'At one place they gave me some milk porridge. But it was no good. Haven't you any sort of powder for children?'

I go on farther, through the thicket.

Another cut-down space, a little larger.

Three camp-fires in a row.

Several families are seated there.

And again, the sudden appearance of an unknown man does not call forth any curiosity.

The people are not interested in anything.

It's all the same to them.

Once more they give the courteous reply: 'Good evening, sir'.

466

Much as I have gone about among the fugitives, amongst those suffering most severely, never have I heard anything but kind, polite, pitiful words.

'Father!' an old man sitting crouching over the fire squeaked rather than said. 'Father, haven't you any stomach drops? The pain's like a knife, father!'

I go on further.

A bonfire. Near it lies a man, immovable.

'What's the matter with him?'

'Rheumatism, sir.'

'But how can you let him lie on the ground?' I ask, repeating the question of the village policeman not long before.

'At the fire, sir, he can warm himself. It's got into his jaws. He can't open his mouth. Can't eat, can't talk. Oh sir, haven't you something for rheumatism?'

I go on further still.

Again there is a man lying by the fire.

'What's the matter with him?'

'Everything passes through him.'

'Blood?'

'That's it, sir. Blood.'

The peasant lifts his head, and says sadly in a weak voice, with a deathly sadness, 'My blood is flowing out of me. It flows out. I'm cold inside me. All my blood is going out of me.'

And calmly, just as if he were not there, the people around say: 'Yes, that's so, he passes blood. He's no strength left – and look at him! That's the sort of state he's in.'

And there is a chorus: 'Oh sir, haven't you any sort of medicine with you?'

'Sir! *Pan!* Master! Stop my blood from flowing away!'

'Medicine! Medicine! Medicine! Haven't you any medicine?'

And there are more and more camp-fires in the forest.

Here a dark strip, then again, as if it were a town – then again a dark strip.

About ten *versts*[1] from Roslavl there is a red glow in the sky.

'A fire?'

'And a large one.'

The nearer we approach the brighter and clearer becomes the glare.

Only one thing is strange: the glare does not waver. It's not like the glare of a fire.

The glare becomes enormous.

467

It stands apparently right over the town.

'What is it? Roslavl on fire?'

'And there . . .'

What a wonderful picture!

We get to within three *versts* of Roslavl.

On the right, on the left, wherever you look, bonfires, bonfires, bonfires.

A whole sea of bonfires.

It is damp. The smoke settles downward.

It is impossible to breathe along the road for the smoke.

It stops the breathing, makes the eyes smart.

The lights of the relief cars cannot penetrate this thick smoke.

And all around in the smoke are crimson fires.

Showers of sparks fly about in the sky.

This great glare is the necessary outcome of all these camp-fires.

Possibly only in the times of the Tartar invasion were there such pictures.

All around in the forest is the unceasing chatter of some gigantic crowd.

Saws are creaking. As in an Old Believers' settlement in the woods when people are called to prayer with a wooden clapper is the sound of the axes, the axes ring soundingly in the night air upon the cold trees.

A sort of continuous forest-clearing.

And the whole shore of the river Oster is spread before us and below us in a bright opal smoke with purple spots in it.

And when we drive over the railway bridge, and see below the blue and red lights, and hear the whistle of the steam-engines, we involuntarily ask: 'Is this really the twentieth century?'

1. *Verst*: a Russian measure, about two thirds of a mile.

FLORENCE FARMBOROUGH

Florence Farmborough (1887–?1980). First went to Russia in 1908. Taught English in a Moscow family. When the war broke out she trained for Red Cross work in a Moscow hospital. Accompanied Russian front-line troops in Poland, Austria and Romania. Wrote for *The Times*. Became a university lecturer in Spain. Her *Diary* was kept, sometimes in note form, between 1914 and 1918, and reached about 400,000 words. The following excerpts from 1916 cover the period when the Russians were attempting to counter-attack in an area that had been part of the Austro-Hungarian Empire. After initial successes (the Russians took a quarter of a million prisoners) they were forced into retreat and suffered over one million casualties. Farmborough's descriptions are vivid, uncompromising and humane. John Reed (*q.v.*) had travelled in the region during the previous year.

Source: Florence Farmborough, *Nurse at the Russian Front: A Diary 1914–18*, London, Constable, 1974.

1916, THE ADVANCE

Wednesday, 24 February [1916]
Chortkov

The position of the Hebrews living in Chortkov is most pitiful. They are being treated with vindictive animosity. As Austrian subjects they enjoyed almost complete liberty, experiencing none of the cruel oppression constantly poured out on to the Russian Jew. But under the new government their rights and freedom have disappeared and it is obvious that they resent the change keenly. Our hostess, a black-eyed, sweet-faced Rebecca, sometimes imparts a few of her woes to me.

A few days ago we had a very heavy fall of snow, which continued incessantly for three days and nights. When the blizzard had blown itself out, the roads were blocked up, wall-high, by enormous drifts. The Jews were at once ordered out to clear the snow and every family was forced to send at least one representative to take his share in the task. Should a family consist only of females – as was the case with our hostess – and there was no man they could send, the penalty for that family would be one rouble per diem. No matter how rich the family, money would not exonerate them from work; *one* male was forced to join the labour-squad. This explains the unusual scene I noticed yesterday – among the groups of Jewish townsfolk clearing the snow off the streets, that there were several well-dressed men whose faces revealed their intelligent and cultured background, working, shovel in hand, side by side with disreputable-looking old Hebrews in long kaftans and conventional side-curls. Near them stand Russian soldiers, knout in hand, whose sharp reprimand – and still sharper lash – provide effective guarantees against negligence or slackness . . .

28 May [1916]
Buchach

. . . We reached our quarters and prepared the bandaging-room without delay. Three or four wounded were brought before we were actually ready for them. We had bandaged those men and were busily engaged in unpacking our own necessary belongings and the first-aid equipment, when an urgent message reached us: 'Prepare for burnt soldiers.' Laconic wording, but elaborated in some detail by the staff messenger. A disastrous fire had gutted a wine-cellar; several soldiers had been burnt to death; some were being brought for instant treatment. It seems that the men of the 101st Permski Regiment had that day marched through Buchach, singing lustily, on their way into reserve. During the evening, several had gone on a tour of exploration. They found a distillery in which casks of alcohol were still stored. They drank their fill and then, inebriated and elated, turned on the taps. But someone must have struck a match, for the cellar was suddenly swept with fierce flames. About a dozen men perished on the spot; others crawled out, but collapsed and died soon afterwards. Only two of them were able to stand and they were brought to us.

They came, both of them, *walking*: two naked red figures! Their clothes had been burnt off their bodies. They stood side by side in the large barn which we had converted into a dressing-station, raw from head to foot. Injections were immediately ordered, but we could find no skin and had to put the needle straight into the flesh. Their arms were hanging stiffly at their sides and from the finger-tips of the men were suspended what looked like leather gloves; these we were told to cut off which we did with surgical scissors. They were the skin of the hand and fingers which had peeled off and was hanging from the raw flesh of the finger-tips. Then we showered them with bicarbonate of soda and swathed their poor, burnt bodies with layers of cotton wool and surgical lint. We laid them down upon straw in an adjoining shed. In an hour or two, the cotton wool was completely saturated, but we could help them no further, save with oft-repeated injections of morphia which, we prayed, would deaden their sufferings. They died, both of them, before morning. And neither of them had spoken a single word! I don't think that anything which I had ever seen touched me so keenly.

The sisters' room was small and the night brought little rest. I dozed off at intervals, but the thought of those two suffering, burnt bodies would not leave me. There was, too, a horrible smell: some dead horses lay not far from the house – and the wind was blowing in the wrong direction. In the distance one could hear noisy singing and faint accordion music. So many soldiers had perished in that foolhardy escapade and yet – here were their comrades once again drinking and revelling! Victory must have deprived them of their senses! . . .

Sunday, 31 July
Monasterzhiska

As we journeyed [from Barish] the scenery became more and more beautiful; to the right and left ran long, undulating ranges of wooded hills; behind them rose majestic mountain-peaks. We came to various places where enemy batteries had stood; and to other sites where our cannon had been hastily stationed. We drove through the little villages of Bertniki and Cherkhov, where the narrow streets had been disfigured and rent asunder by makeshift trenches and where buildings of every description had been demolished, or so badly mutilated as to leave them mere piles of disintegrated brick and wood. We saw the 'ditches' where our men had dug themselves in before the attack. The attack itself must have been of a most terrifying kind on account of the difficult terrain on all three sides. On the hill facing our hastily contrived 'trenches', were the fortified, many-lined Austrian escarpments, and to occupy those enemy strongholds much dangerous manoeuvring would have been necessary, seeing that our men were obliged to descend their hill and ascend the one opposite *in full sight of the enemy*. All over the downward and upward sides of the two opposing hills were branches of trees which, in their own poor way, had helped to disguise the attack and to shelter the attacker. We drove on and came to the upper slopes of the fortified hill; they were spread with mangled heaps of the Austrian barbed-wire protective fences which had lost all their protective capacity under the powerful battering which they had received from our guns. Enormous craters had churned up the earth and left gaping, jagged holes on all sides and a medley of indescribable objects littered the ruptured ground.

On a levelled piece of land near the lower spur of the hill, several small wooden crosses were seen; it was, obviously, a temporary cemetery for the Austrian dead. We walked among the debris caused by the recent conflict and in some of the trenches we saw – scarcely believing our eyes – human figures. They were, we felt sure, Austrian soldiers, whom retreating comrades were unable to remove, and whom the pursuing Russians would have neither time nor will to heed. In one trench there were three men huddled together, their contorted forms proving beyond doubt that they were lifeless; in another lay the figure of a soldier stretched at full length among the broken fragments of a once strongly constructed dug-out. His face was unmarked and his skin still clear; he might have been resting, were it not for the chaotic condition of his surroundings. So this was ADVANCE! Wherein lay its glory? Only these forsaken, mouldering bodies could testify to the Russian Victory.

As we continued our journey, we passed more than one battlefield. The dead were still lying around, in strange, unnatural postures – remaining where they had fallen: crouching, doubled up, stretched out, prostrate, prone ... Austrians and Russians lying side by side. And there were lacerated, crushed bodies lying on darkly stained patches of earth. There was one Austrian without a leg and with blackened, swollen face; another with a smashed face, terrible to look at; a Russian soldier, with legs doubled under him, leaning against the barbed wire. And on more than one open wound flies were crawling and there were other moving, thread-like things. I was glad Anna and Ekaterina were with me; they, too, were silent; they, too, were sorely shaken. Those 'heaps' were once human beings: men who were young, strong and vigorous; now they lay lifeless and inert; shapeless forms of what had been living flesh and bone. What a frail and fragile thing is human life! A bullet passes through the living flesh and it ceases to live. But a bullet cannot kill the soul; one knows, most assuredly, that the Spirit – God's breath in man – returns to God who gave it. Oh! one *must* believe and trust in God's mercy, otherwise these frightful sights would work havoc with one's brain; and one's heart would faint with the depth of its despair.

Dinner was brought to us soon after our arrival. We sisters were still feeling affected by the awful sights which we had witnessed during that memorable journey. There was a heaviness within us difficult to throw off and although the menfolk of our contingent carried on a cheerful conversation we could take but little part in it. We had received instructions to delay the unpacking of all surgical equipment because we might have to continue the journey on the following day. We were still surrounded by gruesome remnants of the recent conflict. Not far from our tent, there was a slight incline with a couple of dug-outs; a dead man was lying near them, half-buried in the piled earth thrown up by a shell. Mamasha took a cloth and threw it over the discoloured face. To our right was a plain; there, too, was a litter of bombs, hand-grenades, cartridges, rifles, spades, pickaxes, gas-masks, shells exploded and unexploded. From where we stood, we could clearly espy the crumpled forms of dead soldiers. I took one or two photographs, but a feeling of shame assailed me – as though I were intruding on the tragic privacy of Death.

On another part of the plain, many bodies were strewn; all in different attitudes – many on knees; others lying prone, with arms flung out; some had fallen head-first and buried their face in the soil; while still others were lying on their side, arms crossed as though they had found time to compose themselves before Death had released them from their sufferings . . . It was a terrible battlefield; a sight which one could never erase from one's memory. There was another dreadful aspect – that of the ghastly smell of decaying human flesh. The sight of so many dead soldiers, left to decay in the hot sun and at the mercy of marauding flies, made a deep impression on us all. Our medical staff were highly indignant; they were taking the matter up immediately with the military authorities of the district and insisting that these forsaken bodies should be buried at once.

Farther away one could see long rows of devastated houses; another village laid desolate by our shells. God help the inhabitants! There was not one home left standing. It seems that some effort had been made to bury the dead, for to the north of that village a pit had been dug, in which some fifty soldiers had been deposited; the pit had not yet been filled in and here too the sight and smell of the decaying bodies were terrible. We left this gloomy halting-place and on the road, we passed a strikingly beautiful Austrian cemetery. The Austrians were particularly solicitous over their war-graves. This one was a neatly fenced-in plot with a rustic gateway, surmounted by a wooden cross and an inscription reading: '*Hier ruhen die für ihr Vaterland gefallenen Helden*' [Here rest the heroes fallen for their Fatherland]. Each grave bore a cross on which was inscribed the name of the soldier. Russian and German soldiers were buried there too. And a grave of a Jewish soldier bore a Star of David which the Austrians had scrupulously erected instead of a cross . . .

ERNEST HEMINGWAY

Ernest Hemingway (1899–1961). After a brief spell as a journalist Hemingway joined the Red Cross as an ambulance driver
in 1918. Met Dos Passos (*q.v.*) in Italy. Shot in both legs while
carrying an injured man. This experience, described in the
letter below, was to form the basis of much of *A Farewell to
Arms*. Hemingway was eighteen. 'Brummy': Ted Brumback.

Source: Ernest Hemingway, *Ernest Hemingway, Selected Letters
1917–1961*, ed. Carlos Baker, London, Granada, 1981.

To His Family   21 July 1918
                                                 Milan

Dear Folks:

I suppose Brummy has written you all about my getting bunged
up. So there isn't anything for me to say. I hope that the cable
didn't worry you very much but Capt. Bates thought it was best
that you hear from me first rather than the newspapers. You see
I'm the first American wounded in Italy and I suppose the
papers say something about it.

This is a peach of a hospital here and there are about 18
American nurses to take care of 4 patients. Everything is fine
and I'm very comfortable and one of the best surgeons in Milan
is looking after my wounds. There are a couple of pieces still in,
one bullet in my knee that the X-Ray showed. The surgeon, very
wisely, is after consultation, going to wait for the wound in my
right knee to become healed cleanly before operating. The bullet
will then be rather encysted and he will make a clean cut and go
in under the side of the knee cap. By allowing it to be completely
healed first he thus avoids any danger of infection and stiff knee.
That is wise don't you think Dad? He will also remove a bullet
from my right foot at the same time. He will probably operate in
about a week as the wound is healing cleanly and there is no
infection. I had two shots of anti tetanus immediately at the
dressing station. All the other bullets and pieces of shell have
been removed and all the wounds on my left leg are healing

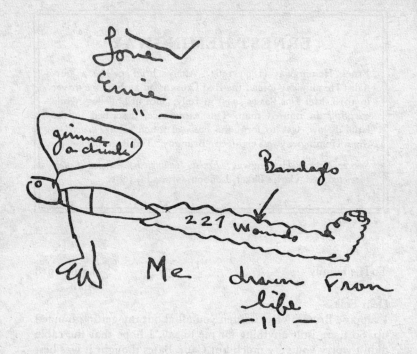

Love
Ernie
— " —

gimme
a drink!

Bandages

2 2 1 Wounds

Me   drawn From
              life
           — " —

finely. My fingers are all cleared up and have the bandages off.
There will be no permanent effects from any of the wounds as
there are no bones shattered. Even in my knees. In both the left
and right the bullets did not fracture the patella; one piece of
shell about the size of a Tinker's roller bearing was in my left
knee but it has been removed and the knee now moves perfectly
and the wound is nearly healed. In the right knee the bullet
went under the knee cap from the left side and didn't smash it a
bit. By the time you get this letter the surgeon will have operated
and it will be all healed, and I hope to be back driving in the
mountains by the latter part of August. I have some fine photographs of the Piave and many other interesting pictures. Also a
wonderful lot of souvenirs. I was all through the big battle and
have Austrian carbines and ammunition, German and Austrian
medals, officer's automatic pistols, Boche helmets, about a dozen
Bayonets, star shell pistols and knives and almost everything you
can think of. The only limit to the amount of souvenirs I could
have is what I could carry for there were so many dead Austrians

and prisoners the ground was almost black with them. It was a great victory and showed the world what wonderful fighters the Italians are.

I'll tell you all about everything when I get home for Christmas. It is awfully hot here now. I receive your letters regularly. Give my love to everybody and lots to all of you.

Ernie

ERNEST HEMINGWAY
see also p. 475

Hemingway's *A Farewell to Arms*, 1929, was a bestseller rivalled only by Remarque's *All Quiet on the Western Front* (*q.v.*), which appeared at the same time. Lieutenant Henry, an American serving as an ambulance driver on the Italian Front, meets Catherine Barkley, an English nurse. After being wounded in the legs (see Hemingway's letters) and a long convalescence, Henry returns to the front. He has to desert after being falsely accused of treachery. He and Catherine, now pregnant, escape to Switzerland. The excerpt below describes Henry's arrest and escape. Catherine later dies in childbirth, which confirms Henry's disillusion after the short-lived success of his initiation into the masculine world of War.

Source: Ernest Hemingway, *A Farewell to Arms*, New York, Charles Scribner's Sons, 1929; Granada edn, 1977.

... I looked over the side and watched the river. Now that we could not go our own pace I felt very tired. There was no exhilaration in crossing the bridge. I wondered what it would be like if a plane bombed it in the daytime.

'Piani,' I said.

'Here I am, Tenente.' He was a little ahead in the jam. No one was talking. They were all trying to get across as soon as they could: thinking only of that. We were almost across. At the far end of the bridge there were officers and carabinieri standing on both sides flashing lights. I saw them silhouetted against the skyline. As we came close to them I saw one of the officers point to a man in the column. A carabiniere went in after him and came out holding the man by the arm. He took him away from the road. We came almost opposite them. The officers were scrutinizing everyone in the column, sometimes speaking to each other, going forward to flash a light in someone's face. They took someone else out just before we came opposite. I saw the man. He was a lieutenant-colonel. I saw the stars in the box on his sleeve as they flashed a light on him. His hair was grey and he was short and fat. The carabiniere pulled him in behind the line of officers. As we came opposite I saw one or two of them look at me. Then one pointed at me and spoke to a carabiniere. I saw the carabiniere start for me, come through the edge of the column towards me, then felt him take me by the collar.

'What's the matter with you?' I said and hit him in the face. I saw his face under the hat, upturned moustaches and blood coming down his cheek. Another one dived in towards us.

'What's the matter with you?' I said. He did not answer. He was watching a chance to grab me. I put my arm behind me to loosen my pistol.

'Don't you know you can't touch an officer?'

The other one grabbed me from behind and pulled my arm up so that it twisted in the socket. I turned with him and the other one grabbed me around the neck. I kicked his shins and got my left knee into his groin.

'Shoot him if he resists,' I heard someone say.

'What's the meaning of this?' I tried to shout but my voice was not very loud. They had me at the side of the road now.

'Shoot him if he resists,' an officer said. 'Take him over back.'

'Who are you?'

'You'll find out.'

'Who are you?'

'Battle police,' another officer said.

'Why don't you ask me to step over instead of having one of these airplanes grab me?'

They did not answer. They did not have to answer. They were battle police.

'Take him back there with the others,' the first officer said. 'You see. He speaks Italian with an accent.'

'So do you, you —,' I said.

'Take him back with the others,' the first officer said. They took me down behind the line of officers below the road towards a group of people in a field by the river bank. As we walked towards them shots were fired. I saw flashes of the rifles and heard the reports. We came up to the group. There were four officers standing together, with a man in front of them with a carabiniere on each side of him. A group of men were standing guarded by carabinieri. Four other carabinieri stood near the questioning officers, leaning on their carbines. They were wide-hatted carabinieri. The two who had me shoved me in with the group waiting to be questioned. I looked at the man the officers were questioning. He was the fat grey-haired little lieutenant-colonel they had taken out of the column. The questioners had all the efficiency, coldness and command of themselves of Italians who are firing and are not being fired on.

'Your brigade?'

He told them.

'Regiment?'

He told them.

'Why are you not with your regiment?'

He told them.

'Do you not know that an officer should be with his troops?'

He did.

That was all. Another officer spoke.

'It is you and such as you that have let the barbarians on to the sacred soil of the fatherland.'

'I beg your pardon,' said the lieutenant-colonel.

'It is because of treachery such as yours that we have lost the fruits of victory.'

'Have you ever been in a retreat?' the lieutenant-colonel asked.

'Italy should never retreat.'

We stood there in the rain and listened to this. We were facing the officers and the prisoner stood in front and a little to one side of us.

'If you are going to shoot me,' the lieutenant-colonel said, 'please shoot me at once without further questioning. The questioning is stupid.' He made the sign of the cross. The officers spoke together. One wrote something on a pad of paper.

'Abandoned his troops, ordered to be shot,' he said.

Two carabinieri took the lieutenant-colonel to the river bank. He walked in the rain, an old man with his hat off, a carabiniere on either side. I did not watch them shoot him but I heard the shots. They were questioning someone else. This officer too was separated from his troops. He was not allowed to make an explanation. He cried when they read the sentence from the pad of paper, and they were questioning another when they shot him. They made a point of being intent on questioning the next man while the man who had been questioned before was being shot. In this way there was obviously nothing they could do about it. I did not know whether I should wait to be questioned or make a break now. I was obviously a German in Italian uniform. I saw how their minds worked; if they had minds and if they worked. They were all young men and they were saving their country. The second army was being re-formed beyond the Tagliamento. They were executing officers of the rank of major and above who were separated from their troops. They were also dealing summarily with German agitators in Italian uniform. They wore steel helmets. Only two of us had steel helmets. Some of the carabinieri had them. The other carabinieri wore the wide hat. Airplanes we called them. We stood in the rain and were taken out one at a time to be questioned and shot. So far they had shot everyone they had questioned. The questioners had that beautiful detachment and devotion to stern justice of men dealing in death without being in any danger of it. They were questioning a full colonel of a line regiment. Three more officers had just been put in with us.

Where was his regiment?

I looked at the carabinieri. They were looking at the newcomers. The others were looking at the colonel. I ducked down, pushed between two men, and ran for the river, my head down. I tripped at the edge and went in with a splash. The water was very cold and I stayed under as long as I could. I could feel the current swirl me and I stayed under until I thought I could never come up. The minute I came up I took a breath and went down again. It was easy to stay under with so much clothing and my boots. When I came up the second time I saw a piece of timber ahead of me and reached it and held on with one hand. I kept my head behind it and did not even look over it. I did not want to see the bank. There were shots when I ran and shots when I came up the first time. I heard them when I was almost above water. There were no shots now. The piece of timber swung in the current and I held it with one hand. I looked at the bank. It seemed to be going by very fast. There was much wood in the stream. The water was very cold. We passed the brush of an island above the water. I held on to the timber with both hands and let it take me along. The shore was out of sight now . . .

R. H. MOTTRAM

R. H. Mottram (1883–1971). Lived mostly in East Anglia. Galsworthy encouraged him. Bank clerk before the war. Served in France 1914–19. The three war novels which are included in *The Spanish Farm Trilogy* were enormously successful. He returned to the war in *Ten Years Ago* (1929), in which Skene also features, *Three Personal Records of the War* (1929), *A Journey to the Western Front 20 Years After* (1938) and various autobiographies. The Ferme l'Espagnole stands on French soil in an area fought over by foreign powers for centuries. The farm is worked by **Jerome Vand**erlynden and his daughter Madeleine. The first two books concern an English officer, Skene, and his liaison with Madeleine who also yearns for her first lover, Georges d'Archeville, aristocratic son of the owner of the land on which the farm stands. In the last book, *The Crime at Vanderlynden's*, Skene is replaced by Dormer, who begins to unravel the 'Crime' in words very similar to Mottram's own at the beginning of 'A Personal Record'. While never losing sight of the war, the *Trilogy* remains one of the few English works to succeed as a complex fiction. It is also unique in sympathetically portraying French people and their resentment against all intruders, including the British.

Source: R. H. Mottram, *The Crime at Vanderlynden's*, London, Chatto & Windus, 1926. Published, with *The Spanish Farm* and *Sixty-Four, Ninety-Four*, as *The Spanish Farm Trilogy, 1914–1918*, Chatto & Windus, 1927; Penguin Books, 1979.

From
THE CRIME AT VANDERLYNDEN'S

They were at the corner of the big pasture before the house. There was an ordinary hedge, like an English one, thickened at this angle into a tiny copse, with a dozen young poplars. Madamoiselle soon found a gap in the fence and led them through, remarking, 'The troops made this short cut!'

They found themselves in Vanderlynden's pasture, like hundreds of others over a hundred miles of country. There were no troops in it at the moment, but it had the air of being continuously occupied. In long regular lines the grass had been trampled away. Posts and wire, and a great bank of manure marked the site of horse-lines. Nearer the house, tents had been set up from time to time, and circles, dotted with peg and post holes, appeared half obliterated. At the corners of the field were latrines, and at one spot the cookers had blackened everything.

'Billets for the troops!' reflected Dormer, to whom the idea of lodging in the open had never ceased to be a thoroughly bad joke. 'Stables for horses, stables for men!' Obviously enough the machinery of war had been here in full swing. Dormer (a man of no imagination) could almost see before him the khaki-clad figures, the sullen mules, the primitive vehicles filing into the place, tarrying ever so briefly and filing out again to be destroyed. But Mademoiselle Vanderlynden was occupied with the matter in hand, and led to the other side of the coppice, where there had been built by some previous generation of pious Vanderlyndens a little shrine. It was perhaps eight feet high, six feet thick, and had its glazed recess towards the main road. But the glazing was all broken, the altar torn down, and all those small wax or plaster figures or flowers, vases, and other objects of the trade in 'votive offerings' and *objets de piété* which a Vanderlynden would revere so much more because he bought them at a *fournitures ecclésiastiques*, rather than made them with his own hands, were missing. Army wire had been used to fasten up the gaping aperture.

'There you are,' said Mademoiselle. She added, as if there might be some doubt as to ownership: 'You can see that it is ours. Here is our name, not our proprietor's!'

Sure enough, on a flat plaster panel was a partially effaced inscription: 'Marie Bienheureuse – prie pour – de Benoit Vanderl – femme Marthe – Juin 187–'

The APM lighted a cigar and surveyed the ruins. He was feeling extremely well, and was able to take a detached unofficial attitude. 'Oh, so that's the Virgin, is it?'

'No. That is the place for the image. The image is broken, as I told you, and we removed the pieces.'

'Very good. Then I understand you claim a thousand francs for the damage to the brickwork and the – er – altar furniture which was – ah, broken – it seems too much, you know!'

'Perhaps, sir, you are not well ack-vainted with the price of building materials!' (Ah, thought Dormer, she speaks pretty good English, but that word did her.)

'Oh, I think so, I'm a bit of a farmer myself, you know. I have a place in Hampshire, where I breed cattle.'

Mademoiselle's voice seemed to rise and harden:

'Yes, sir; but if you are rich, that is not a reason that you should deny justice to us, who are poor. I do not know if I can get this altar repaired, and even if I can there is also the question of the *effraction* –'

'The what?'

'Legal damages for breaking in – trespass, sir,' put in Dormer, alarmed by the use of French. He could see she was getting annoyed, and wished the APM, the lunch, the claim, the farm and the war, all the blessed caboodle, were with the devil.

'Oh, I see.'

'*Et puis*, and then there are *dédommagements* – what would you say if I were to knock down your mother's tomb?'

'What's that. Oh, I can't say, I'm sure. I really can't go into all this. Captain Dormer, there is obviously no arrest to be made. It is purely a claim for compensation. I will leave it to you. I must be getting back. *Comprenez*, Mademoiselle, this officer will hear what you have to say and will settle the whole matter with you. Famous lunch you gave us. *Au revoir*. If you care for a game of bridge this evening, Dormer, come round to B Mess!'

Dormer took out his field notebook and conducted the inquiry partly in English, partly in French.

They sat in the cavernous old tiled kitchen, half-filled with the stove and its stupefying heat, half with the table, scrubbed until the grain of the wood stood out in ribs.

Mademoiselle Vanderlynden had dismissed the APM from her mind with the remark that he was a droll type, and gave Dormer her full attention, rather as if he had been a dull boy in the lowest class, and she his teacher.

'When did this occur?'

'Why, in April. It was wet, or he would not have done it!'

'Did you see it done?'

'Yes. I even tried to stop it!'

'Where were you?'

'Why naturally I was at that hole in the fence. One cannot always hire a boy to keep the cattle from straying.'

'Well?'

'Well, then the troops came in. They were not pretty to see!'

'What troops were they?'

She turned over a dirty dog-eared memorandum book.

'469 Trench Mortar Battery.'

'So they had had a bad time?'

'One gathered that. They were very few, and some of their material was missing. At the last came this man with his two mules. One was sick, one was wounded. Most of the men, as soon as they had put up their animals, fell down and slept, but this one kept walking about. It was almost dark and it was beginning to rain. I asked him what he wanted.'

'What did he say?'

'"To Hell with the Pope!"'

The shibboleth sounded so queer on her lips that Dormer glanced at her face. It was blank. She had merely memorized the words in case they might be of use to her. She went on:

'He did not like the images on the altar! Then he began to break the glass, and pull down the woodwork. One saw what he wanted. It was shelter for his mules.'

'You cautioned him that he was doing wrong?'

'I believe you. I even held him by the arm.'

'That was wrong of you, Mademoiselle. You should have informed his officer.'

'Oh, you must understand that his officer was asleep on the kitchen floor. But so asleep. He lay where he had fallen, he had not let go the mug from which he drank his whisky. So much – (she held up four graphic fingers) – ah, but whisky you know!'

'I see. You were unable to report to the officer in charge of the party. But still, you should never touch a soldier. He might do you an injury, and then, at a court of inquiry, it would be said against you that you laid hands on him.'

'Oh, you understand, one is not afraid, one has seen so many soldiers these years. And as for the court of inquiry, we have had four here, about various matters. They all ended in nothing.'

'Well, well, you endeavoured to prevent the damage, and being unable to report to the proper authority, you made your claim for damage in due course. But when the officer woke up, you informed him that you had done so?'

'Why necessarily, since we had the Maire to make a *procès-verbal!*'

'So I hear, from the Maire himself. But apparently the Maire did not do so, for the *procès-verbal* is not included with the other papers.'

'No, the Maire was prevented by the troops.' (A grim smile broke for a moment the calculated business indifference on the face of one who excluded emotion, because it was a bad way of obtaining money.) 'Oh, la-la! There was a *contretemps*!'

'Do you mind telling me what occurred?'

She seemed to regret that brief smile, and apologized to herself.

'All the same, it was shameful. Our Maire is no better than any other, but he is our Maire. One ought to respect those in power, ought not one, sir?'

'In what way were the troops lacking in respect?'

'They sang. They sang – *casse-tête* – enough to split your head, all the way to the village!'

'Oh, they were on the move, were they?'

'It was pitiable, I assure you, sir, it was shameful to see. *Ces pauvres êtres*. They hardly had any sleep. Only a few hours. Then it seems the Bosche made a counter-attack, and paff! here comes a motor-cyclist, and they were obliged to wake up and fall in. Some of them could only stand up with difficulty. But at length, they were ready; then the Maire came. We had sent for him *d'urgence*, when we saw the troops were going, because you can't make a *procès-verbal* of a person who is no longer there!'

'No, quite right. But why did they sing?'

'Ah, *ça tombait d'accord*. Just as the officer gives the word, the Maire arrives. We had informed him it was a crime of violence, and he had taken it very serious. He is old, our Maire. He had put on his – *écharpe*.'

'What is that?'

She made a vivid gesture with her hands.

'It goes so! It is tricolour. It is the Maire's official dress!'

'Ah, his official scarf!'

'That is it. Also, he had mounted his hat!'

'How did he do that?'

'The usual way. But it was a long hat, a hat of *grande tenue* – like a pot of *confiture*.'

'Mademoiselle, this will not do. I cannot settle this matter here and now, I must pass on all the papers to my superior officer, who will place them with the proper authority. They will ask "Is there no *procès-verbal*?" Am I to say: "The Maire went to make one. He put on his hat and the troops began to sing." It sounds like a joke.'

'Ah, you others, you are always the ones to laugh. It was just exactly as I have said. They sang!'

'But you told me just now that they were tired out!'

'Quite true!'

'It will never sound so. What did they sing?'

'Old Hindenburg has bought a hat!'

In a moment Dormer was convinced. The words painted, framed and hung the picture for him. He had just been beginning to hope that the whole thing would break down from sheer improbability. He now saw it stamped and certified with eternal truth. There was no need for her to add: 'They were not gay, you understand, they were *exalté*!'

'Excited!'

'Ah! Excited, like one is after no sleep and no food and then something very strange. They were excited. They called the Maire "Maréchal Hindenburg", and "Bosche", and "Spy". Those are words that ought not to be used between allies!'

'No, Mademoiselle, they ought not.'

But for a moment, the hardness left her face, she became almost impersonal.

'It was curious. They sang that – *sur un air de psaume*, to a church tune.'

'Yes, yes!' agreed Dormer. Out of the depth of his experience as a churchwarden welled up the strains of Whitfield, No. 671, and out of the depths of his experiences as a platoon commander came a sigh: 'They will do it.'

He went through his notes to see if there were anything more he wanted to know, but from business habit he had already possessed himself of the essentials. He did not like the way the thing was shaping. He knew only too well what happened in the army. Some individual being, besides a number on a payroll, a human creature, would do something quite natural, perhaps rather useful, something which a mile or two farther on, in the trenches, would be worth, and might occasionally gain, the Military Medal. This business of breaking down a bit of wood and plaster, to shelter mules, had it occurred a little farther on, had it been a matter of making a machine-gun emplacement in an emergency, would have earned praise. It showed just that sort of initiative one wanted in wartime, and which was none too easy to get from an army of respectable civilians. But at the same time, in billets, there was another set of rules just as important, which in their essence discouraged initiative and reduced the soldier to a mere automaton. The otherwise excellent thing which he did broke those rules. That again did not matter much, unless it was brought into accidental prominence by colliding with some other event or function – this Maire and his dignity for instance, would play the very devil, make a mountain out of a molehill, such was the perversity of things. Fascinated against his better judgement which told him 'The less you know about the business, the better', he found himself asking:

'What was this man like, Mademoiselle?'

There was no answer, and he looked up. She had left him, gone into the back kitchen to some job of her own. She had left him as though the war were some expensive hobby of his that she really could not be bothered with any longer. On hearing his voice she returned and he repeated his question. He never forgot the answer.

'Like – but he was like all the others!'

'You couldn't pick him out in a crowd?'

'Perhaps. But it would be difficult. He was about as big as you, not very fat, he had eyes and hair like you or anyone else.'

'You didn't, of course, hear his name or number?'

'They called him "Nobby". It was his name, but they call every one "Nobby". His number was 6494. I saw it on his valise.'

'On his pack?'

'Yes.'

'Thank you, Mademoiselle. You have told me all I want.' In his heart he feared she had told him much too much, but she had gone on with her work. He rose to go, but passing the dark entry of the back kitchen, he stopped, as though to avoid a shell. He thought he saw a headless figure, but it was only a shirt which Mademoiselle Vanderlynden had flung over a line before putting it through the wringer. He went out. She did not accompany him. She was busy, no doubt.

R. H. MOTTRAM

see also p. 482

R. H. Mottram, in this 'Personal Record', published after *The Spanish Farm Trilogy*, describes his job of sorting out claims for damages made by the local inhabitants against the British Army. The French and Belgian officers involved in similar jobs are strikingly similar to characters in *The Spanish Farm*. The last passage describes the aftermath of the war in 1919 and Mottram makes some very astute comments on modern warfare. 'Pop' is Poperinghe.

Source: R. H. Mottram, 'A Personal Record', from R. H. Mottram, John Easton and Eric Partridge, *Three Personal Records of the War*, London, The Scolartis Press, 1929.

With a mind perfectly blank, I knocked on the door of the Salle des Mariages of the Mairie of 'Pop', which had a large Q on a placard, and entering, completely blinded by the lamplight, came to attention in front of a table, at which was seated the AAQMG, a colonel by rank, an officer of Indian experience by his ribbons. I gave my name and regiment, and he gave me a good stare. I kept perfectly still, as neither I nor F. had the faintest idea why I had been ordered to report. The only thing I could think of was that the affair of the court of inquiry on the company pay I had lost when buried, months before, had cropped up. But instead of placing me under arrest, he hunted among the papers on his table, and said:

'You say you can speak French?'

'Yes, sir!'

'Are you sure?'

'Yessir!'

'Look at the stuff on that table!' and as I went he added: 'It's a horrible business!'

The table in the corner was covered with a mass of papers, prominent among which were blue forms printed in French, backed up by *procès-verbal*, letters from very humble, and a few from very important personages, in Flemish or French. It amounted, in brief, to claims for compensation for depredations of the British army in the divisional sector, drawn up under the French billeting law of 1877 and the corresponding Belgian enactments. It was an astounding mass of information on the habits of a population, the actual impact of modern war, and a satiric commentary on the superficial battle history of the previous year. It amused me, among other things, making me think of that incident in *Charles O'Malley* when the Iron Duke lectures the troops on the iniquity of plundering, and the cockerel in the quarter-master's pocket crows after the third denial. And there was the imminent chance that I might find some necessitous foray of my own set down as '*dégâts occasionnés par les troupes britanniques*'. But the colonel was waiting:

'Can you make it out?'

'Yes, sir, I think so!'

'Then you'd better take it completely off my hands.'

'Yes, sir. Now?'

'You can begin in the morning!'

That was all I wanted. I took off my equipment, lay down with my head on my pack, and was half asleep, when he came back to say:

'You'll mess in B Mess!' He was not used to junior officers going to sleep on the floor of his office, I expect, but didn't know what to do with me.

I thanked him, and knew nothing more until the signallers changed over in the morning. I fancy the colonel was more astonished than I was when I saw him next . . .

———

We started early and splashed along the irretrievably ruined roads through a landscape of Hobbema, but Hobbema framed so as to form the back of a shower-bath. We lost twenty minutes getting our horses past a light railway. Then a great humpty-shouldered church appeared above the elms, for all the world like Hingham, Norfolk, and we found the Mairie (over an estaminet, of course) and pushed through a crowd of villagers trying to get their sons exempted from conscription, and their places on the list of applicants for artificial manure unfairly promoted. In a tiny office, waist deep in official papers of all descriptions, sat an old man in a Dutch cap, smoking a clay pipe.

De G., glorious in strawberry and blue, shouted: '*Monsieur le Maire, nous sommes venus tirer au clair cette sombre histoire!*' The old man looked puzzled. I insisted on seeing the broken door or window through which the barrel had been removed. Then, with the help of some English and some Flemish (the Maire spoke rather less French than I did), we did 'drag to light this sordid story', while de G. ordered lunch. The barrel was there. You could see it and test its emptiness. Nor was there much need. I sympathized thoroughly with the gunners, and was able to reconstruct the crime in which, alas, I had failed to participate. When the brigade, numbering, I suppose, five hundred men, even after months of hammering, had watered and fed and set guards, they all made for the place, demanding drink. The old man had started laboriously filling glasses and mugs while those lasted, and then billycans, and no doubt was soon stumped for change. Of course he got shoved aside and the men simply filled every receptacle they had about them until the barrel was empty. Some paid, he admitted, but the claim was for the difference between the amount received and the value of the contents of the barrel, and may have been two hundred francs. After adjusting this valuation to reality, I settled the claim by the present of a ton or so of manure.

———

At Morbecque, that January, I found a 'meeting' being held by the rank and file of a heavy artillery brigade. The officers, quite helpless, kept out of sight. Senior NCOs were in the chair (the box of a GS wagon), questions were being asked, and a resolution formulated, setting out grievances over demobilization proposals. And why not? The proceedings were perfectly orderly and quite logical. Great Britain had had the services of all those men (and in such a formation, a relatively high proportion of skilled labour). The leadership had not, to speak charitably, been anything brilliant. The camouflage of press and platform utterance failed to convince that great mass of decent, peace-loving citizens, who never wanted to be, and never were 'soldiers', that they had won anything except the right to exploit the opportunity, according to the example set them from high places. Intelligent mechanics and clerks were under no illusion as to the nature of the 'fighting' in which they had been engaged. They made no revolution, as their like across more than half Europe did. They just wanted to go home, before someone pinched their jobs. I sympathized with them, the more so as I suffered nothing in the way of indignity. There were, I have heard, cases of maltreatment of officers, but I have wondered if the victims did anything to attract it. I made no difference in my bearing towards the rank and file, and none of them ever attempted to disregard my orders.

It was only too clear to what pass years of dishonest or inept politics, new industrial methods, and the obliteration of the individual had brought us. I doubt if Napoleon or Marlborough could have done any better, had they been resurrected in modern circumstances. The general level of intelligence and efficiency of the ranks had risen, and the commonplace types at the head of affairs were thus even more noticeably dwarfed by comparison with the average humanity over which they were given such unwarrantably despotic power, than in the nearest historical parallel situations. After South Africa Kipling wrote:

> Ye that tread triumphing crowned, to your meed
> Worthy God's pity, ye best who succeed.

The length of the war had broken down all patience, and most other virtues, in fact. Germany's mistakes had thrown such resources into the scale against her that she had succumbed. This is what 'Victory' amounted to; the dumb equilibrium of an iceberg that rights itself, according to the laws of gravity.

There remained, most serious of all, the moral exhaustion of civilized peoples. It was obvious to me when I got home, and found a whole way of life gone out of fashion. Even then I did not know the worst. I should never have believed, in 1919, that the silly creeds of violence and greed could hold so conspicuous a place in Europe for nearly ten years. A new vision is already overdue. We must hope that it may not be long retarded, for in spite of vapourings about ex-combatants imaginatively 'fighting their battles o'er again', we are not yet saved. We are on reprieve. One more slip-back into that negation of the social contract that 1914-1918 was, and we can hardly hope that the slow but sure logic of existence will give us another chance.

On the whole, the attempt of the civilized nations of the twentieth century to return to barbarism was a failure. Again and again the most deliberate steps had to be taken to procure an artificial ferocity that human beings no longer readily feel. The difficulty lies, I think in the weakening of the fascination which, as I have said, War exercises on account of its great moments, in common with Religion and Love. Just as religious observance is falling into disuse, if not under suspicion, just as the *grande passion* is no longer lightly excused and is subjected to an impersonal scrutiny, so the few great moments of battle are insufficient to obscure the dreary monotony and brainlessness of soldiering. And there is a further and apposite deterrent. If human beings are less deliberately warlike, the necessity for accumulating, nowadays, great mountains of machinery and supplies before a small percentage of the men engaged can 'fight', re-introduces the cold-blooded calculations of murder, at the expense of the generous sacrifice that used to sanction Christian armies. A sword-cut is forgivable, slow poisoning is not.

What conclusion, then, is the citizen of Western Europe to draw from his personal experience? Let him, if possible, like myself, be neither permanently maimed nor embittered, nor deluded by the attempts of our would-be Napoleons and imitation Pitts to exculpate themselves by inculpating their fellows in war-guilt. And let him feel, if possible, like myself, that last phase of military justification, a warm comradeship with those slim, erect figures, helmeted, belted and booted, owning nothing save a few letters in the breast pocket, or a locket, and devoid of any relationship except the common dedication to early and unnecessary death. He cannot feel it impossible that the nations among whom he lives might be stampeded once more into the use of violence to settle some dispute. Nor can he doubt that it will, when it comes, be a national war – not an affair of professional soldiers, but a struggle into which the entire strength of peoples will be thrown, deliberately. Even if 'voluntary' methods of recruitment are admitted, they only make matters worse, in view of the startling disparity between the sacrifice demanded of the individual and the personal result to him, eventually.

There is little hope that a swift conclusion by surprise will be more effective, as means of communication improve and war machinery grows more grotesquely impressive, than in 1914–1918. We must therefore be committed to a series of 'offensives', efforts to dissipate the deadlock. I am convinced that no offensive can succeed. Ypres, Verdun, the 1918 display of the Germans, Arras, Champagne of the French, the Somme, Passchendaele, Vimy of the British, all failed, not because of the defence they met, but because the methods of attack employed today stultify themselves. The machine is of such size and complexity that it soon gets beyond human control. Thus there is, in my belief, no means of avoiding the war of attrition, which, in turn, inevitably brings a complete contempt of the social, political and industrial leaders, the military ones having such insignificant influence. Herein lies the great menace to our civilization. Can anything be done to forestall it that is not already being done?

I can only suggest that it should be explained to the would-be recruit for the next war, that under no possibility can he 'fight'. Of the million enlistments of the late war, very few ever saw a German, fewer still can be sure of having personally done any injury to one, and I never met in the field any real hatred of the enemy. Next time fewer still will operate, across great distances, complicated engines directed against centres of population as per map. To call this 'fighting' and thus associate it with Homeric (or even Crimean) traditions, is to perpetrate a fraud upon the public, upon a large scale. And modern nations can only be stampeded or deluded for short and decreasing periods. When they discover for what they have sacrificed their high standards of comfort and liberty, they become ominously resentful. It might be as well not to give them reason to be so. Such is the conclusion of my personal record of the war.

RICHARD ALDINGTON

Richard Aldington (1892–1962). Born in Hampshire and educated at Dover College and London University. He was a member of the Imagist group of poets and contributed to *Blast* (see Wyndham Lewis, p. 118). He joined the infantry in 1916 and was shell-shocked. *Death of a Hero* was published in 1929 in a censored version with a design by Paul Nash (q.v.) on the cover. It had been started on the Mediterranean island of Port Cros in 1928 while D. H. Lawrence was a guest. He was married to Hilda Doolittle (H.D.), the important Imagist poet. His *Complete Poems* was published in 1948. The first complete version of *Death of a Hero* (by now a bestseller in Russia) was published in 1965. After an 'epic contest' between George Winterbourne, his wife, Elizabeth, and his mistress, Fanny, George joins the army. Anthony Burgess claims (*Observer*, 21 October 1984) that Aldington was hinting at his own situation: Elizabeth represents H.D. and Fanny is Dorothy Yorke. H.D.'s brother was killed in action. In the episodes below, Winterbourne discusses contemporary art while on leave, and meets his death at the end of the novel.

Source: Richard Aldington, *Death of a Hero*, London, Chatto & Windus, 1929; London, Consul, World Distributors Ltd, 1965.

'. . . What I mean to say is, if you get time, come round to my studio and have a look at my new pictures. Are you still writing for periodicals?'

Winterbourne smiled.

'No. I've been rather busy, you know, and in the trenches one –'

'What I mean to say is, I'd like you to do an article on my Latest Development.'

'Suprematism?'

'Good Lord, NO! I finished with *that* long ago. How extraordinarily ignorant you are, Winterbourne! No, no. I'm working at Concavism now. It's by far the greatest contribution that's been made to twentieth-century civilization. What I mean is . . .'

Winterbourne ceased to listen and drank off a full glass of

wine. Why hadn't Evans written to him? Died of the effects of gas, probably. He beckoned to the waiter.

'Bring me another bottle of wine.'

'Yessir.'

'George!' came Elizabeth's voice, warning and slightly reproving. 'Don't drink too much!'

He made no answer, but sat looking heavily at his coffee-cup. Blast her. Blast Upjohn. Blast the lot of them. He drank off another glass of wine, and felt the singing dazzle of intoxication, its comforting oblivion, stealing into him. Blast them.

Mr Upjohn grew tired of improving the mind of a cretin who hadn't even the wits to listen to him, and slid away. Presently Mr Waldo Tubbe took his place.

'Well, my dear Winterbourne, I am very happy to see you again, looking so well. The military life has set you up splendidly. And Mrs Winterbourne tells me that at last you have received a commission. I congratulate you – better late than never.'

'Thanks. But I may not get it, you know. I've got to pass the training-school.'

'Oh, that'll do you a world of good, a world of good.'

'I hope so.'

'And how did you spend your leisure in France – still reading and painting?'

Winterbourne gave a little hard laugh.

'No, mostly lying about, sleeping.'

'I'm sorry to hear that. But, you know, if you will forgive my saying so, I always doubted whether your Vocation were really towards the arts. I felt you were more fitted for an open-air life. Of course, you're doing splendid work now, splendid. The Empire needs every man. When you come back after the Victory, as I trust you will return safe and sound, why don't you take up life in one of our colonies, Australia or Canada? There's a great opening for men there.'

Winterbourne laughed again.

'Wait till I get back, and then we'll see. Have a glass of wine?'

'No-oeh, thank you, no-oeh. By the way, what is that red ribbon on your arm? Vaccination?'

'No; company runner.'

'A company runner? What is that? Not runner away, I hope?'

And Mr Tubbe laughed silently, nodding his head up and down in appreciation of his jest. Winterbourne did not smile.

'Well, it might be under some circumstances, if you knew which way to run.'

'Oh, but our men are so splendid, so splendid, so unlike the Germans, you know. Haven't you found the Germans mean-spirited? They have to be chained to their machine-guns, you know.'

'I hadn't observed it. In fact, they're fighting with wonderful courage and persistence. It's not much of a compliment to our men to suggest otherwise, is it? We haven't managed to shift 'em far yet.'

'Ah! but you must not allow your own labours to distort your perspective. The navy is the important arm in the war; that and the marvellous home organization, of which you, of course, can know nothing.'

'Of course, but still . . .'

Mr Tubbe rose to move away.

'Delighted to have seen you, my dear Winterbourne. And thank you for all your interesting news from the front. *Most* stimulating. *Most* stimulating.'

Winterbourne signed to his wife to go, but she ignored the signal, and went on talking earnestly and attentively with Reggie Burnside. He drank another glass of wine, and stretched his legs. His heavy hobnailed boots came in contact with the shins of the man opposite.

'Sorry. Hope I didn't hurt you. Sorry to be so clumsy.'

'Oh, not at all, nothing, nothing,' said the man, rubbing his bruised shin with a look of furious anguish. Elizabeth frowned at Winterbourne, and leaned across to get the bottle. He grabbed it first, poured himself another glass, and then gave it to her. She looked angry at his rudeness. He felt pleasantly drunk, and cared not a damn for any one.

Coming home in the taxi she reproved him with gentle dignity for drinking too much . . .

———

CRASH! Like an orchestra at the signal of a baton the thousands of guns north and south opened up. The night sprang to flickering daylight with the gun flashes, the earth trembled with the shock, the air roared and screamed with shells. Lights rushed up from the German line, and their artillery in turn flamed into action. Winterbourne could just see a couple of his sections advancing as he started off himself, and then everything was

497

blotted out in a confusion of smoke and bursting shells. He saw his runner stagger and fall as a shell burst between them; then his corporal disappeared, blown to pieces by a direct hit. He came to a sunken road, and lay on the verge, trying to see what was happening in the faint light of dawn. He saw only smoke, and pushed on. Suddenly German helmets were all round him. He clutched at his revolver. Then he saw they were unarmed, holding shaking hands above their heads.

The German machine-guns were tat-tat-tatting at them, and there was a ceaseless swish of bullets. He passed the bodies of several of his men. One section wiped out by a single heavy shell. Other men lay singly. There was Jameson, dead; Halliwell, dead; Sergeant Morton, Taylor and Fish, dead in a little group. He came to the main road, which was three hundred yards short of his objective. A deadly machine-gun fire was holding up his company. The officers and men were lying down, the men firing rifles, and the Lewis guns ripping off drums of bullets. Winterbourne's second runner was hit, and lay groaning: 'Oh, for God's sake kill me, *kill* me. I can't stand it. The agony. *Kill* me.'

Something seemed to break in Winterbourne's head. He felt he was going mad, and sprang to his feet. The line of bullets smashed across his chest like a savage steel whip. The universe exploded darkly into oblivion.

RICHARD ALDINGTON

see also p. 495

Aldington's *Roads to Glory* was published in 1930. As in the case of R. H. Mottram (*q.v.*), one major work, *Death of a Hero*, was not enough to 'use up' the material of wartime experience and Aldington returned to the war in this group of short stories conceived in various narrative modes. The concluding section, 'Farewell to Memories' illustrates an interesting clash of literary and personal loyalties: on the one hand his fascination with the brute facts of war and with the language and experience of the ordinary soldiers, on the other hand, the desire to use the more distanced and sophisticated vision of an Imagist poet. Whether or not the experiment is judged successful, the juxtaposition of the two styles alerts us to the *problem* of style in an area in which the 'realistic' mode is assumed to be inevitable.

Source: Richard Aldington, *Roads to Glory*, London, Chatto & Windus, 1930.

FAREWELL TO MEMORIES

II

. . . Brandon worked with Holme, carrying the bales of hay from the train to the men stacking them on the barge. As Perks foretold, the officer disappeared. The bales of hay, tightly compressed and held by wire and ropes of twisted straw, were deliciously fragrant but dirty and very heavy. Brandon and Holme found it heart-breaking and back-breaking, but the scent of the hay stirred old poignant memories. The rain dripped from the groundsheets worn cloak-wise, the sweat started from their bodies, their faces were dirty, their fingers grimed and bruised.

The weariness of this dirt and labour, of this dirty melting sky!
   For hours we have carried great bundles of hay from train to barge . . .
The weariness of this dirt and labour!
   Last June those heavy dried bales waved and glittered in the fields of England:
   Cinquefoil and clover, buttercups, fennel, thistle and rue, daisy and

ragged robin, wild rose from the hedge, shepherd's purse, and long sweet nodding stalks of grass.

Heart of me, heart of me, be not sick and faint, though fingers and arms and head ache; you bear the gift of the glittering meadows of England. Here are bundles from Somerset, from Wales, from Hereford, Worcester, Gloucester – names we must love, scented with summer peace.

Handle them bravely, meadowsweet, sorrel, lush flag and arid knapweed, flowers of marsh and cliff, handle them bravely.

Dear crushed flowers, dear gentle, perished sisters, speak, whisper, and move, tell me you will dance and whisper for us in the wind next June . . .

IV

Grant that nothing ignoble may render me base to myself.

The weeks and months passed on. Perks was dead, Huxtable wounded, Holme had a job at the base. Thus loneliness was added to despair. Only when they had gone did Brandon realize how much that coarse human relationship had comforted him. A Cockney bar-tender, a commercial traveller, a Devonshire ploughman, for a time had been the centre of his affections. He mourned for poor little Perks, regretted Holme and Huxtable, did not even despise Holme for wangling his Base job.

In June 1918, Brandon was on guard at battalion headquarters when the great gas attack happened. He had reached a stage where he did not care whether he lived or died. All that was left of human in him was a tenacious determination not to lose his inner integrity, not to do anything which would lose his self-respect. Therefore he carried out all duties thoroughly, but with a sort of dull despair. His face was quite expressionless, his eyes dull but haunted – he had seen too much.

The moon, high-seated above the ridge, fills the ruined village with tranquil light and black broken shadows – ruined walls, shattered timbers, piles of rubbish, torn-up ground, almost beautiful in this radiance, in this quiet June air.

Tonight the air blows cleaner and sweeter – the chemistry of earth is slowly purifying the corrupting bodies, the waste and garbage of armies. Sweetness, darkness, clean space – the marble rock of some Greek island, piercing its sparse garments of lavenders and mints like a naked nymph among rustling leaves.

Heavy scented the air tonight – new-mown hay – a pungent, exotic odour – phosgene!

And tomorrow there will be huddled corpses with blue horrible faces, and foam on their writhed mouths.

Battalion headquarters were in the cellars of a ruined village about eight hundred yards behind the front line. The ground rose sharply up to a long crest, silhouetted against the clear moonlit sky. There ran the front line with its valuable observation posts looking far across the enemy's country. Brandon stood on the edge of the village street beside what had once been the entrance to some industrial building – a brewery perhaps, judging from the boilers and wrecked tangled machinery. The sides of the road were bordered by neat piles of stones and bricks, remnants of houses cleared from the *pavé*.

Brandon could see up and down the road – one end of which vanished into no man's land – and commanded quite a large sector of the front. Occasionally, he walked up and down his beat, but mostly he stood still, leaning on his rifle and fixed bayonet, and gazing at the beauty of the night. It was growing towards dawn, but the stars and moonlight were still splendid, filling the soft blue-green sky with delicate light. Except for a light breeze from the enemies' line the night was perfectly still. He heard limbers rattling back to the transport lines in the distance; the clink of picks and shovels from a returning working-party was perfectly sharp and clear. Not a gun was in action.

Suddenly the whole horizon within his gaze rushed up into a sheet of flame, the air whistled and roared with projectiles, which landed with a terrific crash and splutter of fire all along the front line. Brandon half stepped back in amazement and horror. For a moment he thought it was the first discharge of a battle barrage. Then, as no more came, the truth flashed across him – gas containers, thousands of them! He leaped to the Klaxon horn and gave the alarm: 'Gas.' Already the officers had rushed from the cellars and were questioning him through the bellow of the mechanical horn:

'What is it, Brandon, what's happened?'

'Gas containers, I think, sir. The whole front line's smothered with them.'

It was only too true. On the crest of the hill they could see the low cloud of gas, beginning to creep into the valley, and the air was already tainted with phosgene. The colonel ordered every one to wear gas masks, and himself went to the front line to see what had happened. Three working-parties from the battalion had been involved, and many of the men had been too slow in getting on their masks in the surprise. Those, also, who had been wounded by splinters of the containers had inevitably been victims.

In the confusion they forgot to relieve Brandon, and he remained at his post until long after dawn. Stretcher after stretcher passed him with ghastly agonized figures on them, foaming madmen clutching and fighting for breath, or inert figures covered with blankets. As the stretchers passed, the bearers shouted to him the names of those they were carrying.

I am haunted by the memory of my dawns. Not those earlier dawns when I saw for the first time the bell-towers of Florence in the lucid air, or the hills of Ravello violet and mist-wreathed against the gold sky; not those dawns when I rose from some exquisite and beloved body, the brain still feverish with desire, lips and eyes heavy with kisses, to watch the cool waves of light gliding over the silvery roofs of London while the first sparrows twittered in the heavy plane-trees. Not those dawns, but others, tragic and pitiful.

I remember harsh wakenings of winter-time in old French barns, through whose broken tiles at night one saw the morose glitter of the stars, and at dawn the sterile glitter of snow, dawns when one's breath was frozen to the blanket, and the contact of the air was anguish.

I am haunted by sombre or ironically lovely dawns seen from some bleak parade ground, by misty spring dawns in the trenches, when the vague shapes of the wire seemed to be the forms of crouching enemies, by summer dawns when the fresh immeasurably deep blue was a blasphemy, an insult to human misery.

Yet one among them all is poignant, unforgettable. As the shapes of things grew out slowly from the darkness, and the gentle grey suffusion of light made outlines visible, little groups of men carrying stretchers on their shoulders came slowly, stumbling and hesitating, along the ruined street. For a moment each group was silhouetted against the whitening east; the steel helmets (like those of medieval men-at-arms), the slung rifles, the strained postures of carrying, the useless vacillating corpse under its sepulchral blanket – all sharply edged in black on that smooth sky. And as the groups passed they shouted the names of the things they carried – things which yesterday were living men.

v

The last months of the war were a strange hallucination. Almost every week brought news of 'victories' and 'advances' to armies which were now utterly indifferent to victory or defeat. What in 1915, or even in 1916, would have been received with delighted enthusiasm, now scarcely caused the least tremor of interest. The war had lasted long enough to show the inanity of war. All that terrific effort had resulted in nothing but indifference . . .

===

We pass and leave you lying. No need for rhetoric, for funeral music, for melancholy bugle-calls. No need for tears now, no need for regret.

We took our risk with you; you died and we live. We take your noble gift, salute for the last time those lines of pitiable crosses, those solitary mounds, those unknown graves, and turn to live our lives out as we may.

Which of us were the fortunate — who can tell? For you there is silence and the cold twilight drooping in awful desolation over those motionless lands. For us sunlight and the sound of women's voices, song and hope and laughter, despair, gaiety, love — life.

Lost terrible silent comrades, we, who might have died, salute you.

FORD MADOX FORD

Ford Madox Ford (1873–1939). Born Ford Madox Hueffer in Kent. Related to Ford Madox Brown and other Pre-Raphaelites. Part of *The Good Soldier* (not directly about the war) was published in *Blast* (see Wyndham Lewis, p. 118). Although above military age he served on the Western Front in the Welch Regiment. The Tietjens books, *Some Do Not* (1924), *No More Parades* (1925), *A Man Could Stand Up* (1926) and *The Last Post* (1928) were later collected as *Parade's End*. Along with Dos Passos's *U.S.A.*, Faulkner's *A Fable* and Mottram's *Spanish Farm Trilogy* (excerpts from all of which appear elsewhere in this volume) this is arguably some of the finest fiction of the war. Much of Ford's 'war' poetry is less successful. The excerpts are taken from *A Man Could Stand Up* and include Ford's famous evocation of Tietjens being blown up and the post-war celebration which concludes the novel.

Source: Ford Madox Ford, *A Man Could Stand Up*, London, Duckworth, 1926; included in Ford Madox Ford, *Parade's End*, Penguin Books, 1982.

From
A MAN COULD STAND UP

... There was so much noise it seemed to grow dark. It was a mental darkness. You could not think. A Dark Age! The earth moved.

He was looking at Aranjuez from a considerable height. He was enjoying a considerable view. Aranjuez's face had a rapt expression – like that of a man composing poetry. Long dollops of liquid mud surrounded them in the air. Like black pancakes being tossed. He thought: 'Thank God I did not write to her. We are being blown up!' The earth turned like a weary hippopotamus. It settled down slowly over the face of Lance-Corporal Duckett who lay on his side, and went on in a slow wave.

It was slow, slow, slow ... like a slowed-down movie. The earth manoeuvred for an infinite time. He remained suspended in space. As if he were suspended as he had wanted to be in front of that cockscomb in whitewash. Coincidence!

The earth sucked slowly and composedly at his feet.

It assimilated his calves, his thighs. It imprisoned him above the waist. His arms being free, he resembled a man in a life-buoy. The earth moved him slowly. It was solidish.

Below him, down a mound, the face of little Aranjuez, brown, with immense black eyes in bluish whites, looked at him. Out of viscous mud. A head on a charger! He could see the imploring lips form the words: 'Save me, Captain!' He said: 'I've got to save myself first!' He could not hear his own words. The noise was incredible.

A man stood over him. He appeared immensely tall because Tietjens's face was on a level with his belt. But he was a small Cockney Tommy really. Name of Cockshott. He pulled at Tietjens's two arms. Tietjens tried to kick with his feet. Then he realized it was better not to kick with his feet. He was pulled out. Satisfactorily. There had been two men at it. A second, a corporal had come. They were all three of them grinning. He slid down with the sliding earth towards Aranjuez. He smiled at the pallid face. He slipped a lot. He felt a frightful burning on his neck, below and behind the ear. His hand came down from feeling the place. The finger tips had no end of mud and a little pinkishness on them. A pimple had perhaps burst. He had at least two men not killed. He signed agitatedly to the Tommies. He made gestures of digging. They were to get shovels.

He stood over Aranjuez, on the edge of liquid mud. Perhaps he would sink in. He did not sink in. Not above his boot tops. He felt his feet to be enormous and sustaining. He knew what had happened, Aranjuez was sunk in the issuing hole of the spring that made that bog. It was like being on Exmoor. He bent down over an ineffable, small face. He bent lower and his hands entered the slime. He had to get on his hands and knees.

Fury entered his mind. He had been sniped at. Before he had had that pain he had heard, he realized, an intimate drone under the hellish tumult. There was reason for furious haste. Or, no . . . They were low. In a wide hole. There was no reason for furious haste. Especially on your hands and knees.

His hands were under the slime, and his forearms. He battled his hands down greasy cloth; under greasy cloth. *Slimy*, not greasy! He pushed outwards. The boy's hands and arms appeared. It was going to be easier. His face was now quite close to the boy's, but it was impossible to hear what he said. Possibly he was unconscious. Tietjens said: 'Thank God for my enormous physical strength!' It was the first time that he had ever had to be thankful for great physical strength. He lifted the boy's arms over his own shoulders so that his hands might clasp themselves behind his neck. They were slimy and disagreeable. He was short in the wind. He heaved back. The boy came up a little. He was certainly fainting. He gave no assistance. The slime was filthy. It was condemnation of a civilization that he, Tietjens, possessed of enormous physical strength, should never have needed to use it before. He looked like a collection of meal-sacks; but, at least, he could tear a pack of cards in half. If only his lungs weren't . . .

Cockshott, the Tommy, and the Corporal were beside him. Grinning. With the two shovels that ought not to have stood against the parapet of their trench. He was intensely irritated. He had tried to indicate with his signs that it was Lance-Corporal Duckett that they were to dig out. It was probably no longer Lance-Corporal Duckett. It was probably by now 'it'. The body! He had probably lost a man, after all!

Cockshott and the corporal pulled Aranjuez out of the slime. He came out reluctantly, like a lugworm out of sand. He could not stand. His legs gave way. He drooped like a flower done in slime. His lips moved, but you could not hear him. Tietjens took him from the two men who supported him between the arms and laid him a little way up the mound. He shouted in the ear of the corporal: 'Duckett! Go and dig out Duckett! At the double!'

He knelt and felt along the boy's back. His spine might have been damaged. The boy did not wince. His spine might be damaged all the same. He could not be left there. Bearers could be sent with a stretcher if one was to be found. But they might be sniped coming. Probably, he, Tietjens, could carry that boy; if his lungs held out. If not, he could drag him. He felt tender, like a mother, and enormous. It might be better to leave the boy there. There was no knowing. He said: 'Are you wounded?' The guns had mostly stopped. Tietjens could not see any blood flowing. The boy whispered 'No, sir!' He was, then, probably just faint. Shell-shock, very likely. There was no knowing what shell-shock was or what it did to you. Or the mere vapour of the projectile.

He could not stop there.

He took the boy under his arm as you might do a roll of blankets. If he took him on his shoulders he might get high enough to be sniped. He did not go very fast, his legs were so heavy. He bundled down several steps in the direction of the spring in which the boy had been. There was more water. The spring was filling up that hollow. He could not have left the boy there. You could only imagine that his body had corked up the spring-hole before. This had been like being at home where they had springs like that. On the moors, digging out badgers. Digging earth drains, rather. Badgers have dry lairs. On the moors above Groby. April sunlight. Lots of sunlight and skylarks.

He was mounting the mound. For some feet there was no other way. They had been left in the shaft made by that projectile. He inclined to the left. To the right would take them quicker to the trench, but he wanted to get the mound between them and the sniper. His breathing was tremendous. There was more light falling on them.

Exactly! . . . Snap! Snap! Snap! . . . Clear sounds from a quarter of a mile away . . . Bullets whined. Overhead. Long sounds, going away. Not snipers. The men of a battalion. A chance! Snap! Snap! Snap! Bullets whined overhead. Men of a battalion get excited when shooting at anything running. They fire high. Trigger pressure. *He* was now a fat, running object. Did they fire with a sense of hatred or fun! Hatred probably. Huns have not much sense of fun.

His breathing was unbearable. Both his legs were like painful bolsters. He would be on the relatively level in two steps if he made them . . . Well, make them! . . . He was on the level. He had been climbing: up clods. He *had* to take an immense breath. The ground under his left foot gave way. He had been holding Aranjuez in front of his own body as much as he could, under his right arm. As his left foot sank in, the boy's body came right on top of him. Naturally this stiffish earth in huge clods had fissures in it. Apertures. It was not like regular digging.

The boy kicked, screamed, tore himself loose . . . Well, if he wanted to go! The scream was like a horse's in a stable on fire. Bullets had gone overhead. The boy rushed off, his hands to his face. He disappeared round the mound. It was a conical mound. He, Tietjens, could now crawl on his belly. It was satisfactory.

He crawled. Shuffling himself along with his hips and elbows. There was probably a textbook way of crawling. He did not know it. The clods of earth appeared friendly. For bottom soil thrown to the top they did not feel or smell so very sour. Still, it would take a long time to get them into cultivation or under grass. Probably, agriculturally speaking, that country would be in a pretty poor condition for a long time . . .

He felt pleased with his body. It had had no exercise to speak of for two months – as second-in-command. He could not have expected to be in even the condition he was in. But the mind had probably had a good deal to do with that! He had, no doubt, been in a devil of a funk. It was only reasonable. It was disagreeable to think of those Hun devils hunting down the unfortunate. A disagreeable business. Still, we did the same . . . That boy must have been in a devil of a funk. Suddenly. He had held his hands in front of his face. Afraid to see. Well, you couldn't blame him. They ought not to send out schoolgirls. He was like a girl. Still, he ought to have stayed to see that he, Tietjens, was not pipped. He might have thought he was hit from the way his left leg had gone down. He would have to be strafed. Gently.

Cockshott and the corporal were on their hands and knees digging with the short-handled shovels that are known as trenching tools. They were on the rear side of the mound.

'We've found im, sir,' the corporal said. 'Regular buried. Just seed his foot. Dursen't use a shovel. Might cut im in arf!'

Tietjens said:

'You're probably right. Give me the shovel!'

Cockshott was a draper's assistant, the corporal a milkman. Very likely they were not good with shovels.

He had had the advantage of a boyhood crowded with digging of all sorts. Duckett was buried horizontally, running into the side of a conical mound. His feet at least stuck out like that, but you could not tell how the body was disposed. It might turn to either side or upwards. He said:

'Go on with your tools above! But give me room.'

The toes being to the sky, the trunk could hardly bend downwards. He stood below the feet and aimed terrific blows with the shovel eighteen inches below. He liked digging. This earth was luckily dryish. It ran down the hill conveniently. This man had been buried probably ten minutes. It seemed longer but it was probably less. He ought to have a chance. Probably earth was less suffocating than water. He said to the corporal:

'Do you know how to apply artificial respiration?'

'To the drowned?'

Cockshott said:

'I do, sir. I was swimming champion of Islington baths!' . .

. . . He said:

'Hullo, Aranjuez! Better?'

It was like a whale speaking to a shrimp: but still more like an uncle speaking to a favourite nephew! Aranjuez blushed with sheer pleasure. He faded away as if in awe before tremendous eminences. For him she too was an eminence. His life-hero's . . . woman!

The VC was in the mood to argue about politics. He always was. She had met him twice during evenings at friends' called Prinsep. She had not known him because of his eyeglasses: he must have put that up along with his ribbon. It took your breath away: like a drop of blood illuminated by a light that never was.

He said:

'They say you're receiving for Tietjens! Who'd have thought it? you a pro-German, and he such a sound Tory. Squire of Groby and all, eh what?'

He said:

'Know Groby?' He squinted through his glasses round the room. 'Looks like a mess this . . . Only needs the *Vie Parisienne* and the *Pink Un* . . . Suppose he has moved his stuff to Groby. He'll be going to live at Groby, now. The war's over!'

He said:

'But you and old Tory Tietjens in the same room . . . By Jove the war's over . . . The lion lying down with the lamb's nothing . . .' he exclaimed 'Oh, damn! Oh damn, damn, damn . . . I say . . . I didn't mean it . . . Don't cry. My dear little girl. My dear Miss Wannop. One of the best I always thought you. You don't suppose . . .'

She said:

'I'm crying because of Groby . . . It's a day to cry on anyhow . . . You're quite a good sort, really!'

He said:

'Thank you! Thank you! Drink some more port! He's a good fat old beggar, old Tietjens. A good officer!' He added: 'Drink a *lot* more port!'

He had been the most asinine, creaking, 'what about your king and country', shocked, outraged and speechless creature of all the many who for years had objected to her objecting to men being unable to stand up . . . Now he was a rather kind brother!

They were all yelling.

'Good old Tietjens! Good old Fat Man! Pre-war Hooch! He'd be the one to get it.' No one like Fat Man Tietjens! He lounged at the door; easy; benevolent. In uniform now. That was better. An officer, yelling like an enraged Redskin, dealt him an immense blow behind the shoulder blades. He staggered, smiling, into the centre of the room. An officer pushed her into the centre of the room. She was against him. Khaki encircled them. They began to yell and to prance, joining hands. Others waved the bottles and smashed underfoot the glasses. Gypsies break glasses at their weddings. The bed was against the wall. She did not like the bed to be against the wall. It had been brushed by . . .

They were going round them: yelling in unison: 'Over here! Pom Pom! Over here! Pom Pom! That's the word, that's the word. Over here . . .'

At least they weren't over there! They were prancing. The whole world round them was yelling and prancing round. They were the centre of unending roaring circles. The man with the eyeglass had stuck a half-crown in his other eye. He was well-meaning. A brother. She had a brother with the V C. All in the family.

Tietjens was stretching out his two hands from the waist. It was incomprehensible. His right hand was behind her back, his left in her right hand. She was frightened. She was amazed. Did you ever! He was swaying slowly. The elephant! They were dancing! Aranjuez was hanging on to the tall woman like a kid on a telegraph pole. The officer who had said he had picked up a little bit of fluff . . . well, he had! He had run out and fetched it. It wore white cotton gloves and a flowered hat. It said: 'Ow! Now!' . . . There was a fellow with a most beautiful voice. He led; better than a gramophone. Better . . .

Les petites marionettes: font! font! font! . . .

On an elephant. A dear, meal-sack elephant. She was setting out on . . .

EDITH WHARTON

Edith Wharton (1862–1937). Born into an aristocratic New York family. Educated at home. From 1906 lived mainly in France where she helped the unemployed, French and Belgian refugees, and children. Frequently went to the front and witnessed an attack at Verdun. Awarded the cross of the Légion d'Honneur in 1915. Friend of Henry James. She approached the war as a liberal but also, in accepting that there were European values worth fighting to preserve, she distanced herself from some other American writers who may have used the war for the purpose of self-dramatization. The passage below is from her non-fiction account of the early stages of the war, *Fighting France*.

Source: Edith Wharton, *Fighting France*, New York, Charles Scribner's Sons, 1915.

. . . That evening, in a restaurant of the rue Royale, we sat at a table in one of the open windows, abreast with the street, and saw the strange new crowds stream by. In an instant we were being shown what mobilizaiton was – a huge break in the normal flow of traffic, like the sudden rupture of a dyke. The street was flooded by the torrent of people sweeping past us to the various railway stations. All were on foot, and carrying their luggage; for since dawn every cab and taxi and motor-omnibus had disappeared. The War Office had thrown out its drag-net and caught them all in. The crowd that passed our window was chiefly composed of conscripts, the *mobilisables* of the first day, who were on the way to the station accompanied by their families and friends; but among them were little clusters of bewildered tourists, labouring along with bags and bundles, and watching their luggage pushed before them on hand-carts – puzzled inarticulate waifs caught in the cross-tides racing to a maelstrom.

In the restaurant, the befrogged and redcoated band poured out patriotic music, and the intervals between the courses that so few waiters were left to serve were broken by the ever-recurring obligation to stand up for the 'Marseillaise', to stand up for 'God

Save the King', to stand up for the Russian National Anthem, to stand up again for the 'Marseillaise'. *'Et dire que ce sont des Hongrois qui jouent tout cela!'* a humourist remarked from the pavement.

As the evening wore on and the crowd about our window thickened, the loiterers outside began to join in the war-songs. *'Allons, debout!'* – and the loyal round begins again. *'La chanson du départ!'* is a frequent demand; and the chorus of spectators chimes in roundly. A sort of quiet humour was the note of the street. Down the rue Royale, toward the Madeleine, the bands of other restaurants were attracting other throngs, and martial refrains were strung along the Boulevard like its garlands of arc-lights. It was a night of singing and acclamations, not boisterous, but gallant and determined. It was Paris *badauderie* at its best.

Meanwhile, beyond the fringe of idlers the steady stream of conscripts still poured along. Wives and families trudged beside them, carrying all kinds of odd improvised bags and bundles. The impression disengaging itself from all this superficial confusion was that of a cheerful steadiness of spirit. The faces ceaselessly streaming by were serious but not sad; nor was there any air of bewilderment – the stare of driven cattle. All these lads and young men seemed to know what they were about and why they were about it. The youngest of them looked suddenly grown up and responsible: they understood their stake in the job, and accepted it.

The next day the army of midsummer travel was immobilized to let the other army move. No more wild rushes to the station, no more bribing of concierges, vain quests for invisible cabs, haggard hours of waiting in the queue at Cook's. No train stirred except to carry soldiers, and the civilians who had not bribed and jammed their way into a cranny of the thronged carriages leaving the first night could only creep back through the hot streets to their hotels and wait. Back they went, disappointed yet half-relieved, to the resounding emptiness of porterless halls, waiterless restaurants, motionless lifts: to the queer disjointed life of fashionable hotels suddenly reduced to the intimacies and makeshift of a Latin Quarter *pension*. Meanwhile it was strange to watch the gradual paralysis of the city. As the motors, taxis, cabs and vans had vanished from the streets, so the lively little steamers had left the Seine. The canal-boats too were gone, or lay motionless: loading and unloading had ceased. Every great architectural opening framed an emptiness; all the endless avenues stretched away to desert distances. In the parks and gardens no one raked the paths or trimmed the borders. The fountains slept in their basins, the worried sparrows fluttered unfed, and vague dogs, shaken out of their daily habits, roamed unquietly, looking for familiar eyes. Paris, so intensely conscious yet so strangely entranced, seemed to have had curare injected into all her veins.

EDITH WHARTON

see also p. 511

Edith Wharton's *A Son at the Front* (1923), although written after the war, draws particularly on her feelings about the earlier part of it. It opens in the summer of 1914. John Campton, an American painter living in Paris, has a son, George, by a former marriage, who was born in France and is therefore subject to mobilization. John Campton, who has an outsider's lack of interest in the war and a father's concern for his son's safety, is surprised to find that George seems to relish the prospect. He joins his regiment, apparently in a 'safe' job, but, without telling his father, he soon moves to the front and is severely wounded. John Campton hears the truth from a friend, Boylston, and goes with George's step-father, Brant, to visit his son. George recovers, eventually returns to the front, is wounded again and dies early in 1917, the year the Americans entered the war. John Campton now finds himself in sympathy with the aims of the war and with the young soldiers who defend the 'idea' of France. The novel was written in France between 1918 and 1922.

Source: Edith Wharton, *A Son at the Front*, New York, Charles Scribner's Sons, 1923.

. . .The vision of Fortin-Lescluze's motor vanished, and in its place Campton suddenly saw Boylston's screwed-up eyes staring out at him under furrows of anguish. Campton remembered, the evening before, pushing the letter over to him across the office table, and stammering: 'Read it – read it to me. I can't –' and Boylston's sudden sobbing explosion: 'But I *knew*, sir – I've known all along . . .' and then the endless pause before Campton gathered himself up to falter out (like a child deciphering the words in a primer): 'You *knew* – knew that George was wounded?'

'No, no, not that; but that he might be – oh, at any minute! Forgive me – oh, do forgive me! He wouldn't let me tell you that he was at the front,' Boylston had faltered through his sobs.

'Let you tell me –?'

'You and his mother: he refused a citation last March so that you shouldn't find out that he'd exchanged into an infantry regiment. He was determined to from the first. He's been fighting for months; he's been magnificent; he got away from the Argonne last February; but you were none of you to know.'

'But why – why – why?' Campton had flashed out; then his heart stood still, and he awaited the answer with lowered head.

'Well, you see, he was afraid: afraid you might prevent . . . use your influence . . . you and Mrs Brant . . .'

Campton looked up again, challenging the other. 'He imagined perhaps that we *had* – in the beginning?'

'Oh, yes' – Boylston was perfectly calm about it – 'he knew all about that. And he made us swear not to speak; Miss Anthony and me. Miss Anthony knew . . . If this thing happened,' Boylston ended in a stricken voice, 'you were not to be unfair to her, he said' . . .

———

. . . On a landing Campton heard a babble and scream: a nauseating scream in a queer bleached voice that might have been man, woman or monkey's. Perhaps that was what the French meant by 'a white voice': this voice which was as featureless as some of the poor men's obliterated faces! Campton shot an anguished look at his companion, and she understood and shook her head. 'Oh, no: that's in the big ward. It's the way they scream after a dressing . . .'

She opened a door, and he was in a room with three beds in it, wooden pallets hastily knocked together and spread with rough grey blankets. In spite of the cold, flies still swarmed on the unwashed panes, and there were big holes in the fly-net over the bed nearest the window. Under the net lay a middle-aged bearded man, heavily bandaged about the chest and left arm: he was snoring, his mouth open, his gaunt cheeks drawn in with the fight for breath. Campton said to himself that if his own boy lived he should like some day to do something for this poor devil who was his room-mate. Then he looked about him and saw that the two other beds were empty.

He drew back.

The nurse was bending over the bearded man. 'He'll wake presently – I'll leave you'; and she slipped out. Campton looked again at the stranger; then his glance travelled to the scarred brown hand on the sheet, a hand with broken nails and black-ened finger-tips. It was George's hand, his son's, swollen, disfigured but unmistakable. The father knelt down and laid his lips on it . . .

. . . The sense of it had first come to Campton when the bearded man, raising his lids, looked at him from far off with George's eyes, and touched him, very feebly, with George's hand. It was in the moment of identifying his son that he felt the son he had known to be lost to him for ever.

George's lips were moving, and the father laid his ear to them; perhaps these were last words that his boy was saying.

'Old Dad – in a motor?'

Campton nodded.

The fact seemed faintly to interest George, who continued to examine him with those distant eyes.

'Uncle Andy's?'

Campton nodded again.

'Mother – ?'

'She's coming too – very soon.'

George's lips were screwed into a whimsical smile. 'I must have a shave first,' he said, and drowsed off again, his hand in Campton's . . .

'The other gentleman –?' the nurse questioned the next morning.

Campton had spent the night in the hospital, stretched on the floor at his son's threshold. It was a breach of rules, but for once the major had condoned it. As for Mr Brant, Campton had forgotten all about him, and at first did not know what the nurse meant. Then he woke with a start to the consciousness of his fellow-traveller's nearness. Mr Brant, the nurse explained, had come to the hospital early, and had been waiting below for the last two hours. Campton, almost as gaunt and unshorn as his son, pulled himself to his feet and went down. In the hall the banker, very white, but smooth and trim as ever, was patiently measuring the muddy flags.

'Less temperature this morning,' Campton called from the last flight.

'Oh,' stammered Mr Brant, red and pale by turns.

Campton smiled haggardly and pulled himself together in an effort of communicativeness. 'Look here – he's asked for you; you'd better go up. Only for a few minutes, please; he's awfully weak.'

Mr Brant, speechless, stood stiffly waiting to be conducted. Campton noticed the mist in his eyes, and took pity on him.

'I say – where's the hotel? Just a step away? I'll go around, then, and get a shave and a wash while you're with him,' the father said, with a magnanimity which he somehow felt the powers might take account of in their subsequent dealings with George. If the boy was to live Campton could afford to be generous; and he had decided to assume that the boy would live, and to order his behaviour accordingly.

'I – thank you,' said Mr Brant, turning toward the stairs . . .

WILLA CATHER

Willa Cather (1874–1947). Born in Virginia, probably in 1874. Educated at home, like her contemporary, Edith Wharton, and at a Nebraska high school. She attended the University of Nebraska. Worked as a teacher and journalist till 1911 when she became a full-time writer. Started to publish poetry in 1903 and stories in 1905. Her first novel, *Alexander's Bridge*, was published in 1912. Broadly speaking, Willa Cather supported American entry into the war. *One of Ours* was based partly on the experience of her cousin, G. P. Cather, who was killed at Cantigny in 1918. She visited France in the spring of 1920 to gain firsthand knowledge of France after the war. The novel received mixed reviews from, amongst others, H. L. Mencken (who had previously praised her), Sinclair Lewis and Edmund Wilson (*q.v.*), who compared it adversely with Dos Passos's *Three Soldiers*. However, it won the Pulitzer Prize. *One of Ours* opens in the years just before the outbreak of war. Claude Wheeler has been brought up in the culturally narrow environment of a Nebraska farm. He begins to break free by attending a religious college and then the state university. He makes an unsuccessful marriage but has the conviction 'that there was something splendid about life, if he could but find it'. He joins up when America enters the war in 1917. In France, he is introduced to Mlle Olive de Courcy, who helps him to realize his true feelings for France. After reaching the front line he is injured. Later, during a desperate defence action, he sees the Germans advance and pause before they explode an enormous mine. Claude fights bravely but is shot and killed. The final scene confirms the ambiguity of the novel: has Claude really found anything 'splendid' either for himself, his family, America or France?

Source: Willa Cather, *One of Ours*, New York, Alfred Knopf, 1922.

. . . 'You have found a flower?' She looked up.

'Yes. It grows at home, on my father's farm.'

She dropped the faded shirt she was darning. 'Oh, tell me about your country! I have talked to so many, but it is difficult to understand. Yes, tell me about that!'

Nebraska – What was it? How many days from the sea, what did it look like? As he tried to describe it, she listened with half-closed eyes. 'Flat – covered with grain – muddy rivers. I think it must be like Russia. But your father's farm; describe that to me, minutely, and perhaps I can see the rest.'

Claude took a stick and drew a square in the sand: there, to begin with, was the house and farmyard; there was the big pasture, with Lovely Creek flowing through it; there were the wheatfields and cornfields, the timber claim; more wheat and corn, more pastures. There it all was, diagrammed on the yellow sand, with shadows gliding over it from the half-charred locust trees. He would not have believed that he could tell a stranger about it in such detail. It was partly due to his listener, no doubt; she gave him unusual sympathy, and the glow of an unusual mind. While she bent over his map, questioning him, a light dew of perspiration gathered on her upper lip, and she breathed faster from her effort to see and understand everything. He told her about his mother and his father and Mahailey; what life was like there in summer and winter and autumn – what it had been like in that fateful summer when the Hun was moving always toward Paris, and on those three days when the French were standing at the Marne; how his mother and father waited for him to bring the news at night, and how the very cornfields seemed to hold their breath.

Mlle Olive sank back wearily in her chair. Claude looked up and saw tears sparkling in her brilliant eyes. 'And I myself,' she murmured, 'did not know of the Marne until days afterward, though my father and brother were both there! I was far off in Brittany, and the trains did not run. That is what is wonderful, that you are here, telling me this! We, – we were taught from childhood that some day the Germans would come; we grew up under that threat. But you were so safe, with all your wheat and corn. Nothing could touch you, nothing!'

Claude dropped his eyes. 'Yes,' he muttered, blushing, 'shame could. It pretty nearly did. We are pretty late.' He rose from his chair as if he were going to fetch something . . . But where was he to get it from? He shook his head. 'I am afraid,' he said mournfully, 'there is nothing I can say to make you understand how far away it all seemed, how almost visionary. It didn't only seem miles away, it seemed centuries away.'

'But you do come, – so many, and from so far! It is the last miracle of this war. I was in Paris on the fourth day of July, when your Marines, just from Château-Thierry, marched for your national fête, and I said to myself as they came on, "*That is a new man!*" Such heads they had, so fine there, behind the ears. Such discipline and purpose. Our people laughed and called to them and threw them flowers, but they never turned to look ... eyes straight before. They passed like men of destiny.' She threw out her hands with a swift movement and dropped them in her lap. The emotion of that day came back in her face. As Claude looked at her burning cheeks, her burning eyes, he understood that the strain of this war had given her a perception that was almost like a gift of prophecy ...

... When his hostess came back, he moved her chair for her out of the creeping sunlight. 'I didn't know there were any French girls like you,' he said simply, as she sat down.

She smiled. 'I do not think there are any French girls left. There are children and women. I was twenty-one when the war came, and I had never been anywhere without my mother or my brother or sister. Within a year I went all over France alone; with soldiers, with Senegalese, with anybody. Everything is different with us.' She lived at Versailles, she told him, where her father had been an instructor in the military school. He had died since the beginning of the war. Her grandfather was killed in the war of 1870. Hers was a family of soldiers, but not one of the men would be left to see the day of victory.

She looked so tired that Claude knew he had no right to stay. Long shadows were falling in the garden. It was hard to leave; but an hour more or less wouldn't matter. Two people could hardly give each other more if they were together for years, he thought.

'Will you tell me where I can come and see you, if we both get through this war?' he asked as he rose.

He wrote it down in his notebook.

'I shall look for you,' she said, giving him her hand.

There was nothing to do but to take his helmet and go. At the edge of the hill, just before he plunged down the path, he stopped and glanced back at the garden lying flattened in the sun; the three stone arches, the dahlias and marigolds, the glistening boxwood wall. He had left something on the hilltop which he would never find again ...

Suddenly the advance was checked. The files of running men dropped behind a wrinkle in the earth fifty yards forward and did not instantly reappear. It struck Claude that they were waiting for something; he ought to be clever enough to know for what, but he was not. The colonel's line man came up to him.

'Headquarters has a runner from the Missourians. They'll be up in twenty minutes. The colonel will put them in here at once. Till then you must manage to hold.'

'We'll hold. Fritz is behaving queerly. I don't understand his tactics . . .'

While he was speaking, everything was explained. The Boar's Snout spread apart with an explosion that split the earth, and went up in a volcano of smoke and flame. Claude and the colonel's messenger were thrown on their faces. When they got to their feet, the Snout was a smoking crater full of dead and dying men. The Georgia gun teams were gone.

It was for this that the Hun advance had been waiting behind the ridge. The mine under the Snout had been made long ago, probably, on a venture, when the Hun held Moltke trench for months without molestation. During the last twenty-four hours they had been getting their explosives in, reasoning that the strongest garrison would be placed there.

Here they were, coming on the run. It was up to the rifles. The men who had been knocked down by the shock were all on their feet again. They looked at their officer questioningly, as if the whole situation had changed. Claude felt they were going soft under his eyes. In a moment the Hun bombers would be in on them, and they would break. He ran along the trench, pointing over the sandbags and shouting. 'It's up to you, it's up to you!'

The rifles recovered themselves and began firing, but Claude felt they were spongy and uncertain, that their minds were already on the way to the rear. If they did anything, it must be quick, and their gun-work must be accurate. Nothing but a withering fire could check . . . He sprang to the fire-step and then out on the parapet. Something instantaneous happened; he had his men in hand.

'Steady, steady!' He called the range to the rifle teams behind him, and he could see the fire take effect. All along the Hun lines men were stumbling and falling. They swerved a little to the left;

he called the rifles to follow, directing them with his voice and with his hands. It was not only that from here he could correct the range and direct the fire; the men behind him had become like rock. That line of faces below, Hicks, Jones, Fuller, Anderson, Oscar . . . Their eyes never left him. With these men he could do anything. He had learned the mastery of men.

The right of the Hun line swerved out, not more than twenty yards from the battered Snout, trying to run to shelter under that pile of debris and human bodies. A quick concentration of rifle fire depressed it, and the swell came out again toward the left. Claude's appearance on the parapet had attracted no attention from the enemy at first, but now the bullets began popping about him; two rattled on his tin hat, one caught him in the shoulder. The blood dripped down his coat, but he felt no weakness. He felt only one thing; that he commanded wonderful men. When David came up with the supports he might find them dead, but he would find them all there. They were to stay until they were carried out to be buried. They were mortal, but they were unconquerable.

The colonel's twenty minutes must be almost up, he thought. He couldn't take his eyes from the front line long enough to look at his wrist watch . . . The men behind him saw Claude sway as if he had lost his balance and were trying to recover it. Then he plunged, face down, outside the parapet. Hicks caught his foot and pulled him back. At the same moment the Missourians ran yelling up the communication. They threw their machine-guns up on the sand-bags and went into action without an unnecessary motion . . .

═══

. . . By the banks of Lovely Creek, where it began, Claude Wheeler's story still goes on. To the two old women who work together in the farmhouse, the thought of him is always there, beyond everything else, at the farthest edge of consciousness, like the evening sun on the horizon.

Mrs Wheeler got the word of his death one afternoon in the sitting-room, the room in which he had bade her goodbye. She was reading when the telephone rang.

'Is this the Wheeler farm? This is the telegraph office at Frankfort. We have a message from the War Department, –' the voice hesitated. 'Isn't Mr Wheeler there?'

'No, but you can read the message to me.'

Mrs Wheeler said 'Thank you', and hung up the receiver. She felt her way softly to her chair. She had an hour alone, when there was nothing but him in the room, – but him and the map there, which was the end of his road. Somewhere among those perplexing names, he had found his place.

Claude's letters kept coming for weeks afterward; then came the letters from his comrades and his colonel to tell her all.

In the dark months that followed, when human nature looked to her uglier than it had ever done before, those letters were Mrs Wheeler's comfort. As she read the newspapers, she used to think about the passage of the Red Sea, in the Bible; it seemed as if the flood of meanness and greed had been held back just long enough for the boys to go over, and then swept down and engulfed everything that was left at home. When she can see nothing that has come of it all but evil, she reads Claude's letters over again and reassures herself; for him the call was clear, the cause was glorious. Never a doubt stained his bright faith. She divines so much that he did not write. She knows what to read into those short flashes of enthusiasm; how fully he must have found his life before he could let himself go so far – he, who was so afraid of being fooled! He died believing his own country better than it is, and France better than any country can ever be. And those were beautiful beliefs to die with. Perhaps it was as well to see that vision, and then to see no more. She would have dreaded the awakening, – she sometimes even doubts whether he could have borne at all that last, desolating disappointment. One by one the heroes of that war, the men of dazzling soldiership, leave prematurely the world they have come back to. Airmen whose deeds were tales of wonder, officers whose names made the blood of youth beat faster, survivors of incredible dangers, – one by one they quietly die by their own hand. Some do it in obscure lodging-houses, some in their office, where they seemed to be carrying on their business like other men. Some slip over a vessel's side and disappear into the sea. When Claude's mother hears of these things, she shudders and presses her hands tight over her breast, as if she had him there. She feels as if God had saved him from some horrible suffering, some horrible end. For as she reads, she thinks those slayers of themselves were all so like him; they were the ones who had hoped extravagantly, – who in order to do what they did had to hope extravagantly, and to believe passionately. And they found they had hoped and believed too much. But one she knew, who could ill bear disillusion . . . safe, safe . . .

LOUIS-FERDINAND CÉLINE

Louis-Ferdinand Céline (Louis-Ferdinand Destouches, 1894–1961). Born in a lower-middle-class family in Paris. Joined the army in September 1912 and served in the cavalry. Severely wounded in November 1914 and awarded the Military Medal. Invalided out with 75 per cent disability. Travelled to England, then Africa. Returned to France in 1917 and qualified as a doctor in 1924. Spent time in Germany at the end of the Second World War and was charged with collaborating. Published anti-Semitic writings. *Journey to the End of the Night* was his first novel. Ferdinand Bardamu volunteers. He is wounded and, while convalescing in Paris, meets Lola, an American helping the war effort by supervising the cooking and distribution of apple fritters to the troops in hospitals in Paris. This passage comes early in the novel and gives a very different view of American involvement, and the 'idea' of France, from that given by Edith Wharton and Willa Cather (*qq.v.*). Céline's cynicism may be compared with that of Drieu la Rochelle (*q.v.*). There seem to be no English counterparts. His experience of the war and his injury is directly used in *Journey* and later works.

Source: Louis-Ferdinand Céline, *Journey to the End of the Night* (translated from *Voyage au bout de la nuit*, Paris, Denoël & Steele, 1932, by John H. P. Marks), London, Chatto & Windus, 1934; London, Vision Press, 1950.

Morals, in fact, were a dirty business. If I had told Lola what I thought of the war, she would only have taken me for a depraved freak and she'd deny me all intimate pleasures. So I took good care not to confess these things to her. Besides which, I still had other difficulties and rivalries to contend with. More than one officer was trying to take her from me. Their competition was dangerous, armed as they were with the attraction of their Legions of Honour. And there was beginning to be a lot about this damn Legion of Honour in the American papers. In fact, I think that after she had deceived me two or three times, our relationship would have been seriously threatened if just then the minx had not suddenly discovered something more to be said in my favour, which was that I could be used every morning as a substitute taster of fritters.

This last-minute specialization saved me. She could accept *me* as her deputy. Was I not myself a gallant fighting man and therefore worthy of this confidential post? From then onwards we were partners as well as lovers. A new era had begun.

Her body was an endless source of joy to me. I never tired of caressing its American contours. To tell the truth, I was an appalling lecher – and I went on being one.

Indeed, I came to the very delightful and comforting conclusion that a country capable of producing anatomies of such startling loveliness, and so full of spiritual grace, must have many other revelations of primary importance to offer – biologically speaking of course.

My little games with Lola led me to decide that I would sooner or later make a journey, or rather a pilgrimage, to the United States; and certainly just as soon as I could manage it. Nor did I ever find respite and quiet (throughout a life fated in any case to be difficult and restless) until I was able to bring off this supremely mystical adventure in anatomical research.

Thus it was in the neighbourhood of Lola's backside that a message from a new world came to me. And she hadn't only a fine body, my Lola, – let us get that quite clear at once; she was graced also with a piquant little face and grey-blue eyes, which gave her a slightly cruel look, because they were set a wee bit on the upward slant, like those of a wildcat.

Just to look into her face made my mouth water like a sip of dry wine, of silex, will. Her eyes were hard and lacking the animation of that charming trademark vivacity reminiscent of the Orient and of Fragonard, which one finds in almost all the eyes over here.

We usually met in a café around the corner. Wounded men in increasing numbers hobbled along the streets, in rags as often as not. Collections were made on their behalf. There was a 'Day' for these, a 'Day' for those, Days above all for the people who organized them. Lie, copulate and die. One wasn't allowed to do anything else. People lied fiercely and beyond belief, ridiculously, beyond the limits of absurdity: lies in the papers, lies on the hoardings, lies on foot, on horseback and on wheels. Everybody was doing it, trying to see who could produce a more fantastic lie than his neighbour. There was soon no truth left in town.

And what truth there was one was ashamed of, in 1914.

Everything you touched was faked in some way – the sugar, the aeroplanes, shoe leather, jam, photographs; everything you read, swallowed, sucked, admired, proclaimed, refuted or upheld – it was all an evil myth and masquerade. Even traitors weren't real traitors. A mania for lying and believing lies is as catching as the itch. Little Lola knew only a few phrases in French but they were all jingo phrases: *'On les aura', 'Madelon, viens!'* ... It was enough to make you weep.

She hovered over the death which was confronting us, persistently, obscenely – as indeed did all the women, now that it had become the fashion to be courageous at other people's expense.

And there was I at that time discovering in myself such a fondness for all the things which kept me apart from the war! I asked her again and again to tell me about America but she only answered with vague, silly and obviously inaccurate descriptions, which were meant to make a dazzling impression on me.

But I distrusted impressions just then. I'd been had that way once before; I wasn't going to be caught so easily again. Not by anybody.

I believed in her body, I didn't believe in her mind and heart. I considered her to be charming and cushily placed in this war, cushily placed in life.

Her attitude towards an existence which for me was horrible, was merely that of the patriotic press: *Pompon, Fanfare, ma Lorraine et gants blancs* ... Meanwhile I made love to her more and more often, having assured her that it would make her slim. But she relied more on our long walks to do that. I hated these long walks myself. But she was adamant.

So for several hours in the afternoon we would stride along in the Bois de Boulogne, around the lakes. Nature is a terrifying thing and even when well domesticated as in the Bois she still inspires a sort of uneasiness in real town dwellers. They are pretty apt in such surroundings to take you into their confidence. Nothing like the Bois de Boulogne, wet, railed-in, sleek and shorn as it is, for calling up a flock of stubborn memories in the minds of city folk strolling amid trees. Lola was a prey to this mood of melancholy, confidential unease. As we walked along, she'd tell me, more or less truthfully, a hundred and one things about her life in New York and her little friends there.

I couldn't quite disentangle what was convincing from what was doubtful in all this complicated rigmarole of dollars, engagements, dresses and jewellery, which seems to have made up her life in America.

That day we were going towards the race course. At that time one still came across children on donkeys there, and horse-cabs, and more children kicking up the dust, and cars full of men on leave, hunting all the time in the little paths, as fast as possible, between two trains, for women with nothing to do; they raised even more dust, in their hurry to go off and have dinner and make love, agitated and oily, with roving eyes, worried by the passage of time and the wish to live. They sweated with desire as well as with the heat.

The Bois was less well-kept than usual, temporarily neglected by the authorities.

'This place must have been very pretty before the war,' Lola remarked. 'It must have been awfully smart, wasn't it, Ferdinand? Tell me. Were the races like those in New York?'

To tell the truth, I'd never been to the races before the war myself, but I at once made up a colourful description of them for her benefit, basing myself on what I'd often heard about them from other people. Beautiful dresses . . . smart society women . . . splendid four-in-hands . . . They're off! The gay trumpets . . . the water jump . . . The President of the Republic . . . The excitement of changing odds . . . And so on.

She was so delighted with these idealized vignettes of mine that my remarks brought us closer together. From that moment on Lola felt she had discovered a taste which we had in common, a taste, for my part well dissimulated, for the gay social round. She even kissed me there and then in her excitement, a thing which seldom happened with her, I must confess. And then the sadness of fashions dead and gone overcame her. We all mourn the passage of time in our own particular way. For Lola it was the passing of fashion which made her perceive the flight of years.

'Ferdinand,' she asked, 'do you think there will ever be races held here again?'

'I suppose there will, when the war is over, Lola.'

'It's not certain, though, is it?'

'No, it's not certain.'

The possibility of there never being any more races at Longchamps upset her. The sadness of life takes hold of people as best it may, but it seems almost always to manage to take hold of them somehow.

'Suppose the war goes on for a long time, Ferdinand, for years perhaps. Then for me it will be too late . . . to come back here . . . Don't you understand, Ferdinand? You see, I'm so fond of lovely places like this . . . that are so smart . . . and attractive. It will be too late, I expect. I shall be old then, Ferdinand, when the meetings begin again. I shall be already too old . . . You'll see, Ferdinand, how it'll be too late. I feel it will be too late.'

And then once again she was filled with despair, as she had been before about the two pounds' added weight. I said everything I could think of to reassure her and give her hope. After all, she was only twenty-three, I told her . . . And the war would be over very soon. Good times would come again. As good as before, better times than before . . . For her, at least, an attractive girl like her . . . Lost time was nothing: she'd make it up as easily as anything . . . There'd be people to admire her, to make a fuss over her, for a long time yet. She put on a less unhappy face, to please me.

'Must we go on walking?' she asked.

'But you want to get slim?'

'Oh, I'd forgotten that . . .'

We left Longchamps, the children had gone away. Only the dust was left. The fellows on leave were still looking for Happiness, but out in the open now. Happiness was to be tracked down among the café tables around the Porte Maillot.

We walked towards Saint-Cloud along the river banks hazy with autumn mist. Near the bridge several lighters pressed their bows against the arches, lying deep in the water, loaded with coal to the bulwarks.

The park foliage spread itself like an enormous fan above the railings. These trees are as detached, magnificent and impressive as one's dreams. But I was afraid of trees too, since I had known them to conceal an enemy. Every tree meant a dead man. The avenue led uphill towards the fountains flanked by roses. Near the kiosk the old lady who sold refreshments seemed slowly to be gathering all the shadows of evening about her skirts. Further away in the side alleys great squares and rectangles of dark-coloured canvas were flapping; the canvas of the tents of a fair which the war had taken by surprise and filled with silence.

'They've been away a whole year now,' the old lady reminded us. 'Nowadays only a couple of people will come along here in all the day. I come still, out of habit . . . There used to be such a crowd . . .'

The old lady had understood nothing else of what had happened: that was all she knew. Lola had a curious desire to walk past the empty marquees, because she was feeling sad.

We counted about twenty of them, big ones full of mirrors, and a greater number of small ones, sweet stalls, lotteries, and a small theatre even, full of draughts. There was one to every tree; they were all round us. One in particular near the main avenue had lost its canvas walls altogether and stood empty as an explained mystery.

They leaned over towards the mud and fallen leaves, these tents. We stopped close to the last one, which was further aslant than the rest, its posts pitching in the rising wind like the masts of a ship with wildly tugging sails about to snap the last of its ropes. The whole tent swayed, its inner canvas flapping towards heaven, flapping above the roof. Its ancient name was written in green and red on a board over the door. It was a shooting alley. 'The Stand of All Nations' it was called.

There was no one to look after it, either. He himself was away shooting along with the rest perhaps, the proprietor shooting shoulder to shoulder with his clients.

What a lot of shot had struck the targets of the booth! They were all spotted with little white pellet marks. There was a funny wedding scene, in zinc: in front the bride with her bouquet, the best man, a soldier, the bridegroom with a big red face, and in the background more guests – they must all have been killed again and again when the fair was on.

'I'm sure you're a good shot, aren't you, Ferdinand? If the fair was still here, I'd take you on . . . You shoot well, don't you, Ferdinand?'

'No, I'm not a very good shot.'

Further back, beyond the wedding, was another roughly painted target – the town hall with its flag flying. You shot at the town hall, when it was working, into the windows, and they opened and a bell rang, and you even shot at the little zinc flag. And you shot too at the regiment of soldiers marching up a hill near by, like mine in the Place Clichy; amid all these discs and uprights, all there to be shot at as much as possible, now it was I who was to be shot at – who had been shot at yesterday and would be shot at tomorrow –

'They shoot at me too, Lola!' I cried out. I couldn't help it.

'Come on,' she said. 'You're being silly, Ferdinand – and we shall catch cold.'

We went on towards Saint-Cloud down the Royal Avenue, avoiding the mud. She held my hand in hers, such a small hand, but I could think of nothing else but the zinc wedding of the

'Stand of All Nations' which we had left behind us in the gathering darkness. I even forgot to kiss her; it was all too much for me. I felt very strange.

In fact, I think it must have been from that moment that my head began to be so full of ideas and so difficult to calm.

When we got to the bridge at Saint-Cloud it was quite dark.

'Would you like to eat at Duval's, Ferdinand? You like Duval's ... It would cheer you up ... There's always a lot of people there. Unless you'd rather have supper in my room?' She was being very attentive that evening, in fact.

We finally decided on Duval's. But we'd hardly got our table than the place struck me as ludicrous and horrible. All these people sitting in rows all around us seemed to me to be sitting there waiting, they too, to be shot at from all sides as they ate.

'Run, all of you!' I shouted to them. 'Get out! They're going to fire! They'll kill you. They'll kill us all.'

I was hurried back to Lola's hotel. Everywhere I could see the same thing happening. All the people in the Paritz seemed to be going to get themselves shot and so did the hotel clerks at the reception desk. There they were, simply asking for it, and the porter man down by the door of the Paritz in his uniform of sky blue and his braid as golden as the sun, and the soldiers too, the officers who were wandering about, and those generals – not so grand as he, of course, but in uniforms nevertheless – it was all one vast shooting alley from which none of them, not one of them, could possibly escape.

'They're going to shoot!' I shouted to them at the top of my voice, in the middle of the main hall. 'They're going to shoot! Clear out, all of you, run away!' Then I went and shouted it from the window too. I couldn't help myself. There was a terrible scene. 'Poor boy,' people said.

The porter took me along, very gently, to the bar. With great kindness he made me drink, and I drank a lot and then finally the gendarmes came to fetch me; they were rougher about it. In the 'Stand of All Nations' there'd been gendarmes too. I remembered having seen them. Lola kissed me and helped them to handcuff me and lead me away.

After that I was feverish and fell ill; driven insane, they said in hospital, by fear. They may have been right. When one's in this world, surely the best thing one can do, isn't it, is to get out of it? Whether one's mad or not, frightened or not.

PIERRE-EUGÈNE DRIEU LA ROCHELLE

Pierre-Eugène Drieu la Rochelle (1893–1945). Published war poems (*Interrogations*, 1917) and initially accepted the war. Disillusion and pacifism came later (as did his fascism). Committed suicide 1945. He led the charge at Charleroi described in the novel. In the following passages the narrator revisits the battlefield with a dead comrade's mother, who hopes to find her son's grave and identify the body. The narrator relives the battle.

Source: Pierre-Eugène Drieu la Rochelle, *The Comedy of Charleroi* (translated from *La Comédie de Charleroi*, Paris, Gallimard, 1934, by Douglas Gallagher), Cambridge, Rivers Press, 1973.

. . . 'If you wouldn't mind, Madame Pragen, I should like to go over to that brick wall.'

All this time my gaze had kept coming back in fascination to the brick wall. Although Madame Pragen on her frail legs of a Parisian of 1900 did not walk very fast, and although the mayor suffered from gout, making our way through the new barbed-wire fences and across the rises in the ground, we approached the wall which had seemed to me so far off and inaccessible.

'Ah, there's the quarry.'

I had stopped dead in front of a huge hole.

'What about it?' asked Madame Pragen, impatiently.

'Well, that's the hole we fell into when the regiment charged.'

'Claude as well?'

'I saw him for the last time at midday, Madame Pragen, I've already told you. I wonder if he was in the charge.'

'If he was alive . . .'

'Yes.'

Madame Pragen continued on her way, paying no attention to my hole. That lovely hole, that hole in which my life had taken refuge, to emerge totally changed, that hole in which such odd incidents had taken place. For me, and for a few others, that was where our charge had died, mown down by the German machine-gun. That was where Captain Étienne and Jacob had come to terms, and where I had come to terms with Captain Étienne. What else? That was where, for me, the tide of the battle had turned.

But Madame Pragen was calling me in her impatient tone of voice.

'Let's go to your brick wall.'

She was expecting some miracle from that brick wall.

'So, what's so special about this brick wall?' she said to me, flashing her lorgnette at that piece of stage scenery made for *The Last Bullets*. Still riddled with bullet holes, our bullets. So some of them had reached their target. Yes, of course, several times the German machine-gun had fallen silent . . .

It was like this. Beside the brick wall, there was a sort of huge pigeon-loft or old tower where the Germans, towards midday, had very shrewdly installed a machine-gun. For two hours we had fired at that hide-out, not just with our rifles; we were supported by our own machine-gunners on our left, with our few wheezy machine-guns that jammed so easily and fell silent for long, deadly minutes – deadly for us, that is.

Two or three times, with a barrage of bullets, shovelfuls, sackfuls, cartfuls of bullets, we managed to silence the Germans who were in the pigeon-loft. Then, for the others, it was the moment of heroism; it was a question of running along in front of the brick wall to pick up the corpses of the men we had killed. At the beginning of the war – and no doubt at the end of the war it would still be the same – volunteers jostled with each other, like in a theatre queue. Many were called, only a few were chosen. As I looked on, it was like a succession of shadow puppets, with one puppet after another toppling down on to the wall. And once up in the pigeon-loft, those chosen gradually turned into sieves. But as long as they survived they really hurt us, with their angled fire raking the entire plain where our regiment was. So we did not just want to shoot them, we wanted to rip them open and tear them to pieces . . .

———

Madame Pragen was in a rage of impatience with me. She was not the slightest bit interested in this battlefield, where I was keeping her waiting.

She had wanted, almost in an abstract fashion, to see the spot where her son had died; not the spot where he had been killed.

She did not know what war was, and she did not want to know. War was part of that world of men about which women feel scarcely any curiosity. Honours were the only things that interested Madame Pragen in the world of men. Her husband was an important businessman, he had the *Légion d'honneur*; her son had died on the field of honour. For one reason or another, once the conduct of women is no longer dictated by their instinctive feelings, all they can find to guide themselves are stereotyped images that they worship with even greater abandon than men.

Yet she must have thought of the sufferings of her son, she must have tried to imagine them.

But just what sort of picture could she conjure up? That was what I kept asking myself with a piercing curiosity. How can one tell what any particular suffering is like, when one has never felt it oneself? One's own forgetfulness, following so quickly after the ordeal, makes one wonder about the impotence of the imagination. And yet, after the battle, a month later, I was reading *La Débâcle* by Zola, and several times I found my own feelings evoked. But then, Madame Pragen was far from sharing Zola's love for things and for men.

Several times I tried to probe her, unable to reconcile myself to this barrier between human beings.

'I hope he didn't suffer,' she repeated constantly.

I could sense so clearly that she had reached the stage of convincing herself that he had not suffered, that one day, no longer able to bear this hypocrisy (which none the less is nature's law, since by this means she was defending herself just like an animal), I protested:

'Perhaps he did suffer.'

And this is what she replied:

'He had such a fine career in front of him: he must have suffered at the thought of sacrificing all that.'

I looked at this woman sweeping the battlefield with the rapid and superficial flash of her lorgnette. And I shuddered with the shudder that I had felt throughout the war: no woman can ever share my suffering. But are we capable of knowing what they feel when they are pregnant, or when they give birth?

She had another reason for being in a hurry; she wanted to go to the cemetery where there was a grave thought to be that of Claude. Leaving my brick wall, we set off towards the cemetery.

The cemetery had been set up by the Germans in the wood, the famous wood we had had at our backs, where it had seemed to us that we would be under cover. A delightful cemetery, where the Nordic touch could easily be seen. It was a large square, laid out discreetly beneath the trees. In the middle, an isolated gravestone. They had left nearly all the trees and a lot of grass around the simple crosses.

What peace! That was the banal word that rose to my lips as I entered the cemetery. I was struck by the contrast between this silence and the terrifying din that had engendered it, and that had once more filled my ears.

I knew well, however, that there is no difference between life and death, that the latter, with its crackling of gas, is just as active as the former, and just as noisy. I could hear the explosions of chemistry at the bottom of the graves, of this communal labyrinth where five hundred Normans and five hundred Saxons – people of the same race, probably; oh, the absurdity of national boundaries – no doubt joined and mingled with each other.

But that did nothing to alter the illusion of silence that hung over the cemetery. Illusion of silence, of nothingness. Could I surrender to this charm of soft grass and dreaming trees? No, because I could remember that on that day of fighting, when life was so agonizing, I had not wished for that nothingness one commonly wishes for when one wishes for death. That is the saving grace of action.

Moreover, how could I have felt what I am incapable of conceiving? Everything in me that is thought, that is, my essence, rebels against the idea of nothingness. For me, death is not nothingness, it is the continuation of life; heaven and hell will never be separated.

The only time when I can remember having come near to this idea of nothingness was when I decided to kill myself. A few days before the battle, not sure that it would ever take place, I had looked at my rifle. That soothing, excruciating voluptuousness flooding through my limbs as I looked down that little black hole, was that the invasion of nothingness? No, it was merely the seductive illusion of suicide. With the venom of that idea, one's soul can manufacture a balm. The idea of suicide, for someone who does not actually commit it, is a galling balm. After that moment of release, he is ready to start anew.

And as I strolled in the deceitful shadows of that little Saxon cemetery, I could also remember the moment when, running towards the self-same wood, towards this cemetery, I had been hit on the head by a piece of shrapnel. At first I thought I had been killed. There was a heavy blow, a total feeling of silence (my legs continued galloping towards the wood) but immediately afterwards, and it seemed to be at the exact moment of impact, I said to myself: 'Ah! what bliss!' But not because I would be rid of all that, of that unbearable hell-fire, of myself, but because I was at last destined to find out: 'I'm going to know what death is like.' That was the thought that blazed through my brain. A thought of pure, lofty curiosity, a metaphysical thought, a totally intellectual reaction.

No doubt I reacted in that way because it was only a superficial wound, because I did not feel the hand of death and its preliminary torture on me, because on the contrary, my wound presented me with all sorts of rights and opportunities – above all, and in particular, because I did not feel any pain. Oh, under the torture suffered at Verdun, I was not the same, good Lord no. Then I repudiated everything in the universe – to no avail as it happened. From that overall, absurd revolt was to come a more particular, more precise revolt, the condition of life for those men who reached maturity.

Madame Pragen was strolling through the cemetery with her lorgnette. Charming cemetery. A gentle breeze rustled through the softly swaying trees, and the graves of this young cemetery were just the same as those of an old cemetery. The havoc of battle had wrought the same destruction as that of time. Most of the graves were without names and thus abandoned; only a few had flowers on them. Three of my friends from university, who like me had expected a soft option in that Paris regiment, were buried side by side. A single shell had demolished all three of them. The mayor told me that what was left of them took up less room in the coffins than their name-plates on the outside; those three coffins were empty.

There were five hundred Germans there, against five hundred Frenchmen. All in all, the 75s had done as much damage as the heavy artillery and the machine-guns, and the grey trousers had saved no more lives than the red trousers had cost. In the middle of the cemetery, there was General Baron von Z. 'Well done, General, you managed to die like they used to in the good old days.' But the mayor pointed out to me that he had been killed by a bullet in the stomach from a wounded Senegalese who had been crawling along the roadside, the evening after the battle.

What had they done, those thousand men? What had they done together? What had their concerted effort accomplished?

There had been a moment in the middle of the day when, in that inert army, pinned down in the mud ever since daybreak by enemy fire, squirting bullets like someone with diarrhoea – I had the impression that my platoon was the most inert – something none the less had stirred.

Where had it come from? From elsewhere, or from ourselves? From High Command, or from our own wills?

First of all a rumour had run through the ranks, along the trenches, along the lines of faces: we had won. The whole front was advancing. We too were going to advance . . .

———

. . . I was shouting – I was standing in the middle of the battlefield. I was running. I was stumbling, shouting. Oh! that war-cry has remained in my throat and hurts like a wound.

They were running. We were running, we were stumbling, falling. We were not equipped to run and fight and conquer. Loaded down with clothes, packs and weapons. Trussed up like bureaucrats, like so many duck-hunters, with this mass of utensils and bulky clothes. We were not dressed like men. We could not overcome. Barrack animals released totally unprepared and then shut up once more, we could not overcome. I would have liked to strip naked.

Yet I picked myself up, I kept running, shouting, calling. I was calling, I was calling the Germans and the French.

I remember two years later that giant of a German officer standing there in the midst of the agony of Verdun, Fritz von X, who was standing there, and calling, calling me. And I did not reply. I potted him from a safe distance.

In this war everyone called out, but no one replied. I became aware of that at the end of a sprint that lasted a century. Everyone became aware of that. I was only waving feebly and moaning.

I had practically stopped running forward. I kept stumbling, falling.

They were all stumbling, falling.

I could sense it. I could sense the man in me dying.

The Germans, enchanted by the facility of it all, started firing again. In earnest. A hail of bullets. It is so simple to rip open an inch of flesh with a ton of steel.

I was waving feebly, moaning.

I stumbled, fell.

Suddenly a few of us, companions for that minute – for ever companions in the eternity of that minute – fell into a shell-hole.

We had to take a breather, get our breath back. In order to start off again, only better. For we were going to start again.

We are still in that hole, we never left it . . .

———

. . . I looked at the captain, with his enormous moustache, shame-faced and hateful. This great fat oaf, who wanted to stick to his duty, in other words, just where he was. Oh, I had always detested my officers and teachers. What right has some mediocre individual to come and give me orders, vaunting the privilege of a hierarchy that one can always knock for six? He knows that I should be the one to give him orders, and that in fact I do. I remember one of my teachers, of below-average intelligence, who took advantage of his age and title to teach me what Plato was all about. He wasted no time in hating me, in telling me just what he thought, while I had to listen to him. The spite of petty officials, safe behind their counters, who keep you waiting for minutes on end.

You can put up with mediocrity when it is wholesale, but when you come down to the individual case, each individual humiliation, you begin to get angry. And your anger is never far from pushing you into the system yourself. It's only a step from there to the ambition to become a general, a minister, a dictator, to incite a revolution in order to have them all under your own heel. A step that I have always very carefully avoided taking. I understand you, Trotsky – and you too, Mussolini – but I do not approve of you.

This captain had no hold over me.

Suddenly, I sprang out of the hole. And I set off towards the wood.

A new charge, my very own charge. The charge that every proud man when the urge takes him . . .

I was running off, joyfully, through the whistling bullets.

Suddenly – bang, on the back of the neck!

Ah, I'm dying.

In the evening we returned with brands and torches. We returned to that cemetery which, through the charm of its Nordic inspiration, was an idyllic park, sheltering beneath its evenly spaced trees, beneath its smooth, soft grass, its deep, vital

537

melancholy. A little Valhalla, where the silent purity of manhood reigns.

We were searching for some tiny, chimerical object – an identity, a personality, a regimental number. With our torches, Jews and Christians alike, we were hunting for that talisman which is the corner-stone of European life, a name. Madame Pragen was searching for the name of Pragen. Madame Pragen, whose maiden name was Muller, was searching for the name of Pragen, as something that belonged to her. She wanted to exert her right to inscribe the name of Pragen here, to imprint this spot with the name Pragen – with the name that had left its indelible imprint on her, and that she had made her own quite fortuitously. She was not looking for her son.

Along with our torches we had brought picks and pliers. We had the money to do what we were doing and the necessary authorization. Madame Pragen had the *Légion d'honneur*. She would have liked to have obtained it for her son as well, but he had been killed too soon. And so we set about jostling all those people in the half-light, searching them, asking for their identity papers in the strange dampness of the night and the earth.

That mass of people sunk beneath the level of society, inter-twined in the common nobility of death, in the subtle chemistry of the grave – we were burgling them, we were trying to resurrect them, in the flickering light of the oil lamps borrowed from the local police station. We did two or three corpses the honour of taking them for Claude Pragen. We were petty and foolish, a bunch of amateur spiritualists.

I have always maintained that passion can render any moment sacred, lift it to a plane where it becomes eternal, but Madame Pragen, devoid of passion, exuded an odour of the ephemeral wherever she went. What do women do in society? These savages seize our amulets and give them new life at their breasts. But Madame Pragen's breasts were without warmth.

'There's no telling whether that's a Frenchman or a German,' someone muttered darkly, as the first coffin was opened.

Madame Pragen fingered her medal, as if to protect herself from that pathetic threat.

The last plank of wood cracked open. We all agreed that it was impossible to give the name of Claude Pragen to that horrible pulp. The mis-shapen shape was much too long.

'That's big enough to be a German,' said the same ridiculous voice, which seemed to be taking the part of a Greek chorus. As for me, it reminded me of Matigot, Matigot the butcher, the first one I had seen killed, stretched out on the ground, killed cleanly and neatly. How big he was, how surprised he had looked!

As I have said, our search was limited. Madame Pragen's money had been working for her for some considerable time in the district. The five graves that we were busy exploring were the only ones to have been marked out; each one contained a piece of doubtful evidence.

'You see, this one here can't be Claude, can't be Matigot, since he's wearing a gold bracelet,' someone might have said to me.

'But it's possible,' I might have replied, 'that Matigot, the good-looking butcher, was a queer or a pimp.'

They were breaking open the lid of another coffin.

'That's him,' said Madame Pragen.

In the middle of the pulp, a grin, one front tooth slightly shorter than the other, just as Claude had. The perfect set of circumstances for judicial error, on which all that impious pity was heaped.

'There's no point in looking at the others.'

'Just as Madame Pragen wishes,' replied the mayor, delighted at having got it over so quickly.

But no sooner had she said it than she decided that she wanted her money's worth, and got them to open up the other coffins. She did not stop to look at what was inside . . .

C. E. MONTAGUE

Charles Edward Montague (1867–1928). Born in London, and educated there and at Oxford. He enlisted in the army when war started in 1914, and was in France until his health failed. His not entirely anti-establishment book of social criticism, *Disenchantment*, from which the excerpts below are taken, was published in 1922. The interested reader may also consult *Fiery Particles* (1923).

Source: C. E. Montague, *Disenchantment*, London, Chatto & Windus, 1922.

TEDIUM, v

The men who could not shirk the choice of Hercules, for other people, were the doctors. The stay of every NCO or man at a base depot was on probation. Each had to go before a medical board soon after he came. It adjudged him either TB (Temporary Base) or PB (Permanent Base). If marked TB he went before the board again once a week, and each time he might be marked TB again, or, if his disablement was thought graver or more likely to last, PB; or he might be marked A (Active Service), and then he would join the next draft from home going up to his own battalion or another battalion of his regiment. When once a man was marked PB he only went before the board once a month, and each time he, too, might be marked either PB, TB, or A.

Chance relegated me once for some weeks to a base and gave me the job of marching parties of crocks, total and partial, real, half-real, and sham, across the sand dunes to the place where the faculty did its endeavour to sort them. A picture remains of a hut with a long table in it: two middle-aged army doctors sitting beyond it, like dons at a viva, and each of my party in turn taking his stand at attention, my side of the table, facing the board, like so many Oliver Twists. The presiding officer takes a manifest pride in knowing all the guile and subtlety of soldier-men. No taking *him* in – that is proclaimed in every look and tone. He has had several other parties before him today, and the lamp of his faith, never dazzling while these rites are on, has burnt low.

'Well, my man – cold feet, I suppose?' he begins, to the first of my lamentable party. As some practitioners are said to begin all treatments with a prefatory purge, so would this psychologist start with a good full dose of insult and watch the patient's reaction under the stimulus.

'No, sir, me 'eart's thrutched up,' says the examinee. Then, while the board perforates him from head to foot for some seconds with a basilisk stare of unbelief, he dribbles out at intervals, in a voice that bespeaks falling hope, such ineffective addenda as 'Can't get me sleep' and 'Not a smile in me.'

'Very picturesque, indeed,' says the senior expert in doubting. 'We'll see to that "thrutched" heart of yours. Kardiagraph case. Next man.'

The suspect, duly spat upon, slinks out. The next man takes his place at the table. The president gives him the Dogberry eye that means: 'Masters, it is proved already that you are little better than false knaves; and it will go near to be thought so shortly.' What he says is: 'Another old hospital bird? Eh? Now, hadn't you better get back to work before you're in trouble?'

The target of this consputation is almost convinced by its force that he must be guilty of something, if only he knew what it was. Still, he repeats authority's last diagnosis as well as he can: 'Mine's Arthuritic rheumatism, sir. *An'* piles.'

'Fall out and strip. Next man.' While the next is taking his stand the presiding M O has been making a note, and does not look up before saying 'Well, what's the matter with *you* – besides rheumatism?'

'No rheumatism, sir. And nothing else.' The voice is as stiff as it dares.

The presiding M O seems taken aback. Why, here is a fellow not playing up to him! Making a nasty break in the long line of cases that fed his darling cynicism so well! Flat burglary as ever was committed. The second member of the board comes to life and begins in a tone that savours of dissatisfaction: 'Well, you're the first man –'

'I'm an NCO, sir.' The young lance-sergeant's voice is again about as stiff as is safe. Quite safe, though, this time. For the presiding M O is a Regular. Verbal points of military correctitude are the law and the prophets to him. He cannot be wholly sorry when junior colleagues, temporary commissioners, slip up on even the least of these shreds of orange-peel. Like Susan Nipper, he knows his place – 'me being a permanency' – and thinks that 'temporaries' ought to know theirs. So he amends the outsider's false start to: 'You're the first NCO or man who has come before us this morning and not said he had rheumatism.'

The sergeant, whom I have known for some days as a choleric body, holds his tongue, having special reasons just now not to risk a court martial. 'Well,' the president snaps as if in resentment of this self-control, 'what *is* the matter with you?'

'Fit as can be, sir.'

'What are you doing down here, then, away from your unit?'

'Obeying orders of Medical Board, sir. No. 8 General Hospital, 8 December.'

'Not sorry, either, I daresay,' the president mutters, wobbling back towards his first line of approach to the business. 'Not very keen to go back up the line, sergeant, eh?'

'It's all I want, sir, thank you.' The sergeant puts powerful brakes on his tongue and says only that. But he has sadly disconcerted the faculty. A major with twenty years' service has cast himself for the fine sombre part of recording angel to note all the cowardice and mendacity that he can. And here is a minor actor forgetting his part and putting everything out. From where I am keeping a wooden face near the door I see opposition arising in the heart of the outraged psychologist beyond the table.

A sound professional instinct reinforces the personal one. Whenever a soldier goes before a medical board it is soon clear that he wants to be thought either less fit than he is or more fit. The doctor's first impulse, as soon as he sees which way the man's wishes tend, is to lean towards the other. And this, in due measure, is just. We all understate or overstate symptoms to our own family doctors according to what we fear or desire. The doctor rightly tries to detect the disturbing force in the patient's mind, and to discount for it duly – just like 'laying-off' for a side-wind in shooting. So now the president sees light again. The board is now out to find the lance-sergeant a crock. 'Hold out your wrist,' says the senior member. The pulse is jealously felt.

'Rotten!' the senior member says to the junior. Then, penetratingly, to the sergeant: 'What's that cicatrice you've got on the back of your hand? Both hands! Show me here.'

Two spongy, purplish-red pads of new flesh are inspected.

'Burns, scarcely healed!' says the president wrathfully. 'Skin just the strength of wet tissue-paper! Man alive, you've a bracelet of ulcers all round your wrists. Never wash, eh?' When liquid fire flayed a man's hands to the sleeve, but not further, the skin was apt to break out, as he recovered, in small, deep boils about the frontier of the new skin and the old. The sergeant does not answer. He wants no capital punishment under the Army Act.

'Man's an absolute wreck,' says the major. 'Debility, wounds imperfectly healed, blood-poisoning likely. Not fit for the line for two months to come. P B – eh?' he turns to his junior.

'That's what *I* should say, sir,' the junior concurs, in a tone of desperate independence.

'Next man,' says the major. Before the lance-sergeant has quite stalked to the door the major calls after him 'Sergeant!'

'Sir?' says the sergeant, furious and red but contained.

'You're a damned good man, but it won't do,' says the major. 'Good luck to you!' Great are the forces of decent human relentment after a hearty let-out with the temper.

The inquisition proceeds, still on that Baconian principle of finding out which is a man's special bent and then bending the twig pretty hard in the other direction; still, too, with the dry light of reason a little suffused, as Bacon would say, with the humours of the affections, of vanity, ill-temper and impatience. Nearly everybody is morally weary. Most of the men inspected have outlived the first profuse impulse to court more of bodily risk than authority expressly orders. Most of the doctors, living here in the distant rear of the war, have outlived their first generous belief in an almost universally high *moral* among the men. In the training-camps in 1914 the safe working presumption about any unknown man was that he only wanted to get at the enemy as soon as he could. Now the working presumption, the starting hypothesis, is that a man wants to stay in, out of the rain, as long as you let him. Faith has fallen lame; generosity flags; there has entered into the soul as well as the body the malady known to athletes as staleness.

THE OLD AGE OF THE WAR, IV

Sir Douglas Haig came to Cologne when we had been there a few days. On the grandiose bridge over the Rhine he made a short speech to a few of us. Most of it sounded as if the thing were a job he had got to get through with, and did not much care for. Perhaps the speech, like those of other great men who wisely hate making speeches, had been written for him by somebody else. But once he looked up from the paper and put in some words which I felt sure were his own; 'I only hope that, now we have won, we shall not lose our heads, as the Germans did after 1870. It has brought them to this.' He looked at the gigantic mounted statue of the Kaiser overhead, a thing crying out in its pride for fire from heaven to fall and consume it, and at the homely, squat British sentry moving below on his post. I think the speech was reported. But none of our foremen at home took any notice of it at all. They knew a trick worth two of Haig's. They were as moonstruck as any victorious Prussian.

So we had failed – had won the fight and lost the prize; the garland of the war was withered before it was gained. The lost years, the broken youth, the dead friends, the women's over-shadowed lives at home, the agony and bloody sweat – all had gone to darken the stains which most of us had thought to scour out of the world that our children would live in. Many men felt, and said to each other, that they had been fooled. They had believed that their country was backing them. They had thought, as they marched into Germany, 'Now we shall show old Fritz how you treat a man when you've thrashed him.' They would let him into the English secret, the tip that the power and glory are not to the bully. As some of them looked at the melancholy performance which followed, our press and our politicians parading at Paris in moral *Pickelhauben* and doing the Prussianist goose-step by way of *pas de triomphe*, they could not but say in dismay to themselves: 'This is our doing. We cannot wish the war unwon, and yet – if we had shirked, poor old England, for all we know, might not have come to this pass. So we come home draggle-tailed, sick of the mess that we were unwittingly helping to make when we tried to do well.'

H. M. TOMLINSON

Henry Major Tomlinson (1873–1958). Born in East London, he began work in a shipping office and became intimately acquainted with the Thames-side dockland. He was a war correspondent in Flanders and France. This experience, as well as his early life in London, is reflected in his novel *All Our Yesterdays*. Edmund Blunden, who felt that Tomlinson wrote 'the best prose in England now', recalls that his reports from Flanders were attacked on the grounds that they were 'too human' and that he returned to England to become literary editor of the *Nation*. His 'A Footnote to the War Books' published in *Out of Soundings* in 1931 contains interesting judgements on Montague, Duhamel, Zweig, Mottram, Blunden and Owen (*qq.v.*). The excerpts below begin as one of Tomlinson's main characters, Charley Bolt, on his way from Dublin to London, reads of the growing tension in Europe. Jean Jaurès was the French socialist leader who had argued against the war; he was assassinated in a Paris restaurant in July 1914.

Source: H. M. Tomlinson, *All Our Yesterdays*, London, William Heinemann, 1930.

... The opening of that paper was as startling to Charley as the loosing of a maniacal yell at his ear. The morning broke into a senseless clangour, as with the cries of lunatics in multitudes terrified and contentious, and the beating of brass and iron. The magnified headlines bawled the excitement of the gathering of millions of armed men, with the alarms of Paris, Berlin, London, Brussels, and St Petersburg. He could hear under it all, in paragraphs more obscure, the protesting cries of the workers in the capitals; though the alarm of Berlin was cut short in its record, as though stifled. It was consternation smothered before it was articulate. And, he then noticed, as though it were a symbolic act, the forewarning of what now would be done in darkness, that the benign and enlightening mind of Jean Jaurès had been put out. Peace, sitting at its dinner in its accustomed seat, had been shot through the head by a madman. Peace was dead ...

... The uncomfortable and stringy quality of the gentleman; own up, pay up, and shut up! Our train came to a stand in a junction. Another train was there, composed of cattle trucks like our own, though not, like ours, bearing a burden of the completely living. I gave it no attention till Jim frowned in wonder, and then dropped hurriedly to the ground. A French soldier, trailing a leg with its foot improperly reversed, was escaping from the other train on his hands and knees across the tracks towards us. His twisted mouth was slavering; he made Bedlamite noises when there was an attempt to get him to safety. That train bore a load of battle wreckage, but nothing was near to give it ease. These wounded men had been travelling for two days, we heard, and were not there yet, wherever it was they were going, if that were known. The relentless sun made a glaring desert of the steel lines and the gravel, and the dying men waited in the heavy heat for whatever their country would do with their last hours. They stank. They drew the blow-flies. Their clothes were glued to them with ordure and dried blood. One man on his back near a door, his face that of a child in its pallor, had a darkened hole in his thigh, stuck full of floor rubbish and straws. He opened his eyes once to us in the sunlight, and shut them again. Beside him were two of his field-grey enemies, but he and they were reconciled. One was a boy who stared at the roof, and he was alive, for he blinked at a fly; the other was his senior, with a blond beard, but he had found peace ...

... There Langham was. 'Are we downhearted?' he cried. He beamed on Maynard. 'Haven't you just come across? You're the very man I want to see. Come over here. What about this great victory? Are we being lied to as usual? This is my brother. He is going over to France today to save souls; isn't that so, Francis?'

His brother did not reply, but gravely disapproved. The Reverend Francis Langham might have been in the dress of a British officer, to a careless inspection, except for the collar he was wearing. His uniform was so very new that his leathery complexion of aged and meditating sorrow appeared to be a mistake in his embellishment. Soon, and with easy authority, he rejected a few of Maynard's more pointed allusions to the things to be seen in France as of little consequence. They were hardly relevant to the great issue. Maynard turned sharply upon him.

'Then you don't think we need bother about this casual slaughter?'

'No. Isn't there something more important than that?'

'And you are going to attend to it?'

The new chaplain was silent. It could be inferred that so much was manifest. He broke bread, and continued seriously to chew.

His brother laughed uneasily. 'Francis really is for salvation. We're only for death. He knows their souls cannot die, so nothing can happen to them, if they are Christian soldiers. Isn't that so, Francis? That's all right,' continued the elder Langham cheerfully to us. 'We can't lose this war if we can only get men into it like my brother.' He patted him on the back. 'The more we have killed, the more intercessors we shall have with God . . .'

———

. . . The ugly but intermittent sound of unseen bodies lumbering through the air was more frequent when we reached another group of buildings, scattered among trees at a road crossing. The trees were motionless in the sleeping afternoon. The walls of one of the barns, a structure so weathered that its rufous brickwork had the surface of crumbling grey stone, were riven, and the raw edges of the gaps were bright red. From somewhere came a noise which might have been made by an idle boy rattling a stick along a fence. An officer, to my surprise, then appeared at the door of a barn I had thought was empty. 'Come in,' he urged us. 'They spray that road with a machine-gun. Can't you hear it?' But for that distant rattling the silence was so deep that I imagined I could hear a frog I saw flopping across the road. A pair of swallows were circling about, and their familiar celerity and accuracy, as they pitched on their nest built under the eaves of a house on the point of collapse, had been regarded by me in confidence as tokens of the world I used to know.

Under the rafters of that partially dismantled barn was a man who laughed when he saw me. His amusement was caused, most likely, by my unexpected appearance, which he had to take as another absurd feature in a fantasy. He himself, an oriental scholar, as a soldier in that place, was not easily believable. He laughed again because his quizzical temper, I suppose, thoroughly relished the waywardness of this coincidence.

'What brings you here? Have you gone potty, too?' he asked.

He gossiped disjointedly about our circumstances. 'You may have noticed there is a war on up here, but who is making it, except ourselves, beats me. It's between us and the spooks, I think. You haven't noticed any so-called Germans hanging about, have you? I haven't seen one yet' – he flinched and grimaced at an explosion outside – 'but that sort of thing all day has to be accounted for.'

We left that barn . . .

———

. . . 'Presently he rolled up, this French johnny – a big fellow, with a tummy on him, in a blue uniform and brown bulging gaiters. Behind him was a slender young officer, very stiff and correct. The French colonel had one of those hunting horns round his shoulder – you know the sort of thing – you see it in comic prints of French sportsmen – a curly trumpet – they go out after partridge with it, don't they? Well, he didn't take that trumpet off him. Only his cap. His bald head was pale, but his big round face was rosy and very happy, with lots of chin, and a long grizzled moustache which would have been straight and fierce if he hadn't laughed so much. He did laugh. He stamped with one foot, and patted his tummy with both hands, and laughed very free and hearty, and then hummed and pulled out his moustache. A cheery card. But his young officer was prim. He didn't laugh at anything. Never said a word. Smiled faintly and loftily when spoken to. "Yes," he said. Only that. He was supercilious. Thought we were rather a bore, I believe.

'Not a word did they give us about the object of their visit – just rich laughter from the colonel over nothing in particular. We began dinner. The French colonel wore his hunting horn. Of course, we pretended not to see the thing – sort of behaved as though we were used to that at dinner – custom of the country, you know. The young officer, he hardly looked up, or if he did it was only to screw his eyes at the wall over the head of the man opposite. That chap ate our food as if he had to do it. Duty was duty, and we were only British, and didn't know any better.

'But his colonel was all right. He was different. He enjoyed himself – we happened to have a Burgundy of a good year – and our fellows played up to him for the good of the regiment. After one burst of merriment, which was so hearty that we all joined in, that big Frenchman rose, put one foot on his chair, and tootled his hunting horn.

'Not likely we took any notice of it. Not likely. Too well-trained. Pretended we heard nothing. The young Frenchman, he took no notice of it. I supposed this tootling might be the custom of the regiment of our visitors, an ancient right won in battle. It was the proper thing for the colonel of that regiment to do – blow his blessed horn at intervals during dinner. He had to maintain a link with the glorious past.

'He was a lusty chap, our important guest. Full of beans and funny stories. At the end of a cheery one, when he'd got us all going, he'd rise from his chair, and solemnly let go a tantara. Our servants were good lads – they did seem a bit surprised, but they never laughed. As for our own old man, he was so polite that he might have been as deaf to that hunting horn as the young French officer.

'After dinner the fun got very lively. I must say our youngsters thoroughly enjoyed this Gascon, who certainly was enjoying himself. He approved our whisky. Then he got into a sentimental mood; he mentioned his wife. Ah! He would show why France would fight, gentlemen, till not a German was this side of the Rhine; that or death. He became serious. Gentlemen, you shall observe this. He put a hand inside his tunic, and tugged at what I thought was a pack of cards. But the pack was tight, and he tugged too hard. The cards shot across the table. Well, I was a bit shocked. I'll admit it. Photographs of women! And some of them! You never saw such a collection of bosoms and behinds. Do you think that fine old fellow was embarrassed? Not a scrap. It was the sort of thing that might happen to any good man, if he were clumsy with his pocket-book. He began to sort them, coolly and indifferently, sort of shuffling the pack, perhaps looking for the queen of hearts – I dunno.

'Then for the first time that evening the severe young Frenchman condescended to take an interest in what was going on. He rose, and leaned over the table, intently inspecting the pictorial assortment of ladies. His curiosity was genuine. Suddenly he pointed sharply at a photograph. He spoke at last. "That is my wife," he said to his colonel.

'He punched his colonel in the eye. The big fellow collided with a chair behind him, and over it went, and so did he, with a frightful banging of brassware on the stone floor. Our own colonel was horrified. We were all alarmed. We stared at one another. What happened when a French officer punched his colonel in the eye? What ought we to do when they were our guests? There's nothing in the King's Regulations about that, is there?

'One of our fellows was assisting the jolly Frenchman to his feet, but he sprang up, shook with laughter as he pulled his tunic straight, and went out into the yard. Outside, we heard him play a bold fanfare on his horn – a salute to all stags, I suppose. He was soon back.

'As he entered he was met by his junior. They embraced each other, and kissed . . .'

———

. . . 'It is likely that the country whose civilian riff-raff gets the most grievous hacking about of its jolly expectations loses the war.'

'I hope nobody loses it,' commented a young officer cheerfully, a major and a stranger to me, whose lack of decorative colour and honours suggested that he belonged to the trenches.

'Nobody?' asked the general, turning to him mystified. 'One side must win?'

'I suppose so, sir, and I hope it's us. But sometimes I think it would be better if nobody won it. It's sure to be a beastly business if one side can get glorious over victory. I think it would be nicer if the whole war jammed into a complete silly stark foozle. That would give everybody who wasn't dead a chance to sort it over in a sensible way.'

Most of the poised cocktails shook in amused approval of the idea. Even the general smiled grimly, as though never before had he glanced in that direction, but now could make out there an item of remote and impossible good sense . . .

———

. . . But in France we had grown used to opinions which, had they been exposed carelessly in daylight to civilians at home, might have caused alarms from police whistles. London had not arrived at the point where we were; not yet. It no longer shocked us to see Law and Religion derelict, as were other honoured things, on the flood which had left traditional bearings below the horizon of 1914. The talk at most mess-tables in France wandered freely and with slight deference even to the presence of august military rank. Generals were generals, with the privileges due to their degree, yet even they shared the common lot of a day wherein the wreckage of Society's moral safeguards was like the policeman's battered helmet in the gutter the morning after the joy of Mafeking night. We were looking for clues to a new order, if there were any, because a new order might not be easy to find since most of Europe's younger men had a duty, as good soldiers, to deride and destroy all that priest and schoolmaster had once advised them was of divine ordination. Our elders, in the desperation of their fears, had allowed youth to see how much society had ever deserved its respect and fidelity. That peep, as into the interior of a hitherto revered and tabooed family sarcophagus, made even the enemy's machine-guns the less terrible to face. Before the last shot was fired, ancient thrones and altars would be tottering through the work of worms unsuspected. We already knew, out there, that we must begin anew, but nobody knew where, nor with what.

The deep interest of those strange days, in which the value of so much had gravely altered, and even old commonplaces were hardly recognizable, swept our table. The talk was eager, as though we were alert to a new time in which suffering had become an honour, and abhorrence of evil a joke. It surprised me that Langham's banter, springing as it did from a cunning man's acquaintance with news withheld from vulgar eyes, though still a pleasant addition to a dinner-table, was quite alien now, with its London origin, in the common air of France. He was merrily unconscious of it. He did not know he had become inapplicable. The most miserable example of a Hun prisoner in a barbed-wire enclosure was more akin to some of us at that table, than that sprightly and well-informed administrator fresh from Whitehall. The general, it was evident, listened to him at first in hard-featured doubt, for Langham was a clever Radical, and then in surprised approval . . .

HUMPHREY COBB

Humphrey Cobb (1899–1944). Born in Florence of American parents, and educated in the US. Served in France with the Canadian forces in the war. Wounded and gassed. His experiences on the Western Front gave him the basic material for *Paths of Glory* (1935), from which the excerpt below is taken. A film of the same title, based on Cobb's novel, was made in 1957. Langlois and two other men are chosen at random to face summary court martial *pour encourager les autres* after an attack on the German lines has failed. Langlois writes home before his execution. Cobb notes that such events did happen. Men were posthumously exonerated and their widows awarded damages of between 7 cents and 1 franc in 1934; the insult, implicit in these awards was, presumably, to ensure that the 'others' remained encouraged.

Source: Humphrey Cobb, *Paths of Glory*, London, William Heinemann, 1935; Bath, Cedric Chivers, 1974.

LANGLOIS'S LETTER

At the front

My darling wife,

How can I begin to tell you of what has happened to me? It is too cruel, but when you read this letter I shall be dead, fallen under the bullets of a French firing-squad. I am bewildered and so lonely. You must forgive my incoherence. Thoughts and feelings rush in upon me so fast they carry me away.

If Sergeant Picard or Captain Étienne should ever come to you, you can believe them. They were friends, and Picard is the priest who promises to see that you will get this letter. Colonel Dax, too, I think was a friend, though a remote one. They will tell you how it was done. Briefly, this is what happened. We failed to take our objectives in an attack this morning. It seems ages ago now. It was not our fault. No human being could have advanced through that fire. Somebody wanted some examples made, and I am one of them. There are two others besides myself. We have been court-martialled and we're going to be shot in the morning. We were charged with cowardice and the court martial was a steam-roller. I was not a coward, I swear it to you. But they want examples. I don't say I wasn't afraid. There's no man who hasn't been afraid.

Oh, my darling, dearest one. Words, words, how pitifully they fail me. The president of the court was a Colonel Labouchère, and his name sounds like what he was, a butcher, though I suppose he thought he was doing his duty.

The speed of time appals me. At any moment now I may hear the tread of the guards come to take us out. No, that is not true. It is still night and they won't shoot us till daylight. They've got to have light to take aim by. It is so difficult to remain honest, especially in a time of crisis. What I mean is that I feel as if they might come at any minute. In truth, I have some hours left to live. They will go so slowly, they will go so fast. Already I feel numb inside, as if my intestines were filled with lead. They will be, soon enough. Forgive the cheap and cruel sarcasm. Perhaps in writing to you I may get some control over myself. I shall try not to inflict the pain of my heart on yours for, by the time you learn of it, mine will be all over. I never knew that time could exert such a terrific pressure.

What will become of you, my dearest, what will become of that new life which must already be stirring within your body, that body that I loved so much and that I'll never see again? But it is not of your body that I think now. Already half disembodied myself, I have lost all capacity for sensuality. On the other hand, my mind feels intensified to a point which is nearer to bursting. My yearning for you is an anguish which I can hardly bear. Every fibre of me is straining to you in a pitiful, hopeless attempt to bring you to me so that we might comfort each other. But I am alone, and my only means of communication is to leave you this sorrowful letter to read after I am gone.

That, I think, is the brutality of death – sudden incommunicability. Then rage rises in me and I wonder if I shall go mad. Then I feel the need of telling life what I think of it, now that I am to be parted from it. Then I realize the futility of that and my rage subsides and I float out for a while on a serene ocean of tolerance and resignation. I have just done so, and for twenty minutes before writing this present sentence, I didn't write anything. I was in a sort of trance, I think. I watched Didier labouring over his letter. I watched Férol, lying in his corner, smoking peacefully as if he had all time before him. Well, he has, at that, although he doesn't seem to realize the form it will take. I envy him his fatalism. I always thought I had it too, but his kind of fatalism seems to work, mine doesn't.

Now, suddenly, the bitterness returns to me. It is brought back this time by the sight of a cockroach which is exploring the cracks in the guard-room floor. That cockroach will be alive, exploring as he has always done, when I am dead. That cockroach will have a communicability with you which I, your husband, am being robbed of – the communicability which is life.

Only yesterday, before the attack, I was talking with the men. I said that I was not afraid to die, only of being killed. That was true, and it still is, though I know that I can face the firing-squad without weakening. But I have learnt now that fear of an appointment with death is a real and terrible thing. And the thought of you, my dearest one, is the only one which gives me strength to live through these hours.

The injustice of this to me is something so obvious that I have no desire to enlarge upon it. Of course, I am in a state of violent rebellion against it. But it is the injustice to you that throws me into a frenzy, if I allow myself to dwell upon it. Here we are, two human beings who have never harmed anybody. We love each other and we have constructed, from two lives, one life together, one which is ours, which is wholly of ourselves, which is our most precious possession, a beautiful, satisfying thing, intangible but more real more necessary than anything else in life. We have applied our effort and intelligence to building, expanding, and keeping the structure in repair. Somebody suddenly steps in, not caring, not even knowing who we are, and in an instant has reduced our utterly private relationship to a horrible ruin, mangled and bleeding and aching with pain.

Sweet and adored other part of myself. I ramble on. I do not, I cannot say a half of what I feel or mean. If we could be in each other's arms, if we could look into each other's eyes, that is all the communication that would be necessary. But I cannot bring myself to end this letter. It is the only means I have of talking to you. When I stop, as I shall have to, the silence, for all I know, will be everlasting. Do you blame me for lingering over a conversation which may never be resumed? Do you blame me for trying to delay a parting which will be absolute? Do you blame me for trying to make my inarticulateness articulate?

I love you so.

I was drawn by lot. The sergeant-major bungled the drawing, so it had to be made again. It was on the second drawing that I was chosen. Just a confusion about numbers, and here we are, you and I, put to the torture. I don't try to understand it.

Please, please, get a lawyer and have my case investigated. Your father will help you. Get all the influence you can, borrow money if necessary, carry it to the highest court, to the President himself. See that my murderers pay the penalty of murder. I have no forgiveness in my heart for them, whoever they are, only revenge, a deep desire for revenge which I hand on to you as a duty which you must fulfil.

How I love you, my only one. The pocket-book you gave me is in my hand. I touch it. It is something you have touched. It will be sent to you. I kiss it all over, a sad attempt to communicate some kisses to you. Poor, worn, greasy little piece of leather. What a surge of love pours from me upon this forlorn object, the only tragic, personal link I have with you. Tears rise and I cannot hold them back. They pour upon the pocket-book, make it more limp and ugly than ever. How glad I am I didn't bring that photograph of you. Do you remember, when you gave it to me, how I wept because it was so lovely and your expression was so sad. It would kill me to have it here now, and yet, if I did, I couldn't keep my eyes off it.

The bounds of my soul seem to be bursting. I am choking with grief and longing. Férol goes on smoking. Didier has finished his letter and I must tear myself from mine, too, so that the thought of you shall not weaken me.

Goodbye, my dearest, dearest one, my darling wife. Have courage. Time will help you. I have control over myself now. I am no longer afraid. I shall face the French bullets like a Frenchman. The priest has just come back. How I love you, how I need you. Dearest, I have always loved you, always needed you. You have always satisfied me in every way. Goodbye, goodbye. I don't care what our child is now. I think I hope it will be a boy, for your suffering when you read this letter will be far greater than mine when I wrote it. All my love is for you alone . . .

LAURENCE STALLINGS

Laurence Stallings (1894–1968). Born in Georgia. Became a captain in the Marines. Like the hero of his novel, *Plumes*, he volunteered eagerly for the war and had a leg amputated after distinguished service. Like Richard Plume he was disillusioned and wrote several anti-war books including *The First World War* (1933), a collection of photographs with a commentary. Richard Plume leaves for the war not knowing that his wife, Esme, is pregnant. He returns after his injury to try to make sense of his own life and to understand post-war American attitudes.

Source: Laurence Stallings, *Plumes*, New York, Harcourt Brace, 1924.

. . . Esme Plume, wife of Richard, recalls to this day the morning her husband left for overseas. There had been a rally that morning at chapel, for Richard was resigning his instructorship in biology. Esme sat well back in the gallery, with not a tear in her eyes. Esme's husband was going to war, and Esme's colleagues were glad he was going. Not that they were jealous of him. The boy only held a $1,800-a-year instructorship. Esme would have ventured that they liked her husband personally, but they felt that Richard's going gave them a glad sense of sharing in a very noble thing.

'If the Lord has chosen, in His infinite mercy and wisdom, to call one of us to the flag,' said Dean Baylor, sonorously, 'it is fit that Richard Plume should be called. He is strong, he is worthy, he is young.'

Esme, though she was very unhappy, smiled at this deification of Richard's impulsiveness. Dean Baylor, who was professor of Old Testament literature, thought her face drawn in pain. 'God cherish,' the Dean continued, 'and keep his little wife, and return him safely to her.' Dean Baylor had been at Appomattox.

The gentlemen of the faculty, Esme observed, could not fix their eyes upon her. They stared in the sun-pierced gloom of the chapel as so many preachers of the gospel immemorialized upon the festooned walls in dull, full-length oils. 'Those dreadful oils,'

Esme reflected. Mrs Richard Plume noted, too, that her husband was extremely uncomfortable. The boots upon which he poured gallons of polishing cream shone cheap and glossy when they rested in a window's shafted light. He had detested this ceremony, and Esme had made him come. 'It will injure father's feelings if you don't, Richard . . .' The president of the student body was speaking now . . . 'Professor Richard Plume's great example to us . . .'

Esme's lips curled. That was why she had insisted that he attend the chapel ceremony . . . To shame those yellow students. 'Do you think,' she wanted to scream, 'that I want him to go? He is only a child. It would ruin his life if he didn't go. If he fought a draft board he'd never get over it. I'm not proud of him, you fools.'

They were singing 'Onward Christian Soldiers' and Richard was almost running as he moved up the aisle. She arose to join her husband. He was such a child. He was so young. He was so thin. She loved him . . .

———

Esme for the first time was conscious of strain, when the orderly motioned for her to follow him. 'Sorry y'have to wait, Miz Plume,' he said, without taking the cigarette from his mouth or the hands from the pockets of his dirty white jacket, 'but they were dressing the lieutenant.'

'Did they give him some uniforms?' she said.

'No, lady,' said the orderly, 'I mean they were dressing his wounds.' Christ! These officers' wives were dumb.

Esme grasped Dickie, who had become the embodiment of a bed of wild violets. Her white cuffs shone with starching. She tried to powder Dickie's nose again, but the orderly moved too quickly down the long, covered corridors. She passed two men in white caps, short veils, overall jumpers and flannel buskins, who wheeled a cart on which a blanket covered a log that reeked of nitrous oxide and gave off a faint, droning sound. Glass doors, swirling past, gave paneled vistas of a forest of white beds with high, rough wood trellises reared above them, on which were trained human legs and arms to grow again. Unshaven men in bathrobes struggled with impetuously propelled wheelchairs. Iodine in a thousand uncanny smells came to the mother's nose and she sickened, as one does when an odor recalls a scene in sculptured clarity. Dickie almost slipped from her arms as she remembered the ether cone of his birth night. She would not relinquish the baby to the orderly. She would bear him to Richard, and he should first see them thus.

'Is Lieutenant Plume in a private room?' she asked the orderly, who was gallantly making faces at Dickie to amuse him while she staggered under the load.

'Oh, no lady. Y'have to be a colonel to get a room in this dump.'

Esme was outraged. She was about to say so. The orderly checked up at a ward door. Esme's feet groped. She gasped and followed the soldier down the aisle, the blood rushing to her cheeks. 'How will he look . . . how will I look to him . . .?' Her legs trembled. She staggered.

'Here,' said the soldier in the dirty white coat, taking Dickie from her. Esme looked.

A white iron bed and from its center a huge swathed leg reared upward toward two wooden transversals over which were cords, pulleys, sand bags. Esme's heart shrunk to a dry pod, and her knees broke.

A man she had never seen before lay flat upon his back, his head turned towards her, and his eyes closed more from weariness than pain. The thin, acrid smell of chlorine fouled the air, and many red rubber tubes ran from an enameled reservoir overhead to the covers. The sick man's faded red hair was straggly and the back of his head was rubbed more bald than Dickie's from moving upon a thousand pillows. The face was immobile, hawk-like, dead putty white, and the mouth was drawn, the mouth of a man about to be flogged. On a cradle-like chest hung the silver miniature locket she had, thousands of centuries past, given Richard Plume. The man on the bed opened Richard's eyes. She sank down and put her hot, shaken cheek to his dry parchment face. He raised two bony arms, the gown-sleeves tumbling back unimpeded past the peeling, yellowed skin of a fevered Ivanhoe. Esme wept as they circled her, trembling, and with no pressure. The orderly set Dickie down by the wounded man's free shoulder. The baby caught at a sandbag and swung it, drolly.

Richard Plume felt the cheek against his. He was weak, and at the odor of her skin so buoyant his pulse jumped as though he were a gas patient under an oxygen bell. Every wound in his body, and there were seven, was painted with a cool liquid fire. He could have cried out with the anguished happiness of the contact from his cheek. For six months he had lain thus, days and nights, sane and insane, awaiting this consummation of agony. Somewhere in the dim centers of his twisted, wrenched brain he knew the pain that lay ahead for her and for himself. But the prospect was dwarfed and shrunken in the realization of her past sufferings. She had no words for him. There were no words. She knew that he was realizing her own agony, as she was immersed in his. They clung thus and went shares in sufferings.

The baby rolled its rounded, padded little bottom over upon his shoulder. A creator beheld his son. 'Oh, Esme,' a voice cried in the wilderness of white bed, 'God forgive me for my folly.'

HERBERT SULZBACH

Herbert Sulzbach (1894–1985). Volunteered in 1914 and served until 1918. The diary entries below are from 1918. Germany's defeat is recorded without exaggerated nationalism or self-pity. In 1937, two years after publication, Sulzbach had to leave Germany because of his Jewish origins. He served in the British army in the Second World War and helped to re-educate German prisoners of war. He worked till the age of eighty-six in the German embassy in London and broadcast about his experiences on BBC Radio in 1983. Sulzbach recalls the battle of Sedan (1 September 1870), when the German army inflicted a heavy defeat on the French; nearly 100,000 were killed or wounded or surrendered.

Source: Herbert Sulzbach, *With the German Guns, Fifty Months on the Western Front, 1914–1918*, (translated from *Zwei lebende Mauern*, Berlin, Bernard & Graef, 1935, by Richard Thonger), London, Frederick Warne, 1981.

1918, THE ST QUENTIN OFFENSIVE

3 March

The final peace treaty has been signed with Russia. Our conditions are hard and severe, but our quite exceptional victories entitle us to demand these, since our troops are nearly in Petersburg, and further over on the southern front, Kiev has been occupied, while in the last week we have captured the following men and items of equipment: 6,800 officers, 54,000 men, 2,400 guns, 5,000 machine-guns, 8,000 railway trucks, 8,000 locomotives, 128,000 rifles, and 2 million rounds of artillery ammunition. Yes, there is still some justice left, and the state which was first to start mass murder in 1914 has now, with all its missions, been finally overthrown. Courland, Livonia and Estonia are ours, and Finland and the Ukraine have become independent states. While on this subject I recall the words of a song, and if I mention it here, I do so because many Germans do not themselves realize to what extent France, which is always putting the blame for the World War on to us, has been agitating for decades, preaching revenge for Sedan in 1870. The song I remember was one I heard on my journey to the North African colonies in 1913; its chorus ran: '*Alors, petit soldat de la république, préparez-vous pour le combat!*' ('Now, little soldier of the Republic, prepare for the battle!'). You can hardly imagine the hullabaloo and general enthusiasm at the end of the song. This event is highly significant in proving the agitation for a war of revenge, which thus reached right into the furthest corners of the French colonies . . .

———

1918, THE END

11 November, 1918

The order arrived in the morning:

Hostilities will cease as from 12 noon today.

This was the order which I had to read out to my men.

The war is over . . . How we looked forward to *this* moment; how we used to picture it as the most splendid event of our lives; and here we are now, humbled, our souls torn and bleeding, and know that we've surrendered. Germany has surrendered to the Entente!

Apart from the Kaiser and the Crown Prince, all ruling princes of the German Federation have abdicated. Our Kaiser has transferred all his powers over the German Army to General-Field-Marshal von Hindenburg. Hindenburg is staying, out of love for his soldiers, who have achieved such an endless number of great deeds in four years and four months. In fourteen days we must have evacuated the entire occupied area up to the Rhine, and this means that the millions of men, with all the huge stores of equipment and supplies held in the rear, must be transported back or abandoned to the enemy.

A few pages back I copied out Ebert's appeal for peace. Hindenburg warns his comrades:

You did not forget your Field-Marshal in battle – and from now on I rely on you in the same way!

It is a great, a really great, achievement, and a marvellous piece of self-control, that Hindenburg is not deserting us.

This very day I find a little poem in a magazine, entitled *Dem*

Letzten – 'To the Last Man'. It is for the last man who falls for his Fatherland. The last three lines read:

> *Er, der das Todestor verriegelt*
> *mit seinem Tod den Frieden siegelt,*
> *in Auserwählter wird er sein . . .*

> He who has locked the gates of Death
> And sealed the peace with blood and breath,
> He shall be one of the chosen . . .

General von Hutier warns his 18th Army to expect a feeling of sadness, bitter tears in fact, when reading the words: 'Even if the war is lost . . . you can be proud of your achievements!'

Then, in an order of some length, he writes:

> Undefeated by the enemy but forced to this by external circumstances, we have to abandon the territory which we occupied after so fierce a contest. Even if the armistice conditions prescribed by the enemy constitute a monstrous hardship for our nation, we can nevertheless march back to our beloved country with heads held high.

He goes on to utter a warning that order and discipline must be preserved, especially so that this great army's ration supplies should not be held up. He reminds us that feeding a single army for one day requires five ration trains and 600 head of cattle. He reminds us further that four armies are waiting along one railway track beyond Namur, that therefore at least twenty ration trains have to pull in if we are to be properly fed, so no interruptions in the railway service must be allowed to occur; further, that large numbers of the land forces will have to march home on foot. His appeal ends with the words:

> Keep the German army's bright shield of honour clean to the last, and then, in spite of the unhappy way this war has ended, you will be able to look back full of pride, to the very end of your days, upon your heroic deeds.

The armistice conditions, which are not yet official, are supposed to be: surrender of 5,000 guns and all our U-Boats; release of all prisoners; occupation of Western Germany as far as the Rhine. – That would be more than a humiliated nation can bear.

Whereas our men still have the old front-line spirit in them, further to the rear one comes across undisciplined hordes.

What is this dispute over our oath to the colours really about?

I took my oath to the black, white and red colours and to the Kaiser. But Ebert rightly says that at the present time we should disregard the details of our oath, continue to do our duty, and protect the Fatherland from destruction.

Shop stewards' committees are now being formed in all units, each consisting of one officer, one NCO and two other ranks, with a small committee in addition. No one in the regiment feels inclined for such things, but we are still ordered to have them.

12 November

To Sart Eustache: We did not find anything very pleasant there. The fanatical Belgians ran up the Belgian flag over our heads. The bells are ringing for the French marching in behind us. We have to keep calm and swallow this provocation.

13 November

On further to Sart-St Laurent.

We now keep meeting small or large parties of British or French prisoners moving west on their way home. What a splendid mood they must be in compared with us!

But then, now and again, you do get filled with a feeling of happiness to be going home for good, and an inexpressible thankfulness as well that in all these years, in those countless battles and actions, absolutely nothing has happened to me. I was stationed at the front four years and two months, and all but a fortnight of that in the murderous west. I believe now, as I believed from the first day of my service, in destiny and providence. I do not believe that there are many soldiers who were stationed at the front for fifty months and are coming home, as I am now, unwounded!

Our regiment has to surrender five guns to the French. As late as 4 November, that frightful day of heavy fighting, we defended our guns like heroes and recovered and saved those which we lost. We did not lose a single gun to the enemy, and now we have to give them up!

We are now near Namur; the war is ending for me at the place where it started. Thus we come full circle after over four years, as though the beginning and the end were shaking hands. But you shouldn't think back to the strength we had in us at Namur in 1914, or remember how happy we were then, or compare all that with today.

In spite of it all, we can be proud of the performance we put up, and we shall always be proud of it. Never before has a nation, a single army, had the whole world against it and stood its ground against such overwhelming odds; had it been the other way round, this heroic performance could never have been achieved by any other nation. We protected our homeland from her enemies – they never pushed as far as German territory.

Now comes the order which moved us most of all:

To my Armies!
Now that His Majesty the Kaiser has relinquished the Supreme Command, I too am forced by circumstances, now that hostilities have ceased, to resign the command of my Army Group.

As always in the past, I can today express most heartfelt thanks to my brave armies, and to every single man, for their heroic courage, their spirit of self-sacrifice and self-denial with which they have looked all dangers in the eye and willingly endured all privations for the Fatherland both in good times and bad.

The Army Group has not been defeated by force of arms! We have been forced to this by hunger and bitter necessity! Proudly, and with heads held high, my Army Group may now leave that territory of France which was fought for and won with the best of German blood. Your shield, your soldiers' honour, is bright and unspotted. Let every single man take care that it remains so, here, and later, at home!

Four long years I was privileged to be with my armies, in victory and adversity, four long years I belonged with a full heart, and my whole heart, to my faithful troops. Deeply moved, I take my leave of you today, bowing in respect to the overwhelming greatness of your deeds, those deeds which History shall one day make known in words of flame to later generations.

Now keep true, as before, to your leaders, until their orders can release you to return to wife and child, to hearth and home!

God be with you and with your German Fatherland!

The Commander-in-Chief
(signed) Wilhelm
Crown Prince of the German Reich
and of Prussia

———

4 December
... I said goodbye to my horse and to my faithful Fritz.[1] I took leave of my regimental CO, and I had the feeling that saying

goodbye like this was much more terrible for each of us than a large-scale battle. I went over once again to my old No. 2 Battery and said goodbye to the few remaining faithfuls from the old days whom I still knew – and who were still alive.

In the evening, for the last time, I wrote my signature at the bottom of battalion orders, and then came the farewell which was of course the most difficult of all, from my faithful, well-beloved, courageous comrade Hans-Ado von Seebach.

I am travelling to Frankenberg, alone, and meanwhile feel I must mention something of particular interest: Corps of volunteers are being formed for the *Grenzschutz Ost*[2] to protect Germany against the Poles in the east; now just imagine this, soldiers who have been engaged in heavy fighting for years are volunteering straight away, thousands and thousands of them, and a large number of them from my regiment. Could there be more splendid proof of spirit and conviction than this?

After a night spent with fifteen soldiers in one compartment, I travelled through Marburg and arrived at Frankfurt on the morning of *7 December*, after four and one third years! Alone and without my Regiment. Huge posters shouting appeals are no longer able to please me. I can't get used yet to the word 'Republic'. Well, here I am in the new Germany. I take my parents by surprise, but they expected me to arrive in the next few days anyway. They are very happy.

What does it all seem like to me now! Home at last, and not having to go away again!

On 8 December I went for a walk in my beloved uniform for the last time to report my discharge to the local military office, the *Bezirkskommando*.

I felt as though I were walking to my own funeral.

---

1. My batman.
2. One of the post-Armistice formations of paramilitary volunteers formed in 1918. [RT]

PAUL KLEE

Paul Klee (1879–1940). Swiss painter, born near Berne. He trained in Munich, where he settled in 1906. He was called up in 1916 and wrote in his diary, 'Now I have a new position in life: I am Infantry Reservist Klee.' Klee was not in the front line. The excerpts below are taken from the *Diaries*, which were edited by his son, Felix Klee. Each section has a number and date (day and month).

Source: Paul Klee, *Diaries: 1898–1918* (translated from *Tagebücher von Paul Klee 1898–1918*, Cologne, Verlag M. Du Mont Schauberg, 1957/Zurich, Europa Verlag, 1957, by Pierre B. Schneider, R. Y. Zachary and Max Knight) London, Peter Owen, 1965.

LANDSHUT 1916

987.   6.4. Singing instructions are no longer given by the clear-voiced sergeant, but by Corporal Bruckner. A neat man with a slight squint that doesn't look bad. First we all read the text together, then he sings the first stanza, fearfully off-key, so that our ears cringe. Then *we* sing it. Today we learned a horrible piece of trash called 'Flag Song', music-hall stuff.

I am living with apes. I realize this seeing them take this unadulterated rubbish with such seriousness. And yet, we are all brothers. Everybody wants to go home. Even the officers.

How Corporal Weidl laughed at the fat, rosy Jew Karlsen because at last a rich man was caught.

7.4. Announced my absence at the orchestra rehearsal of *Creation* on account of a long hike . . .

9.5. Marksmanship competition. Take it easy: this time, I didn't hit anything. At a distance of four hundred yards my slight nearsightedness begins to tell a bit. I talked myself out of it and was allowed not to lug along any special sights. We finally ate at three o'clock. On the rifle range I talked to Schinnerer and – talked to him at great length. He gave me an apple to quiet my hungry stomach.

1011. 20.7. . . . I was in no hurry at all about my marksman-ship. An instinct bade me to be fatalistic about it.

SECOND TRANSPORT

6.12. In the morning, arrived at Cambrai-Annexe. Pasted on new stickers to Cantimpré, Cambrai's other auxiliary station. Apparently our destination. We again have more time than we need and stroll off to town, a pitifully miserable, hungry village. Pleasant market. Plenty of endives. Lunch at the canteen in the station annexe. Then back to the city, into a pastry shop with cakes and fruit. A battalion from the Somme marches up with music, an overwhelming sight. Everything yellow with mud. The unmilitary, matter-of-fact appearance, the steel helmets, the equipment. The trotting step. Nothing heroic, just like beasts of burden, like slaves. Against a background of circus music. The drummer outdoes himself. The worn faces convey only a distorted reflection, if any, of the joy of being replaced and sent off to rest.

Had a look at the airplanes below. Waited for a long time and then at last moved on to a little station. Again waited and waited in the waiting-room of the main station, among a group of Saxons (brr!). And finally, moved on to another station, to Cantimpré. Here, out in the street at 3 a.m.

GERSTHOFEN 1917

1089. 22.10. Arrived safely here, was glad I took the next to last train. Found much work waiting for me. Paymaster away on a trip. 'It must be done and shall be done. We'll manage it.'

24.10. Just enough work. The doctor went on leave yesterday, amid much fussing and protracted preparations. I hurry so as to have some free time, since the office is now very peaceful and makes a good studio in the evening.

26.10. I again work more in black and white than in colour. Colour seems to be a little exhausted just now; new reserves have to accumulate. If it weren't for the duties, this might be a good time to push my plastic experiments further. This is probably the only damage inflicted on me by the war. For whether I'll catch up on it later is questionable; perhaps I shall then stand at a point outside of this domain.

1098.   3.1. Arrived safely. The train left Munich an hour late and did not arrive in Augsburg until nine o'clock. A few passengers left the train in desperation; as a result, I was able to sit down. Sitting, you can take a lot more; besides, you can nap. Augsburg quite pretty and friendly. A fine dish of lung and potatoes at Ost's did its share. On my way, had a sense of total contentment about the past ten beautiful days.

Outside of Augsburg some more serious thoughts came to me, evoked by the horrible snowy wastes and the chaotic darkness. This mood became even more marked in the countryside as time passed, and *Kyrie eleison* became my dominant theme. The village of Gersthofen brought a measure of relief for a quarter of an hour; then a fierce snowstorm started. The crucifix stood on my right, black and forbidding. At camp I threw myself on the straw pallet without a word, realizing that I would be faced with a heavily loaded desk tomorrow.

I have still not reached the point of loving England our enemy and of including it in my prayers. Perhaps I'll find peace once I have learned to do so . . .

1100.   14.1. The mails are moving again. It's no use guessing about whether we'll have peace. No one knows anything. But it is coming to that point with Russia, because both parties need it. What kind of a peace will it be, we don't care, since we don't play the game of politics.

1106.   21.2. Yesterday the golden wedding anniversary of Their Majesties, we were on duty, with the usual crash. Tonight the entire camp is without light. Went to bed with the chickens. Nothing more consoling in sight.

21.2. This week we had three fatal casualties; one man was smashed by the propeller, the other two crashed from the air! Yesterday, a fourth came ploughing with a loud bang into the roof of the workshop. Had been flying too low, caught on a telephone pole, bounced on the roof of the factory, turned a somersault, and collapsed upside down in a heap of wreckage. People came running from all sides; in a second the roof was black with mechanics in working clothes. Stretchers, ladders. The photographer. A human being pulled out of the debris and carried away unconscious. Loud cursing at the bystanders. First-rate movie effect. This is how a royal regiment celebrated a golden wedding. In addition, three smashed airplanes are lying about in the vicinity today. It was a fine show.

24.8. ... The *Leipziger Illustrierte*, the old aunt, wants to reproduce something by me under the heading of Expressionism. In reply, I asked who was writing the article, what artists were being considered besides me, and whether I would receive a fee.

I believe we can face the future now with confidence. And we'll hire a maid too and pay fitting wages.

If only the country's chances were as good as mine!

1128.   2.10. ... Come, holy spirit!

The war happenings are all too worldly! One thinks about the Bulgarians, who hold the war's issue in their hands, and whether the Turks will now be smashed? Will the Western Front soon fall back to the Rhine?

Then we shall go home, a theme worthy of a hymn! But now total collapse must actually occur. No one must be allowed to recover. The psychological moment has come.

1130.   30.10. Austria and the Turks are acting as they should. I am filled with high spirits. I only hope the tension will end soon, because all this world history makes you too worldly.

I mounted my watercolours, six of them, right here, and in so doing used up my cardboard (and my official government paste).

Finished *Robinson*; it grows less inspired as the action rises. But still very good.

What a moment this is – the Reich stands all alone now, armed to the teeth and yet so hopeless! Will my hope also be shattered that inner dignity will be preserved and that the idea of destiny will keep the upper hand over common atheism? We would now have an opportunity to be an example of how a people should endure its downfall. But if the masses go into action, what then? Then the usual things will happen, blood will flow, and still worse, there will be trials! How banal!

At the moment everything still seems peaceful.

1132.   14.11. I had a definite attack of the grippe, had a fever, and coughed the day before yesterday. But a fancy-filled night cured me. It was too obvious that the illness wanted to break out but couldn't.

After the enormous confusion that went with the collapse, when nobody did anything but curse, our duties have resumed as usual. Various units from the front are announced, and also the entire Flying School 2, Speyerdorf (Pfalz). Flying squadrons from the front, Bogohls, etc. It will be quite a mess, but exciting.

19.11. Had a very good trip on the 7.45 express (morning), ate a big, warm breakfast in Augsburg, then calmly put on my disguise again and set out for the walk through the sunny countryside, which was covered with a light layer of snow. Here, brisk activity on account of the arriving flying divisions from the front. Hair-raising stories about the débâcle, out there. My little room now seems twice as peaceful in all this chaos.

The military commission is adding three marks a day to our pay. It is impossible to spend anything, so we become rich.

16.12. 'My dearest Lily. Arrived safely; this time, walked all the way, but in this mild, clear weather it doesn't matter at all. Today I was shown an order from headquarters requesting that the payroll personnel be kept in the army for the time being. But that doesn't change my plans at all. I am acting on my inner urge; for now every man must ruthlessly take care of himself; I visualize with great interest the results of the paymaster's and my leaving here. The doctor will miss us. The auxiliary lasses will weep. But this time it will pay to obey my inner voice, I know it. After all, fate has delivered its verdict, and in the midst of this gigantic collapse, there is no sense in remaining loyal at one's little post. But I want to do this gracefully, and not just rudely run away. Modestly accept my Christmas furlough from the hands of the gentlemen on the commission and then . . . à la Leporello . . . Yours, Paul.'

'The soldier of Bavarian Flying School 5 begs to be released as soon as possible from the army and to be replaced by a substitute paymaster. (Class of 1879.) The said soldier would incur great damage by being retained any longer in the army, owing to the fact that the employment which he is awaiting as teacher at an art school in Berlin and as artistic adviser of a modern theatre in Munich could not materialize, in the event his military service continues. In his position as head of a family, he feels it his duty to call the attention of the military commission to these circumstances and to ask them to solve this difficulty by replacing him, as soon as possible, by a substitute paymaster. Private first-class Paul Klee.'

PAUL ALVERDES

Paul Alverdes (1897–1979). Son of an officer. Volunteered in 1914. Wounded in the throat in 1915. After the war he studied at the universities of Jena and Munich and became a journalist as well as writing poems, plays and stories. His own experience in hospital was used in *The Whistlers' Room*, 1929. Three German soldiers, Pointner, Kollin, and Benjamin have to breathe through metal tubes since their throats are closed by scar tissue. The bond caused by their particular wounds makes them reject an English prisoner similarly affected who is placed in their ward. Eventually the Englishman is accepted. He and Benjamin are cured (the others die) and the Englishman decides to stay in Germany rather than be exchanged. Although Arnold Bennett described it as the most 'harrowing' war book he had read he added that it was 'a beautiful thing'.

Source: Paul Alverdes, *The Whistlers' Room* (translated from *Die Pfeiferstube*, Frankfurt, Rütten & Loening Verlag, 1929, by Basil Creighton) London, Martin Secker, 1929.

I

The large room with the wide terrace in front and the view over the park and fields and a glimpse of the Rhine in the distance beneath a brown cloud of smoke was known throughout the hospital as the Whistlers' Room. It was named after the three soldiers who had been shot in the throat and awaited their recovery there. They had been there a long while; some said since the first year of the war. The stretcher-bearers who were the first to bandage them under fire in the shelter of ruined houses or in dug-outs roofed over with planks and turf, pronounced on them a sentence of speedy death; but in defiance of all precedent and expectation they came through, for the time at any rate.

The process of healing, however, overshot its mark: for the bullet holes were covered over on the inner side of the windpipe by new flesh in such thick rolls and weals that the air passage was speedily blocked, and a new channel had to be made to meet this unforeseen threat of suffocation. So the surgeon's knife cut a small hole in the neck below the old wound, which was causing a more and more impassable block. At this point a tube was sunk into the windpipe, and the air then passed freely in and out of the lungs.

The tube was a small silver pipe of the length and thickness of the little finger. At its outer end there was a small shield, fixed at right angles, not larger than the identity disc that everyone at the front wore next his skin. The purpose of it was to prevent the tube slipping into the gullet; and to prevent it falling out, there was a white tape passing through two eye-holes in the shield and secured behind round the neck by a double slip knot. In fact, however, the pipe was of two parts, closely fitted together, the innermost of which was held in its place by a tiny winged screw. Three times a day it was pulled out by two small handles to be cleaned; for since they could not now breathe through the nostrils, the tubes had become as it were the whistlers' noses, and when they were not actually bedridden they gladly cleaned them for themselves with the little round brush provided for that purpose.

After it was cleaned the entrance of the tube had at once to be protected against dust and flies by a clean curtain. This was about the size of the hand and rectangular in form. It was cut from a thick roll of white muslin and attached to the tape with pins. It recalled the clerical band that forms part of the official garb of evangelical clergymen. Thus it was that the whistlers, with their spotless white between chin and chest, had always a ceremonial air. They were well aware of it. There was something of this in their whole bearing, and gladly they changed their bibs and tuckers several times a day for even cleaner and whiter ones. When they breathed quickly or laughed, a soft piping note, like the squeaking of mice, came from the silver mouth. Hence they were called the neck whistlers, or the whistlers simply.

Talking, after being for a long while practically dumb, gave them great trouble at first, and they were glad to avoid it, particularly before strangers. When they wished to speak they had to close the mouth of the pipe with the tip of the finger. Then a thread-like stream of air found its way upwards through the throat and played on the vocal cords, or what remained of them; and they, very unwillingly roused from their torpor, emitted no more than a painful wheezing and croaking.

It was not, however, for their cracked notes that the whistlers blushed, but for this to-do with lifting their bibs and feeling with their fingers for their secret mouthpiece; and this predicament they tried every means to disguise. Were a stranger to address them on the roads through the park, or in the wide passages and halls of the great building where in bad weather they sometimes took their walks, they usually forbore returning an immediate answer. They looked in meditation down at their toes, or with head courteously inclined and raised eyebrows gazed into the face of him who accosted them as though earnestly seeking within themselves for a suitable response. Meanwhile, quite without any particular object, they put up a hand to their breasts and after a moment proceeded as though to dally with a shirt button that might be concealed beneath the white pinafore. After this they began to talk and sometimes, if they gained sufficient confidence, their first silence might be exchanged for a cheerful loquacity. It was as though they wished to show that, in the very natural and, indeed, most everyday matter of being hoarse, they were not any different from other men. Why they did this they could not themselves have said; and they did not speak of it to each other. Yet they all behaved as though sworn to secrecy by oath; and when a fourth was added to them, he, from the very first, did likewise.

It was just the same, moreover, with the others in the room upstairs who had lost an arm or a leg. They felt no shyness at being seen by strangers with an empty sleeve or a trouser leg dangling loose and empty; indeed some of them vaunted their docked limbs and even went so far as to instil a kind of grizzly veneration in those who had come off more lightly by a display of their sad stumps. Yet the scraping and creaking of the sometimes not very successful appliances with which they had to learn to walk again, caused them acute embarrassment before strangers. At once they came to a stop and tried to disguise the grasp for the lever that enabled them to fix the artificial joint by catching or pulling at their trousers, or by any other apparently trivial movement. They never, either, displayed an unclothed false hand or foot, and at night when they undressed for bed they concealed the arm they had screwed off by hanging the coat over it, or the leg by leaving it carefully in a corner inside the trouser. For they were always afraid of being surprised by outsiders, and would have liked best being always by themselves.

Sometimes, however, visitors from outside came to distribute gifts – to the whistlers as well in their room. They made presents of wine, fruit and cakes, and especially of all kinds of scent with which the whistlers gladly and copiously besprinkled themselves. It is true that their sense of smell was for the time in abeyance; but they were all the more gratified to feel that they carried a pleasant aroma about with them. For all that, these occasions of munificence did not long continue. For too often the visitors came to a hasty conclusion that he who could not utter a sound, or only in a treble voice, must necessarily be stone deaf as well, and they proceeded to shout at the whistlers without mercy; and some even pulled out notebooks and wrote in enormous letters what they might just as well have said; or they tried from the very outset to make themselves intelligible by gestures of the most exaggerated description. For the whistlers this was gross insult. The defect which they had now adopted as a peculiarity of their own, seemed to them in a sense a merit, and no longer really a defect at all. But the one that was thus falsely laid to their door wounded them to the quick. And so, no sooner had the unknown visitors entered at one door than they took flight by another. But if they were caught in bed they pretended to be asleep, or put their fingers warningly to their lips, shook their heads with a pretence of regret, and enjoined upon the intruders an alarmed and guilty retreat.

Among themselves the whistlers held lively and intimate talks. They could do so easily in a wordless clucking speech that, in default of a stream of air to make words with, they formed by means of their lips and tongues and teeth. Their powers of comprehension had arrived at such a pitch that in the night, when lights were out and when there was no help from gestures of the hands, they held long talks between three from bed to bed. It sounded like an incessant clucking and splashing in a water-butt under the changing quick patter of heavy drops. For the low fever that seldom left the whistlers, or the effect of the drugs they were given, kept them often long awake. They never talked of a future and seldom of a past before the war. But of their last day at the front and of the exact circumstances in which they were wounded they never tired of giving vivid and stirring accounts; and with such leisure for recollection there was always more and more to add, and sometimes, indeed, an entirely new story was evolved and told for the first time. But not one of them showed any surprise at that.

IX

In the third autumn of the war, however, a fourth comrade was added to the whistlers in earnest. One afternoon Sister Emily, a red-cheeked Valkyrie of uncertain age, came in and laid a heap of clean clothes on the fourth bed that since Fürlein's departure had stood unmade up in the corner.

'Early tomorrow there's a new whistler coming, and a real one this time,' she said in her robust tones, as she turned down the sheet over the heavy blanket, 'and what d'you think – it's an English prisoner.'

The whistlers pricked up their ears and shook their heads. Pointner noisily pushed back his chair and laid down his spoon. 'No,' he said loudly, and the other two showed their indignation in their faces.

'It's not a bit of use,' said Sister Emily emphatically, and shook up the pillow. 'He has been shot through the throat like you, and there's nowhere else for him to go for treatment. So you must just put up with him.'

Herewith she pulled a piece of chalk out of the pocket of her apron and wrote on the nameplate at the head of the empty bed. 'Harry Flint' was now to be read there; and below, where in other cases a man's rank was stated – 'Englishman'. Pointner still signified his distaste with one or two gestures of his hands, and brought the coffee jug threateningly down on the table. Then he rammed his cap down on one side and went out into the garden, spitting with rage like a cat.

The next morning when the whistlers were sitting over their breakfast, the door slowly opened and there entered a round-faced boy with large brown eyes and thick blue-black hair. In his hand he held a small bundle about the size of a head of cabbage. He wore the hospital uniform of blue and white striped linen, and over it a kind of round cape. On his head was an utterly washed-out cap of the same material and far too small for him. It was Harry Flint, in German Heini Kieselstein, or simply Kiesel, of the Gloucesters. He stood blushing in the doorway, and, putting his hand to his cap by way of greeting, made at the same time something like a slight bow. After that he remained fixed in an appealing attitude, his hands laid one over the other at the level of his waist, and looked steadily at the three whistlers with a mixture of shame, pride and fear.

The whistlers did not appear to see him. Each looked straight in front of him over his cup, and so contrived to avoid the eyes of the others. After a while Harry once more saluted, and his eyes began to fill with tears. Pointner sat mouthing a large piece of soaked bread with a long knife in his hand, and at this he jerked the knife over his shoulder in the direction of the vacant bed. Harry Flint betook himself there at once and sat down gingerly on the edge of it, as though he desired to show that he made the least possible claim on the air space of the room. Directly afterwards the whistlers got up all together for a walk in the garden, and left the rifleman to himself without deigning to cast him a glance.

When they came back again at midday they found Harry sweeping out the room with a broom and shovel that he had found for himself. It was now apparent that he wore his tube in his neck without any protective covering and secured only by a thin cord. It looked as though he had a large metal button or a screw stuck in the front of his throat. Kollin shook his head and went up to him, and, leading him by the sleeve to the cupboard at his bedside, took a clean piece of muslin out of the drawer and pinned it carefully and neatly under his chin. Harry, who had stood without a movement, took a small looking-glass from his pocket and looked at himself with delight. Then he rummaged in his bundle and produced a stick of chocolate and offered it to Kollin. Kollin gave it a passing glance and quietly shook his head. Harry bit his lip and turned away.

At this time food was scarce in Germany, and white bread, cake, meat and imported fruit had vanished. Harry, however, had no lack of them. Soon after his arrival a large parcel of otherwise unprocurable food came for him from an English Prisoners of War Committee in Switzerland, and regularly every third and fourth day came another. Harry handed it all round in the friendliest way – smoked bacon, *Wurst* in cans, butter in tin tubes, biscuits with nuts and almonds, and white bread with brown and shining crust. But though the whistlers had long forgotten their hatred of Great Britain, they obstinately refused to touch even a morsel of it.

It was not always their loss. For sometimes the parcels were a long time on the road, and then there was a dangerous hissing and effervescing when Harry stuck in the tin-opener. The meat smelled like bad cheese, and the bread was not to be cut with any knife. This put the whistlers in the best of moods. They surrounded the table on which Harry had spread his treasures, and in the mixture of German and English that had become meanwhile the common whistler lingo, passed the severest criticisms on England and English products. 'What muck!' they croaked, and showed their disgust by holding their noses. This was always a disconcerting moment for Harry. He could not admit that Britain presented a Briton with bad fare. With indignant eyes he soaked his bread in his soup and rubbed salt in the putrid meat. And then he swallowed it all down, and patting his stomach endeavoured to show by his face how much he enjoyed it. Often, however, he turned pale and hurried out and vomited long and painfully for the honour of Great Britain.

The originator of the common German-English whistler-language was Benjamin. After he had overcome his first modesty he brought forward his grammar-school English and initiated Harry into the usages and rules of the hospital, and in particular of the whistlers' room. He instructed him also in the art of speaking, or rather croaking, by stopping the mouth of the tube with the finger-tip, and began to teach him a little German. Harry was a quick pupil, and soon transformed himself from the dumb and constrained foreigner into a friend who was always ready for a talk. The whistlers got to be very fond of him.

One day he confided to Benjamin that he was married. A war-marriage, he called it. He was twenty and Mrs Flint of Gloucester a little over sixteen. Benjamin had often found him seated on his bed in the act, apparently, of smelling, or indeed tasting, a sheet of notepaper, and had been at a loss for the explanation. And now Harry revealed it. Mrs Flint was allowed by the censorship to send no more than four sides of note paper to her prisoner husband every week. But writing was no easy task for her; she had, as Harry confessed, first to set about learning how to do it. For this reason each letter contained no more than one or two laboured sentences, traced in large letters on lines previously ruled out. The remaining space, three and a half sides, was covered with small neatly formed crosses. Each one of them, Harry explained, betokened a kiss of wedded love. Harry loyally responded to each. Even in the darkness of the night his lips often met those of his far-distant wife on the paper. Benjamin, whose bed was opposite his, could hear the rustling folds and the sighs of the prisoner. Once he got up and groped his way across to console him with a joke. But Harry quickly pulled the bedclothes over his head because his face was wet with tears.

EDMUND WILSON

Edmund Wilson (1895–1972). Born in New Jersey. Graduated from Princeton and started military training in 1916. After working as a reporter in New York he enlisted when the US entered the war in 1917. Stationed in Vittel as a stretcher-bearer. Transferred to military intelligence in 1918. Despite the appalling conditions and the terrible injuries he had to deal with he read two hundred books between August 1917 and November 1918. After the Armistice he went to Trier (Trèves) with the occupying forces. 'Lieutenant Franklin', written shortly afterwards, is autobiographical. In Trèves, Franklin sees the 'abandoned armor of the Empire which irreverent pygmies now came to explore'. He does not know German but is assigned to work in the censor's office checking the press for anti-American sentiments. Billeted with the burgomaster and his attractive daughters he is accused of fraternizing and immediately posted back to France.

Source: Edmund Wilson, 'Lieutenant Franklin', in *Travels in Two Democracies*, N.Y., Harcourt Brace, 1936; and in *A Prelude*, London, W. H. Allen, 1967.

. . . Coming home late one afternoon thus – he had been billeted in the burgomaster's own house – he was surprised to find Captain Scudder.

'Well, old chap,' the captain greeted him, 'how goes it? I've just been out for a little hike and I thought I'd look in and see how you were. How are you getting along out here?'

'All right,' replied Lieutenant Franklin, 'but it gets to be pretty monotonous. Nothing to do except eat.'

'What do you do?' asked the captain. 'Have a mess just for one?'

'Oh, no,' said Lieutenant Franklin. 'I eat with the family here.'

'You don't have to, you know,' said the captain. 'You could have them bring you your mess in your room – or make them serve you first.'

A lady appeared in the sitting-room door but, seeing the captain, did not enter.

'Oh, I beg your pardon,' she apologized in French. 'I didn't know you had a visitor!'

'This is Madame Hoffer,' said Lieutenant Franklin, rising and coming to meet her. '*Je vous présente le capitaine Scudder.*'

Madame Hoffer bowed; the captain rose, as if perfunctorily.

'What became of you?' asked the lieutenant. 'I looked for you everywhere. I went to all the *Konditorei* in the square.'

'Oh, it's not a *Konditorei*,' she said smilingly. 'It's a little restaurant. You thought it was a *Konditorei* on account of the cakes! – Well, you shall have some *Baumkuchen*, after all! We brought some back with us for you.' She held up the paper bag and smiled: her amiable eyes and easy manners carried off the dowdy taste of her dress and the dullness of her mealy complexion.

She nodded to the captain and withdrew.

'Not French, is she?' asked the captain, who had been watching the dialogue with attention.

'Oh, no,' said the lieutenant, 'but she usually talks French because I don't know much German and she doesn't know much English. They all talk French here – the whole family: she's the burgomaster's daughter. They're quite interesting. They give me German lessons in the evenings.'

'Look here, old chap,' advised Captain Scudder, 'I wouldn't get too much mixed up with these people, if I were you. Remember you can never trust a German: that's been proved a thousand times!'

'Oh, they're all right,' said the lieutenant. 'Really very nice, in fact.'

'I wouldn't let them get too pally. Just keep your distance!'

'Well, after all –' demurred the lieutenant: he felt more and more hostile to Captain Scudder, 'I mean, the war's over now –'

'Don't be too sure of that,' cautioned the captain. 'Remember this is only an armistice!'

They talked about the German food and wine, but as the captain got up to go, he returned to his former subject. 'Just let me give you a tip,' he said, lowering his voice and holding the front door half open so that the outer cold came into the hall and blasted its already feeble warmth. 'Better be careful with the natives! The French have been complaining lately about the American troops getting too friendly with the Germans. I have it direct from GHQ that the C-in-C's taking the matter up. You'll hear something about it very soon!'

'Well,' the lieutenant cut him short, 'let's not worry till we hear something definite.'

'All right, old chap: I'm simply telling you.'

'Thanks a lot for coming out.'

'Not a bit: good to see you again!'

'Don't miss the path: the third street to your left.'

'Right-o!' He saluted. 'Goodnight.'

Lieutenant Franklin closed the hall door and pushed out the overpowering blackness.

They sat at first only five at dinner; Lieutenant Franklin felt the empty place. There were Frau Hoffer and her youngish husband, a schoolmaster, with cropped bristling head and a black shiny alpaca coat; the burgomaster, whose white upturned mustaches still followed the fashion set by the Kaiser; and an American sergeant, all in one chunkish piece, who had been assigned Lieutenant Franklin as interpreter on the strength of fifty or sixty words of German handed down from Michigan grandparents and lopped in the transit of most of their inflections. Frau Hoffer found the sergeant amusing and always spoke of him as 'Monsieur Schwab'.

'Well,' announced the lieutenant triumphantly, 'I see that Clemenceau has come out for a League of Nations.'

'That will be a League of Nations for the Entente and not for anybody else,' said the schoolmaster, 'if it's Clemenceau who is organizing it. The Entente is already a League of Nations. No doubt, it's that he means.'

'But America,' protested Lieutenant Franklin, 'will insist upon a league for the whole of Europe! –'

The burgomaster's second daughter appeared and took her place at the table. She was a small but sturdy girl of twenty-two, whom the rest of the family called Bäbchen – red cheeks, dark serious eyes and a straight profile almost American.

'It was so stupid of me to miss you today!' said Lieutenant Franklin eagerly. 'I'd been counting on it. I'm so terribly sorry!'

'We were sorry, too,' she smiled. 'However, we brought you some cake.'

'That was very nice of you: I don't deserve it.' And he returned to the international situation with an ardor stimulated by her presence. 'That's precisely the reason,' he insisted, 'that the President has come to Europe. He isn't merely working for the Entente: he's working for justice for everybody!'

The schoolmaster shrugged his shoulders: 'I don't think it's possible to have justice in Europe. The nation who wins will never consent to it.'

The old woman who waited on the table told the burgomaster there was someone to see him, and he excused himself and went away.

The liveliness which had revived with the oil-lamps of dinner declined when the *Baumkuchen* had been finished. The conversation suddenly lapsed; all stared blankly into their plates. The terrible ennui of evening was upon them . . .

———

. . . Sweet and deep he drew it from her eyes, the romantic longing of the music. How much he would like to kiss her! Those merry young fellows in Dreimäderlhaus with the *Konzertmeister*'s daughters! – so free and gay, in blue brass-buttoned coats, in the fresh Viennese spring . . . drinking under the lilac trellis, drinking to the lindens and their loves! – But it wouldn't, he thought, be correct to – besides, she mightn't like him enough.

But he came out with a bold proposal: 'Won't you let me take you to the theater in Trèves some night?'

'Thank you: I should like to very much. – If it is possible.' She smiled.

Possible? Why shouldn't it be possible? Who were the Scudders to bully him?

'It's not very amusing here,' she went on. 'We don't have much music now. In Dresden, they have good music in all the cafés. We used to go to the opera every week.'

'Dresden must be a marvellous city!' exclaimed Lieutenant Franklin.

'Yes: it is a fine city. I like Dresden very very much. – We used to go out very early Sunday morning – my husband and I, with our friends – and have breakfast in the Grosser Garten. We would have breakfast on the shores of the Carola-See – a beautiful little lake. We'd feed the swans with the crumbs. They have beautiful swans in the Grosser Garten. I liked Dresden very much.'

He saw her sent back to her provincial sewing – that old threadbare couch in the burgomaster's house – no more music, no more friends, no more outings in the Grosser Garten!

'But even Dresden,' she added, 'is not the same since the war.'

'Nothing is the same anywhere since the war!' He suddenly took fire. 'Everybody has lost by the war! Nobody has anything to gain from war! – Nobody really wants it. I don't suppose you wanted it any more than we did! – And now that everybody knows they don't want it, there must never be another! – That's why America came into it – so that there should never be another war!'

'Yes,' she looked up at him with strong soft eyes. 'I don't think that the Americans hate us.'

Of course not! How proud he felt that she knew it! He was aware of his cleanness, his blondness, his straightness – he was exalted to know himself an American: heir to the War of Independence, soldier of the American Republic! They had left the intrigues, the antagonisms, the greeds of the old world behind – and now they had come back to save it! *He* was not pledged to hate the Germans – he was pledged to Humanity and Justice. And he loved them all! – he loved Herr Hoffer, who had read through the whole of French literature in a French prison-camp and had found it polished but superficial; Sergeant Schwab, who had been stricken speechless by the sun and oleanders of Galveston; dear Bäbchen, who had liked to take breakfast out of doors and to feed the beautiful swans.

Everything in him that had been kicked and kept under during the months he had spent in the army – by the naggings and snubs of superiors, by the months of suffocating boredom, by the brutalities of the artillery school at Langres, by the intolerable horror of artillery itself: blowing people to shreds whom you had never seen, so that you had to try to occupy your mind with the mathematical and technical end, all culminating in Captain Scudder! – his spirit rose proudly to reject the army and everything that made it possible, to affirm human solidarity! Now for ever there must be no more hatred, no more slaughter, among Christian peoples! – men who were moved by the same music, made gay by the same wine!

All about them, outside this room, the desolation of Europe opened: the starved fatigue of the living, the abyss – one could not look into it! – of the dead; that world which had been cursed for four years with the indictment of every natural instinct, the abortion of every kindly impulse. And tonight in this bright-lit room, where still the wine from Moselle grapes was yellow, where still Schubert's music swam in sun, the fellowship of men was reviving after the bitterness, the agony, the panic! Had young German girls like Bäbchen – and young French and young English and young Americans – been cheated of spring-time and music and youth? Well, the Americans were there to see to it that the children of the future should never again be so cheated! ... The Americans and Germans were much alike ... they were all speaking that fine language, French ... He wondered whether he couldn't do something about that poor old man and his cow. It would make Bäbchen admire him ... What if he should marry her and take her home? ...

He watched her lips, so good-natured and full, finishing words he had not heard her speak. A sudden utterance took shape in his thought: it demanded expression in German.

'*Sie sind sehr schön!*' he said suddenly, earnestly, and took her hand under the table.

'*Sie sind sehr freundlich das zu sagen,*' she answered with grave eyes, leaving her hand in his.

Herr Hoffer and the sergeant had been driven by the wine to the toilet; Frau Hoffer, at the piano, had her back to them. He kissed Bäbchen's lips with grave tenderness.

A deep blush flooded her face and flooded her pretty round neck and spread under her plain blue beads and beneath the black border of her mourning.

JOHN DOS PASSOS

John Dos Passos (1896–1970). Born in Chicago and educated abroad and at Harvard. Opposed the war although he tried to join the army to get firsthand experience of it. Rejected because of poor eyesight, he joined the Norton-Harjes Ambulance Corps. Served with the Red Cross in Italy but sent back to the US *inter alia* for singing '*Deutschland über Alles*' during an air-raid. After two early books on the war, *One Man's Initiation*, 1917, and *Three Soldiers*, 1921, he based his great trilogy *U.S.A.* on American society about the time of the war. *The 42nd Parallel* (1930), *1919* (1932), and *The Big Money* (1936) appeared together in 1938. *U.S.A.* used both fact and fiction, realism and modernism in setting Dos Passos's personal experiences and observations in the context of a cross-section of fictional events and characters. John Reed (*q.v.*) and Randolph Bourne (*q.v.*) are amongst the real characters given memorable modernist portraits. The various technical and narrative strands are constantly inter-cut, as in the excerpts from *1919* which follow. 'Joe Williams', a deserter from the US navy, sails in British and American merchant ships with false papers. While on a British freighter docked in Liverpool he is arrested as a spy by the British, who are both suspicious and scornful of the Americans who have not yet entered the war. On a later voyage, described below, his ship is sunk by the Germans.

Source: John Dos Passos, *U.S.A.*, New York, The Modern Library, 1938; London, Constable, 1938; Penguin Books, 1966.

JOE WILLIAMS

. . . Next morning they raised the Hebrides to the south. Cap'n Perry was just pointing out the Butt of Lewis to the mate when the lookout in the bow gave a scared hail. It was a submarine all right. You could see first the periscope trailing a white feather of foam, then the dripping conning tower. The submarine had hardly gotten to the surface when she started firing across the *North Star*'s bows with a small gun that the squareheads manned while decks were still awash. Joe went running aft to run up the flag, although they had the flag painted amidships on either side of the boat. The engineroom bells jingled as Cap'n Perry threw her into full speed astern. The jerries stopped firing and four of them came on board in a collapsible punt. All hands had their life preservers on and some of the men were going below for their duffle when the fritz officer who came aboard shouted in English that they had five minutes to abandon the ship. Cap'n Perry handed over the ship's papers, the boats were lowered like winking as the blocks were well oiled. Something made Joe run back up to the boat deck and cut the lashings on the liferafts with his jackknife, so he and Cap'n Perry and the ship's cat were the last to leave the *North Star*. The jerries had planted bombs in the engine-room and were rowing back to the submarine like the devil was after them. The Cap'n's boat had hardly pushed off when the explosion lammed them a blow on the side of the head. The boat swamped and before they knew what had hit them they were swimming in the icy water among all kinds of planking and junk. Two of the boats were still afloat. The old *North Star* was sinking quietly with the flag flying and the signal-flags blowing out prettily in the light breeze. They must have been half an hour or an hour in the water. After the ship had sunk they managed to get on to the liferafts and the mate's boat and the Chief's boat took them in tow. Cap'n Perry called the roll. There wasn't a soul missing. The submarine had submerged and gone some time ago. The men in the boats started pulling towards shore. Till nightfall the strong tide was carrying them in fast towards the Pentland Firth. In the last dusk they could see the tall headlands of the Orkneys. But when the tide changed they couldn't make headway against it. The men in the boats and the men in the rafts took turn and turn about at the oars but they couldn't buck the terrible ebb. Somebody said the tide ran eight knots an hour in there. It was a pretty bad night. With the first dawn they caught sight of a scoutcruiser bearing down on them. Her searchlight glared suddenly in their faces making everything look black again. The Britishers took 'em on board and hustled them down into the engineroom to get warm. A redfaced steward came down with a bucket of steaming tea with rum in it and served it out with a ladle.

The scoutcruiser took 'em into Glasgow, pretty well shaken up by the chop of the Irish Sea, and they all stood around in the drizzle on the dock while Cap'n Perry went to find the American consul. Joe was getting numb in the feet standing still and tried to walk across to the iron gates opposite the wharf house to take a squint down the street, but an elderly man in a uniform poked a bayonet at his belly and he stopped. Joe went back to the crowd and told 'em how they were prisoners there like they were fritzes. Jez, it made 'em sore. Flannagan started telling about how the frogs had arrested him one time for getting into a fight with an orangeman in a bar in Marseilles and had been ready to shoot him because they said the Irish were all pro-German. Joe told about how the limeys had run him in in Liverpool. They were all grousing about how the whole business was a lousy deal when Ben Tarbell the mate turned up with an old guy from the consulate and told 'em to come along.

They had to troop half across town through streets black dark for fear of airraids and slimy with rain, to a long tarpaper shack inside a barbedwire enclosure. Ben Tarbell told the boys he was sorry but they'd have to stay there for the present, and that he was trying to get the consul to do something about it and the old man had called the owners to try to get 'em some pay. Some girls from the Red Cross brought them grub, mostly bread and marmalade and meatpaste, nothing you could really sink your teeth into, and some thin blankets. They stayed in that damn place for twelve days, playing poker and yarning and reading old newspapers. Evenings sometimes a frousy halfdrunk woman would get past the old guard and peek in the door of the shack and beckon one of the men out into the foggy darkness behind the latrines somewhere. Some of the guys were disgusted and wouldn't go.

They'd been shut up in there so long that when the mate finally came around and told 'em they were going home they didn't have enough spunk left in 'em to yell. They went across the town packed with traffic and gasflare in the fog again and on board a new 6,000 ton freighter, the *Vicksburg*, that had just unloaded a cargo of cotton. It felt funny being a passenger and being able to lay around all day on the trip home.

Joe was lying out on the hatchcover the first sunny day they'd had when old Cap'n Perry came up to him. Joe got to his feet. Cap'n Perry said he hadn't had a chance to tell him what he thought of him for having the presence of mind to cut the lashings on those rafts and that half the men on the boat owed their lives to him. He said Joe was a bright boy and ought to start studying how to get out of the focastle and that the

American merchant marine was growing every day on account of the war and young fellers like him were just what they needed for officers. 'You remind me, boy,' he said, 'when we get to Hampton Roads and I'll see what I can do on the next ship I get. You could get your third mate's ticket right now with a little time in shore school.' Joe grinned and said he sure would like to. It made him feel good the whole trip. He couldn't wait to go and see Del and tell her he wasn't in the focastle any more. Dod gast it, he was tired of being treated like a jailbird all his life . . .

RANDOLPH BOURNE

Randolph Bourne
    came as an inhabitant of this earth
    without the pleasure of choosing his dwelling or his career.

He was a hunchback, grandson of a congregational minister, born in 1886[1] in Bloomfield, New Jersey; there he attended grammarschool and highschool.

At the age of seventeen he went to work as secretary to a Morristown businessman.

He worked his way through Columbia working in a pianola record factory in Newark, working as proof-reader, pianotuner, accompanist in a vocal studio in Carnegie Hall.

At Columbia he studied with John Dewey,
    got a travelling fellowship that took him to England Paris Rome Berlin Copenhagen,
    wrote a book on the Gary schools.

In Europe he heard music, a great deal of Wagner and Scriabine
    and bought himself a black cape.

This little sparrowlike man,
tiny twisted bit of flesh in a black cape,
always in pain and ailing,
put a pebble in his sling
and hit Goliath square in the forehead with it.

War, he wrote, *is the health of the state*.

Half musician, half educational theorist (weak health and being poor and twisted in body and on bad terms with his people hadn't spoiled the world for Randolph Bourne; he was a happy man, loved die Meistersinger and playing Bach with his long hands that stretched so easily over the keys and pretty girls and good food and evenings of talk. When he was dying of pneumonia a friend brought him an eggnog; Look at the yellow, its beautiful, he kept saying as his life ebbed into delirium and fever. He was a happy man.) Bourne seized with feverish intensity on the ideas then going around at Columbia, he picked rosy glasses out of the turgid jumble of John Dewey's teaching through which he saw clear and sharp

the shining capitol of reformed democracy,

Wilson's New Freedom;

but he was too good a mathematician; he had to work the equations out;

with the result

that in the crazy spring of 1917 he began to get unpopular where his bread was buttered at the New Republic;

for *New Freedom* read *Conscription*, for *Democracy*, *Win the War*, for *Reform*, *Safeguard the Morgan Loans*

for Progress Civilization Education Service,

Buy a Liberty Bond,

Straff the Hun,

Jail the Objectors.

He resigned from *The New Republic*; only *The Seven Arts* had the nerve to publish his articles against the war. The backers of *The Seven Arts* took their money elsewhere; friends didn't like to be seen with Bourne, his father wrote him begging him not to disgrace the family name. The rainbowtinted future of reformed democracy went pop like a pricked soapbubble.

The liberals scurried to Washington;

some of his friends plead with him to climb up on School-master Wilson's sharabang; the war was great fought from the swivel chairs of Mr Creel's bureau in Washington.

He was cartooned, shadowed by the espionage service and the counter-espionage service; taking a walk with two girl friends at Wood's Hole he was arrested, a trunk full of manuscript and letters was stolen from him in Connecticut. (Force to the utmost, thundered Schoolmaster Wilson)

He didn't live to see the big circus of the Peace of Versailles or the purplish normalcy of the Ohio Gang.

Six weeks after the armistice he died planning an essay on the foundations of future radicalism in America.

If any man has a ghost
Bourne has a ghost,
a tiny twisted unscared ghost in a black cloak
hopping along the grimy old brick and brownstone streets
still left in downtown New York,
crying out in a shrill soundless giggle:
War is the health of the state.

1. Actually 1896 – see p. 349.

WILLIAM FAULKNER

William Faulkner (1897–1962). Born in New Albany, Mississippi. In 1918 joined the (British) Royal Flying Corps at a training camp near Toronto, Canada, as a cadet posing as an Englishman from Finchley, Middlesex. He was given a Canadian serial number. Despite rumours, which he encouraged, that he flew, crashed and was rewarded by the British, his biographer, Joseph Blotner, leaves it open as to whether he ever flew at this period. Even the supposed crash on Armistice Day after a drunken celebration flight may not have taken place. He never reached Europe and was soon discharged after the war was over. He returned to the University of Mississippi as its rather inefficient post-master and enrolled as a special student. However, he was deeply affected by the war, which is the subject of several of his novels and short stories. While he was training in Toronto, his brother, Jack, was being gassed in France. During 1925 he visited Europe and 'Victory' was probably started at this time. A young Scot, Alec Gray, from a proud shipyard worker's family, enlists. The passages below describe how he is ridiculed by his sergeant-major and, unobserved, takes his revenge. Although he rises to become a successful officer he finds no permanent work after the war. The last passage describes an encounter with an old comrade while he sells matches.

Source: William Faulkner, 'Victory', in *These Thirteen*, New York, Cape & Smith, 1931; reprinted in *Collected Stories*, New York, Random House, 1950.

... The battalion stands at ease in the rain. It has been in rest billets two days, equipment has been replaced and cleaned, vacancies have been filled and the ranks closed up, and it now stands at ease with the stupid docility of sheep in the ceaseless rain, facing the streaming shape of the sergeant-major.

Presently the colonel emerges from a door across the square. He stands in the door a moment, fastening his trench coat, then, followed by two ADCs, he steps gingerly into the mud in polished boots and approaches.

'Para-a-a-de – 'Shun!' the sergeant-major shouts. The battalion clashes, a single muffled, sullen sound. The sergeant-major turns, takes a pace toward the officers, and salutes, his stick beneath his armpit. The colonel jerks his stick toward his cap peak.

'Stand at ease, men,' he says. Again the battalion clashes, a single sluggish, trickling sound. The officers approach the guide file of the first platoon, the sergeant-major falling in behind the last officer. The sergeant of the first platoon takes a pace forward and salutes. The colonel does not respond at all. The sergeant falls in behind the sergeant-major, and the five of them pass down the company front, staring in turn at each rigid, forward-staring face as they pass it. First company.

The sergeant salutes the colonel's back and returns to his original position and comes to attention. The sergeant of the second company has stepped forward, saluted, is ignored, and falls in behind the sergeant-major, and they pass down the second company front. The colonel's trench coat sheathes water on to his polished boots. Mud from the earth creeps up his boots and meets the water and is channelled by the water as the mud creeps up the polished boots again.

Third company. The colonel stops before a soldier, his trench coat hunched about his shoulders where the rain trickles from the back of his cap, so that he looks somehow like a choleric and outraged bird. The other two officers, the sergeant-major and the sergeant halt in turn, and the five of them glare at the five soldiers whom they are facing. The five soldiers stare rigid and unwinking straight before them, their faces like wooden faces, their eyes like wooden eyes.

'Sergeant,' the colonel says in his pettish voice, 'has this man shaved today?'

'Sir!' the sergeant says in a ringing voice; the sergeant-major says:

'Did this man shave today, Sergeant?' and all five of them glare now at the soldier, whose rigid gaze seems to pass through and beyond them, as if they were not there. 'Take a pace forward when you speak in ranks!' the sergeant-major says.

The soldier, who has not spoken, steps out of ranks, splashing a jet of mud yet higher up the colonel's boots.

'What is your name?' the colonel says.

'024186 Gray,' the soldier raps out glibly. The company, the battalion, stares straight ahead.

'Sir!' the sergeant-major thunders.

'Sir-r,' the soldier says.

'Did you shave this morning?' the colonel says.

'Nae, sir-r.'

'Why not?'

'A dinna shave, sir-r.'

'You dont shave?'

'A am nae auld enough tae shave.'

'Sir!' the sergeant-major thunders.

'Sir-r,' the soldier says.

'You are not . . .' The colonel's voice dies somewhere behind his choleric glare, the trickling water from his cap peak. 'Take his name, Sergeant-major,' he says, passing on

The battalion stares rigidly ahead. Presently it sees the colonel, the two officers and the sergeant-major reappear in single file. At the proper place the sergeant-major halts and salutes the colonel's back. The colonel jerks his stick hand again and goes on, followed by the two officers, at a trot toward the door from which he had emerged.

The sergeant-major faces the battalion again. 'Para-a-a-de –' he shouts. An indistinguishable movement passes from rank to rank, an indistinguishable precursor of that damp and sullen clash which dies borning. The sergeant-major's stick has come down from his armpit; he now leans on it, as officers do. For a time his eye roves along the battalion front.

'Sergeant Cunninghame!' he says at last.

'Sir!'

'Did you take that man's name?'

There is silence for a moment – a little more than a short moment, a little less than a long one. Then the sergeant says: 'What man, sir?'

'You, soldier!' the sergeant-major says.

The battalion stands rigid. The rain lances quietly into the mud between it and the sergeant-major as though it were too spent to either hurry or cease.

'You soldier that dont shave!' the sergeant-major says.

'Gray, sir!' the sergeant says.

'Gray. Double out 'ere.'

The man Gray appears without haste and tramps stolidly before the battalion, his kilts dark and damp and heavy as a wet horse-blanket. He halts, facing the sergeant-major.

'Why didn't you shave this morning?' the sergeant-major says.

'A am nae auld enough tae shave,' Gray says.

'Sir!' the sergeant-major says.

Gray stares rigidly beyond the sergeant-major's shoulder.

'Say *sir* when addressing a first-class warrant officer!' the sergeant-major says. Gray stares doggedly past his shoulder, his face beneath his vizorless bonnet as oblivious of the cold lances of rain as though it were granite. The sergeant-major raises his voice:

'Sergeant Cunninghame!'

'Sir!'

'Take this man's name for insubordination also.'

'Very good, sir!'

The sergeant-major looks at Gray again. 'And I'll see that you get the penal battalion, my man. Fall in!'

Gray turns without haste and returns to his place in ranks, the sergeant-major watching him. The sergeant-major raises his voice again:

'Sergeant Cunninghame!'

'Sir!'

'You did not take that man's name when ordered. Let that happen again and you'll be for it yourself.'

'Very good, sir!'

'Carry on!' the sergeant-major says.

'But why did ye no shave?' the corporal asked him. They were back in billets: a stone barn with leprous walls, where no light entered, squatting in the ammoniac air on wet straw about a reeking brazier. 'Ye kenned we were for inspection thae mor-rn.'

'A am nae auld enough tae shave,' Gray said.

'But ye kenned thae colonel would mar-rk ye on parade.'

'A am nae auld enough tae shave,' Gray repeated doggedly and without heat . . .

―――

. . . They are in the trench. Until the first rifle explodes in their faces, not a shot has been fired. Gray is the third man. During all the while that they crept between flares from shellhole to shellhole, he has been working himself nearer to the sergeant-major and the Officer; in the glare of that first rifle he can see the gap in the wire toward which the Officer was leading them, the moiled rigid glints of the wire where bullets have nicked the mud and rust from it, and against the glare the tall, leaping shape of the sergeant-major. Then Gray, too, springs bayonet first into the trench full of grunting shouts and thudding blows.

Flares go up by dozens now; in the corpse glare Gray sees the sergeant-major methodically tossing grenades into the next traverse. He runs toward him, passing the Officer leaning, bent double, against the fire-step. The sergeant-major has vanished beyond the traverse. Gray follows and comes upon the sergeant-major. Holding the burlap curtain aside with one hand, the sergeant-major is in the act of tossing a grenade into a dug-out as if he might be tossing an orange hull into a cellar.

The sergeant-major turns in the rocket glare. ' 'Tis you, Gray,' he says. The earth-muffled bomb thuds; the sergeant-major is in the act of catching another bomb from the sack about his neck as Gray's bayonet goes into his throat. The sergeant-major is a big man. He falls backward, holding the rifle barrel with both hands against his throat, his teeth glaring, pulling Gray with him. Gray clings to the rifle. He tries to shake the speared body on the bayonet as he would shake a rat on an umbrella rib.

He frees the bayonet. The sergeant-major falls. Gray reverses the rifle and hammers its butt into the sergeant-major's face, but the trench floor is too soft to supply any resistance. He glares about. His gaze falls upon a duckboard upended in the mud. He drags it free and slips it beneath the sergeant-major's head and hammers the face with his rifle-butt. Behind him in the first traverse the Officer is shouting: 'Blow your whistle, Sergeant-major!'

In the citation it told how Private Gray, on a night raid, one of four survivors, following the disablement of the Officer and the death of all the NCOs, took command of the situation and (the purpose of the expedition was a quick raid for prisoners) held a foothold in the enemy's front line until a supporting attack arrived and consolidated the position. The Officer told how he ordered the men back out, ordering them to leave him and save themselves, and how Gray appeared with a German machine-gun from somewhere and, while his three companions built a barricade, overcame the Officer and took from him his Very pistol and fired the colored signal which called for the attack; all so quickly that support arrived before the enemy could counter-attack or put down a barrage . . .

———

. . . Among the demobilized officers who emigrated from England after the Armistice was a subaltern named Walkley. He went out to Canada, where he raised wheat and prospered, both in pocket and in health. So much so that, had he been walking out of the Gare de Lyon in Paris instead of in Piccadilly Circus on this first evening (it is Christmas Eve) of his first visit home, they would have said, 'Here is not only a rich milord; it is a well one.'

He had been in London just long enough to outfit himself with the beginning of a wardrobe, and in his new clothes (bought of a tailor which in the old days he could not have afforded) he was enjoying himself too much to even go anywhere. So he just walked the streets, among the cheerful throngs, until suddenly he stopped dead still, staring at a face. The man had almost white hair, moustaches waxed to needle points. He wore a frayed scarf in which could be barely distinguished the colors and pattern of a regiment. His threadbare clothes were freshly ironed and he carried a stick. He was standing at the curb, and he appeared to be saying something to the people who passed, and Walkley moved suddenly forward, his hand extended. But the other man only stared at him with eyes that were perfectly dead.

'Gray,' Walkley said, 'don't you remember me?' The other stared at him with that dead intensity. 'We were in hospital together. I went out to Canada. Don't you remember?'

'Yes,' the other said. 'I remember you. You are Walkley.' Then he quit looking at Walkley. He moved a little aside, turning to the crowd again, his hand extended; it was only then that Walkley saw that the hand contained three or four boxes of the matches which may be bought from any tobacconist for a penny a box. 'Matches? Matches, sir?' he said. 'Matches? Matches?'

Walkley moved also, getting again in front of the other. 'Gray –' he said.

The other looked at Walkley again, this time with a kind of restrained yet raging impatience. 'Let me alone, you son of a bitch!' he said, turning immediately toward the crowd again, his hand extended. 'Matches! Matches, sir!' he chanted.

Walkley moved on. He paused again, half turning, looking back at the gaunt face above the waxed moustaches. Again the other looked him full in the face, but the glance passed on, as though without recognition. Walkley went on. He walked swiftly. 'My God,' he said. 'I think I am going to vomit.'

WILLIAM FAULKNER

see also p. 590

A Fable, one of Faulkner's last works, published in 1954, returns
again to 1918. This fine, underrated novel was greeted with
considerable official recognition (the Pulitzer Prize and the
National Book Award) but also some critical controversy. It has
been seen as obscure, mechanically allegorical and 'liberal' at
the expense of 'literary' values. An entry in one companion to
literature suggests that it is 'deeply flawed by reason of unsuccessful parallels that were drawn between events of AD 33 and
1918'. It has also been adversely and unfairly compared with
Humphrey Cobb's *Paths of Glory* (*q.v.*). A corporal (the Christ
figure) and twelve ordinary soldiers have been spreading the
word that it would be possible to stop the war simply by
refusing to fight. The novel opens with a French general's
reaction to his best regiment's refusal to go over the top. The
rest of the novel moves back and forwards over the events
leading up to the mutiny, the apparently inexplicable fact that
the Germans do not take advantage of the French (they had
been tipped off) and the trials of the corporal and the general.
Eventually, after both have been executed, the war is successfully
re-started by the 'cooperation' of both sides. In the passages
below from 'Monday' and 'Tuesday Night' the general considers
his failure and an English runner learns of the thirteen soldiers'
subversive activities. The runner tries to influence a sentry and
is beaten up for his pains.

Source: William Faulkner, *A Fable*, New York, Random House,
1954.

Monday

... Then he didn't even have a failure. He had a mutiny. When
the barrage lifted, he was not even observing the scene beneath
him, but was already looking at his watch-face. He didn't need
to see the attack. After watching them from beneath his stars for
three years now, he had become an expert, not merely in
forecasting failure, but in predicting almost exactly when, where,
at what point in time and terrain, they would become void and

harmless – this, even when he was not familiar with the troops making the attack, which in the present case he was, having selected this particular regiment the day before because he knew, on the one hand, not only the condition of the regiment but its colonel's belief in it and the record of his success with it; and on the other, its value as measured against each of the other three in the division; he knew it would deliver the attack near enough to the maximum demanded of him, yet if the foreordained failure meant its temporary wreckage or even permanent ruin, this would weigh less in the strength and morale of the division than that of any of the other three; he could never, breathing, have been convinced or even told that he had chosen the regiment out of his division exactly as the group commander had chosen the division out of his armies . . .

———

Tuesday night

. . . 'Yes,' the runner said.

'Right,' the colonel said. 'Carry on. Just remember.' Which he did, sometimes when on duty but mostly during the periods when the battalion was in rest billets, carrying the unloaded rifle slung across his back which was his cognizance, his badge of office, with somewhere in his pocket some – any – scrap of paper bearing the colonel's or the adjutant's signature in case of emergency. At times he managed lifts from passing transport – lorries, empty ambulances, an unoccupied sidecar. At times while in rest areas he even wangled the use of a motorbike himself, as if he actually were a dispatch rider; he could be seen sitting on empty petrol tins in scout- or fighter- or bomber-squadron hangars, in the material sheds of artillery or transport parks, at the back doors of field stations and hospitals and divisional châteaux, in kitchens and canteens and at the toy-sized zinc bars of village estaminets, as he had told the colonel, not talking but listening.

So he learned about the thirteen French soldiers almost at once – or rather, the thirteen men in French uniforms – who had been known for a year now among all combat troops below the grade of sergeant in the British forces and obviously in the French too, realizing at the same moment that not only had he been the last man below sergeant in the whole Allied front to hear about them, but why: who five months ago had been an officer too, by the badges on his tunic also for ever barred and interdict from the right and freedom to the simple passions and hopes and fears – sickness for home, worry about wives and allotment pay, the weak beer and the shilling a day which wont even buy enough of that; even the right to be afraid of death – all that confederation of fellowship which enables man to support the weight of war; in fact, the surprise was that, having been an officer once, he had been permitted to learn about the thirteen men at all.

His informant was an ASC private more than sixty years old, member of and lay preacher to a small nonconformist congregation in Southwark; he had been half porter and half confidential servant with an unblemished record to an Inns of Court law firm, as his father had been before him and his son was to be after, except that at the Old Bailey assizes in the spring of 1914 the son would have been sent up for breaking and burglary had not the presiding judge been not only a humanitarian but a member of the same philatelist society to which the head of the law firm belonged; whereupon the son was permitted to enlist instead the next day and in August went to Belgium and was reported missing at Mons all in the same three weeks and was accepted so by all save his father, who received leave of absence to enlist from the law firm for the single reason that his employers did not believe he could pass the doctors; eight months later the father was in France too; a year after that he was still trying to get, first, leave of absence; then, failing that, transfer to some unit near enough to Mons to look for his son, although it had been a long time now since he had mentioned the son, as if he had forgot the reason and remembered only the destination, still a lay preacher, still half night-watchman and half nurse, unimpeachable of record, to the succession of (to him) children who ran a vast ammunition dump behind St Omer, where one afternoon he told the runner about the thirteen French soldiers.

'Go and listen to them,' the old porter said. 'You can speak foreign; you can understand them.'

'I thought you said that the nine who should have spoken French, didn't, and that the other four couldn't speak anything at all.'

'They dont need to talk,' the old porter said. 'You dont need to understand. Just go and look at him.'

'Him?' the runner said. 'So it's just one now?'

'Wasn't it just one before?' the old porter said. 'Wasn't one enough then to tell us the same thing all them two thousand years ago: that all we ever needed to do was just to say, Enough of this – us, not even the sergeants and corporals, but just us, all of us, Germans and Colonials and Frenchmen and all the other foreigners in the mud here, saying together: Enough. Let them that's already dead and maimed and missing be enough of this – a thing so easy and simple that even human man, as full of evil and sin and folly as he is, can understand and believe it this time. Go and look at him.'

But he didn't see them, not yet. Not that he couldn't have found them; at any time they would be in the British zone, against that khaki monotone, that clump of thirteen men in horizon blue, even battle-stained, would have stood out like a cluster of hyacinths in a Scottish moat. He didn't even try yet. He didn't dare; he had been an officer himself, even though for only five months, and even though he had repudiated it, something ineradicable of it still remained, as the unfrocked priest or repentant murderer, even though unfrocked at heart and reformed at heart, carries for ever about him like a catalyst the indelible effluvium of the old condition; it seemed to him that he durst not be present even on the fringe of whatever surrounding crowd, even to walk, pass through, let alone stop, within the same air of that small blue clump of hope; this, even while telling himself that he did not believe it, that it couldn't be true, possible, since if it were possible, it would not need to be hidden from Authority; that it would not matter whether Authority knew about it or not, since even ruthless and all-powerful and unchallengeable Authority would be impotent before that massed unresisting undemanding passivity. He thought: *They could execute only so many of us before they will have worn out the last rifle and pistol and expended the last live shell,* visualizing it . . .

———

Tuesday night [cont.]

. . . 'One regiment,' the runner said. 'One French regiment. Only a fool would look on war as a condition; it's too expensive. War is an episode, a crisis, a fever the purpose of which is to rid the body of fever. So the purpose of a war is to end the war. We've known that for six thousand years. The trouble was, it took us six thousand years to learn how to do it. For six thousand years we labored under the delusion that the only way

599

to stop a war was to get together more regiments and battalions than the enemy could, or vice versa, and hurl them upon each other until one lot was destroyed and, the one having nothing left to fight with, the other could stop fighting. We were wrong, because yesterday morning, by simply declining to make an attack, one single French regiment stopped us all.'

This time the sentry didn't move, leaning – braced rather – against the trench-wall beneath the vicious rake of his motionless helmet, peering apparently almost idly through the aperture save for that rigidity about his back and shoulders – a kind of immobility on top of immobility – as though he were braced not against the dirt wall but rather against the quiet and empty air behind him. Nor had the runner moved either, though from his speech it was almost as if he had turned his face to look directly at the back of the sentry's head. 'What do you see?' he said. 'No novelty, you think? – the same stinking strip of ownerless valueless frantic dirt between our wire and theirs, which you have been peering at through a hole in a sandbag for four years now? The same war which we had come to believe did not know how to end itself, like the amateur orator searching desperately for a definitive preposition? You're wrong. You can go out there now, at least during the next fifteen minutes, say, and not die probably. Yes, that may be the novelty: you can go out there now and stand erect and look about you – granted of course that any of us really ever can stand erect again. But we will learn how. Who knows? In four or five years we may even have got our neck-muscles supple enough simply to duck our heads again in place of merely bowing them to await the stroke, as we have been doing for four years now; in ten years, certainly.' The sentry didn't move, like a blind man suddenly within range of a threat, the first warning of which he must translate through some remaining secondary sense, already too late to fend with . . .

———

. . . the faint glare washing over the runner's lifted face and then, even after the light itself had died, seeming to linger still on it as if the glow had not been refraction at all but water or perhaps grease; he spoke in a tense furious murmur not much louder than a whisper:

'Do you see now? Not for us to ask what nor why but just go down a hole in the ground and stay there until they decide what to do. No: just how to do it because they already know what. Of course they wont tell us. They wouldn't have told us anything at all if they hadn't had to, hadn't had to tell us something, tell the rest of you something before the ones of us who were drawn out yesterday for special couriers out of Corps would get back in tonight and tell you what we had heard. And even then, they told you just enough to keep you in the proper frame of mind so that, when they said go down the dug-outs and stay there you would do it. And even I wouldn't have known any more in time if on the way back in tonight I hadn't blundered on to that lorry train.

'No: that's wrong too; just known in time that they are already up to something. Because all of us know by now that something is wrong. Dont you see? Something happened down there yesterday morning in the French front, a regiment failed – burked – mutinied, we dont know what and are not going to know what because they aren't going to tell us. Besides, it doesn't matter what happened. What matters is, what happened afterward. At dawn yesterday a French regiment did something – did or failed to do something which a regiment in a front line is not supposed to do or fail to do, and as a result of it, the entire war in Western Europe took a recess at three o'clock yesterday afternoon. Dont you see? When you are in battle and one of your units fails, the last thing you do, dare do, is quit. Instead, you snatch up everything else you've got and fling it in as quick and hard as you can, because you know that that's exactly what the enemy is going to do as soon as he discovers or even suspects you have trouble on your side. Of course you're going to be one unit short of him when you meet; your hope, your only hope, is that if you can only start first and be going the fastest, momentum and surprise might make up a little of it.

'But they didn't. Instead, they took a recess, remanded: the French at noon, us and the Americans three hours later. And not only us, but Jerry too. Dont you see? How can you remand in war, unless your enemy agrees too? And why should Jerry have agreed, after squatting under the sort of barrage which four years had trained him to know meant that an attack was coming, then no attack came or failed or whatever it was it did, and four years had certainly trained him to the right assumption for that; when the message, signal, request – whatever it was – came over suggesting a remand, why should he have agreed to it, unless he had a reason as good as the one we had, maybe the same reason we had? The same reason; those thirteen French

601

soldiers apparently had no difficulty whatever going anywhere they liked in our back-areas for three years, why weren't they across yonder in Jerry's too, since we all know that, unless you've got the right properly signed paper in your hand, it's a good deal more difficult to go to Paris from here than to Berlin; any time you want to go east from here, all you need is a British or French or American uniform. Or perhaps they didn't even need to go themselves, perhaps just wind, moving air, carried it. Or perhaps not even moving air but just air, spreading by attrition from invisible and weightless molecule to molecule as disease, smallpox spreads, or fear, or hope – just enough of us, all of us in the mud here saying together, Enough of this, let's have done with this . . .

———

. . . 'So you see what we must do before that German emissary or whatever he will be can reach Paris or Chaulnesmont or wherever he is to go, and he and whoever he is to agree with, have agreed, not on what to do because that is no problem: only on how, and goes back home to report it. We dont even need to start it; the French, that one French regiment, has already taken up the load. All we need is not to let it drop, falter, pause for even a second. We must do it now, tomorrow – tomorrow? it's already tomorrow; it's already today now – do as that French regiment did, the whole battalion of us: climb over this parapet tomorrow morning and get through the wire, with no rifles, nothing, and walk toward Jerry's wire until he can see us, enough of him can see us – a regiment of him or a battalion or maybe just a company or maybe even just one because even just one will be enough. You can do it. You own the whole battalion, every man in it under corporal, beneficiary of every man's insurance in it who hasn't got a wife and I O Us for their next month's pay of all the rest of them in that belt around your waist. All you'll need is just to tell them to when you say, Follow me; I'll go along to the first ones as soon as you are relieved, so they can see you vouch for me. Then others will see you vouch for me when I vouch for them, so that by daylight or by sun-up anyway, when Jerry can see us, all the rest of Europe can see us, will have to see us, cant help but see us –' He thought: *He's really going to kick me this time, and in the face.* Then the sentry's boot struck the side of his jaw, snapping his head back even before his body toppled, the thin flow of water which sheathed his face flying at the blow like a thin spray of spittle or perhaps of dew or rain from a snapped leaf, the sentry kicking at him again as he went over backward on to the fire-step, and was still stamping his boot at the unconscious face when the officer and the sergeant ran back around the traverse, still stamping at the prone face and panting at it:

'Will you for Christ's sake now? Will you? Will you?' when the sergeant jerked him bodily down to the duckboards. The sentry didn't even pause, whirling while the sergeant held him, and slashing his reversed rifle blindly across the nearest face. It was the officer's, but the sentry didn't even wait to see, whirling again back toward the fire-step though the sergeant still gripped him in one arm around his middle, still – the sentry – striking with the rifle-butt at the runner's bleeding head when the sergeant fumbled his pistol out with his free hand and thumbed the safety off.

'As you were,' the officer said, jerking the blood from his mouth, on to his wrist and flinging it away. 'Hold him.' He spoke without turning his head, toward the corner of the down-traverse, raising his voice a little: 'Two-eight. Pass the word for corporal.'

The sentry was actually foaming now, apparently not even conscious that the sergeant was holding him, still jabbing the rifle-butt at or at least toward the runner's peaceful and bloody head, until the sergeant spoke almost against his ear.

'Two-seven . . . for corporal,' a voice beyond the down traverse said; then fainter, beyond that, another:

'Two-six . . . corporal.'

'Use yer boot,' the sergeant muttered. 'Kick his ——ing teeth in.'

GENERAL SIR IAN HAMILTON
and
ERICH MARIA REMARQUE

General Sir Ian Hamilton (1853–1947). Born in Corfu. Joined the army in 1873. Served in the Boer War. In charge of the Gallipoli landings. Kitchener and others were suspicious of him. According to Hugh MacDiarmid (C. M. Grieve), he was known as 'that b—y poet' (sic). This quotation is taken from a sympathetic portrait by MacDiarmid in *Contemporary Scottish Studies* (1926), where he also praised the general's poetry, his dispatches from the front and his Scots nationalism. Constant Huntington sent bound page proofs of Remarque's *All Quiet on the Western Front* to interested parties (including Henry Williamson, *q.v.*, who thought it 'like a fart on a curtain pole', Preface to *The Patriot's Progress*). Hamilton's views drew Remarque out of the silence he had maintained after his book was published. The reader may find Hamilton's *Gallipoli Diary* (1920) both readable and humane.

Source: General Sir Ian Hamilton, 'The End of War?', *Life and Letters*, Vol. III, No. 18, November 1929.

THE END OF WAR?

A correspondence between the author of *All Quiet on the Western Front* and General Sir Ian Hamilton, G C B, G C M G

I

2 April 1929

My Dear Huntington,
Thank you for the advance copy of *All Quiet on the Western Front*: I am glad you have found so capable a translator, clever enough to pick up Remarque's bomb and fling it across the Channel. We here just needed this bit of wakening up.

The tale is that of a generation who have been destroyed by the war: we who fought 'are forlorn like children, and experienced like old men, we are crude and sorrowful and superficial –

I believe we are lost'; or, more tersely, 'the war has ruined us for everything'.

This is the keynote of the diary – in which form the revelations are cast: it is struck firmly in the opening half-dozen lines and recurs again and again, until, at the end, the last chord dies softly away into the unknown.

There was a time when I would have strenuously combated Remarque's inferences and conclusions. Now, sorrowfully, I must admit, there is a great deal of truth in them. Latrines, rats, lice; smells, blood, corpses; scenes of sheer horror as where comrades surround the deathbed of a young *Kamerad* with one eye on his agonies, the other on his new English boots; the uninspired strategy; the feeling that the leaders are unsympathetic or stupid; the shrivelling up of thought and enthusiasm under ever-growing machinery of an attrition war; all this lasting too long – so long indeed that half a million souls, still existing in our own island, have been, in Remarque's own terrible word, 'lost'. Why else, may I ask, should those who were once the flower of our youth form today so disproportionate a number of the down and out?

All the same, this German goes too far. As there is more in Easter than hot cross buns, so there is more in Patriotism than 'beans and bacon'. Even in the last and most accursed of all wars – the war 'on the Western Front' – was there not the superb leading of forlorn hopes; the vague triumphs, vague but real, of dying for a cause? Was there not also that very patriotism which Remarque treats much as he treated the goose his hero murdered in the officers' mess? Above all, is there not the victory of those, and they were many, who survived everything; profited even by Passchendaele; and afterwards still found courage enough to turn themselves to making the world a better place for themselves and everyone else, including their ex-enemies?

Remarque seems to me a writer who could do anything. He says some incredibly coarse things, but he lets slip sometimes, as if by accident, astonishingly true things hitherto unsaid. As, for instance, his answer to those who with their clumsy questions grope and rummage about his heart, seeking for his innermost feelings upon the happenings of the Western Front: 'a man cannot talk of such things; I would do it willingly, but it is too dangerous for me to put these things into words. I am afraid they might then become gigantic, and I be no longer able to marshal them'.

Im Westen Nichts Neues is a masterpiece of realism, but not a perfect war book; for war, as well as life, holds something more than realism.

Yours sincerely,
(*Signed*) Ian Hamilton

11 [1]

1 June 1929

Dear Sir Ian Hamilton,

An extract from your letter to Mr Huntington concerning my book, *All Quiet on the Western Front*, was very kindly sent on to me by the publishers, Messrs Putnam. I intended to write to you about it at once, but was prevented from so doing during long weeks of illness which denied me the quiet hour I needed for my reply.

I cannot even now tell you which feeling was uppermost in me on receipt of your letter – whether that of personal pleasure, or of amazement and admiration at having been so clearly, so completely, so justly understood. Probably both were equally strong. You will be able to appreciate that I was entirely unaware what effect my work might produce outside Germany – whether I should have succeeded in making myself intelligible to all, or not.

A book on the war is readily exposed to criticism of a political character, but my work should not be so judged, for it was not political, neither pacifist nor militarist, in intention, but human simply. It presents the war as seen within the small compass of the front-line soldier, pieced together out of many separate situations, out of minutes and hours, out of struggle, fear, dirt, bravery, dire necessity, death and comradeship, into one whole mosaic, from which the word Patriotism is only *seemingly* absent, because the simple soldier never spoke of it. His patriotism lay in the *deed* (not in the *word*); it consisted simply in the fact of his presence at the front. For him that was enough. He cursed and swore at the war; but he fought on, and fought on even when already without hope. And of this there is, I believe, for those who can read, enough in my book.

But you, Sir Ian, have in a few words, exposed the very heart of my book, namely, the intention of presenting the fate of a generation of young men, who at the critical age, when they were just beginning to feel the pulse of life, were set face to face with death. I thank you for that most sincerely, and am delighted to hear these words from a man of high military rank. Your words are prized by me as those of a voice speaking clearly from England. In Germany it has never been forgotten how *fair* the English were, even in the midst of the battle, and so I am particularly pleased to find it confirmed in letters from English soldiers and English officers, that the background, the little things, but things so important for the individual soldier, were apparently similar on all the fronts.

I have not felt myself called upon to argue about the war. That must be reserved for the leaders, who alone know all that it is necessary to know. I merely wanted to awaken understanding for a generation that more than all others has found it difficult to make its way back from the four years of death, struggle and terror, to the peaceful fields of work and progress. Thousands upon thousands have even yet been unable to do it; countless letters from all countries have proved it to me. But all these letters say the same thing: 'We have been unable, because we did not know that our lethargy, our cynicism, our unrest, our hopelessness, our silence, our feeling of secession and exclusion arose from the fact that the regenerative power of our youth had been dissipated in the war. But now we will find the way, for you in your book have shown us the danger in which we stand, the danger of being destroyed by ourselves. But the recognition of a danger is the first step towards escape from it. We will now find our way back, for you have told us what it was that threatened us, and thereby it has become harmless.'

You see, Sir Ian, it is in this vein that my comrades write to me, and that proves that my book is only *seemingly* pessimistic. In reality, as it shows how much has been destroyed, it should serve as a call to them to rally for the peaceful battle of work and of life itself, the effort to achieve personality and culture. For the very reason that we had so early to learn to know death, we now want to shake off its paralysing spell – for we have seen it eye to eye and undisguised – we want to begin once again to believe in life. This will be the aim of my future work. He who has pointed out the danger, must also point out the road onward.

I have as yet never spoken my mind so fully; but your charming, appreciative letter compelled me to take up the pen in order to emphasize the two things in my book which, though not there in any very explicit way, are nevertheless there implicit – I mean, in the first place, the quiet heroism of the simple soldier, which lay precisely in the fact that he did not speak of it, that he did not perhaps so much as once realize it himself – speaking only of 'beans and bacon', while all the time so much more lay behind that was other than this; and secondly, the fact that my book does not desire to preach resignation but rather to be an SOS call.

You are right, Sir Ian, my book is not a 'perfect war book'. But such a war book, in the comprehensive sense, may not be written for yet another ten, perhaps even another hundred years. I restricted myself to the purely human aspect of war experience, the experience through which every man who went up to the front had to make his painful way: the fighting, the terror, the mastery, the power, the tenacity of the vital forces in the individual man faced with death and annihilation.

I like to regard that as the universal, fundamental experience; and I have aimed at describing without rhetoric and without political exploitation, this fundamental experience alone. And to this, I believe, may be attributed the success of my book, which in Germany has been read not merely in literary circles, but by those also who almost never take a book in their hands – by artisans, labourers, business people, mechanics, postmen, chauffeurs, apprentices, and so on; for many hundreds of letters all say: '*It is my own experience.*' The *outward* experience was, perhaps, in each case merely similar (though, as far as possible, I described only typical, standard situations, such as constantly recurred), but the decisive factor undoubtedly was that the book represented a part of the *inner* experience – Life confronting and fighting Death.

In conclusion, Sir Ian, allow me to thank you once again for your letter, and you may judge from the length of this how highly I valued it. I am happy to have met with such appreciative understanding.

Yours sincerely,
(*Signed*) Erich Maria Remarque

III

19 June 1929

Dear Mr Remarque,
Yours of 1 June has given me much pleasure. I can well imagine the postman pouring out the best part of his heavy bag whilst you look at the pile of letters in despair, saying to yourself: 'So, because I have written well I must go on writing for ever!' All

the more then am I grateful to you for having found time to write so fully and indeed so important an epistle to an ex-enemy commander.

I fear I have been a long time in answering, and one reason is that I have so much work on my hands as President of the British Legion in London and in trying to help old soldiers who fought under me in the war. You see, in England we have over one million unemployed. More than half of these are old soldiers. When they went to the war they were the flower, not the dregs, of our people. Always I have tried to rouse them and stir them up by explaining to them the reason; namely, that education is most valuable from the age of eighteen to twenty-two and that, just during those very years, when the stay-at-homes were mastering their trades, they were standing in mud under a rain of shells. Therefore, when they came back they were at a disadvantage. Therefore, when trade was slack they were the first to be discharged. But all this lost ground, I have been careful to add, could be, by courage and perseverance, recovered. First of all the Legionaries must bind themselves into a body professing, as such, no politics, so that they must carry weight with any government. Secondly, they must work to save their old comrades and the widows and orphans of their late comrades. Thirdly, they must strive for some high ideal, the highest being peace: for this, as ex-service men they could do with far better grace than professed pacifists: especially they could work wonders for the cause of peace by holding out the hand of friendship to ex-enemy associations of soldiers. For all the people of the world would then say to one another: 'Surely, if these soldiers who threw bombs at one another can shake hands, we, who never struck or were stricken in our own persons can also afford to be friends!'

These things I tell you not (I hope) from conceit, but because you should thus understand better how your work has appealed to me. For you have explained to your war heroes (no longer *die Gemeine*) that the war not only robbed them of their education, but actually burnt up in its fiery furnace the energy and regenerative power which was intended by God to see them through the early struggles of their careers as citizens.

But when we come to practice, how difficult! Easier it will be to put a hook into the nose of leviathan than to draw the Stahlhelms and the Reichsbanner into one non-political Legion for the battle against war.

Five years ago, I was almost voted out of the Presidency of the Legion in London because I wanted them to shake hands with the Germans, and because I pointed out that they would thus show the way to the timorous, manoeuvring politicians and *Beamten* at Geneva, who depend for their livelihood upon the absence of the peace they are paid heavy sums to secure.

Yet still the pen is mightier than the sword. So write another book, my dear Mr Remarque. As one who has served in eight campaigns, I say, take up thy pen and write. For you possess the gift of genius and you may not wrap it up in a napkin. That magical scene where you sit in your old room and pray in vain to your old gods, the books. That unforgettable moment when you breathe in again the acid smell of the cold water of the Mill – *In einem kuhlen Grunde!* Yes; you have the touch; the sure touch, and you can do it as no other can. But you will need all the power of your persuasive pen. For great and terrible is the counter-power of the romance and beauty of war, to which you wisely make no reference in your book. But there it is – entrenched somewhere – latent in your soul. Have you seen a German army corps, colours flying, march past, the earth shaking to the tramp of the parade step? Lord Roberts told me in his old age, that the most superb picture he preserved in his mind's eye was that of two Highland battalions, in their kilts and feather bonnets, advancing in perfect line against the walled city of Lucknow, the round shot hopping and skipping over the plain, sometimes over them, sometimes into them, yet all keeping step as on an inspection parade. These are the legends and illusions you have got to transfix very quickly with your pen.

For the boys of today are just the same as you were twenty years ago, and as I was sixty years ago.

Yours very truly,
(*Signed*) Ian Hamilton

1. Translated by A. W. Wheen, translator of *All Quiet on the Western Front* and *The Way Back*.

FURTHER READING

Note: There is little criticism in English of European war literature as such. It is hoped that the surveys of French and German literature will provide the reader with some further leads. The war prose of the great American writers tends to be dealt with as a prelude to their later works. English war prose is hardly better served and it tends to be dealt with as an adjunct to study of war poetry. This list is necessarily incomplete and tentative.

Peter Aichinger, *The American Soldier in Fiction, 1880–1963*, Ames, Iowa State University Press, 1975

Anthony Babington, *For the Sake of Example, Capital Courts Martial, 1914–18, the Truth*, London, Leo Cooper/Martin Secker & Warburg, 1983

Correlli Barnett, *The Sword-bearers, Supreme Command in the First World War*, New York, William Morrow, 1963

Bernard Bergonzi, *Heroes' Twilight*, London, Constable, 1965

Edmund Blunden, Cyril Falls, H. M. Tomlinson and R. Wright, *The War 1914–1918, A Booklist*, London, The Reader, 1929

J. K. Bostock, *Some Well-Known German War Novels 1914–1930*, Oxford, Blackwell, 1931

Leon Bramson and George W. Goethals, eds., *War, Studies from Psychology, Sociology, Anthropology*, New York, Basic Books, 1964

Malcolm Brown, *Tommy Goes to War*, London, Dent, 1978

Kenneth Burke, *The Philosophy of Literary Form*, Baton Rouge, Louisiana State University Press, 1941

Mary Cadogan and Patricia Craig, *Women and Children First*, London, Gollancz, 1978

Guy Chapman, ed., *Vain Glory*, London, Cassell, 1937

P. E. Charvet, *A Literary History of France*, Vol. 5, London, Ernest Benn, and New York, Barnes & Noble, 1975

Richard Cobb, *French and Germans, Germans and French*, Hanover, University of New England Press, 1983

Stanley Cooperman, *World War 1 and the American Novel*, Baltimore, The Johns Hopkins Press, 1967

Malcolm Cowley, *The Literary Situation*, London, André Deutsch, 1955

Malcolm Cowley, *A Second Flowering, Works and Days of the Lost Generation*, London, André Deutsch, 1973

John Cruikshank, ed., *French Literature and its Background*, Vol. 6, London, Oxford University Press, 1970

John Cruikshank, *Variations on a Catastrophe: Some French Responses to the Great War*, Oxford, The Clarendon Press, 1982

John Ellis, *Eye-Deep in Hell*, London, Croom Helm, 1976

A. G. S. Enser, *A Subject Bibliography of the First World War*, London, André Deutsch, 1979

Cyril Falls, *War Books: A Critical Guide*, London, Peter Davies, 1930

Marc Ferro, *The Great War, 1914–18*, London, Routledge & Kegan Paul, 1973

Frank Field, *Three French Writers and the Great War: Barbusse, Drieu la Rochelle, Bernanos*, Cambridge, Cambridge University Press, 1975

Mary Sargant Florence, Catherine Marshall, C. K. Ogden, *Militarism versus Feminism: Writings on Women and War*, London, Virago Press, 1987

C. J. Fox, 'The Wind in the Rampart Trees, War Thoughts 60 Years after Ypres', *P. N. Review*, No. 4, 1977

Paul Fussell, *The Great War and Modern Memory*, London, Oxford University Press, 1975

Ronald Gray, *The German Tradition in Literature*, Cambridge, Cambridge University Press, 1965

M. S. Greicus, *Prose Writers of World War 1*, London, Longmans, for the British Council, 1973

William H. Harrison, *Seeing Through Everything, English Writers 1918–1940*, London, Faber, 1977

Alisdair Horne, *The Price of Glory, Verdun 1916*, London, Macmillan, 1962; Penguin Books, 1964

Samuel Hynes, *Edwardian Occasions*, London, Routledge & Kegan Paul, 1972

Robert Rhodes James, *Gallipoli*, London, Batsford, 1965

Douglas Jerrold, *The Lie about the War*, London, Faber, 1930

John Keegan, *The Face of Battle*, London, Jonathan Cape, 1976; Penguin Books, 1978

Holger Klein, ed., *The First World War in Fiction*, London, Macmillan, 1976

Dave Lamb, *Mutinies: 1917–1920*, Oxford and London, Solidarity, (no date)

Eric Leed, *No Man's Land, Combat and Identity in World War 1*, Cambridge, Cambridge University Press, 1979

B. H. Liddell Hart, *History of the First World War*, London, Cassell, 1970; Pan, 1972

Rosa Luxemburg, *Letters from Prison*, translated from the German by Eden and Cedar Paul, Berlin–Schoenenberg, Publishing House of the Young International 1923

Lyn Macdonald, *They Called it Passchendaele*, London, Michael Joseph, 1978

Lyn Macdonald, *The Roses of No Man's Land*, London, Michael Joseph, 1980

Arthur Marwick, *The Deluge*, London, Macmillan, 1965

Arthur Marwick, *Women at War, 1914–1918*, London, Fontana, 1977

Martin Middlebrook, *The First Day of the Somme*, London, Allen Lane, 1971

Martin Middlebrook, *The Kaiser's Battle*, London, Allen Lane, 1978

Harry T. Moore, *Twentieth Century German Literature*, London, William Heinemann, 1971

Michael Moynihan, ed., *A Place Called Armageddon, Letters from the Great War*, Newton Abbot, David & Charles, 1975

Michael Moynihan, ed., *Greater Love, Letters Home 1914–1918*, London: W. H. Allen, 1980

George A. Panichas, ed., *The Promise of Greatness: The 1914–1918 War*, with a Foreword by Sir Herbert Read, London, Cassell, 1968

Roy Pascal, *From Naturalism to Expressionism, German Society 1880–1918*, London, Weidenfeld & Nicolson, 1973

Edgell Rickword, *Literature and Society* (Essays and Opinions, 11), Manchester, Carcanet, 1978

Andrew Rutherford, *The Literature of War*, London, The Macmillan Press, 1978

Denis Saurat, *Modern French Literature, 1870–1940*, London, Dent, 1947

Jon Silkin, *Out of Battle*, London, Oxford University Press, 1972; Routledge & Kegan Paul, 1987

Hilda D. Spear, *Remembering, We Forget*, London, Davis Poynter, 1979

Ronald Steele, 'Where Modern Politics Began', *New York Review of Books*, Vol. xxxi, No. 2, 16 Feb. 1984 (review of John Milton Cooper, jr, *The Warrior and the Priest*, The Belknap Press of Harvard University Press, 1983)

A. J. P. Taylor. *The First World War: An Illustrated History*, London, Hamish Hamilton, 1963; Penguin Books, 1966

Ronald Taylor, *Literature and Society in Germany, 1918–1945*, Brighton, The Harvester Press, and Totowa, N. J., Barnes & Noble, 1980

Richard Thoumin, *The First World War*, London, Martin Secker & Warburg, 1963

John Toland, *No Man's Land*, London, Eyre Methuen, 1980

H. M. Tomlinson, 'A Footnote to the War Books', *Out of Soundings*, London, Heinemann, 1931

Barbara Tuchman, *August 1914*, London, Constable, 1962

Peter Vansittart, *Voices from the Great War*, London, Jonathan Cape, 1981; Penguin Books, 1982

Jeffrey Walsh, *American War Literature*, London, Macmillan, 1982

Richard M. Watt, *Dare Call it Treason*, London, Chatto & Windus, 1964

C. E. Williams, *The Broken Eagle, The Politics of Austrian Literature from Empire to Anschluss*, London, Paul Elek, 1974

Denis Winter, *Death's Men*, London, Allen Lane, 1978; Penguin Books, 1979

Leon Wolf, *In Flanders Fields*, London, Longmans, 1959; Penguin Books, 1979